Dance for the Dead

Dance for the Dead

THOMAS PERRY

RANDOM HOUSE NEW YORK

Library of Congress Cataloging-in-Publication Data
Perry, Thomas.
Dance for the dead / Thomas Perry.
p.   cm.
ISBN 0-679-44911-6
1. Seneca Indians—Fiction.   I. Title.
PS3566.E718D36   1996
813'.54—dc20   95-32716

Printed in the United States of America on acid-free paper
24689753
First Edition

For Jo

with love to
Alix and Isabel

The common aim of all war parties was to bring back persons to replace the mourned-for dead. This could be done in three ways: by bringing back the scalp of a dead enemy (this scalp might even be put through an adoption ceremony); by bringing back a live prisoner (to be adopted, tortured, and killed); or by bringing back a live prisoner to be allowed to live and even to replace in a social role the one whose death had called for this "revenge."

Anthony F. C. Wallace, *The Death and Rebirth of the Seneca*, 1969

Dance for the Dead

1

The tall, slim woman hastily tied her long, dark hair into a knot behind her head, planted her feet in the center of the long courthouse corridor, and waited. A few litigants and their attorneys passed her, some of them secretly studying her, more because she was attractive than because she was standing motionless, forcing them to step around her on their way to the courtrooms. Her chest rose and fell in deep breaths as though she had been running, and her eyes looked past them, having already dismissed them before they approached as she stared into the middle distance.

She heard the chime sound above the elevator thirty feet away. Before the doors had fully parted, three large men in sportcoats slipped out between them and spun their heads to stare up the hallway. All three seemed to see her within an instant, their eyes widening, then narrowing to focus, and then becoming watchful and predatory, losing any hint of introspection as they began to move toward her, one beside each wall and one in the middle, increasing their pace with each step.

Several bystanders averted their eyes and sidestepped to avoid them, but the woman never moved. She hiked up the skirt of her navy blue business suit so it was out of her way, took two more deep breaths, then swung her shoulder bag hard at the first man's face.

The man's eyes shone with triumph and eagerness as he snatched the purse out of the air. The triumph turned to shock as the woman slipped the strap around his forearm and used the momentum of his charge to haul him into the second man, sending them both against the wall to her right. As they caromed off it, she delivered a kick to one and a chop to the other to put them on the floor. This bought her a few heartbeats to devote to the third man, who was moving along the left wall to get behind her.

She leaned back and swung one leg high. The man read her intention, stopped, and held up his hands to clutch her ankle, but her back foot left the ground and she hurled her weight into him. As her foot caught him at thigh level and propelled him into the wall, there was the sickening crack of his knee popping. He crumpled to the floor and began to gasp and clutch at his crippled leg as the woman rolled to the side and sprang up.

The first two men were rising to their feet. Her fist jabbed out at the nearest one and she rocked him back, pivoted to throw an elbow into the bridge of his nose, and brought a knee into the second man's face.

There was a loud slapping sound and the woman's head jerked nearly to her left shoulder as a big fist swung into her cheekbone. Strong arms snaked around her from behind, lifted her off her feet to stretch her erect, and she saw the rest as motion and flashes. The first two men rushed at her in rage, aiming hard roundhouse punches at her head and face, gleeful in the certainty that she saw the blows coming but could do nothing to block them or even turn to divert their force.

Two loud, deep voices overlapped, barking for dominance. "Police officers! Freeze!" "Step away from her!" When her opponents released her and stepped away, she dropped to her knees and covered her face with her hands. In a moment, several bystanders who had stood paralyzed with alarm seemed to awaken. They were drawn closer by some impulse to be of use, but they only hovered helplessly nearby without touching her or speaking.

The judge's chambers were in shadow except for a few horizontal slices of late-afternoon sunlight that shone through the blinds on the wood-paneled wall. Judge Kramer sat in his old oak swivel chair with his robe unzipped but with the yoke still resting on his shoulders. He loosened his tie and leaned back, making the chair's springs creak, then pressed the PLAY button on the tape recorder.

There were sounds of chairs scraping, papers shuffling, and a garble of murmured conversation, so that the judge's empty chamber seemed to be crowded with invisible people. A female voice came from somewhere too close to the microphone. "This deposition is to be taken before Julia R. Kinnock, court stenographer at 501 North Spring Street, Los Angeles, California, at ten . . . seventeen A.M. on November third. The court's instructions were that if there is an objection to the use of a tape recorder, it will be turned off." There was silence. "Will the others in the room please identify themselves."

"David M. Schoenfeld, court-appointed counsel to Timothy Phillips." Schoenfeld's voice was smooth, and each syllable took too long to come out. Judge Kramer could almost see him leaning into the microphone to croon.

"Nina Coffey, Department of Children's Services, Los Angeles County, in the capacity of guardian for a minor person." Kramer had read her name on a number of official papers, but he had never heard her voice before. It was clear and unapologetic, the words quick and clipped, as though she were trying to guard against some kind of vulnerability.

"Kyle Ambrose, Assistant District Attorney, Los Angeles." As usual, the prosecutor sounded vaguely confused, a pose that had irritated Kramer through six or seven long trials.

Then came the low, monotone voices that were at once self-effacing and weighty, voices of men who had spent a lot of time talking over radios. They started quietly and grew louder, because the last part of each name was the important part.

"Lieutenant James E. Bates, Los Angeles Police Department."

"Agent Joseph Gould, Federal Bureau of Investigation."

There was some more shuffling of papers and then Julia Kinnock said, "Mr. Ambrose, do you wish to begin?"

Ambrose's parched, uncertain voice came in a beat late. "Will you state your name for the record, please?"

There was some throat clearing, and then the high, reedy voice of a young boy. "Tim . . . Timothy John Phillips."

Schoenfeld's courtroom voice intoned, "Perhaps it would be a good idea to ask that the record show that Lieutenant Bates and Agent Gould here present have verified that the deponent's fingerprints match those of Timothy John Phillips, taken prior to his disappearance."

The two voices muttered, "So verified," in the tone of a response in a church. Amen, thought Kramer. Schoenfeld had managed to sidestep onto the record with the one essential fact to be established in the case from Schoenfeld's point of view.

Ambrose's voice became slow and clear as he spoke to the boy. "You are to answer of your own accord. You are not to feel that you are in any way obligated to tell us things you don't want to." Judge Kramer could imagine Ambrose's dark eyes flicking to the faces of Schoenfeld, the lawyer, and Nina Coffey, the social worker. It was a confidence game, as Ambrose's legal work always was. The kid would have to answer all of the questions at some point, but Ambrose was trying to put the watchdogs to sleep. "Mr. Schoenfeld is here as your lawyer, so if you have any doubts, just ask him. And Mrs. Coffey will take you home if you're too tired. Do you understand?"

The small, high-pitched voice said, "Yes."

"How old are you?"

"Eight."

"Can you tell me, please, your earliest recollections?" Judge Kramer clenched his teeth.

"You mean, ever?"

"Yes."

"I remember . . . I guess I remember a lot of things. Christmas. Birthdays. I remember moving into our house in Washington."

"When was that?"

"I don't know."

A male voice interjected, "The lease on the Georgetown house began four years ago on January first. That was established during the murder investigation. He would have been four." The voice would be that of the F.B.I. agent, thought the judge.

"Do you remember anything before that, in another house?"

"No, I don't think so."

"When you moved in, was Miss Mona Turley already with you?"

"I don't know. I guess so."

"Who lived there?"

"My parents, me, Mona."

"Did you have relatives besides your parents? Cousins or uncles?"

"No, just my grandma."

"Did you ever see her?"

"Not that I remember. She lived far away. We used to send her a Christmas card every year."

"Did you?" There was the confusion again, as though Ambrose were hearing it for the first time and trying to fathom the implications.

"Yeah. I remember, because my daddy would put my handprint on it. He would write something, and then he would squish my hand onto a stamp pad and press it on the card, because I couldn't write yet."

Ambrose hesitated, then said gently, "Do you remember anybody else? Any other grown-ups that you were with?"

"You mean Mr. and Mrs. Phillips?"

"Yes."

"I know about them. I don't think I ever saw them."

"So when you say your 'parents' you mean Raymond and Emily Decker?"

"They were my mother and father."

Judge Kramer's brows knitted in distaste. This was typical of Ambrose. Get on with it, he thought. An eight-year-old's distant recollections weren't going to get Ambrose anything in a criminal investigation. Such meticulous, redundant questioning had bought him an inflated reputation as a prosecutor—laying the groundwork for an unshakable, brick-hard case. It looked like magic to juries, but to Judge Kramer and the opposing attorneys who knew where he was going, it was like watching an ant carrying single crumbs until he had a hero sandwich.

"So you lived in Washington from the time you were four until . . . ? We'll get back to that. Tell me what it was like in Washington. Did you like it?"

"It was okay."

"Were your parents . . . nice to you?"

There was a hint of shock in the boy's voice. "Sure."

"How about discipline? Rules. Were there rules?"

"Yeah."

"Can you tell me some?"

"Ummm . . . Pick up the toys. Brush your teeth. My father always brushed his teeth when I did, and then he'd show me his fillings and tell me I'd need some if I didn't brush the ones in the back."

"What happened when you didn't follow the rules?" Ambrose was casual. "Did they hit you?"

Now the little voice was scandalized. "No."

"Did you go to school?"

"Sure. The Morningside School. It wasn't far, so sometimes we walked."

"So life was pretty good in Washington?"

"Yeah."

"What did you do when you weren't in school?"

"I don't know. Mona used to take me to the park when I was little, and then later sometimes I'd go with my friends. She would sit in the car and wait for me."

Ambrose paused and seemed to be thinking for a long time, but then Judge Kramer recognized the sound of someone whispering. After a second exchange it sounded angry. He knew it was Nina Coffey. The lawyer Schoenfeld said, "I must point out that this is not an adversarial proceeding, and this part of the story adds no new information to any of the investigations in progress. Miss Coffey has consented to this questioning because she was assured its purpose was for the safety and future welfare of the child. She has a right to withdraw the consent of the Department of Children's Services if she feels this is unnecessarily traumatic. The child has been over this ground several times with the psychologist and the juvenile officers already. Perhaps we could depart from our regular habits of thoroughness and skip to the recent past."

Ambrose sounded defensive. "Then would one of you care to help us in that regard to make the record comprehensible?"

Nina Coffey said, "Timmy, tell me if anything I say isn't true."

"Okay."

"Timmy was raised from the time of his earliest recollections until the age of six by Raymond and Emily Decker. They hired Miss Mona Turley as a nanny when they came to Washington, D.C. He has no direct knowledge of earlier events. He was told he was Timmy Decker. From every assessment, he had a normal early childhood. It was a loving home. Miss Turley was a British citizen and a trained nanny, a legal resident alien. There are no signs of physical or psychological abuse, or of developmental difficulties that would indicate deprivation of any kind." She said pointedly, "This is all covered in the caseworker's report, so it already is part of the record."

Judge Kramer felt like applauding. His finger had been hovering over the FAST FWD button, but he knew that he wouldn't have let it strike. Either you listened to all of it or you were just another politician in a costume.

Ambrose went on. "All right. Now, Timmy, we have to talk about some unpleasant things, and I'll try to keep it short. What happened on the afternoon of July twenty-third two years ago?"

"I don't know."

Schoenfeld prompted. "That was the day when they died."

"Oh," said Timmy. "Mona and I went to the shoe store after school. Usually we came home at three, but that day we didn't. After we bought the shoes we walked in and everything had changed. I remember Mona opened the door, and then she stopped and went, 'Uh!' Like that. Then she made me wait outside while she went in alone. She was inside a long time. I thought it was a surprise, and she was telling my parents I was there so they could hide. So I went around to the side of the house and looked in the window. And I saw them." His voice cracked, and the judge could hear that he was trying to keep the sob from coming out of his throat in front of all these strange adults, so it just stayed there, with the muscles clamping it in place. Judge Kramer had heard a lot of testimony that had to be forced out through that kind of throat, so he had become expert.

"They were covered with blood. I never knew so much blood came out of a person. It was everywhere. The walls, the floor. I could see Mona was in the next room on the telephone. Then she hung up and walked into my bedroom. I ran around to that window, and it was broken. All my stuff was gone."

"What do you mean 'stuff'?"

"My toys, my clothes, my books, everything. They stole my stuff. She kept looking around my room and frowning."

"What then?"

"She looked up and saw me. She ran out of the house and grabbed me. She took me to the car and we drove away."

"What did she say about it?"

"She started to say that my parents were called away, but I told her I saw them."

"What did she say then?"

"She said that awful things sometimes happen, and a bunch of stuff about how they wanted me to be safe more than anything. I didn't hear a lot of it because I was crying and wasn't really listening."

"Where did she take you?"

"She had a friend. A man. He used to come to the house to pick her up sometimes. She said he was a lawyer. She took me to his house."

"For the record, do you know his name?"

"Dennis."

"Was his last name Morgan?"

"Yes."

"Do you know the name of the street?"

"No. It wasn't anyplace I ever was before. We drove a long time on a big road, and then at the end there were a lot of turns. By then it was night."

"What happened there?"

"She put me to sleep on the couch, but I could hear them talking in the kitchen."

"What did they say?"

"She told him about my parents. She said it looked like an abuttar."

Abattoir, the judge translated. No wonder Nina Coffey was all over Ambrose. This kid had looked in his own window and seen his parents—or the ones he knew as parents—lying on the floor butchered, and Ambrose was asking him about spankings and dental hygiene. The man was a dangerous idiot.

"What did he say?"

"He said she did the right thing to call the police, and the wrong thing to leave. Then she said a lot of things. She said it looked as though whoever came in wasn't even looking for them. They were looking for me."

"What made her say that?"

"They broke into my room at a time when I was usually home and my parents weren't. She said it looked like they tried to make my parents tell them something. And then the only things they took were my stuff, and all the pictures."

"What pictures were those?"

"My father used to take a lot of pictures. Like when we were at the beach . . ." Here it comes, thought the judge. The sob forced its way out, and there was a squealing sound, and then the tears came in volume.

"Come on, Timmy," said Nina Coffey. "Let's go take a break."

Amid the sounds of chairs scraping and feet hitting the floor, Ambrose said redundantly, "Let the record show that we recessed at this point."

There was another click, and the recording began again. "We will continue now. It is six minutes after eleven," said the stenographer.

Ambrose said, "Timmy, I'm sorry to ask so many sad questions."

"It's okay," said the little voice. There was no conviction behind it.

"You were at the lawyer's house. They didn't agree, right?"

"He told her to go to the police. Mona said they would just

make me stay in a place where I wouldn't be safe. They talked for a long time, and I fell asleep."

"What happened when you woke up?"

"The lawyer—Dennis—he was talking on the telephone. I couldn't hear what he was saying. When he hung up, he and Mona talked some more. He gave her some money. He had a lot of money inside of books on the bookshelf, and some in his pocket. He gave her that too."

"Then what?"

"The phone rang and Dennis answered it, and talked to somebody else. Then we all got in the car and Dennis drove. This time we drove all night and all the next day, almost. Then we got to Jane's house."

"What is Jane's full name?"

"I don't know."

"Where does she live?"

"I don't know."

"Tell me about her."

"We went to her house. She put us in a room upstairs, and we went to sleep. When I woke up, she made us breakfast. Mona was already awake."

"I mean about Jane. What was she like?"

"I was afraid of her at first."

"Why?"

"She was tall and skinny and had long black hair, and she seemed to listen to people with her eyes."

Ambrose paused. "I see. What did she do?"

"She and Mona talked for a long time. Then I heard her say she would make us disappear."

"Is that why you thought she was scary?"

"No . . . maybe."

"How long did you stay with Jane?"

"A long time. I think Mona said it was three weeks, but it seemed like a year. Then we all got in Jane's car and she drove us to Chicago."

"What did she do then?"

"She stayed for a day or two, and then one morning I woke up and she was gone."

"Was Mona surprised?"

"No. Mona acted like it was normal, and didn't talk about her again. Mona and I lived in Chicago after that. Mona was Diana Johnson, and I was her son. She wanted me to be Andrew, but I didn't like it, so I got to stay Tim."

"How did you live?"

"Like people do."

"I mean, did Mona have a job—did she go to work?"

"Yes. While I was in school."

"They called you Tim Johnson at school?"

"Yes."

"When did you start—what grade?"

"Kindergarten. I had already been in kindergarten, so it was the second time."

"And you're in the second grade now?"

"Yes."

"Were you afraid in Chicago?"

"At first I was. It was different. I was afraid the bad people would get Mona, and then I would be all alone. But after a while I made some friends, and got used to it, and I didn't think about that part much anymore. I was sad sometimes."

"And Mona pretended to be your mother for over two years?"

"I guess so."

"What else did she do? Did she still see anybody you knew from Washington?"

"No. She used to talk on the phone a lot."

"To whom? Jane?"

"No. Dennis."

"Did you ever hear what she said?"

"Once in a while, but it wasn't really okay. She would go in her bedroom and talk to him. Sometimes she would tell me what she said."

"Then a little over a week ago something changed, didn't it?"

"Yes. Everything."

"You found out who you were, didn't you?"

"Yes."

"Excuse me, Mr. Ambrose." It was Schoenfeld's resonant

voice again. "Maybe we should let Timmy tell us exactly what happened in his own words from here on. I believe you've done an admirable job in laying the groundwork, but now we're in new territory, and I have no objection to letting Mr. Phillips speak freely and tell us whatever he can that will aid in the possible prosecutions." Of course not, thought the judge. Schoenfeld could be magnanimous. He had already established that Timmy was Mr. Phillips, and nothing else that anyone said or did from there on was of any consequence for Schoenfeld.

"Thank you," said Ambrose. "Timmy, tell us what happened."

"I came home from school, and Mona was there, and so was Dennis the lawyer, and so was Jane. Dennis said he had spent two years trying to figure out why anyone would want to hurt my parents and me, and now he knew."

"This was in Chicago?"

"Yeah," said Timmy. "He told me that when my mother died they had special doctors look at her, and that she had never been to the hospital to have a baby. He said he got to look at a copy of the birth certificate they had at my school, and it wasn't real. He said I wasn't adopted. They just drew a picture of a birth certificate and said it was mine. He said that the reason they did that was because they loved me very much and had always wanted a little boy."

Judge Kramer stopped the tape and backed it up to listen to the last exchange again. It was a hell of a way to explain a kidnapping. In spite of everything, he had to admire Dennis Morgan. After what he had seen, this little boy was going to be an annuity for the psychiatrists for the next fifty years. There was no reason to make it worse.

The tape kept running. "Then he told you about your other parents?"

"Yes. Mr. and Mrs. Phillips. They died when I was one."

"And your grandma?"

"I knew about her already, but I didn't know she had died like all my parents. She had been dead for three years."

"Did Mr. Morgan tell you that she had left you some money?"

"Yeah. He said that when Mr. and Mrs. Phillips died she put all the family money in a big pot and said it could only go to me. And when I was gone she hired a company to take care of the money and keep looking for me forever."

"Did she say what they were called?"

"Trusty."

Judge Kramer prayed that Ambrose wasn't about to drag an eight-year-old on a field trip through a morass of legal terminology. What could the child possibly know about trustees and executors?

"What happened last week to change that? Did he tell you?"

"He said that the Trusty had gotten tired of looking and waiting, and they were going to say I wasn't alive anymore. So he called Jane again."

"I'm very curious about this Jane. I understand about Mona. She was your nanny, and she loved you. The lawyer, Mr. Morgan, was a very close friend of Mona's, right?"

"Yeah. They were going to get married when the people came and got my parents. Then they couldn't because we'd get caught. That was why he looked so hard to find out where I was really supposed to be—so Mona could go back to being Mona and marry him."

"But why was Jane doing it? Did she know your parents?"

"No. Mona had to tell her about them that time when we went to her house. Mona thought they worked for the government, so the people who hurt them must be spies. It took Jane a long time to find out that my parents didn't work for the government."

"Then Jane was Mona's friend?"

"I don't think so. Dennis was the one who called her."

Judge Kramer could imagine the F.B.I. agent. He was going to make his career sorting all this out. Not the least interesting question was why a prominent Washington defense attorney had the telephone number of a woman who made people disappear. They would be going over the record of Morgan's former clients right now to see if there were any on their Most Wanted List.

Even Ambrose seemed to sense that he had crossed the trail of an unfamiliar creature. "The lawyer knew her?" he repeated. "Did he pay her?"

"No. Dennis said he tried, but she had decided that so many people loved me that I must be a fine boy."

"Hmmmm . . ."

Judge Kramer had a vision of Ambrose's raised eyebrows, as he had seen them during cross-examinations.

"Did anybody say anything else about her?"

"Dennis. He said that from then on we had to do everything that Jane said, exactly. It didn't matter what anybody else said, we should listen to her."

"So she was the boss."

"He said that he had done everything he could to find out things, but the only way to solve this was to walk into court and surprise everybody and say who I was. He said the bad people knew I must be alive, so they would be expecting me to come. Jane was the one who knew how to get us past them."

"So you all took an airplane to California?"

"No. Jane said we had to drive all the way or the bad people might see us. Every day we got a new car. She would go to a place where they rented them, and then drive all day and then leave it and rent another one. Then we were in California."

"What then? Did you stay in a hotel?"

"No. Jane said that if people were after me, they would be watching hotels near the courthouse, because they would be expecting us to do that. So we went to the courthouse right away."

"What time was it?"

"About dinnertime. Jane opened the lock on an office and we stayed there all night. I fell asleep on a couch."

"What happened when you woke up?"

"I heard Dennis come into the office. He had been out in the building by himself. He said they had pulled a trick on us, and now we had to go to a different building. So we ran out and got into our car and drove again. Jane said on the way that it didn't feel right."

"Did she say anything else?"

"She asked Dennis if there was any way of doing this besides actually showing up in court. Could we call and ask for a delay or something. He said that he didn't know who was honest and who wasn't. A phone call wouldn't stop the case for sure, but it would tell the bad guys I was coming for sure. Then he said if they fooled the judge they could do something that day, right away. I don't know what. Jane drove for a long time without saying anything. Then she said, 'Is there any way to know what's in the building?' "

"What did she mean by that?"

"She said, 'We want to fade in. If Timmy's the only boy in the crowd, we're in trouble.' She said something about adoption and custody."

"I see," said Ambrose. "Did Mr. Morgan know the answer?"

"We stopped at a phone booth and he looked in the book and made a call. He came back and got into the car and made Jane scoot over, so he could drive. He said he and Mona would be getting a divorce before they got married, and Jane would carry his briefcase like she was their lawyer. But we would go to Courtroom 22 on the fifth floor instead."

"Did Jane agree?"

"At first. But then we got near the courthouse, and Jane said two men in a car were following us. They kept coming faster and faster, and then they tried to get in front of us, and they bumped the car."

"What did Mr. Morgan do?"

"He got all nervous, and kept trying to go fast and keep the car straight. Jane said to him, 'Well? What's it going to be?' and he said, 'I can't get them into the building. It's got to be me.' He was scared. He looked pale and sick and sweaty."

"And Jane?"

"She was quiet. He drove to the parking lot and stopped. Mona kissed him, and Jane yanked me out the door and we started running."

"Did you see what Mr. Morgan did after you were out of the car?"

"I heard this loud bang, and I turned around and it looked like what he had done was go backwards into the other car. One of the men jumped out and started hitting him. He tried to fight but he wasn't good at it. And the other man got out of the car and ran after us, so Dennis tried to tackle him, but the man kicked him, and the first one grabbed him around the neck. I didn't see any more because Jane and Mona and I were running and I tripped, but Jane held my hand and kept me from falling. We ran up the steps."

"Did anyone try to stop you?"

"There was a man on the other side of the glass door, and he saw us and put his foot against it so it wouldn't open. Jane didn't stop. She let go of me and hit it with her shoulder and stuck her purse in it when it opened a little. The man put his arm there to push the purse out, but as soon as his arm was in there she jerked the purse out by the strap and shut the door on his arm. When he pulled the handle to get his arm out, she pushed the door into his face and we ran on."

"Anybody else?"

"There were men right by the elevator, and they started coming toward us. We ran up the stairs. I counted four flights, but there was a door and it only had a two on it. We ran through it, and when we passed the elevator Jane pushed the button and ran to another staircase, and we got up to the third floor. We got to the fourth floor, and we heard a door below us slam open against the wall, and some men were running up after us. Mona was breathing hard and then she was crying too. She touched my arm at the top of the next landing and said, 'This is my stop. Keep going. I love you, Timmy.' "

"What did Jane say?"

"Nothing. She just looked at her, and then we ran up to the fifth floor. Just when we got to the top, I looked back and saw Mona on the stairs. She was holding on to both railings and kicking at these men. I saw one of them reaching out like he was trying to hug her. But right then, the door that said five swung open right in front of us. It was one of the men that was by the elevator. He looked surprised, and Jane just punched him and kept going."

"She hit him in the jaw?" The judge could sense Ambrose's raised eyebrow again.

"No. In the neck. Then we were on the fifth floor, and we ran down this long hallway. When we got to the corner I could see 'TWENTY TO THIRTY' painted on the wall with an arrow pointing to the left, but the door we had used to get there opened up again and three big men were running after us. Jane jerked me around the corner and said, 'Run to the room that says twenty-two. Don't stop for anybody until you're right in the front where the judge sits, and yell, "I'm Timothy Phillips." ' I tried to say something, but she said, 'Don't talk, just run.' "

Judge Kramer pushed the STOP button and sat in his dark office. He had been on the bench when the little boy had burst through the doors and run up the aisle screaming. The bailiff had made a reasonably competent attempt to head him off, but he had actually touched the bench and yelled, "I'm Tim Phillips." What had happened in the hallway Judge Kramer had heard from one of the policemen who had piled out of the adjoining courtrooms to quell the disturbance.

Judge Kramer pressed the intercom button on his telephone.

"Yes, Judge?" came his assistant's voice.

"Where are they holding this 'Jane' woman?"

"I think they took her for medical treatment to County-USC. I'll find out if she's in the jail ward and let you know."

"No," Kramer said. "Just call the precinct and tell them I want to see her."

"Would you like a conference room at the jail?"

"Have them bring her here."

The male police officer was tall and rangy, and the female was short and blond with her hair drawn up in the back and cinched in that way they all knew how to do. The department never had all-male teams transport a female prisoner anymore, so the judge should have been used to it, but the pairs still seemed to him like married couples from a planet where people wore uniforms. They ushered the prisoner into his chambers. When her face came into the light he felt his breath suck in. He had never gotten used to seeing a young woman's face with bruises and cuts and blackened eyes. He tried to see past them.

She was not quite what he had heard described on the tape. She was tall, as tall as he was if he stood up, and this realization made him intuit that it was better not to, so he stayed down behind his big desk. Her hair was black and hung loose to a place below her shoulder blades, but that probably wasn't the way she wore it; they had combed it out because they always searched women's hair. He could see that Timmy's description was not wrong, just uninformed. This woman had the strange, angular beauty he associated with fashion models: it was striking, but geometric and cold. The judge's taste ran more to women like his late wife and the little policewoman, who looked round and soft and warm. The woman's hands were cuffed in front of her instead of behind, which meant they weren't taking all the precautions, but the police officers were wary: the policewoman kept a hand at her left elbow, and the man was a step behind and to her right, leaving just enough room to swing his club.

Judge Kramer said, "Thank you very much, officers. We've got some coffee in the outer office, and I keep soft drinks in the little refrigerator under the water cooler. I'll be finished with the prisoner in about fifteen minutes."

The policewoman said, "Your Honor, we should mention—"

He interrupted, "I know. I spoke with the arresting officer. Has she hurt anyone since she's been in custody?"

"No."

"Then I'll chance it."

The prisoner held out her hands, and the male officer unlocked the cuffs, took them off, and said to no one in particular, "We'll be right outside."

When they had closed the door, Judge Kramer said to her, "Sit down, please."

The woman sat in the chair in front of the desk.

Judge Kramer probed for a way to break the silence. "I hear you're one of those people who could kill me with a pencil."

She said simply, "If I am, then I wouldn't need a pencil." She looked at the tape recorder on his desk. "Is that running?"

He said, "I want to assure you that no record will be made of this conversation. I just listened to a deposition of Timothy Phillips, and I decided that the only person left who can answer the questions I have is you. Mona Turley and Dennis Morgan are dead."

She nodded silently and watched him.

"What do you know about the child's situation?"

"Who are you? Why are you the one who has questions?"

His eyes widened involuntarily, as though someone had thrown a glass of water in his face. "I'm sorry," he said. "When you've been a judge for a few years, you're used to being the only one in the room everyone takes at face value. My name is John Kramer. I'm the judge who was presiding in Courtroom 22. We hadn't gotten to the petition to declare Timothy Phillips legally dead when he ran in and disrupted my court. For the moment, the matter is still undecided, and I've left it that way."

"Why?"

"First I had to recess while the officers took you away. Then I had to adjourn for a few days to give time to the authorities who can verify Timothy's claim. In a day or so, oddly enough, I have to set a date to give the petitioners the opportunity to refute the claim—fingerprints, blood tests, and all. Then I have to rule on it."

"Will you be the one who decides what happens to him after that?"

He shook his head. "Not directly. At the moment he's in the care of a very protective woman from Children's Services named Nina Coffey. After a time there will be criminal cases—probably several of them. There will be a family court case to decide who is granted guardianship of Timmy. There will be some sort of civil action to settle the disposition of the trust. I can influence the direction some of those cases take if I find out the truth and get it on the record so it can't be ignored. I'm asking what you know because I don't have much time and I need to know where to begin. Once I rule on the petition that's before me, it's out of my hands."

"Is any of this legal?"

"What I'm doing is so contrary to legal procedure that it has no name."

She sat erect in the chair and met his gaze steadily while she decided. "He was a ward of his grandmother because his parents were killed in a car crash. She was old at the time—about eighty. Whoever she hired to watch him didn't. Along came Raymond and Emily Decker, and he disappeared. I have no way of knowing what was going on in their minds at the time. They may have been kidnappers who stalked him from birth, or they may have been one of those half-crazy couples who create their own little world that doesn't need to incorporate all of the facts in front of their eyes. If you read the old newspaper reports, it sounds as though maybe they just found him wandering around alone in a remote area of a county park, picked him up, and then convinced themselves that he was better off with them than with anybody who let a two-year-old get that lost. I've tried to find out, and so did Mona and Dennis, but what we learned was full of contradictions."

"What sorts of contradictions?"

"Timmy says they sent pictures of him to his grandmother, sometimes holding a newspaper, sometimes with his fingerprints. He doesn't know what the letters said. If the Deckers knew where to send the letters, then they knew who he was. But I can't tell whether it was a straight ransom demand or they were trying to keep him officially alive so he could claim his inheritance when he grew up, or whether they were just being kind to an old lady by letting her know her grandson was okay."

"What do you know about the grandmother?"

"From what Dennis Morgan said, the police stopped looking. That means they never saw the letters. Grandma kept looking, so maybe she got them. She must have believed he would turn up eventually, because she tied up all the family money in a living trust for him and made a business-management firm named Hoffen-Bayne the trustee. She died a few years ago."

"Before or after Raymond and Emily Decker?"

"Before. But I'm not the best source for dates and addresses. I'm sure if you don't have it in the papers on your desk yet, it'll be in the next batch. Anyway, I don't think she hired somebody to kill them for kidnapping her grandson."

"You're the only source of information I have right now. Who did kill them?"

"I don't know."

"Who do you *think* did it?"

"When someone killed the Deckers, they also stole all of Timmy's belongings, every picture of him, and a lot of paper. If you're looking for somebody, you would want the photographs. But they took his toys, clothes, everything. That's a lot of work. The only reason I can think of for doing that is to hide the fact that he was alive—that a little boy lived there. Maybe they did such a good job of wiping off their own prints that they got all of his too, as a matter of course. I doubt it."

"Who would want to accomplish that?"

She hesitated, and he could tell she was preparing to be disbelieved. "What I'm telling you is not from personal knowledge. It's what Dennis Morgan told me. This company, Hoffen-Bayne, got to administer a fortune of something like a hundred million dollars. They would get a commission of at least two percent a year, or two million, for that. They also got to invest the money any way they pleased, and that gave them power. There are some fair-sized companies you can control for that kind of investment. As long as Timmy was lost, the trust would continue. You're a judge. You tell me what would happen if Timmy turned up in California."

"The court would—will—appoint a guardian, and probably in this case, a conservator, if you're right about the size of the inheritance."

"That wouldn't be Hoffen-Bayne?"

"We don't appoint business-management companies to raise children, or to audit themselves."

"Then the power and money would be in jeopardy."

"Certainly they would have to at least share the control."

"And they did try to have him declared dead."

"That's a legal convenience. It relieves them of responsibility to search for him, and also protects them if someone were to ask later why they're administering a trust for a client who hasn't been seen for seven years."

"Then it would have been even more convenient if he were really dead. They wouldn't have had to go to court at all."

"Filing a motion is a little different from hiring assassins to hunt down a six-year-old and kill him."

"Maybe. I think filing the motion was a trap. I think Dennis Morgan was poking around, and somebody noticed it. It's not all that hard to find out what you want about people; the trick is to keep them from knowing you're doing it. Dennis was a respected lawyer, but investigating wasn't his field; lawyers hire people to do that. I think they sensed that if a Washington attorney was interested, then Timmy was going to turn up sometime soon."

"And you—all of you—got caught in the trap?"

"Yes." She stood up. "You asked me what I think, so you would know where to begin. I've told you. Dennis couldn't find anybody but Hoffen-Bayne who would benefit from Timmy's death—no competing claims to the money or angry relatives, for instance. Nobody tried to break the will during all the years while Timmy was missing. But I don't know what Dennis got right and what he got wrong, and I can't prove any of it. I only saw the police putting handcuffs on four of the men in the courthouse, and there won't be anything on paper that connects them with Hoffen-Bayne or anybody else. I know I never saw them before, so I can't have been the one they recognized. They saw Timmy." She took a step toward the door. "Keep him safe."

The judge said, "Then there's you." He watched her stop and face him. "Who are you?"

"Jane Whitefield."

"I mean what's your interest in this?"

"Dennis Morgan asked me to keep Timmy alive. I did that. We all did that."

"What are you? A private detective, a bodyguard?"

"I'm a guide."

"What kind of guide?"

"I show people how to go from places where someone is trying to kill them to other places where nobody is."

"What sort of pay do you get for this?"

"Sometimes they give me presents. I declare the presents on my income taxes. There's a line for that."

"Did somebody give you a present for this job?"

"If you fail, there's nobody around to be grateful. My clients are dead." After a second she added, "I don't take money from kids, even rich kids."

"Have you served in your capacity as 'guide' for Dennis Morgan before?"

"Never met him until he called. He was a friend of a friend."

"You—all three of you—went into this knowing that whoever was near this little boy might be murdered."

She looked at him as though she were trying to decide whether he was intelligent or not. Finally, she said, "An innocent little boy is going to die. You're either somebody who will help him or somebody who won't. For the rest of your life you'll be somebody who did help him or somebody who didn't."

The judge stared down at his desk for a few seconds, his face obscured by the deep shadows. When he looked up, his jaw was tight. "You are a criminal. The system hates people like you. It has special teeth designed to grind you up."

As she watched him, she could see his face begin to set like a death mask. He pressed his intercom button. "Tell the officers to come in." He began to write, filling in lines on a form on his desk.

The two police officers swung the door open quickly and walked inside. The man had his right hand resting comfortably on the handle of the club in his belt.

The judge said, "I've finally straightened this out. Her real name is Mahoney. Colleen Anne Mahoney. She was attacked by those suspects on the way into the courthouse. Apparently it was a case of mistaken identity, because she had no connection with the Phillips case. I'm giving you a release order now, and I want all records—prints, photographs, and so on—sealed ... no, destroyed. Call me when it's been done." He handed the female officer the paper. "I want to avoid any possibility of reprisals."

"Will do, Judge," said the policewoman. Kramer's instinct about her was confirmed. She had a cute little smile.

The policeman opened the door for Jane Whitefield, but this time nobody touched her. She didn't move. "You should have those teeth checked."

He shrugged. "The system was never meant to rule on every human action. Some things slip through."

She stared at him for a second, then said simply and without irony, "Thank you, Your Honor," turned, and walked out of his office.

2

Jane Whitefield drove her rental car down Fairfax past
the high school, the old delicatessens and small grocery stores and
the shops that sold single items like luggage or lamps, beyond the
big white CBS buildings and then into the hot asphalt parking lot
at Farmers' Market, where she found refuge from the Southern
California sun in the cool shadow between two tour buses. The
market was crowded on Saturdays, and it took her a few minutes
of threading her way among the hundreds of preoccupied people
to find the pet store. There were two glass enclosures out front
where puppies lay sleeping with their smooth little potbellies in
the air.

She bought two cubical birdcages that had one side that could
be opened for cleaning, and a two-pound bag of bird feed that was
peppered with sunflower seeds. She walked across the market to a
craft store where people bought kits for making bead jewelry. She
drove out of the market and headed northward toward the hills,
but then stopped only a few blocks up when she saw a secondhand

store that looked as though it might have the right kind of teddy bear. Then she drove the winding road over Laurel Canyon to the San Fernando Valley, and on across the flats to the campus of the California State University at Northridge. She had been past the school once years ago, and carried a picture of it in her mind. It was the right kind of habitat.

Jane had not done this in years, but she was very good at it. She drove around the nearly empty campus until she found a long drive with a row of tall eucalyptus trees beside it and a few acres of model orchard beyond them. She parked her car in the small faculty parking lot behind some kind of science building and carried her cages to the eucalyptus trees. Nearly everyone on campus seemed to be in a library or dormitory, so she had the luxury of silence while she worked.

She propped open the sides of the cages with sticks that had fallen from the trees, took the food cups from their slots on the bars and filled them with bird feed, then ran thin jewelry wire from the cups to the sticks. She balanced a stone on the open wall of each cage so it would come down fast and stay shut. She sprinkled a handful of bird feed over the carpet of fallen eucalyptus leaves in front of the cages, and went for a walk. She used her sense of the geography of university campuses to find the Student Union, and sat at a table in the shade of a big umbrella at the edge of a terrace to drink a cup of lemonade.

Even at this time of year, Southern California seemed to her to be parched and inhospitable. The broad lawns in public places like this were still a little yellow and sparse from the eight-month-long summer, with its hundred-degree stretches. Back home people would be telling each other stories about years they remembered when the snow didn't stop until May, and wondering if this would be another one. When her lemonade was finished she walked back across the campus to the row of eucalyptus trees. Before she turned the corner of the science building she heard a squawk, and then some fluttering, and she thought about the difference between birds and human beings. No matter how many times it had been done, each new generation of birds flew into the trap as though it had never before happened on earth. Maybe they weren't so different.

She approached the traps, but they didn't look the way she had expected. One of them was just as she had left it, and the other one had two big blue scrub jays in it together. When she moved closer she could see that one was a male and the other female, slightly smaller with more brown on top and less blue. As she stepped to the cage, the questions began. *"Jree?"* asked the male. *"Jree?"* The female scolded, *"Check check check!"*

They weren't like the birds at home, but they were quick and greedy for survival, so territorial and aggressive that they had probably crowded in together without hesitation. It was too late in the year for them to be feeding hatchlings, and having one of each seemed right. They were already mated.

She poured in some more seed to give them something to think about, lifted the cage, put it in the back seat of the car, and covered it with a silk blouse from her suitcase.

Jane drove to the county office building and wiped her face clean of the thick makeup she had been using to hide the bruises, then walked to the Department of Children's Services. The people in the office were busy in a way that showed they had given up hope of ever doing all they were supposed to do but were keeping on in the belief that if they worked hard enough they would accomplish some part of it. There were two empty desks for each one that had a person behind it, so they moved from one to another picking up telephones and slipping files in and out of the piles like workers tending machines in a factory. She waited for a minute, then saw a woman hang up her telephone and pause to make a note in a file.

Jane stepped forward. "Excuse me," she said. "I need to leave something for Nina Coffey."

The woman's eyes rolled up over the rim of her glasses and settled on Jane; her head, which was still bent over the papers on the desk, never moved. Jane could tell that her bruises had identified her as an abused mother. "How can I help you?"

"It's this teddy bear," said Jane. "Timmy Phillips left it in my car."

The woman showed no recognition of the name. She snatched a gummed sticker out of the top drawer and put her pen to it. "Spell it," she said.

"P-H-I-L-L-I-P-S. I'd appreciate it if you got it to her, because it's important to Timmy." Jane handed the woman the small, worn brown teddy bear.

The woman turned her sharp gaze through the glasses at the bear. "I can see that," she said. "Don't worry. I'll give it to her."

"Thanks," said Jane warmly.

The telephone rang and the woman held up one finger to signal that Jane was to wait while she answered it, but Jane turned away. She heard the woman call, "Mrs. Phillips?" but she was out the door.

Jane waited down the street from the parking garage. She had seen the row where the employees' parking spaces were, and now she parked at the curb where she could watch them.

It was not long before she saw the woman she had been waiting for. Nina Coffey was in her forties and very slight with red hair that was fading into a gray that muted it. Jane saw that she had the habit of holding her keys in one fist when she came out of the elevator, so she suspected that this was a woman whose profession had given her a clear-eyed view of the planet she was living on. In her other hand she held a hard-sided briefcase and a teddy bear.

Jane waited for her to start her car, drive to the exit, and move off down the street before she pulled her own car out from among the others along the block. She followed Nina Coffey at a distance, and strung two other cars between them so she wouldn't get too accustomed to the sight of Jane's. Coffey turned expertly a couple of times, popped around a corner and then up onto a freeway ramp, and Jane was glad she had put the other cars between them so that she had time to follow in the unfamiliar city.

She pushed into the traffic and over to the same lane that Coffey chose and stayed there, letting a couple of other cars slip in between them again. Coffey turned off the freeway in a hilly area that the signs said was in Pasadena, and Jane had to move closer. There seemed to be stoplights at every intersection, and Nina Coffey was an aggressive driver who had a knack for timing them. After the third one, Jane had to stop while Coffey diminished into the distance. She turned right, then left, then sped up five blocks of residential streets that had no lights, turned left, then right again to come out three blocks behind her.

Finally Nina Coffey came to a street where she had to wait to make a left turn, and Jane caught up with her again. When Coffey stopped in front of a modest two-story house with a brick facade, Jane kept going. As she passed, she studied the car that blocked the driveway and knew it was the right house. The car was a full-sized Chevrolet painted a blue as monotonous as a police uniform.

The authorities had done exactly as Jane had hoped they would. They were protecting Timmy from everybody, without distinction—the people who wanted him declared dead, the reporters, people who were sure to search the family tree to suddenly discover they were relatives—and without comment. They had put Timmy in the home of a cop while the mess around him was sorted out.

She spent fifteen minutes driving around the neighborhood to look for signs that anyone else had found the house. She saw no parked cars with heads in them, no nearby houses with too many blinds drawn, and no male pedestrians between twenty and fifty. She came back out on Colorado Boulevard satisfied and drove up two streets before she found the place where she wanted to park her car.

She had to climb over the fence at the back of the yard and crouch in the little cinderblock enclosure where the pool motor droned away and stare in the back window until she saw Timmy. She watched him eat his dinner in the kitchen with two other children, and then begin to climb the carpeted stairway to the second floor. Upstairs, a light went on for a few minutes and then went out. The other children weren't much older than Timmy was but they were still downstairs. She supposed he was still living on Chicago time, where it was two hours later.

The sun was low when Jane decided how she would do it. She walked quietly to the back of the house. In a moment she was up the fig tree and on the roof of the garage. She walked across it to a second-floor window of the house, tied a length of the jewelry wire into a loop, inserted it between the window and the sill, and slowly twirled it until she had it around the latch. She gave a sharp tug to open the latch, quietly slid the window up, and slipped into the upstairs hallway.

When she opened the bedroom door Timmy was lying on his

side looking at her, his coffee-with-cream eyes reflecting a glint of the light coming from the hallway, his child-blond hair already in unruly tufts from burrowing into the pillow. Somebody had bought him a new pair of pajamas with pictures of fighter planes in a dogfight all over them, and had at least looked at him closely enough to be sure they fit his long legs. He held the teddy bear on the sheet beside him. "Jane?" he said.

"Hello, Timmy," she whispered. "Can't sleep?"

"I'm tired, but it's still light, and I keep thinking about them. Mona and Dennis."

"I thought you might want to go to their funeral."

"I did want to, but they said I couldn't."

"So we'll have our own."

The shadows of the trees at the edge of the vast cemetery were already merging into the dusk, but the sky to the west had a reddish glow. Jane had sent two big displays of white roses in case she and Timmy arrived after dark, but the flowers weren't necessary. It was still light enough to find the two fresh graves on the hillside.

The bodies of Dennis and Mona would be shipped to London and Washington for burial, but Jane had searched the funeral notices in the newspaper and found a pair of brothers who had been killed in a car accident and had been buried today. As they walked up the hill Timmy said, "What are we going to do?"

Jane shrugged. "We can only do what we know. The kind of funeral I know best is the kind my family did for my father, my mother, and my grandparents."

They stopped at the head of the graves. Jane said, "One thing we always did was to have close friends or relatives say something to them."

"How?"

"Just talk to them."

Timmy looked down at the two mounds of dirt for a moment, then said, "I don't know what to say."

"Then I'll go first," Jane said. "Dennis and Mona? We're here to say goodbye to you, and to tell you that there are people who know and understand who you were and what you did. We saw it. You spent your lives protecting and caring for people who needed help: little children, and people who were going to court and didn't have anybody to speak for them. You died fighting enemies you knew were bigger and stronger, trying to give us time. We're here because we want you to see that we're okay. You won." She nudged Timmy. "Ready to say something?"

Timmy said, "Mona, I'll . . . I'll miss you. It's lonely here. I didn't know you weren't coming back. I would have said something . . ." His voice trailed off.

"What would you have said?" asked Jane.

"I . . . guess . . . 'I love you.' "

"That's good."

"And I would have thanked her. But I can't now. It's too late."

"You just did," said Jane. "Those are the two things that had to be said."

Jane knelt on the grass and used her hands to dig a hole in the soft mound of earth over the first grave. Then she reached into her purse.

"What are you doing now?"

"Well, the Old People believed that after somebody died, he had to make a long trip to a place where he would be happy all the time. They figured it took a long time to get there, so they tried to give him presents that would make the trip easier. Weapons, food, that kind of thing."

She held up a new Mont Blanc fountain pen and said, "This is like the one Dennis carried in his briefcase, but the police have that. We'll let it stand for the weapon." She pulled out a credit card and put it beside the pen. "This is the way people travel now."

At the other grave she dug a second hole and placed a credit card and four granola bars in the bottom.

"What's that?" asked Timmy.

"Mona wasn't the sort of person who thought much of weapons. She loved to feed people, so she would like this better." Jane stood and brushed the dirt off her hands. "Now cover them up."

As Timmy worked to pack the dirt over the little holes, Jane went to the car and brought back the birdcage.

"What's in there?"

She took the blouse off the cage and the scrub jays glared around them suspiciously, the white streaks above their shining black eyes looking like raised eyebrows.

"Birds!" said Timmy.

"The Old People did this, so maybe it works." She spoke to the birds. "Mr. and Mrs. Bird, we have the souls here of two very brave and noble people. They had a lot of reasons why they must have wanted to run away from danger, because they loved each other very much, just like you do. But they did the hard thing instead. I want you to carry them up to Hawenneyugeh. Will you do it?"

The birds jumped back and forth on the perches calling *"Check-check-check,"* uneasy about the low level of the sun.

Jane said, "Mona, it's time to go. Have a short trip. You did your work well. You were a wonderful woman." She grasped the female scrub jay gently, holding her on her back and stroking her breast feathers as she stood over the grave, then tossed her into the sky. She fluttered about and then flew fifty feet to light on a limb of a magnolia tree.

Jane reached into the cage again and caught the male. "Dennis," she said, "you were a great fighter. Now I wish you peace. Mona is waiting."

The scrub jay flew up and joined the female on the branch of the magnolia. They looked down at Jane and Timmy for a few seconds as though they wanted to be sure there was no plan afoot to molest them further, then flew off to the west toward either the setting sun or the college campus.

"Goodbye," said Timmy. He waved as the birds flew, and kept waving long after they were invisible.

"Ready to go now?"

"I guess so."

They walked back to the car in silence, got inside, and coasted down the hill and out of the cemetery.

"Do you think they heard us?" asked Timmy.

"There's no way to know," said Jane. "The Old People will tell you that they do. What I think is that it doesn't really matter. Funerals aren't for the dead."

"They're not?"

"They're for us, the ones who have to go on."

"You did all this for me, didn't you?"

"For you and for me." She drove on for a few seconds, then admitted, "But mostly for you. For somebody your age you've seen a lot of heartache. Some of it you don't remember already, but you'll remember this. I wanted to be sure you remember it right."

"What should I remember?"

"That you got to live when there were still heroes. Real heroes that feel scared and bleed, and that's the part that gets left out of the books. That's a privilege. Nobody has to read you a story. You saw it."

"I wish they hadn't done it," said Timmy.

"Me too."

Timmy started to cry. At first it was just a welling of tears, but Jane knew the rest of the tears that he had been too exhausted to cry were behind them. She drove to the freeway and kept going beyond Pasadena into bare and unfamiliar hills. After half an hour Timmy stopped crying, and Jane drove until he spoke again. "What's going to happen? They're all gone."

"You don't have to worry about that, because some very smart people are spending all their time taking care of it. Judge Kramer said the court would study your story, learn all they can about you, and appoint somebody to take care of you."

"Will it be you?"

"No," she said. "It will be a family. Somebody like the people you're staying with now. Are they nice?"

"Yes," he said.

Jane let out a breath before she realized she had been holding it. "Well, I've got to get you back there so you can get some sleep."

"Will I see you?"

"Probably not for a long time."

She drove back to Pasadena and parked behind the street where the policeman and his family lived. She climbed to the top of the fence, lifted Timmy and lowered him to the lawn. She could see that the other two children were still watching television downstairs. She led him to the tree, hoisted him to her back, and climbed. When they walked to the open window, Timmy was seized with a panic. "I don't want you to leave."

"I have to, Timmy," she said.

"But what am I going to do? I mean after you're gone."

Jane hesitated, then accepted the fact that she had to try. "Go to school. Make friends. Play games. Try to grow up strong and decent and healthy. That's plenty to do for now." She helped him in the window and sat on his bed while he put on his pajamas.

"But what happens after that? What will I be then?"

"I think that's why it takes so much time to grow up. You don't really make a decision; you just find out when the time comes."

"What would you do?"

Jane shook her head and smiled sadly. "I'm not a good one to ask."

"Who is?"

Jane had an urge to tell him everything she knew, because this would be the last time. No words came into her mind that were of any use, but she had to push him in the right direction. "Well, when I was in college I knew a boy who was in a position sort of like yours. He didn't know what to do, but he knew that if he wasn't careful, he would be lazy and wasteful and selfish."

"What did he decide?"

"He decided to become a doctor. It was the hardest thing he could think of to be, so he knew that would force him to study. And when he had done enough studying, he would know how to do something worthwhile. At the time I thought he was being very sensible. I still can't find anything wrong with the idea."

"Is he a doctor now?"

"As it happens, he is, but that isn't the point. The real reward was that he got to be the kind of person he wanted to be. It doesn't matter whether he ended up a doctor or something else. He had decided to try. That made him special."

There were noises. She heard the first complaints from little voices downstairs. The children were being sent to bed.

"I've got to go now or I'll get caught," she said. She leaned down and kissed his cheek. "Sleep well, Timmy. Remember that people have loved you before and others will love you again, because you're worth it."

As she slipped out the window she heard a whisper. "Jane?"

"Yes?" She stopped and leaned on the sill.

"Thanks for the bear. I knew it was from you."

"I thought you would."

"Are you one of the people? The ones who love me?"

"Of course I am."

"Will you marry me?"

"Sure."

She drifted across the garage roof like a shadow, and seemed to Timmy to fly down the tree without moving a leaf. He watched the back fence, but even in the light of the moon he didn't see her go over it. After listening for a few minutes, he fell asleep.

3

J ane returned the car to the airport rental lot and caught the shuttle bus to the terminal. As she stepped off, she smiled perfunctorily at the efficient skycap offering to check her luggage through to her destination and shook her head. She didn't have luggage and she didn't have a destination. She had made a stop at a Salvation Army office on the way to the airport and disposed of the clothes that had remained in her suitcase that weren't torn or bloodstained, and then had donated the suitcase too. She had known that she would never wear any of the clothes again because they would have reminded her of all that had happened.

She had spent her three days in the county jail ruminating on failure, and her nights remembering the faces of dead people. She should have been quick-witted enough to save Mona and Dennis. There had to be some better way to stop a court case. If nothing else had come to mind, she should have called in a bomb threat to make the police evacuate the courthouse, then arrived during the confusion and attached Timmy and Mona to a squad of policemen. She had not thought clearly because she was so busy trying to get Timmy to the building on time; she had not seen the ambush because she was too busy dragging her clients into it.

In the nighttime, after a day of reliving her failure in her mind, gripped by the shock over and over again as each of her mistakes was repeated, old ghosts crept into her cell. The one she knew best was Harry the gambler. She had hidden him, then made the mistake of believing that the man who had been his friend would not also be his killer. Harry had visited her so often over the years that he had almost become part of her.

One of the ghosts was a man she had never met. She kept remembering the newspaper picture of John Doe. The police artists had needed to touch it up so much that it was more a reconstruction than a photograph. A cop had found him three years ago sprawled among the rocks below River Road. He had five thousand dollars in cash sewn into his suit, a pair of eyeglasses with clear glass lenses, a brand-new hairpiece that didn't match his own hair, and three bullet holes in his head. Jane had watched the newspapers for months, but the police had never learned who he had been or why he was running. Maybe he had not been trying to reach her; perhaps he was just heading for the Canadian border. But his death within a few miles of her house still haunted her.

On the third day in jail, one of the ghosts came to life. The guards had let Jane out into the exercise yard with the other prisoners and she had seen Ellery Robinson. Years ago Jane had taken Ellery Robinson's sister Clarice out of the world to escape a boyfriend who was working his way up to killing her. Jane could remember Ellery's eyes when she had tried to talk her into disappearing with her sister. Ellery had said, "No, thank you. He's got nothing to do with me." For the next few years Jane had often thought about those clear, innocent eyes. Ellery had waited a couple of days while Jane got Clarice far away, then killed the boyfriend. Later Jane had made quiet inquiries for Clarice and learned that Ellery's life sentence meant she would serve four to six years.

After the six years, Jane had kept the memory quiet by imagining Ellery Robinson out of the state prison and living a tolerable life. But here she was, back in county jail. In that moment ten or twelve years ago when Jane had not thought of the right argument, not said the right words, not read the look in those eyes, Ellery Robinson's life had slipped away. Jane looked at her once across the vast, hot blacktop yard, but if Ellery Robinson recognized her, no hint of it reached her face. After that, Jane had not gone out to the yard again. Instead she had sat on her bunk and thought about Timothy Phillips.

As she stepped into the airport terminal she had a sudden, hollow feeling in her stomach. She still had not freed herself of the urge to take Timmy with her. She had recognized the madness of the idea as soon as she had formulated it. The whole purpose of this trip had been to bring Timmy under the protection of the authorities. They weren't going to let him disappear again easily. Even if she succeeded in getting him away, it might be exactly the wrong thing to do. It might make her feel as though she had not abandoned him, but Timmy would lose all that money, and with it, the protection. Maybe in ten years he would hate her for it—if he lived ten years. Jane had not even been good enough to keep Mona and Dennis alive. No, Timmy was better off where he was, with the cops and judges and social workers. She was tired, beaten. It was time to go home, stop interfering, and give the world a vacation from Jane Whitefield.

She walked to the counter and bought a ticket for New York City because it was the right direction and there were so many flights that she didn't expect to have to wait long to get moving again. She used a credit card that said Margaret Cerillo. As the man at the counter finished clicking the keys of the computer and waited for the machine to print out the ticket, she noticed his eyes come up, rest on Jane's face for an instant, and then move away too fast. Jane explained, "I had a little car accident yesterday. Some idiot took a wide left turn on La Cienega and plowed right into me." The last time she had looked, the makeup had covered her injuries well enough, but with the heat and the hurry, the scrapes and bruises must be showing through.

"It must have been . . . painful," said the man.

"Pretty bad," said Jane. She took the ticket and credit card and walked up the escalator and through the row of metal detectors. She kept going along the concourse until she found an airport shop that had a big display of cosmetics. She selected an opaque foundation that matched her skin tone and some powder and eye shadow. When she caught a glimpse of herself in the mirror at the top of a revolving display, she reached below it and picked out a pair of sunglasses with brown-tinted lenses. Then she took her purchases with her into the ladies' room. Her face was still hot and tender from the punches she had taken, and her right hand was aching from the hard blows she had given the men in the hallway, but a little discomfort was better than being noticed.

She looked under the stalls and found she was alone. She was glad, because she wouldn't have to pretend that what she was doing was easy. She leaned close to the mirror and dabbed on the foundation painfully. The result looked tolerable, but it stung for a few seconds. She stopped until the pain subsided a little, and had just begun to work on her eyes when she heard the door open and a pair of high heels cross the floor behind her. She had a pretty vivid black eye from the big guy with the yellow tie who had piled in at the end. It was hard to cover it and make both eyes look the same with a hand that hurt.

"Can I help you with that?"

Jane didn't turn around, just moved her head a little to verify what she guessed about the woman behind her in the mirror. She wasn't surprised that the woman was attractive. Makeup was a personal issue—not quite a secret, but almost—and you had to be pretty spectacular to have the nerve to tell somebody you could do her makeup better than she could. This one was tall—almost as tall as Jane—and almost as thin, but her face had that blushing china-figurine skin that women like her somehow kept into their forties. They were always blond, or became blond, like this one. Every last one of them had switched to tennis after their cheerleading coaches had put them out to pasture, but they must have played it at night, because their skin looked as though it had never seen sunlight.

Jane said, "No, thanks. I can handle the painting. It's the repairs that are hard."

"You don't remember me, do you?" There was tension in the voice.

"No," said Jane. "If I should, then you must be good at this. Maybe I should let you do my makeup after all."

The woman whispered, "I was in the county jail when you were."

Jane turned to look at the woman more closely, this time with a sense that she ought to be watching her hands, not her face. "Well, congratulations on getting out."

Jane waited for her to leave, but the woman just smiled nervously and waited too. "Thanks."

Jane decided that she could do the finishing touches in another ladies' room or even on the plane. "Well, I've got a plane to catch."

"No, you don't. It doesn't leave for an hour. Four-nineteen to New York. I'm on it too. My name is Mary Perkins."

"Are you following me?"

"I was hoping to do better than that."

"What do you mean?"

"There's not much to talk about when you're in jail. There was a girl who had been in court when you were arrested. There was a rumor you had hidden somebody. That sounded interesting, so I asked around to find somebody who could introduce us, but sure enough, all of a sudden they were letting you go under another name. How you managed that I don't want to know."

"You don't?"

"No. I want you to do it for me."

"Why?"

"When I got arrested there were some men following me. That was thirty days ago. I just saw two of them here."

"Why do they want you?"

The woman gave her a look that was at once pleading and frustrated. "Please, I don't have time to tell you my life story and you don't have time to listen to it right now. I have to get out of Los Angeles now—today—only they're already here, and it can't be a coincidence. They're looking for me."

"But who are you?"

"The short answer is that I'm a woman who needs to disappear and has the money to pay whatever it is you usually get for your services."

Jane felt exhausted and defeated. Her head, face, hands, and wrists were throbbing and weak. She looked at the woman who called herself Mary Perkins, and the sight of her face made Jane tired. She had said almost nothing, but Jane was already picking up signs in her eyes and mouth that she had lied about something. She was genuinely afraid, so she probably wasn't just some sort of bait placed in the airport by the people Jane had fought outside the courtroom. But if men were following her at all, they were undoubtedly policemen. Jane thought, No. Not now. I'm not up to this. Aloud, she said, "Sorry."

"Please," said the woman. "How much do you want?"

"Nothing. You have the wrong person. Mistaken identity."

Mary Perkins looked into Jane's eyes, and Jane could see that she was remembering that Jane was injured. "Oh," the woman said softly. "I understand." She turned and walked toward the door.

As she opened the door, Jane said, "Good luck." Mary Perkins didn't seem to hear her.

Jane looked at her face in the mirror. The bruises were covered, but the thick makeup felt like a mask. When she put the glasses on, they reminded her that the side of her nose had been scraped by the buttons on the big guy's sleeve when he missed with the first swing.

She walked out to the concourse and strolled along it with the crowds until she was near Gate 72. She saw the woman sitting there pretending to read a magazine. If she was being hunted, it was a stupid thing to do. Jane walked closer to the television set where they posted flight information. Mary Perkins's eyes focused on Jane, and then flicked to her left. Jane appreciated not being stared at, but then the eyes came back to her, widened emphatically, and flicked again to the left. Jane stopped for a moment, opened her purse, turned her head a little as though she were looking for something and studied the two men to Mary Perkins's left. If they were hunters they were doing a fairly good job of keeping Mary Perkins penned in and panicky. The short one was sitting quietly reading a newspaper about fifty feet from Mary Perkins, and the big one was pretending to look out the big window at the activity on the dark runway. She could see he was watching the reflection instead, but that wasn't unusual. Her eyes moved down to the briefcase at his feet. It was familiar, the kind they sold in the gift shop where she had bought the makeup.

The smaller man had no carry-on luggage. He sat quietly with his newspaper, not looking directly at Mary Perkins. He had to be the cut-off man, the one she wasn't supposed to notice at all until the other man came for her and she bolted. They couldn't be cops, or they would already have her. She had already bought her ticket, and a plane ticket was proof of intent to flee.

Jane felt spent and hopeless. She admitted to herself that if she got home safely she would find herself tomorrow going to a newsstand and picking up a *Los Angeles Times* and the New York papers to look for a story about a woman's body being found in a field. These two were going to follow Mary Perkins until, inevitably, she found herself alone.

Jane walked back down the concourse, raising her eyes to look at the television monitors where the departing flights were posted, never raising her head and never slowing down. By the time she had passed the third monitor she had made her selection. There was a Southwestern Airlines flight leaving for Las Vegas five minutes after the flight to New York. She went down the escalator, walked to the ticket counter and paid cash for two tickets to Las Vegas for Monica Weissman and Betty Weissman. Then she returned to the gate where Mary Perkins was waiting. She sat down a few seats from her, counted to five hundred, then stood up again.

She walked close to Mary Perkins on the way to the ladies' room. As she did, she waggled her hand behind her back, away from the two watchers.

She waited inside the ladies' room in front of the mirror until Mary Perkins came in. "Did you check any luggage onto the plane for New York?"

"I don't have any," said Mary Perkins. "As soon as I got out I came here."

"Good," said Jane. "When we get out of here, stay close but don't look at me. You never saw me before. One of those guys will be standing between you and the exits. The other one will have moved to a place where he can see his buddy signal him." She handed Mary Perkins the ticket for Las Vegas.

She looked down at the ticket. "Las Vegas? How does this change anything?"

"Just listen. When it's time to board, one of them will go to a telephone to tell somebody at the other end that you're on the plane. It's a five-hour flight with a stop in Chicago, and that gives them time to do everything but dig your grave before we get there. The other will sit tight until the last minute."

"But what are we going to do? What's the plan?"

Jane looked at her wearily. "The plan is to go to Las Vegas and make them think you've gone to New York. Now give me about the time it takes to sing the national anthem before you come out. Then go sit where you sat before."

Jane swung the door open. Instead of looking toward the waiting area, she glanced behind her for the one watching the exit. The man with the paper was loitering a few yards away at the water fountain. She turned and saw that the other one had taken a seat where he could watch his friend. There was a certain comfort in seeing that they were predictable.

Jane sat a few yards behind the man with the briefcase and studied him. He couldn't be armed with anything worse than a pocketknife. Three inches or less, if she remembered the regulation correctly. They weren't going to do anything in an airport anyway. People you didn't know wouldn't commit suicide to kill you. These were hired help for somebody.

The woman at the boarding desk was joined by a second woman, who said something to her. Then the one who had given Jane her boarding pass picked up a microphone and cooed into it, "Flight 419 for New York is now ready for boarding." People all over the waiting area stood up. "Will those passengers with small children, or who need help boarding, please come to the gate now. . . ."

That invitation seemed to apply to no one, so as the woman went on—"Passengers in rows one through ten may board now"— the taller man walked to the row of telephones beside the men's room.

Mary Perkins stirred, but Jane gave her head a little shake and picked up a newspaper someone had left on a seat near her. The woman went on calling out rows of seats, then said, "Passengers in the remaining seats may board now." Still Jane sat and stared at the newspaper. There were four minutes left. When there were three minutes, she closed the newspaper and began to walk toward the gate.

In her peripheral vision she saw Mary Perkins stand up and follow, then saw the taller man hurriedly punch some numbers into the telephone. Jane stopped to glance up at the clock on the wall, and saw the smaller man walking along behind Mary Perkins. The man at the telephone had hung up, and he walked straight to the gate, handed the woman his ticket, and entered the tunnel. Jane walked a few feet past the last set of seats in the waiting area slowly, letting Mary Perkins catch up with her. At the last second, she turned to her.

"Why, Mary," she said. "It *is* you."

Mary Perkins stopped and stared at her in genuine shock. "Well . . . yes."

"You don't remember me, do you?"

The man who had been following Mary Perkins stopped too, standing almost behind them. Jane seemed to notice him for the first time. "Oh, don't mind us. Go ahead." She pulled Mary Perkins aside. "It's me, Margaret Cerillo. I thought I recognized you before, but I wasn't sure . . ."

The man hesitated. He obviously had orders to follow Mary Perkins onto the airplane, but he also had been instructed to be sure he wasn't caught doing it. He could think of no reason to stand and wait for these two women while they talked, so he stepped forward, handed his ticket to the woman at the door, and stepped past her into the boarding tunnel.

Jane moved Mary Perkins away from the gate casually. "Slowly, now, and keep talking," Jane whispered. "You seem to be worth a lot of expense."

"I guess they think I am," said Mary Perkins.

"If you have something they want, you'll never have a better time to come up with it. We can go right into the plane and make a deal. The lights are on and everybody's been through metal detectors. There's no chance of other people we can't see."

"If I had anything to buy them off with, what would I need you for?"

Jane stopped and looked at her. "I'll still help you shake them afterward in case there are hard feelings."

"Thanks, but I can't get rid of them that way."

"What did you do?"

Mary Perkins turned to look at Jane, leaning away from her as though she had just noticed her there and found it displeasing. "Why do you assume I did something?"

"I know you did. If you didn't, what would you need me for?"

Jane began to walk again. Any woman whose claim to trust was that she had picked up some gossip in the L.A. county jail didn't inspire much confidence, and this one struck her as a person who had done some lying professionally. But Jane could see no indication of what she was lying about. She was being followed by two men who had not taken the sorts of steps that anybody would take if they wanted to stop her from jumping bail or catch her doing something illegal. They had seen her waiting for a flight to a distant state, and they had gotten aboard. The local cops couldn't do that, the F.B.I. wouldn't be prepared to do it on impulse, and if none of them had stopped her from leaving the county jail, then they didn't know of any reason to keep her there.

Jane had to admit to herself that the only possibility that accounted for the way these men were behaving was that they wanted to keep her in sight until there weren't any witnesses. "A little faster now," she said. "We've got a plane to catch."

They started across the waiting area and Jane caught a peculiar movement in the edge of her vision. A man sitting at the far end of the waiting area stood up, and two men who had been conferring quietly at a table in the coffee shop did the same. It wasn't that any of them would have seemed ominous alone. It was the fact that their movements coincided with Jane's and Mary's starting to walk fast. "Did you hear them announce a flight just now?"

Mary winced. "Please don't tell me you hear voices."

"I don't. There were two men on that flight. Do you have some reason to believe there wouldn't be others?"

"Well . . . no."

Jane's jaw tightened. "Let me give you some advice. Whatever it is you've been doing that makes people mad at you, cut it out. You're not very good at getting out of town afterward."

Mary Perkins let Jane hurry her along the concourse in silence until they reached Gate 36. They slipped into the tunnel with the last of the passengers, just as the man at the gate was preparing to close the door. Jane heard running footsteps behind her, so she stopped at the curve and listened.

"I'm sorry, sir," said the airline man's voice. "You'll need a ticket. We aren't permitted to accept cash."

"Can't I buy one?"

"Yes, sir, but you'll have to go to the ticket counter. I have no way to issue a ticket."

"But that's way the hell on the other end of the airport. Can you hold the plane?"

"I'm sorry, sir, but passengers have to catch connecting flights, and we have a schedule. There are five flights a day from LAX to McCarran. You could—"

Jane walked the rest of the way up the tunnel and through the open hatch, and she and the woman took their seats. Mary Perkins said, "What do you call that?"

"Airport tag," said Jane. "I haven't played it in years." She sat back, fastened her seat belt, and closed her eyes. "I hope I never do again."

"**W**hat are you thinking?" asked Mary Perkins.

"I'm not thinking. I'm resting," said Jane.

"Does resting mean you've already thought, and you have a plan? Because if it does, I'd sure like to know what it is."

"No, it means I want you to be quiet."

Jane closed her eyes again. The plane was flying over the Southwest now, toward the places where the desert people lived: Mohave, Yavapai, Zuni, Hopi, Apache, Navajo. Some of them believed that events didn't come into being one after another but existed all at once. They were simply revealed like the cards a dealer turned over in a blackjack game: they came off the deck one at a time, but they were all there together at the beginning of the game.

What Jane needed to do now was to find a way to reveal the cards in the wrong order: go away, then arrive. She reviewed all of the rituals that were followed when an airplane landed. The fact that they were known and predictable and unchanging meant that they already existed, even though the plane was still in the air. The flight was a short one, and she felt the plane begin to descend almost as soon as it had reached apogee. It was just a hop over the mountains, really, and then a long low glide onto the plateau beyond.

Jane reached into the pocket on the back of the seat in front of her and examined the monthly magazine the airline published. She leafed past the advertisements for hotels and resorts and the articles on money, cars, children, and pets. At the back she found the section she was looking for. There were little maps of all of the airports where the airline landed, so people could find their connecting gates. She studied the one for McCarran, then tore the back cover off, reached into the seat pocket in front of Mary, and tore that back cover off too.

"What are you doing?" asked Mary.

Jane pulled her pen out of her purse and began printing in bold capital letters. "Here's what you have to do. When the plane lands, everybody is going to get off except you. You take as much time as you can. You're sick, or your contact lens fell out. I don't care what it is."

"How long?"

"Try to stretch it out long enough to get at least one flight attendant to leave the plane first. It may not work, but I've seen it happen, and when it does, people watching for a passenger get confused."

"Okay," said Mary. "Then what?"

"Then you come off the plane. Walk out fast, don't look to either side. Head for the car-rental desk. Rent a car. Make it a big one, not a compact. Something fat and luxurious and overpowered. They'll probably have lots of them in Las Vegas. Drive it around to the edge of the building where you can see the Southwest baggage area. When I come out the door, zoom up fast and get me."

"What if something goes wrong?"

Jane was busy going over and over the printing on her two sheets, making the letters bigger and bolder. "Here's what it will be. They'll follow you to the car desk. They'll stick around long enough to be sure what you're doing, and then they'll leave to try to get to the lot before you do. The lot will be the first time you're alone and away from airport security. They'll want to get into the car with you."

"Then what do I do?"

Jane looked at her in disappointment. "As soon as they're gone, cancel the car and go to the next desk, of course. Rent from a different company. They'll take you to a different lot."

"Just let me get it straight. Stay on the plane, get off quick, rent a big car, pick you up at baggage."

"Right." She looked up at Mary critically. "Come to think of it, even if you don't spot anybody behind you at the rental counter, cancel the car and go to the next desk anyway."

"You don't think I'll see them, do you? That's it, isn't it?"

Jane stuck the two magazine covers into her belt under her coat at the small of her back. Then she leaned back and closed her eyes again. "Bet your life on it if you want. Either way I'll come out of the baggage door and look for you. If you don't come, I can probably find a cab."

When the pilot's voice came on the intercom and said something inaudible that contained the words *Las Vegas,* Jane opened her eyes. People ahead of her in the plane were looking out their windows and nudging each other. Probably they were beginning to see the lights. Flying into Las Vegas after dark was always a strange experience. The world below the plane was as black as the sky above it, and then suddenly, with no warning, there was a light like a frozen explosion in the middle of it: not just a lot of dull yellowish bulbs like the lights of other cities, but crimson, aquamarine, veridian, gold, and bright splashes of white. As the plane descended, the lights moved, blinking, flashing, and sweeping, and a line of fan-shaped beams of car headlights were visible flowing up and down in the middle of it. The explosion had gotten even crazier in the past couple of years, she noticed.

Mary was staring out the window like the others. "God, I love this place," she said. "Are we going to be here long?"

"Not unless you're held over by popular demand," said Jane, and closed her eyes again. She listened and let her body feel the machinery of the plane work. The ailerons moved to tilt and swing the plane around, and then the right one went down with the left and the plane leveled to skim over the desert. There was the odd whistling noise of the wind holding the plane back, and the engines cut down, and then the noise seemed to get louder for no reason she had ever understood, and then the hydraulic system pushed the wheels down until they locked with a thump, and there was the long sickening feeling of the plane losing altitude. She said, "You okay on everything?"

"Yes," said Mary.

Jane nodded. The best part of the plan was that if Mary Perkins, or whatever her real name was, panicked and ran, they would both have a pretty good chance. Mary Perkins would be behind the wheel of a big, fast car with a good head start. Most of the watchers would still be following Jane.

The plane bounced along the runway, slowed, and taxied to a stop at the terminal. Jane stood up and joined the line of impatient people opening overhead compartments and shuffling along between the seats. She stepped into the boarding tunnel and picked out a man a few paces ahead of her. He was tall and in his mid-forties and had the preoccupied, bored look of a salesman making his rounds.

She hurried until she was at his side, then matched his pace to make it look as though they were together. As soon as they were out of the tunnel and around the corner she separated herself from him and ducked into the gift shop. She took two steps past the entrance and found a baseball cap with LAS VEGAS on the crown in sequins and gold thread, and a sweatshirt with a picture of a hand holding five aces. She walked across to the other side wall and picked out a pair of running shorts. The little store didn't sell shoes, but it had some foldable slippers for people whose feet bothered them on long flights. The whole shopping spree took less than a minute, and then she was at the cash register.

She came out the door with her bag of purchases and slipped into the ladies' room. She changed in the stall, dropped her clothes into the trash can, picked up her magazine covers, and then came out again, this time to join the crowd going toward the arrival gates.

As she walked, she checked her watch. Only four minutes had passed since she had stepped off the plane and come out of Gate 10 with the salesman. This time she was in her shorts and sweatshirt, two and a half inches shorter than she had been in her high heels, her tinted glasses gone and her hair in a ponytail through the back strap of her Las Vegas baseball cap.

She moved to Gate 12, directly across the open hallway from Gate 10. The sign over the desk at Gate 12 said, ARR: NORTHWEST FLT 907 LOS ANGELES. She sat down in the side row of seats where other people were waiting for Flight 907 to arrive and put the sign she had made on her lap, where it could be seen if somebody were looking. It said in big, black letters, MARY PERKINS.

She saw the two men notice her. They were in the positions they should be in—apart, but watching the people coming off the Southwest flight from Los Angeles at Gate 10. They both wore sportcoats that might have covered the guns they couldn't have on them now. They noticed Jane within a few seconds. They kept glancing across the hallway at her, but neither moved.

At last Jane saw two stewardesses come out of the tunnel at Gate 10 and walk past the two watchers. They were wearing their little uniform jackets and were towing their overnight bags on little carts. Jane's heart began to beat more quickly. Whatever Mary Perkins had done to delay getting off the plane must have been good. If she could only hold out a little longer, Jane would be able to tie the knot in time.

The two men were staring at each other now, silently conferring. The departure of the flight attendants struck them as evidence that they had already watched all the passengers get off the plane at Gate 10. The two women they had been told to watch for had not been among them. But there was a person waiting at Gate 12 holding a sign that said MARY PERKINS. A second flight from Los Angeles was going to arrive at that gate any minute. Obviously they had been given the wrong airline and flight number. The men silently agreed. First one man went to the drinking fountain. When he came back up the concourse, it was to Gate 12, where Jane waited. She pretended not to see him. She looked at her watch, at the clock on the wall, at the carpet.

At last the second man moved. He walked along the window, pretended to see something out on the runway, and moved closer to get a better angle. Then, without seeming to have made a decision, he was in Jane's waiting area. He guessed maybe he hadn't seen anything after all. He looked at his watch and sat down.

Now there was only one more thing. If they were trained, or even if they had an instinct for this sort of work, they would be anxious not to spook her. A woman limousine driver who picked up strangers at airports probably often drove alone at night, and she would be careful to avoid being stalked. The sensible place for them to be was behind her, and fairly far away.

Jane turned to face Gate 12, so the men would move to the spots where she wanted them to be. She let her eyes go up under the brim of her cap and used the reflection in the darkened window to check. Yes, they were perfect now, watching her from behind, not able to see the first gate at all.

She picked up movement behind them. Mary Perkins was not a novice. She was coming out of the accordion tunnel fast. Ten steps across the waiting area, around the corner, and gone.

Jane needed to keep their attention on her, so she stood up and walked toward the gate. She sat down in the closest seat she could find to the gate and held her sign in her lap. She felt her heart begin to beat more slowly. Now time had a little knot in it, and the longer the rest of it took the better. The men were convinced that Mary Perkins's plane was about to arrive, but she was already on her way down to the car-rental counter.

A woman much like the one who had presided over the arrival of Jane's flight announced, "Flight 907 from Los Angeles will be arriving at Gate 12 in approximately four minutes." Jane could already see the lights of the plane shimmying along at the end of the runway. She kept her head motionless so the two men wouldn't get the urge to move again. She could see that the plane was a big one, and this improved her chances considerably.

The plane slowly rolled to the terminal and nuzzled up to the doorway. The ground crew chocked the wheels, the boarding tunnel extended a few feet to touch the fuselage, and the engines shut down. People near Jane began to stand up and congregate near the doorway. Most of the passengers flying into McCarran were strangers, so the crowd of relatives and friends was small.

Jane stood among them. She held up the MARY PERKINS sign

while she watched the first few passengers come out. There were some middle-aged couples, some men traveling alone, a couple of grandmothers. Then there were about ten people of both sexes who seemed to be the age of college students, and she remembered there was a college here. Then she saw a pair of women in their early thirties, and one of them was blond.

She had been cradling the MARY PERKINS sign under her chin, and now she flipped the sign over without letting the move be visible from behind. She stepped out where the two women could not help seeing her, and tried to look at them winningly. They read her new sign: PRIVATE LIMO: ANY HOTEL, THREE DOLLARS.

The blond woman stopped and asked, "Three dollars for both of us, or three each?"

Jane smiled. "If you're both going to the same place, I'll take you for four."

The blonde said, "Caesar's."

"No sweat," said Jane.

The three women walked down the concourse quickly. Jane didn't look behind her to see if the men were following. She knew they were. She said, "You've been to Vegas before?"

The blonde had appointed herself to do the talking. "Once in a while. Just when we get really sick of behaving ourselves. We gamble, stay up late, and never grade a single paper."

"You're teachers?"

"Yes," said the other one, who had curly brown hair. "As if you couldn't tell by looking."

Jane felt guilty about what she was going to do next, but the truth was that both of them were attractive in a scrubbed-and-deodorized way. "No," she said. "Everybody comes to Vegas. I just drive them around. Once you're here, you're whoever you say you are—at least until your money's gone. I wouldn't have guessed teachers, though. Most people wouldn't."

"Sure," said the blonde.

"Really. Those two guys who gave you the wall-to-wall and roof-to-foundation when you got off the plane. I bet they don't think you're teachers."

The quiet one said, "That's a laugh." As though to prove it, she laughed.

Jane had put the itch in them, and that was enough. At some point in their walk to the baggage area, each of them would turn and look at the two men, trying very hard and very clumsily to be sure she wasn't caught at it. Looking had nothing to do with real interest. It didn't matter if they were nuns, or lesbians in the tenth year of a lifelong relationship. If they were human, they would look. The idea that they were being watched might frighten them or disgust them or make their weekend, but they would look, and when they did, the two men would be sure.

Jane led them to the baggage claim and waited while they tried to spot their suitcases. The dark one said, "Are those the ones? Don't look."

Jane didn't look. She said, "Tall, muscular guy with dark hair and cowboy boots. Shorter one with curly hair. Both in coats, no ties."

"Yes," said the blonde. "The very ones."

Her companion turned to her in surprise. "You looked?"

"Of course I did," said the blonde. "As soon as I heard about it. But I have a feeling they're not our type. Worse luck."

There was more to the quiet one than Jane had expected. "Maybe my type in Las Vegas isn't the same as my type in Woodland Hills." She was joking, but some part of her mind was agitated.

Jane decided not to let them get too curious. "A lot of ugly things happen in this town. Nobody you want to know hangs around in airports looking for a nice date."

The two bags came down and the blonde soberly scooped them both off the track. Jane picked them up and walked toward the exit with the two women at her back. She used the seconds to prepare herself. If Mary Perkins had failed to rent the car in time, or more likely, had rented it and decided not to drive it back into the light and danger of the airport, Jane was going to be left at the curb with two innocents and some men who might consider this a good opportunity to push them into the back of a car.

She stepped out the door into the cool desert air, set the bags down on the sidewalk, and looked around her. She was careful not to look behind her for the two men, but she knew they must be coming closer. Then a car swung out from the loading zone for

United Airlines a hundred yards away and glided toward them. It was a black Lincoln Town Car, and as it drew nearer, she could see Mary Perkins behind the wheel, her face set in an expression of intense discomfort. She stopped two feet from the curb in front of Jane.

The order and economy of Jane's movements were critical now. As soon as the car stopped she swung open the back door and said, "Hop in." As soon as the two women were inside she pushed the button down and slammed the door. Scooping somebody off a curb was easy, but dragging them out of a locked car took time and force. She snatched the suitcases off the pavement, scurried to the back of the car, and banged on the trunk. Mary Perkins leaned out the window and tossed her the key. She set the suitcases inside, closed the lid, and looked around her as she ran to the driver's side. She couldn't see them anywhere, which meant they were somewhere nearby getting into their own car. "I'll drive," she said.

Mary Perkins barely had time to slide to the passenger seat before Jane was inside and wheeling the big car out into the loop. She drove fast to be sure the two men thought it was worthwhile to keep her in sight. She swung to the right on Las Vegas Boulevard. The Strip began just past the airport entrance, and already she was gliding past big hotels: Excalibur, Tropicana, Aladdin, Bally's on the right, the Dunes on the left. They stopped for the light at Flamingo Road, but she still couldn't pick out the car that must be following somewhere in the long line of headlights. The light changed and she drove the two hundred yards with the bright moving lights of the Flamingo Hilton on her right and Caesar's parking lot on the left, then pulled into the long approach to the front entrance.

The blonde said, "How do you make any money on four dollars a trip?"

Jane shrugged. "Lots of hotels, lots of flights, and nothing shuts down, so we work long hours. We take turns driving." She turned to Mary Perkins. "That reminds me. If you want to take a nap, this is a good time."

Mary took the hint and leaned back in the big front seat. "Thanks," she said. She arranged herself so that her head didn't show over the headrest.

Jane stopped the car at the Caesar's front entrance and ran to open the trunk. The doorman opened the back door for the two passengers while a bellman picked up their suitcases. The doorman made a move to reach for Mary Perkins's door, but Jane stopped him. "She's not getting out."

The blond woman said "Thanks" to Jane, handed her seven dollars, and followed the suitcases toward the lobby.

Jane said to the doorman, "I saw a couple of creeps pick those two out at the airport and follow us. I didn't want to scare them, but you might want to tell Security."

The doorman said seriously, "Yeah. Thanks. I'll do it." He went to his station at the side of the door and picked up a telephone.

Jane slipped behind the wheel and started the car. "Keep your head down," she said. "No matter what happens, stay down and out of sight." She watched for the two men as she glided back along the driveway to the strip. When she saw a dark blue car stop at the side of the building, she kept it in the mirror until she saw the men from the airport get out. They would waste the next few hours trying to find the two women in the enormous hotel complex, then watch them for a while. They would receive no help from anybody who worked at the hotel, and sooner or later two or three polite men in dark suits who had been watching them through the network of video cameras and the see-through mirrors in the ceilings would ask them what they wanted.

"Can I get up yet?" asked Mary Perkins.

"Yeah," Jane said. "I guess it's okay now."

Mary Perkins sat up and looked through the windshield. "That's the airport up ahead. I thought we were going to drive out."

"We're not."

"Why not? It's dark and empty, and we could go a hundred."

Jane sighed. "It's the logical thing to do."

They returned the car to the rental lot, walked into the terminal, and bought two tickets for the next flight out. It happened to be to New York with a stop in Chicago. They had to walk quickly to get to the gate in time. It was almost three A.M. now, and any watchers would have had to be disguised as furniture to escape Jane's notice.

As soon as they had taken their seats, Mary Perkins whispered, "I can't believe it. By now those guys don't know where they are, let alone where we are."

"We're alive," said Jane quietly. "Now I'm going to sleep. Don't wake me up until we're in Chicago."

She closed her eyes and prepared herself for the unpleasant experience of having the past few days run through her mind all over again. There were a few bright, crackling images that flashed in her vision, but they weren't in order or coherent, so they didn't cause her much pain. After she had dozed for a short time, she saw the fist coming around just before she had flinched to take the force out of it. The spasmodic jerk woke her up, but when she relaxed her muscles again, she dropped into a deeper animal sleep that put her in darkness far out of reach of recent memories.

5

W hen the plane began to descend, the pressure on Jane's ears increased and she woke up. The engines changed their tone, and she pushed the button to let her seat back pop up again. The sleep had left her feeling stiff in the shoulders, but she was alert. The Old People believed that the place to obtain secret information was in dreams. Sometimes a dream would be an expression of an unconscious desire of the soul, and at other times a message planted there by a guardian spirit. Those were two ways of saying the same thing. If there were such a force as the supernatural, then the soul and the guardian both would be supernatural. If there were no such force, then the soul was the psyche, and the guardian spirit was just the lonely mind's imaginary friend.

This time Jane could not remember any impression that had passed through her mind in three hours. Maybe that was the message from her subconscious: enough. She had stored enough tragedy and violence in her memory during the past few days to trip the circuit breaker and turn the lights out. The rest had helped:

she was thinking clearly again. As they walked into the terminal at O'Hare she glanced up at a monitor that had the schedule of arrivals and departures on it.

"More tag?" asked Mary Perkins.

Jane kept her moving. "Once a game starts, you have to play to win. That means remembering all the moves. We sent two men to New York with a stop in Chicago. The two we left in Las Vegas can look at the schedule and see that a plane left for Chicago about the time we did. When you start sending the chasers across your own path, it's time to get off the path."

They walked along with the crowd heading for the baggage claim until it passed the car-rental counters, and then Jane led Mary Perkins aside. Within minutes they were in a white Plymouth moving along the 294 Expressway toward Route 80.

Jane drove fast but kept the pace steady, always in a pack of cars that were going the same speed. She counted as she drove: two men fooled into boarding the flight to New York, three left at the gate in L.A., two following the wrong woman in Las Vegas. Seven. The one who had made a phone call before he had boarded the plane to New York must have been reporting to somebody, so it was more than seven. Who were they, and why was Mary Perkins worth all this trouble?

"Where are we going?" asked Mary Perkins.

"Detroit," said Jane. "It's about three hundred miles." She turned her head and pointedly studied the right-hand mirror to check for headlights coming up in the right lane. "In the airport you said you didn't have time to tell me anything and I didn't have time to listen. We've got about five hours."

Mary Perkins sat in silence for a long time. They passed an exit where a blazing neon sign towered above a building much bigger than the gas stations around it. Mary gave a little snort that was the abbreviation for a laugh. "Jimmy Fugazi's End Zone Restaurant. Did you ever notice that all those guys who get too old to play buy restaurants?"

This time Jane did look at her. Mary was probably in her thirties, but she was already paying too much attention to her hair and skin and clothes. "I guess they have to invest their money somewhere," she said.

"All professional athletes want to own restaurants," Mary Perkins pronounced. "It doesn't have to do with money. It has to do with not being able to give up having people look at them and pay attention. Even the dumbest jock in the world knows he can do better by putting bets on any ten mutual funds, but all professional athletes want a restaurant. Every crook already has one. What he wants is a casino. A crook is basically lazy, and that way people come to him to get robbed, and they bring it in cash so he can take it and screw the government at the same time. There's only one game bigger than that."

Jane could sense that Mary Perkins was backing closer to whatever she had been concealing, so she waited patiently.

"What happened to me," said Mary Perkins, "well, not exactly to me—but what happened was that one day in 1982 Congress passed the Garn–Saint Germain Act. It pretty much got rid of all the rules for savings and loan companies. They could charge what they wanted, pay what they wanted, buy and sell what they wanted, take deposits in any amount from anywhere, and then lend it to whomever they wanted, or even forget about lending and invest it themselves. I could see that this was maybe the first great opportunity in American life since the discovery of gold at Sutter's Mill, so I jumped at it."

She glanced at Jane to see if her expression had changed, but it had not, so she went on. "It wasn't only that the rules had changed, but that there was nobody to enforce them. That was part of the program. If you don't have regulations, you don't have to hire regulators. Reagan was cutting the size of the government payroll."

Jane had finally learned something true about Mary Perkins. She was a thief. But until she knew more about what Mary Perkins had stolen, there would be no way to know who was after her. "What did you have to do with savings and loans?"

"I started working in one right out of college. When I got there, the regulators still knew all the players and all the rules were fifty years old. The money coming in was all from local people with passbooks, and the money going out was for mortgages on local one-family houses."

"I take it you were one of the ones who changed all that?"

"No, not little me. I just came to the party. That's what it was like—a party. You have to understand what was happening. One day the rules change, so each savings and loan sets its own rates. The next day, deposit brokers start taking money from everywhere in the world, breaking it down into hundred-thousand-dollar chips and depositing the chips in whatever institution anywhere in the country had the highest interest that day. So if Bubba and Billy's Bank in Kinkajou, Texas, gives an extra quarter point, suddenly it's got millions of dollars being deposited: Arab oil money, skim-off money from business, drug money from L.A. and Miami, Yakuza money from Japan, money the C.I.A. was washing to slip to some tyrant someplace, and lots of tax money."

"Wait. You did say 'tax money'?" Maybe Jane had been wrong about the men in the airport. If they were federal agents of some kind, they might be prepared in advance to follow a woman like this.

"Sure. You think they keep it in a big box under the president's bed? Say there's a billion-dollar budget for some program. It's got to be in short-term CDs so they can use it when they need it. A loan broker pops it in wherever the interest is highest. Half a year's interest on a billion dollars at eight percent is forty million, right?"

"If you say so."

"And this is money that can't rest. It can't stay put if there's another bank that's offering higher interest. One point of interest on one billion is ten million dollars. There were all kinds of city-government funds, college budgets, whole states that got their money a few months before they spent it. They counted on the timing and figured the interest in as a way to stretch it. And it didn't matter if the money was in the Bank of America or the Bank of Corncob, Iowa, because it was all insured."

"How did this create an opportunity for you?"

"Forget about me for a minute. A few other things had to change first. Glockenspiel City Savings is suddenly a happening thing."

"What's Glockenspiel City Savings?"

"You know, the little storefront with a million in assets built up over twenty years. One day they offer a nice rate on their CDs;

the next week they've got four hundred million in deposits. That happened a hell of a lot more often than you'd think. There are little pitfalls, though. They're offering, say, nine percent. That means they've got to turn maybe ten, even twelve to make a profit. There's very little in Glockenspiel City that you can invest in that pays ten percent, and nothing at all that you can invest four hundred million in. So you've got to invest it the way you got it, in the great wide world outside Glockenspiel City."

Mary Perkins was telling all this with relish, as though she weren't sitting in a car speeding across the dark Midwest to keep her alive. She seemed to be calming herself by wandering in territory that was familiar to her, a place that was filled with numbers. Jane let her talk.

"Glockenspiel Savings is run by a guy named Cyrus Curbstone. He goes along for years and years, paying three percent on savings, charging six percent on loans. He knows his limits because they've been written down in a law since the thirties. He's honest. He was born there, and he's got two plots in the cemetery for him and Mrs. Curbstone, right behind Great-grandma and one row over from Colonel Curbstone, who got shot in the ass at Gettysburg. But I know Cyrus Curbstone is vulnerable."

"You said he was honest. What's his weakness?"

"One day Cyrus wakes up and finds himself on another planet. He's got to pay nine percent and charge twelve. His million-dollar bank suddenly has four hundred million in deposits. He can't invest it fast enough in the usual way to make the forty or fifty million he needs to turn a profit. In walks a nice person: maybe me. Maybe I've been referred to him by a deposit broker who's been putting lots of those hundred-thousand-dollar chips in the bank. Or I simply happened to meet one of his regular customers socially. Anyway, I'm a developer, or the general partner in a limited partnership. I've got a piece of land that's been appraised for twenty million, I want to develop it as a resort, and I need a loan of ten million to finance it."

"Is the land real?"

"Sure. That doesn't mean I own it, or that it's worth anything like twenty million."

"Didn't they look at deeds?"

"Sure. The owner is Pan-Financial Enterprises of San Diego, or Big Deals of Boca Raton. I'm an officer."

"How did you make it look like it was worth twenty million?"

"In those days there was no licensing law for appraisers anywhere in the country. So I'd get an appraisal that said what I wanted. Then we'd do a land-flip."

"What's that?"

"Buy it for a million. Sell it to your brother-in-law for six million. He sells it back to you for ten. You sell it to Big Deals, Inc. for twenty."

"That worked?"

"Of course it worked. They've been doing it since the Romans."

"If it was that stale, wasn't it risky?"

"You've heard of the term 'motivated seller'?"

"Yes."

"Well, the day after Cyrus Curbstone starts getting these brokered deposits, he becomes a motivated lender. He's got four hundred million to lend out. If he makes ten percent, that's forty million a year. He pays his depositors nine percent, or thirty-six million, pays his overhead, and he's got maybe two million left in profit. He's part owner, or at least a big stockholder. The others are local people, friends of his. He wants that profit. But if he lets the deposits sit in the vault, he's losing three million a month. That's a hundred thousand a day. That's almost forty-two hundred an hour. I mean, it's costing this guy thirty-three thousand dollars to sleep eight hours."

"You're saying Cyrus fooled himself."

"No. Cyrus had never played for big numbers before, but he wasn't stupid. I was a nice, personable businesswoman. I dressed well. I smelled good, I smiled, I had money. I had a hot business and I wanted to expand. Hot businesses need banks. Banks need hot businesses. He got fooled because he was doing exactly what he was supposed to do: for the first few years, a great company looks exactly like the company I was showing him. So he cut a check."

"But what if—"

"What if he said no? If Cyrus didn't bite, I'd leave him to

somebody who had a pitch he liked better, and I'd go after his buddy Homer in the next town, who by now has five hundred million to move. But we hardly ever had to do that. Cyrus would have had to hunt pretty hard for a reason to turn me down, and he knew he didn't have time to hunt. He had to find jobs for his dollars."

"So you got a loan. What then?"

"Big Deals, Inc., got a loan. Big Deals spent it: building expenses, salaries, et cetera. But Big Deals neglected to pay the interest."

"What did Cyrus do about it?"

"I'll skip a few phone calls, meetings, and threats. Usually that went on for months. At some point Cyrus sees that he's got a problem. He can do several things. One is to foreclose on the land. Fine with me. I just sold a one-million-dollar chunk of Manitoba for ten million. Another is to accept my excuses and roll over the loan into a new one that includes the interest I owe him. Now it's a new loan for eleven million. Some of these banks carried loans like that for five years."

"What for?"

"Because Cyrus hasn't lost any money until he reports the loan as nonperforming. If he makes a new loan, he not only hasn't lost the ten million, he can put out another million as an asset. This satisfies the regulators, if any should ever get around to Cyrus with all the work they've got. It keeps the bank looking healthy, so Cyrus has breathing space."

"Why does he need such expensive breathing space?"

"Because he didn't make the forty million he needed to turn a profit. If he was a very quick learner, he made maybe thirty-five million: eight and three-quarters percent. He's still got to pay nine percent to the depositors, so he's maybe a million in the hole at the end of the first year. From one point of view that's not bad. It cost a million dollars to make his bank four hundred times as big as it was last year. But now he's on a treadmill that's going faster and faster. He needs to attract more brokered deposits so he can make more loans. If he gets another two hundred million, he can bring back maybe fifty or sixty million next year and easily absorb the million dollars he lost. As I said, he's not stupid. He knows that he looks great on paper as long as he's moving fast. But if somebody takes a photograph—that is, stops the action and studies it—his bank is insolvent. So now he's interested in keeping the system in motion."

There was still something missing from the story Mary Perkins was telling: who were the seven men following her? "By then he must have known you weren't going to pay the money back."

"In a way they all knew too much. See, Cyrus has been around long enough to have seen problems come and go—the oil crisis and the stock market slide in the early seventies, the inflation after that. He's a survivor. There was no question this wasn't going on forever. If he rode it out, then when it ended he'd be on top of a big company and could count the change later. But if he stopped now, he was out of business. Sometimes these guys would do anything to keep the money moving through—loan anything to anybody and then cook the books to keep the loan from going bad."

"So you got big loans and walked away with the money."

"That was my specialty. There were other people who made a lot of headlines by building screwy empires—lending themselves money to build ghost communities in the desert and paying themselves and their families fifty million in salaries for doing it. But what I'm trying to tell you is that it was all going on a long time, and the ones you've read about weren't the only ones who did it. They weren't even the only ones who got caught. They were just the ones who got convicted. They were very unlucky."

"Why unlucky?"

"It meant that one of these overworked low-level federal accountants had to get around to looking at all the loan papers, spot yours, notice there was something really wrong with the loan, ask questions, get the wrong answers, and convince his supervisor to do something about your loan instead of about somebody else's. Even then the procedures were amazing. That stuff we've all heard about the cold-eyed bank examiners popping in at dawn and padlocking everything is a myth. It never happened that way. Not once."

"You're saying it was staged for the television cameras?"

"No, the pictures were real. What you didn't see was what happened first. The regulator asks questions. Six months go by while somebody at the bank dances around. The supervisor sends his first-level letter."

"What's that?"

"They all have names like Notice of Discrepancy or Letter of Caution or Admonition. The letter describes what they found and says they want it fixed. Another six months go by, and the regulator checks the bank again and sees that you didn't fix it. He looks deeper for other problems, or he forces you to agree to move the loan over to the debit column instead of the credit column. Another six months go by and you get the Caution. Then the Admonition."

"That's ludicrous."

"Of course. The regulating procedures were left over from the days when everybody in the business was Cyrus Curbstone. If he got a letter pointing out a discrepancy, he would have been after it like it was a gaping hole in his own roof. The system was set up to say, 'Please look into this,' then 'Have you fixed it?' then 'Okay, here's how you fix it,' then 'If you don't fix it, I will,' and finally, 'Here I come.' "

"You have to wonder how any of these people got caught."

"It was like being chased by a glacier. You could live a whole life without seeing it get any closer. It was coming, sure. But there was so much time to get out of the way."

"And some waited too long."

"Only a few. About a thousand people actually got to the point where they went to trial. This meant that their savings and loans were so out of control that the government put them at the top of the list for closure. They had to be losing millions a day for that. Then a couple of agents had to figure you were so obviously guilty that it was worth spending four years of their lives preparing the case. A U.S. attorney had to be sure the case was a slam-dunk, so it wouldn't ruin her won-lost record. Then her boss would have to be convinced that you had stolen so much that when the case was over they could recover enough millions in civil court to repay the millions all this prosecution was costing, and enough millions more to make it look to Joe Taxpayer like they'd gotten his money back, and enough millions more so it would look like they put your head on a pole to scare off the other high rollers."

"How did that work out?"

"Not so great. In order to convict, they had to take the judge and jury through all these loan papers, land-flips, asset appraisals, and files. The average person can barely follow his own taxes. All this paper was written up to fool qualified accountants. The paper made most of these guys look like victims. For all I know plenty of them were. About a third got off, and of the others only about half got convicted of anything that carried jail time. The average sentence was three years."

"You said they were picked so there could be civil suits. Didn't they still have to face that?"

"Sure, but they all said they were broke. Even if they had a hundred million dollars in a box under their bed, they also had papers to show they owed somebody two hundred million."

"I know the government confiscated land and buildings and things. They've been selling them off for years."

"If you read that much, you don't have to ask me how that's going. The savings and loans the government took over were the worst, because that was all they had enough money for. The worst were ones where somebody had pulled land-flips to jack up an acre in the middle of a toxic waste dump from a thousand dollars to a million, and had a shady contractor put a substandard building on it so they could jack up the price of the land all around it."

"It's an interesting story," said Jane, "but it's history. It's been over for years."

"Oh?" said Mary Perkins. "Then let me ask you something. Where is it?"

"What?"

"The money?"

"It wasn't real to begin with, was it? If you take something that's worth a thousand dollars and say it's worth a million, and then it goes back to a thousand, nothing happened."

"Something happened. Somebody walked out the door clutching a check for a million dollars he didn't have before, so he got a profit of nine hundred and ninety-nine thousand. The collateral wasn't real, but the money he got from the bank was. He didn't even have to pay taxes on it. A loan isn't income. It's a deduction."

"I forgot about that for a second."

"Sure you did. You're supposed to. Everybody gets used to the idea that money is gooey, flexible stuff. They talk about it inflating and deflating and flowing and being liquid. No reason why it can't evaporate."

"Somebody got it, but if nobody can put his hand on it, then it did evaporate. So that part of it is over."

"It's not over," said Mary Perkins. "We're just moving into the second round now."

"What's the second round? The ten thousand who got away are still doing it?"

"No. Let's say a lull has settled over the borrowing industry. There's no such thing as a savings and loan anymore. The ones that are left are just banks that haven't changed their names yet. That goose has been killed. Scams always work best in boom times, when everybody's too busy to do much checking, almost any business you say you're in might make a profit, and the value of any kind of collateral is going up. But there's still unfinished business."

"Then what's unfinished?"

"I'll give you another typical case: a guy who got into the borrowing business right after the law changed. He didn't amount to much before that. The government shuts him down in 'eighty-nine or 'ninety when they take over the S and L he was borrowing from. He weasels around during the four years it takes to prepare a noose for him. His lawyer and the prosecutor work out a plea bargain. He'll cooperate in the investigation, do six months for one count of making a false statement on a loan form, and settle for twenty million in damages."

"The government bought that?"

"Would you?"

"No."

"Neither did they. If he's offering twenty, he's got forty. The only way he could have gotten it is by stealing it. They take him to court. He's convicted. He gets his standard three-year sentence and is ordered to repay fifty million dollars. He says he's broke. They say, 'No way is this man broke.' They lock him up and look for hidden accounts, fake names, the rest of it. They find nothing. He serves his three years. Some time during those three years the statute of limitations runs out on everything he did at the bank."

"You mean he's free? Nobody can do anything?"

"He can never be charged again by the government for the crimes he committed in getting the money. Of course he still can't show that he's got twenty or forty or a hundred million. He's still got the judgment against him for that much, and swearing he didn't have it was a new crime. But generally speaking, his legal problems are over. Now he's got illegal problems."

"What are those?"

"Well, let's study this guy. He got only a three-year sentence for the following reasons." She ticked them off on her long, thin fingers, the nails looking like knife points. "He has never committed any offense before. He is clearly not armed or violent or dangerous. He has no known connection with organized crime or the drug trade. Everybody who ever heard his name thinks he's got a fortune, but federal investigators who sniff out money for a living didn't find it. What does all that mean to you?"

"It means he's got the money pretty well hidden."

"Good for you. You win a trip to the Caribbean."

Jane looked closely at Mary Perkins. "I think I know what his illegal problems are."

"Yes," said Mary Perkins. "He's not violent enough to scare anybody off and he's got no connections that are worth anything. If you steal his umpteen million he can't even call the police because he'd have to tell them he had that kind of money, and this time his sentence wouldn't be three years; it'd be more like thirty. He's the perfect victim." After a long pause Mary Perkins added, "He's a lot like me."

6

J ane drove along the dark highway skillfully, sometimes lingering in the wake of a big eighteen-wheel truck for many minutes if the driver was pushing to make time, and sometimes moving out into the other lanes to slither between drifting cars where the truck wasn't nimble enough to navigate. Always she stayed within a few miles an hour of the rest of the traffic to keep from tempting the state police, but almost always she was the one who was passing. It was difficult to study and recognize the headlights coming up from behind, so she kept them back there. Now and then she would see one of the exceptions coming up fast in the rearview mirror, and she would evacuate the lane he seemed to prefer and find a space in the center, where she could move to either side if he swerved toward her, and waited there until he had gone on his way.

"Why aren't you saying anything?" asked Mary Perkins.

"I'm waiting to hear your story."

"I told you."

"You told me a lot of stuff about how you used to steal money. You didn't tell me anything about yourself. I thought you were just warming up to it."

"What do you want to know?"

"What's your name?"

"Mary Perkins," she answered, the annoyance making her voice strain. "I told you that in the ladies' room in Los Angeles."

"Okay," said Jane quietly. She drove in silence for a long time.

"Oh," said Mary Perkins brightly. "You mean the one I was born with. I haven't used it in years, so it sounds strange when I say it: Lily Smith."

"What made you pick Mary Perkins?"

"Well, I was in a business where it didn't seem to be a good idea to use the name on my birth certificate. Smith is okay, but it sounds like an alias. Perkins is the kind of name that makes the mark think good thoughts. Mary Perkins is Mary Poppins, with 'perk,' which is peppy and cheerful instead of 'pop,' which is unpredictable. And 'kins' is sweet and innocent, like babykins and lambkins. Also, all names that end with 'kins' are Anglo-Saxon in a homespun straight-from-the-farm sort of way, not in the my-ancestors-were-on-the-*Mayflower* way."

"And Mary is just from Mary Poppins?"

She smiled. "It's kind of hard to find anything that sounds more innocent."

"The word *immaculate* comes to mind," said Jane.

"Well, there's that side of it, of course," said Mary Perkins. "But there are other things that aren't quite as obvious. First, Mary says 'mother.' In fact, it says 'mother of somebody important.' And it's common and feminine. See, if you're going to rob banks—" She stopped, as though she realized it was going to be hard to make herself understood, then started over. "Did you ever take a look at the way your bank is set up?"

"I think I have," said Jane.

"You've got the open floor, which is just there to make you think the bank is big and solid. Then you see the people. At the tellers' counter there are twenty women and a couple of men too young to shave. Then there are a few desks behind that, where everybody is always on the phone. Those are usually women in their fifties. They look like chaperones, there to supervise the twenty women and two boys up front, and to smooth over mistakes."

"I take it those aren't the people you were trying to impress."

"Not if what you came for is money. When you get behind those desks, there are offices. Sometimes they're not even on the same floor. But somewhere down a long, quiet, carpeted hallway there will be a huge wooden desk with nothing on it except a couple of those old-fashioned black pens that stick up out of a marble slab, and a lamp with a green shade. Behind that desk will be a middle-aged man. See, banks are in layers. You can meet fifty-two senior executive vice presidents, and all of them are women. You've got to resist the temptation to tell them enough so that they can say no, and hold out until you see this man."

"And Mary was for him?"

"Yes. It's straightforward, short, and unpretentious. It's not a nickname. It's not a boy's name that was supposed to be cute on a girl. A lot of women in businesses use initials: M. H. Perkins, or M. Hall Perkins. They think it makes them serious. They're wrong. It does not endear them to that man in the back office, and that is the only game being played."

"It is?"

"You must impress the man who has the power to say yes. He doesn't want to be fooled, or to be in business with any person of either sex who is insecure enough to hide things. The only thing worse is a hyphenated name—the woman is married, which is a fact that has very big pluses and minuses that have to be managed carefully. But the hyphenation implies some kind of nonconformist convictions about men and women that she wants to advertise. The man in the back office is not interested in thinking about that. He's interested in getting more money. He wants to deal with somebody who is going to get lots of money and pay him some of it."

"Okay, so Mary Perkins makes it in the door, and M. H. Perkins doesn't."

"Right. She's at the door now. She's energetic and cheerful and well scrubbed, and she has hair that's a bit on the long side and high heels and subtle makeup, but not so subtle that he can't tell she bothered. She wears good jewelry, but very little of it, and it's small. If Mary is married for this meeting, it's a solitaire diamond that's just a little bigger than an honest banker can afford, and that's all. If she's not, maybe a lapel pin. Why? Because that's the way the women who end up with the most money look. The most common way to get it is still to marry it, so Mary is feminine."

"It doesn't sound as though he's thinking about Mary Perkins as a business partner."

"I'm not talking about the deal. I'm talking about the first impression—unconscious, probably—the five seconds from the door to the chair. Finance is a tough business. The guy is smart, and above all he's patient. He's seen a lot on the way to the corner office. In order to automatically get back ten percent of his loan each year, he has to lend the money to somebody who will win—who will use his money to make fifteen percent. What I'm describing for you is the sort of woman he can be made to believe will win."

"How did Mary Perkins get to the point where people are hunting for her?"

Mary Perkins shook her head as though she were marveling at it. "There was a lot of wild stuff in the papers when I went to trial. My lawyer told me that if I went for the plea bargain, it didn't matter how much I agreed to admit I took, because I was already broke. The prosecutor could use a ridiculous number to help her look good, and I would declare bankruptcy and never have to pay a dime. It didn't work that way. Now people think I was one of the ones who ended up with the big money. They want it. I don't have it."

"Who are these people?"

"That's part of the problem. It could be anybody."

Jane looked at her for a moment. Mary was slouching in the passenger seat, looking out the window at the darkness. When she turned to meet Jane's gaze her eyes were wide with wonder and a touch of injury. What she was saying coincided with the truth in one spot: there was no way of limiting the number of people who might be interested in robbing a woman who had stolen millions of dollars. But this did not alter the fact that Mary Perkins knew who was after her tonight, and that she insisted she didn't. Jane said, "Why were you in county jail?"

Mary Perkins shrugged. "Parole violation. I saw those men and tried to leave town."

Jane stifled the annoyed response that rose to her tongue. Mary obviously was experienced enough to know that the best lies were short and simple. Where did the lie begin? She might have noticed that men were following her, but she had not tried to leave town because of that. Something else must have happened first—something that told her what they wanted. All of the hours Jane had spent hustling this woman around the country settled on her chest like a weight. "Where do you think you could go where there would be the smallest chance you'd be recognized?"

"Smallest chance?"

"That's what I said."

"Let's see. We just left California, so that's out. Texas is also out."

Jane concentrated on the mechanical details for the next few minutes. At Ann Arbor she took the Huron Street exit. She said, "When was the last time you slept?"

"I slept maybe four hours last night. Jails never seem to quiet down until you start to smell breakfast."

"We'll sleep now."

There was a motel just after the exit. Jane pulled into the lot and walked into the office by herself to rent a room. She opened the door with the key, locked the door, checked each of the windows, tossed the key on the table by the door, undressed, and lay down on the nearest bed without speaking. Mary Perkins had no choice but to imitate her. When she awoke, the sun was glaring through a crack between the curtains and Jane was sitting on the other bed reading a newspaper. Mary sat up and said, "What time is it?"

"Ten. Checkout is twelve. We've got a lot to do."

Mary Perkins rubbed her eyes. "I guess we'll make it." She smiled. "It's not as though we had to pack, is it?"

"No."

Mary Perkins swung her feet to the floor and stood up. She had been surprised to see that Jane was dressed, but the newspaper suddenly caught her attention. "You've been out."

"Yes," said Jane, not looking up. Mary Perkins could see that she had circled some little boxes in the want ads. Jane also had set a medium-sized grocery bag on the table beside the key.

"I never heard you," said Mary on the way to the bathroom. "You must be the quietest person I ever met in my life."

"I figured you needed to sleep."

Mary examined the shower and found that the knobs were hot and the tub was wet. She thought about the woman in the other room. A lot of people could tiptoe around pretty well, just like little cats. But how did this one get everything else to be quiet—appliances and fixtures and things?

Mary Perkins got the water to run warm and stepped under the spray. She felt good, she had to admit. Here she was in a clean room with a clear head a couple of thousand miles away from danger, and taking a shower. Once again whatever it was that had always kept the luck coming had not failed.

But now that she was alert and not particularly frightened, she had time to think about that woman out there on the bed. What she sensed about Jane Whitefield was not comforting. No, the animal wasn't a cat. Just because it looked like it had soft fur and the eyes were big and liquid and it didn't make any noise at all didn't mean it was cuddly and gentle. Mary was not the sort of person who lost fingers at zoos. Whatever this one was, it had that look because it happened to be the female of its species, not because it was something you wanted around the house.

The person who had recognized Jane Whitefield in jail was a short black woman named Ellery Robinson. The word on Ellery Robinson was that she had been pulled in on a parole violation. That didn't make her seem interesting until Mary learned that the conviction was for having killed a man in bed with an old-fashioned straight razor. She had served six or seven years of a life sentence in the California Institution for Women at Frontera, one of those places in the endless desert east of Los Angeles. She was in her fifties now, small and compact with a short, athletic body like a leathery teenager. She never spoke to anyone, having long ago lost interest in whatever other people gained from listening, and having gotten used to whatever it was they expelled by talking. But sometimes she still answered questions if they weren't personal.

Mary was in the mess hall one morning when another woman

pointed out Jane Whitefield and asked Ellery Robinson if she knew anything about her. Ellery Robinson had actually turned her whole body around in the chow line to stare at her before she said, "She makes people disappear." Then the conversation was over. Ellery Robinson turned back to eye the food on the warming tables. When a young woman down the line on her first day inside saw the same food and started crying, she looked at her too for a second, not revealing either sympathy or contempt, but as though she just wanted to see where the noise was coming from.

Mary Perkins had come upon Ellery Robinson sitting in the sunshine in the yard, a headband around her forehead and the sleeves of her prison shirt rolled up to make it fit her child-sized frame. Mary Perkins smiled, but Ellery Robinson said only, "What do you want?"

"I heard you know who that woman is that came in yesterday. Tall, black hair, thin?"

"Yes."

"Is it true that she hides people?"

Ellery Robinson closed one eye and tilted her head up to look at Mary Perkins. "Why aren't you talking to her?"

"I thought I'd better find out what I could first."

Ellery Robinson abruptly lost interest in Mary Perkins. She seemed determined to end the conversation, so everything came out quickly in a monotone. "I heard that if a person is in trouble— not the kind of trouble where the cops take them to court, but the kind where the cops find their head in a Dumpster—the person could do worse than see her."

Mary Perkins stared at Ellery Robinson, but her face revealed nothing. "You sure nobody made her up?"

Ellery Robinson nodded in the direction of the cellblock. "There she is."

"If you know her, why haven't you talked to her?"

For the first time Ellery Robinson's facial muscles moved a little, but it wasn't a smile. "I don't have that kind of trouble. If you do, go meet her yourself."

Mary Perkins looked uncomfortable. "This is all new to me. It's the first time I've been arrested."

"No, it isn't." It wasn't an accusation. There was no trace of reproof or irony. There was nothing behind it at all. Then she seemed to acknowledge that her words were what had made Mary Perkins take a step backwards. "Lots of bad girls in here. You aren't the worst." She closed her eyes and moved to the side a little so she would be in the full sun again and Mary's shadow would be gone.

Now Mary stood in the shower in Michigan, feeling safe. She had begun to relax when she sensed something had changed again. She tensed and swung around to see the shape outside the shower curtain.

"Dry off," said Jane, "but leave your hair wet."

Mary turned off the water, snatched a towel off the rack, pulled it inside the curtain with her, and turned away to dry herself. "Why?"

"Why what?"

"Why leave my hair wet?"

Jane reached into the paper bag and pulled out a box with a picture of a fashion model on it. "We'll dry it after it's dyed."

"Dyed? What if I don't want it dyed?"

"Then don't dye it," said Jane. "You've got easy ways to stay lost, and hard ways. Changing the color of your hair is one of the easy ways."

Mary glared at the model on the box. Whatever color her hair had been when the picture was taken, an artist had painted it over a hedgehog brown. "That color?"

Jane set the box on the sink just under the mirror. "What's wrong with it?"

"I've just always been blond."

Jane's eyes lifted to glance at her in the mirror, and then Mary saw them move to the picture on the box. She said nothing, but Mary saw what she was comparing the color on the box to. She angrily snatched another towel off the rack, wrapped it around her and tucked it under her arm like a sarong. "I meant I've always *felt* blond. I've been blond for a long time."

Jane didn't turn to face her. "We've got less than two hours before checkout time. If you want to look different, the time to do it is before you rent an apartment, not later, after everybody has seen you already. I'll be out there. Think it over."

Mary sat on the edge of the tub and stared at the mirror. It was just high enough so that all she could see of herself was the glowing blond hair at the crown of her head. It was bright, shiny, almost metallic when it was wet like this. She walked to the door and called, "Okay, let's get it over with."

Jane came back in, slipped on rubber gloves, pulled a chair up next to the sink, and went to work on Mary's hair. The acrid smells and the mess on the counter were all familiar to Mary, but it had been years since she had endured them outside of a hairdresser's shop.

Jane worked in silence and with extreme care, glancing at her watch every few minutes. Then it was over, and she was brushing Mary's hair out.

Mary said, "You've done this quite a bit, haven't you?"

"Sure," Jane said. "If you do all of the easy things, the hard ones work better. Dyeing your hair, buying new clothes, using glasses to change the way your eyes look—those are easy. You can do all of them in a day, and none of them has any risk. If you think about what you're trying to accomplish, you can do it as well as I can."

"What am I trying to accomplish?"

Jane looked at her in the mirror impatiently. "You put in a lot of time trying to be Mary Perkins. You had it all worked out. Just do it in reverse. For the time being, you have nothing in common with Mary Perkins. She liked Las Vegas. You hate it; the lights give you a headache and everybody on the street looks like a zombie to you. Mary Perkins made businessmen think about her and remember her. Lose everything you did to accomplish that. Be the one who doesn't catch their eye. That's easy to do, and if you don't do at least that much, you're finished. Anybody who wants to find you can knock on doors and show your picture."

Mary Perkins studied her reflection. The effect wasn't as bad as she had expected. The woman who stared back at her wasn't dowdy or mousy. She was mildly, quietly attractive, and with a little makeup she could be made better than that. What she looked most like was a woman who had never existed; she looked like a grown-up version of Lily Smith. "All right," she said. "What do we change next?"

"That will have to do for now. Come on."

Checking out consisted of sitting in the car while Jane went into the motel office and set the key on the counter. When she returned, she started the car and said, "All right. Now we start getting into the hard parts. Do you have identification in any name besides Mary Perkins?"

"Lila Samuels," said Mary.

"Throw her away with Mary Perkins. You've been in county jail. Although you haven't exactly said so, you've been investigated, and probably arrested more than once. The authorities know your aliases, and so can anybody else who wants to."

Mary Perkins said, "I've got to be somebody."

"I've got some papers with me that you can use. Your name is Donna Kester. You're thirty-five."

Mary Perkins stared at her. "You have fake I.D. with you? But you were arrested too. They went through your purse."

Jane pulled the car out of the parking lot and drove up the street. "It wasn't in my purse." Jane had brought the papers for Mona and kept them taped under the dashboard of each car they had used while traveling across the country. After Dennis had wrecked the last car, she had gone to the lot where it had been towed and found the papers untouched. "You can be Donna Kester without worrying about anything for a while."

They looked at three different apartments before they found the right one. It was in a building in the middle of a large modern apartment complex on Huron Street that seemed to contain a high proportion of single people, but it was far enough from the University of Michigan campus to be vacant. The fact that Donna Kester had a credit card was enough to get her a lease that began in two days. The fact that she had no local employer only confirmed her story that she had just gotten to town.

That afternoon Jane checked them into another motel at the edge of Ann Arbor, past the place where Huron Street crossed Route 94 and became Liberty Road. Jane sat in the motel room on the twin bed across from Mary. It was dusk, and the cold wind was beginning to blow outside to announce that the short fall days were fading into winter nights here. The tree branches that scraped and rattled the gutters of the building were bare, and the wet pavement of the parking lot outside the window would be frosted by morning.

Jane said, "This is a good place to be. There are about thirty-five thousand students here, just about all of them strangers. Figure five thousand faculty, all from other places. Most of them are married, so they're really ten thousand, and another five thousand staff. Most of those people just returned here for fall semester. You're one of fifty thousand people who just got to town in a community with a year-round population that can't be much over a hundred thousand."

"Are you trying to sell me a condo?" asked Mary.

"No," said Jane. "I'm trying to teach you something. If you're going to be a fugitive you'd better get good at it. I've heard a couple of versions of who isn't chasing you, but not who is. It doesn't matter. This isn't the sort of place where they'll look first. That's the best you can do in choosing a place to be invisible. There are always about five likely places to look for anybody. If you're stupid, you'll be in one. Once you move beyond those, every place is about as likely as any other, so the odds of finding you drop dramatically."

"Where would you look? You said five places."

"I haven't studied Mary Perkins as thoroughly as they have. You've been to Las Vegas and liked it. You'd be too smart to go back, and Reno's too close, so I might try looking in Atlantic City. You said you had worked in Texas and California, so people know you. But that leaves lots of cities in between that would appeal to Mary Perkins: I'd try Scottsdale, Sedona, Santa Fe. You like to be around money and sunshine." As she watched Mary, she could see that the list was making her frightened. "The fifth place is somewhere in the South."

Mary Perkins looked like a woman who had paid to have her palm read and heard that she had no life line. "Where?"

"You have just a trace of a southern accent. Since I know you've been arrested, I'd check the arrest record to find the city where you were born. That's always the fifth place."

Mary looked at Jane with an expression that was meant to be intrigued puzzlement, but the surface never set properly; her face only formed itself into pie-faced hurt. "Why is that?"

Jane's eyes were tired and sad. "I don't know. Some people will tell you it's because they know the territory better than a stranger could, but they say that even if every inch of the place was bulldozed and rebuilt the day they left. Some of them say it's because they can get help from friends and relatives, but half the time they don't ask for it when they're there. They go there even if everybody they ever knew is dead and buried."

"You're telling me what you don't believe. What do you believe makes them go back?"

"I'm telling you I don't think the people who do it know why. Maybe it's just some feeling that people have because we're animals too. You go to ground where you once felt most safe, and that's wherever your mother was." She watched Mary Perkins for a moment. "It's a lousy instinct, and it will get you killed."

"So what now?"

"This is a place where nobody is searching for you. You look a little different, and if you work at it you can change more. You have identification as Donna Kester that should hold up. The credit cards are real. You'll get the bills. The driver's license is from New York, but it's good too. Somebody actually took the road test. You can get a new one here with the old one and the birth certificate. That's real too." A man Jane knew had found a job in a small-town courthouse and added forty or fifty birth records that hadn't been there before. He sold about one name a year, so the odds were good that nobody would catch one and start looking into the rest.

Mary Perkins looked increasingly alarmed. "How long do we have to stay here?"

"It's up to you. If you want my advice, I'll give it to you. Spend your time around the university, where there are crowds of strangers of every description and all the thugs wear helmets and shoulder pads. Buy yourself a long, warm coat with a high collar and wear a hat and scarf."

"You're telling me you're cutting me loose, aren't you?" said Mary Perkins with growing anxiety. "I thought you were going to protect me and get me settled."

Jane framed her words carefully, making an effort to keep the frustration out of her voice. "You came to me in trouble, with two men on your back. I got you out of that trouble because you asked me to and I didn't think you could do it yourself. Now you're reasonably safe if you want to be. That's as far as I go with you."

"It's because you think I can't pay, right? Well, I can. I've got money with me, and I can get more when it's safe to travel. Enough to make it worth your time, anyway."

"Keep it," said Jane. She picked up her purse and the keys to the car. "The more you have, the longer it will be before you do something foolish." She walked to the door, stopped, and added, "Take care."

"I have a right to know why."

"No, you don't," said Jane. She stepped outside, closed the door, and walked across the cold lot to the car. She started it and drove around the block and past the motel twice. When she was certain that nobody was watching the motel and nobody had followed the car, she continued straight to Route 94 and headed east toward the junction with 23 to Ohio.

7

When Jane reached Toledo she swung east across the vast flat lake country toward home. In the morning when she passed into the southwestern tip of New York, she felt as though she had left enemy territory. Three hours later, she drove the rented car to the Rochester airport and turned it in at the lot to make it look as though the driver had continued east on a plane. Then she took a commuter flight seventy miles west to the Buffalo airport, where she had left her own car.

She drove up the Youngmann Expressway to Delaware Avenue and turned north into the city of Deganawida in the late afternoon. The sun had already moved to a position in the west where its feeble glow did little to blunt the bite of the wind off the Niagara River. She drove onto Main Street near the old cemetery that had filled up before the Spanish-American War, took the shortcut along the railroad tracks and down Erie to Ogden Street, then turned again to her block. The house was one of a hundred or more narrow two-story wooden buildings placed beside the street that ran the length of the city from one creek to the next one, two miles away.

Jane pulled the car into the driveway and her eyes instantly took in the state of the neighborhood. She had been looking at these same sights since she had first stood upright and been able to see over the hedges to survey the world while she was playing. The houses in this block had been built before the turn of the century for the people who worked in the factories and shipyards that were no longer here, and the trees were tall and thick, their roots pushing the blocks of the sidewalks up into rakish tilts that had made roller skating dangerous. Her front yard looked lush and green and needed cutting, the blades thick and wet from the rain she had missed while she was away. The clapboards of the narrow two-story house always had looked soft and organic to her because the dozens of layers of paint spread on by generations of Whitefields had made the corners rounded. She saw the curtain on Jake Reinert's corner window twitch aside and she knew he had heard the car's engine in the driveway next door.

She walked to her front door, unlocked it, and slipped inside to punch the code on her alarm keypad before the alarm could go off. She left her front door open so Jake would know that she was willing to talk. She walked into the kitchen, poured coffee into the filter of the coffeemaker, opened the freezer and unwrapped a frozen square of corn bread and a package of blueberries, and started to defrost them in the microwave oven.

Jane heard Jake on the porch, his footsteps heavy and a little stiff. "Come on in," she called, then went back to the cupboard for honey. The microwave bell chimed, and she had the corn bread, berries, and honey on the kitchen table before Jake was comfortably seated. She heard him strain a little to ease himself down with his arms.

"I brought your mail," said Jake. He set a pile of letters on the table.

"Thanks. Arthritis acting up?"

"It's just the winters," said Jake.

"Cold nights getting to you?"

"Yeah, too damned many of them."

He watched her bustling around getting cups, plates, and silverware. Nothing escaped his notice. She was wearing heavier makeup than usual, and her right eye was half closed and the high cheekbone on that side seemed tight—not puffy, exactly, but swollen. She still moved quickly and gracefully, but she didn't pick up things in groups: she lifted each one and set it down before she picked up the next. He judged it was probably a sprained wrist.

Jake had known Jane Whitefield for all of her thirty-two years, had known her mother for a few years before that, and her father all his life. He had come into this same kitchen as a child and watched her grandmother lay out corn bread, berries, and honey for him on this same table. Seneca women obeyed some ancient law that said that anybody who came in at any time of the day or night got fed.

He had not merely known Jane Whitefield, he had been around to see her coming, but it had been only two years ago that he had accidentally discovered what little Janie had grown up to do with herself. From the look of her, it had gotten harder lately. He said, "Rough trip this time?" He had suspected he would feel like an idiot if he said it this way, and he did; a woman who made her living by taking fugitives away from their troubles and into hiding probably didn't have any kind of trips but rough ones. He had said it that way because it acknowledged that he knew the nature of her business and implied that he wasn't shocked by it anymore. He considered this a necessary piece of hypocrisy.

To Jake's surprise Jane didn't take the chance he had given her to shrug it off or make a joke out of it. "Yeah," she said. "It was awful." She set a plate of corn bread in front of him and started to eat her own, but then set the fork back down. "I always thought the way it would end was that one day I would get sick of people and decide they weren't worth the trouble anymore. That probably won't be how it happens. I lost two of them, Jake."

"Lost them?" he said. "You mean you can't find them?"

"No." She spoke clearly but with the quiet voice that made him know what she was going to say, because people spoke in low voices about the dead. "I got them killed."

"How?"

"I don't know, exactly. I mean, I know what happened, but not how. We—the three of us—were taking a little boy to California. There was an ambush. I didn't read it in time because it wasn't a dark alley or a lonely road. It was a courthouse. The other two had to stop and buy me time to get the boy inside where he would be safe."

"I'm sorry," Jake said. That was what people said when somebody died. A man his age ought to have thought of something better than that by now, but if he had, he never remembered it when he needed it.

"Somebody outsmarted me. He knew what bait to use, and somehow he must have figured out a way to be sure that this lawyer—the one who died—knew it was there. But the trap he set wasn't for a lawyer. It was for someone like me."

"How do you know that?"

"He knew that I would find a way to get the boy into the courthouse before it opened in the morning, or at least study the building so I knew the entrances and exits and who was supposed to be where. So at the last minute he had them transfer the case to a different court."

Jake ate some of the corn bread and honey, and thought about what she had said. "Who is he, a cop?"

She said, "He was tracking the boy all over the country for years. If you run into a crooked cop, you can almost always avoid him by driving past the city line. There's hardly ever a good enough reason to follow you beyond it. On one side of the line he's just about invulnerable. On the other, he has no legal power and the local police wonder what he's up to. No," she said. "I think he's something else."

Jake stopped pretending not to stare at her face. "How did you get hurt?"

When she lifted her hands out of her lap and picked up her coffee cup he saw her knuckles and fingers. "At the courthouse," she said.

Jake ate his corn bread, drank his coffee, and considered. What she had wrong with her looked like one shot to the side of her face, but there was a lot of damage to her hands and wrists and probably elbows from somebody's teeth and facial bones. It was possible somebody was dead that she hadn't mentioned. "Should I be listening for sirens?"

"No. There was a judge who made sure I got out before it got to that stage." She noticed his puzzled look. "There are people like that. I don't know if I ever told you about that part of it. People who have no reason to take risks will do it. He knew he could get into trouble—probably get disbarred or something—but he did it anyway."

Jake answered, "People one at a time are a lot more appetizing than you would think if you look at them all at once." He shrugged. "So you came home."

She shook her head. "I was trying, but something else happened on the way home. There was a woman I ran into. She heard somebody talking about me in jail in California. She needed my help to get out of trouble. I started to do it. Then I realized I couldn't. I gave her some identification and some advice and left."

"Was she in danger when you left?"

"No."

"Then that's a good place to stop," he said.

She looked at him over the rim of her coffee cup. He couldn't see her mouth, just the deep strange blue of her eyes against her olive skin. To Jake it was like looking at both of Jane's parents at once. The skin and the long black hair that wreathed her face were all Seneca. But there was her mother too, the liquid blue eyes that had originated somewhere far from here in northern Europe. He tried to talk to the eyes because he had some superstitious feeling that he had something in common with them, some hope of talking to somebody behind them who shared at least one or two assumptions. But even before he began, he knew that it was nonsense. It was like thinking she was her mother because she was wearing her mother's dress. "I don't want to start giving you advice," he lied. "I never have, in spite of the fact that if everybody listened to me they'd all be a hell of a lot less erratic, since I seldom contradict myself. But I know something about how time works. No matter what you do with yourself, the day comes when it ends. You die or go into something else. If you spent your time catching fish, no matter how long you stuck at it, on the day you quit there would still be some fish out there somewhere. Not only can you not go back out and get them, but you shouldn't try."

Jane stood up and changed into the young woman next door

again. She picked up the plates carefully, one at a time, and put them in the sink. She stood tall and straight, with her long black hair naturally parting to hang down her back, and began to clean her kitchen.

Jake stood up too and signified that he understood that their meeting was over. "Well, thanks for the snack, but I've got a lot to do in the yard before supper. It gets dark so damned early now, I barely have time to wake up before the streetlights go on."

Jane turned to him and gave him a small kiss on the cheek. "Thanks, Jake."

"I'll be home if you need anything," he said as he walked to the door. "I don't imagine much of what's in your refrigerator bears looking at by now." He stopped and glared suspiciously at the keypad on the wall by the door. "Can I open this without going deaf?"

"Yes," she said. "It's turned off."

He walked outside. "Don't forget to turn it on again."

Jane closed the door and stood beside it to listen to his foot-steps going down the wooden steps and scraping on the sidewalk before she moved away. She walked back into the kitchen, washed the dishes, wiped the counters, and turned off the lights. She had cleaned the oven and emptied the shelves of the refrigerator before she had left to pick up Timmy and Mona in Chicago, so she could think of no justification for doing anything more in here. She walked out into the living room. She had given the whole house a nervous cleaning before she had left, and it had been closed tight with the furnace thermostat set to 50 degrees just to keep the pipes from freezing if the winds coming out of Canada turned fierce early, so there wasn't even any dust.

She climbed the old varnished staircase and walked into her bedroom. The telephone answering machine glowed with a steady, unblinking zero. She stripped off the clothes she had been wearing since she had left Michigan, stuffed them into the laundry bag she kept in her closet, then walked into the bathroom. She ran the water so that it cascaded into the tub hot, turned the air steamy, and condensed on the mirrors.

She stepped into the tub and let the water rise until it was close to the rim, then turned it off, leaned back, and closed her eyes. She had slept very little for the past few days, waiting until Mary Perkins was settled and breathing deep, regular breaths before she stood up, moved a chair to the best window, and sat watching the street outside the motel. Whenever she had begun to doze off, she had found herself sinking into a dream about Timothy Phillips.

She sat up, washed her hair, then lay back down and submerged her head to let the hot water soak away the shampoo and sting the bruises and abrasions on her cheek and jaw. She held her breath for a minute and a half, hearing the old, hollow sound of the pipes, feeling her hair floating up around her face and shoulders like a cloud of soft seaweed. Then she slowly lifted her head above the surface and arched her back to let the long, heavy hair hang down her back, draining along her spine. She lay back to feel the water cleaning every part of her body, slowly dissolving away the feeling of dirt, like a stain, that she always felt when she had been locked in a jail. The showers they had in jails could never wash it out. It had to come off in water she found outside.

Jane stayed in the water until it was cold, and then got out and dried herself gingerly with a big, thick towel, wrapped it around her, and brushed out her hair. Her skin was tender now, as though all of her pores had opened and the grime of the trip had been taken away, and then beneath that, a whole layer of skin cells had come off. She felt new.

She put on a clean gray sweatshirt, some soft faded blue jeans, and white socks, then lay on her bed facing the ceiling, her arms away from her body. She consciously relaxed each muscle, first her feet, ankles, calves, knees, thighs, then her fingers, hands, wrists, forearms, biceps, then her back muscles one pair at a time, from the waist to the shoulders, and fell asleep.

Jake Reinert raked the leaves in his back yard and put them into a new bushel basket. The problem with planting trees when you were young was that the damned things got bigger and more vigorous while you got older and stiffer, until you found one day that you were too old to pick up all the leaves. His problem was worse than most, because his grandfather had planted the one over his head right now. It was absurd to keep picking up sycamore leaves, but it was the first task that had presented itself while he was looking for a way to keep himself from thinking about Jane. The problem was that raking took so little thought that he kept coming back to her.

He remembered the day he had started worrying full-time, when Jane was ten or eleven. Jake had been working in the chemical plant up in the Falls. It was good money for those days, but it was heavy and hard, and the danger of it was constant. There were caustic chemicals that would have to be poured from the big vats a few times each day, and tiny droplets might hit your overalls without your noticing it. By the end of the shift there would be men in the shop whose clothes were already disintegrating, with pinholes through their pants and shirts that were getting big enough to meet each other. In those days nobody said much about it because this was a part of the country where most people worked in the heat of open-hearth steel mills, risked their limbs beside drop-forges or hydraulic presses, or worked in the lumberyards, where anything that made a noise had the capacity to cut you in two.

There were a number of Indian fellows in the part of the plant where Jake worked. There were a few Tuscaroras from the reservation in Lewiston, two or three Mohawks who came over the Rainbow Bridge before dawn every morning from Brantsford, Ontario, and four Senecas—two from Cattaraugus and two from Tonawanda. They were always playing practical jokes on each other and shouting across the shop in their languages and then laughing. At lunchtime they all sat around one of the long workbenches that was covered with butcher paper and played as many hands of euchre as they could in half an hour, slapping cards down so fast that sometimes it was hard to see them. There were about ten in the shop but only eight played, so there were two games going at a time. They made tally marks on the butcher paper to keep score. Euchre usually went to ten, but they played to a hundred.

Jake had watched them for his first couple of shifts on the job when one day he heard an enormous roar of laughter. One of their interminable games had ended. The two losers sat in their places looking as solemn and wooden as any movie fan would have liked. The two winners stood over them and gleefully flipped the cards against their noses while everybody else pointed and laughed. If the loser was caught laughing or even let a muscle of his face change, the penalty was doubled. Jake didn't need to have it explained to him. They were playing for Nosey, just like kids had when he was growing up. Later, after he knew them better, they had corrected him. The name of the game was some Indian word—they all sounded like "yadadadadadada" to him. So he said, "What's it mean?" and one of them thought for a second, and then said, "Nosey."

They accepted Jake without appearing to notice that they had, and during the summer, when people took their vacation time, he would be the one they asked to sit in for the absent player. One late July he had sat down with his lunch and eyed the tally marks on the butcher paper, pretty certain that if he and his partner, Doyle Winthrop, didn't get lucky this was their day to go home with red noses. Or redder, in Doyle's case.

One of the Mohawks came in from the loading dock looking grim. He talked to two of the others in low tones and then one of the others talked to three more on the other end of the shop. Finally Doyle Winthrop looked back at the bench, stared at Jake for a moment, and then came to sit down.

Doyle leaned on his elbows across the table, stared directly into Jake's eyes, and said, "You were a friend of Henry Whitefield's, weren't you?"

After that the details didn't much matter, but Jake listened to them anyway. Henry was an ironworker. He had been part of a gang, all of them Iroquois, who had been out west someplace building a big bridge. Doyle said a cable that was holding the girder Henry was walking on had snapped, and down went Henry. Theirs was the generation that had fought in Europe and the Pacific, and the memory of it hadn't gotten hazy in the few years since. The Iroquois Confederacy had officially and independently declared war on Germany, and all of this little band that had somehow come to include Jake Reinert had seen friends blown apart by heavy weapons. They were all acquainted with the feeling, but none of them spoke again that day.

Jake had gone home early and found his wife, Margaret, already next door with Jane and her mother. Over the years after that he had tried to be helpful, but they weren't the sort of women who needed much help. Jane had been good at schoolwork, and had never had the sort of critical shortage of boys that would have required a fatherly man to come over and tell her the story of the ugly duckling. She managed to get herself a scholarship to Cornell and apparently did whatever they required of her, because they gave her a diploma at the end of it.

Jake had only begun to worry about Jane in earnest again a year or so after that, when her mother died. Here she was a young, strikingly attractive girl with a college degree and the whole world out there waiting for her. She came back, moved into the old house next door, and lived there all alone. She had always held jobs in the summers when she was home from school, but now, as nearly as he could tell, her movements weren't regular enough to accommodate any job he had ever heard of. She was not merely secretive about what she did, she was opaque.

If he managed to plant himself so that he was impossible to ignore while she was out front mowing her lawn and ask her a question like, "What are you doing these days?" she would say in her friendliest way, "Mowing my lawn." Then she would flick the conversation out of his hands, fold it into a joke, and toss it back to him. "When I get done with this one I'm heading over to your house to do yours. You're turning that place into an eyesore and lowering property values from here to Buffalo."

It was around this time that Jake had begun to notice the visitors. Maybe they had been coming for a long time, and he hadn't noticed because he was still going to work every day. But there they were. The strangers would come to her front door. Some were women, but most of them were men. The door would open and they would disappear inside. Sometimes late at night he would hear a car engine and then they would be gone. A lot of the time Jane would be gone too, and not return for a month or more.

After a couple of years of this he pretended he didn't know where the boundary was between small talk and prying. He asked her where she was getting the money to live. She said she had a "consulting business." That pushed Jake four or five steps past the boundary and made him determined to find out what was going on. Various theories suggested themselves. She obviously had plenty of money that she wasn't prepared to account for in a way that might set anyone's mind at ease.

He had worried himself five years closer to the grave before he heard her burglar alarm go off one night. He rushed to his corner window and flipped the switch to turn on the porch light that he used so seldom he wasn't even sure the 250-watt bulb was good anymore. There, caught in the sudden glare, were not one or two but four men. The one nearest him reached into his coat and produced a pistol. It wasn't the standard revolver the Deganawida police carried. It was big and square like the .45 Colts they used to issue in the army. Jake still considered it a great piece of fortune that the man's second reaction to the light had been to turn his face and then his tail rather than to open fire.

After that night he had sat Jane down and demanded answers to the questions he had been asking less and less politely for years. The ones he got weren't the sort that would induce a reasonable person to sleep much better. A man who had the sort of enemies other people only dream about had managed to get himself tracked to her door, and the four of them had tried to break in to see if there was anything in there to help them learn where he was.

Now Jake took his bushel basket and dumped the leaves into the big barrel by the garage. This part of the country was different from other places because the Indians had never left. There were so many differences between groups—the English from Massachusetts who had fought here in the Revolution and seen how much better this land was; the Irish recruited from their bogs to dig the Erie Canal, supposedly because somebody figured they could survive the swamps but maybe because nobody cared if they didn't; the German farmers who arrived as soon as there was enough water in the ditch to float their belongings here on canal boats—that the Indians weren't much stranger to them than they were to each other. After that the rest of the world arrived.

The names of most places stayed pretty much whatever the Seneca had called them, and the roads were just improvements of the paths between them. The cities were built on the sites of Seneca villages beside rivers and lakes, plenty of them with Senecas still living in them, at first just a trading post and then a few more cabins, and then a mill.

Even now things that people thought of as regional attitudes and expressions came straight from the Senecas. When anybody from around here wanted to say they were still present at the end of a big party, they would say they had "stayed until the last dog was hung." Most of them probably had no idea anymore that they were talking about the Seneca New Year's celebration in the winter, where on the fifth day they used to strangle a white dog and hang it on a pole. Nobody had done that for at least a hundred years.

It was easy to forget about Indians as Indians or Poles as Poles most of the time, so people did, but whenever Jake got to the point where he was pretty sure everybody was just about the same, one of them did something that was absolutely incomprehensible unless you compared it with what her great-grandpa used to do.

$\mathcal{8}$

J ane awoke suddenly in the darkness. Her hands could feel the stitched outlines of the flowers on the quilted bedspread her mother had made. She was puzzled. It took her a moment to remember why she was in Deganawida, sleeping fully dressed. She could tell that her mind had been struggling with something in the darkness, but whatever it was, she had not been able to bring it back with her this time. There was a sound still in the air, maybe left over from the dream, and then she heard it again: the ring of the doorbell.

She stepped to the window and looked down at the front steps. She could see the faint glow of the porch light on Carey McKinnon's high forehead. He was carrying a big brown shopping bag. She hurried to the mirror, turned on the light, brushed her hair quickly, then rushed into the bathroom and reached for the handle of her makeup drawer, but the ring came again. She had no time.

She came down the stairs, crossed the living room, and swung the door open. She stayed back out of the reach of the bright light on the porch and said, "Oh, too bad. I was hoping it was Special Delivery."

"No, you weren't," said Carey. "They don't come at eleven o'clock at night. I happened to be passing by on the way home from work, and I saw your car was back."

"No, you weren't," she said. "Deganawida is north of the hospital. Amherst is due east."

"I had to stop near here to buy myself these flowers." He opened the bag and held up a dozen white roses. "Since you're up anyway, could you do me a favor and put them someplace?"

"Oh, all right." She reached out and took them. "I suppose you'd better come in while I do it. I don't want you scaring Mrs. Oshinski's Dobermans."

He stepped in and closed the door behind him. She knew she had imagined he had ducked to come through the doorway; he had just looked down to plant his feet on the mat. But he had always given the impression that he was a big boy and still growing, and it had never gone away, ten years after college, when his sandy hair was already thinning a little at the crown.

He followed her into the kitchen. "So how was your trip?"

"Who said I was on a trip?"

"Oh. Then how did your car like its month in the shop?"

"I was on a trip," she conceded. "California. It's pretty much as advertised."

He nodded. "Warm."

"Yeah. What's a doctor doing coming home this late? House calls?"

"Dream on. I'm working the emergency room. Night is the time when roads get slippery, fevers go up, people clean loaded guns."

Jane snipped the stems of the roses and skillfully arranged them in a cloisonné vase that had been her grandmother's, then placed the vase on the dining room table.

"Beautiful," said Carey. "Good place for them, too."

"They're right where you won't forget them when you leave."

"No, you might as well keep them. They're all wet." He pretended to fold up his shopping bag. "Oh, I forgot. They gave me this too." He held up a bottle of champagne. "Two-for-one sale or something. I couldn't understand the lady in the store. Thick Polish accent."

"Your mother was Polish."

"Was she? I couldn't understand her either." He walked to the sink, popped the cork on the champagne, and plucked two glasses out of the cupboard. "Explains a lot. Maybe that's what she was trying to tell me. Nice woman, though."

Jane had to step into the light to take her glass. Carey clinked it gently with his, then followed her into the living room.

"So why are you working the emergency room?" she asked as she curled her legs under her on the couch. "Finally piss somebody off?"

A change came into his voice as it always did when he talked about his work. "I decided I needed a refresher course, so I took over the evening shift a couple of weeks ago. If Jake asks, I've still got plenty of time to check my regular patients for suspicious moles."

"Why does a young quack like you need a refresher course? Doze off in medical school?"

"I guess I should have said 'a reminder course.' It's basic medicine. The door at the end of the hall slides open, and in walks Death. You get to look him in the eye, spin him around, and kick his ass for him. It's exhilarating. Besides, the regular guy asked me to help him out. E.R. doctors last about as long as the average test pilot, and he's approaching the crash-and-burn stage. They don't always win." He seemed to notice her listening to him. "You look awful, by the way."

"Sweet of you to say so. That's how women look when you wake them up."

He turned his head to the left to call to an invisible person. "Nurse! More light!" Her eyes involuntarily followed his voice, and he turned on the lamp above him with his right. "Wow. Pretty good contusions and abrasions. Finally piss somebody off?"

She knew she wasn't going to get the car accident story past Dr. Carey McKinnon. "I was mugged outside my hotel."

"I'm sorry, Jane," he said, tilting his head to see her more clearly. "What happened?"

"It was nothing, really. He came out from behind one of those pillars in the garage under the hotel to grab my purse. I yelled and the parking attendant came. He got away."

"Is he all right?"

She frowned. "Why would anybody say that?"

"Your hands."

"Oh," she said. "Well, I did resist a little. I'm not dumb enough to die for a purse, but he scared me."

Carey was already on his feet and moving toward the door.

"Where are you going?"

"I left my bag in the car. I always have one with me in case there's a chance to bill somebody."

"You're a dear friend, but I like you because your big feet tromp my snow down in the winter so I can get my car out. Who said I wanted medical treatment from you?"

"I just need to bring it in. Old Jake probably recognized my car, and he's handy enough to break in for the drugs."

Carey stepped outside. She heard his trunk slam, and then his feet coming back up on the porch. In a moment he was inside, the black bag was open at her feet, and he was sitting beside her turning her head gently from side to side. He took a bottle out of his bag and poured something out of it onto a ball of cotton. He swabbed her face with the cold liquid and then stared into her eyes with a little flashlight. He took her hands in his and studied them, then bent her wrists a couple of times, staring as though he could see through to her bones.

"Doctor?" she said. "Just tell me, will I be able to play the piano?"

"Heard it. You couldn't before." He didn't smile. "The wrist is only a mild sprain," he said. "It'll be okay in a few days. The lacerations on the knuckles look good already—probably because you didn't put makeup on them. You're lucky. Human teeth are an incredible source of infection." He took a small aerosol can out of the bag and sprayed her hands. It felt colder than the disinfectant, but as it dried, the pain seemed to go away. He lifted her hand and kissed the fingertips. "I just like the taste of that stuff." He looked at her cheerfully. "You want to know the truth, it helps things heal. We don't tell people that, of course."

Jane couldn't think of a retort. In all of the twelve or thirteen years she had known Carey McKinnon, they had been buddies. They had kissed hello and goodbye, but he had been the friend she could call so she didn't have to go to a movie alone or eat at a table for one. The champagne was a pleasant surprise, but the roses brought with them a new ambiguity, and it was growing and getting more confusing.

"Stand up," he said. She stood up. He moved her arms and felt the elbows, pressed the radius and ulna between his fingers. He put his big hand under her rib cage and poked her a couple of times with the other. "Does that hurt?"

"Uh! Of course it hurts. Cut it out," she said. At another time she would have poked him back, but now he was being a doctor—at least she thought he was.

"Your liver didn't pop loose, anyway," he said. "You can have champagne without fear of death."

"Oh?" she said. "How long have I got?"

"What do I care?" He sipped his champagne. "I'll have been dead for twenty years. You pamper yourself like a racehorse, and women handle the wear and tear better than men." His eyes swept up and down her body with a frankness that she wasn't positive was detachment. "It's just a better machine."

"Then you must really be walking around in a piece of junk," she said. She stretched her sore arms and rubbed her shoulders.

"That's only muscle pain," he said.

"Well, don't sound disappointed. It's the best pain I can manage right now."

"A big shot of adrenaline comes in and your muscles go from rest to overperformance in a second or two, and they feel the strain. In two days you'll be back out there teaching truck drivers to arm wrestle, or whatever it is you do."

"Consulting."

"Insulting them—whatever," he said. He started to close his bag, but then spotted something. He picked up a clear bottle with a liquid in it that looked like vinegar. "Try this stuff."

"What is it?"

He handed it to her. "Don't look free samples in the mouth. Doctors get an incredible number of them, and once in a while you get something you can give your friends legally. This stuff is terrific."

"What's it for?"

"It's not medicine. It's just glorified massage oil. It's got a very mild analgesic in it, so it puts a deep warmth on sore muscles."

Jane opened the bottle and sniffed it. "You're not lying, anyway. It smells too good to be medicine."

He took it back. "Come on," he said. "Lie down and I'll put some on you."

"Lie down, Carey?" she asked. "Could you be a little more specific, please? Or maybe less specific?"

"I assure you, madam, I am a qualified physician. Board-certified. Climb up there on the board." He pointed to the dining room table.

She walked uncertainly in that direction and stared at the table skeptically. "The table? Are you sure?"

"Well, if I asked you to lie down on your bed, would you do it?"

"Maybe," she said. Then she wondered how much she had actually meant by that. If it wasn't what she was afraid it was, why had she hesitated?

He said, "Okay, if it's not occupied, let's use it." He walked to the stairs.

Jane took a big gulp of her champagne. They had been friends for so long that the possibility of a sudden change was unsettling. She didn't want to lose him. She picked up the bottle and followed. "I was thinking about you a few days ago," she said. "I was talking to a little boy."

"Tall or short?"

"Uh . . . tall, I guess, for his age. He's eight."

"Tell him surgery, then. Dermatologists are short, as a rule. Surgeons are tall."

He stopped at the door of her bedroom, and she edged past him and sat on the bed. She looked up at him. "Are you sure you're not just trying to get funny with me?"

Carey sipped his glass of champagne thoughtfully. "It's crossed my mind. Always does. We never have before, and this may not be the best time to start. I sure don't want to lose you just because we disagreed on how to go about it. It's kind of tricky, and you're a very critical person."

"I am not," she said. "But what if it turned out to be an awful mistake? Would you still be able to call me up when you wanted to go someplace where no respectable person would go with you?"

"It's hard to know. How about you? If you needed somebody to make fun of, would it still be me?"

She stared at him for a moment. "I don't know. I guess we should talk about it sometime when we're not exhausted and the bottle's still corked." She flopped onto the bed on her stomach with her arms bent and her hands under her chin. "Right now I need an old friend who's willing to rub my sore back."

He sat on the bed beside her, lifted the sweatshirt a few inches, poured a little of the oil in his hand, and then slowly and gently rubbed it into the small of her back in a circular motion.

"Ooh," she sighed. "That's good."

He worked patiently, his strong hands softly kneading the sore muscles in exactly the right spots, working up higher on her back now, to the shoulder blades. She could feel the tight, hard knots of muscle relaxing under his touch. The hands kept moving inward toward the tender muscles along the spine. When he stopped to pour more oil into his palm, Jane pulled the sweatshirt up almost to her shoulders, hesitated, then slipped it up over her head and set it beside her. She was naked to the waist now, but it had seemed that making him work under a shirt was idiotic. If Carey saw her breasts, he saw her breasts.

His hands were on her shoulders, and then the connecting muscles to her neck and then along the back of her neck to her scalp. She felt goose bumps and shivered, then relaxed again. She was so loose and at ease now that all the muscles on the top half of her body were on the edge of some kind of sleep, a paralysis of laziness, so happy not moving that they didn't quite belong to her anymore. They were just there waiting for him to touch them again.

Carey said, "How's it going so far?"

"I'm ready to die now," she announced. "Just give me more champagne and keep rubbing, and you can tell them to pull the trigger whenever."

He worked back down her spine, and she began to imagine that she could see him clearly from the position of his hands on her skin. She remembered telling Timmy about him. She had said he was special, and he was. Without warning, the word *angel* appeared in her mind, and she laughed.

"What's funny?"

"Nothing," she answered with the smile still in her voice. "You're being an angel."

"How about your legs?"

"What about them?"

"Do they hurt?"

She considered the implications. He couldn't rub oil on her through a pair of blue jeans. He knew that. "Not at the moment." When she had said it she felt a sense of loss that she didn't have the time to analyze if she was going to fix it. "You can't be too careful, though." She reached under her stomach to unbutton the jeans and give a tug on the zipper.

He slipped the jeans down her legs and off her ankles, and she felt tension in her throat. Then his hands were on the soles of her feet, squeezing them with tiny circular movements, until she began to imagine she was feeling him sending messages up the nerves to her shoulders and neck. The tension didn't go away, but it wasn't unpleasant anymore. He worked up the Achilles tendon, the calves, and very softly the backs of her knees, and then slowly and carefully up the hamstrings. She was calm and happy, and she wasn't thinking at all anymore, just following his touch. But then the circular movement of his hand passed for a moment between her thighs and she caught herself arching her back to spread them apart the tiniest bit.

He kept working on her legs and back, but she could feel that the hands weren't alternating anymore, so he was undressing with the other. Then she felt the panties being peeled off, and he turned her over to gently kiss her bruised face, and they slowly joined in the embrace that she had always known would come.

Everything began with a slow inevitability, a luxurious ease and simplicity that made her feel warm, then eager, and then glad. But the feeling didn't fade. It built and intensified. After that, every second, every heartbeat expanded into a moment of its own. Suddenly she became aware that she was hearing a woman's voice, and she wondered how long she had been doing that, moaning and making little cries that she couldn't have silenced if she tried. Then she went beyond thinking into a place where every sensation seemed to go up one notch on the scale to the highest frequency—colors, sounds, movements. She was almost afraid when the intensity kept building, and the word *angel* came back to her, but this time she didn't laugh, because everything was bright and fever-clear and immediate, with no distance left at all, no will inside her but his.

The whole night passed without her knowing the time, because she had the sense that she would have to give up something in order to think. They would pause and let their heartbeats slow, lying together still clasped in the same embrace but not the same now, somehow friends simply passing together into sleep. But then one of them would stir, and the other would silently say yes, each time the question and the answer completely different, because every time the last time had not faded or gone away, so it was like going up another step on a stairway.

At dawn they were lying on the bed, eyes closed, when he said, "What do you think about getting married?"

Jane's breath caught in her throat. Have beautiful tall children. Live here—not in this house, but at least close by, in the big old stone one in Amherst with him. Maybe that was where all of this had been taking her, leading her away from death the way she had taken other people. She would never have to tell him what a guide was because it would all be over—already was over when you started losing.

"No answer?" he asked.

"Every girl's fondest wish," she said. "Think the guy who owns the Buffalo Bills might be interested in marrying me? Maybe the one who fathered those quintuplets. There's a guy who knows his way around a diaper."

"I mean it," said Carey. "We should get married."

Jane sat up, then leaned over and kissed him, letting her hair hang down on both sides of their faces like a curtain. She lay back down. "Thank you," she said. "I guess we ought to have a serious talk about it sometime."

"Does that mean yes? That's what you said last night."

"Don't be an idiot."

"Meaning?"

"I've always loved everything I knew about you."

"So why are you saying no?"

"I didn't say no." She sat up again and ran her fingers through her hair to find imaginary tangles. "I said we should have a serious talk sometime. I'll start any time you want to, but I'm not going to say yes right now."

He sat up too. "I can do that."

She sighed. "When was the last time you had sex, Carey?"

He pursed his lips and said reluctantly, "The other night."

"You mean the night before last night. The last time you came off a shift."

"It was a colleague. It wasn't a routine procedure. She's a terrific diagnostician, a person of the highest—"

"I don't want to know."

"What is this? You pry and then pretend you're not interested?"

"You'd make a lousy husband."

"Jane, this thing with my colleague. It's not anything to get jealous about. It was a single, isolated event. Two patients died at the end of the shift after we did everything we could. I think we were just comforting each other. There's something buried deep in the cerebral cortex that gets triggered when you lose a life, some primitive forgotten instinct that says 'Fuck while you can, because one of these times that is going to be you.' It's the practical animal reaction that evolved to keep the species alive after prehistoric kill-offs. She's probably mystified that we did it. Next time we do a shift together we'll be perfectly professional."

"I'm sure you will. You're a good doctor, and you'd know if she weren't. But I assure you, if you had her in the sack, she's not going to let herself get too mystified. She's probably waiting on your doorstep. If she isn't, it doesn't matter, because there will be another along shortly. There is, in fact, isn't there? Me. The world is full of women—an endless supply—and every last one of them has something about her: a little smile that makes you want to smile too, or breasts like two perfect grapefruits. Remember her?

That's probably why she hung around your supermarket—so you could make the comparison."

"That's not fair," he said. "You want me to start quoting you?"

"No," Jane answered. "It isn't fair. That's part of what I'm talking about. What we know about each other looks a little different if marriage rears its ugly head. And I'm not criticizing you."

"You aren't?"

"No. I never thought for a second that there was anything wrong with anything you do. I still don't. But the only way it would make any sense to marry you is if I had some reason to believe you had become monogamous."

"You actually think I can't do that?" Carey asked.

She smiled and lay down with her head on his shoulder. It was surprising how good it felt. In a moment she said, "Want some breakfast?" and was up and heading for the kitchen. She slipped her bathrobe on as she walked down the hall. Then she heard the *beep-beep-beep-beep,* stopped, and walked back to the bedroom doorway. He was sitting on the bed staring sadly at the pager attached to the belt on the floor. "Your alarm's going off," she said. "Somebody seems to be breaking into your pants."

Carey picked up the beeper, slipped on his pants, walked to the telephone by the bed, and cradled the receiver under his chin as he dialed. "It's the hospital," he said, and buckled his belt. As she walked back down the hallway she heard him say, "Dr. McKinnon."

Jane went into the kitchen and packed him a little lunch while he talked on the telephone. She could hear him thumping around up there, probably not doing a very good job of making himself presentable. When she heard his feet on the stairs she came out and handed him the little brown bag.

"Sorry," he said. "I'll call you as soon as I'm off and get some sleep."

"Thanks," she answered, then added, "If I'm not around, don't worry. I may have to go out of town."

"See?" He grinned. "Nothing's changed. You always say that." He gave her a long, gentle kiss, picked up his black bag, and hurried out to his car.

Jane thought about what she had said. She had no plans to go anywhere. It was simply the old habit: never give anyone a reason to ask the police to look for you.

She considered going back to bed, but if she did she would be out of step with the sun and moon, and she hated that feeling more than being tired. She spent the day cleaning her clean house, cutting her lawn, and weeding her flower beds. She tried not to think about what Carey McKinnon was doing, or about being Mrs. Carey McKinnon, or about finding the right way of loving a particular person. What she needed to know wasn't something that could be figured out in advance. She had to wait until she was sure she wasn't taking an old friend and converting him into the consolation prize for failure. It was only after night had come that she went back up to bed and allowed herself to sleep.

9

Jane sat in the kitchen and drank coffee. The sun was beginning to come up, the light now diffused and gray beyond the window. She wasn't sure how long she had been hearing the birds, but they were flitting from limb to limb now, making chirrups. She used the hot coffee and the silence to work her way back through her dream, and she knew where every bit of it had come from.

She had been running at night through the woods, trying to make it to the river. She must have been a child, because her parents were with her. There was something big and dark and ferocious chasing them, but she wasn't able to catch a glimpse of it through the trees. Every time she tried to look over her shoulder it seemed to be closer, but she could only discern a shadow that blotted out some of the stars, or see branches shaking as it trampled through a thicket.

She walked to the middle of the living room and cleared her mind while she began the one hundred and twenty-eight movements of Tai Chi, one flowing into the next without interruption.

She decided her muscles weren't as sore as they had been yesterday. Maybe Carey's liniment had worked after all—or something else had. Her body borrowed part of her consciousness as it had learned to do through long years to move through positions with names like "Grasp Sparrow's Tail" and "Cross Hands and Carry Tiger to Mountain," and ended as it had begun, almost floating. Then she slipped on a sweat suit, hung her house key on a chain around her neck, went down the front steps, and began to run.

She started slowly and easily in the cold dawn air and gradually lengthened her strides as her body warmed and her muscles relaxed. She ran down to the river and along the open grassy strip toward the south. Deganawida was alive this morning with people just up and driving along Niagara Street toward their jobs, the men's hair wet from their showers and plastered to their heads, the children dressed in their second-heaviest coats already, their mothers hustling them down the sidewalk and making sure they were at least pointed in the direction of the school when they started off. She ran up as far as the Grand Island bridge and then turned back. The run home would give her just the right stretch of time to shower, change, and eat before the library opened.

Inside the library she walked to the desk and collected all of the past month's issues of the *Los Angeles Times,* then hid in the small room in the corner surrounded by the reference books that nobody ever used unless they wanted to settle a bet, and sat down to read.

The first one that caught her eye was two days old.

INVESTIGATION OF COURTHOUSE DEATHS IS INCONCLUSIVE

VAN NUYS—In the latest development in the strange saga of Timothy Phillips, kidnap victim and heir to a San Francisco fortune, an L.A. Police spokesman conceded today that the investigation has so far produced no charges against anyone. The bizarre events at the Van Nuys courthouse which caused the deaths of two persons and the arrests of five others last month are still under investigation, said Captain Daniel Brice.

Details are still sketchy, but the police have put together this much of the puzzle: Just as the courts began session on the morning of the 15th, attorney Dennis Morgan, 38, of Washington, D.C., stopped his car in front of the courthouse to let off his eight-year-old client, Timothy Phillips, and Mona Turley, 29, the woman posing as Phillips's mother. The rented car then apparently slipped into reverse and slammed into an oncoming vehicle. Driver Harold Kern, 23, and passenger James Curtain, 26, both of Los Angeles, suffered minor injuries, but Morgan was (See *Inconclusive*, A 29)

Jane impatiently searched page 29 and found the rest of the article in the lower left corner.

pronounced dead at the scene.

Kern and Curtain ran into the courthouse, apparently seeking assistance for Morgan. Mona Turley, police theorize, may have believed the two men were pursuing her with hostile intent. A struggle ensued, in which numerous bystanders took sides. The confrontation erupted into a fight in a fifth-floor hallway, where bailiffs in a nearby courtroom responded to the disturbance.

Arrested with Curtain and Kern were Roscoe Hull, 22, Max Corto, 28, both of Burbank, and Colleen Mahoney, 29, of Orlando, Florida.

After police restored order, the body of Mona Turley was discovered at the bottom of a stairwell, an apparent victim of a fall from an upper floor. Police sources confirm that a maze of conflicting allegations have been made, but eyewitnesses have established that none of the five persons arrested could have left the hallway once the fighting began.

Captain Brice explained that in the absence of evidence that any of the combatants had ever met the deceased, had any motive to harm her, or were in the stairwell at the time of her death, they could not be considered suspects. He said that foul play has not been ruled out, but that Turley might have been overcome with anxiety or remorse because of possible kidnapping charges and taken her own life.

Jane sat and stared at the orderly rows of thick volumes on the shelves in front of her. They had killed Mona, but the best she could do was to go into court as Colleen Mahoney, lie and say she saw them, then watch twenty witnesses parade to the stand and say she was wrong. The ones who had been in the car had certainly broken Dennis's neck with a choke-hold after the crash, but she hadn't seen that either.

If the police hadn't found a connection between any of them and the Timothy Phillips case, then they were hired hands. No doubt the police and the F.B.I. were quietly looking for Colleen Mahoney, but there was no reason to let them find her. She was finished.

She looked through the newspapers for more articles about Timothy Phillips. Finally she found one that was only a day old.

HOFFEN-BAYNE NOT SUSPECTED OF WRONGDOING, D.A. SAYS

A spokesman for the District Attorney's Office issued a statement today denying rumors that Hoffen-Bayne Financial, Inc., is under suspicion of attempting to defraud kidnapped heir Timothy Phillips of the multimillion-dollar estate of his late grandmother.

"The rumor has no merit," said Deputy D.A. Kyle Ambrose. "All you have to do is read the conditions of the trust. If Mr. Phillips were deceased, Hoffen-Bayne did not stand to benefit. All the money was to be donated to charities. I'm convinced that they filed to have the child declared dead because it was the proper procedure under the trust instructions, and consistent with the behavior of a good corporate citizen. There's very little benefit to society from having vast fortunes tied up in trusts with no beneficiaries. The intent of the grandmother was to provide for her grandson, not to build a perpetually-growing pyramid of unused money." Ambrose noted that Hoffen-Bayne had reason to be delighted with the news that Timothy Phillips had been found. "If the estate went to charities, the company would have lost large annual fees as trustee and executor, which now legally must continue until the boy reaches eighteen, and could continue as long as he wishes."

Jane read the article twice. Dennis had been certain that the men who were after Timmy had been hired by Hoffen-Bayne. Dennis was a lawyer, and there had been something in the documents that had convinced him that Hoffen-Bayne had a rational reason for doing it. But the Los Angeles D.A.'s office was full of lawyers, criminal lawyers at that. Were they just convinced that companies like Hoffen-Bayne weren't in the business of killing their clients?

She tried to look at it in a logical way. Hoffen-Bayne had chosen this time to have Timmy declared dead. If they were capable of murder, they could have waited until they had actually killed him, left his body where it would be found, and let the coroner do the paperwork. Or they could have waited and filed the papers at the best possible time for them. No, she had to assume that they had already waited, and that this was the perfect time. There was nothing external to make them do it now. There were ten more years until Timmy could take control of the money and fire them, ten more years of the "large annual fee" the D.A. had mentioned.

Jane stood up, walked out to the librarian's counter, and caught Amy Folliger's eye. "Can I make a couple of copies on the machine?"

"Sure," said Amy. "A dime a copy. But I'm afraid you'll have to sign this sheet," she added apologetically. "It relieves the library of liability if you violate a copyright."

Jane glanced at the papers on the clipboard. The first page was a summary of the copyright law of 1978. She signed the second page and handed it back.

"Sorry," said Amy. "Did you ever wonder how we ever got to this point?"

"What point?"

Amy's big eyes widened behind the silver-framed glasses that Jane had never seen her wear except on duty at the library. "Where everything is lawyers. Of course they get to write the laws. Did you ever hear of a lawyer missing the chance to give himself perpetual fees?"

"Once or twice," said Jane. "Maybe if we all behave ourselves for a hundred years, they'll go away." She copied the articles, then walked to the newspaper rack and carefully replaced the stack of L.A. Times.

Jane put the copies into her purse and walked out of the library. As she approached her car, she composed the note that she would write to Karen the lawyer to explain what was bothering her, but it didn't feel right. What was bothering her was that she wanted to know now.

Jane passed the telephone booth beside the building and then walked back to it. She dialed the number and said to the secretary who answered, "This is Jane Whitefield. She knows me. Tell her I'm going to fax something to her."

"Would you like an appointment for a consultation or—"

"No, thanks," she said. "She can call me." Jane hung up and walked up Main Street to the little stationery store that Dick Herman had run for the last few years since his father retired. The growing collection of signs in the window announced there were post office boxes, copiers, and a fax service now.

When she had sent the clippings Jane drove home, walked inside, and heard the telephone ringing. She closed the door and hurried to the phone. Maybe Carey wasn't with the great diagnostician. She snatched up the receiver just as her answering machine started. "You have reached—" said the recording, and clicked off. "Hello?"

"Hi, Jane." It was Karen's voice. The last time Jane had heard it Karen had wondered aloud—in a purely speculative way— whether there was any way to protect a witness who had just saved a client of hers. "I got your message. But what is it?"

"Did you read the articles?" said Jane.

"The second woman—I take it that was you?"

"You don't want to know."

"It's okay. Attorney-client privilege."

"I'm not a client."

"If you're in trouble you are."

"I'm not," said Jane. "I just need advice. How are they stealing the money?"

"I don't have the slightest idea," said Karen. "If it were obvious, I certainly wouldn't be the only one who could figure it out. Without reading the documents that established the trust I'd only be guessing anyway."

"All right," said Jane. "Let me fish, then. What's the statute of limitations on stealing money from a trust fund?"

"That's breach of trust as a fiduciary. Here it's four years. I'd have to look up California."

"Suppose they robbed Timmy the day the old lady died. They have Timmy declared dead and it's over? Nobody can do anything?"

"No," said Karen. "He's a minor, right? The statute time doesn't start running until he's eighteen, when the money goes to him. If he doesn't spot it after four years, they're in the clear, as long as they didn't do anything worse."

"What if he were dead?"

"Then the next heir gets the money—presumably some adult—and the clock starts again. Who is it?"

Jane was silent for a minute. "The charities," she said. "That's it, isn't it?"

"That's what?"

"That's the answer. That's why they wanted Timmy dead—legally or really. So that the heir isn't a person."

"I'm not sure I follow that."

"Timmy's grandmother set up this trust fund. It was supposed to go to her son. The son died. The next beneficiary was her infant grandson. That's Timmy. There weren't any other relatives, or if there were, Grandma wasn't interested. The D.A. mentioned it in that article. The money goes to charities."

"It can't be that. Charities aren't generally run by stupid people. They receive bequests all the time, and their counsel are very sophisticated about making sure they get what the benefactor wanted them to. The charity is a corporation, and that's like a person in law. The charity would have four years before the statute time ran. The lawyers would go over the will and the trust papers the day they heard about it."

"No," said Jane. "The trust doesn't go to the charities. Only the money does."

Karen was silent for the space of an indrawn breath. "Oh, no," she said. "You're telling me the old lady didn't specify the charities?"

"Nobody has ever mentioned any," said Jane. "And Dennis— another lawyer who did read the papers—said it was just 'charities.' He was sure they were going to steal the money, but he didn't say how."

Karen's voice sounded tired, but she spoke quickly, as though she were reading something that was printed inside her eyelids. "Then I can think of a lot of ways to do it. Here's the simplest. Timmy becomes deceased—either in fact or in law—and they get a death certificate. They then disperse the money to a charity of their choice, or even of their own making, which kicks most of the money back in some way: ghost salaries and services, paid directorships, whatever."

"Is that the way you would do it?"

Karen's voice was a monotone. "Thank you very much."

"You know what I mean. Is it the smartest way? They picked this time to have Timmy declared dead. They could have waited forever. There must be a reason why they did it now."

"What I just told you is the dumb way. The smartest way is always to stay as close to legality as possible. If they were sole trustee and executor, they could have been draining the fund since it was started. They could set enormous fees, charge all sorts of costs to the trust, and cook the books a little here and there to show losing investments. They wouldn't steal it all. They would leave a substantial sum in there. How much is there?"

"I don't know. I get the impression it's tens of millions, maybe hundreds."

"Okay. Say it's a hundred million. They could get away with four or five percent a year as trustee and executor. They could also do virtually anything with the principal. There are written guidelines in every state I know of, but they're broad, and they're open to interpretation. They could invest in their friend's chinchilla ranch and have their friend go bankrupt, if nobody knew the connection. If they were smart enough to steal it slowly and vary the investments to make it look inconclusive, they could do a lot."

"Inconclusive?"

"You know. The trust has lots of stock in fifteen hundred companies, twenty million in federal bonds and a five-million-dollar write-off on the chinchilla ranch, and it's tough to prove they were anything but mistaken on the issue of chinchilla futures. Not dishonest."

"So then what?"

"They do it a few more times over the years, always making sure that the proportions are right—nine winners, one loser. They're stealing a lot, but some of it is hidden by the fact that most investments are making money. You have to remember that even the good investments go up and down too, so the bad ones are hard to spot. When they've got all they can, they call it quits."

"How do they call it quits?"

"They fulfill the terms of the trust—that is, they disperse the money to charities. Only now it's not a hundred million. It's twenty million."

"And nobody notices that eighty million is gone?"

"If the trust doesn't change hands, nobody looks. If you have twenty million, you can create quite a splash in the world of charity. You don't write a twenty-million-dollar check to the United Way and close the books."

"What do you do?"

"You divide it into ten-thousand-dollar tidbits and dole it out. Now you have two thousand checks from the Agnes Phillips Trust, which nobody ever heard of. Each year, you send four hundred different charities all over the country ten thousand dollars each. That's more than one a day. You do it for five years. The first year, when the Children's Fund of Kankakee gets a check from the Agnes Phillips Trust, what does it do?"

"You've got me."

"It sends a thank-you note. They're not going to demand an audit of the trust that sent them ten grand. It would never occur to them, and if it did, they couldn't make it stick. They're not heirs named in a will. They're a charity that got a big check at the discretion of the people who sent it. They're grateful. They have no idea of the size of the trust, and they hope they'll get another check next year so they can help more children."

"So at the end of five years, the money is all gone, and the statute of limitations has run on the eighty million they stole?"

"If they get only five percent return on the money while they dole it out, they get a couple of extra years. What's working most in their favor is that during all that time—figure eight years—nobody is asking any questions. That's the main thing. If at the end of that time there's a full-scale audit, the auditors won't be able to find a single instance of mistaken judgment that isn't at least eight years old, and no theft at all. As long as it's more than four since the payout began, nothing much matters."

"So what do I do now?"

"I'll tell you one thing I'd do. I'd make sure Timothy Phillips isn't alone much. None of this works if the heir is alive."

10

Jane went to the pay telephone at a market a few miles from her house, dialed Los Angeles Information to get the number of the Superior Court in Van Nuys, then asked to be transferred to Judge Kramer's office. It was still early in the morning in California and Judge Kramer's secretary sounded irritable and sleepy. "Judge Kramer's chambers."

Jane said, "Could you please tell him it's Colleen?" The last name he had given her had slipped her mind.

"One moment. I'll see if he can be disturbed."

The name came back to her. "Mahoney."

"Pardon me?"

"Colleen Mahoney."

Jane's mind could see the secretary pushing the hold button, walking to the big oak door, giving a perfunctory knock, and walking into the dim room with the horizontal blinds. She allowed a few seconds for the secretary to tell him, but before she expected him to remember and pick up, he was on the line. "Judge Kramer."

"Hello, Judge," she said. "Remember me?"

"Yes. This is an unexpected pleasure," he said. "At least I hope it is."

"I found out something that you need to know."

"What is it?"

"Well, I read that the D.A. has taken a look at Timmy's trust and said Hoffen-Bayne couldn't be anything but honest. He missed something."

"What did he miss?"

Jane spoke with a quiet urgency. "If Timmy was dead, the trust was to go to charities, so the D.A. assumed everything had to be okay. But in the trust Grandma didn't say, 'If Timmy dies, dissolve the trust right away and divide its assets among the following charities,' or 'Let the trust continue forever and the income go to the following charities.' She simply said, 'Give it away.' So there was no specific organization named in the trust who could demand the right to see the books."

"You're saying that someone at Hoffen-Bayne planned to plunder the trust fund, give the residue to charities, and nobody would be the wiser?" he asked. "I don't see how they could imagine they would get away with it."

"A lawyer friend of mine thinks it would have worked fine if Timmy hadn't turned up. If there are no heirs, there's nobody with the right to demand an audit."

"Except the state of California."

"Let me ask you this. When the grandmother died, wouldn't the trust have either gone through probate or been declared exempt?"

"Well, yes."

"And doesn't it have to file tax returns each year?"

"Certainly."

"My friend seems to think that there's no other occasion when the state automatically takes a look, unless the trust changes hands. Somebody with a legitimate reason has to ask. And the statute of limitations for embezzling the money is something like four years."

The judge blew some air out through his teeth. "Your friend seems to have worked this through more carefully than I have. If they filed the standard annual forms, declared Timmy legally dead, and took their time about the disbursement to charities, then yes, they could probably avoid scrutiny until it was too late to prosecute the theft. Your friend must practice in another state. The statute of limitations here isn't four years. It's two."

"Great," she muttered.

"But they can't do what they planned. They never got the death certificate."

Jane spoke slowly and quietly. "If they've already robbed him, then they still need to get one. I think they're committed."

"It's all right. Timmy is under police protection."

"I know," said Jane. "I went into his bedroom, talked to him, took him for a ride, and brought him back."

"I'll order him moved," said the judge.

"Moving him increases the danger. Just tell them you're not keeping him incommunicado, you want him protected, and they'll do their best. I'm sure you know they can't keep somebody from killing him if the person tries hard enough."

"Then what the hell do you want me to do?"

"Remove the motive."

"How?"

"The reason to kill him is to hide a theft, so uncover it. He's a ward of the court. Order an audit of his assets. Open everything up."

"All right."

"And, Judge," Jane said, "can you make it a surprise? You know—like a raid?"

"Yes. I'll have to do some preliminary probing first, and I'll have to find probable cause for a search, but I'll do it. Now what else are you waiting for me to stumble onto?"

"Nothing." Then she added, "But, Judge . . ."

"What?"

"I don't know if it's occurred to you yet, but if they realize you're going to do this, then Timmy isn't the big threat to them anymore. You are."

"I'm aware of that," he snapped. "Now I've got sixty-three litigants and petitioners and all their damned attorneys penned up in a courtroom waiting for me, so if you'll excuse me . . ."

"Keep safe. You're a good man."

"Of course I am," he said. "Goodbye."

Jane hung up the telephone and drove home. She climbed the stairs, opened her closet, and then remembered that she had given the suitcase she was looking for to the Salvation Army in Los Angeles. She went downstairs into the little office she had made out of her mother's sewing room, looked in the closet, and found the old brown one. It was a little smaller, but she wasn't going to bring much with her. She stared at the telephone for a moment, then dialed his number. His answering machine clicked on. "Carey, this is Jane. I'm afraid I was right about the trip. I'll call when I'm home. Meanwhile you'll have to make your own fun. Bye." She walked upstairs to her bedroom and began to pack.

As Jane set down her suitcase and walked through the kitchen to be sure that all the windows were locked and the food stored in the freezer, she saw the pile of letters that Jake had brought her. She had not even bothered to look at them. She leaned against the counter and glanced at each envelope, looking for bills. There were several envelopes from companies, but they were all pitches to get her to buy something new.

Finally she opened the one at the bottom. It was thin and square and stiff, from Maxwell-Lammett Investment Services in New York. Inside was a greeting card. It was old, the picture from a photograph that had been hand-tinted. There was a stream with a deer just emerging from a thicket, so that it was easy to miss at first. All the leaves of the trees were bright red and orange and yellow. The caption said "Indian Summer." When she looked inside, a check fluttered to the floor. The female handwriting in the card said, "You told me that one morning after a year or two I would wake up and look around me and feel good because it was over, and then I would send you a present. I found the card months ago and saved it, but you're a hard person to shop for. Thanks. MaRried and PrEgnant." *R* was Rhonda and *E* was Eckerly, or used to be.

Jane picked up the check and looked at it. The cashier's machine printing on it said "Two Hundred and Fifty Thousand and 00/100 Dollars." The purchaser was the investment company, and the notation said "Sale of Securities." She put the check into her purse and took one last look at the card. Rhonda had probably felt clever putting her name in code. If the people her ex-husband had paid to hunt her had known about Jane they could have identified Rhonda's prints from the paper and probably traced her through the check.

She switched on the ventilator on the hood over the stove, set out a foil pan, lit the card at a gas burner, and set it in the pan to burn. There would come a time when an uninvited guest would go through this house. Maybe it would be some bounty hunter, or maybe it would be the policemen investigating her death. Whoever it was would not find traces of a hundred fugitives and then turn them into a bonanza for his retirement. When the card was burned, she turned off the fan, then rinsed the ashes into her garbage disposal and let it grind them into the sewer. She dropped the rest of the mail into the trash can, picked up her suitcase, set the alarm, and stepped out onto the porch.

As she locked her door and took a last look at her house, she thought about the old days, when Senecas went out regularly to raid the tribes to the south and west in parties as small as three or four warriors. After a fight they would run back along the trail through the great forest, sometimes not stopping for two days and nights.

When they made it back into Nundawaonoga, they would approach their village and give a special shout to tell the people what it was they would be celebrating. But sometimes a lone warrior would come up the trail, the only one of his party who had survived. He would rest and eat and mourn his friends for a time. Then he would quietly collect his weapons and extra moccasins and provisions and walk back down the trail alone. He would travel all the way back to the country of the enemy, even if it were a thousand miles west to the Mississippi or a thousand miles south beyond the Cumberland. He would stay alone in the forest and observe the enemy until he was certain he knew their habits and defenses and vulnerabilities. He would watch and wait until he had perceived that they no longer thought about an Iroquois attack, even if it took a year or two.

It occurred to Jane as she got into her car that Rhonda's present had come at a good time. If she stopped to deposit it on her way to the airport, it would buy a lot of spare moccasins.

11

J ane took a flight to Dallas–Fort Worth under the name Wendy Simmons, and another to San Diego as Diane Newberry. Then she took a five-minute shuttle bus ride from the airport to the row of tall hotels on Harbor Island. She stepped off at the TraveLodge, but walked down Harbor Island Drive to the Sheraton East because it seemed to be the biggest.

She checked in with a credit card in the name of Katherine Webster. She had gotten the card in the same way she had obtained the five others she had brought with her: she had grown them. Now and then she would take a trip to a different part of the country just to grow new credit cards. She would start with a forged birth certificate, use it to admit her to the test for a genuine driver's license, and then would go to a bank and start a checking account in a new name. If the amount she deposited was large enough, sometimes the bank would offer her a credit card that day. If it did not, she would use the checks to pay for mail orders. Within a few months, the new woman would begin receiving unsolicited mail.

Among the catalogs and requests for contributions would inevitably be offers for credit cards. She used the credit cards carefully, a new one in each town, so that when Katherine Webster disappeared, she didn't reappear in the next city. Instead, a woman named Denise Hollinger took her place.

The banks that issued their own credit cards were happy to pay themselves automatically each month from her checking account, so all she had to do was to keep the balance high. For the others, she simply filled in the change-of-address section on the third bill and had future ones sent to a fictitious business manager named Stewart Hoffstedder, C.P.A. One of Mr. Hoffstedder's services was paying clients' bills. He had a post office box in New York City to receive the bills, and he issued neatly typed checks from a large New York bank to pay them. The imaginary Mr. Hoffstedder was so reliable that each year most of his clients would have their credit limits increased.

Sometimes Jane would grow a different kind of credit card. It would begin with her opening a joint checking account for herself and her husband, who was so busy that she had to bring the signature card home and have him sign it and return it by mail. Months passed while the husband paid for his mail-order goods with the checks and got his credit card. Then Jane would close the joint checking account and make sure the imaginary Mr. Hoffstedder got her imaginary husband's bills. She could use the man's card to pay expenses if she made reservations over the telephone, and when traveling let people guess whether she was wife, lover, or colleague without having to give herself any name at all.

After Katherine Webster checked into the hotel, she bought the San Diego newspapers, went directly to her room, ordered dinner from room service, and made the preparations she had planned during her long trip across the country. First she ordered a rental car by telephone, the keys to be delivered to her room for Mr. William Dunlavey, and the car left in the hotel parking lot. She spent a few minutes reading the society page of the *San Diego Union,* then set her alarm for six A.M. and went to bed.

When the alarm woke her, she checked the name she had found on the society page again: Marcy Hungerford of Del Mar, co-chair of the Women of St. James Fund-raising Committee and honorary chair of this year's ball, was headed for the family's eastern digs in Palm Beach. That was the best name in the columns. Honorary chairs were either famous or had money, and Marcy Hungerford wasn't famous. She was doing fund-raising and was active in that world, so she might have one telephone number that people could find. Jane checked the telephone book and found it listed, with the address beside it.

Jane took the stairs to the swimming pool, went out the garden gate, and skirted the building to the parking lot. She had no difficulty finding the rented car. She had told the woman on the telephone that Mr. Dunlavey liked big black cars, and this one had a small sticker on the left rear bumper that had the right rental company's name on it. She walked farther along the line of cars until she found one with an Auto Club sticker, peeled it off with a nail file, and stuck it over the one on her car's bumper.

She drove out to the Golden State Freeway, headed north to the first Del Mar exit, went over a high mesa and came down onto the road along the ocean. The houses on the west side of the street were big and far apart, and she could see vast stretches of flat beach on the other side of them. When she found Marcy Hungerford's house she was satisfied. It was two stories with a long, sloped roof and stilts on the beach side, a four-car garage under it on the street side, and about eight thousand square feet in the middle. She drove past it at thirty miles an hour and studied the exterior. The establishment was too complicated for Marcy Hungerford to have given all of the servants the week off or taken them with her, but they would cause no trouble. By the time they realized something was wrong, it wouldn't be wrong anymore.

At nine A.M. Jane found a little shop in San Diego that rented post office boxes, and she took a key and paid for a month in the name of Marcy Hungerford. Then she drove back to Del Mar and found the post office. She filled out a change-of-address form and had all of Marcy Hungerford's mail sent to her new post office box beginning the next day.

At ten A.M. Jane went to a pay telephone in a quiet corner of Balboa Park and dialed a Los Angeles number. As she put the coins into the slot, she checked her watch again.

"Hoffen-Bayne," said the receptionist.

"I'd like to speak to a representative for new customers, please," said Jane.

"Your name?"

"Marcy Hungerford."

"Please hold and I'll transfer you to Mr. Hanlon." There were a few clicks and a man said "Ronald Hanlon" in a quiet, calm voice. "What can I do for you, Ms. Hungerford?"

Jane said, "It's Mrs. I'm considering new financial management and I'm shopping around. I'd like to know more about Hoffen-Bayne."

Mr. Hanlon said, "Well, we've been in business in Los Angeles since 1948 and handled a full range of financial affairs for a great many people. We offer investment specialists, tax specialists, accountants, property-management teams, and so on. If you could give me a rough idea of your needs, I think I could give you a more focused picture."

That was the money question. "Well," said Jane, "my husband's affairs are managed by Chase Manhattan." This established that she wasn't somebody who had just dialed the wrong number; banks seldom managed anything less than a few million. "But I have some assets I like to hold separately." She kept her voice cheerful and opaque. Maybe there were problems with the marriage, and maybe not. If there were, California was a community-property state, and this meant she might be talking about some money the husband didn't know about and half of what he had at Chase Manhattan. She was giving Mr. Hanlon a small taste. "I'm interested in having somebody I trust manage my money conservatively so that it pays a reliable income each year." "Conservative" meant she didn't need to gamble to make more, and the income was another hint of divorce.

Hanlon rose to the bait slowly and smoothly. "Yes, that sounds wise," he said. "That would mean setting you up with our accountants and tax people, and a financial planner."

"And property management," she added. "Do you have arrangements to handle foreign real estate? France and Italy?"

That did it. He wasn't talking to a lady with a couple hundred thousand in passbooks. "I think the best thing to do would be to make an appointment and we can talk it all over in detail with advisers from some of our departments. When are you free?"

"That's a problem," said Jane. "I live in San Diego and I'm leaving for Palm Beach today." She checked her watch again to see how long she had been talking.

"When will you be back?"

"I'm not sure. It could be a month. I'm asking for information from several companies. I'm going to look it over while I'm away, and when I'm back I'll have the choices narrowed down." The element of competition would help. "I'd like to have you send me whatever material you've got that will help me know whether your company is the right one for me." She decided Marcy Hungerford had no reason to be vague, and making her naive wouldn't help. "I'd like to know the backgrounds and qualifications of your investment people, financial planners, and so on."

Mr. Hanlon seemed a little surprised. Maybe she had gone too far. "I think we have some things we can send you. What's your address?"

"It's 99233 The Shores, Del Mar, California 91182." She glanced at her watch again. She had only twenty seconds left before the operator came on and asked for more quarters.

"Phone?"

Jane gave him Marcy Hungerford's telephone number. The answering machine or the maids would tell him she was out of town.

"Got it," he said. "I'll get that right out to you."

Ten seconds left. "Fine. I'll watch for it. And thanks." She hung up and walked across the lush green grass of the park in the direction of the zoo. She felt satisfied. Hanlon would make a serious attempt to impress her with Hoffen-Bayne's operation. The main issue would be whether he had caught the hint about backgrounds. Whoever had gone after Timmy Phillips had been in the company seven years ago and was still there.

The next morning when Jane went for her run on the beach, she considered the ways of taking the company apart so that she could see what was inside. If Hoffen-Bayne had been around since 1948, then they had almost certainly been sued. She could drive up to U.C.L.A. and hire a student to research the county records for the cases. The least that would give her were the names of the people at Hoffen-Bayne who had been served with subpoenas, and almost any lawsuit would provide a lot more.

But that would mean dreaming up another story to tell the law student that would make him feel comfortable about doing it but not comfortable enough to talk about it freely. It would also place the student in a public building where someone might notice that he had an unusual curiosity about one particular company. He might be helping somebody build a case. That sort of information might easily get back to Hoffen-Bayne. Certainly when Dennis Morgan had been doing his research, somebody at Hoffen-Bayne had learned about it. She decided not to bring anybody else into this mess.

At four o'clock Jane drove back along the Golden State Freeway to Del Mar and stopped at the little store where her post office box was. She saw through the little window that Marcy Hungerford had lots of mail. She sorted through the letters and bills and catalogs until she found the packet from Hoffen-Bayne, then drove to the post office and filled out another change-of-address form so that Marcy Hungerford's mail would start being delivered to her house again.

She considered scrawling "misdelivered" on today's mail and slipping it into the nearest mailbox, but she decided that the safest way was to ensure that there was no interruption in service. She waited until eight P.M., when it was dark along the beach, walked past Marcy Hungerford's house, left the mail in her box, returned to her car, and drove on.

At the hotel Jane opened the packet from Hoffen-Bayne and began to study it. She could see immediately that Mr. Hanlon had not missed any of her hints and that he had been convinced that her account was worth having. There was a printed brochure that included little descriptions of the various arms of the company and a cover with a touched-up photograph of their building on Wilshire Boulevard. Inside were graphs and tables purporting to be proof of high returns for their clients, mixed with a text that promised personal service. Mr. Hanlon had also dictated a cover letter to Mrs. Hungerford, and stapled to it was a little stack of computer-printed résumés.

The next morning Jane checked out of the hotel and drove up the freeway toward Los Angeles. The coast of California had always made her uneasy. The air was lukewarm, calm and quiet, as though it were not outdoors. On the left side of the road the blue-gray ocean rose and fell in long, lazy swells, looking almost gelatinous where the beds of brown kelp spread like a net on the surface. The low, dry, gentle yellow hills to the east always made her sleepy because they were difficult for the eye to define, not clear enough to tell whether they were small and near or large and far. Behind them she could see the abrupt rising of the dark, jagged mountains like a painted wall.

The land along this road always looked deserted. She had to remind herself that it had been the most densely populated part of the continent when the Spanish missionaries and their soldiers arrived. The Indians here had not been at war for centuries the way the Iroquois had, so they weren't fighters. The first Europeans they saw herded them into concentration camps where they forced them to build stone missions and work the fields, and then locked them up at night in barracks, the men in one and the women in another. They were chained, whipped, starved, tortured, and executed for infractions against the priests' authority, and they died from diseases that flourished in their cramped quarters until they were virtually exterminated.

California was a sad place, a piece of property that had begun as a slaughterhouse and could never be made completely clean. It was perpetually being remodeled by new tenants who could not explain why they were doing it. They bulldozed the gentle hills into flat tables where they built hideous, crowded developments that encrusted the high places like beehives. They gouged and scraped away at the surface and covered it with cement so that every town looked like every other town, and the rebuilding was so constant that every block of buildings in the state seemed to be between ten and twenty years old and just beginning to show signs that it needed to be bulldozed and rebuilt again.

Jane drove along the Golden State Freeway for three hours until she came to the Hollywood Freeway, took the exit at Ver-mont, then swung south again for the few blocks to Wilshire Boulevard, where the tall buildings that sheltered corporations instead of people rose abruptly out of the pavement.

The things that had been happening had a very impersonal quality to them: a respected corporation had managed an account, and it had decided it was time to file a petition to declare a client deceased. But somewhere behind the opaque and anonymous veneer there was a person. Money was stolen by human beings. Sometimes thieves worked together and sometimes separately, but most successful embezzlers worked alone. It was time to find the man.

12

Ⅰn the late afternoon, Jane began to watch the Hoffen-Bayne building from the window of a restaurant across Wilshire Boulevard. It was small for this part of Los Angeles, only five floors. The bottom floor was rented out to a travel agency and a coffee shop, and the second floor was a reception area for Hoffen-Bayne. After an hour she moved to the upper tier of the parking ramp for the tall insurance building beside Hoffen-Bayne and studied the upper windows to determine which ones were small, functional offices for accountants, brokers, and consultants, and which ones were big pools for bookkeepers and secretaries. She paid special attention to the desirable corner offices.

At six P.M., when she saw people inside taking purses out of desk drawers and turning off computers for the day, she strolled along the quiet side street near the driveway and studied the men and women who came out and got into cars in the reserved-for-employees spaces in the parking lot. She wrote down the license numbers and makes and models, and matched the cars to the people she had seen in the windows.

Tall-Thin-and-Bald wanted to be noticed. He drove a gray Mercedes 320 two-door convertible that retailed for about eighty-five thousand and was too sporty for him. Woman-with-Eye-Trouble, who had the habit of putting on her sunglasses while she was still inside the office, drove a racing-green Jaguar XJ6, which was only about fifty thousand, but she was still a possibility, as was Old Weight-Lifter, who drove a Lexus LS 400, which sold for even less. Eye-Trouble might have chosen her car because it was pretty, and Weight-Lifter might be the sort of person who bought whatever the car magazines told him to.

Jane made four grids on a sheet of paper to represent the windows of the upper floors, labeled them "N," "S," "E," and "W," and made notes on each window about who had appeared in it and what went on when he did. A supervisor might pop in on a subordinate, might even deliver sheets of paper to the subordinate's desk, but when several people met in an office, it was usually the office of the ranking person.

An hour later, after the upper windows were dim but there were still people in the coffee shop and travel agency, she went into the lobby, took the elevator to the second floor, and stood outside the locked glass doors to the Hoffen-Bayne reception area. She was looking for a directory of offices posted on the wall, but there was none. The reception area was all smooth veneer and expensive furniture that made it look like a doctor's waiting room. There was no easy way into the complex, and there was a small sticker on the glass door that said "Protected By Intercontinental Security," and under that, "Armed Response." She didn't particularly want to bet that she could fool the sort of security system a company that handled money for a lot of rich people might consider a good investment, so she turned and went back to the elevator and took it to the basement of the building, on the level with the parking lot, and found a door with a NO ADMITTANCE sign. The door had a knob with a keyhole to lock it and it wasn't wired, so she had little trouble slipping her William Dunlavey MasterCard between the knob and the jamb and pushing the catch in. Inside the room were circuit breaker boxes and a telephone junction box. She opened it and studied the chart pasted inside the door. It gave the extensions of the various offices in the building, so she copied them and returned to her car.

She checked into a hotel two miles down Wilshire Boulevard and compared her office chart with the telephone extensions. Some of the offices must be the big ones she had seen through the third-floor windows, where people sat at computers and worked telephones in a pool. Nobody important had a single number with fifteen extensions. The offices she wanted were on the fourth and fifth floors, so she concentrated on them. She dialed each number and listened to a computerized voice-mail system telling her what part of the company it belonged to—investment, property management, billing, accounting—but not the name of the person. She used the information to eliminate more of the offices. The person who had been robbing the trust fund would have to be in a position to exert power over where the money was placed and how the company kept track of it. He didn't share an office, or send out bills for services, or manage real estate, or answer other people's phones. She consulted the résumés that Mr. Hanlon had sent her, and filled out more of the chart before she went to sleep.

The next morning Jane went to the Hollywood lot of the car-rental agency, told them Mr. Dunlavey didn't like the car he had rented in San Diego and that he had instructed her to exchange it for a different model. She drove out with a white Toyota Camry and sat on the side street watching the west side of the building while the Hoffen-Bayne executives arrived for work.

She watched and worked on her chart of the company for three more days. Each morning she turned in the car she had rented the day before and went to a different agency to rent a new one under a new name. Each evening she would choose one of the likely executives and follow him home when he left the office. Each night she slept in a different hotel in a different part of the city.

On the afternoon of the fifth day, Jane was reasonably sure that the man she was after was Blond Napoleon. His name was Alan Turner, and he had the office on the southeast corner of the fifth floor. This afforded him the best view of the city and made people walk a long way to get to him, past secretaries and intermediaries. The car he drove, a dark blue BMW 740I, cost about sixty thousand dollars. It was not the most expensive, but like only four others in the lot, it had a license plate holder from Green Import Auto, a leasing company in Beverly Hills. To Jane this meant that he was one of only five people who were entitled to company cars.

Whoever had been robbing Timmy would have needed to be high enough in the hierarchy seven years ago to make decisions about the Phillips trust's portfolio without much fear of second-guessing. He would also need to remain in that position long enough to see the cover-up through to the end. Of the five people who drove company cars and occupied the right sort of offices in the building, two had joined the firm within the past four years. Of the others, one was a tax attorney and another the head of the Property Management Division. There was nothing in either man's résumé to suggest that he had ever served in another capacity or had the background to handle a trust fund. The only one who had been with the company long enough and who had a specialty that sounded promising was Alan Turner, head of the Investment and Financial Planning Division.

Jane decided to test-drive a car from Green Import Auto. She selected a gray Mercedes with a telephone in it and drove directly to the side street below the southeast corner of the Hoffen-Bayne building. She waited until three o'clock, when even the important people were back from lunch meetings and the sun was on the west side of the building so that Turner's blinds would be open. She turned the corner off Wilshire and cruised toward the building, dialed the number of Mr. Hanlon, the salesman, and set the receiver in the cradle so she could use the speaker and keep her hands free.

"Hanlon," he said. She knew he was at his desk on the other side of the building.

"This is Marcy Hungerford. We spoke a few days ago, and you sent me some material." She pulled over and parked on the quiet, tree-lined street.

"Yes. Did you have a chance to look it over?"

"I did, and I think yours is one of the firms I should talk to."

She wanted to make it clear there was no commitment. She was not in the bag yet.

"Good," he said. "I've been thinking about what you've told me, and I think I'd like to get you together with one of our partners for a talk." Salesmen didn't make decisions like that; partners did. He had told his boss about her call. "Are you back in Del Mar?"

"No," she said. "I won't be back for another week. I just thought I should tell you I got your information and am still considering it."

Hanlon went on cheerfully as though he hadn't heard her. "The man I'd like you to meet is very experienced. He's been with the company for twelve years, and he's knowledgeable about all aspects of personal management."

Jane listened carefully. While she had been investigating them, they had been investigating Marcy Hungerford. The name had rung some bell or other. She had chosen well, but from here on she had to be cautious. They knew more about Marcy Hungerford than she did. She decided to stop flirting. It would do her no good to convince people Marcy Hungerford was an idiot. "Fine," she said. "I'll be happy to drive up there and meet him as soon as I'm back in California. Can you connect me with whoever keeps his calendar?"

"Let me see if he's free to talk to you himself right now. I know he'd like to if he can."

"Even better."

She heard a cascade of annoying music pour out of the speaker, and watched the man in the corner window. She saw him pick up the receiver. He talked to Hanlon for a few seconds, reached across his desk, picked up a file, opened it, and then pushed a button on his telephone.

"Hello, Mrs. Hungerford," he said. "My name is Alan Turner."

"Hello," she said. She started the car and pulled away from the curb.

"I understand you're considering us to manage your assets."

"Yes, I am," she said. She drove up the street away from the building, turned right at the corner, and kept going west. "I'm considering several companies. I'd like to find someone who will take responsibility for handling things."

"Well, that's what we're in business to offer," said Turner. "We have experts on the staff in every aspect of financial management, and—"

"I know," she interrupted. "Mr. Hanlon said the same thing. But let me explain. I want to know who would be the one person coordinating everything. I don't want to have to call thirty people every time I have a question."

"I understand perfectly. With your approval, I would manage your account myself. I don't do much of that anymore, but I still have a few."

"That's very kind."

"Here's what I propose. I'll sit down with you when you return from Palm Beach. We'll take an inventory of your current assets. I'll examine what you have and come back with a hypothetical portfolio that's sufficiently diversified to ensure you a good income. We can arrange to have it continue in perpetuity for your heirs, if you wish."

Jane had to be sure. "That sounds like a trust fund."

"That's what it is," Turner said. "In my experience, people who are busy—as I know you are, with your charity work and so on—don't want to waste their lives micromanaging their wealth. Over the years I've helped quite a few of our clients establish trusts, and so far we've done very well for them."

Now she was sure that they'd had Marcy Hungerford investigated. She had never mentioned charities. "What do you charge for all this?"

"Our commission is five percent of income," he said. "Of course there would be incidental fees from time to time for brokers, front-end loads on certain purchases, and so on, but you're familiar with those and they don't go to Hoffen-Bayne. They might be quite high in the first year while we're developing a group of haphazard assets into a coordinated portfolio, and there will be legal fees if you choose to establish a trust, but the costs taper off as the years go by."

"That all sounds good," said Jane. "What you've said in the

last few minutes has done a lot to convince me that you're the one I'm looking for. I'll call you as soon as I'm back home."

"Wonderful," he said. "I look forward to meeting you."

"Goodbye," she said, and tapped the button to disconnect, then drove the Mercedes back to the dealer's lot. She looked at a few more models, then let the salesman know that she hadn't found anything she was really comfortable in. She got back into her rented Honda Acura and drove over the pass to the Hilton on the hill above Universal City and took another room. It was a comfortable hotel, and she didn't mind staying there a few days while she did the paperwork. After she was settled and had dinner she left instructions with the concierge to have both the morning and evening editions of the *L.A. Times* delivered to her room each day, and went for a walk.

She strolled around the complex of buildings at the top of the hill and across the parking lots to a row of pay telephones outside the gate of the Universal Studios tour. She reviewed what she was about to do. There was no way anyone could trace to Jane White-field a call made from a public telephone at a place that had millions of visitors a year. It was safe. With the three-hour time difference, she would catch him just after he had come home. She felt a little uncomfortable. She had told herself that she was doing it now because she was afraid of waking him up early in the morning, and there was no point in calling while he was out. But she also knew that if he had decided to do something other than come home from work, this would be the time a person might call and find out. She had no choice but to behave the way she would if she were trying to check up on him, and she hated that. She pushed a quarter into the slot and dialed Carey McKinnon's number. The operator came on to tell her how many more quarters were needed, and she dropped them in.

"Hello?" he said. His voice seemed a little thin, as though he were winded.

"Hi, Carey," she said. "It's me."

"Well, hello," he said. He sounded delighted, and she felt glad. "Are you back from your trip?" When she noticed he had not yet said "Jane," it occurred to her that there might be a reason.

"No, I won't be able to get through this job right away. I just felt like hearing your voice."

She wanted him to say "And I felt like hearing yours," maybe because if he said it she would know there wasn't another woman in the room with him. The thought made her feel contempt for herself. He said, "My sentiments exactly. I must have just missed you the other day. When I came in there was your message on my machine. When will you be back in town?"

"I'm not sure."

She heard the *beep-beep-beep* of his pager in the background. "Oh, shit," he said. "That's my pager."

"I heard it."

"Look, give me the number where you're staying, and I'll call you when I'm back from the hospital."

"Oh, I'm sorry," she said. "I'm out and I don't have it with me. I'm never there anyway. I'll have to try you again in a day or so, when things cool down."

"Do that."

"Goodbye."

"For now," he said.

As Jane stepped away from the bank of telephones she had to dodge a group of Asian teenagers who swept past laughing and talking. She wished that she didn't have the kind of mind that always suspected deception. She reminded herself that it was ridiculous even to think of Carey that way—as though she had a right to expect that he would never see another woman. He had offered, and she had not agreed, had only said "We'll talk about it." There was no proof that a woman was in the room with him, anyway. She was just inventing a way to make herself miserable. As she walked back to her hotel, she wished that she hadn't known that when a pager was clicked off and then on again, it beeped to signal that it was working.

She spent the late evening trying to think about Alan Turner, but found her attention slipping back to Carey McKinnon. She was angry at herself for being suspicious, and angry at him for being the sort of person who made her suspicious. He was probably innocent, and if she cared about him enough to be this uncomfortable, what was she doing thousands of miles away from him, forming agonizingly clear pictures of what he might be doing with some other woman? She should be there. She was surprised by the strength of her urge to be with him. She wondered why it was stronger now than it had been yesterday. Was it because his voice had triggered some unconscious longing for him—maybe love, but maybe just some crude sexual reflex, the equivalent of Pavlov's dogs' hearing a bell and salivating—or because it had set off an even cruder instinct to gallop back and defend her mate from the competition? Twice she was tempted to call the hospital to see if he was on duty but fought down the impulse.

When the hour was late enough so that she could not imagine a good excuse to call any of Carey's numbers, Jane managed to remind herself of what she was doing in Los Angeles. She had decided it was necessary to find out who had been trying to kill Timmy Phillips. If that was true a week ago, then it was still true. Turner was the prime suspect, and anything she could figure out about him might save a little boy's life. Thinking about anything else was a waste of time. When she had reached this conclusion, she promptly fell asleep.

As the morning sun came up over the next ridge in a blinding glare, Jane laid all of her information about Alan Turner on the table of her room and studied it. She had Turner's name, the license number of the car he drove, the address of his office, and the address of his house on Hillcrest in Beverly Hills where she had followed him two nights ago. The résumé that Hanlon had sent to Marcy Hungerford said that Turner was a 1969 graduate of the University of Pennsylvania, and that he had an M.B.A. from the University of Southern California.

She forged a letter from Turner to the U.S.C. registrar's office requesting that a transcript of his graduate work be sent to the personnel manager of Furnace Financial, Ltd., in Chicago. The Furnace corporation was a business she had founded some years before. It had a genuine legal existence, but the ownership was cloudy and the physical plant consisted of a post office box that she had rented in a small Chicago mini-mall, with the arrangement that everything that arrived was to be sent unopened to another post office box in Buffalo. Then she called the owner of the little shop where the box was and asked him to call the Hilton when anything with a U.S.C. return address arrived.

As soon as she hung up she dialed Carey's number. When his machine clicked on, she tried to think of the right kind of message. She knew he wasn't working now, or she thought he wasn't. It occurred to her that if there had been a woman with him last night, she would still be there. She simply said, "It's Jane Whitefield." She paused to let him change his mind or go to an extension where the woman wouldn't hear. "I guess I missed you again." As she hung up, she closed her eyes and felt a headache building. All right, she thought. I said I would call him, and I've called him. Enough. I have work to do.

She drove to the Department of Motor Vehicles office in Glendale and filled out a form. On a line near the top, she provided the license number of the BMW Turner drove, and in the big space at the bottom she said he had scraped her car in a parking lot. The DMV answered with the name and address of the owner, which was only the leasing company Green Import Auto, but it also listed the lessee, Alan Turner, and included his driver's license number.

After only two days, the U.S.C. transcript arrived in Chicago. Jane asked the owner of the shop to open it and read it to her. From this she got Turner's Social Security number. With the driver's license number and Social Security number, she was able to have Furnace Financial request a credit report on Alan Turner.

The credit report told her he was paying a mortgage of one million, eight hundred thousand dollars to Southland Mortgage. This must be the house on Hillcrest. He had several credit cards and paid the balances each month to avoid interest charges. He had checked the box on his mortgage papers that said "Divorced," which made things simpler: he didn't have a wife with a second income. But there was also a surprise. Turner was repaying another loan of six hundred thousand dollars to the Bank of Northern California. It was a mortgage on a second home.

She looked in the telephone book for the Bank of Northern California and found listings for several branches, as well as a Bank of Northern California Mortgage Services in San Bernardino. She called the mortgage office and asked for the credit department.

Anybody who loaned money must have a credit department. In a second a woman answered.

"This is Monica Butler at the San Francisco office," Jane said. "I've got a loan application here from a customer who lists a mortgage from us already for six hundred thousand. I'd like to know what the property is."

The young woman said, "The name?"

"Alan R. Turner. Need his Social Security number?"

"No," the woman said. She was typing the name into a computer. If the person on the other end of the line thought you were from the same company, none of the privacy rules applied. She was merely transferring information from one internal file drawer to another.

"The property is at 1522 Morales Prospect, in Monterey."

"Do you have a zip?"

"Sure. It's 93940."

"Thanks." Jane hung up and wrote down the address. The picture she was forming of Turner was coherent and consistent: he made a lot of money and he was cautious and premeditated. He saved some by driving a leased company car. He used his high income and stability to take out big deductible mortgages on two of the most desirable addresses in the Western Hemisphere, so he probably didn't pay much in taxes. But those were relatively modest prices for their neighborhoods, so he wasn't taking big risks. He wasn't in love with debt, because his credit cards had never carried a balance to the next month. He didn't look like an embezzler. If he had been quietly robbing the Phillips trust fund for years, he must have had the foresight to know that some day a stranger might take a look at his assets. Either he was extremely sophisticated or she had chosen the wrong man at Hoffen-Bayne.

The following morning Jane rose before dawn, walked to the door of her room, picked up her copy of the *Los Angeles Times*, and unfolded it to reveal the second page, where the summary of major articles was printed. On the lower left side was a box that said, "Judge Seizes Hoffen-Bayne Records (See E-1, Business)." She had run out of time.

13

Jane had checked out of the Hilton and had her car on Laurel Canyon Boulevard by five A.M. She hadn't dared stop to read the whole article, but she had scanned it on the walk down the hallway to the desk, and took a longer look while she was waiting for the valet to bring her car to the entrance. The judge had been devious. He had issued requests for specific documents, which Hoffen-Bayne had dutifully provided a week ago. Probably he had done this to give them the impression that he was just going to take a cursory glance at a couple of carefully cooked annual reports. If he hadn't asked for something, they would have suspected trouble. Then, last night after business hours, he had issued a warrant and sent cops with a truck down to Wilshire Boulevard. She moved her eyes down the column of print, but could see no names.

She decided to avoid Wilshire Boulevard. The office would already have reporters and cops and, as soon as the clients got up and read their papers, enough panicky investors to keep them all busy. She needed to go to Beverly Hills.

She reached Sunset and turned right. Even at five in the morning the street was busy, but the cars were moving quickly. She made her way in the intervals between cars, the skyline in front of her dominated by enormous lighted billboards with pictures of pairs of giant actors looking stern and fearless, and actresses with moist lips the size of watermelon slices.

The judge had done his work. Timmy was, at least for the moment, as safe as anyone could make him. He had already told the authorities everything he knew. The judge had taken away the incentive for anybody at Hoffen-Bayne to kill him. It would be like killing a witness who already had testified. There was only Turner to occupy her mind now. She had calculated that she would have a few more days to study him, and her feeling of frustration surprised her. It wasn't that she had any real hope that she could do any more than the authorities could to get Timmy's money back. She wasn't even sure how she felt about the money. She had to fight the conviction she had been raised with that accumulating wealth was a contemptible activity.

This wasn't something that her parents had invented. It was an old attitude that had never gone away. In the old days no family ever built up disproportionate surpluses of food. Whatever they had was shared with scrupulous equality. Each longhouse was owned by the women of the clan, and each woman had a right to live there and raise her children and sleep with her husband when he was around. A man was a warrior and hunter, out in the forest for most of the year, and he seldom owned anything he couldn't carry. If he wanted respect, he would bring back lots of meat and plunder for the village. A person's status was a measure of how good he was at obtaining things to share, not how much he was able to take and hoard. After the white people arrived they advised each other that the way to find the leaders of the Iroquois was to look for the men in rags.

Whatever would happen to Timmy's money would happen whether she was here or in Deganawida. It was Turner she was interested in. She had to know if his careful accounting and his conservative, respectable manner of living had all been part of a scheme to disguise a greed strong enough to make him kill people.

She turned down Hillcrest and cruised slowly past Turner's

house. She had to be alert and careful this morning. The richest parts of Los Angeles were guarded with a strange, subtle vigilance. There were small, tasteful signs with the trademarks of security patrols on every lawn, small, unobtrusive surveillance cameras on the eaves of the big houses, and lots of invisible servants watching. The sound of a helicopter overhead probably meant a cop was looking down with night-vision binoculars. An unfamiliar car parked in the wrong place, a stranger walking down the street, and particularly anybody doing anything before sunrise, were ominous signs to be remembered and reported.

She drove across Sunset onto the slope on the north side, parked her car on a side street next to a medical building in a space that was shielded from the intersection by a big tree and a Land Rover, and ducked down in the seat while she changed into her sweat suit and sneakers. She pulled her hair behind her head, slipped a rubber band around it to make a ponytail, and began to jog slowly down onto the flats.

The sidewalks here were wide and even, and the street was lined by two long rows of coconut palms. The air was warm for five-thirty A.M., and she could hear traffic above and below her but saw no cars driving down Hillcrest yet. She ran slowly and easily, less to keep from pulling a muscle than to keep anyone who saw her from looking twice. A woman trotting painfully along a residential street at dawn was just another local girl in the dull business of keeping her waist and thighs attractive; a woman loping along like a track star was something else.

Jane took her time and looked closely at the houses. Few of them showed any interior lights at this hour. The garages were all hidden far back behind the houses at the ends of long driveways, and nobody left his car parked on the street. When she approached Turner's block she slowed to a walk, as though she were catching her breath.

The house had lights on behind the drawn blinds. She watched the windows for a few seconds and glanced at her watch. It was five-thirty now. When she looked up, one of the lights had gone off. She began to jog again. If he was turning lights off, he must be coming out. She passed the house, keeping her head forward but moving her eyes to the left to scan the house and the yard. As she came abreast of the house, another light went off.

She saw the newspaper lying on the front porch. As she trotted on down the street she wondered about it. By now there was no chance he didn't know that his office had been raided. If he hadn't been behind his desk at Hoffen-Bayne when the cops came in and started padlocking filing cabinets, then somebody certainly would have told him. Reporters would call him. Was it possible that he wouldn't bother to read what the newspapers said about it the next morning?

She stopped running again at the end of the block and looked back at the house as she crossed the street. Two lights were still on. She started moving again, this time down the street toward Wilshire, glancing back now and then to see if anything had changed. Maybe he had gone out in the night to buy the paper as soon as it had come off the presses. No, that didn't make sense; the newsstands carried only the early edition that had been printed the previous afternoon, before the raid.

She turned and ran toward her car. The sun would be up before long, and there would be people out even in this quiet neighborhood. Inside her car she quickly changed into a pair of jeans and a blouse.

She drove back down onto Hillcrest. As she passed the house, the other two lights went off. She checked her watch. It was exactly six o'clock. She was positive now that the lights were on timers. The ones they sold in hardware stores had crude dials on them, so it was difficult to set them for any time but an hour or half hour. She had always used them in her house when she went on a trip, and had solved the problem by setting the present time on them not to correspond with what her watch said. Turner wasn't as good at this as she was. He might be a thief, but he had not learned to think like one. He had not even timed them to be sure they didn't click off before the sun was up.

Still, it was conceivable that he had set them but hadn't left yet. She stopped at a small convenience store with an iron grate across the door, walked to the pay telephone, and dialed his number. There was no answer and no machine to record a message. She hung up after ten rings and got back into the car. As she started it, she checked the rearview mirror and saw a car coming that had lights on the roof like a police cruiser. It had blue and yellow stripes, and the shield on the door said "Intercontinental Security." She pulled out and followed it at a distance. The car swung up and down a couple of side streets above Sunset, and then came down to Hillcrest, gliding along, the driver glancing casually at all of the houses with blue-and-yellow security signs. He pulled up at the curb in front of Turner's house and got out. He was young and broad-shouldered and wore a tight uniform like a cop's with a gun belt that made him hold his arms out a little from his sides as though he were carrying two buckets. He opened the gate, ran a flashlight over a couple of side windows, and picked up the news-paper. Turner was gone.

Jane drove on, turned left on Sunset Boulevard and continued west to the entrance for the 405 freeway near U.C.L.A. This was the way Turner would have come after he had heard the news. He could have turned south toward the airport, but she was sure he had not done so. He was a conservative, judicious man. He had taken the second ramp, the one that got him safely out of town but didn't incur the risk of appearing to flee the country. He had gone north to his house in Monterey.

14

J ane came up over the hill that separated the city from the San Fernando Valley and edged to the right onto the Ventura Freeway, then stayed on it as far as Santa Barbara before she stopped for breakfast in the restaurant of a sprawling hotel complex along the beach. By the time the food was cooked she was too impatient to eat, so she had the waitress put it in a Styrofoam container and took it with her in the car. North of the city at the Santa Barbara airport, she turned in the rented car and took a commuter flight to San Francisco, then rented another car there to drive down the coast to Monterey. It was early evening when she checked into a small motel a mile inland from the ocean, showered, and wrapped herself in a towel.

She sat on the bed and dialed Carey McKinnon's number, then hung up before it rang. She had been waiting, listening to the static while the telephone company's computers threw switches to move the call across the country to Carey's house, and she sensed in herself a feeling that was not right. She had not been calling because she wanted to give him a message of love before he dropped off to sleep, or even to soothe herself with the sound of his voice. These were the only legitimate reasons for calling Carey tonight. If the eagerness she had been feeling was morbid curiosity or the grim satisfaction of confirming a suspicion, then the only decent thing to do was leave him alone.

She opened her suitcase and looked at her clothes. She decided that evening in Monterey was an occasion for basic black. She put on a black turtleneck sweater, a matching jacket, and black pants, then tied her hair back. The accessories were what would make such an outfit. She laid out the few items of female paraphernalia she had brought and made her selections. She fastened her hair with a black ring and a thin five-inch-long peg that had a T-shaped handle at one end and was sharpened at the other. Before she put the perfume bottle into her purse she opened it and sniffed cautiously. It had a soft wildflower smell with a little touch of damp earth that tickled the nose a little. It was a mixture of mayapple and water hemlock roots that she had mashed and strained into a clear concentrate. Eating the roots was the customary Iroquois method of suicide.

For her feet she chose a pair of twenty-dollar black leather Keds. They had gum soles like sneakers, but the soles had no distinctive lines or patterns. They were merely plain, flat, and rough, a texture that could make it hard to distinguish the prints they left as a human track, let alone identify them as the prints of a particular woman's shoe.

She left the lights on in her motel room in case she returned, but put her suitcase in the trunk of the car in case she didn't. She made her preparations carefully because she could not have said what she was preparing for. As she started the car and pulled out of the lot, she began to feel uneasy. If she had seen another woman adorning her hair with a spike designed to be driven into a person's chest, or popping a vial of hemlock extract into her purse, she would have said that the woman was on her way to to kill someone. People who brought along weapons without knowing why had a tendency to find out why after they arrived.

She ran a quick inventory of the thoughts she had about Turner. She suspected that he was a man who stole from children, but she had not discovered any evidence that he had ordered the deaths of Timmy and his parents, or told anybody to kill Mona and Dennis rather than let them into the courtroom. She wanted to watch him and study him. He didn't seem to be a physical threat, and she was not suddenly feeling the urge to go and supply herself with a gun; that would have been a bad sign. The poison proved nothing. Over the years she had promised clients that she would die rather than reveal where she had taken them. To say this without keeping within reach the means to accomplish it would have made it a lie.

Jane drove down Morales Prospect past the address and took a long, careful look. The house was set far back on the deep lot, partly concealed by a few tall pine trees that had been left standing when the house was built. The second floor was fake Tudor, with a high, steep mansard roof that didn't go with it, and the ground floor had a brick facade about six feet high. There were dim lights on in the second-story windows, but the bottom-floor windows were dark. Even the porch light was off. As she passed, she could see that the house was sheltered on three sides by the remnants of the pine grove. The trees ran right up to the edge of the driveway and nearly touched the garage.

She drove up the road looking for a place to leave her car. A half mile farther she found a closed gas station with five or six cars lined up along the side waiting to be fixed. One of them had its hood off and in its place was a tarp of heavy-gauge plastic taped down to keep the sea air out of its engine. She pulled into the lot with her lights off, parked next to this car, and moved the tarp to her own hood.

She walked back along the road, keeping in the shadows of hedges and trees inside the property lines of the big front yards so that any headlights unexpectedly shining on her would fall on her black hair and black clothes and not on her face and hands. But this part of Monterey was a winding seventeen-mile scenic route, so people probably drove it in the daytime when they could see it.

In ten minutes Jane was standing among the trees in the side yard of the house. She felt the soft, cushioned layer of long needles on the ground and smelled the pine scent in the dark, still air. She made her way to the garage and looked in the window. She could see the gleaming finish of the black BMW inside. This was the place where Turner had come to wait out the scandal, leaving the questions and cameras to his lawyer. She walked slowly and quietly around the house, staying back among the trees.

She studied the lower windows, then the upper ones. She scanned the eaves and gutters for spotlights that might automatically come on if she made a noise, but she saw nothing that worried her.

She wanted to see Alan Turner. She returned to the spot where she felt most sheltered by the trees, at the back corner, and watched the lighted upper windows on two sides of the house. There was no glow of a television set, no shadows on the ceiling from anyone walking across any of the rooms. She felt a strong urge to see what he was doing and what he looked like tonight. Maybe she had come too late, and he had lain down to rest with the lights on and fallen asleep. He had driven much farther than she had, and had probably done a lot of it at night, so he would be tired.

She felt drawn to the light. When she walked to the side of the house to peer into a window, she saw the little yellow-and-blue sticker of Intercontinental Security. It made her take a step backward while she tried to analyze the uneasiness this gave her. It had begun to seem that every building she had seen since she started looking into Timmy's problems had one of these stickers on its window. Alarm systems didn't surprise her—she had one herself— but California seemed to be blanketed with Intercontinental stickers. Had it been that way for years without her seeing it?

But of course Turner's houses would be protected by the same company that Hoffen-Bayne used. He probably hid the cost of the alarm systems for both houses in the monthly fee for Hoffen-Bayne. She decided that her uneasiness was only the result of having her attention focused on the signs. If somebody she knew got a disease she had never heard of, suddenly she would notice articles in the newspapers about it and overhear people talking about it until it seemed that the whole world had been infected.

She pushed the security company out of her mind and forced herself to think about the sticker in a way that was of more immediate use. It warned her that Turner had an alarm system. Whatever interior traps and gadgets the system had, they would probably be turned off if he was still up and walking around, or he would risk setting them off himself. The perimeter circuits would certainly be turned on.

She studied the building for its weakness. The alarm system would protect the windows and doors. The high, steep roof didn't have skylights or big vents, and if he were in an upstairs room, he would hear her walking up there. She looked down. This house was like most in California. The ground never froze, so they had no basements. Houses were bolted to three-foot foundations with a crawl space under the floors for pipes and wires. Near the side door by the kitchen was a little wooden trap to cover a two-by-three-foot concrete access well. She lifted the cover off quietly. As she looked down she had a momentary foreboding of spiders and rats, but she pretended there were no such things. She crawled under the house and pulled the trap back over the opening.

Beneath her was bare, powdery dirt. It was dark under the house, but she could see moonlight coming through little screened openings placed at intervals in the foundation. She found the gas pipe from the kitchen overhead and followed it slowly toward the center of the house, making out thick drain pipes and thinner water pipes here and there. Finally she reached the place where the gas pipe jointed and went upward. There was a square opening in the floor beside it about three feet wide.

She reached up to touch the place where the opening ended. It was a big square fabric filter. She pushed up on it and tilted it, then brought it down under the house with her. She reached up again and felt the row of burners. There was only about a foot and a half of space between the business part of the gas furnace and the floor, but she estimated that she could probably fit. She felt carefully around the inside of the furnace until she found the panel that slipped off so the filter could be removed and cleaned. That must be the front.

Jane placed her fingers on the lip and the top of the panel and slowly pushed upward. The panel slid up a quarter inch, when suddenly there was a flash and a click, and the pilot light came on. The burners just above her head began to hiss as the gas came out of them. She ducked down quickly and lay on her back as the gas ignited and the level blue flame spread across the top of the row of burners. Now she could see in the weird blue light. She could tell that she had estimated the shape and structure of the furnace only slightly wrong. She studied it, moving her head from side to side and lifting it as far as she dared.

There had to be some kind of safety button to kill the furnace when the door was off so that it didn't start up and burn the house down. As she searched, the blower motor went on and the fire grew hotter. She couldn't let it run for long, or all the metal around it would get hot too. She kept her head low, slipped her fingers under the bottom of the panel, and pushed upward again. The panel lip was freed, and the furnace went off. Carefully she pushed the panel higher until it came off, then leaned it on its side to keep from making noise, and lay down again.

A few minutes later she judged the air was cool enough to let her reach up through the space where the panel had been and feel around. There was a wooden door in front of the panel: the furnace must be in a space disguised as a closet. She ran her fingers up the side of it until she felt a hinge.

She sat on the ground and waited until she could touch the burners with her fingers before she made her attempt. She squatted cautiously, rose to a crouch, straightened to raise the upper part of her body into the furnace, reached out the front to find the doorknob, and opened the door a crack. She pulled herself up, slithered under the burners and out the front of the furnace, crawled out of the closet, and closed the door behind her.

She was in a dim hallway with a bleached oak floor and a long row of small framed drawings of sailing ships on the white walls. As she looked down the hall she could see the foyer. There was an alarm keypad on the wall near the front door. A small red light was glowing to indicate that the system was armed. At the other end of the hall was a staircase. If she herself had installed the security system, this was where she would have put an interior trap. Whatever a burglar stole down here, you didn't want him getting up those stairs where the bedrooms were. She stepped slowly to the side of the staircase, grasped the railing, and sidestepped between the posts up along the outside of it. She was ten feet up, just below the center of the staircase, before she found the electric eye mechanism. It was a foot above a step, so a crawling intruder couldn't slide under it, and even one who took three steps in a stride would break the beam. There were probably pressure pads under the carpet on some of the steps in case an intruder saw it in time.

She kept outside the railing beyond the top of the stairs and then climbed over the railing into the hallway. There might be other traps on the second floor, but if Turner was up here, this alarm zone was probably turned off.

There were lighted rooms on both ends of the second-floor hallway. The house was absolutely quiet. She could hear no movement or snoring or the shifting of a person in a chair. She wondered for a moment if she had been lucky and entered while he was out, but then she remembered the car in the garage.

She looked at the glowing doorway of each room and chose the one to her left. It was slightly closer to the stairway, and if she had to run she didn't want to have Turner three steps closer to the only way out. Slowly she edged along the hallway with her shoulder almost touching the wall. When hardwood floorboards creaked, it was usually the ones in the center.

At the doorway she leaned out just far enough to use the dark windows in the room as mirrors to search for Turner. When she found him she jerked backward. She had been looking for a human form, and when she found it lower and closer to her than she had expected, her reflex was to duck back quickly to evade the blow or the shot. But even as her body was protecting itself, the feeling had already turned into something else.

His blond hair was wet with blood, and under the body, the thick beige rug had soaked up the first of it and saturated, then let a pool of it form and spread. She could see that the outer edge of the pool was already drying into a dark maroon ring, the carpet tufts hardening into twisted bristles. She craned her neck to look for the gun, and found it where it was supposed to be, beside the right hand. She knew enough about the way policemen treated the scenes of suicides to know it was a bad idea to enter the room. If she lost a strand of hair or a fiber from her clothes, she would be somebody they wanted to talk to.

She leaned inward far enough to verify that there was a discoloration that looked like a powder burn on Turner's right temple around the entry hole. The other temple was pressed to the carpet, and she decided it was just as well. The exit hole would be bigger and harder to look at.

It hadn't occurred to her that he would kill himself. If he hadn't doctored the records well enough he was about to be revealed as a thief, but a lot of people in his business had suffered that kind of publicity, and a fair percentage of them had never gone to jail. If he had been likely to be charged with the murders it would have made more sense, but the authorities had made no progress on the first ones in over two years, and they hadn't even been able to hold the men who had broken Dennis's neck and thrown Mona down the stairwell. Nobody was offering those men a deal in exchange for his name.

The raid on Turner's office must have made him panic. She looked down at him and felt something like sympathy for his fear and his forlorn death, but then she decided that she was only feeling the immediacy of it. The sweat and blood were still fresh, and the smell of his fear was probably still trapped in the air of the room and had set off some basic physical reaction in her brain that was stronger than the disgust he had aroused when he was alive.

She took off her shoes and stepped back along the same path that she had taken to reach the door, shuffling her feet a little to obscure any invisible marks her sneakers had made. At the stairway she hesitated and looked at the second room on the far end of the hallway. Why was the light on in there too? She reminded herself that he was beyond caring about electric bills, but then why had he turned off all the lights downstairs?

As soon as she was at the door, she could see the two sheets of paper on the desk. They were placed on the surface in the pool of light from the desk lamp like an exhibit. She stepped into the room.

They had been typed on the computer in the corner of the room and printed on the printer beside it. She looked at the second sheet, the one with the signature. All it said was "I take full responsibility for my actions. Alan Turner."

Then she looked at the first page. It began, "This is my last message to the rest of the world. When you read it I'll be gone, out of your reach." She had never seen a suicide note before, but somehow she had assumed they were addressed to family members or friends, like personal letters.

"The reason I have decided to end my life is that I have not been able to resist the temptation to steal from one of my accounts. I believed Timothy Phillips would never be found alive, so I was harming no one. Later it became apparent that Timothy Phillips was not dead. The people who had been posing as his parents were sending letters, and I knew that if I allowed them to go on, I would be caught. I went to Washington, D.C., where the letters were coming from, and agreed to a meeting. I hired two men to follow the couple from the meeting and find out where they were living with the boy. I am not certain, to this day, what I would have done if they had followed my instructions, but they did not. They formed some plan of their own, probably to take the boy and use him to take control of his money. Whatever it was, it failed. The next thing I knew, the supposed parents were dead and the boy had disappeared. I regret having proceeded in this fashion. Because I hired those men, I was, and am, technically guilty of arranging two murders. I should mention that none of my associates or colleagues benefitted in any way from my actions, and none of them had any knowledge of my theft or any of the things I did to cover it up. I do not know the names of the two men I hired to find the boy in Washington. I met them in a bar and made the deal in the parking lot outside. There is nothing more to say."

Jane studied the sheet without touching it. The printing went right to the bottom of the page. Then there was the second page with "I take full responsibility for my actions" and the signature. The handwriting experts would certainly find that the signature was genuine. It was only the first page that she suspected was a forgery.

She had sensed that it was odd to write a suicide note on a computer, but now she could see the purpose of it. Once Turner was dead, they had simply gone into the file, deleted whatever had been on the first page, typed a new one, and printed it out. Computer printers placed an extra step between the typist and the paper. There were no keys to hit unevenly, no distinctive characteristics to reveal that one page had been typed by Turner and the other by someone else. Maybe he had signed a blank sheet before they shot him, and they had simply run that through the printer too. It didn't matter. He had been shot in the right way and fallen in the right way. Everything was in the right place. The security system was on, so the police would assume there was no way anyone could have come in, killed him, and left. Unless they found something that wasn't perfect—a wrong chemical residue on his right hand, or a different set of prints on the brass casings of the bullets—he was a suicide.

She stood still for a moment. She could feel that the man who had done this was the one who had fooled her at the courthouse. Turner probably had earned his death, but he wasn't the one she should have been thinking about all this time. The one to worry about wasn't the inside man who took a share and didn't ask enough questions about what was going to happen if the plan didn't work. The one to look for would be the one who would still be left standing if everything went wrong. He had been in this room. If she had been smelling fear, she now knew it had been fear of him. His cunning had arranged everything around her to disguise his presence, but the perfect positions of the objects in the room only made his presence more pervasive.

Jane did not stop to form a clear, logical plan about what she was going to do. She simply knew that whatever arrangements the enemy had made must be to his benefit. She snatched up the forged suicide note, walked to the room where the body was lying, picked up the pistol, put it into her belt, and slid down the banister to the ground floor. Then she made her way back through the furnace to the crawl space, closed the closet door above her, replaced the metal panel, and crawled back out from under the house.

Within ten minutes she was back at the gas station taking the plastic tarp off her rented car. She dropped her room key in the mail slot at the motel office and drove south. She didn't know the enemy's name and she didn't know where he lived, but now she knew something about him. He wasn't some accountant who had hired a few head-bangers to block a courtroom so his embezzling wouldn't get noticed by the authorities. He was a pro.

15

J ane drove for the rest of the night. As soon as she was over the last big hill into Los Angeles County at Thousand Oaks, she ate breakfast at an enormous coffee shop surrounded by brown gumdrop-shaped hills. Just as she was taking her first sip of coffee the clock reached seven and men with heavy machinery began assaulting the mounds, shaving the tops to make level building lots.

She waited in a shopping mall until noon and then checked into a brick hotel in Burbank with a glass elevator that ran up the outside of the building to give future guests a view of whatever was going to be built in the empty, weed-tufted lot under it. She was glad that whatever was in the master plan for the lot had not yet been started, because she needed to sleep. She closed the curtains, undressed, and turned off the lamp. She knew that the dreams would probably come, but she was too tired now to fight them. She lay in the bed staring up at the single red light of the smoke detector on the ceiling, then relinquished her will and slept.

In her dream she found herself kneeling on a bare earth floor in a dark enclosure. Her ears told her that the space was about fifteen feet square. As her eyes slowly became more used to the dark she could see the texture of the inner side of the elm bark that had been shingled together to make the walls and roof of the ganosote. It was a large one built in the old style, about a hundred and twenty feet long with compartments like this one on either side. She counted ten cooking fires at intervals down the center aisle. She could see dark shapes of men, women, and children huddled at the fires or walking past them.

One of the children pushed aside the bearskin that was hanging at the east end of the longhouse to cover the door, and she had to look down to avoid the glare. She knew from the bright sunlight that it must be morning. When the child scampered out and the bearskin swung shut again she didn't raise her head because she was thinking about what the light had shown her. She was wearing a leather skirt and moccasins, and she could feel that the reason the bare ground didn't bother her knees was that they were protected by a pair of leggings. She reflected in a detached way that all of her clothes were soft deerskin, and this confirmed her impression that the day that was beginning was in the Old Time.

She could see that around her neck was a necklace woven from fragrant marsh grass, and she reached up to touch it. Every few inches there was a little disk of marsh grass covered with shell beads. She could smell the fresh, grassy scent, and she knew that the perfume made the smoke, cooking meat, and the twenty or thirty bodies in the ganosote easier on her nostrils.

She heard a noise and turned to see that behind her there was the big shape of a man on the lower platform along the wall of the compartment, and that he was stirring, about to wake up. She didn't know who he was, but stored on the platform five feet above him were her things—the extra moccasins she would use to replace the ones on her feet now, the elm bark gaowo tray she used to prepare corn bread, her collection of ahdoquasa with the bowl ends polished smooth for eating soup and the handles carved in the shapes of men and women embracing. She knew he must be her husband, but he stayed asleep in the shadows with his face to the wall because it was not time for her to see him yet.

She heard someone calling her name outside, and in the logic of dreams, she knew that the voice was the reason she was here. She stood up and walked past the fires to the bearskin flap. A strong hand gripped her arm, and she turned. A man whose face she did not quite see in the dim light said in Seneca, "If you don't want to dream about the dead, you don't have to. If the women sing the Ohgiwe, they'll leave." She knew this voice.

"I know, Jake," said Jane. She lifted the corner of the bearskin and ducked out into the light.

"Jane!" said a voice. It was harsh and high, not quite human, like the screech of a parrot. "Jane!"

She looked around her, and her eye caught a flash of deep blue above her on a maple tree, and then another flitted across the open air from an old sycamore. It flew in spurts, a dip and a wing-flap to bring the bird up, then a dip and a wing-flap and claws clutching the branch of the tree beside the first one. Jane could tell they were the two scrub jays she had captured in California.

The two birds dropped to the lowest branch of the maple just above her. The male tilted his head to the side and glared at her with one shiny black eye. "Jane!"

"What?" she asked.

The female jay hopped to reverse her position on the branch, her head where her tail had been, and leaned down. "We did what you asked," she said. "We took Dennis and Mona to Hawenneyugeh."

"Thank you," said Jane. "But you have to go home now. You can't survive in this climate, and winter is coming."

The male shifted back and forth on the branch nervously, and she could hear its claws scratching the bark. "We came for you."

The jays eyed her without moving. Jane felt a small, growing fear. "Am I going to die too? So many people, all dying for nothing."

The female dropped to the grass at her feet and jerked her head from side to side to bring first one eye and then the other to bear on Jane. "It's not supposed to be *for* anything," she said. "It's what we are."

"What we are?"

"Hawenneyu, the Right-Handed Twin, creates people, birds, trees. Hanegoategeh, the Left-Handed Twin, makes cancer, num-

ber-six birdshot, Dutch Elm disease. For every measure, a coun-
termeasure: Hawenneyu creates the air, Hanegoategeh churns it
into the cold wind; Hawenneyu makes fire and houses, Hanegoategeh makes the fire burn the houses."

"Are you here to tell me it's my turn to be used up?" asked
Jane.

"To warn you. If you want to be alive and breathe the air and
drink the water, then look and listen. Nothing has changed since
the beginning of the world. You're still walking through wild
country. No sight or sound is irrelevant. Learn about your enemy."

She studied the two birds. "Who is my enemy?"

"Think about how he works," said the female jay.

"He's been killing people," Jane said. "There's nothing special about it at all. It's just brutal: cutting up the Deckers—"

"Without leaving any sign in the house that a little boy had
ever lived there," the male reminded her.

"How about Mona and Dennis?" she asked. "He hired some
men to beat Dennis to death and throw Mona down a stairwell."

"He waited until you had made your preparations for one
building, and got the case moved to another. You had to go to a
new place where a dozen men were waiting for you and court was
already in session."

"And what about Alan Turner?" asked the female jay.

"What about him?" Jane asked.

"We know how you got into Turner's house past the alarm
system and out again. How did he do it?"

"I don't know," said Jane. "I suppose he rang the doorbell.
Alan Turner let him in. They must have known each other."

"You're not listening," said the female jay. "Anybody could
get *in* by ringing the doorbell. How did he get *out* without tripping
the alarm after Turner was dead?"

"How?" she asked.

Jane awoke and listened to the sounds of the cars on the freeway a few blocks away. Rush hour must have begun, but then she
remembered that the term had no meaning around Los Angeles.
There were cars clogging the roads every hour of every day. She sat
up and looked around her, then stood and walked into the shower.

She had only needed some sleep. She still didn't know the

man's name, but while she slept she had figured out something else about him. He might have gotten into the house in Monterey without setting off the alarm because Turner had let him in. But the only way he could have gotten out and left the alarm on after he had killed Turner was to know the alarm code.

16

Ellery Robinson opened the apartment door and looked out past her with wary eyes. "Come in," she said quietly. "This isn't a neighborhood for standing in a lighted doorway."

Jane stepped inside and watched the thin, hard arms move to close the steel door and then turn the dead bolt.

"I been waiting for you," said Ellery Robinson. "I knew you saw me in jail because I saw you. How did you find me? I'm not in the phone book."

"I went to your old apartment and asked around until I found somebody who still knew you. . . . You're in trouble again."

"No big thing. My parole officer thinks I have an attitude, so he forgot to write down when I came to see him."

"You don't have an attitude?"

Ellery Robinson shrugged her thin shoulders. "When a black woman gets past the age where they stop thinking about her big ass, they remember they didn't like her very much to begin with."

"Can you do anything about it?"

"He turned out to be unreliable, so his reports aren't enough to send anybody to jail anymore."

"He must have been really unreliable."

"Yeah. While I was in jail I heard they caught him in his office with a Mexican girl going down on him. He's been getting what he wanted regular like that for years. All he had to do to get them deported was check a box on a form, so they did a lot of favors."

"Does he know who set him up?"

For the first time Ellery Robinson smiled a little, and Jane could see a resemblance to the young woman she had met years ago. "Could be anybody. Everybody knew."

Jane sat in silence and stared at her. She had aged in the past eleven years, but it seemed to have refined and polished her. Ellery Robinson tolerated the gaze for a time, then said, "How about you? Have you been well?"

"I can't complain."

"You mean you can't complain to me, don't you?" said Ellery Robinson. "You're thinking I should have gone with you."

"I don't know. Nobody can say what would have happened."

"Don't feel sorry for me. I had a life, you know. My sister Clarice and I had one life. When I was in prison I would sit in the sun in the yard and close my eyes and follow her and the baby around all day with my mind. The women in jail thought I'd gone crazy, that I sat there all day in a coma, but I wasn't there at all. I was living inside my head."

"You don't regret it?"

"I regret that I'm a murderer. I don't regret that he got killed. He needed it."

Jane nodded. "You doing okay now?"

"I'm contented. I know what's on your mind. It's that woman in county jail, isn't it?"

"Mary Perkins?" said Jane. "No. She's far away now."

"What, then?"

"I know people hear things—in jail, the parole office, places like that."

"Sometimes."

"What have you heard about Intercontinental Security?"

Ellery Robinson's clear, untroubled face wrinkled with distaste. "If you're hiring, hire somebody else. If they're looking for you, don't let them find you."

"They seem to have a lot of business."

"Oh, yeah, it's a big company. And it's old, like Pinkerton's or Brinks or one of them. I think they used to guard trains and banks and things. For all I know they still do; I'm not a stockholder."

"Have you heard anything about burglaries in places they're supposed to protect—as though they might be fooling their own alarm systems or something?"

"No. What I hear most about them now is they hunt for people."

"What sort of people?"

"The usual. Skip-trace, open warrants, wanted for questioning, runaways. Somebody jumps bail, the bail bondsman is on the hook. Some clerk takes a little money out of the till and runs. The police don't look very hard, so the company hires Intercontinental."

"What's different?"

"The ones they bring in seem to fall down a lot. Maybe a broken arm, maybe a leg. Maybe their face doesn't look too good."

"It's an old company. Did they always have that reputation?"

Ellery Robinson shrugged. "I didn't always know people who got chased. Then I was away for a few years. It's since I got back that I've been hearing things."

"Who have you been hearing them from? Can you help me get to one of them?"

The little woman leaned back on her worn couch and looked up at the ceiling for a moment. She seemed to be searching for names and addresses up there, but Jane could tell that she was rejecting some of them for reasons that she would not reveal.

The young man stood beside a car in the darkness. He was tall and heavy, with a jacket that was too thick for this weather and baggy blue pants. Jane could see that there was a streetlight directly above him, but the lamp was a jagged rim of broken glass.

Ellery Robinson followed the angle of Jane's eyes. "The street dealers shoot them out at night, and the city replaces them in the day. Everybody gets paid." She stopped walking and held Jane's arm. The young man looked up the block for three or four seconds, then down the block. When he was satisfied, he came away from the car and walked across the sidewalk onto the lawn.

Ellery Robinson looked up and said to him, "This is the woman." Then she turned to Jane. "He won't hurt you." Then she turned and walked away across the packed dirt of the big gray project toward her room.

Jane turned to the young man. "Thank you for coming."

The young man started walking, and she stepped off with him. "Got to keep moving or everybody starts to notice you're not going about your business."

"All right."

"She said you want to know about Intercontinental."

"Yes," said Jane. She waited for the logical question, but it did not come. He didn't consider it his business why she wanted to know, just as Ellery Robinson had not taken it on herself to tell either of them the other's name.

He said, "I worked for them."

"How long?"

"About two weeks." He anticipated the next question. "In October. They put out ads in this part of town. They wanted store security for two big malls in time for Christmas. You know, they didn't want a couple of white kids in uniforms in front of a store on Crenshaw. They'd just get hurt."

"What happened?"

"They made me a trainee. That means they don't have to pay regular wages. They put me through a lie detector test, a couple of days in a classroom, and turned me out. I worked the malls for a week and a half."

"Why did they fire you?"

The young man's eyes shot to hers and then ahead again. "Security check turned up my priors. Couldn't get bonded."

"What did you find out before you left?"

"Now you're not going to believe me, right?" he asked. "I got priors, and I'm a 'disgruntled former employee.' "

Jane looked up at the sky, then sighted along the wall of the complex. "It's a cold, clammy night for L.A. It'll probably rain soon, from the way it feels. And you may not believe it, but I hardly ever find myself in this part of town after midnight in any weather."

"I can believe that," he said.

"If I thought you were going to lie to me, I'd be pretty stupid to be here, wouldn't I?"

"Yeah."

"Then tell me what it was like."

"They're looking for young men with strong motivation and they'll give them the skills to succeed. Like the army. They got this guy who comes in and tells you how to be a thief in a big store so that you know what to look for."

"Did he get it right?"

"There were plenty of people in that room who could tell you for sure, but I wasn't one of them. I think it was pretty close, though, because they were all listening. Probably got some new ideas for the off-season."

"The skills to succeed. Can you tell me anything about this guy? Who was he?"

"His name was Farrell. Sort of an old guy with gray hair that's all bristly like a brush and spit-shined shoes. They called him the training officer. After he told us how to spot thieves, he told us what to do about them."

"Take them to the back of the store and call your supervisor?"

"Yeah," he said. "He says the system doesn't do any good. They get a court date and in a day they're back for more. So the supervisor would take them someplace and scare them."

"How scared?"

"Farrell says that comes under initiative. The company judges supervisors on the results."

"What are the results?"

"He says there are three kinds: the ones who don't need it and are doing it for some kind of kick, the ones in a crew that sells it, and junkies. There's no way to make any of them stop, but you can make them go to another store next time."

"Did you get to see any of this?"

"Once. A woman got caught with a bag that had a big box in it with a trapdoor cut in it, and she was shoveling stuff into it. The supervisor took her in the back for a while, then shoved her out the loading dock door. She ran."

"I've heard this before. Stores do it themselves. What else did you see?"

"The next week my background check comes in, so I'm out. I turn in my blues and go home. Two days later I get a phone call. It's Farrell. He says he's sorry to hear what happened, but maybe he can do something for me. I got initiative and motivation and I'm not afraid to do what needs to be done. He says sometimes there are jobs for people who can't make it through a background check. I'd still be working for Intercontinental, but they'd pay me in cash. Kind of an undercover job, and it paid a lot more."

"Did he say what you would be doing?"

"I'm twenty-two. Never had a job before because I'm dragging a five-page rap sheet. Got two convictions. Aggravated assault—did three for that in youth camp. Assault with a deadly weapon—did three more for that in Soledad. I figure he was looking for a brain surgeon."

"You said there were a lot of people in the training class who had the same problem. Did anybody else get the same offer?"

"I don't know."

"What did you tell him?"

They reached the sidewalk on the other side of the complex. He moved to the outside and looked carefully up and down the street before he ventured out of the shelter of the big buildings. "I told you I couldn't get another job."

"So you signed on."

"He had me come to another office. Not the big place where they hire and train people. This one was out in Van Nuys. There were eight or ten men hanging around—white guys, black guys, a couple of Mexicans. Everybody dressed good, but not really doing much. The sign on the door said 'Enterprise Development.' "

Jane remembered the men at the courthouse. They had all been wearing suits or sportcoats, and none of them had been carrying anything that could connect them with Intercontinental Security. "Where in Van Nuys?"

"The address is 5122 Van Nuys Boulevard. Big building, small office."

"What did you do there?"

"Farrell came and talked to me for a while."

"What did he tell you?"

"Pretty much what anybody tells you when you're doing something you get paid in cash for. If something goes wrong they'll slip you bail money, but if you tell anybody anything, there are a bunch of them and only one of you."

"And he still didn't tell you what he wanted you for?"

"Yeah, he did," said the young man. "Hunting."

"What?"

"That's what he said. The way it works is, the company has a list of people they want. The company does whatever is legal to find them. That's all in the open. It's a big company with offices in fifty places and a lot of people on the payroll. But then there's some cases that are off the books. Like maybe a guy disappears at the same time as a computer chip or a famous painting or something. The company knows it, they know he's got it, or he's got the money from it. Somehow he got away with it."

"So they hunt him."

"Yeah. The rest of it was just about the head guy."

"What about him?"

"How he did all of it. He went to work in the L.A. office a few years ago and set all this up. He was born off in the woods someplace way north of here, and he's a tracker. He thinks like a hound. Once he's got the scent, he never gives up. Farrell says he used to go after killers all by himself just for the kick it gave him. He gets a rush out of it, like a hunter."

"When?"

"When what?"

"When did he go after killers?"

"Before. When he was a cop."

Jane felt increasingly tense. "What's his name?"

"Bearclaw."

It wasn't exactly a surprise, but she felt a sensation like an electric shock. "Barraclough?"

"B-A-R-R-A-something. He's—"

"I've heard of him," Jane interrupted. She tried to clear her mind of the thoughts that were crowding in. She could almost see Danny Mittgang's face eight or nine years ago when she had asked him why he was running. He had not said the Los Angeles police wanted him as a material witness; what came out of Danny's mouth was "Barraclough." He had actually begun to sweat and gulp air. The name was already so familiar in certain circles that he had expected her to know it.

She had heard it many times after that, and each time there was something odd about the story. A fugitive's friends who had refused to betray him the first time they were questioned talked to Barraclough. A middle-aged man who had committed a white-collar crime would uncharacteristically forget there was no evidence against him and burst out at Barraclough with guns blazing. Barraclough would use information that could have come only from a wiretap to find a suspect, but no wiretap evidence would be introduced at the trial. She had filed the name with a few others, policemen in various parts of the country who were willing to do just about anything to catch a suspect. But the difference between Barraclough and the others was that when his name was mentioned, the person who said it was always afraid.

Jane tried to concentrate. She was not likely to get a second interview with this young man. "How did you get out of the job?"

"No problem. I told Farrell I didn't want in."

"Why not?"

"I didn't like him."

"It was the job you didn't like, wasn't it? The first one he wanted you to do?"

The young man shrugged. "Ellery said you might be interested in the picture they gave me, and I just told you I got no job."

Jane held out her hand. In the palm were two fresh green bills that had been rolled into her fingers since she'd come out of the shadows to meet him. They unrolled enough so that he could see the hundreds in the corners.

He reached inside his jacket and pulled a photograph out of

his breast pocket. He handed it to her and then gently plucked the two bills off her palm.

Jane held the picture up, trying to catch the dim glow of the distant street lamp. She didn't want to wait to know whether it was one of the Christmas snapshots the Deckers had mailed to Grandma or one of the family mementos the killers had taken from the Washington house. She caught a flash of blond hair, and held it higher to be sure. It wasn't a picture of Timmy at all: it was Mary Perkins.

17

Mary Perkins had spent most of her month in Ann Arbor learning about Donna Kester. She had discovered that Donna was not comfortable in the apartment that Jane Whitefield had helped her to rent. It was not Jane Whitefield's fault, although she was tempted to sweep up whatever annoying particles of blame were lying around and heap them on her. Mary had assumed that Donna Kester was going to be someone who would like the long, clean lines of the modern apartment complex. It reminded Mary of the hotels where she had stayed for most of her adult life.

But as the winter came on, the building seemed hastily built and drafty, as though the carpenters had left something undone that she couldn't see. The exercise room that the tenants shared was a big box with a glass wall where women a lot younger than Mary went to display the results of many earlier visits to young men who seemed to be too intent on lifting large pieces of iron to notice what was being offered. The pool in the courtyard promised more of the same in the distant summer without the chance to hide the mileage under a good pair of tights. And the dirty snow that had drifted over its plastic cover began to contribute to her feeling that summer wasn't something that was still to come.

As Donna Kester explained her position to herself, the place wasn't congenial. She moved closer to the university and rented the top floor of a big house that had been built in the 1920s. It was the sort of house where she had grown up in Memphis, with a lot of time-darkened wood in places where they didn't put wood anymore, and a layer of thick carpet that covered the stairway and muffled the creak and was much cleaner at the edges than at the center.

Her apartment had a small, neat little kitchen and a bedroom with a brass bed in it that wasn't a reproduction of anything, but wasn't good enough to be an antique. The closet was small, but it was big enough for the sort of wardrobe that Donna Kester was likely to acquire. The living room had a bad couch and a good easy chair that was aimed as though by a surveyor directly at a twenty-year-old RCA television set that picked up only two channels she had trouble telling apart. But the two channels had forecasters who did a fair job of predicting the weather, and this was about all she required of them for the moment because it let her know what to wear while she was out looking for a job.

Mary began to feel more comfortable as Donna Kester soon after she moved into the old apartment. She had no trouble suppressing the landlords' curiosity with a vague reference to a divorce. In the future, whenever they had a question in their minds about her lack of a work history and shallow credit record, she could be too sensitive to talk about it. They could chew on the divorce and come up with plausible answers until they found one that satisfied them. It sometimes seemed that Donna Kester knew everything about people that Mary Perkins knew, only it hadn't cost her as much.

Donna walked into the hallway, threaded her new scarf into the sleeve of her big goose-down coat, stuffed her new gloves into the pockets, and hoisted the coat onto the peg. She sat down on the steps to take off her boots, and felt the distressing sensation of having the melted snow from her last trip soak through the seat of her pants. She stood up quickly, set the boots on the mat, and carefully made her way up the stairs in her socks. She felt unfairly punished. She thought she had learned about tracking snow on the steps early enough. The carpet would have dried by now if there had been heating ducts near the entrance at the foot of the stairs.

If she owned this place, she would damned well have a contractor in by tomorrow noon. She would put a big old brass register right by the door where a person could get hugged by that breath of hot air as soon as she made it inside, and then leave her coat and boots in front of it to get toasted before she went out again. She had a brief fantasy about buying the house from the Monahans and getting the contractor on the phone before the ink on the deed was dry.

She reached into her purse and grasped her key. That made her feel better. It was the big old-fashioned kind that was a shaft of steel four inches long with an oval ring on one end and the teeth on the other. It looked like the key to a castle and it made her feel safe. She had some justification for the feeling. The lock set into the thick, solid door looked about the size of a deck of cards, with big steel tumblers and springs that snapped like a trap when she locked it, and it was easy to see that it had been in there for a long time. If there had ever been a break-in they would have replaced it.

She reached the top, put her hand on the yellowed porcelain doorknob, pushed in her key, and felt the door swing open. The lights were on. She turned and tried to step back down the stairs as quickly and quietly as she could, but she knew she was making too much noise—already had made too much noise just coming in and climbing the stairs—so she began to take the steps by leaning on the railing and jumping as many as she could to land with a thump.

She burned with a hatred for her stupidity. When she had felt the cold wet spot on the stairs she should have known someone else had been here. It wasn't as though it were a faint clue; it was a warning sign practically branded on her ass. She regretted all of it: leaving the sprawling, noisy, busy apartment complex for this old house where they didn't even have to think hard about how to get her alone because she was always alone; letting herself rent a second apartment at all, because showing the false documents twice raised the risk by exactly one hundred percent; trusting like a child to big locks and keys—no, hiding the way a child did, not by concealing herself but by covering her own eyes with her hands.

As she reached the bottom and realized with a pang that common sense required that she race through the door into the snow without stopping for her boots, the voice touched her gently.

"It's me," said Jane Whitefield. "Don't run. It's only me."

Mary stopped with her face to the door. She turned and looked up. She could see the silhouette of the tall, slim woman in front of the dimly lighted doorway at the top of the stairs. The shape was dark, a deeper shadow, and for a second a little of the fear came back into her chest like a paralysis in her lungs. Then the woman at the top of the stairs swung Mary's door open and said in the same quiet voice, "Sorry to startle you."

Mary climbed back up her stairs slowly and deliberately because she wanted to let her heart stop pounding. The way Jane had said it was an invitation to join a conspiracy. People who were startled jumped half an inch and said, "Oh." They didn't vault down twenty-foot staircases and dash into the snow in wet socks. That was what people did who were terrified, running for their lives. We'll let your cowardice pass without comment, and we'll call it something else. That was what Jane was saying. No, it was even worse than that. She knew it wasn't merely cowardice. It was the only sane response for a woman who was guilty of so much that any surprise visitor was probably there because he wanted to put her in a bag. That was what Jane was passing without comment.

Mary reached the top of the stairs and stepped into her living room. She looked around for Jane but couldn't see or hear her, which made her remember the strangeness about the woman that had always irritated her. It was that erect quietness that made other people feel as though they talked too much without getting anything in return, like they were emptying the contents of their brains into a deep, dark hole, where it wasn't deemed enough to amount to much. She drifted around like she was the queen of the swans, and it was okay with her if anybody with her suspected she thought they were dumb, short, and pasty-faced and their voices were too loud.

Mary heard the sound of the teakettle steaming in the kitchen; then it stopped, so that was where Jane must be. She felt tension stiffen the back of her neck and shoulders. This was her place, and there was some primal insult in having another woman walk in and go through her cupboards. She hated owing this woman so much that she had to endure it.

Mary moved toward her little kitchen just as Jane came out with the tea tray, already talking. "I'm really sorry I had to come in like this. It would make me angry if anyone did it to me, but it seemed best. In the first place, I didn't know you well enough to be able to predict whether you were likely to have gotten your hands on a gun. You've had plenty of time to do it."

Mary felt the words dissolve what remained of her confidence like a sugar cube in a rainstorm. She had been here a month, and it had never occurred to her to obtain the most obvious way of protecting herself. The decision she would have made was by no means certain, but that didn't help; it made her even more frightened, because she had not given it even enough thought to reject it.

But Jane was going on, and Mary hadn't been listening. ". . . didn't want to get my head blown off, and I figured if your landlord heard a woman coming up the steps he would assume it was you. I've been very careful not to cause trouble by coming here. Nobody followed me and nobody had a chance to see me outside waiting. I saw you coming up the sidewalk, so I made tea." She held out a cup so Mary could take it.

Mary sniffed it and said, "It's different."

"I picked it up in L.A.," said Jane. "It's mixed with blackberry leaves. I've got a weakness for nonsense like that."

Mary sipped. At least this woman had not come in and put her hands into the cupboards looking for things. The teakettle and the water were in plain sight. She resisted the feeling. Whatever this woman wanted, she was not going to get it by dropping a teabag into a cup of water. She smiled. "Me too."

Mary's smile was like a cat purring while it rubbed its fur against a person's leg. Jane could see that the smile had not just been practiced in front of a mirror. It had about it the cat's ease and grace that could only have come from bringing it out and using it to get what the cat needed. She looked around. "I like your apartment," she said.

Mary longed for her to say something insincere about the furniture.

"You got everything right," said Jane. "It would be pretty hard for somebody to get all the way up that stairway if you really wanted to stop him. The building looks like a single-family house from the outside, so nobody would look for a stranger here. That's the important thing. Not what you'll do if they find you, but being where they won't look."

"How did you find me? Or were you here all the time watching me?"

"Why would I do that?"

"I don't know. Maybe to see what I did." Mary realized that she had not said anything. She resolved not to make this mistake again. "To see if I was good enough at it to have a chance."

Jane said, "No, I don't play games."

"Then you changed your mind about me." Without any reason at all, Mary thought.

"No again," said Jane. "I expected you to be good at it."

Mary was tired. She had spent the day trying to get personnel managers to give her a competitive test of business skills when all they wanted was references, then to give her the benefit of the doubt based on her ability to speak knowledgeably, the promise that references could be obtained, and finally just to give her a break because she was pleasant, well-groomed, and eager. Now she was sitting in a pair of pants with a wet seat. "Let me try to be more direct," she said. "You helped me, and I thank you for that. Then you walked out on me. Rather mysteriously, I might add. Now you're back. You tell me I played a good game of hide-and-seek, but here you are. You seem to have had no trouble finding me, or opening the lock to my door to get in and make yourself a cup of tea. I've never had any difficulty believing you're better at this than I am, but now I'm not just awed, I'm scared to death. So what do you want?"

Jane put down her tea. "You shouldn't be scared to death. I found you because I knew where to look. If you had been stupid, you would have left Ann Arbor, put yourself in the airports and hotel lobbies again, and inevitably found your way to one of the places where they're looking. I knew you weren't stupid, so I was pretty sure you must still be in this town. So what would you be doing? If you had wanted to give up on life you would have stayed put and done nothing. A person can sit in the right locked room forever without getting found if she has enough to pay the rent. I figured you would be too lively to go that way, so I tried the job route."

"What's the job route?" Mary asked.

"I knew you had the sense to figure out that the more you do with a fake identity, the better it gets because after a while it's not exactly fake anymore. You're not the only woman in town with records that only go back a few years. Pretty soon it will take a lot of digging to detect whether you're entirely rebuilt or just went through the usual changes—a couple of marriages that brought new names, a couple of moves from one state to another, a career change or two. Having eliminated the possibility that you had left or gone into a coma, I knew you would be applying for jobs. It's the best way to start a new life."

"That was enough?" asked Mary.

"The biggest and safest employer in Ann Arbor is the university. I called the personnel office and said I was a member of a faculty committee trying to hire someone to do the accounting and clerical work for a big research grant in the medical school."

"Why that? Why not something else?"

"Faculty members aren't hired by the university personnel office. They're hired by the faculty, so there was very little chance she would look for a personnel file on me and not find it. Medical schools are semi-autonomous, so I could play an insider without knowing anything about her operation. I asked her to send me copies of applications with a bookkeeping background, since I figured that would be your strength. I asked how long it would take to bring them to my office. She said a day or two, so I offered to come over and pick them out myself. That way I didn't need an office."

"You got this address off my application. God, it's easy."

"Not that easy," said Jane. "Nobody knows what I knew—

your new name, the city, and where you'd have to apply for work if you wanted any." She stared at Mary Perkins over the rim of her teacup. "Not even Barraclough."

Mary felt her spine stiffen. She considered her options. She could pretend the name had made no impression on her, and later find a chance to slip away quietly. She could create some kind of disturbance—throw the cup at Jane and run. But even if she got out the door, the only way of taking the next step was to fall back on the name and the credit that Jane had given her. She wasn't ready. She should have been ready. "How do you know that name? I never told you."

"Why didn't you?" asked Jane. "You told me you didn't know who was looking for you."

Mary Perkins's mind stumbled, held back from the conclusion it was about to reach. That was right. She had come to Jane White- field, and Jane Whitefield kept nagging her about who it was. She hadn't known. She couldn't have been working for Barraclough. At least a month ago she couldn't. "I wanted you to help me," said Mary. "I only provide the arguments for what I want. You have to supply your own arguments against."

"All right," said Jane. "Then let's take the whole issue off the table. I have decided to help you."

"In spite of Barraclough?"

"Because of Barraclough."

"Do you know him?"

"I've seen his work." She looked at Mary closely. "Has he ever seen you?"

The question didn't make any sense unless the way Jane Whitefield wanted to make money was to sell someone else to Bar- raclough and say she was Mary Perkins. "I suppose he has lots of pictures of me."

"Not pictures," Jane said. "Has he actually looked at you face-to-face?"

"Is that important?"

"Yes. Tell me."

"We never met," said Mary Perkins. "When I got out of the federal prison eight months ago, he somehow heard about it. He knew where I was living. How he got that I don't know. They said it was going to be a secret to help in my rehab—you know, help me fit into the community, keep my old cronies away, and all that."

"He used to be a cop. He knows how to use the system. He didn't come for you himself?"

"He sent two men," said Mary Perkins. "They explained to me about Barraclough."

"What did they tell you?"

"He's the director of the Los Angeles office of Intercontinental Security. He's got a huge organization and a lot of power, and connections with every police department. You can't get away from him and you can't fight him. He had read about me."

"Read what?"

"Everything. Newspaper reports, the transcript of my trial, the investigation reports. I don't know how he got those either. He had decided that I had a whole lot of savings and loan money hidden someplace. He wanted it. I couldn't call the police and say he was taking it because I wasn't supposed to have it."

"You told me the pitch. You just didn't tell me where you heard it. Since you're still running and they're still chasing, you must have gotten away. How?"

"They didn't put a gun to my head and say 'Pay or die.' I told them I didn't have it. But they said Barraclough knew I did because he had followed my case." She chuckled sadly. "You know how prosecutors are. They rave around in front of the jury, flinging enormous, impossible numbers around. This is how much is missing from savings and loans in this great, tormented state of Texas. This is the woman caught with ten dollars of it. All that nonsense doesn't simply go into the jury's subconscious; it goes into the transcript. Even if your lawyer proves it's silly, once it's been said it exists. It had convinced Barraclough I had some insane amount of money—like fifty million."

"So Barraclough sent them to pick you up and take you with them, right?"

"What else? If I had that kind of money I couldn't haul it around in a suitcase. It would take a couple of freight cars. It would have to be in a numbered account in Switzerland or someplace. They said they'd have to hold on to me until I had led them to the accounts."

"What was the up side?"

"Does this sound like it has an up side?"

Jane said, "When it was all over, what did they promise to leave you? Would you have any money left, or just your life?"

"They said Barraclough had done this quite a few times before. He just took half from each one he caught and let him go."

"Did you believe them?"

Mary Perkins smirked. "Do I look younger than I am, or what? It was like having a man ask you to take off half your clothes."

"What happened then?"

"They each took one of my arms and led me outside to their car. It was a two-door, so you had to kind of squinch in behind the front seat. They had the passenger seat already tipped forward when they opened the door. They had turned off the dome light so it wouldn't go on when the door opened. I remember looking in and thinking, I'm going to die. I had just read one of those articles they have in magazines about serial killers and rapists, and it said whatever you do, don't get in the car. Once you're in, nothing is up to you anymore; it's up to them. They pushed me in and I started crying."

"Because you thought you were going to die?"

"Knew it. I knew I would die if I didn't do something. The crying was all I could think of. It made them nervous and nasty. One of them said if I didn't stop he'd hurt me, so I stopped. I could see that made them get overconfident. It was a long drive, and they had been waiting outside my apartment for hours. They had to make a pee stop. They were talking about going to a gas station, but they had a full tank, so they didn't want to stop and have the gas guy stare at them and maybe remember they had a woman with them. So they waited until they were on the Interstate and pulled into a truck stop. One of them was going to go in, and then the other while the first one stayed with me. I kept looking for a chance to get in there, so I could scream my head off, even make one of them hit me, but they didn't give me any chance. I tried saying I had to pee too. I tried saying I had to change a tampon. I begged, I promised."

"How did you manage it?"

"Did I mention it was a two-door car?"

"Yes."

"They kept the motor running so they could get away fast if something went wrong. I waited until the first one got back. He was the driver. He comes to the left door to open it, and the other one opens the right-side door to get out. I pushed the driver's seat forward, flopped over on it on my belly, set the transmission in gear, ducked down, and punched the gas pedal with the palm of my hand. The car goes. Not real fast, just jerks ahead and coasts at maybe ten miles an hour. The one trying to get into the driver's side gets his foot run over. The other one jumps back into his seat. The car moves in this sort of stately pace right into the front of the restaurant—*crash!* When it hit, it kind of jammed me head-first under the dashboard onto my elbows with the brake pedal pressing on my forehead and the steering wheel holding my butt down and not enough room for a somersault anyway. The one in the seat kind of belly-flopped next to me, only his face hit the glove compartment."

Jane frowned. "Why are you making this up?"

Mary Perkins looked angry, but she seemed to be holding her breath. Finally she let it out. "I'm not sure. I guess I wanted to sound brave."

"What really happened?"

"A Highway Patrol car pulled in beside us. I was too scared to even look at them. The cop saw I had been crying, so he knocked on my window and asked if there was something wrong. I told the cop I was turning myself in—that I left Los Angeles in violation of my parole."

"Why did you tell him you were on parole?"

"I thought it was a stroke of genius. If I said I'd been kidnapped, they'd keep me there to testify. They could do it; I really was out on parole. Even if I did get these two convicted, what good was that going to do me? They might not have been telling the truth about Barraclough, but they were working for somebody. On their own, these two couldn't have known all that about my trial transcripts and everything. They were maybe twenty-one or twenty-two years old, and dumb."

"So what happened?"

"I figured the C.H.P. would just ship me back to L.A. for a lecture, and when that was over I could hop on a plane and disappear. Only wouldn't you know it, when they identified these two characters, they both turned out to be convicted felons, so instead of a little scolding, I get to do ninety in L.A. County Jail. Consorting with convicted felons is apparently more serious than going out of town without telling your parole officer."

"That was what you were in for when you saw me?"

"Yes. They let me out two weeks early, or else those guys would have had me before I got to the airport. But they must have a way of knowing when somebody is released early."

"Not them. Barraclough does." They sat for a time in silence, sipping their tea. The cold wind outside the old house was stronger up here on the second floor. The snow was falling harder now, as it sometimes did after nightfall, and the white flakes came tumbling into the light and ticked the window as though it were the windshield of a moving car.

Mary Perkins said, "What do you know about Barraclough?"

Jane stopped watching the snowflakes and turned to her. "He's not what they all think he is. They think he's a hunter, so he's entitled to hunt. That's the chance you take: if you run, there will be somebody like him who gets paid to bring you back. But he's not that anymore. He's a cannibal."

"What do you mean?"

"He's not working for the system anymore, catching people and bringing them in and then getting his reward. He's living by gobbling people up."

"Who else?"

"The last one I know about is an eight-year-old boy."

"Why was he after a little boy?"

"The boy inherited some money and disappeared. Barraclough heard about it and killed at least four people just because they were between him and the boy—killed them just to get them out of his way so he could get the money."

"Did he get it?"

Jane shrugged. "The lawyers still have to do their audits and studies and sort out at least eight years of paper. When they finish, they'll probably learn enough to charge an accountant who's already dead with breach of trust or something. They'll also find out that the money is gone. They don't know that yet, but it is. Barraclough would never have killed the accountant if he didn't already have it."

"Why did you come back here?"

"Because I was one of the people who let him do it. I don't want him to do the same thing to you."

18

The night was cold and the oil furnace hummed in the basement two stories below them. Jane sat quietly in the corner of the room looking out the window and watching the feathery snow falling, first to fill in the icy ruts on the road and then to lay a blue-white blanket over it. No cars passed on the street to disturb it, and nobody had been out to leave human footprints, so it began to seem that she and Mary Perkins were the only ones left, adrift in a place where there was no motion and no time.

Mary stirred and walked into the kitchen. After more snow fell, Jane could smell food cooking and hear plates rattling onto the table. The roasting smell grew thicker in the air, and steam that carried the scent of vegetables fogged the window. There was the creak of the oven door opening and then the thump of it closing. Mary's footsteps reached the doorway and she said, "Time to eat."

On the table were a roasted chicken, asparagus, carrots, and potatoes, an excess of food cooked absentmindedly without regard to the number of people at the table. They ate sparingly and with formality. When they were finished they cleared the table and washed the dishes without speaking. They were like two strangers stranded together in the only way station in the empty wilderness, surrounded by hundreds of miles of howling winds and drifting snow—not because they had decided to be together but because there was no other shelter.

Mary walked into her bedroom for a few minutes and came out to set a pillow and a thick quilt on the couch, then went inside again and closed the door. Jane went back to the window to watch. The snow fell for another two hours before she stood up and walked to the couch, pulled the quilt over her, and fell asleep.

In her dream a light, powdery snow was falling while she trotted ahead of her companion through the forest. It was cold, but she didn't feel the cruelty of it because she had worked up a light sweat. She ducked her head under spidery branches frosted with snow, knowing that if she bumped one, the snow would shower off onto the ground. Then pursuers would read that as clearly as a track, and the wind would be slower to cover it.

They were making their way south from Ann Arbor and she was watching for the rivers that fed into Lake Erie. First would be the Raisin, then the Maumee, then the Sandusky. This forest was wild country. Hunters from tribes from every direction came to get bear, deer, and beaver in the winter and passed through it in the summer on their way to kill each other. It had been full of armed men for a thousand years.

She listened to the breaths of the woman trotting along behind her, and at each breath there was more of her voice, more of a cry. Jane stopped and looked back. Mary Perkins had slowed down to a stagger, too tired to plant her feet in the trail Jane had broken for her, and now and then meandering to waste her strength fighting the deep drifts. Jane walked back in her own tracks and held Mary's arm as they walked. Mary tried to say something, but Jane pulled her near and whispered, "They could be close, so save your breath. Nothing does us any good but moving."

Mary didn't try to answer, so she returned her attention to the trail. It was important that they cover as much ground as they could while the snow was still falling to hide the signs of their passing. As soon as she had completed the thought, the snow stopped.

The air was frosty and still, and their feet made loud crunching sounds each time they stepped on the unbroken snow.

The ones who were following them would be able to keep up a fast pace, running in their footsteps in the flat places where the going was easy, and avoiding the depressions where their tracks had sunk in deep. Jane was always looking ahead, using the glow of the moon on the snow to search for any irregularity in the terrain that she could use to hide their trail—a thicket or a fallen log or a frozen streambed leading to the next river.

Far behind, she heard the first call of the hunters. "Coo-wigh!" reached her in the still air, and it was answered by a whistle somewhere closer and to their left.

"We've got to run now," she whispered to Mary Perkins.

They stepped into a jog with Jane at the front again, keeping her strides short to push aside the snow and make the going easier for Mary. She heard more whistles, and then the report of a rifle off to the left, and there were faint voices behind. She stepped into a deep drift and fell, then scrambled out of it and saw the stream. They ran along it for about a mile. As Jane came around a bend she saw the platform. It stood alone on the bank, a row of poles lashed ten feet above the ground between two saplings. She could see that its surface had something on it, so she hurried to the thicker sapling and began to climb.

"What are you doing?" hissed Mary impatiently. "They're coming."

"We can't outrun them," Jane whispered. "They never get tired and they never give up. All you can ever do is fool them."

The sapling was smooth and half frozen, with a layer of frost on the northwest side that held the snow to it, but she hoisted herself up high enough to see what was on the platform. There was a haunch of venison with the hide still on it, and a fat chunk of flesh that could only be bear meat. Some hunter had stored it there to keep it frozen and high enough to be out of the reach of animals. Then she found the two pairs of snowshoes. She tossed them to the ground and dropped beside them.

She knelt in the snow and tied one pair on Mary Perkins backward, so the long narrow shaft was at the toe end. "Stay here. Don't move," she said, then ran along the streambed and into the woods where the hunters' trail began. She tied her own snowshoes on backward, made her way back to Mary Perkins and said, "Come on."

They stepped along more easily now, the snowshoes holding them on the surface of the snow. Jane followed the stream to the right for a hundred yards to the first place where the low plants penetrated the snowpack enough to complicate their trail, then turned right again, toward the east. They made a trail that looked as though it led in the opposite direction and belonged to the hunters who had cached their game on the platform.

When the first sunlight caught them, they were in a flat, open valley. Their trail stretched behind them for miles, and as soon as the sun was high enough to stir the morning wind, much of it would be blown away. She said to Mary Perkins, "Just one more run, to get out of the open before they see us."

They began to run due east, where Jane could see a row of evergreen bushes tall enough to hide the shape of a standing woman. She was tired now too. They had been moving silently for the whole night, never speaking for hours at a time, only concentrating on the awkward business of walking in snowshoes. They could see the end now, and it made Jane run faster. As soon as they reached the shelter of the bushes they would be able to sit and rest, maybe even sleep in turns while the wind blew across the valley and erased the shallow marks of their snowshoes. "Faster," she said to Mary. Everything would depend on how they behaved for the next few minutes. They ran until their breath came in short gasps and their legs were numb.

The sun was rising now right behind the row of evergreens, glaring through the upper branches and making it hard for Jane to focus her eyes on them to tell how far they were. She clenched her teeth and kept running, and then they were there. Jane dragged Mary between the first pair of trees, then five more steps into thicker cover where the trees were small and close together, and they both let themselves collapse into the soft snow.

Jane lay there, breathing deeply, feeling the cold flakes against her cheek but not caring. She started to raise herself to her elbows, and her eyes rested on the bushes. All around her, they began to topple over. The men who had been holding them let go, and they fell to the snow with a low, whispery, ugly swish. All of the bushes seemed to change into men as warriors stood up from behind the clumps of brush they had tied into blinds or shouldered aside the small trees they had stuck into the snow.

Rough, hard hands clutched her arms, a heavy, leather-clad body threw itself across her legs, and another pressed her face into the snow so that she nearly smothered. They bound her hands behind her, dragged her to her feet, and jerked her ahead. One of her snowshoes came off, but when she tried to stop and look down a push that felt like a punch propelled her forward, so she limped along a few steps before the other one came off too. She tried to glance behind her to see what had happened to Mary, but a hand on the small of her back shoved her on with such force that for an instant she saw the sky.

They marched them to a path that led up over the hill into the next river valley. As Jane climbed, she tried to get her strength back, but they kept her moving too fast. She heard a language that meant nothing to her. The sounds were gruff, gutteral, and alien. When she reached the crest of the hill her heart stopped for a moment, then began to beat hard.

Stretched out below was a squalid, sprawling settlement that seemed to have been laid out by a madman. There were a few long-houses that looked as though Hurons or Eries had built them with no intention of living there long, interspersed with Algonquin wig-wams made of bark and thatch, a few hide tents like the wander-ing plains people had, and in the center a clump of shanties made of boards. It was as though enemies of all of the wars of the Nun-dawaono had somehow survived in debased remnants and gath-ered here for the winter hunt.

As she stumbled down the steep path to the huge collection of ramshackle dwellings, she could see small shapes of people below, their shadows long in the bright dawn sunlight. One of them pointed upward and yelled something, and then men began to stream out of the shelters and gather in the center of the village. She could see them talking and pointing, and she could feel their excitement growing until, when she was dragged to the edge of the village, their voices rose in a shout that was harsh and deafening, full of hatred and glee. It grew louder as she moved closer to it, until she could feel her stomach vibrating with it, and the men started to fire their guns into the air, a ragged *powpow pow pow-pow*, like popcorn popping.

They prodded Jane and Mary across the dirty, mud-caked snow between the huts and pushed them into a big pen made of upright pine logs sharpened at the tops. Jane looked around her and saw to her surprise that there were dozens of other people already inside—men clinging to their wives and children, trying in vain to reach around all of them with their arms, other men who looked as though they had run the gauntlet on the way into the little pen, with limbs broken and faces streaked with blood from blows above the hairline, women with eyes swelled shut and missing teeth.

"What's going to happen?" asked Mary.

Jane said, "The fighting has gone on forever. So many people get killed that the main reason for it now is to get prisoners to adopt."

"Adopt? We're grown women."

"When people are killed they capture someone to take their place—their name, their work, their family."

The gate across the pen opened and about fifty warriors streamed in, painted and armed as though they had just returned from battle. They were agitated and angry, some of them in a frenzy, dancing from one foot to the other like boxers and shouting in the incomprehensible languages of enemies. One by one and with reluctance, they took notice of something behind them and stepped aside to let the one Jane had been watching for pass among them to the front.

Jane hung her head like the captives around her to give her a chance to study him without attracting his attention. She looked from his feet upward. He was big and muscular, wearing a clinging, whitish leather shirt that seemed to have been stitched together from many small pieces. Around his neck and shoulders hung a gateasha of six rows of small white wampum beads. When she forced her gaze to move upward, she nearly fainted.

He was wearing a Face. It was a scalp mask, painted bright red, with round staring copper eyes and the clenched teeth that made it resemble both the rage of battle and the ghastly grin of a rotting corpse. It was terrifying to see a Face here. She could tell that this was an old Face, the features that a supernatural being had shown to some virtuous Seneca ages ago in a dream. The Seneca had carved to free the Face from the trunk of a living basswood tree, given it presents of tobacco, rubbed it with sunflower oil, and fed it the same mixture of cornmeal and maple sugar that the warriors ate on the trail to battle. It didn't merely represent the supernatural being; it *was* the supernatural being. It gleamed with power strong enough to cure disease and change the weather, but on this man that power became the force of evil and witchcraft and death.

The Face approached and stared at her with its round, empty eyes. Jane could see now that the necklace was made not of little white shells but of human teeth. As he moved on, she realized with revulsion what the leather must be: strips of skin flayed from human beings. The Face walked around the pen, stopping in front of each captive to turn its round-eyed, unreadable gaze on him for a second or two, then moving on.

Finally the Face came back to where Jane was standing. The Face stopped and pointed at Mary. At once a warrior appeared out of the mob and poured a bucket of black, greasy paint over Mary Perkins's head. The paint streamed down to her shoulders and ran along her arms to her fingertips.

Mary gasped and sputtered. "Why did he do that? What is it, some kind of joke?"

"No," said Jane. She could feel waves of nausea that started in her chest and moved down to grip her belly.

Mary shivered with cold. "It must be an initiation, right?" Her voice was tense and scared now, and a little sob was audible in it. "Why me?" she wailed. "What do they want me to do?"

Jane tried to speak, but what she would have to say was impossible to put into words. The black paint was the sign that a captive had been selected to be burned.

19

J ane awoke in the darkness with her heart pounding. She walked to the window. The snow had stopped sometime during the night, and now the sidewalks and streets were white and still, but in the east the sky had changed enough to tell her there was no point in going back to the couch. She raised her hand to touch her forehead and rubbed away the beads of sweat that had formed there. She had been denying what she knew about Barraclough, and the knowledge was fighting its way to the surface in dreams.

She moved quietly into the kitchen and put the coffee on. Then she sat and listened to Mary waking up and remembering and making her way toward the smell of the brewing coffee. The door opened and Mary walked out into the kitchen, poured a cup of coffee, and stood at the sink to drink it. "I've been thinking," she said. "I've been on my own most of my life and I think I can stay out of Barraclough's way if I don't do anything stupid." It was a question.

"It can be done." Jane sat still. It was time already. She would have to work up to it gradually, tell Mary what she knew and let her draw her own conclusion. "You just have to avoid doing anything stupid."

"Like getting my picture in the papers," Mary offered.

"Right," said Jane. "You might want to keep it off things like credit cards and driver's licenses too. Barraclough is the regional head of a very big detective agency, so he can probably find a way to have your picture circulated. You know, a reward for a missing person."

"I guess I can," Mary said. "And keep from getting arrested."

"Or fingerprinted."

"That's what I said."

"You've got to keep from being a victim, too. If your house is burglarized or your car is stolen, they fingerprint the owner so they can identify prints that aren't supposed to be there. Some states take your prints for a driver's license. And a lot of employers require it; if you need to be bonded or licensed or need a security clearance, it's hard to avoid. Most companies hire a security service to handle the details and report the results—a service like Intercontinental."

Mary Perkins glared at her. "You're trying to scare me."

"Yes," said Jane. "It's better. I don't want to hear you sometime saying, 'Why me?' "

"All right," said Mary. "What else?"

Jane stared at the wall. "Well, they're not just passively waiting for you to turn up. They're searching. I know that because I talked to somebody who was hired to help. But the easiest way is to get you to come to them. You know—an announcement in the paper says some rich aunt of yours died and the following eighty people are named in the will. Or the help-wanted section says there's a job for a blue-eyed woman age thirty-four and a half and five feet four and seven eighths who's good at arithmetic. Or a personal ad says a wealthy widow with a large secluded mansion wants a roommate: a quiet female nonsmoker from the South who plays cribbage, or whatever else you do but not everyone does. Barraclough is perfectly capable of renting houses in the ten most likely places and having ten women sit there for a month waiting for you to show up."

"He'd do that?"

"Sure," said Jane. "It's quick, it's easy, and it's cheaper than the alternatives."

"What are those?"

"Well, you have a history. There are people you were close to. They'll go see them. Maybe watch to see if you come for a visit, or maybe bully them into telling what they know. If you ever left clothes anywhere when you started running, they'll have translated the labels into places where you might buy the next batch. The more expensive they were, the fewer places to buy them, and they know you'll need spring clothes or risk standing out. They'll also use them to construct a projection of how you're likely to look now, so they don't miss you in a public place: exact height, weight, style, and color preference. Then there's chemical analysis."

"What do they have to analyze?"

"If you wore perfume or cosmetics when you wore the clothes, they'll identify them and add them to your profile. If you love Thai food or going to the zoo, they'll know that too."

"That's crazy."

Jane shrugged. "No crazier than having people meet us in airports all over the western half of the country. Intercontinental is an enormous detective agency, much bigger than most police departments. There isn't a city in the country that doesn't have a crime lab with a trace-analysis section. There's a machine called a gas chromatograph that vaporizes whatever substance they find and identifies it. There's no question Intercontinental has one, and probably an emission spectrometer and an electron microscope. If you're in the business of tracking people for money, that stuff pays for itself quickly."

"You're making it sound hopeless."

"Not hopeless. It just takes some thought."

Mary protested. "But there are thousands of people in this country nobody can find."

"Millions," said Jane.

"Well, who are they? You can't tell me they all get caught."

"It depends on who's looking for them and how hard. A lot

of them are divorce fugitives: the man who doesn't want to pay alimony or the parent who loses custody and takes the child out of state. Somebody else runs up a debt or embezzles a few bucks. Unless the person is foaming at the mouth and shooting people at freeway rest stops, the only ones who are very interested are the local police back home. Then there are a few million illegal aliens. There's not much reason to look for them because nobody gets any benefit from finding them. There are also personal cases: some woman breaks up with her boyfriend and he threatens her. There's practically no place where the police will do anything to help her, so she moves away and changes her name. There are millions of people hiding under assumed identities, and the reason most of them don't get found is that nobody's looking."

"What you're saying is that if anybody tried, they would."

"No," said Jane. "What I said is that it depends on who's looking and how hard."

"You think I'm going to get caught, don't you?"

Jane hesitated. "You can take that chance, or you can choose to take other chances."

"What does that mean?"

"He's not going to give up. He has lots of trained people at his disposal in offices all over the country, and he can probably dream up a charge to get the police looking for you too, if he wants to. If you learn fast and never make a mistake, he might not find you." Jane looked at her closely. "Or you could make a mistake—intentionally."

Mary's eyes widened and the color seemed to drain from her face. "You want to use me for—"

"Bait. Yes. What he's doing isn't just evil; it's also illegal."

"I can't. I don't have the money. You're wrong. He's wrong."

"It doesn't matter. He thinks you do, and he wants it. That makes him predictable, and that can be turned into a weakness. Your chance of trapping him and getting him convicted might be better than your chance of hiding from him."

"No. I won't do it." Mary looked at Jane defiantly.

"Suit yourself."

"Are you leaving this morning?"

"I said I'd help you get settled."

"But I told you I wouldn't do it. You can't use me as bait."

"I heard you."

For the next six days, Jane Whitefield waited. When Mary woke up she would find the quilt folded neatly and stowed beside the couch. Jane would be in the middle of the only open space in the small living room going through the slow, floating movements of Tai Chi.

On the sixth day, Mary Perkins said, "Why do you do that?"

"It keeps my waist thin and my ass from getting flabby."

Mary repeated, "Why do you do that?"

"It helps me feel good. It keeps me flexible. It helps me think clearly and concentrate."

"Don't worry," said Mary. "I'll shut up."

"You don't have to," said Jane. "Part of the idea is that after a while the body makes the movements flow into each other without consulting the conscious mind much."

"What's that one?"

"What do you mean?"

"They all have names, right?"

"Oh. 'Cloud Hands.' " Then her body was in a radically different position without much apparent movement. " 'Golden Cock Stands on Leg.' " Her body continued to drift into a changing pattern of positions.

Mary watched for a long time. "Where did you learn to fight?"

"By fighting."

"No," said Mary. "I mean fight like that."

"This isn't exactly about fighting. It's about not fighting. Your opponent is fighting, but you're watching. He attacks, but you've already begun to yield the space. He strikes, but you're not really there. You only passed through there on your way to somewhere else. You bring his force around in a circle, add yours to it, and let him hurt himself."

"The mystic wisdom of the mysterious East."

"It's practical. I'm a very strong woman, but no matter what I do, I'm going to be smaller than any man who's likely to try to hurt me. If I fight him for the space between us, I'll get hammered. He's using one arm and maybe his back foot to throw the punch.

I'm bringing my whole body into one motion to add force to his punch and alter its direction just a little. For that fraction of a second I have him outnumbered."

Mary put on her coat, walked toward the door, opened it, turned, and said, "You should have let your ass get flabby. It might have made you more human." She went out and closed the door. That night she came home late and tiptoed past Jane on the couch.

Two hours later Jane opened her eyes and acknowledged that she had heard Mary come out of her room again. It was three A.M. and she was sitting in the big easy chair staring at Jane.

Mary said, "You're trying to wear me down. You're staying in the corner of my room and not saying anything to convince me, just putting yourself in front of my eyes wherever I look so I'll have to think about it."

Jane said, "You've spent time with people who take what they want."

"I was one of them."

"Then you can predict what Barraclough is thinking as well as I can. You don't need any arguments from me."

Mary sat back in the big chair with her hands resting on the arms. "Why haven't you mentioned the little boy?"

"Why should I?"

"I've lived by convincing people to do stupid things they didn't want to do, so I know how it's done. The little boy is an overlooked resource. Here I am, unmarried and alone, and anybody who is alive can feel her biological clock ticking away. I've reached the age where women start getting too many cats. The little boy is alone and probably scared. Barraclough has already robbed him, and now he'll kill him."

"Will he?"

"You know he will, and that's why you're here. If the kid's dead, the cops will run around bumping into each other for a couple of months and then forget him. If he's alive, there's always the chance that Barraclough will wind up sitting in a courtroom across the aisle from an innocent ten-year-old."

"Not much chance."

"But as long as the kid is alive, there's also the chance that he'll live another ten or fifteen years and find out who killed his four best friends and left him broke. Barraclough will be thinking he doesn't want to wake up some night and find a young man who looks vaguely familiar holding a gun against his head." Mary waited a few seconds. "So why didn't you mention him again?"

Jane sat up and stared at her. "People are killed every day. Why would I imagine you would pick him out of all the thousands and say, 'You're the one I've chosen. I've trained myself since I was a baby to ignore the screams of the dying because if I let even a little of the sound in I couldn't hear or think of anything else. But for you I'll risk my own life.'"

"You're right, I wouldn't." She leaned forward. "But not saying it is the argument, isn't it? I'm supposed to think of doing it, and if I think of it, I have to admit a second later that I'm not the kind of person who does that, and wonder why not."

"I apologize for telling you about him."

"But he's the reason why you're doing this, isn't he?"

"There's not much more I can do for him. I was in a fight, and all of the people on my side except Timmy are dead. That's all."

"I don't suppose the money has anything to do with it."

"For me? Not this time."

"You're above that kind of consideration."

"Hardly," said Jane. "I have enormous expenses. But money is not a pressing problem. Once you have what you need, it's hard to get yourself to lean over a cliff to reach for more. And I can't even spend what I have. A fancier house or a lot of expensive jewelry raises my profile and maybe gets me killed."

"Then why does this kid's money matter to you?"

"Or your money either? It's important only because it's what Barraclough wants. He uses it to grow stronger. I don't want him to succeed. I don't want to feed him."

"Why do you care?"

"I'm the rabbit, he's the dog. I run, he chases. He's good at it, and he's getting better. He's using Intercontinental to recruit young guys with nothing much to do and criminal records that make it unlikely that anybody else will ever pay them to do anything. He's picking out the ones with a certified history of violence and training them to hunt."

"We're finally getting down to a reason that means something. You're afraid he might get to be a problem, aren't you? Not just to people like me, but to you."

"He already is. If I let him get stronger, eventually he'll kill me."

Mary slumped back in her chair and breathed a deep, windy sigh. "At last. Thank you."

"You haven't changed your mind, have you?"

"No, but now maybe I can sleep. You're no better than I am."

When Mary came out into the living room again it was nearly noon. She looked at Jane and her face seemed to deflate. "You're still here."

"Even if you won't help me get Barraclough, it's still to my advantage to make sure he doesn't get you."

"How long do I have to live like this?"

"After we get you working, it will be easier," said Jane. "We'll study the other women here—shop where they shop and buy what they buy. Everything you do has to keep your head down where there are lots of other heads."

Mary looked as though she were considering it. "How long do I have to do this?"

Jane shrugged. "The longer you do it, the safer you'll be. Most women live quiet, private lives, and most women are basically happy. It helps to make new friends and be part of a community. If you look at the way your friends live, you'll feel better, and that will keep you from getting lazy."

"Lazy?"

"The average person sets an alarm to get up early, goes to work, has a little leisure time, sets the alarm, and goes to bed. The weeks get long, and people don't get paid what they deserve. There will come a day when you can't get your mind off some fantasy— a week in the Bahamas, or maybe only a dress you saw in a magazine. It doesn't matter what it is. Live within your means. I mean your visible means."

Mary's face turned hard and her eyes glittered. "I'm not sure I understand."

"Don't touch the money that's in Zurich or Singapore."

"I told you: there is no money." She stared at Jane for a long time, waiting for the contradiction.

Jane sat motionless and returned her stare evenly. Finally Mary angrily jumped to her feet, threw on her coat, and walked out the door. When Jane heard the dull thump of the door at the bottom of the stairs, she stood up, put on her coat, and prepared to go out too. She had a lot of work to do.

20

The Detroit–Wayne County airport was only twenty-six miles east of Mary Perkins's apartment on Route 94. The flight was not even three hundred miles, so when Jane Whitefield emerged from the gate at O'Hare, the clock on the wall said 3:10. The taxi took her to the State Street mall and she walked two blocks along East Madison Street. On another day she might have had the taxi driver leave her farther away, but last night's snow had reached Chicago by morning, and today the wind was picking it up and moving it along between the big buildings in horizontal sheets. Most pedestrians were just scurrying across the open to get from one building to another, and she saw none who might have followed her.

She reached the Bank of Illinois before four o'clock and was behind the counter in a quiet cubicle opening her safe-deposit box within five minutes. Months ago she had come to Chicago to pay the bill for the Furnace corporation's post office box, shop for clothes, and store Catherine Snowdon's papers. She took them out and studied them. Catherine Snowdon had a birth certificate, a driver's license, a Social Security card, a Visa card, and an ATM card from the Bank of America in case she needed cash. Jane examined the other papers in the box. That left only Wendy Lewis, Karen Gottlieb, and Anne Bronstein. She examined their papers to reassure herself that she had not let any of the expiration dates go by. Then she put them back under the savings passbook and the nine-millimeter Beretta pistol, closed the box, and rang for the lady who would go with her to return it to its slot in the vault.

A guide needed more insurance policies than any of her clients, but she could spare Catherine Snowdon for Mary Perkins. She would hide the Catherine Snowdon papers with ten thousand dollars in cash somewhere within walking distance of Mary's apartment in case she had to bail out.

Jane caught a cab from the Dirksen Building on East Adams and flew back to Detroit to do some shopping. At a Toys "R" Us she found a toy called Musical Moves. If the child stepped in the right places on a brightly colored mat, he could play a tune electronically. Jane would redirect the wire so that instead the pressure on the mat would send current to a small lightbulb. Two would be better—one mounted inside the apartment and one somewhere outside—maybe in the mailbox, if it could be done without alarming the letter carrier. If the bulb was lit, Mary Perkins would know that somebody was in her apartment waiting for her.

At a hardware store she bought the tools, wires, electrical tape, and a rope ladder designed for getting out a second-floor window in an emergency. She decided these purchases would be enough for the present. Mary had a lot to get used to in a short time, and she would be less likely to make mistakes in a crisis if she wasn't distracted by complexity.

Jane stopped at a pay telephone and dialed her own number. She heard the telephone ring four times and then heard her own voice. "Hello. Please leave a message at—" Jane quickly punched in her two-digit code, then heard the machine rewind. It seemed to be taking a long time. Then there were a couple of clicks and Carey McKinnon's voice.

"Jane? It's Carey. I know you're probably calling in for messages, and this is the only way I have to reach you. I'm sorry I had to go back to the hospital the other night. Give me a call when you can—at home or the hospital or my office. If I'm in surgery or something, leave me a number where I can reach you." The machine's computer voice said, "Tuesday, ten-fifteen A.M."

Carey's voice came on again. "Hi, Jane. Just me again. It's been a few days and you still haven't called me. Am I imagining that you said you would? I'm in my usual haunts." "Saturday," said the machine, "two thirty-six P.M."

The next one said, "I'm beginning to think you're mad at me or something. If you are, please call me up and yell at me. Two weeks is a long time to sit around wondering." "Friday, six fifty-two P.M."

Jane hung up the telephone and then dialed Carey's number. When his machine came on, she said, "Hi, Carey. It's me. I'm sorry I couldn't get back to you. This job has turned out to be just awful. I'm trying to help a woman make her business profitable, and her business is promoting products all over the country. I've been in more airports than . . . a couple more than my suitcase has, anyway. I always seem to be strapped into an airplane seat when you're home, and then we have to sit down and run figures for the next meeting the minute we're in a hotel, and get to the meeting by breakfast time. Enough whining. I'm not mad at you. I'll call you when I'm home." She caught herself before she said "I love you" because he had never said it to her, but then she felt foolish for being petty. She changed it into "I miss you," then hung up. She tested the sound of it in her mind and decided it was true, as far as it went. She did miss him.

There had been two or three friends in college who had known that she had a knack for hiding people, but Carey McKinnon had not been one of them. Each year thereafter it would have been harder to tell him, but that was not why she had avoided it. She had been saving him for herself. She needed to keep home a safe place where she could talk to people who cared about her and forget that the next day she might have to take a fugitive out of the world. But she had planted a lie that had grown thick enough to choke her. Now that he had asked her to marry him, she could barely stand to talk to his answering machine.

As she stepped off the curb, she realized that the only solution she had thought of was to perpetuate the lie—tell him the profession she was quitting was the consulting business—and not admit to him that she was not the person he thought he knew. She would only be doing what she had taught dozens of other people to do—pick the life you want and lie fifty times a day to get it—so she felt ashamed that the prospect seemed so empty and hopeless to her.

Then she recognized that she was thinking about it as though she had decided to marry Carey. She had not decided. The time to decide about marriage was when you had reason to assume you would be alive on your wedding day.

Jane took a bus back to Ann Arbor and got off at the university. She did not begin the walk down Huron Street back to the apartment until after midnight. She had taken a longer time than necessary to give Mary Perkins a day alone. The more time Mary had to think, the better she would be.

As Jane walked up Huron in the cold, still air, listening to her feet crunching the snow, she began to hear another sound, far off behind her. It started low and quickly moved up an octave a second until she recognized it as a siren. She walked along, listening to it grow louder and closer, until she heard it pass her on a parallel street. A minute later, she heard another set of sirens coming toward her from somewhere ahead and to her right.

She watched the intersections ahead and saw the blinking lights of a fire engine swing around a corner and head out Huron Street. After another block she began to smell the smoke in the air. It was a thin, hanging haze like the smoke from somebody's fireplace in the windless night. She began to walk faster, and at the next corner she turned down a side street. It was a two-alarm fire so far, and there was no point in walking into the middle of a lot of firemen and policemen after midnight carrying shopping bags. At the first corner she turned right along the street behind Huron and hurried on.

When she was still two blocks from the big old house where Mary lived, she could see the sky suddenly begin to glow. She dropped her bags and broke into a run. It must be the house. As she ran up the quiet residential street, she began to see other people coming out of apartments and houses and walking toward the fire.

When Jane turned back onto Huron, she could see the trucks lined up in front of Mary's house. The coats of the firemen were glowing, their wet helmets reflecting the flames that were now coming out of the lower windows and licking up the wooden clapboards toward the upper floor.

Jane forced herself to slow her pace to a fast walk, looking carefully at every human shape illuminated by the fire. She tried to recognize one that might be Mary, already almost certain that she would not see her. The fire didn't make sense unless they had made a mistake and killed her. They had set a fire not because it would fool a coroner—Farrell, the training officer, would have taught them that much—but because fire got rid of fingerprints and fibers, and because water and firemen's boots obliterated footprints.

She moved into the curious crowd and began to study the faces of the people who had gathered in a big circle around the fire. She wasn't looking for Mary anymore; she was looking for any face that she had seen before.

She heard the loud *blip-blip* of another siren and saw another set of lights sweep around the corner and stop at the curb thirty feet behind a fire truck. The new vehicle was an ambulance. Jane moved toward it, weaving her way between spectators who were so intent on the fire that they seemed to be unaware of her passing.

She edged closer to the ambulance and watched the two paramedics haul their collapsible stretcher out the back and rush, not to Mary's house but up the other side of the hedge to the lawn of the house next door. Jane felt a tiny resurgence of hope that she could not suppress. Maybe that was where the firemen had taken the victims—out of their way and out of danger—and if the paramedics were in a hurry, they must believe they had a patient waiting for them, not a corpse.

Jane followed the paramedics. They hurried up the lawn until they reached a pair of firemen in gas masks who were kneeling over somebody lying prone on the snow beyond the hedge. One of the firemen had an oxygen tank on his back like a scuba diver, and he was holding the mask over the face of the person on the ground. Jane held her breath as the four men slid the victim onto the stretcher. When they lifted it to unfold the legs, she let her breath out in disappointment. The person on the stretcher was wearing a black rubber turnout coat and high boots. One of the firemen must have collapsed from the smoke.

She turned away and looked at the house. The top floor had caught now, and she could see the flames eating their way through the inner walls. In a few minutes the roof would collapse into Mary Perkins's apartment and the killers would have accomplished what Barraclough's training officer had taught them to do when things went wrong.

She watched the firemen straining to hold the hoses steady while they sprayed enormous streams of water into the upper windows. She glanced at a couple of firemen coming around the house carrying long pike poles. Their faces had dark, grimy smoke stains around the eyes and on the foreheads where their masks had not covered, their coats and pants glistened with water and dripped on the snow as they trotted toward their truck. She whirled around in time to see the four men pushing the stretcher toward the back of the ambulance. The injured fireman's turnout coat wasn't wet. He had been in there long enough to succumb to the smoke, but he didn't have a drop on him. The two firemen who had been kneeling over him were dry too.

Jane moved quickly in a diagonal path toward the ambulance, keeping her eyes on the stretcher. They had the tie-down restraints strapped over a blanket they'd draped over the turnout coat, and the mask still over the face. She couldn't see the hair because they had a pillow under the head and their bodies shielded it from view. As they reached the lighted street she stared hard at the side of the blanket, where a couple of the victim's fingers protruded an inch. The red, whirling light from the fire truck just ahead passed across them and glinted off a set of tapered, polished fingernails. It was Mary Perkins.

Jane stepped around the front of the ambulance, slipped into the driver's door, and crouched on the floor. She heard the back doors open, the sliding of the metal wheels of the stretcher, and then the back doors slammed. She climbed into the seat, threw the transmission into gear, stepped on the gas pedal, and veered away from the curb to avoid the fire engine parked thirty feet ahead.

Then she straightened her wheels and roared down the block. She glanced in the rearview mirror. The four men took a couple of steps after her, then seemed to see the futility of it and stopped in the street. Before she turned the corner at the first traffic signal she looked again, but she couldn't see them anymore.

She drove fast for five blocks, letting the siren clear the way for her, and then turned into a smaller street, flipped off the flashing lights and siren, and went faster.

"Mary!" she called. There was no answer. It occurred to her that the gas in the fireman's tank had probably not been oxygen. It could as easily have been medical anesthetic. If it was, Mary was about as likely to die as recover. Jane drove on for another minute, then pulled the van to a stop in the lot behind a school. She ran to the back of the ambulance, opened the door, climbed inside, and looked down at Mary. She could see that her eyes were wide open, and then they blinked.

"You're alive after all," said Jane. She pulled at the oxygen mask and saw that it was held by a piece of elastic behind the head, so she slipped it up and off. There was a wide strip of adhesive tape across Mary's mouth. She undid the top straps on the stretcher.

Mary quickly sat up and fumbled to free her own feet. She was sobbing and shaking, and kicking at the strap so hard that her own hands couldn't hold on to it. Jane undid that strap too. "You'd better take the tape off your own mouth," she said.

Mary clawed at it and gave a little cry of pain as she tore it off. "They trapped me!" she sobbed. "There was no other way out." She shook the heavy turnout coat off, and Jane could see they had slipped it over the jacket she had put on to escape the fire. "There was smoke, and they banged on the door, and they looked like firemen. One of them gave me an oxygen mask, and—"

"I know," said Jane. "Come on. We've got to get out of here."

"Can't you just keep going?" Mary looked at the driver's seat, willing Jane into it.

"No. We're already pushing our luck. They'll be looking for the ambulance. I assume it's stolen, so the police will be too." She pulled Mary to her feet, pushed her out the back door, and said, "Run with me."

Mary stood against the ambulance. She took a step in the fireman's boots, her beige pants bloused over the tops just below her knees, then stopped and pulled her jacket around her. "I can't."

"Try," said Jane simply. She slung her purse across her chest and started off across the lot at a slow, easy trot. After a few steps she heard Mary running too.

Jane jogged onto the broad back lawn of the school. It seemed to be a high school because all of the athletic fields were full-sized and elaborate, with wooden bleachers beside them. The grass under the snow was level and clear, with no chance of any unseen obstacles. Even better, there were tracks on it where she could place her feet. When she was in the open away from the building she could feel the wind blowing tiny particles of snow against her cheeks. Now was the time to set a quick pace, before some cop arrived to find the ambulance. She waited until she thought Mary Perkins was warm and loose, then lengthened her strides a bit. The playing fields were an advantage because she could lead them out a quarter of a mile away on a street far from the path of the ambulance. But while they were out here they would be the only black spots on an ocean of empty white snow.

She looked over her shoulder at Mary and saw that she interpreted the look as permission to slow down. Jane turned ahead again and quickly worked her way up to a comfortable lope. She listened to Mary's footsteps and timed her breathing. She was not used to running, but she seemed to be doing it.

When Jane reached the goalpost at the end of the football field, she stopped and ran in place until Mary caught up. She said, "We'll be able to walk as soon as we reach cover," and started off again. This time it seemed to be a soccer field because it was longer. She could discern what was at the end of the school property now. There was a high chain-link fence, and beyond it some tall, leafless trees. She ran ahead to look for the gate.

She found it in a few seconds, but it had a thick chain and a serious padlock on it. She looked back to see Mary struggling to catch up. She could see that there were tracks all over the field. Unless kids had changed a lot since she was in high school they would never walk an extra quarter mile just to get around a fence. She moved along the fence and saw the answer. There was a city parking lot beyond the fence, filled with plows, dump trucks, tractors, and a forage harvester parked beside a building that looked like a warehouse. The parking lot was empty of cars, but it was clear of snow because they had used the plows to push an enormous pile of snow up against the fence nearly to its top eight feet up.

Mary came up behind her, breathing deeply but not in distress. Jane said, "How are you at climbing fences?"

"Take a guess."

"I'll help you," said Jane. "All we have to do is get to the top. We can walk down." She took Mary's arm and pointedly placed her hand on a chain link above her head. She began to climb, and Jane waited for the moment to come when she decided she couldn't do it.

Mary stopped. "I don't think—"

Jane reached up, put both hands on her thighs, and boosted her higher. "Do the work with your legs. Toes in the spaces, step up. Just use your hands to hold on. Step up. Good. Step up." She climbed up after her, and when Mary reached the intimidating part, where the packed snow was above the top of the fence, she said, "Step up," held on to the fence with one hand, and pushed Mary hard with the other so that she rolled up onto the mountain of snow.

When Jane reached the top and flopped onto the snow she found Mary still lying there, breathing deeply and trying to get her heart to slow. Jane sat up for a second, then ducked down and burrowed into the snow. "Stay down," she said.

A beam of light moved across the field. Jane could see it pass above their heads, lighting up thousands of tiny snowflakes that had been blown into the air by the wind. The police car was beside the ambulance, so the beam widened in the thousand feet of empty fields and became enormous, but it was still so bright that she could see the line of adhesive the tape had left on Mary's cheek.

Mary asked, "Is it—"

"Cops," said Jane. "In a minute they'll shut the light off. When they do, don't move."

The light swept across the field, came back, continued around the horizon, and then went out. "Rest," said Jane. "Use this time to rest." They lay in the darkness and she listened. Suddenly the light came on again, swept over their heads, and shot back and forth around the field. She listened for the sound of the engine, but it didn't come. Finally the light went off. "Okay," said Jane. "Now we move." She sat up a little, slid down the hill, and waited while Mary followed.

They hurried to the far side of the lot, where the gate to the street was, and stopped. This gate was locked with the same kind of padlock and chain as the first one. She looked up at the fence. It was as high as the first, but it had coils of barbed wire strung along the top. They couldn't go back because the police wouldn't leave until they had a tow truck hooked up to the ambulance. She looked around her. There were sure to be cutting tools in the low building at the side of the lot, but breaking in would be harder than getting over a fence, and at least the fence didn't have an alarm. There were trucks, tractors, and plows all over the place, but even if she managed to hot-wire one of them to crash the gate, the sound of the engine would bring the police car across the field in twenty seconds. Then her eyes sorted out the strange shapes at the other end of the yard.

"All right," she said. "I hope you're strong, because I'll need your help."

She ran to the corner of the little compound, past the swing sets stored for the winter and the playground merry-go-rounds and over to the slides. The first two had frames of welded steel pipes that made them too heavy. The third was made of thin fiberglass in the shape of a tube, and Jane could lift the end of it by herself. They dragged it to the fence, lifted it so that the ladder was on their side and the tube went over the barbed wire and out to the street. "Want to go first?" asked Jane.

Mary climbed the ladder, slipped her legs into the tube, and flew out the other end onto the snow. Then Jane slid down and fell in the same spot. Mary was impatient to get away from the fence now, but Jane said, "If we don't move it, the cops will figure it out without having to get out of their car. Help me." They pushed the tube back over into the compound, then started down the street.

"Where are we going?" asked Mary.

"The university."

They jogged the last mile in silence. Jane set the pace again and listened for Mary's footsteps. She glanced at her watch. It was after two A.M. now, and even close to the university there were no pedestrians. Twice she saw headlights far down the street and pulled Mary with her into the dark space between two houses until the car had passed. When they finally reached the university campus, Jane slowed to a walk. She heard Mary's footsteps hit hard for two or three more steps, and then they sounded softer and slower too.

Jane walked on, studying the buildings for a long time. Finally she pointed to a long four-story building. The name on the facade was Helen Mileham Hall. Jane stopped a hundred feet away. "That wouldn't be a bad place to get out of the cold."

Mary Perkins said, "What is it?" She was so exhausted that her voice sounded almost detached.

"I think it's a women's dormitory," said Jane.

"It's the middle of the night. Won't it be locked?"

"Of course," said Jane. She wished she hadn't mentioned the cold. They were both heated from their run, but the night air was already beginning to dry the sweat on her face and leave it numb. The front door was out of the question. It led into a reception area that looked like a hotel lobby. She could see that there was an intercom and some kind of electronic locking system on the glass door. She supposed she had been in the last generation of coeds who had curfews, so probably there was no old bat to take the names of girls who came in late, but the world had gotten more dangerous for women since then, so they would have something worse, like an old bat in a guard's uniform with a .357 Magnum strapped to her hip. She walked around the building once looking for the fire doors while Mary waited. Then she heard the sound of the dryer.

As Jane walked toward it she walked into her memory. When a girl was eighteen and away from home for the first time, nights like this came now and again. The term papers and the laundry had piled up at about the same rate, and it was a Friday night near the end of the fall semester. The music and the shouting in the dorm had died out, but she wasn't ready to lie in the dark yet because even though morning would come with nauseating punctuality in a few hours, she was still eighteen and restless. She would convince herself that what she was doing was eminently practical. She could use all the laundry machines at once if she had enough quarters, and the silence and the solitude would make the term paper better.

The girl was sitting across from the dryers with her feet on a chair, underlining passages in a textbook. The laundry room was hot and humid from the washers and dryers, and she had the door propped open to let the steamy air out.

Jane hurried to the corner of the building and beckoned to Mary. Then she moved to the wall of the building, stepped close to the door, and looked at it. There was a crash bar that pulled a dead bolt out of a hole in the floor, and there was a standard spring latch that fit into the jamb. She opened her purse, pulled six dimes out of her wallet, and leaned behind the door to reach out and slide them into the hole in the floor. Then she came over to Mary and whispered, "What did you do with the tape they put over your mouth?"

"What?" whispered Mary.

"I didn't see you throw it away. Where is it?"

Mary said, "I don't know. I guess I . . ." She reached into her pocket. "Here it is." It was in a wad.

Jane took it, stepped far back from the door and away from the light, came back to the doorjamb, and stuffed it into the hole where the latch would go when the door shut. Then she beckoned to Mary and they both went across the dormitory lawn to sit on a curb and wait.

In fifteen minutes the girl's dryers stopped and she folded her clothes, kicked the doorstop up, and closed the door slowly and quietly. It was almost three in the morning and she didn't need a couple of hundred neighbors waking up angry.

Jane waited a few minutes longer before she opened the door, pulled the adhesive tape out of the doorjamb, dug the dimes out of the hole, and pulled Mary inside. She shut the door, and they made their way up the back stairs to the second floor, away from the public areas to the long corridors lined with students' rooms. Jane walked quietly through the halls of the dormitory, looking at the doors of all of the rooms. At each corner she stopped and listened for other footsteps, but she heard none. Finally she stopped at a door where there was a folded note taped at eye level. She pulled it off carefully and read it.

Cindy—
Your mother called like eight times!!! I told her you were in
the library. Call her as soon as you get back from Columbus.
Lauren

Jane slipped the Catherine Snowdon credit card between the
doorknob and the jamb until she found the plunger, then bowed it
a little to push the plunger aside and open the door. Before she
closed it behind Mary she put the note back. Cindy was going to
need time to prepare a comforting story for her mother.

Jane felt for the single bed by the wall, pulled the thick blanket off it and draped it over the rod behind the curtains so that no
light would escape, then turned the switch on. She went to the
closet and studied the clothes for a moment, then started taking
things out. "She's about your height, but she wears her tops big."
She tossed a sweater on the bed. "Put it on." She took off her own
blouse and slipped another sweater over her head. Then she
glanced at Mary's rubber boots. "Those aren't going to help us either. Try some of hers."

Within a few minutes they were both dressed in Cindy's
clothes. There was one short fall coat and one University of Michigan jacket. It was reversible, so Jane pulled it inside out and put it
on. There were places where she could still pass as a college girl,
but a college was not one of them. She counted a thousand dollars
out of her purse and set it on the desk. "Sorry, Cindy," she wrote
on Cindy's pad. "I needed clothes." She turned to Mary. "You
look good, considering. Let's go."

Jane led Mary out through the laundry room, then found the
Student Union by walking toward the center of the campus. The
Ride Board was something she remembered from her college days,
and she found it in a big hallway off the entrance. There were
index cards posted in long lines on a cork bulletin board. She ignored the "Ride Wanted" cards and looked closely at the "Going
to . . ." cards. Most of them offered rides for Thursday night or
Friday, so they were obsolete already. She selected one that said,
"Going to Ohio State. Leaving for Columbus Saturday 5:oo A.M.
Return after game. Share driving and gas. Doug," and gave a
phone number. She glanced at her watch. It was four A.M. now. If

Doug wasn't an idiot he was at least awake. She walked to the pay phone across the hall and dialed the number.

At five o'clock the car pulled up in front of the Student Union. Doug was big and smiled easily. He was the sort of boy who would shortly flesh out and play a lot of golf. His two passengers were a surprise to him. While he was driving from his room to the campus he had planned to say he was glad that they had turned up at the last minute because he loved company. He also liked making a road trip without having to pay all of the expenses himself, but better than either, he liked women. He liked looking at them and hearing their voices and smelling the scents that hung in the air around them. When he saw the two women walking down the steps of the Student Union he thought that this was turning out to be a very fortunate day. But when they got into the car and the light came on he realized that they were old. They weren't old like somebody's mother, but they were still too old to be any more interested in Doug than his female professors were.

Near the ramp for the 23 Expressway at Geddes Avenue, Doug started to signal for a turn into the all-night gas station, but the dark one said, "Can we stop for gas later? There's nobody on the road now and we can make good time. Later on we'll be dying to stop."

Doug could live with that. The gauge said they had half a tank, so it didn't really matter. But for a second it seemed to him that she had some other reason for not wanting to stop until she was out of Ann Arbor. It was as though her husband was cruising around looking for her or something. They didn't stop until Toledo, and then the dark one insisted on paying for the gas and driving the next hundred miles.

It turned out that the one in the back was a graduate student in the business school. She had worked for ten years and then decided to go back. She was asleep most of the time. The dark one was a lot more talkative. She was a friend of the graduate student, and had talked her into going down for the game. Maybe she wasn't really that talkative, because afterward he couldn't remember learning anything else about her in the four-hour drive. Maybe she had just prompted Doug to talk and smiled a lot.

When they were on the outskirts of Columbus, the dark one

announced that they still had to go scrounge tickets to the game, because she had talked Alene into coming at the last minute on a whim. She had him drop them off on the Ohio State campus so they could check the bulletin boards for offers of unused tickets.

Doug hated to relinquish the fantasy he had been developing for four hours, revising and refining it at each turn in the long road. He had envisioned himself ending up in a hotel in Columbus with the two older women, celebrating Michigan's victory on a king-sized bed. But he had not been able to invent any plausible set of circumstances that might lead to the fulfillment of this fantasy, nor could he imagine how one went about proposing such a thing. He left them with a regret that hung about him until later in the day, when he met a girl named Michele who called herself Micki with an *i*. She had seen him on the Ohio State campus with the two older women and convinced herself that there was a melancholy sophistication about him. He did not think about the two older women again until Sunday night, when he was driving back to Michigan with Micki. It had occurred to him that they might not have been able to get tickets to the game, but he would not have guessed that instead they had bought airline tickets from Columbus to Boston under assumed names and disappeared during the stopover in Cleveland.

21

$\mathbf{M}$ary lay on her bed in the motel room and listened to the airplanes passing overhead. She had already unconsciously perceived their rhythm. They would growl along for four minutes somewhere far beyond the eastern end of the building, then roar overhead and into nothingness. There would be a pause of forty-five seconds before she heard the next one growling and muttering at the starting line.

Mary was tired of waiting for the question. She turned her head to look at Jane. "It was the medical records," she said.

Jane was sitting at the round table under the hideous hanging lamp sorting small items she had taken from her purse. There was a lot of cash, and cards that seemed to have been taped to the lining in rows. "What medical records?" She didn't look up.

"You were the one who made me think of it. I wanted to do it the way you would. I went to a doctor in Ann Arbor. I asked for the form people send to their old doctors to get their records forwarded. I signed it and changed the doctor's address so they would send it to me."

"Why did you do that?" asked Jane. "Do you have some condition that needs to be watched?"

Mary Perkins shook her head. "It just seemed like the right thing to do—to have them. Now, before something happened. I was going to change my name on them and bring them to the new doctor on the first visit. I couldn't think of a reason why a woman my age wouldn't have records somewhere, and I knew I could never make some up. And they're confidential; they're supposed to be protected."

Jane sighed. "They are. The address where they're sent isn't."

"Oh. But how did Barraclough's people get it?"

"There are a lot of ways. You pose as Mary Perkins's probation officer and ask. Or you get a person hired to work in the office so she can watch for the right piece of paper to come in the mail. They might have wanted a copy of your records anyway to see if you had a condition that meant you had to keep seeing one of fifteen specialists in the country, or needed a particular kind of surgery or something. They could even do the same thing you did: send a note from a real doctor requesting the records. The old doctor's secretary would say they'd already been sent to such and such an address. I don't know, and it doesn't matter very much. Did you get them?"

"Get what?"

"The medical records."

"Oh. Sure." She looked uncomfortable. "They got burned up."

"Good." Jane went back to her sorting. "It's one more avenue Barraclough had that he doesn't have anymore."

Mary's voice began in a quiet tone that was low-pitched and tense, as though she were flexing her throat muscles to keep her vocal cords from tightening. "They started the fire while I was asleep in the house, you know. They didn't do it so nobody would know they had been there. They made me come out to them because they were dressed like firemen who were there to save me. I couldn't see their faces, just the masks and helmets and raincoats."

"I know," said Jane.

"I'm not trying to tell you what happened," said Mary Perkins. "I'm trying to tell you what happened to me." She said more softly, "To me." She stared at Jane's face for a reaction, and what she saw told her Jane was waiting. "I'm new at this," she said again. "For you it's like herding cattle around. It's not just taking care of them; it's making sure they don't stampede off a cliff or eat poison or drink so much water that their stomachs rupture."

"There's nothing to be ashamed of," said Jane. "They had you. It wasn't something you imagined."

"They do that too. They talk softly to the cattle and say, 'Come on, girl. It's okay.' But it's not exactly true and it's not exactly for the cow's benefit." Mary took a deep breath. "I'm not used to being the only one who doesn't know things, and I'm not used to this way of looking at the world. I guess I should have had enough imagination to figure out what it was like. I once knew some people slightly who were supposed to be very tough, but I never saw any of them actually *do* anything. I keep looking back and wondering how I ever got from being eighteen and smart and pretty all the way to being twice that and having men I never saw before burning me out of a house."

Jane shrugged. "You told me how it happened."

"No," said Mary Perkins. "No, I didn't. I told you what happened to some savings and loan companies. Not what happened to me."

Jane stopped sorting and began to string together credit cards and licenses with strips of adhesive tape. She did not dare look at Mary for fear there would be something in her eyes that gave Mary permission to stop talking.

"In the summer of 1981 I was twenty-two. I had just graduated from Florida State. I was good at interviews—I could tell that they liked me—but I couldn't seem to get a job. I remember coming home and closing the door to my bedroom upstairs. I would take off my outfit and hang it up carefully so my makeup wouldn't ruin it when I flopped down on the bed to cry. Then I would get newspapers from other places and write letters to answer the ads. Finally in October I got a job. Winton-Waugh Savings in Waco, Texas, wanted a management trainee. I went to work in the loan department at just about the time when things started heating up.

I remember I was making two hundred and seventy-two dollars a week. Pretty soon I started noticing that a lot more money was coming into the bank, and a lot more going out as loans. That was the start."

"What did you do?"

"I went to a party." Her face had an ironic smile, as though she had thought about it so many times that she expected Jane to understand. "The bank had a giant bash for its big customers, and I got introduced to some of them. There were men there who had tens of millions of dollars. And I was with them, talking futures and options with them as if I was one of them. There was one in particular who was really nice. His name was Dan Campbell. Not Daniel. When he signed papers he wrote 'Dan.' He had everything: a big house in Houston, a cattle ranch in Oklahoma, and a plane for flying back and forth. I knew all about them because the loan papers were in a filing cabinet right behind the desk where I sat every day.

"There was this big candlelight dinner on tables set up in the bank lobby, and dancing. I'd never seen so much liquor, all the bottles lined up on this portable bar with the lights behind them so they looked pretty, like perfume bottles or something. When the formal party was over and most of the people went home, the night wasn't over. There was a small private party just for maybe twenty people like Dan Campbell in the executive suites down the hall. We all started in Mr. Waugh's office, but people wandered out into the garden outside the sliding door and into some of the other offices, carrying their drinks. Somehow Dan Campbell and I ended up in my office. After a few minutes he switched off the light and locked the door. A person would have had to be retarded not to have it occur to her that if we didn't make any noise people would never know we were in there."

"You don't have to tell me this."

"Yes, I do," said Mary. Her face was set and insistent. "So then Dan Campbell is saying, 'Come on, Lily. Just touch it. I promise it won't bite.' I was not an innocent young thing. I don't want to give you that impression or imply that I was drunk or something. I wasn't left breathless and swept off my feet by a charming older man. If I was dazzled by anything, it was by being near all that money. Also, I liked him and was impressed with him, so I did it.

"The next day I was back at my desk as usual, feeling a little bit amazed when my eyes would happen to fall on some particular piece of furniture, and then a little depressed and foolish, and in comes a delivery guy with twenty-four long-stemmed red roses in a beautiful crystal vase and puts them on my desk. I see them, and for a second I think maybe I wasn't just this stupid girl who got talked into something. Maybe this was just what I had convinced myself it was for a few minutes last night when I forgot it was the bank that took me to dinner. Then I opened the card, and it was signed by Mr. Waugh, my boss. There was a check for a thousand dollars from the bank that said 'Employee Incentive Bonus.' "

"Did you quit?"

"No," said Mary. "I didn't. I started to, I thought about it, but I didn't do it. You hear a lot about people doing that, but you don't see it much. People say they walked out, threw their jobs away or something, but at least they have their principles. But it's almost never like that. It almost never happens right away, just like you never think of the clever thing to say to somebody when it would have mattered. And I couldn't think of a way to tell Mr. Waugh I resented getting a check for it without coming out and announcing exactly what it was that he and I both knew I had done. I decided I wasn't about to face that conversation, and there was nothing else I could do to change things. All I could do was cash the check and go on with my life.

"The bank was growing then, and pretty soon I'm not working in the loan department, I'm a loan officer. Mr. Waugh tells me we've got to go on a business trip to Houston. I remember the flowers and get all upset, but there just isn't a way to get out of it. By now I understand why the bank needs to move money in and out, and my job is to keep the money going out, and that means meeting with customers. And there were two other women going: Mr. Waugh's assistant and another loan officer. The pay was getting better and better, and I was learning a lot, so I didn't try to get out of it."

Jane could tell that Mary was not lying now. She was trying to push away the excuses. This was a confession.

"We meet with a group of twelve investors who have formed a limited partnership for a real estate development. You know, right now I can't even remember what they were calling it, but it was the usual thing, something like Sunnydale Vistas or Meadowgrove Heights. Anyway, the first session is in an office they've set up near River Oaks. Not *in* River Oaks, of course, but close enough so people would smell money on their business cards. Things were really tantalizing in that first session. We've got the chance to lend them sixty million, maybe more later. They're willing to keep it deposited until they need it, with the interest in escrow offsetting our costs—which are nil—and release times tied to what gets built. Then we were supposed to go out and see the land. It was near La Porte, right by Galveston Bay. The plans called for canals, with boat slips for each house, malls, and all that.

"We don't drive, though. We go out to get the best view on this big boat that's leased to the company's sales department for impressing the customers. We see it through binoculars and talk business until dark, but still no papers get signed. We have a catered dinner, and still no agreement comes out of Mr. Waugh's briefcase. It just degenerates into a cocktail party on the upper deck. Everybody's talking about money and their favorite things that it buys and how great they're all doing. They're getting tipsy and optimistic. Pretty soon I start to hear music coming from somewhere down below, and laughing and loud talk. One by one, people start to disappear. It goes on awhile until it's just me and Waugh and maybe three of these investors. It's getting cold up on deck. I say to Waugh, 'Maybe I'll go down below.' He says, 'If you like.' So I make my way down those steps in the dark in high heels carrying a martini."

"The others didn't go down?"

"One did. I had to help him, because he was getting drunk. So I go down and open the door to this big room they called the saloon, and the music is deafening. What I see at that moment makes me drop my drink. It's Waugh's assistant. Her name was Marla. She's dancing, doing a strip for these four investors, and I do not mean a tease. When I came in she was already down to her panties, and she's got her thumbs in the waistband, as though they were about to move south. I start to back out, but the drunk behind me pushes me in, and Marla sees me. She kind of wriggles over to me without losing a beat, puts her arm around me with a big smile, yells into my ear, 'Come on. Get with the party,' and starts pulling me into the saloon with her. I pushed her arm off me and said, 'Stop it. I'm not some hooker.' "

"What happened?"

"She got really angry—shot me a look that would knock a pigeon off a telephone wire—and said, 'Don't kid me, honey. Who do you think made out your last bonus check?' But then there's one of these investors behind her, and he's impatient for the show to go on, and he pulls the panties down to her feet. She grins, steps out of them, kind of sticks out her rear end, gives it a little wriggle, and starts to dance with him. I turn and walk out of the saloon. I don't know where to go. I open the door to one of the staterooms, and there's the other loan officer. She's doing one of the investors on the bed while a couple of others watch. I shut the door, go back up the hallway toward the steps, and there's Mr. Waugh. He opens the door of the saloon so he can glance in, and I can see that Marla has gone way beyond the strip. It's an orgy. He opens the door a little wider, holding it for me to go in first. Then he sees the expression on my face, kind of shrugs, and goes inside. I spend the next four hours alone up on that freezing deck."

"Did he fire you?"

"No. I took a plane back by myself and came in Monday morning to find the loan papers, all signed, on my desk. All of a sudden the account was mine and I had to make the deal work—get it through the loan committee and the lawyers, and set up the schedules, and all that. And I had to make out the bonus checks: ten grand each. Nobody said a word about it. Marla was invisible for weeks. The other loan officer—her name was Kathy—was no friend of mine. She never spoke to me again. I started looking for jobs. The bank was growing out of control by then, so we were all busy enough not to have to look right at each other."

"Nothing else happened?"

"About a month later, I come into work and there are these strange women in the office. Both of them are young—twenty or twenty-one—and gorgeous. Marla comes in with them, and her face is absolutely empty. She says to me, 'We're really running short of space around here. Mr. Waugh wants you to move back out to your old desk to make room for the new loan officers.' Out front was the pool of low-level clerical people and beginners. I cleaned out my office—pictures, plants, and paper clips—carried everything out, and put it all on my old desk, and something happened. I knew they wanted me to quit, and I wanted to quit, but up until then I had also wanted to outlast them, take whatever they had to offer for as long as it took and then end up with a better job somewhere else. I had been operating on the theory that I made them more uncomfortable than they made me. But it was too much. I closed the desk drawer and walked into Mr. Waugh's office. He was on the phone and he said into it, 'Excuse me. I have something I have to take care of. I'll call you right back,' all the time with his eyes on me. He hung up. I said, 'You didn't have to hang up. I just wanted to say goodbye.' I reached over the desk and shook his hand and said, "Thank you for hiring me.' He was surprised. I thought at first that he was just relieved because it wasn't a horrible scene, but before I was across the lobby I realized that all along he had been expecting me to come around."

"You didn't have another job. Where did you go?"

Mary Perkins gave a sad little laugh. "I went nowhere. I couldn't find another job in town. I couldn't find one anywhere, so I moved to California. Just getting there took about the last of the money I had saved. I was out of work for six months. I was twenty-four, looking better than I ever have in my life because I didn't have enough money to eat regularly. I'm not trying to make you feel sorry for me. The fantasy I had wasn't about getting a nicer place to live and having enough food. It was getting rich—really rich. I had been on the party boats, done the big real estate deals, and flown in the private planes, and I wanted them again. So I thought of how to get them, and I got started."

"How did you get started?"

"I used to spend a lot of time at the unemployment office, and I got used to seeing the regulars. One was a guy who had tried to talk to me. You have to picture this. There's a guy about forty, in there to collect his unemployment check, and he sees a woman who turns him on, so he goes up to her and tells her not to worry. He's a successful contractor, and as soon as spring comes he's going to be doing more big projects and he'll hire her. But he was good-looking and cheerful and, oddly enough, he wasn't stupid, so I decided to get to know him. I went into the unemployment office and smiled at him. When he hit on me, I said, 'Why don't you take me out for coffee?' We walked out to the lot, and he's driving a three-year-old BMW with a brand-new lock on the trunk. I'd had enough experience making loans to know that locks don't wear out in three years. They get drilled out because the original owner didn't hand over the keys. It turns out that even though he's a liar, he really does have a contractor's license, but no capital, no crew, and nothing going for him. He was perfect."

"Perfect for what?"

"I had decided to use what I knew about savings and loans. I promoted him from contractor to developer. I was his wife. We called ourselves the Comstocks or the Staffords or the Stoddards. We would go to a new city where nobody knew us. Sometimes we'd rent a house in a quiet, upscale part of town and do nothing but get to know our neighbors. Eventually there would be somebody who would invite us to his club, or to a summer home, or just to a party. Once we were accepted, the bankers would find us. Sometimes all it took was to let our new friends know we were happy there and wanted to buy a fancy house. By 'eighty-three a lot of savings executives were dying to lend a couple of million to just about anybody who wanted it for something as normal as a house, and they listened for leads."

"What then?"

"It varied. Sometimes we'd get somebody to sell us a hundred-thousand-dollar house for a million, kick back five hundred thousand, and leave town on the same day. The best was when we got to know the savings and loan executive and his wife—saw them socially. I would find a way to get the man alone—happen to go alone to the place where he always ate lunch, or drop in to see his wife on a Saturday afternoon when I knew she would be gone. I would convince him that he was so irresistible that I didn't plan to try. If that worked I would turn it into a full-blown affair and concentrate on making sure he didn't want it to end just yet. Eventually the subject of my husband's real estate development would come up. I would say he was considering moving to another state and doing the project there because the local money people didn't see the potential. Bobby would get his loan. When Bobby didn't make payments, the bank would issue a new loan to cover the interest, or buy into the project. I learned all the tricks that a banker could think of just by watching these guys trying to keep Bobby busy and stupid."

"It always worked?"

Mary Perkins shook her head. "Nothing *always* works. But I designed it so that if the banker wasn't interested, the worst he could do to me was to tell my husband. But if he once sunk it into me, that option was gone, and he was in for the ride of his life." She stopped and stared at Jane. "You're thinking that I invented a scheme to turn myself into a whore, don't you? To do what I wouldn't do for Mr. Waugh."

Jane shrugged. "I'm not in the habit of making that kind of judgment."

"Well, that's exactly what I did. At one point I was doing both the husband and wife at once, and the three of us were conspiring to keep Bobby too busy to notice by pumping money into his business. Of course I had to keep Bobby happy too. We were living as a married couple, and I couldn't have him going off tomcatting around the country club. This went on for about three years."

"What ended it?"

"I got enough money and enough inside information to do the stunts I told you about. It was essentially the same, except that Bobby had enough to retire, so I let him. I would get the loan myself, and would default on it myself, but first I made sure that Cyrus Curbstone had seen enough of me so that he didn't want my loan brought to the police."

"How did you get caught?"

"I bought a savings and loan," Mary said. "Big mistake. I thought I knew more than I did. I didn't know when to set fire to the place and get on a plane."

"Why are you telling me all this now?"

"I want you to know," Mary said.

"Know what?"

"Why I held on to the money when I was caught and the feds wanted it back. Why I told you I didn't have it when I needed your help and any sane person would have given it up to stay alive. It wasn't because I needed to have a lot of money hidden someplace where I'll probably never see it again; it's because of what I had to do to get it."

"But why now?"

"Because now that I know enough to want to give it up, I can't give it up. He wouldn't take it and let me go, would he?"

"No."

"He would take it and insist there was more, and when I couldn't give him any more, all he could do was kill me."

"Yes."

"And he'll never give up, will he?"

"No," said Jane. "He won't."

"And if I go to the police and tell them he's been chasing me, what I'm telling them is that he might be trying to steal fifty million dollars. That's no crime, but I'm admitting that I still have it. I'm the only one who will go to jail, and he'll still be free to kill me."

"Fifty million dollars." Jane returned to taping her cards into the lining of her purse. "You'll make good bait."

"Yes," Mary said, "I will."

22

When Jane and Mary left Cleveland they were carrying suitcases that were much larger than they needed to hold the few outfits they had bought, because they had more shopping to do in Chicago. The first item they selected at the electronics store was a small video camera with automatic focus and a zoom lens. The second was a directional microphone. The brochure that went with the microphone described the wonderful capability it offered for recording bird songs without coming close enough to disturb the little creatures. The copy obviously had been composed in order to protect the company from becoming a co-defendant in some criminal proceeding. Jane tested a number of voice-activated tape recorders, and when she had settled on the best, she told the salesman to write up a bill for two.

While he was busy doing this, Mary whispered, "Why two?"

Jane answered, "Because I don't think having a conversation with Barraclough is something I'll want to try twice if the first recorder doesn't catch every word."

Jane bought a used Toyota in Chicago under the name Catherine Snowdon. It was five years old, had one previous owner who had kept it greased, oiled, and maintained, but it had a sporty red exterior. She drove it off the lot to a one-day spray shop and had it painted gray for five hundred dollars. Then she picked up Mary at the motel and turned west onto Route 80. It was winter now, and if they were going to travel by road, it had to be a big one.

For six days they drove the interstate through Davenport, Des Moines, Omaha, Grand Island, North Platte, Cheyenne, Salt Lake City. Just before Reno they turned south down 395 along the east side of the Sierras to the desert. Jane checked them into a motel in San Bernardino near the entrance to I-10, rested for a day, and studied the maps of Los Angeles County. The next day she drove to the Department of Motor Vehicles, reported the sale of Catherine Snowdon's car to Katherine Webster, a resident of Los Angeles, and picked up a set of California plates.

She spent two days driving the freeways until she found the spot she wanted, right on the western edge of a confusing knot of interlocking entrances, exits, and overpasses on the Ventura Freeway. If a person drove east, he would immediately come to the fork where half the lanes swung off onto the San Diego Freeway, then divided again to go north toward Sacramento or south toward San Diego. After another mile or two, there was another junction where some lanes went north on the Hollywood Freeway but most swung southeast toward the city. Another mile and there was another fork, with some lanes continuing southeast and the others bearing due east toward Glendale and Pasadena. With a small head start, a car heading eastward could be very hard to follow.

Every mile on the Ventura Freeway there was a little yellow pole with an emergency telephone on it. The small blue marker above the pole Jane chose announced that it was number 177.

That night in the motel Jane tested the equipment. At two A.M. she drove back into the San Fernando Valley. She parked the car on a quiet side street in Sherman Oaks just north of Riverside Drive and walked the rest of the way to the little hill that elevated the Ventura Freeway above the surrounding neighborhoods. She had to lower the equipment over a fence and then climb over after it.

She was hidden from the street by thick bushes, and from the freeway by a low metal barrier along the shoulder. The barrier was supposed to keep a runaway car on the eastbound side of the Ventura Freeway from careening down the hill into the front of somebody's house, and judging by the depth of some of the dents and scrapes, it probably had. She trained the directional microphone carefully across the freeway on a spot twenty feet from call box number 177, then adjusted the breadth of its field until it picked up very little street noise. She threw a stone at the spot and watched the reels of the two tape recorders turn when it hit, then stop again. She set the video camera on automatic focus and aimed it at the same spot. She switched everything off, carefully covered all of the equipment with leaves and branches, then went down the hill, over the fence, and back to her car.

Jane and Mary stayed at the motel for two more days. They rehearsed, memorized, and analyzed until it began to seem as though everything Jane was planning had already happened and they were weeks past it already, trying to recall the details.

"How long do you stay?" asked Jane.

"Ten seconds. Fifteen at the most. Just long enough to pop out the tapes."

"What happens if he pulls out a gun?" Jane asked.

"I leave."

"What if he puts it to my head?"

"I ignore it. There's nothing I can do to stop him, so I leave."

Early each morning they drove along the Ventura Freeway past call box 177, studying the flow of the traffic for ten miles in both directions. They memorized the fastest lanes, practiced making an exit just beyond the junction with another freeway and then coming up a side street to emerge on the new freeway going in another direction.

"Can't you just call him up and record what he says on the phone?" asked Mary.

"No," said Jane. "He's the regional head of a big security company. His phone will have sweepers and bug detectors that even the police can't buy yet. Besides, he won't say anything that will put him away unless he sees you."

On the third day at four in the afternoon Jane Whitefield went to a pay telephone in Barstow and made the call. "I want to speak with Mr. Barraclough," she said. "Tell him it's Colleen Mahoney from the courthouse. I have something he wants to talk about."

"Can you hold?" said the secretary.

"No," said Jane. "I'll call back in two minutes. Tell him if he's not the one who answers, he's lost it." She waited four minutes, then dialed the number again.

This time a man's voice answered. It was deep, as though it came from a big body, but it was smooth, clear, and untroubled. "Yes?" he said.

"Is this Mr. Barraclough?"

"Yes, it is." He held the last word so it was almost singsong.

"This is—"

"I know who it is, Jane," he said. "I heard that's what you like to be called. What can I do for you?"

Her mind stumbled, then raced to catch up. He was far ahead of the place where she had thought he would be. "I have Mary Perkins," she said.

"Who's Mary Perkins?"

"I'm not recording this," she said. "Your phone isn't tapped."

"I know it isn't."

"Then do you want her?"

"If you have her, why do you need me? You like me all of a sudden?"

"If you weren't tracing this call, why would you ask so many stupid questions?" Jane asked. "I'll call this number at five A.M. to-morrow. If you meet me alone and unarmed, you'll get a peek." She hung up, picked up Mary, and drove to Los Angeles, where they rented two identical white cars, then left the gray Toyota at the Burbank Airport. They spent the night in a motel in Woodland Hills.

At four A.M. Jane parked her rented car on the street she had chosen below the freeway, climbed the fence to turn on her cam-era, microphone, and recorders. Then she drove west to the big coffee shop in Agoura and at exactly five A.M. used the pay tele-phone outside the door.

"Yes?" said Barraclough.

"It's me," she said. "In twenty minutes I'll be at the lot on the corner of Woodley Avenue and Burbank Boulevard in the Sepulveda Dam Recreation Area. If you're not there I'll keep going."

"Wait," he said. "I didn't get those streets."

"Then rewind the tape and play it back," she said, and hung up.

Twenty minutes was an enormous stretch of time for a man like Barraclough. Jane thought about all of the preparations he would have made already. He would have all of the trainees on the special payroll of Enterprise Development already awake and standing by. He would have some pretext for using Intercontinental Security's facilities and equipment too. Now he would be frantically ordering all of them into positions around the Sepulveda Recreation Area. No, not frantically: coldly, methodically.

She had selected the meeting place carefully. It was the sort of spot a person might choose who had some fear of ambush but no understanding of how such things happened. It was free of people in the hours before dawn, a flat open lawn that had been built as a flood basin with a vast empty sod farm on one side, a golf course on the other, and nothing much but picnic tables and a baseball diamond in between. The place gave the illusion of safety because she could see a second car coming from half a mile off. So could he, but all he had to do was block two spots on Burbank Boulevard and one end of Woodley and she was trapped.

Jane left the Ventura Freeway and continued eastward on Burbank Boulevard. It would still be another hour before the sun came up. At exactly 5:20 she was driving beside the golf course, and as she came around the long curve, she saw his car. It was a new, dark gray Chevrolet parked beside the road on the small gravel plateau above the empty reservoir. She could see the little stream of exhaust from the tailpipe that showed her the car was running. She took her foot off the gas pedal as she approached, and coasted to a speed of under ten miles an hour. She made a left turn onto the lot, then pulled up ten feet away from his car and stared into the side window.

It was difficult to tell how tall he was when he was seated in the car, but he gave her the impression of being big. His hands on the wheel were thick and square-knuckled, and his shoulders were much wider than the steering wheel. The white pinstriped shirt he had on seemed a little tight on his upper arms, the way cops wore theirs. He was obviously wearing it without a coat to make her believe he had actually come unarmed.

She looked directly into his face. The corners of his mouth were turned up in a wry half smile. She reminded herself that she had known he would try to rattle her with some intimidating expression, maybe the poker player's look when he raised his bet: my money's on the table, so let's see yours. But his face set off a little burst of heat in her chest that rose up her throat into her jaw muscles. She could not turn away from the eyes. They were light, almost gray, squinting a little because of the false smile, and watching her with a disconcerting intensity. They took in her fear and discomfort, added his savoring of it, and reflected it back to her. His mind was focused utterly on her, on what she was feeling and thinking. His eyes revealed that he felt nothing except some vicarious glow from the anxiety he could inspire in her.

It was time to lose whoever he had brought with him. Jane stamped her foot on the gas pedal and the car's back wheels spun, kicking up gravel. It fishtailed a little as one wheel caught before the other and then it squealed out of the lot onto Burbank Boulevard. She drove to the east, took the ramp onto the San Diego Freeway at forty, and sailed into the right lane at sixty-five. She checked her rearview mirror to be sure he was coming, and saw the gray Chevrolet skid around the curve and shoot off the ramp toward her. She kept adding increments of speed while she held the car steady in the center lane.

She watched the mirror so she could spot his helpers coming up to join him, but no other car on the freeway was traveling as fast as theirs were. She checked the cars ahead, but none of them did anything out of the ordinary either. She waited until the last second to cut back across the right lane to the feeder for the Ventura Freeway, then stayed in the eastbound lane until it was almost too late before she cut across the painted lines to the westbound ramp. She looked into the mirror again, not to confirm that he was still chasing her but to be sure that no other car could have followed him.

She drove westward until she saw the telephone with the blue "177" painted above it, then turned on her emergency flashers and coasted along until she made it to the shoulder and stopped twenty feet past the call box. She got out of her car and walked to the spot where she had aimed her directional microphone and camera. She saw his headlights after five seconds, then the turn signal, and in a moment he was rolling up along the shoulder of the road to stop behind her.

He swung his door open on the traffic side, got out as though he were invulnerable to getting clipped, and walked up to her. His arms were out from his sides, but he was carrying something in his hand. She stepped backward to the door of her car. He saw her move and seemed to understand that she was preparing to bolt. He set the object on the ground and stepped back.

Jane kept her eyes on him as she stepped forward and picked it up. It was a small box with a metal hoop and a thumb switch. She recognized that it was a hand-held metal detector like the ones they used in airports when somebody set off the walk-through model. She ran it over herself from head to foot, then tossed it to him and he did the same, turning around so she could see there was nothing stuck in his belt. The little box didn't beep.

Barraclough's eyes scanned the area around him in every direction, returning to her face abruptly now and then to see if she reacted. He said, "Mind if I look in your car?"

"Go ahead," she said. "Mind if I look in yours?"

The mysterious smile returned. "No." He watched her as he took a step toward her rented car. She never moved. He said, "You driving or am I?"

She said, "I'm not getting into a car with you."

He looked around him again, as though this meant he needed to do a better job of searching the middle distance for witnesses. He said, "What made you panic back there?"

"That's not what I want to talk about. I say it was a trap, you say it wasn't, I say you're a liar."

His smile seemed to grow a little. "What do you want to talk about?"

"You've been chasing Mary Perkins, I've been hiding her. Now I'm ready to sell her."

He squinted a little as he studied her face. "Why?"

She returned his stare. "I've been at this a long time. A lot of people would be dead without me."

"I've heard that," said Barraclough. "Sometime I'll get you to give me a list."

"No, you won't," she said simply. "Mary Perkins isn't the sort of person I want to risk my life for. She's not worth it. I gave her a chance and she disappointed me. I know that she's got a lot of money. You seem to think you can get it. I'm not interested in that kind of work."

Barraclough tilted his head a little to watch her closely. "You know what will happen when I have her?"

"You'll end up with her money. I also know that if you have her she's not coming back to ask me how it happened."

"That's true," he said.

She took a deep breath and blew it out. She had done it. He had agreed on tape that he was going to take the money and kill her. "This is a one-day sale," she said. "Tomorrow she goes up for auction. You want her or not?"

"I want her."

"The price is three million in cash. You hand it over and I give her up three weeks later. I know you'll mark it, so I need time to pass it on before you start tracing."

A laugh escaped him abruptly, as though a small child had surprised him by saying something unintentionally profound. "Done," he said. "Of course, that's assuming I get to see her in person so I know you can deliver."

"You can," said Jane. "She'll be along any minute."

"Here?" he said. She could see his mind working. He wanted to get back to his car to retrieve the weapon he had hidden, but he had not yet thought of a way to do it without Jane's noticing.

"There," said Jane. She pointed across the ten lanes of the freeway at the white car just like hers gliding onto the shoulder on the eastbound side. "That's her now." Mary Perkins's car rolled to a stop just at the spot Jane had shown her. "She'll get out of the car so you can see her. Then she'll pick up something I left for her in the bushes over there. She thinks you're a wholesaler who sells me stolen credit cards and licenses." Jane watched Barraclough's hands. "You're not trustworthy, so I can't pay you until she has them." Mary got out of the car and stepped over the barrier into the bushes.

Jane let her eyes flick up to Barraclough's face. "Well?"

"Hard to tell," he said. "She's so far away."

"Nice try," she said. "I saw you start to drool the second she opened the door. You get one more peek."

Mary Perkins came back out of the bushes. Jane could see the bulge of the tapes from the video camera and the recorders in her purse. Mary nodded and Jane stepped away from Barraclough, closer to her car. Now was the time when it would occur to him to hold her.

Barraclough was smiling again. His arm straightened and he waved happily at Mary Perkins.

"What are you doing?" Jane snapped.

He turned to face her, but his arms were poised in front of him. He looked like a fisherman about to make a grab for a hooked fish. "Just waving to the lady. We don't want her to think I'm not a friendly wholesaler."

Jane's body tensed, not certain whether to run for the car or attack him. He was signaling someone, and it wasn't Mary. What had she missed? She jerked her head to the left to look back up the freeway—and saw the man Barraclough must have been waving to. He stepped out of the bushes and ran back along the shoulder just at the entrance ramp. In another two steps he disappeared around the curve.

He must be getting into another car that had been idling out of sight beside the entrance ramp. Now she saw its lights come onto the freeway and they seemed to jerk upward into the sky before they swung around and leveled on the pavement ahead of it. The car accelerated toward Jane and Barraclough, its right tires already on the shoulder as though it were going to obliterate them.

Jane waved her arm at Mary. "Go!" she shouted.

Mary seemed to be transfixed by the sudden arrival of an unexpected car. She stared across the ten lanes of the freeway and watched the red car rushing up the westbound side toward Jane, knowing it was time for her to leave, but not knowing how.

Jane screamed. "Go! Go! It's a trap!" She started backing toward her parked car, the adrenaline making her legs push too hard so she half walked and half danced, trying to watch the car bearing down on her and Mary and Barraclough at the same time.

Mary dropped her keys, bobbed down to pick them up, then got into her car. Jane took one more look at Barraclough and hurried to the door of her own car.

The headlights of the car Barraclough had summoned dipped down as it decelerated suddenly, moved past Barraclough, and then pulled over. As it slowly moved up behind Jane's car, her heart began to pound. Its headlights went out, the driver's door opened an inch, and the dome light came on. The one in the passenger seat was Timothy Phillips.

Barraclough opened the other door, pulled the little boy out onto the shoulder of the freeway and yelled, "Hey, Jane! How about a trade? Is he worth it?"

These were the first words loud enough for Mary to hear across the freeway. She started the engine and shifted to Drive, but her eyes were on the activity going on across the freeway. The little boy must be the one Jane had told her about. Who else could he be? He was scared, straining to get closer to Jane Whitefield, but the big man in the white shirt had a grip on his thin arm and it was hurting him. Anybody could see it was hurting him. Headlights settled on them, grew brighter and brighter, and then flashed past. Were those drivers blind? Couldn't they see that something horrible was happening?

The knowledge slowly settled on Mary that none of the drivers knew who the big man was, and you had to know that. They probably thought he was a father who was afraid his son might stray too close to the lane where their cars were speeding past. There was only one person here who had any idea of what she was looking at.

Mary turned off the engine, got out of the car, and stood on the shoulder of the road. She could see Jane ten lanes away, caught for a second in the headlights of a speeding car, staring back at Mary, her mouth wide open and her arm in motion, waving her back into the car. Her voice reached Mary faintly across all the lanes, but whatever it was saying was only a distraction.

Mary was concentrating, so there was no room for Jane's voice. She waited for a moment while a truck barreled past and the hot, sulfurous wind from its passing tore at her clothes and stung her face. Then she stepped onto the hard pavement of the freeway. She walked at a normal pace. She never stopped to wait on the dotted line between two lanes, because anything that was not in motion might blend in. It would take only a second of blindness for a driver going sixty miles an hour to travel eighty-eight feet and kill her. She made it across five lanes to the middle island and rested her fear for a moment inside the barrier before she could face walking across another five lanes.

Now Jane was much closer, and Mary could see the anguish on her face. "Run! Go back!" Jane shouted. Mary was disappointed. Jane simply didn't understand.

Mary looked across the last five lanes at Barraclough. They stared into each other's eyes, and she could see that he understood. He pushed the little boy back into the red car that had brought him, then ran back along the edge of the freeway and got into his big gray car.

Mary Perkins's eyes never left Barraclough after that. She could see him glancing in his rearview mirror as he pulled out into the traffic, then crossed over one lane, then another, then another. He had already gone far past her, but she walked in his direction patiently, watching him take the last two lanes and stop far ahead of her on the center island where she walked. Then she saw his back-up lights come on, and he began to move in reverse on the center margin to meet her. She had never seen anybody drive backward so fast. Oh, yes, he had once been a policeman. They all learned how to do things like backing up on freeway shoulders.

Timothy Phillips looked out the window of the red car and watched Jane staring in horror at the other lady. But as the man who had brought him here started the car, Timmy saw Jane's right hand move down beside her leg and beckon to him.

Timmy got the passenger door of the red car half open before the driver lunged across the seat and clutched his shirt to drag him back. The sudden movement was enough. Jane flung the driver's door open, delivered a hard jab to his kidney, and snatched the key out of the ignition.

The driver turned with a pained snarl and started out the door after her. Jane retreated toward the front of the car. The driver heard the boy opening the door behind him again just as his foot touched the ground. He yelled, "Stay there or I'll kill you," but half turning his head to say it made him a microsecond slower. Jane had time to take a running step and deliver a hard kick to the driver's door.

The door caught the driver's leg just above the ankle. He winced at the pain, pivoted with his hip against the door to keep it from coming back at him, and rolled out onto the ground. He scrambled toward the rear of the car to lure Jane into an attack. All he had to do was get his hands on any part of her and swing her onto the freeway.

As she advanced a step, he did his best to look as though he were hurt and vulnerable. He got her to take three quick steps toward him while he hobbled backward, preparing to grasp her and roll back to add momentum as he propelled her into traffic. Jane took one more step, slipped into the car, slammed the door, and hammered down the lock buttons.

The man heard the engine start as he dashed toward her. Just as his fingers brushed the door handle, the rear wheels spun, bits of loose gravel shot out behind, and he had to step back to keep from being dragged out into the traffic as the car shot past him.

23

"**F**asten your seat belt, Timmy, and don't be scared," said Jane. She drove as fast as she dared, threading her way between slower vehicles and accelerating into the clear stretches. Even half an hour before sunrise there were beginning to be places where knots of cars jammed all the lanes at once. She turned off the freeway at Whiteoak, then shot under the overpass and up the eastbound ramp. The traffic was heavier heading into the center of the city. She had intended this as an advantage for Mary, because the slow, close-spaced stream would make it hard for even a superior driver to catch up with her. Now Jane was fighting the inertia herself.

She glanced down at the dashboard. The gas tank was full. Of course it would be. The car didn't seem to have a radio, but there was a black box about the size of one mounted in front of the shifter on the hump for the driveshaft. "Tell me what happened," she said. "How you got here."

Timmy shrugged. "They brought some of my stuff. You

know, from the apartment where Mona and I lived in Chicago. There were things they wanted me to identify that belonged to Mona. Then there was another box with some of my clothes and things. The next day I tried to put on my good shoes, but I couldn't get one of them on because your note was crumpled up in the toe."

"My note?" Once again Barraclough had been thinking faster than she had. Timmy's location had been kept secret, but the Chicago apartment had not. Barraclough had known that the F.B.I. or the Chicago police would search it. Because he had been a cop, he had also known that after they had preserved and labeled everything that could be considered evidence, there would be a lot left. They would release some of Timmy's belongings. Barraclough had even known that if nothing else got to Timmy, his best shoes would. He was going to have to look presentable in court.

"Yeah. So I called the phone number on your note, and the lady told me you weren't home but to call again when I could. And she asked me what the address was. I thought that was kind of odd, but she said you forgot to tell her. So last night when I called, she told me you wanted me to meet you."

Jane held herself in check. It wasn't Timmy's fault. For over two years he had been surviving by following whatever incomprehensible directions some adult—Morgan or Mona or Jane—had given him. "What else did she tell you?"

"That you told her if I could make it to the door by the garden, I could crawl along between the bushes and the house and slip right through the hedge to the next yard without anybody seeing me. You were right about all of it. Nobody saw me go. Then I walked over two streets, found this car right where she said it would be, climbed in the back seat, and lay down to wait. After a long time that man got in and we drove off. He said we were going to meet you."

Jane groped under the seat and beneath the dashboard, and then realized it was a waste of time. If there had been a gun in the car it couldn't be anyplace where the driver could have reached it or she and Timmy would be dead. Barraclough had made sure the assignment had stayed specific. Probably what he had feared most was not that Jane would see a gun and call the meeting off. He would be more afraid that his court-certified violence-prone trainee would show his initiative by using a gun where Mary might get hit.

She studied the inside of the car. "Did you see the driver use this black box?"

"Oh, yeah," said Timmy. "He said it was how he knew where we were going to meet you. See?" He pointed at a dial on the top that looked like the face of a compass. Jane was on a long, straight stretch of freeway, and she could see the needle was moving.

"Timmy," said Jane. "I didn't send the note. If I ever come for you again, I won't send a note or make a telephone call either. I'll make sure you see me. Don't go to some woman with dark hair who waves from a hundred feet away. I'll be up close, so you can tell."

He looked alarmed. "You're taking me back?"

"I can't drive you to a policeman's house in a stolen car," said Jane. "I'll have to drop you off in a safe place."

Jane leaned forward a little to glance at the black box. The needle was moving again. They had swung around to the east, just as she had. She had only the vaguest idea how direction finders worked. There was some kind of transmitter in Barraclough's car, and the black box received the signal and pointed out the direction it was coming from. But what could the range possibly be? A mile? Five miles? As though the machine had read her thoughts, the needle wavered, then swung to a straight vertical position and stayed there. It had already lost touch with Barraclough.

Jane maneuvered through the crush of vehicles. At any minute Barraclough or one of his lieutenants would know that she had the car, and they would take the necessary steps to find it. Probably they would report it stolen and let the police catch her for them. She had only one way to avoid the police. She drove to the parking structure at the Burbank airport.

She parked beside the gray Toyota and took the car keys from under the bumper. For a moment she considered ripping the black box out of the red car and trying to install it in her own car. But by now Barraclough certainly knew she had it. If she got the direction finder to work, eventually she would find that it was following a transmitter Barraclough had placed where she could be ambushed. She ushered Timmy into the gray Toyota and drove out of the parking ramp.

Ten minutes later Jane dialed a pay telephone and listened to Judge Kramer's voice. "Hello?"

She said, "Judge, it's me. Do you know for sure that your phone is not tapped?"

"I have it swept every day. No bugs so far. What's going on? How did you get this number?"

"Listen carefully. I'm with Timmy. They found him and lured him out. They know I've got him back and they're about to start looking for us, if they aren't already. I'm leaving him in the waiting area of the emergency room at Saint Joseph's Hospital in Burbank. He's faking a stomachache, so they'll have to keep him at least long enough for a doctor to be sure it's not his appendix. The guard inside thinks I'm calling his father to say we got here. Say that's who you are when you come for him."

"But what—"

"He'll tell you. Bye." She hung up and looked in through the glass doors of the emergency room at Timmy for a heartbeat, then hurried to her car.

As Jane got back on the freeway she had to struggle against the feeling that Barraclough was simply too smart for her. Every time she tried anything, he seemed to have anticipated it and brought it back to bear on her. She pulled off the freeway and made her way to the quiet side street in Sherman Oaks. She climbed the fence with a growing dread. She made her way up the little hill and crouched beside the freeway. The rented car was still where Mary had left it, and across the freeway she could see hers too. She moved to Mary's car, looked in the windows, then under the seats and mats and in the glove compartment. Barraclough had won again. When he had produced Timmy, Mary had gone to him with the tapes still in her purse.

Jane forced herself to move. She slipped away from the freeway, leaving the camera, microphone, and recorders in the brush. She climbed the fence and drove out to Riverside Drive. Everything depended on her ability to use time efficiently now.

She glanced at her watch. It was six-thirty A.M. and the sun glinted on the windows ahead as she drove west. She tried to think of all of the facts that carried with them some bit of hope. Timmy was alive. Barraclough would never have kidnapped him if he had not expected the driver to take him somewhere and kill him quietly as soon as Barraclough had Mary. Mary was also alive, and would stay alive as long as she was able to keep from giving Barraclough the last dime she had stolen. This thought led Jane in a direction she did not want to go, so she forced herself away from it. Even the black box might help. If Barraclough thought Jane had it, he would try to use it to trap her. This would take some of his time and attention, and anything that accomplished that would help to neutralize the enormous advantage he had.

Jane had an advantage too, and she began to concentrate on it. There was no way that Barraclough could know that the young man she had met in the housing project had told her about Enterprise Development. He had said 5122 Van Nuys Boulevard. She turned right on Van Nuys Boulevard and watched for the building.

When it came up on her right, she could see the car Barraclough had been driving. It was parked on the street near the side door of the small, four-story building. Jane took a breath and felt the air keep coming and coming, expanding in her chest with a feeling of joy. Maybe Barraclough had finally done something foolish. She had assumed he would take Mary to a safe house somewhere. Maybe he had gotten overconfident and stopped at Van Nuys Boulevard to direct the search for Jane. Maybe the driver of the red car had not been heard from yet and Barraclough assumed she and Timmy were dead. Even as she formulated the idea she knew it was impossible. Barraclough had stopped here just long enough to change cars. She pulled her car around the corner out of sight, then went across the street into a coffee shop.

She waited in the coffee shop and watched Enterprise Development for half an hour before a man came out the door of the building. She checked her watch. It was exactly eight. Something prearranged was going on. The chance that someone would happen to emerge from the building on the stroke of the hour was exactly fifty-nine to one against. As the man approached Barraclough's car she studied his wiry gray hair, the razorsharp crease of his pants, the cocky toe-out walk and impeccably shined shoes.

He must be Farrell, the one who called himself the training officer at Intercontinental but who ran the undercover operation out of this building. He took a set of keys out of his pocket, pretended to look down to select the right one while his eyes scanned the block, then got in and drove off. Jane was confused for an instant. Of all the people Barraclough had working for him, Farrell was the only one she had been sure would not be here. He would be where Mary was.

Jane made up her mind quickly, hurried to her car, and drove after him. She had gone only a couple of blocks before she noticed the second car. It was black and nondescript, with one man in it. She turned off Van Nuys Boulevard, then left up the parallel street and watched her mirror, but he didn't follow. She pulled back onto Van Nuys Boulevard two blocks behind him. When Farrell turned right on Victory Boulevard and he followed, she realized that the black car had not been following her; it was following Farrell.

After the turn Jane pulled a little closer to the black car. Even if he was the star graduate of the police auto-surveillance team he couldn't follow a car ahead of him and watch his own back at the same time.

Then Farrell's gray car reached its destination. Jane watched the second car pull to the curb ten feet from the entrance. She drove another two blocks before she parked and watched them in her rearview mirror. Farrell was returning Barraclough's gray car to the agency from which it had been rented. A few minutes later he emerged from the little building, walked out to the street, and got into the black car with the other man. Jane drove around a block to come out behind them on Van Nuys Boulevard. They continued south only as far as the Enterprise Development building and turned in at the parking lot.

Even as Jane winced with frustration and disappointment, she knew she had been right. Farrell was the one Barraclough trusted to manage his separate under-the-surface operation. He was the one to select and recruit young thugs, deliver pep talks, and give them the skills to do his hunting. He was the one who talked about potential, initiative, motivation, and all the nonsense that made them think that whatever qualities they had gone to jail for were now going to make them rich. He was the specialist in the psychology of brutality. He would be the one person Barraclough was sure to want with him for the interrogation of Mary Perkins.

24

Mary sat on the bare, ridged, metal floor of a van. The bumps of the pavement were regular, and she was beginning to get used to them now. Her spine was jarred by the *ba-bump* as the front wheels, then the back, went over each crack, then paused and went *ba-bump* again. She had felt a moment of relief when they had dragged her out of the car, but before she had taken a step under her own power they had pushed her into the back of the van and put the bag over her head. It was a burlap sack that had been sprayed with several coats of black paint so she couldn't see through it. The bag went over her head and down her arms to her elbows, and then unseen hands cinched it at the neck. It looked like the black hoods convicts wore in old photographs of hangings—no holes for the eyes or nose, just a gap at the mouth for breathing.

Her heart had stutter-started when she saw it, and then just when she had begun to sense that it wasn't what it looked like, she had felt them pulling her wrists together behind her. This made her remember the article in the magazine about doing anything you could before you got into the car, because afterward it was too late. She had struggled then to save the use of her hands, but she knew she had already missed her best chance to accomplish an escape. She resisted only because her fear was jumping around inside her and making her body move. With the black-painted hood over her head, any one of the three men could have tied her hands while the others went away.

The van was white. She had seen that much before the hood went on. For some time thereafter, while the white van turned sharply a couple of times to topple her over onto the floor, then gathered speed, she wondered why she was no longer afraid. It took her more than an hour in the solitude and darkness of the black-painted hood to detect that it was because none of this was happening to her.

The distinction was a delicate, slippery one that had to be grasped carefully and not squeezed too hard. She was here feeling movement and hearing activity, but even before they had put the hood on, the sights had been distant and the sounds hollow. This didn't feel real. She had been afraid this was going to happen for such a long time that she knew the way it should have felt. It wasn't happening to her; it must be happening to someone else.

The van turned off the big road with the regular cracks on it and went more slowly. Now and then there would be a sharper bump, maybe a pothole, and the hard floor of the van would abruptly jolt her. It was not the bumps that bothered her; it was the fact that the van was moving more slowly, the way people drove when a trip was nearly over.

For the first time she became conscious of everything about the hood over her head. It was hot and rough, and the petroleum smell of the black paint was nauseating. She could feel an itch on the side of her cheek, but her hands were fettered behind her. She tried rubbing the side of her face against the metal strut beside her, but the fabric was so rough and prickly that it seemed to spread the itch from her hairline to her chin. Then the van hit another pothole and the jolt knocked the strut hard against her cheekbone. She let out a little cry and felt tears welling in her eyes.

She hoped the men had not heard it. She knew they had, so

they must be aware of her weakness now, staring at her with critical, unpitying eyes while her hope deteriorated into a bitter wish that she had not been so stupid. The physical pain in her cheek kept insisting that she examine it, so she stopped resisting. She allowed herself to contemplate it and to wait for it each time her heart beat and then experience the throb. It was a small pain, only one of the bumps that the body was made to take, but it brought her bad news: this wasn't happening to somebody else. It was happening to her. She had filed somewhere in the back of her mind the information that a person in this situation might have to face some physical violence. Now she could not ignore what her common sense told her: that the pain was not going to be incidental, but was the whole purpose of this trip. They were taking her someplace to hurt her profoundly. It wasn't going to be her standing outside of herself and watching the tall man slapping her once across the face so she didn't really feel it. She was in a kind of trouble that made her heart release a flow of heat that went up her throat and got trapped under the hood with her so that it felt as though her head were in an oven. She could barely breathe, gasping in air through her mouth and tightening her neck and shoulders to bring the small mouth hole they had cut in the hood closer. The hood was wet now from the humidity of her breath, but this didn't seem important. Every sensation was uncomfortable and unpleasant, and her mind couldn't choose only one to think about.

The van turned and tipped her against the wall again, but she didn't dwell on that either. She was consumed by the fear of the pain that was to come.

As Jane watched the office building on Van Nuys Boulevard she searched her mind for other ways to get Mary back. It was midmorning already, and there had been no further sign of Farrell. She longed to call the police and get them to find Barraclough. The reasons she couldn't do so flooded into her mind. Barraclough would take time to find even if the police did everything right, and usually they didn't. Even then there was no way they could do anything without talking to somebody who worked for Intercontinental or showing up at one of their offices. If Barraclough had a few minutes of advance warning, Mary would disappear forever.

Barraclough would be taking Mary to a safe house somewhere. The property would probably be a place Barraclough owned, but there would be no way to use his name to find it. He had been in the business of kidnapping people for some time now, so his routine would be practiced and efficient, field-tested and refined. The only reasonable way of finding the place where Mary was being held was to get Farrell to lead her there. That was not going to be simple. She thought of trying to find another Intercontinental car with a direction finder installed in it. But this meant figuring out what car Farrell would drive to the safe house, hiding a transponder inside it, and teaching herself how to operate the receiver. Then she would be stuck behind the wheel of a stolen car, probably for some distance. It wasn't a plan; it was a fantasy.

Any preparation she tried to make now would involve taking her eyes off Farrell's door for at least an hour, and in that time he could have a sixty-mile head start in any direction. She would just have to keep him in sight for as long as it took and hope that he would lead her to Mary.

She kept her car parked a block away and around the corner, out of sight of the windows of Enterprise Development. She watched the building, first from the diner across the street, then from the inside of a bookstore two doors away. After she had leafed through every book near the front window twice, she walked to the thrift store across the street and picked over the used clothes. She chose two hats, a tan jacket, a black sweatshirt, and a pair of sunglasses. She put them on the floor of her car and went to eat dinner at the hamburger franchise on the far corner, where she still had a good view of Enterprise Development.

She knew that every thought she had, every movement she made that wasn't directed toward Farrell was a waste and a danger, but she couldn't keep Mary in the back of her mind where she should be. Each time she thought she had her mind focused on Farrell, a few seconds would tick away and the mere passing of time would remind her. A lot could happen to a person like Mary in thirty seconds, enough horror to last an eternity.

Each hour passed so slowly that she couldn't remember what she might have been thinking or doing before the last one, and the meeting on the freeway seemed to have happened weeks ago. She had stared at the office doors and windows for twelve hours, and still Farrell had not emerged.

Something must have happened that she had missed. At ten P.M. she began to prepare herself to enter the building. He might have walked out the door while she was in the ladies' room of the diner hours ago and gotten into a car that someone had brought to the curb for him. That could be why none of the cars parked near the building had been gone when she returned to the window. Maybe she had seen him go. He could have changed clothes with one of his trainees—something simple and rudimentary like that—and fooled her. He had spent his life perfecting the skills of searching and following, and there was no reason to imagine he had not seen all the ways of hiding and deceiving.

This was the other thought that she couldn't seem to get out of her mind. The reason Barraclough had Mary was that he had known what she would do and Jane had not. No, it was even worse. Mary had never met Timmy. He couldn't have known that she would walk into a fire for him. What Barraclough had known was how Jane would react. He had known that she would have to choose one of them, and the one she would choose was the one he had no further use for, the one he could kill.

She dumped her unfinished food and wrappers into the trash can by the door, slid her tray onto the stack, and walked across the parking lot toward the dark stretch of the street where she could cross without coming under any lights. She could hear footsteps on the sidewalk behind her as she stepped into the street, but she had to use this chance to see the building from a new angle, so she ignored them for the moment. She looked up at the building as she crossed, and through the window she saw Farrell. He was sitting behind his desk talking on the telephone. She reached the sidewalk on the other side of the street, stopped walking, and felt her calm return for a second before she remembered the footsteps.

Maybe the footsteps had been behind her when she came out of the restaurant and she had been so distracted that she simply had not heard them. She began to walk and listened carefully; there were three sets of shoes. She felt as though she had put her foot on a step and it had fallen through. She had been so busy watching the office that it had not occurred to her that Farrell might have a few trainees on the streets outside. She walked along more quickly until she could use the darkened window of a store to get a look at their reflection. The three didn't fit the pattern at all. One of them wore a baseball cap backwards and all three wore baggy pants and over-sized jackets. They looked about seventeen or eighteen years old, and not seasoned or desperate enough for Farrell.

She had told Carey she had been mugged in Los Angeles, and now here she was, being considered and evaluated for a mugging in Los Angeles. It was simply out of the question tonight. It was not going to happen.

She took a moment to collect her thoughts, then suddenly turned on her heel and walked toward the three boys. They slowed down and spread apart on the sidewalk. When she stepped directly up to the one in the center, he stopped, not sure what he was going to do, but certain he didn't want to bump into her. "Hold it, all three of you," she said. "I want to talk to you."

The other two stopped, looking at her warily with half-averted faces. "What?" said the one on her left.

As she looked at the three unpromising young men, the idea came to her fully formed. The only question was whether she could convince them. "Are you doing anything tonight?" she asked.

The one on her right said, "We're not doing anything," with no inflection. He didn't know whether she was accusing or inviting, but either way that was the right answer.

Jane reached into her purse and they all tensed to move, as though they expected her to douse them with tear gas, an event that was probably not out of the question on these streets at night. She ran her fingers along the lining of her purse and found the Katherine Webster identification packet. She flashed the business card at them. "Katherine Webster, Treasury Department," she said.

"We didn't do nothing," said the one in the center.

"I didn't ask," she said. "I want to know if you're interested in working for a few hours."

"Doing what?" He was very suspicious now.

She pointed up at the lighted window of the Enterprise Development office. "There's a man in that office who's a suspect. In a while he's going to get into a car and drive out of town. You follow him, I follow you. If he spots you, turn off and go home. If he doesn't, you follow him to wherever he's going, you call a number, leave the address on the answering machine, and go home."

"Why us?" said the one on the left.

Jane quoted from an imaginary field manual. "If in the judgment of the investigating agent it is useful to deputize or otherwise employ private citizens in order to avoid detection by the surveillant, he or she is authorized to do so." She waited for a moment while they deciphered this, then said, "You don't have to do it. I can pay you per diem and a performance bonus if you work out."

"What does that mean?" asked the one on the right.

"A hundred dollars each to cover your expenses on the drive. That's the per diem. It means 'per day,' and you don't declare it on your tax return." She caught the amused glance from the one in the middle to the one on the left when he heard that. "Another two hundred each if he doesn't see you. You could each make three hundred before the sun comes up."

"What makes it worth that?"

"He's armed, he's dangerous, and he's smart. If he stops, you've got to keep going. Don't get yourself into a spot where his car is stopped and so is yours. He'll probably kill you."

The three looked at each other. There were a few shrugs and head tilts, but no smirks. The part about killing seemed to have raised their level of interest considerably. She had forgotten for a moment about seventeen-year-old boys. There had never been a moment in human history when anybody hadn't been able to recruit enough of them for a war. She reached into her purse again and said, "The per diem is in advance." She started to count the bills in front of them.

The one in the middle said to the one on the right, "You want to use your car or mine?"

"You have two?" asked Jane.

"Yeah," said the one in the middle.

"Use them both and you each get an extra hundred."

Mary was leaning against the tiled wall of the shower stall in the big first-floor bathroom of the farmhouse. They had finally left her alone, her right wrist handcuffed to the shower head so that she could never quite sit down. She tried to stand on her own, but she felt faint and unsteady. This was probably why they had chained her that way. If she fell she would hurt her arm, but she probably couldn't kill herself by hitting her head on the tiles.

When she looked down at her legs she could see the bruises were already a deep purple, and the welts were red and swelling. She had tried to kick out at them, but they had not grabbed her or tried to wrestle with her; they had simply clubbed the leg that came up at them, and when she kicked out again they would hit it again, until finally she couldn't get the leg to kick.

The two men had not spoken, even to each other. They went about it in a cold, impersonal silence, like people in a slaughterhouse working on an animal. They left the hood on her head the first time, but not because they didn't want her to see their faces; it was because they had no desire to see hers. Desire had nothing at all to do with it. The next time, when she was thinking that maybe it was better that she couldn't breathe, because dying was just going to sleep and being awake was every nightmare she had ever had, they took the hood off. She could see them doing it, their faces intent but detached, whatever they were feeling not comprehensible to her as emotion. Their faces were not like the faces of men having intercourse, but unself-conscious and empty, as though no other human being were present. She had always thought of rape as a crime of hatred, or the sick pleasure of exerting power over somebody who was helpless. But this didn't seem to bring them even that feeling of triumph; they were just using what was there because it was there.

At first she cried and screamed. She said, "No, please. You're hurting me." The one who was holding her tightened his grip, but the one who was doing it to her didn't pay any attention at all. He didn't seem to be able to understand. Her voice was the call of a bird or the bark of a dog, something he could hear but that carried no meaning at all.

When they left they chained her to the shower, still naked. She tried to take what was left of herself and put it back together, but she couldn't. She was torn apart, a lot of fragments that she couldn't seem to collect. After a long time she started to think again. Her mind kept ticking off an automatic inventory of hurts and injuries that kept being the same over and over, as though it were establishing the boundaries. Then she began to imagine herself telling Barraclough what they had done to her, and saw him decide to kill them for it. She was valuable. But even while she thought about it, there was a small, nagging voice somewhere just below hearing to remind her that she wasn't important. She wasn't really worth anything at all.

It was midnight when Farrell emerged from the back door of the building. He walked a hundred feet to the rear of the parking lot, opened the trunk of a dark sedan at the rear of the lot, took out a large hard-sided briefcase, and then turned and walked back into the building.

Jane waved to her lookout and pointed at the front entrance, then started her car. A moment later, Farrell came out the front door. A young man drove up to the curb in a white station wagon, got out, and stood on the sidewalk while Farrell took his place behind the wheel. Jane watched the boys she had hired. The lookout had been in the narrow space between two buildings, and already he was gone. He had waited long enough to see the car Farrell was driving, and now he was in the back of the building getting into his companion's car.

When Farrell started off and turned right, she saw the boys' black Trans-Am already on the right street, crossing the intersection after him. The second car, a sedate-looking brown Saturn, only joined in after she had counted to eight. She turned around in order to avoid passing the office building, went down the side street, and joined the convoy three blocks later.

She followed the three cars onto the freeway, fell back a quarter mile, and watched the Saturn's taillights. She had given the boys a short course on following cars while they waited for Farrell to move, and now she watched them work. On a freeway all they had to watch Farrell for was an exit. They stayed well back from him. When there were packs of cars on the road ahead they moved up and hid among them. They didn't change lanes when he did. They waited, showing a clear preference for the right lane, where it was difficult for him to notice them, and other cars entered the freeway and slipped in to put a new set of headlights in his mirror for a few minutes.

After they were north of the city and the traffic thinned out a bit, the second car passed the one in front and stayed there until it was possible that Farrell was getting used to the new set of headlights, and then it dropped to the rear again. Jane drove conservatively, watching the taillights of her decoys and holding herself in reserve. She was beginning to feel a little more hopeful now. Every minute that passed, Farrell would come closer to accepting the conclusion that he had not been followed.

Mary had been left alone in the shower stall for hours. She had begun to spend long periods trapped in her own mind. She would try to strengthen herself. "I did this. I chose to trade my life for the life of a little boy. This is the best thing that I have ever done. It's the best that any human being ever does. I'm past the decision, the part where I'd have been weak if I had thought about it, so no matter what happens to me now, I can't fail. I can do this." But there was another feeling, one that didn't respond in its own words. It was just like an echo that revealed the hollowness of the sounds Mary was making. She was a fraud. She was not brave enough. It was self-deception. She had stepped off a cliff and now as she was falling she was regretting it more every second. Then she would wonder. Priests said that if a person made a pure unselfish act of contrition at the very last moment, she would be forgiven, her whole life validated retroactively. But what if she did make the promise, the sacrifice, and then wanted to take it back much more sincerely with every single breath? She wished she had died before she had ever had that moment of madness.

Then there were sounds outside the door, men's voices, big heavy feet on the floorboards, and she tried to stand without holding on to the wall, but she couldn't. It wasn't that she was hurt, but her muscles didn't want to contract when her mind willed them to. They were quivering and weak.

When the door swung open she felt an impulse to scream, but even her throat was paralyzed. Just a harsh, raspy "Huh" came out. The man came into the room and closed the door. It was Barraclough. She cringed and tried to disappear into the corner of the shower as he walked toward her. She tried to cover herself with the one arm she could use.

After a moment she realized that he was paying no attention to her. He walked across the tile floor, looked around, and stopped. He seemed only to be making sure she was alive. Then to her surprise he turned to go.

"Wait," she said. "Don't you want to talk?" She was fighting the fear that he was going out to let the other two come in again.

He said, "What do you want?"

"They raped me," she tried to say, but her face seemed to collapse and shrivel inward, and she couldn't control her voice, so it broke into a sob.

"Don't waste my time," he said. It sounded like a warning. It didn't matter what they did to her because she wasn't a regular person anymore, a being who had the right to keep anything as hers, even her body. She had thrown her rights away. She was a criminal and she had been caught. She longed to change that, or at least hide it from him.

"Look, this has been a mistake. You seem to think I'm somebody I'm not. I didn't do anything or hurt anybody." She pointed to the door. "They hurt me. But I can understand; they didn't know they weren't supposed to. I'll just forget that it ever happened. Like a bad dream. We'll never mention it again. You let me go—anywhere you like. Drive me someplace so I don't know where this house was."

He looked at her with an expression that froze her. It came from a vast distance. It seemed to detect everything at once: her abject fear, her guilt, her lying—no, not just that she was lying but that she was a liar. His expression showed that he knew all of it, and that it inspired disgust and contempt. For the first time he even seemed to contemplate her naked body, but not with lust. It was the way a god would look down at it from a great height. She was dirty, bruised, covered with sweat, and throbbing with pain, a small, unremarkable female creature who would have been unappetizing at any time but was now filthy and cowering.

It made her desperate, as though she were standing alone on a shore and the ship was drifting farther away. "I'm not naive, and I know you aren't. Sure, I have money. That's what you want, and

I've got it. You seem to forget, I didn't get caught. I came to you. Why do you suppose I did that? I know you want some money from me, but I also want something from you. I took lots of banks for lots of money while the time was right. And I wasn't alone. I know people you haven't even heard of who took a whole lot more than I did. I can bring them to you. I can deliver them here."

His expression didn't change, and it made her more desperate.

"You'd really be making a mistake to waste a resource like me." She was sweating and horrified at how unconvincing she sounded, but she couldn't stop, could only go on like a drowning swimmer. "I took the Bank of Whalen for six million dollars on a piece of land I'd bought for half a million a month before. I'm a moneymaker. When I bought out Harrison Savings, I used their own money to leverage an option on a controlling interest and then made the bank pay back the loan as an operating cost. I can do all of it again." His face didn't change. "I can do new things because a person who knows how to make money will always know."

When he turned toward the door and took a step, she tried to stop talking, but she couldn't. "If you don't want to get into business, I understand. You want it quick and clean and simple. So take me to a bank. Any major bank can do an electronic transfer. I'll get the money, hand it over, and everybody can go away."

He was at the door now, and she waited for him to turn and look back at her so that she could read his features. Maybe there would be something false in his expression to let her know that he didn't really intend to kill her. He opened the door without hesitation and walked out.

Jane drove through the night thinking about the station wagon far ahead of her. She knew all of the reasons Farrell had chosen it. There was something benign about station wagons. The drivers were people who hauled kids around and had houses in the suburbs. They were also useful because if you put a good tarp down in the cargo bay you could carry a fairly stiff corpse without breaking any joints or doing any cutting.

Maybe Mary had already broken and told them how to get her money. It took time to do that to a person, but she wasn't coming into this fresh. She was already exhausted and disoriented when she first saw Barraclough. She had been in prison for a month, and then spent the next month running and hiding, getting burned out of a house, and then running some more. The belief that had been nurtured in the human brain that a person could endure physical and psychological torture without revealing secrets was probably accurate. The notion that more than one person in a thousand could do it was idiotic.

Mary had one advantage. She was smart enough to know that within an hour of the moment when Barraclough had her money, she would die. It might make her hold out for an extra couple of hours. There was no doubt in Jane's mind that at some point Barraclough would make dying seem like an attractive alternative to whatever was happening to Mary, but first she would offer all of the stalls that she could imagine—lies, promises, con games. As long as she kept trying new ones instead of giving in and telling the truth, she would keep breathing.

Farrell had driven deep into the San Joaquin Valley. Some time in the past hour the signs marking ways to go east to Bakersfield and Tulare had ended and been replaced by signs for Fresno. Suddenly Jane caught the flashing of taillights ahead as the two follower cars tried to slow down without getting closer to Farrell's station wagon. They slowed to forty and Jane let herself glide up behind them in time to see Farrell turning off the highway.

She watched the first car take the exit ramp to go up the road after Farrell. The sign at the top of the ramp said MENDOTA 20. When Farrell stopped at the lighted island of a gas station, the boys drove past, then pulled over to wait a quarter mile down the road while he filled up his tank. Jane drove up the road, stopped ahead of the boys, and kept her eyes on Farrell's car as she hurried to the driver's window. She held out a handful of hundred-dollar bills. "Here," she said. "This is far enough. Pay your buddies."

The boy protested. "This can't be the end of the road."

"For you it is," she said, and stepped back to her car.

When Farrell had paid the gas station attendant and gotten back into his car, he drove a mile down the road to a motel. Jane watched him go into the lighted office, then come out with a key and go into a room. She pounded the steering wheel in frustration. This wasn't it. He was going to sleep.

Two hours before dawn Mary almost fell asleep. She woke up with a start, gripped by the feeling that she was falling, and slapped her hand against the side of the shower stall to hold herself up. The second day began for her at that moment. She was feeling a dread so deep that there was no difference between the dream and what was happening. The ground was coming up faster and faster, and when she hit she would be dead.

An hour after dawn she saw the doorknob turn. When the door opened she saw it was Barraclough. He was naked too this time. He unlocked her handcuff and left the key in it, turned on the shower, and held her under it for a long time, turning her this way and that as though he wanted to be sure she was clean enough. Then he turned her face to the wall. He never spoke. He just put his foot between hers and kicked each of her feet outward a little so she would know, and put a hand on her back. This time she did not struggle. She stood stiff and still like a dead person while he forced himself into her. After a few moments he slapped her buttock hard with one hand, then grasped her wet hair in the other and gave it three hard tugs. Slowly, a little at a time, she understood what he wanted and began to move her hips with him.

After he had finished with her, he turned on the shower again, washed himself as though she were not there, then turned the water off, refastened her handcuff, and left the room. As soon as the door closed, she began to cry. She had no idea how long it went on, because time was no longer something that had meaning. Finally the tears simply stopped and she was gripped by a fully formed, uncontrollable anger. She wanted them to come in. Her fingers clutched at the air, wanting to claw their eyes. Her jaw clenched, her mouth salivating at the thought of biting a throat and clinging to the man while the others tried to tear her loose.

The anger left her as abruptly as it had come, but as she leaned against the wall in the shower again she discovered that the anger had left something inside her. It was small and hard and clean like the scar from a burn. She studied it, touching it the way her tongue might touch a little sore in her mouth, over and over until it knew the place and the pain and the shape. She knew what she was going to do. Of all the people this might happen to, Mary had the best chance of carrying it off. She had a good head for numbers.

A few hours later Barraclough returned with the tape recorder. He plugged it in at the outlet by the sink for electric shavers, then turned it on. Mary watched him warily. Now must be the time when he was going to get her to talk. But then she heard a sound like the swish of a car going by, then several of them at once, then Jane's voice saying "You've been chasing Mary Perkins, I've been hiding her. Now I'm ready to sell her."

"Why?" That was Barraclough.

"I've been at this a long time. A lot of people would be dead without me."

"I've heard that. Sometime I'll get you to give me a list."

"No, you won't. Mary Perkins isn't the sort of person I want to risk my life for. She's not worth it. I gave her a chance and she disappointed me. I know that she's got a lot of money. You seem to think you can get it. I'm not interested in that kind of work."

"You know what will happen when I have her?"

"You'll end up with her money. I also know that if you have her, she's not coming back to ask me how it happened."

Barraclough stared at Mary for a moment, then turned and walked away into the rest of the house, the part where people who were free could walk.

Mary tried to laugh. She wanted Barraclough to hear her laugh, but it was so low and empty that he couldn't have heard it. She knew why he had played the tape. She was supposed to think that Jane had really been selling her. But how could he expect her to believe that? She had been in on the plan from the beginning.

But then she thought about what she had heard, and she knew. He was playing it to let her know that Jane had caught him on tape, and that she had thrown the evidence away. She was so stupid that she had forgotten to leave the tapes in the car when she had gone to him. She had forgotten there were any tapes. He would have been caught and convicted of her kidnapping, rape, and murder except for her unbelievably stupid mistake. She felt burning humiliation and shame. She was going to die a horrible, slow, degrading, painful death and the last thing she would remember was that she had let her killer go free.

It was another hour before she moved beyond herself and thought about Jane. "Mary Perkins isn't the sort of person I want to risk my life for. . . . I gave her a chance and she disappointed me." The reason Jane sounded so convincing on the tape was that she was telling the truth. Mary knew how to lie, and she had lied the same way. "She's not worth it." Even Barraclough, who caught liars for a living, was fooled because the words were literally true. Then the last part came back to her. "I know if you have her she isn't coming back . . ." That was true too. She was here, chained, injured, and hungry, and it was going to go on and on until she was dead.

For the next six hours Mary tried to work out a way to kill herself. The shower door had been taken out, and they had been too smart to leave the hinges. She experimented with the handcuff to see if there was a way she could get the chain across her throat to hang from the shower head, but the effort hurt her wrist terribly and there was no way to bring any pressure on her windpipe. At some point they would have to feed her, and there would be something—a glass, a knife, or even a china plate—that she could use to slash and stab herself.

But in the end she realized that she was not going to do it. If she killed herself, she would leave the hard, cold, perfect nugget of hatred inside her dead body, stranded like a virus. She had to stay alive to use it.

25

J ane waited until she was positive that Farrell was asleep, drove the mile back to the gas station to fill the tank of her own car, and returned to the motel. She was so exhausted that she was afraid she would doze off and wake up hours later to find Farrell's station wagon gone. She walked close to his car and looked in the windows. For a moment she considered hiding in the cargo section in the back and letting him drive her to Mary, but dismissed the idea. He would have a gun, and she would probably wake up about the time he flipped off the safety to fire it into her head.

Then she saw something lying on the dashboard, a yellow, crumpled piece of paper. She moved closer and recognized that it was a receipt from an American Express card. It was so wrinkled that she could barely read the machine printing on it. She took her pen and a receipt from her purse and wrote down the information—the name David R. King, the expiration date, and the thirteen-digit number—then walked to the pay telephone at the convenience store across the street.

She looked at the back of Catherine Snowdon's American Express card and dialed the number printed on it.

"Customer Service," said the voice. "May I help you?"

Jane said, "Yes. I'm afraid I have a problem and I guess you can tell me what to do. My husband's wallet has been lost, and his American Express card was in it."

"Account number?"

Jane read it off her receipt.

"Expiration date?"

"Next August. He's in the hospital. There was an accident and they brought him in, and his wallet somehow disappeared. I don't know if—"

"I understand," said the woman gently. "We'd better not take a chance. I'm going to cancel the card as of now. He'll be receiving a new one in the mail in a couple of days with a new number."

"But what happens if somebody else has it?"

"That's all explained in detail on the back of your statement. Basically you have nothing to worry about. You did the right thing by calling. Thank you very much. I hope your husband recovers quickly."

"Thank you," said Jane. She took some time walking back to the motel, formulating the details of her story.

She opened the office door with an air of authority and looked around. It was a bright morning already, but the young man behind the desk looked as exhausted as she felt. The hair on the back of his head was standing out in tufts from lying back in his chair while he watched a dreadful dubbed movie on the small television set beside him. At the moment several muscular men in fur kilts were swinging clumsily at each other with swords and taking a terrible toll on the columns of the Parthenon. He stood up and leaned his elbows on the counter. "May I help you?"

"I'm Kit Snowdon," Jane said. "American Express Fraud Division. I'm afraid we've got a little problem."

The young man switched off the swordsmen behind him and looked as though he were glad she had come along. "How can I help?"

"You have a gentleman staying in Room 4 who is in possession of a stolen American Express card. He would be registered under the name David R. King."

The young man was shocked. "But I ran his card on the machine. There's got to be some mistake."

"Run the numbers again." She allowed her voice to betray a tiny portion of the impatience she was feeling.

He picked the receipt out of the drawer, pushed a few buttons to get onto the phone line, then punched the numbers in. After a few seconds the machine rattled off a message from the central computers in North Dakota or someplace. He looked sick. "They want me to confiscate the card."

"The computer always says that. We haven't had a computer beat up yet," she said. "Ignore it."

"But—"

"If you ran the card before, you must have gotten a look at him. Did he look like somebody you want to take a card from?"

"No." He shook his head solemnly, then looked at the telephone on the counter. "Should I call the police?"

Jane sighed wearily. "I'll lay it out for you. He's been traveling for two days. He has two other cards and he's got some charges—maybe fifteen hundred by now. If I apprehend him, he gets charged with petty larceny. If I can get him without making a legal mistake and if the company lawyers follow through, he gets ninety days—tops. If I follow him another day or two and he gets the bill up over three thousand, then it's grand theft, forgery, maybe possession of stolen property, and the judge gets to swing hard. In fact, he has to."

"What do we do?"

"I've been following him for two days," said Jane. "I'm asleep on my feet. I want you to check me into a room and watch his door while I get some sleep. The minute you know he's awake, ring my room."

"What if he checks out? Should I slow him down?"

"Don't do anything you wouldn't normally do, except this time buzz my room. That's all." She handed him the Catherine Snowdon credit card.

The kid slid it across the slot of his machine and handed it back to her with the key. "I'm sorry I messed up with the authorization. I was positive—"

"You didn't mess up," said Jane. "He altered the magnetic strip to change one digit, or the machine would have said 'Tilt.' The real pros know how to do that. Just be sure he doesn't slip away. If you go off duty, make sure the next guy knows what to do."

She went into her room and slept in her clothes. The call came in the evening. When she picked up the receiver there was nobody on the other end. He must be in the office, so the boy could do nothing but press the button for her room. She was on her feet instantly, standing by the window. His station wagon was still in the lot in front of Room 4. She slipped out her door, turned away from the office, walked around the building, got into her car, and followed Farrell down the street past the freeway entrance. He pulled into the parking lot of a supermarket, got out of his car, and walked into the store.

Jane looked at her watch. Some of the mystery of his movements was dispelled. It was eight-thirty P.M. He had left his office in a clean car at midnight and driven through the rest of the night. When he was positive he had not been followed, he had slept through the day in the motel room under a fake name. If he was wrong about being followed, probably the pursuers would have made a move of some kind while he slept. If they had lost him somewhere during the long drive, he would have been invisible for a whole day, while they were forced to widen their search to places he had never been, dispersing and exhausting themselves.

Now he was sure he had nothing to worry about, and he was going grocery shopping. That made sense too. They could not have known they were going to be using the safe house. They probably didn't visit it often enough to keep fresh food there. When Barraclough had gotten Mary, he had simply changed cars and driven her up here.

There was another side to what Farrell was doing, and it made her feel anxious again. He had efficiently changed himself into a nocturnal creature. Jane had taken a few people out of the world who had been held by someone who wanted information, and they had told her what it was like. The captors would wear them down for days, alternately abusing and ignoring them, depriving them of sleep and food until some chemical imbalance occurred and they began to lose themselves in a depressive psychosis that seemed to bounce erratically from guilt to anger, but hopeless guilt and anger. The tormentors who understood the process would begin their final interrogation when the mind was weakest and most vulnerable, between two and five in the morning. Tonight when Mary woke up, starved, exhausted, and probably injured, there would be a new face. He would be fresh and sharp and tireless, and by now it would seem to her that he could read her mind.

Jane could see Farrell through the front window of the store filling a shopping cart. The moment was going by, and when it was gone there would not be another. She got out of her car and walked toward the station wagon. She could see his overnight bag on the seat, the crumpled receipt from the motel on the dashboard. She moved out of sight behind the truck parked beside the station wagon and watched the window of the store until she saw him move around the shelves at the end of the aisle. Then she walked to the front of his car, pretended to drop her keys, and knelt down to pick them up. While she was kneeling she slipped her hand under the front bumper and stabbed the lower radiator hose with her pocketknife, stood up, and walked on to the corner of the building where she could see the checkout aisles.

She watched while the clerk ran Farrell's groceries along the conveyor belt and past the cash register, then put them into bags. The first had quart-sized bottles on the top. The second had round bulges of fruits and vegetables, double-bagged in smaller sacks inside. The third had cartons of orange juice, milk in a plastic jug, and a box of cereal. She turned and made her way back to the truck parked by Farrell's car.

She waited while he slipped his key into the driver's door lock and electronically released the rest of the locks so he could load his groceries, then put the three bags in the cargo bay. He finished, then turned to push his cart back to the collection rack, twenty paces away.

Jane moved along the right side of the car to the back seat door, slipped the rubber band off her ponytail, doubled it, opened the door, slipped the rubber band over the catch in the door lock, then eased it shut again. Then she moved back around the truck out of sight and made her way back to her own car.

Farrell drove out of the lot and turned east across the flat farm country toward Mendota. Jane glanced at her watch, walked into the store, and bought a can of cola and a box of plastic straws. Then she got into her car, waited three minutes, and drove out after him. She could picture what was happening. When the station wagon's engine started, the water pump began to circulate the coolant, taking the water from the leaky bottom radiator hose, while some of it drained from the hole. As soon as the engine reached its optimum temperature, the thermostat would open. He would go a few miles before his temperature gauge went wild, because the expansion tank would empty, keeping the engine cool until that coolant too drained out the hose onto the road.

She drove down the dark road until she saw the car pulled over on the right shoulder. She turned off the road, killed her lights, and watched. There was no sign of him. Far ahead along the road a truck pulled over to the side and she could see him caught in its lights for a moment, waving it down. He climbed into the truck and it drove toward her. She turned on her lights, pulled back onto the road, and passed it, but as soon as it was out of sight she turned around and drove back to Farrell's car.

She opened the backseat door, took the rubber hair band off the latch, and pulled up the button on the driver's side to unlock the tailgate. She had thought it through carefully on her drive, so she had no decisions to make. She put a tiny slit in the plastic milk jug, stuck a plastic straw into her perfume bottle of water hemlock and mayapple, put her finger over the end, inserted the straw into the milk bottle, and let it drain into the milk. Then she moved the gummed price tag to cover the slit.

She did the same to the cartons of orange juice. The flat packages of meat were an experiment because she had no idea what cooking would do to the chemical composition of the clear liquid, but the holes in the cellophane wrappings were easy to hide, so she used them. She was confident about the bottle of scotch because the alcohol would hide any taste. She found the cap could be opened and reclosed by peeling the blue tax stamp off with her knife instead of tearing it, then pasting it down with a little spit. She was certain that even if a bit of the food was intended to reward Mary for talking, the scotch was for the men. Alcohol made people too reckless to be afraid and too stupid to remember, and it dulled pain. She left the vegetables alone because they would be washed and boiled, but she made a tiny incision in each of the apples and pushed the straw far enough into the depression at the bottom to reach the almost-hollow core, so the poison would come out as juice and the white of the apple would not be discolored by contact with the air.

When the perfume bottle was empty Jane closed the tailgate, went to the driver's side, pushed down the button to relock all the doors, and then drove her own car a mile down the road to wait for Mary Perkins's interrogator to return with a new hose for his radiator.

26

It had been nearly forty-eight hours since Mary had walked across five lanes of the Ventura Freeway and gotten into the car. She did not know this because time had already become one more thing that had to do with other people. Sometimes so much happened in a very short time. If one of the men hit her, the bright sharp suddenness seemed to explode into pain and wonder, then bleed on into the next several hours, slowly tapering down into something she knew but didn't feel.

At first she had been most afraid of permanence. There was some instinct that told her it didn't matter if they gave her a sensation that made her scream, not because having it happen so many times had made her used to it but because it left something. It was like dividing her in half. Each time they did it, half of her was gone. Then they would divide the half, and she would be smaller, but no matter how many times they hurt her, some tiny fraction of her would be left. Even if all that was left at the end was the size of a germ, someday it might grow back. But if they blinded her or crippled her, her eyes or legs would not grow back. She had a deep animal urge to keep her body intact.

But even this feeling was faded now. She had gone from fear to despair. She could not force herself to imagine a future. The past was all lies, arrogance, and deception, and she could not think about her life as separate events now. Even Mary Perkins was more filth she had made up and smeared on herself. She was Lily Smith, and she was sorry.

Sometime after the little window high on the wall in the bathroom turned dark again, a man she had never seen before walked in carrying a briefcase. He was older and had gray, bristly hair. He wore a gray suit with a coat that seemed a little too tight in the shoulders, and a pair of shoes that looked as though he polished them a lot. She thought of him as Policeman. He brought with him a straight-backed chair that appeared to be part of a dining room set and sat down on it.

He watched her with eyes that looked serious and alert, but there didn't seem to be anything else behind them. He had no predatory gleam, no cold contempt. He was simply waiting. She wanted to please him, to deal with this new person and win him over to her side.

She began slowly and logically because she had failed so miserably with Barraclough, and this one seemed even more touchy, more likely to dismiss her and go away. "I would like to find a way to make this end." She tried to sound ingratiating, but her voice came out toneless and monotonous.

He pursed his lips and nodded, as though he were giving her permission to go on. "I know."

She ventured a little further. "Nobody has asked me any questions."

He shrugged. "There's no hurry."

This was like a weight tied to her. "Why?"

He said, "We destroyed the tapes you made of the meeting on the freeway—"

"I didn't do that," she interrupted.

He raised an eyebrow as a warning. She winced, forcing herself to keep silent. That was how she had earned Barraclough's contempt, and if she did it to this one, her last chance would be gone. They both knew she was an accessory to the crime, so she accepted it.

He said, "Your girlfriend Jane wrote you off. She turned up yesterday at the L.A. airport. Operatives followed her to Chicago." He opened his briefcase and lifted out a big plastic food-storage bag with a seal on the top like the ones they used for evidence. Inside was a long shock of shiny black hair. He placed it back in the briefcase. "It seems to me that there's nobody else who even knows that you're missing. You've been traveling under false names for some time."

She had not realized until now that she had been living on the assumption that Jane was alive. If she was gone, then Policeman was right. Enduring a day or a year made no difference because nobody in the world knew she was gone. There was no possibility that she could ever leave this room. She repeated, "Is there any way that I can end this?"

Policeman looked at her judiciously. "It all depends on you."

A tiny hope began to return. It was from a different source this time, and it seemed more genuine than imagining that Jane could convince the authorities to break down the door to save her. Now that Jane was gone, she could see how foolish she had been to think of it at all. She said, "What do I do?"

He said, "Let's talk."

"All right."

"Tell me what happened the day you left the Los Angeles County Jail."

"I took a bus to the airport. Then I saw Jane."

"What color was the bus?" He asked her questions without appearing to listen to the content of the answers, just watching to see if she was lying.

"What name did you use in Ann Arbor?"

"Donna Kester. Jane picked it. She had cards and things in that name."

"Where did you go when you left there?"

"Let's see. Ohio. We hitched a ride with a student to Columbus, then Cleveland. The Copa Motel."

"Did you pay cash?"

"No. Credit cards. She had lots of credit cards, all in different names."

"What name did she use at the Copa?"

"I'm not sure. I think it was Catherine Snowdon." She told him the addresses of the hotels and motels, the agencies where they had rented cars, the routes they had driven—everything that came out of her memory. She wanted to please him. He seemed to be rooting for her, hoping she would pass. He wrote nothing down, but he seemed to be listening for mistakes. Each time a detail struck his ear as wrong, he would interrupt.

"How did you get into a women's dormitory at night? They're locked." It would always be something irrelevant, but it would be like a slap because it made her remember something else to prove she was giving him everything.

Finally, when the questions didn't bring any new answers, he stood up and took a step toward the door.

"Wait," she said. "Don't go. I've done everything, given you everything. What do you expect me to do?"

Policeman opened his briefcase again, pulled out a blank piece of paper, took a black felt-tipped pen out of his shirt pocket, closed the briefcase, and set the pen and paper on the chair. Then he walked to the shower, unlocked the handcuff from her wrist, turned, and walked out the door. She heard him locking it behind him.

She could not believe her good fortune. She stepped unsteadily to the chair. She started by printing the names as neatly as she could: Bahamas Commonwealth Bank; Union Bank of Switzerland; Banco de America Central of the Cayman Islands; International Credit Bank of Switzerland. The names themselves brought back the numbers, clear and fresh and clean in her mind, because numbers always were.

When she was finished, she left the pen and the paper on the seat of the chair and went back to her shower stall. After a long time, Policeman came through the door, picked up the chair and the piece of paper, and walked out the door.

It took them a few hours to do whatever they had needed to do to verify that the accounts existed. Then Policeman came in with Barraclough. This time Barraclough carried the papers. They were bank-transfer authorizations. Across the top was the name of one of her banks and the account number. Across the bottom of each one was the account where all of the money was going: Credit Suisse 08950569237. Her hatred clutched the numbers to her and clung to them as though they were the eyeballs of the men in the house.

When she was finished signing the papers they took them and walked out of the room without speaking to her. She had a strange sense of relief now. Her body felt light, as though she could dance or just rise up into the air. She held the numbers in her head and played with them like colored billiard balls that clicked when she moved them. Oh, eight ninety-five, oh, five sixty-nine, two thirty-seven. No fours or ones. First letters, O-E-N-F-O-F-S-N-T-T-S. 08950569237.

Jane sat in the dark and studied the gravel drive beside the house. There were the white station wagon, a white van, and a dark gray Dodge that looked like the same model as the red one they had used to bring Timmy to the freeway meeting. The small white house looked as though it had once been a real farmhouse where a family had lived and worked the broad flat fields around it, probably back in the thirties.

Jane knew she was going to have to do everything as quickly as she could. In an hour or two the sun would be up and one of them would look out a window. She had left the car a mile away by the side of the road, so there was no chance of using it as a blind.

She moved a little closer to the house, slowly and quietly, watching for signs that they had wired the grounds somehow. She had seen a beige box on the back side of the gate that she guessed was a motion sensor, and she had given the long gravel drive a wide berth because of it. She had come in across the empty field and seen nothing electronic since then.

She had imagined the safe house would be something big and fancy and in proportion with Barraclough's ambitions. But if Barraclough owned such a place, he wasn't going to make the mistake of committing crimes there. This house was small, unobtrusive, and run-down. He was too smart to have the fantasy that he could make any building impregnable. This one looked as though he expected to just walk away from it one day. His protection wasn't the delusion that he could keep the police out if they wanted to get in; it was the high probability that they would never try.

As soon as Jane saw the van she knew she was going to have to look inside it. If Mary was dead, they would not leave her body in the house for long. They would wrap it and place it in the back of the van so they could clean the house without any worry that there would be new blood when they moved it. The inside of a van could be washed with a hose. She moved quietly to the back of the van and looked in the rear window. The floor was lit enough by the moonlight through the windshield for her to tell there was nothing big enough on the floor to be a corpse. She could see the spare tire fastened with a wing nut on the right side just inside the rear door. She tried the door handle and found it unlocked, so she reached inside and searched around the tire by touch. When she found the tire iron she took it out and slipped it into her belt, then closed the door quietly and moved back out into the field.

She selected a spot a hundred feet from the house where the alfalfa had grown to about ten inches. Since the farm had not been worked for decades, the land had not been plowed and the thatch from other seasons lay thick on the surface. The tire iron was thick and heavy, and the chisel end that was designed for taking off hubcaps dug through it easily and reached rich, soft, black dirt only an inch down. She broke the earth and softened it, then took off her black sweatshirt, loaded double handfuls onto it, and used it as a sack to help her spread the dirt around the field in the deep grass. When the trench was longer than she was and ten inches deep, she gathered the tufts of alfalfa and thatch she had removed, lay down, and began to bury her legs.

The dawn came slowly, while the low fields were still blanketed with wet fog. It was still half an hour before sunrise when she heard the front door of the house open. She lay still in her shallow grave with the blanket of alfalfa and thatch covering her to her neck, then the sweatshirt above her head with a layer of cut alfalfa over it. She clutched the tire iron. There were two sets of heavy footsteps on the front porch. She heard them clop down the wooden steps, then followed the quiet crunches on the gravel. She heard one car door slam, then another. Then there was the hum of an engine. She listened as the wheels rolled on the gravel toward the highway.

Jane lifted her head only far enough to see that it was the dark gray car that was gone, then lay back for a few minutes considering the implications. Two men were gone. It could mean that they had come to the end of Mary Perkins's interrogation and that she was dead. She decided this was not likely. There would be the body to worry about. Barraclough had more understanding of human nature than to leave the body and the cleaning entirely to some underling, and he certainly wouldn't send his trainees on an errand while he did the messy, stomach-turning work himself. He would supervise while at least two of them wrapped the body, put it in the van, and took it somewhere far from here, then buried it deep. Mary was alive.

Two men were gone. Jane waited for twenty minutes, listening for sounds from the house, before she moved. Jane had to use this time to find out where Mary was and how many men were still in the house. Quietly she rolled over in her trench and crawled out the end of it. She slipped to the side of the house, put her ear against one of the clapboards, and listened. She heard music. In a moment it stopped and she heard the muffled cadence of speech, but it was loud and exaggerated like the voice of an announcer, and then the music came on again. She moved to the front of the house and checked the window. The living room was almost empty. There were two chairs, an old couch, and a portable television set on a coffee table. She followed the sound of the radio around the house to the kitchen door.

She listened for a few minutes, but there were no other voices. She slowly stepped up beside the door and let one eye slide close to the corner of the screened window. Inside were two young men. They were lying on the floor beside the kitchen table. One of them was clutching his belly, and his mouth was open as though he were trying to scream, but his eyes were staring without moving. The other was facing away from her, but he too was still. She could see that they had begun to eat breakfast. Cereal and milk were spilled on the floor, and on the table were two empty glasses with little bits of orange pulp residue almost to their brims.

Jane swung her tire iron and smashed the small window over the door, reached inside and turned the knob. Neither of the men moved. She walked past them into the living room and quietly climbed the stairs to the second floor, holding the tire iron. She looked in the door of each room and saw only four empty, unmade beds. She descended the stairs again and found a closed door off the hallway. She tried the knob, but it was locked. She pushed the flattened end of the tire iron between the jamb and the door at the knob, lifted her foot to step on the lug end to set it, then pushed with all her strength. The door gave a loud creak and then a bang as it popped inward, bringing a piece of the woodwork with it.

The sight of Mary was worse than the sight of the two men Jane had poisoned. She was naked and bruised, one eye swelled so that it was nearly closed, her lips dry and so chapped that when her mouth moved a clotted wound at the corner cracked and a thin trickle of blood ran down to her chin. She didn't seem to have the strength to stand up, so she started to crawl across the bathroom floor toward Jane.

Jane stepped to her and put her arm around her waist to lift her to her feet. "Come on," she said.

"They said you were dead." Jane could barely hear her.

"I'm not, and you aren't either. We have to hurry. Where are your clothes?"

"I don't know." She was seized with tremors, and it was a moment before Jane heard the rest of what she was trying to say. "Just get me out."

"Stay here a minute," said Jane, and quickly went into the kitchen to search for car keys. They were lying on the counter. As she snatched them up, she sensed movement behind her.

Mary was reaching for the bottle of milk on the table. "No!" Jane said sharply, and knocked it to the floor. Mary cringed and stared at her without comprehension.

"I poisoned everything."

Mary seemed to notice the two men on the floor for the first time. They had died in terrible pain and convulsions, and their faces were so contorted that they didn't look quite human. She seemed to marvel at them. "They look so young," she said. "I thought they were older." Then she seemed to remember something she had known before. "The devil is always exactly your own age."

"Come on," said Jane. "We'll forget the clothes for now." She dragged Mary out of the kitchen and onto the porch. She tried the car key in the van, but it didn't fit. It opened the white station wagon, so she eased Mary into the passenger seat, started the engine, and drove up the driveway. "Here," she said, and put the black sweatshirt on Mary's lap. "It's dirty, but it's better than nothing. Put it on."

Jane drove the next mile staring into her mirrors and up the road ahead for signs of Barraclough and Farrell. When she reached the place where she had parked the gray Toyota, she pulled the station wagon up to it, put Mary in the back seat, and drove up the road. She said, "Keep down on the seat and rest. Whatever you do, don't put your head up. Do you need a doctor right away?"

"I don't want one," said Mary. Her voice was raspy and brittle, but it was beginning to sound stronger.

"We'll get you some clothes and some food as soon as we're far enough away. Nothing's open yet."

"Just get the clothes. I can eat on the plane."

"The plane?"

"I have to go to Texas."

Jane felt a reflex in her throat that brought tears to her eyes. She didn't want to let pictures form of what they had done to Mary, but there was no way to avoid thinking about it. She wasn't dead, because her heart was still beating and she could form words with her bruised face, but she could easily spend the rest of her life in a madhouse.

"Ask me why."

The voice was self-satisfied and coy, almost flirtatious. Now Jane was going to have to follow Mary down whatever path her deranged mind was taking. She owed her a thousand times more than this tiny courtesy. "All right. Why?"

"Because I can remember numbers."

Jane tried to keep her calm. "I know, Mary. I noticed you were good with numbers the first time we talked. You're an intelligent, strong woman, and you're going to be okay." It was a lie. She was not going to be okay. Jane had done this to her. Barraclough had taken the bait and chewed it up.

"They finally made me give them the money I stole."

"I know," said Jane. "There's nobody who wouldn't have done what you did. Forget the money."

"Let me finish," said Mary impatiently. "They knew I had stolen it from banks, but they thought I did it by being an insect or a rat or something who crawled in and took it. It didn't even occur to them that the reason I could do it was that I know all about the business, and that I was smarter than the people I took it from. They filled out bank-transfer slips. They listed my bank account numbers and the number of the account where the money was supposed to go. I signed them all, one after another, so I saw it six times."

"Saw what six times?"

"There's no need to write it down. I can close my eyes and read it any time I want. 08950569237. He's transferring all the money into his bank account at Credit Suisse in Zurich. He has a numbered account, and that's the number. I captured it."

27

As Jane drove, Mary lay on the back seat talking at the roof of the car. "It has to be Dallas."

"Why Dallas? You told me once that you couldn't go there because people knew you."

"And I know them," said Mary. "They have you, and you have them. It's like the tar baby."

Jane tried to choose her words carefully. There would be nothing accomplished if she managed to nudge her own agitation into hysteria, but Mary had to know that it wasn't over. "I killed those two men back there. Barraclough wasn't there."

"Yes," said Mary. "He's in San Francisco."

"How do you know that?"

"That's where the big West Coast banks have their main offices. What he's doing right now is riding the jet stream, and you can't get on it very easily in some branch office in Stinkwood, Minnesota. All they can do for you is to ask the big offices to do it for them, and he can't fool around all day and let all those people know what he's doing."

"What do you mean by 'riding the jet stream'? Is he flying to Switzerland?"

"No," said Mary. "That's way too slow. Stock exchanges, bond markets, commodities, currency, the treasury securities of a hundred countries go up and down a hundred times a day. Some tyrant is shot in South America, and before the ambulance reaches the hospital, billions of dollars from Hong Kong are already buying up copper and coffee beans in London and New York. Barraclough isn't going to travel to Europe and then to the Caribbean to hand six tellers withdrawal slips and collect fifty-two million dollars. He's got to move the money the way big money moves— electronically, in thin air. Bonn, Paris, London, New York, Chicago, San Francisco, L.A., Zurich, Melbourne, Singapore, Hong Kong." After a breath she added, "Dallas."

Jane tilted the rearview mirror to get a glimpse of Mary on the back seat. She was bloody, bruised, and exhausted, but she seemed to be describing something that was real. "You mean you want to try to get your money back? Is that what this is about?"

Mary Perkins gave a quiet cough, and Jane realized that it had been a kind of mirthless laugh. "You told me before and I didn't get it, did I? You have to strip yourself clean. Lose everything: friends, clothes, medical records, your name, even your hair. The money was the last thing to go. That's gone, Jane. I had to give it to him, and I put it right in his hands so I could see which pocket he stashed it in."

Jane dressed Mary in a pair of blue jeans because the welts and bruises on her legs were so bright and angry that a dress would not have covered enough of them, and it was impossible in the small store in Gilroy to buy any other kind of women's pants in a length that fit an actual, living woman. The blouse was off another rack in the same store, a plain blue shirt that would attract no attention and was big enough to let her shrink inside it without having much of the fabric touch her skin.

Jane left the car in the long-term lot in San Jose because Mary insisted there was no time for a more elaborate arrangement. "Get me to Dallas," she said. "After that I don't care."

"What don't you care about?"

"Anything."

Mary ate and drank on the plane, then slept the rest of the way to Dallas. At the Dallas–Fort Worth airport, Jane rented a car. As she drove it out of the lot, she asked, "Where is it?"

"Bank of Sanford, corner of Commerce and Field. Turn left here."

"It must be almost closing time," said Jane. "But we may be able to catch your friend coming out."

"We don't want to catch him coming out," said Mary. Her voice was still even and low, as though it were an enormous effort to talk. "We'll catch him on the way in. Everything happens at night."

They waited in the bank lobby until Jane saw that each customer who approached the wide glass doors hurried to give the nearest handle a tentative tug to be sure they weren't locked, then stepped inside with a small sigh of relief, and then during the walk to the tellers' windows, looked up at the clock built into the wall.

At one minute before four a man about forty years old with hair that was combed straight back to emphasize the gray hair at his temples entered the bank. He wore a lightweight suit that had a slight sheen to it, and on his feet were a pair of brightly shined shoes that it took Jane a second to recognize as cowboy boots.

"There he is," said Mary Perkins. She stood up quickly, but the barely audible groan she gave showed that it had cost her something. She stepped in front of the man. "Hello, Gene," she said. "It's me—Mary Perkins."

The man looked at her, puzzled, while he inhaled once, and then puffed the breath out when he remembered. His eyes shot around him in a reflex, as though he were checking to see who was watching. He said uncomfortably, "Well, now, Mary. How are you these days? I heard you had some problems a while back."

"Yes, I've been away," said Mary. "I can see that you're thinking I don't look like the experience did me any good. You're absolutely right."

The man's brow wrinkled a little to tilt his eyebrows in sympathy, and his mouth forced itself into a sad smile. "Well, I can see it's behind you now, and that's the main thing."

Mary said, "Do you still have an office? I'd like to talk to you about some business."

The man reflexively leaned back away from her. "Mary, you have to understand that things don't work the way they once did. It's nice to see you, but—"

Mary turned and nodded to Jane, who was still sitting in the overstuffed chair next to the marble table where the pens were chained. She stepped forward to join them, but she didn't smile. Mary said, "This is Katherine Webster from the Treasury Department. This is Gene Hiller, my old friend."

The man looked from one to the other. "Now wait a minute," he said. "What's going on?"

"Don't worry," said Mary. "If your time is coming, I don't know about it. Let's talk."

Jane began to open her purse and fiddle with the little black wallet, as though she were about to pull out a badge.

Gene Hiller looked around him again, then said quickly, "This way."

His office was small, a place where he could hang his coat while he was out in the computer room. As soon as they were inside, Mary closed the door and stood in a place that made it impossible for him to sit behind his desk where he felt safe. Jane could see that Mary had once been very good at this.

"Here it is, Gene," she said. "I've made a deal with Katherine here. I'm going to give the money back voluntarily." She seemed to notice the sweat forming on his pale forehead. "I'm not—confirm this for me, Katherine—not expected to testify against anyone who may have had anything to do with any of the illegal activities in which I was once engaged."

The muscles in his shoulders seemed to relax so that his neck actually got longer. "What . . . brings you here?"

"It seems I can't go to Zurich, pick up a check with a lot of zeros on it, and fly back here to hand it over." She gave Jane a sarcastic smile. "There's very little trust left in the world."

"I see," said Gene, but all he could see was that in Mary's mind Jane represented what was stopping her.

"My attorney tells me that in order to get past the judge a week from now, it has to be voluntary, and apparently spontaneous, as evidence that I feel remorse and have been rehabilitated sincerely. I can't appear to have bought my way out with the Treasury Department. This puts me in a serious bind. Consequently I have to ask old friends for help."

The threat was not wasted on him. If for some reason she could not give them the money, there was something else she could give them. "What do you want me to do?"

"An electronic transfer," she said. "Receive the money, then send it on a second later. Write this down, and get it right. Credit Suisse, 08950569237. If they need a transfer request, I'll sign one and you can fax it. If they ask for verification tell them I've furnished identification. The name I used was James Barraclough."

Gene looked at her for a moment. "Want to tell me why you put a false name on a numbered account in a Swiss bank?"

Mary said, "I'm rehabilitating myself these days, not giving anybody lessons."

His eyebrows slowly began to rise. He smelled something. "Where exactly do you want these funds sent?"

Mary took a deep breath and blew it out. "Turn on your payroll computer and punch up the account number where you send the money for federal tax withholding. Can you do that?"

"Sure. What then?"

"Transfer all of the money from the Swiss bank into that account without ever having it appear on your computers as a transaction received by this bank. Give it to the I.R.S."

She looked at Jane Whitefield. Her eyes were wet and red and hot. "You think that will do it?"

Jane nodded solemnly.

Gene Hiller took the paper and walked into the computer room. There was a screen with a long list of transactions he was supposed to monitor—money the Federal Reserve was lending the bank overnight, money the bank was moving into accounts all over the world to cover investments it had made during the day, adjustments to the accounts of the various branches, like water being poured from a pitcher to even out the levels of a hundred little cups.

Gene ignored these and went to another terminal, typed in the name of the Swiss bank and waited while their machine signified that it had heard and recognized his machine. Then he told it he had authorization to close a numbered account and transfer the money. He typed in the number and waited. After a moment he said, "You sure this number is right? It doesn't usually take this long."

"It's right," said Mary firmly. "Tell them again."

As he prepared to do it, something happened. Letters and numbers appeared on the screen to fill in blanks. He stared at it for a moment, then looked up at Mary. "Jesus, Mary, two hundred and six million dollars? You stole two hundred and six million?"

Mary almost smiled. "No, Gene. I only stole fifty-two. The rest I inherited. Send it now."

Gene typed in the number of the Internal Revenue Service account and tapped his return key. Before his fingers rebounded from the keyboard, the money was gone. He stared at the screen as though he were having trouble believing what he had seen, and certainly couldn't believe what he had done.

Mary said, "Probably nobody is ever going to ask you about this, but if they do, you don't know a thing. You didn't do it. That's part of the deal I made. There can't be any way in the world for anyone to get a penny of it back." She patted his shoulder. "That means you too, Gene."

"I'm not that stupid," he said. "Anybody who asks the I.R.S. to refund his two hundred and six million dollars is going to get a lot of things, but none of them will be a check."

"Right," said Mary. She leaned down and gave him a peck on the cheek. "Thanks, baby. Now I'll leave you alone for the rest of your life."

She walked out of the computer room with her head high and her shoulders back. Jane could tell that she was in pain, but she stood erect until Hiller had let them out the fire door and they were around the corner getting into the car. As soon as she sat down the strength seemed to go out of her, and her head rested on the seat.

"Mary?" said Jane. "You okay?"

"It was better than I ever dreamed. All the time I was in that house I was so scared, so hurt, that I thought he had opened an account just to take my money. But you have to open a numbered account in person. How could he do it that fast? He had me, but he had no place to put my money except in the account where he kept all the money he had stolen for years. I got to take every penny he had and pour it all into a sewer."

28

Jane drove fast across the flat plains of northern Texas. The night was just beginning, and she knew that she would need to use this time well. The trip from California to the Texas bank had taken them all day.

She tried to imagine what Barraclough was doing now. She was convinced that Mary knew enough about money to be reliable in her guess that Barraclough had driven to a bank in San Francisco that morning. He and Farrell could not have returned before about noon to find Mary gone and his two trainees dead.

He would have found Farrell's white station wagon by one o'clock and figured out that Jane and Mary had gotten into another car. Then he and Farrell would have spent more time disposing of the two bodies, cleaning the farmhouse of evidence that a woman had been held there, and removing any objects or prints that connected him with the property. That still left him with a van and two cars, with only Farrell to help him drive. He needed at least one person, perhaps two more people, he could trust to drive the vehicles back to Los Angeles. The most likely candidates would have to come all the way up from Enterprise Development in L.A.

She guessed that Barraclough would have been finished with all of this by nine or ten in the evening, about five hours after the time when all of his stolen money had disappeared. She said, "Is there some way Barraclough would know his account in Switzerland was gutted?"

Mary didn't answer. Jane glanced over her shoulder and saw that she was curled up like a child, asleep on the back seat. The question would have to wait. Probably the bank would send him some kind of written closing statement.

Jane couldn't risk going back to the airport and flying Mary out of Dallas tonight. If Barraclough had the presence of mind to ask for confirmation that the gigantic deposit he had made was credited to his account, he would be told that his account was closed. Even if the Swiss bank didn't know that the transfer to the Internal Revenue Service had been initiated in Dallas, there would probably be a way to find out. She had to assume Barraclough would have people searching Dallas before the sun came up.

She looked at Mary again, then returned her eyes to the road. She had been holding down the feelings for days, but now she let them surface. What she had done was unforgivable. She had used this woman for bait and let the beast have her. All she could do now was try to preserve what was left. Whatever had been holding Mary together—the delay of physical sensation that came from shock, or maybe merely the energy of sheer hatred—had apparently drained out of her now. Before she had fallen asleep she had been weak and vague enough to make traveling a risk. Jane would have to get her indoors before morning. She used the last eight hours of darkness to run north out of Texas and up the short side of Oklahoma.

It was still dark when Jane bumped up off the road onto the smooth asphalt surface of a gas station and turned off the car's engine. She heard Mary sit up in the back seat, so she turned around to watch her squinting and blinking at the lighted island, then reach up to run her fingers through her hair. Jane watched her slowly begin to remember. She was suddenly agitated. "Where are we? Why are we stopping?"

Jane chose to answer the first question. "Miami, Oklahoma."

"Where are we going?"

Jane was glad to hear the annoyance in Mary's voice. It was a vital sign, like a pulse or a heartbeat. "This is it for now. It's safe here."

At a little past nine A.M. they walked into the gift shop in the Inter-Tribal Council Building. The young woman who was cleaning the display case turned and smiled, then went back to her work. Jane waited until the woman sensed that she wanted to talk. She looked up from her work, let her eyes rest on Jane for a second, then said, "I'll bet you're here visiting relatives."

Mary smiled involuntarily.

"Yes," said Jane. She saw Mary's face turn to hers in surprise. "I was hoping to catch Martha McCutcheon here."

"Oh, Seneca," said the woman.

"That's right," said Jane. She held out her hand. "Jane White-field."

The woman took it and smiled. "Rowena Cloud. Ottawa."

"I'm very pleased to meet you," said Jane. "Is Martha in the back?"

"Martha hasn't been well this week," said Rowena Cloud. "She has arthritis bad in the winter, and it's been bitter cold for a couple of days, so she might be in bed. She didn't mention anything about going anyplace. If she's not home, though, come on back. You can stay at our house. I can give you directions, and the key is over the door."

"Well, thank you," said Jane warmly. "We'll go see if she's up to visitors."

As they walked down the street, Mary asked softly, "Are you really an Indian, or is that some kind of assumed identity too?"

Jane looked at her, amused. "Think I could fool her?" She opened the car door and waited while Mary eased into the seat, then started the car and pulled out onto the road.

"How did she know? You have blue eyes."

"This is Indian country. She's seen about every kind of Indian there is, so she's an expert. There are reservations all around us."

"Seneca?"

"Some. The Iroquois all lived in New York State in the beginning. But there were some Seneca and Cayuga families who used to go into Ohio every fall to hunt. After the Revolutionary War they didn't see any point in going home. They were on reservations at Lewistown and Sandusky until they got pushed out in 1831 and sent to Oklahoma."

"But this isn't your hometown?"

Jane shook her head. "Not me. My family stayed in New York." She watched Mary closely. "Look, Mary. There are going to be a few things you see and hear that won't make sense to you. Like that girl back there saying we could stay with her, when she had never laid eyes on us before."

"It did seem a little odd," said Mary.

"Smile a lot and ignore anything that seems unfamiliar. I didn't want to bring you here, but we've run about as far as we can for now. Barraclough already knows I killed his men, and pretty soon he'll know you took all his money and gave it to the government. He's going to be searching, and this time he won't let anything distract him. He wants us dead."

"I know that," said Mary.

"A few of the people here know me. Most of them don't. A few are—in the way that we figure these things, not the way you're used to—relatives. We need to get you to a doctor, and we need a place to rest. This is it."

They left the car parked on the road and walked along a path to the trailer park. It took Jane a few minutes of searching before she found the mobile home she remembered on the very edge of the lot. There was a small stenciled sign on the door that said "McCUTCHEON." She knocked quietly and listened.

The door of the mobile home opened and an old woman in a cardigan sweater and a flowered dress stood in the doorway three steps above them. Her long straight hair was thick and gray, tied back in a tight ponytail as though it belonged to a much younger woman, but her mouth was toothless and her jaws were clamped together so her chin nearly touched her nose. She said simply, "Hello."

Jane spoke to her in Seneca. "My name is Jane Whitefield, Grandmother. Do you remember me?"

The old woman squinted, smiled happily, then said in English, "Just a minute." She went away and came back with her false teeth in. "I remember you, Granddaughter," she said in Seneca. "I'm glad to see you again."

Jane said in English, "This is a friend of mine, Mary Perkins."

The old woman scrutinized Mary in mock disapproval. "Not another anthropologist."

"No," said Jane. "She's only a safecracker."

Martha laughed happily. "Dah-joh." She repeated it in English, stepping back to make way. "Come in. I'm having trouble with the lock on this door. Maybe you're the one to fix it."

Jane and Mary climbed the wooden steps into the tiny, neat kitchen. Mary could see that the television set was on in the living room, but Martha seemed to notice it at the same time. She reached into her sweater pocket, pulled out the remote control, aimed it carefully, and killed the machine. She said, "Sit down, sit down. I'll get you something."

Mary drew a breath to say "We just ate," but Jane touched her arm and gave her head a single shake.

Corn bread, honey, and strawberry and blueberry preserves appeared so suddenly and with so little preparation that Mary instantly perceived that this was another of the things that she must simply smile at and not question.

Jane and Martha walked out among the dry, frost-flecked flower stalks in the garden and spoke to one another in Seneca. "What happened to her?"

Jane had come here because it was the only place she could think of in this part of the country where she could trust people absolutely, but when the question came she could not relinquish her old habits. She quickly manufactured a story, but when she looked into the old lady's eyes to begin, they seemed already to have penetrated the lie. Telling it would be a waste of time. "She was kidnapped. She had money that wasn't hers. Some men wanted it. They tortured her. She hasn't said so yet, but they raped her."

"Did the police catch them?"

Jane shook her head. "We couldn't even call the police. She's done too much. She'd end up in jail and the men would find her there and make sure she never got out."

"What's a Nundawaono girl got to do with that kind of business?"

Jane looked into her eyes. "It's what I do. Fugitives come to me and I guide them out of the world."

"Why?"

Jane laughed a sad little chuckle. "Because if I didn't, they would give me bad dreams."

"I'll bet a lot of them do anyway," said Martha. She looked at Jane with her bright old eyes and shook her head. "People like me—the old longhouse people who believe in the visions of Handsome Lake—we're always saying the young have forgotten everything. So the one day I stay home from work my own great-grandmother comes to my door. I should learn to shut up. Now I have to help you take care of her, don't I?"

Jane said, "You're a clan mother. You must have learned enough in all those years to make a decision by yourself."

"Has she been to a doctor?"

"Not yet. I'm going to call a doctor friend of mine and have him use his connections to get us one who won't call the police when she walks in."

"I know one who will see her today. Leave her to me," said Martha.

A few days later, Mary opened the trailer door and walked outside to find Martha standing alone in the weeds. The old woman was already looking at her, as though she had been watching the door and waiting for it to open. "Come on," she said, and began to walk.

Mary Perkins caught up with her. "Where are we going?"

"No place. I've been walking like this for seventy-five years, and if I stop doing it, I'll stiffen up and die."

They walked along in silence for a time. Every few minutes Mary found that her steps had started to move toward the highway without her thinking about it, and she had to correct her course. Martha showed no interest in the road. She kept walking straight through the weeds. After a time Mary noticed that

Martha's dress was hemmed precisely a half inch above the weeds so that it didn't get caught in brambles or pick up seeds. "How about you?" the old woman asked. "Have you decided yet?"

"Decided what?"

"To die."

Mary walked a long time. "I don't know. Sometimes I think it's already happened and I missed it. I don't know exactly when. I was beyond noticing things by the time Jane came. After that I concentrated on staying upright long enough to do something I had promised myself to do. That's over now, but nothing has come to take its place."

Martha walked along in the weeds. The cold made the dry stalks snap as her feet pushed them aside to touch the snow. "Each time I walk through here it's different. In four months this will all be wildflowers. Tiny white ones, lots of blue and gold and pink, all mixed together. There are about four hundred acres here that no-body has farmed since I was a kid, and the flowers grow like crazy."

"I'd like to see that," said Mary.

"Then you're not dead yet."

Mary walked stiffly, not paying much attention to the rattling stalks of the weeds. "Maybe that wasn't me. It's been so long since I used my real name that it doesn't sound like me anymore. Maybe Jane didn't tell you, but that's why this happened."

"Whatever you did, what was done to you wasn't the punishment. It was only something else that happened. Now something else will happen."

"That's my problem. It's not that I don't know what will happen, or that I'm afraid. I can't even think of anything that I would like to happen."

"Maybe you need some help. You could spend the rest of your life going to see psychiatrists."

"I take it you don't approve."

"It's okay with me. Some people like drugs, and I think a lot of them just like getting dressed up and having a place to go where they're expected at a certain time."

"Right now I can't see any difference between that and anything else that people do."

"Maybe Mary Perkins got so torn up that she isn't worth much anymore. Maybe you didn't like her much to begin with. Forgive her, because you know that she's suffered. Love her, because you traveled together and shared secrets. Then end her life and bury her."

"Kill myself?"

"Unless you still want to see the wildflowers."

Mary studied her carefully. "You made that up about the wildflowers, didn't you?"

Martha nodded. "Of course I did. This is all thistle and buffalo grass. I'd like to see some wildflowers, though. Most winters I find that's all that's necessary."

Jane waited until Martha McCutcheon had gone to work at the store, then sat beside Mary on the steps of the trailer.

"I didn't ask you to talk much about what happened because I didn't want to upset you," Jane began. "Now I need to."

Mary's voice was tense, but she said, "Okay."

"They probably asked you a lot of questions—things that didn't seem to make any sense, right?"

"Yes. It was the older one, most of the time. It was like he was trying to see if I was telling the truth. Where did we meet the guy to get a ride in Ann Arbor? What did we eat—"

"Names," Jane interrupted. "Did he ask you about the names we used when we were running?"

"Well, yes." She seemed to sense she had made a terrible mistake. "I told them. I was so scared, so tired—"

"It's okay," Jane said. "It's okay. Just think back. Are there any names you know that you left out?"

"No."

Jane nodded and stood up. "You didn't do anything wrong. I just needed to know."

The "older one" must be Farrell. He had waited until she had reached the lowest point and then asked her all of the questions. The answers would have given Barraclough what he needed now. Barraclough could take something as trivial as the room number of a hotel on a particular date, approach the right clerk in the right way, and get the name Jane had used and her credit card number.

If the hotel happened to be one that bought its security from Intercontinental, then they would give it to him without any fuss. Whenever Barraclough wanted to, he could be Intercontinental Security Services.

Jane spent the next few days watching the horizon. The flat, empty fields on all sides should have made her feel safer, but the endless sameness induced a panicky agoraphobia in her. She would sit at Martha McCutcheon's kitchen table for fifteen minutes at a time, staring into the west down the highway, then move to another window to gaze to the south across the winter-bare fields.

On the fourth night she heard a noise and sat up in bed, not waking up, just awake. From the other wall of the trailer Martha McCutcheon whispered, "It's the wind." After a moment she said in Seneca, "Have you thought about what you were going to do if it weren't?"

"Always," Jane whispered. She stood up, put on her coat, and walked outside the trailer into the field and away from the lights of the trailer park. She sat in the weeds in the dark and listened to the wind. It was cold and wild, coming across the plain in sputtering gusts and eddies. She had a scared feeling that it carried something that she couldn't quite hear. It might be something that she would have been able to identify if the air had been calm, and it might be something she should not have been near enough to hear at all, something the wind had brought from far away.

Either way it was the same sound. It was car doors slamming, men's feet trampling the stiff, frozen weeds, the metallic clicks as shotgun slides pumped and pistol magazines locked into place. She looked up into the sky and tried to discern the constellation of the loon that the old runners had used to navigate as they moved along the Waagwenneyu at night, but it was hidden behind trailing clouds.

When she looked back at the little camp, she could see it through Barraclough's eyes. It would not be hard to find the right trailer, with the shiny new car she had rented in Dallas parked beside it. Ordinary .38 ammunition would pierce the trailer wall. A rifle round in a big-game caliber could go through both walls and kill somebody behind the trailer from three hundred yards out.

There was nothing in the flat, empty country that was big enough to hide a running woman.

In the morning Jane went with Martha on her walk. After a time, Martha said, "You're leaving today, aren't you?"

"Yes."

"You want something first, don't you?"

"It might not be safe here much longer. I want you to drive up north with her."

"Where?"

"Nundawaonoga." It was the Seneca word for the western half of New York State. It was like saying "Home." Jane added, "No planes, no buses, no credit cards." She held out a thick stack of hundred-dollar bills. "This will pay for a car."

Martha walked along in silence for a time, then took the money and slipped it into the pocket of her jacket. "There are people up there I haven't seen in ten years. They'll be very glad to see me."

"Thank you, Grandmother."

Martha held Jane in the corner of her eye. "Why aren't you going with us?"

Jane shook her head. "He's not looking for her now. He's looking for me."

29

Farrell paced back and forth in front of the television monitor, the heels of his polished shoes clicking on the old hardwood floor of the Enterprise Development office. "Take another look at her." The picture on the monitor was dim and grainy. The sound had been erased. The woman had been caught in a telephoto lens standing on the edge of a freeway beside Barraclough. Every few seconds a car or truck would flash past in the foreground, shrunk by the lens to look smaller than the people beyond it. The woman was Jane. "Look at the shape of her face, the way she moves. Forget her hair and clothes. She'll change those. Study the things that don't change."

After ten seconds, the picture vanished in a wash of bright, popping static, and then the tape began to rewind. Farrell turned to his audience of young men. They were sitting on desks, leaning against walls, some even crouched on the floor near the screen. Assembled like this, they were an unprepossessing bunch, but he knew something about each of them that made him feel confident. During his years as a cop, Farrell had become very good at spotting a certain kind of young man early. "This is the only picture we have of her at the moment, but when we find something that's a little clearer, we'll try to work up some still shots for you. Let's run the tape again."

As Farrell reached for the PLAY button he could hear the heavy footsteps on the stairs. He straightened as the door swung open and Barraclough walked in. Few of Farrell's trainees had ever seen Barraclough before, but they had just watched the tape, so none of them wondered who he was. Barraclough's empty gray eyes swept the crowd of young men. When a few of the trainees fidgeted involuntarily to correct their posture, the motion seemed to attract Barraclough's gaze to them. He stared, made some secret assessment, and moved on.

The tailored navy blue blazer and gray pants Barraclough wore had the simplicity and precise lines of a uniform. He turned away from the young men, slipped off the coat and tossed it onto Farrell's desk as a simple gesture to make it clear that this place was his, and turned back to them in his starched, Marine-creased white shirt. Strapped under his left arm was a Browning nine-millimeter automatic in a worn shoulder holster, carried muzzle-upward so it could be drawn with little movement. Attached to the strap under the left arm was an extra ammunition clip. The young men could see that this was not the gleaming, compact sidearm of a successful security executive. It was the weapon of a man who had been in gunfights with people who were now dead.

Barraclough judged that his silence had served its purpose. "Mr. Farrell has probably told you a little about me, but we should know each other better. Let me begin by telling you what I'm not. I'm not your friend."

A few eyes that had been hovering in his general direction shot to his face but found no comfort or reassurance there. "If you bring me what I want, I will give you what you want. Simple as that. Mr. Farrell is not your Boy Scout leader. I haven't been spending money on training to make men out of you, as though I gave a shit if you lived or died. I don't. I'm giving you the knowledge and experience to be useful to me. If you want to make something out of yourself, keep your eyes and ears open and you probably can."

A few of the young men seemed to mine some hint of hope from the notion that they could make something of themselves. He appeared to want to oblige them. "I'll even tell you how the business works. If you win, you get to have the prizes—the girls, the big house, the cars, people calling you 'sir' for the rest of your life. If you lose, you're dead. You may still walk around for a while before one of the winners happens to notice you, but that's just a technicality. Whatever you have is his. You're a failure, a victim, a corpse."

Barraclough looked at them with his empty, unreadable eyes for a moment, then spoke again. "I know at least some of you must have noticed that a couple of guys didn't come back after this last trip. I'm here to tell you what happened to them. They're dead. Mr. Farrell and I left them to guard an unarmed, incapacitated prisoner, and they let the woman you saw on the tape sneak in and poison their breakfast." He shook his head in amazement and chuckled. "If she hadn't used enough poison, I would have had to kill them myself."

A few of the trainees exchanged nervous grins, but Barraclough's smile dissolved. "That's the other part of our deal: I will always tell you the truth. If you're stupid, you're a liability. You won't just hurt yourself, you'll hurt me. I am not going to let that happen. Not for them, not for you."

He glanced at Farrell, who was standing near the door. "Mr. Farrell is going to give you specific assignments over the next day or two. But here's the short version. That woman is all I want right now. When I get her, I want her breathing." He nodded to Farrell, picked up his coat, and slipped it on as he walked out the door.

Barraclough went down the back stairs and across the parking lot to the next street, where he had left his car, and began the long drive to the Intercontinental Security building in Irvine. He could not keep his mind off that Jane woman. He wanted to tear her head off with his hands. She had blundered into his way when he was at the edge of a triumph, and the collision had obliterated years of small, painfully won successes: years on the police force, always working harder than the others, taking more risks, gradually building a reputation; more years at Intercontinental Security, always working tirelessly, always looking for a way up.

After he had come to Intercontinental, Barraclough had focused his attention on each of the divisions in turn: Home Security, Retail Security, Detectives. Slowly he had brought each of them up to modern standards, and the management team in Chicago had responded by making him Director of Western Regional Operations. But Barraclough had not been working for a promotion. He had always lived by his ability to see farther down the path than anyone else, and he had already moved ahead of Intercontinental's management. All of his efforts to revitalize the old security company were mere sideshows—preparations for what was to happen in the little Van Nuys office of the separate corporation he had formed called Enterprise Development.

Barraclough had designed Enterprise Development to fit inside the skin of Intercontinental Security. Its costs were hidden within the giant company's overhead, its personnel culled from Intercontinental's applicant pool. When Enterprise Development conducted its business, a pretext was constructed so that the employees and equipment of Intercontinental's offices in twenty-six cities could be set to work identifying fingerprints, searching for cars, analyzing traces, performing surveillance.

Enterprise Development had been invented to specialize in exploiting a small and neglected group of criminals: the successful ones who had gotten away with large amounts of money. Some were already wanted by the authorities in the United States or elsewhere but were not actively hunted; others had not yet been discovered or were merely suspected. Some had been convicted and served sentences but had not made restitution. Barraclough used Enterprise Development to identify them, hunt them down, and turn them into cash.

In his first seven years of hunting, Barraclough had recovered over seventy-five million dollars. This had not been nearly enough, because the purpose of Enterprise Development was not merely to make its owner rich; it was a device for accumulating enough capital to buy control of Intercontinental Security.

Barraclough had made the next eighty million on only one

find, the Timothy Phillips trust fund. Seven years ago he had decided that Intercontinental Security should obtain the Hoffen-Bayne account so that Enterprise Development could have a look at what was going on inside. He had not known about Timothy Phillips; he had simply realized that a company handling the personal fortunes of so many people was a good place to hunt. He had offered Intercontinental's services for a price that competitors could never match because the bid left no margin for a profit.

When he had placed security devices in the Hoffen-Bayne offices and the partners' homes, the customers had been interested in color and design, but circuitry had been beneath their notice. It had never occurred to people like Alan Turner that a little electronic box with glowing lights might be just about anything. It had never even crossed Turner's mind that if his security system had a little microphone he could talk into during an emergency, the microphone could also pick up what he said when there was no emergency. He had sat all day under security cameras and thought he was alone.

Once Barraclough had discovered the account Turner was stealing from, the money belonged to Barraclough. The man had been robbing clients for years, and all of the people who took salaries for catching thieves had missed him. Turner had been there for anyone to take, but only Barraclough had found him.

Barraclough had worked Mary Perkins with the same patience. Anybody could have read about her trial in the newspapers, as he had, but he had waited until the feds had taken their crack at her, and then he had taken his. The feds had come up empty, and Barraclough had walked away with fifty-two million.

His rage deepened. To have a woman like this Jane take it all away from him was more than an insult; it was a violation of the laws of the universe.

At ten o'clock in the evening, Farrell made his way across the polished marble lobby of the Intercontinental Security Services building, thinking about fate. Ten years ago, when he had been a cop for almost ten years and a detective for two, the captain had suddenly assigned him a new partner, a kid named Barraclough. After

Farrell had watched him work for a few days, he had seen the future.

If Farrell kept on the way he was going, the best he could hope for was twenty years with the police department and a pension that wouldn't be enough to convince him that his life had been worth the effort. But ten years ago it was already apparent that Barraclough wasn't going to end up like that, and if Farrell stuck with him, he wasn't either. At thirty, Barraclough was entering his prime, and what he represented was a world that had no limits.

But tonight, as Farrell walked toward the elevator that would take him up to Barraclough's office, he was a little nervous. He had not been able to think of a way that this Jane woman could have found Mary Perkins except by following him to the farm. If he had figured this out, then Barraclough had too. No, he thought. He was not a little nervous. He knew Barraclough better than anyone alive, and he was deeply, agonizingly afraid. When he raised his hand to the elevator button, he saw it start to shake.

Farrell wasn't even sure what made him most afraid. A bullet in the back of the head had its attractions. It was quicker and kinder than most of the ways that lives ended. Slowly he identified what he feared most. He feared Barraclough's displeasure: not the bullet, but Barraclough's impulse to fire it, whether or not the trigger got pulled. This one lapse might have convinced Barraclough that Farrell wasn't like Barraclough—that he was just one of the others, a loser. After all these years, first teaching Barraclough and then following him, Farrell would be lost, abandoned and exiled from the light. He would be denied a share in Barraclough's future.

He stepped out of the elevator, walked to the big wooden door of Barraclough's office, and knocked quietly. No, that had been too quiet. Barraclough might think he was weak and used up, maybe even afraid. Fear disgusted Barraclough. Farrell gave a hard rap with his knuckles, then heard Barraclough call "Come in."

Farrell found him sitting behind the big desk. He only looked up long enough to verify who had come in the door, then went back to signing papers. He muttered, "The fucking home office is waiting on these reports. That's what they do. They sit in that building in Chicago and read quarterly reports. Talk to me."

"The lines are all in the water," said Farrell. "I finally got the last of the boys on their planes. With the ones we had out already, we should have two-man teams in fifty-six airports by morning."

"Are you sure they'll recognize her if they see her?"

"The ones who have seen her in person will. The tape from the freeway should help the others, but it's mostly on you." Farrell felt a chill. He had given in to some subconscious need to remind Barraclough that Farrell was not the only one who made mistakes. He tried to talk quickly, to get past it before the sour taste of it turned Barraclough against him. "But I've got people working on finding a decent picture of her from surveillance footage in the places we know she's been—stores, hotels, and so on."

Barraclough kept signing papers, then moving each one to a pile at the corner of his desk. He seemed to be listening, so Farrell went on. "I've got a couple of technicians traveling around with the teams trying to find her fingerprints where she touched something that might not have gotten wiped off: hotel bathrooms get scoured with cleanser, but prints might survive on a telephone receiver or on anything that was inside a drawer. Rental cars sometimes sit on the lot for a few days before they go out again. Fingerprints are still the best way to find out who you're really dealing with."

Barraclough frowned as he scrutinized a sheet that appeared to be covered with numbers, then wrote something on it and set it beside the pile of papers. He looked up, so Farrell said, "The credit checks on her fake credit cards come in once a day. So far she hasn't used any of them. I figure she's gone under somewhere to wait until Mary Perkins is healthy enough to travel again."

Barraclough looked down at his papers again. Something he was reading caused a look of weariness and impatience. "Is that it?"

Farrell said, "Just about. Of course I'm trying a couple of long shots. We know she met Mary Perkins in the L.A. County Jail. I hired a hooker to get herself inside and ask questions of the other prisoners, to get us a lead on where she lives."

"You said a couple. What else?"

Farrell gave an apologetic shrug. "Do you remember that guy who kept calling up bank tellers and saying he had their kid, so they'd leave money in a bag somewhere?"

"Sure," said Barraclough. "Ronny Prindle. That must be nine or ten years ago. What about him?"

"Well, there was something I tried that time that didn't pan out. I took one of the telephone tapes to a linguistics professor and asked him for an opinion of the accent. We caught Ronny Prindle before the report came back, but I remembered being surprised when I read it because the professor got it right. Prindle was from the east coast of Maryland. So I cleaned up the tape we had from Jane and sent it to the same guy. He thinks I'm still a cop."

Barraclough smiled at the paper he was signing, and Farrell thought he heard a chuckle. "Every time I can't imagine why I'm dragging your dead ass around with me, you surprise me, and I remember. Let me know as soon as you hear from him."

Farrell's hands stopped shaking. He had bought himself more time.

Two days later Farrell hurried across the same lobby, pushed the elevator button, and walked into the same office. Barraclough looked up at him expectantly.

"She's started using the credit cards," Farrell said. "We got a Katherine Webster at a hotel in Saint Louis, a Denise Hollinger renting a car in Cleveland, a Catherine Snowdon in Erie, Pennsylvania—"

"She's heading northeast," said Barraclough. "Start moving people into her path."

Farrell's eyes twinkled. "It's done. Everybody we've got is either up there already or on a plane to northern Pennsylvania or upstate New York. I've got some strung out in rest stops along the big highways, some checking the parking lots of hotels, restaurants, and malls for the car she rented, others waiting at rental offices for her to turn it in. I've got some more—"

Barraclough interrupted. "Can you tell from the reports what she's doing?"

Farrell scanned the credit reports in his hands. "Pretty much what Mary Perkins told us she does. She alternates identities, so the same person never turns up two places in a row. She's paying the single-room rate, and the meal charges don't seem to be enough for two, so she's probably traveling alone."

"But what's she trying to accomplish?" Barraclough snapped. "Where's she going?"

Farrell smiled. "Well, let me tell you what the professor says." He moved another sheet of paper to the top and stared at it. "She's got a little peculiarity. Her lips don't quite touch when she says *m, b,* or *p.* He thinks that means she grew up speaking two languages, but it's not enough to tell him what the other one is." He moved his finger down the paper. "Oh, here's the part I was looking for. Her accent has what he calls an 'intrusive schwa.' It's a marker that places her in a narrow linguistic belt that stretches from Chicago east as far as Syracuse, New York." He shrugged. "If I had to make a bet, I'd say she's had enough and is going home."

It was only twenty hours later that Farrell returned to Barraclough's office, looking exuberant. "She's been spotted."

"Where?"

"She turned in the rented car at the Buffalo airport, went to the long-term lot, got into a parked car, and drove off. We had two guys there."

Barraclough glowered, his eyes narrowing. "They let her get away?"

"No," Farrell answered quickly. "They followed her to a house in a little town on the Niagara River between Buffalo and Niagara Falls."

"And?" Barraclough asked impatiently.

"She put the car in the garage and opened the door with a key," said Farrell. "It must be her house."

30

Barraclough and Farrell arrived in the Buffalo airport after midnight in the beginning of a snowstorm. The Nissan Pathfinder four-wheel-drive vehicle with tinted windows that Barraclough had specified was waiting at the curb with one of Farrell's trainees behind the wheel, but Barraclough stepped into the street to the driver's side and said, "Get in the back."

Barraclough drove the Pathfinder out to the slush-covered gray street and watched the wiper sweep across the windshield to compress the snowflakes into a thin, ruler-straight bar, then slide back for more while the defroster melted the bar away.

Farrell inspected and loaded the two pistols his trainee had brought for them, attached the laser sights, and tested the night-vision spotter scope he had brought with him from California. "Where is she?"

"You get on the Thruway up here and take it west. Get off at the Delaware exit and head north."

Farrell glanced at Barraclough to be sure he had heard, then back at his trainee. "What's the place like?"

"It's a two-story house. We didn't see any sign of anybody else. She went to bed just before I left for the airport."

"You mean her lights went out," Farrell corrected. "Who's watching the house?"

"Mike. Mike Harris."

"From where?"

"He's in a black Dodge. He's parked down the street, facing away, where he can see in the mirror the front door and the door that goes to the driveway."

Farrell felt a slight, pleasurable warmth in his chest. The boys weren't much to begin with—just oversized balls and a mean streak—but by the time he was through with them they knew how the game was played.

When they arrived at the street, Barraclough stopped the Pathfinder a distance from the Dodge. Farrell took out the radios and handed one to the trainee. "You remember how to use one of these, right?"

"Press the button to talk, keep the volume low when anybody might hear it."

"Good," said Farrell. "We're Unit One, you're Unit Two. Anybody picks up the signal, he thinks we're cops. No chitchat over the air."

Barraclough picked up the night scope and turned it on, then swept it slowly up and down the street. Houses, trees, shrubs seemed to burn with a bright green phosphorescence, but there were no signs of movement. He aimed it through the rear window of the Pathfinder. "Is that the house back there on the left?"

"Yeah."

"You been around the other side to check for other exits?"

"Sure."

"Did you check the houses around it?"

"Yeah. Couples with kids on one side and the back, an old guy on the other. Curtains were open long enough so we saw people watching TV."

"Okay. Here's how it's going to be," said Barraclough. "Give Mike one of the radios and tell him to sit tight and watch. Then come back here and get ready to drive this vehicle. Farrell and I are going in. When we come out with her, pull up to the curb quick and pick us up. I want the burlap sack lying where I can reach it so we can get it over her head as soon as she's in the back."

The young man grunted his assent, then took the radio over to the black Dodge and got inside to talk to his partner.

Suddenly Barraclough hissed, "A light just went on. . . . She's coming out."

Farrell ducked his head below the window and spoke into his radio. "Heads down! She's out of the house."

Thirty seconds later Farrell heard a car door slam, an engine start, and the sound of tires on the wet pavement. He saw the red glow of taillights reflected on the dashboard. After a moment the glow receded.

Barraclough started the Pathfinder and pulled out into the street. Farrell said into the radio, "Change of plan. Unit Two, we're following. Stay behind us for now."

Barraclough swung the Pathfinder around the block and stopped with his lights off on the next street until he saw Jane's car pass under the street lamps of the intersection. The color was gray. It was an old Chevy—maybe a Caprice or Impala. "She's going too slow to be running." He waited another few seconds, glanced in the mirror to verify that Farrell's trainees had followed, and then started up after her.

"I'd sure like to know where she's going at this time of night," said Farrell. "She may have spotted the Dodge and decided to see if they'd follow her."

"I don't think so," said Barraclough. "If she had, she would have tried something like that while Mike was alone. If she saw him and us too, she'd have gone out the back window."

"Then what do you think she's doing?"

Barraclough shrugged. "She's been living like a scared rabbit for years. When she moves, it's nearly always at night. If I had to guess, I'd say she got a phone call."

"Mary Perkins?"

"Could be," said Barraclough. "But she might even be meeting new clients by now."

The gray car drove a few blocks, then turned left at the Niagara River. Barraclough waited for a long time before he turned after her. He had to be careful not to get stuck behind her at a traffic signal, where she would be able to get a good look through the rearview mirror.

When he could see her taillights far enough ahead, he gauged her speed and matched it. "She doesn't drive as though she's seen us. We'll wait until she gets to a dark, deserted stretch before we try to take her."

The road wound a bit to stay beside the big, dark river, then straightened and opened up into four lanes. Farrell unfolded the road map on his lap and checked it against street signs. After a few minutes he called the other vehicle on the radio. "Pull ahead of us now, Unit Two. We're going to fade into the background for a while. Give her lots of space and don't spook her."

The black Dodge followed Jane through little towns along the river, past a cluster of oil refineries, then onto the Thruway just before the Buffalo city line. Farrell studied the map, and as they approached each landmark, he would announce it. "There's a big park up ahead. Riverside Park. If she takes the exit, we might be able to pull her over there." She didn't. "Up ahead is the Peace Bridge over to Canada. That could be where she's heading." But it wasn't. The dark water beside them widened into Lake Erie.

Jane turned off the Thruway at Route 5 where it became Fuhrmann Boulevard and hugged the shoreline into the city of Lackawanna. Ahead of Farrell and Barraclough on their right loomed an enormous complex of old brick factory buildings behind a high chain-link fence. "What's that?" asked Barraclough.

"The map calls it the Gateway Metroport Industrial Center. It used to be one of the biggest steel mills in the world. I was here a couple of times in the early sixties, before it closed down. You couldn't breathe unless there was a strong west wind. It goes on like this for four or five miles." He stared through the high fence. "Looks like they're renting a couple of nooks and crannies of it to a few half-assed businesses now."

The radio crackled. "Unit One, this is Unit Two."

"Go ahead."

"We can't see her anymore."

Barraclough's head snapped to the right to stare at Farrell in intense concentration. "She must have made them."

Farrell spoke into the radio. "Is there any chance she just out-ran you?"

"No. We think she must have turned off on one of those little streets on the left."

"Then turn down the next one and circle—"

Barraclough snatched the radio out of Farrell's hand. "Nega-tive. Cancel that. She didn't turn left, she turned right, or we would have seen her go across three lanes ourselves. Go back to where you saw her and look for railroad tracks."

Farrell held on as Barraclough swung the Pathfinder around on the icy street. What had Barraclough seen? They had been bumping over old railroad tracks for a long time. "You're think-ing there's a way into the factory? But all the tracks lead smack into the fence."

"There has to be a line that goes in," said Barraclough. "They might have closed down the spurs that went to different parts of the plant, but to ship coal and ore in and steel out, there must be a regular railroad right-of-way. That doesn't go away just because something beside it stops making money. And they don't put a gate across it."

More than a mile back, Barraclough found the tracks. There was a functional-looking railroad-crossing light at a little rise just beyond a curve in the road. The big brick buildings on both sides of the boulevard would have obscured the view of her car just long enough for her to turn off her lights and coast up the tracks.

Barraclough turned the utility vehicle onto the railroad ties to straddle the tracks and slowly bumped along them. The tracks went only fifty yards into the dark shadow of the mill before they passed through a gap in the fence. "Here it is," said Barraclough. "She lives around here, remember? She's probably driven by here in daylight a hundred times." He wrenched the steering wheel to lurch off the tracks into the freight yard of the factory and waited until the black Dodge caught up.

Barraclough had already found her trail. The snow was clear and unmarked except for two deep parallel lines from a set of tires that ran deeper into the old steel mill. Barraclough trained his headlights on the tire tracks and sped up. He drove past a few small buildings in the complex that had new signs and recent paint on the doors, but as he went farther, immense brick buildings with dark windows loomed on both sides like the ruins of an abandoned city. He judged he had driven nearly a mile before he saw her car.

It was parked in the shadows on the lake side of a brick building, away from the distant lights of Fuhrmann Boulevard. Barraclough pulled to a stop when he was still a hundred feet away from it and let the Dodge pull up beside him. He said into the radio, "Watch the car and the doors of the building. We'll call when we need you." He handed the radio to Farrell and accepted the gear Farrell handed back: pistol, night-spotting scope, flashlight, nylon wrist restraints.

The two men stepped down from the Pathfinder and walked to Jane's car. Barraclough took off his glove to gauge the warmth of the hood of the car, then winked at Farrell happily. Then he studied the footprints leading from the driver's door. They led around the big building. Barraclough paused at the corner to draw his pistol, then quickly stepped beyond it.

He could see that the footprints led along the side of the building. He bent low to walk beside them, staying near the wall and keeping his head below the level of the windows. There were banks of thousands of little panes of glass along the side of the building, many of them broken and all of them opaque from at least thirty years of grime. The footprints led to a place where two of the panes had been hammered in and the frame had gone with them. "She must have heard us coming and gone in."

Barraclough looked ahead of him, but he could not see where the building ended. He stepped outward away from it to get a better view, then lifted the night scope to his eye, but he still could not see the end. The brick wall seemed to go on forever.

Farrell saw it too. "It's a big place. How do you want to work it?"

Barraclough peered cautiously through the broken window with the night scope, then pushed the switch to infrared. There was nothing nearby that gave off body heat. "We'll have to go in after her ourselves. We can't leave the cars unguarded, and if she can lose those two on an empty road, there's no telling what she'd do to them inside the dark building." He slipped the flashlight into one pocket, the wrist restraints into the other where he could reach them quickly. "When you see her, train your laser sight on her right away. She's not stupid; if she sees that bright red dot settle on her chest she'll forget about trying to outrun the bullet." He hoisted himself to the row of bricks that formed a sill below the missing windows, then squeezed himself inside.

When Farrell joined him inside the building, Barraclough drew his pistol again and turned on his night scope. They were in a huge, empty, unheated brick enclosure with a bare concrete floor, a fifty-foot ceiling, and a slight glow of stars above where panes of glass were missing. Barraclough turned his scope to the floor where Jane had entered. A few wet, snowy partial footprints led toward the other end of the cavernous room.

Barraclough walked beside the footprints, under an arch that was big enough for a truck to pass through, and beyond it into another high, empty room. To the right were a set of barn doors that must once have opened onto a loading dock.

They stalked through room after room. At each doorway they would pause, slip through the entrance low, and crouch a few yards apart around the corner. Barraclough would flick on his night scope, rapidly scan the space ahead for the shape of a woman, and only then venture to cross the open concrete floor. When they reached the end of the long building, they found a door open with snow just beginning to drift inside.

The footprints led to the door of another building. There was a half-rotted sheet of plywood on the ground that had once covered the empty upper panel of the door. Barraclough's heart was beating with excitement. They always made some mistake, and she had just made hers. She had gambled that she could drive into the enormous ruin of a factory, wait ten minutes, and then drive back up the river. Now she was alone on foot on a cold, snowy night. She was trying to hide in a complex that had been so thoroughly gutted that there wasn't anything to hide behind. She was running from two old cops who had been trapping fleeing suspects in dark buildings for half their lives. He would be able to see her in the scope as clearly as if she were in daylight, and she would be blind.

Even the physical discomfort Barraclough felt as he entered the next building made him more eager. The air was frigid. The brick walls offered shelter from the bitter wind, but there was a chill trapped in the big spaces, and the icy concrete seemed to send a shock up his shins at each step. The cold would be much harder on her because she was alone and afraid. At some point she was going to come to a door she couldn't open, and he would have her. It was possible he would have to keep her alive for a month or two while she gave him what she owed him. She was a hunter's dream: a woman who had made at least ten years of fugitives vanish. There must be dozens by now, most of them still hiding wherever she had put them. And what kind of person had enough money to pay for that kind of service? Drug dealers, money launderers, second-toughest gangsters, big-time embezzlers. She had taken Mary Perkins away from him, but she might easily have ten more like her. He grinned as he walked through the darkened building; no doubt about it, she was the girl of his dreams.

Farrell stopped at the next doorway and turned to him, but didn't say anything.

"What is it?" Barraclough whispered eagerly. "Did you hear something?"

"No," Farrell whispered apologetically. "But we've been at this for over an hour."

Barraclough glanced at his watch. It was true.

Farrell said, "I think it might help if we brought the two boys into this. We might want to have at least one of them waiting for her at the other end."

Barraclough clenched his teeth to stifle his annoyance. He didn't want to wait for people to move into position—he wanted to finish this himself now—but Farrell was right. She had already led them too far to have any hope of getting back to her car. She was heading for the far end of the factory. "Give me the radio."

He took the radio and pressed the TALK button. "Unit Two, this is Unit One." He listened to the faint crackle of static. He put the speaker against his ear but could detect no voice. "Come in, Unit Two." He looked at Farrell, letting a little of his impatience show.

Farrell said quickly, "It's got to be the buildings. There's a hell of a lot of brick and steel between them and us. Let me try it outside."

Farrell trotted to the next loading dock, slipped the bolt, and pushed the big wooden door aside so he could stand out in the open air. "Unit Two, this is Unit One. Come in." He listened to the static. "Unit Two, come in." In spite of the temperature, he felt a wave of heat begin at the back of his neck and wash down his spine. He knew his two trainees were probably in the car listening to a radio they had turned off by mistake. He walked back into the building and shook his head. "Nothing."

Barraclough's voice was quiet and cold. "Go back for them. I'll be up ahead somewhere."

Farrell handed Barraclough the radio, then set off to retrace his steps through the factory. After four steps, he broke into a run.

As he heard Farrell's steps receding behind him, Barraclough started into the next big room and turned on his night-vision scope. This building was different from the last. The big row of square enclosures built into the side wall must have been furnaces. The cement of the floor had holes at the edges of big rectangles where heavy machines had once been anchored, and overhead were networks of steel beams that must have held chain hoists, and brackets for vanished devices he could only imagine now. This place must have seemed like hell once, he thought—deafening noise, unbearable heat from the open-hearth furnaces, molten slag running into big buckets. He stepped close to the row of furnaces and shone his flashlight into each one as he passed it. He moved through room after room, seeing few relics, only traces that were less comprehensible than the stones of some ancient city dug out of the ground.

After half an hour the radio in Barraclough's coat pocket squawked and startled him. Farrell's voice said, "Unit One, this is Unit Two."

Barraclough crouched against the wall so the noise would not make him vulnerable and kept his eyes ahead of him on the portal to the next room. He pushed the button and said quietly, "Go ahead."

"I'm at the car," said Farrell. "The reason they didn't answer is that they're dead."

"How?"

"It looks like they left the motor running to keep warm. There's a hose running from their own exhaust pipe right back into the cab through the taillight. Looks like she cut the hose from under the Pathfinder."

Barraclough tried to sort out the implications. "Are all the cars still there? Hers too?"

"Yeah," said Farrell. "I don't know how she got all the way back here past us, but—"

Barraclough gripped the TALK button and shouted, "Then get out! She's still there!"

But Farrell had not released his button. Barraclough heard a swish of fabric as though Farrell were making a sudden movement, maybe whirling to see something. Whatever he saw made him voice an involuntary "Uh!"

Barraclough heard the report of the weapon over the radio. He had time to press his transmitter button and say "Farrell?" before the delayed reverberation reached his ears through the air. The sound was fainter this time, but without the speaker distortion he could tell it was the elongated blast of a shotgun.

Barraclough had already begun to put the radio into his pocket before he remembered there was nobody left to talk to. He hurled it into the darkness toward the corner of the big empty room. He was standing in a dark, icy labyrinth three thousand miles from home. The three men he had brought here with him were corpses. But the biggest change was what was standing between him and the cars. He didn't even know her real name, but he had thought he knew what she would do: she would run, and he would catch her.

He flicked on his flashlight and slowly began to walk away from the sound of the shotgun, his mind working feverishly. Where had the shotgun come from? She had not taken a shotgun off the body of either of the dead trainees, so she must have brought it with her. If she had, then she had known he was coming. This was not what he had expected at all.

Maybe she had not made a mistake and turned her car into the first place along the road that was big enough to hide it. It almost seemed as though she had been in this factory before. As Barraclough traced the logic backward, he began to feel more uneasy.

She had been shuffling credit cards and names for ten or twelve years. Why would she suddenly forget how it was done and take the chance of using accounts he might know about all the way to her own doorstep? Because that house in La Salle wasn't her own doorstep. He had not traced her to her hometown and right up to her house. She probably lived a thousand miles from here. He had followed her into an ambush—a killing ground.

Barraclough decided to run. The beam of his flashlight bobbed up and down wildly, making shadows that crouched in his path, then sprung upward to loom fifty feet tall. He had to remind himself over and over that there couldn't be anyone in front of him. What he had to worry about was behind him.

Was running the best thing to do? It was taking him farther away from the cars. But running made use of the only facts he could be sure of. He had heard the shotgun go off within a few feet of Farrell, so he knew where she was . . . no, he knew where she had been for the instant when she had pulled the trigger. His attempt to state it accurately invited doubts to creep into his mind, but he fought them off. She was half a mile behind him, he was sure. She had the shotgun in her hands, and she was walking through the dark line of empty rooms after him.

As he thought about her, a picture formed in his mind, and in the picture she was not walking. She had the shotgun in both hands across her chest, and she was running, taking long, loping strides. He increased his pace. The clapping of his boots echoed in the cavernous spaces and the rasp of his breath grew louder and louder. As he ran, he tried not to think about the shotgun. A double-aught load was twelve pellets, each the size of a .38 round. From across one of these big rooms they would hit in a pattern about twenty inches wide.

Barraclough calmed himself. All he had to do was keep her half a mile behind him and get out of this horrible place. As though a wish had been granted, his flashlight swept up and down the gray wooden surface of a door in the wall ahead of him. He dashed to it and tried the knob, but it spun in his hand without moving the catch. He pulled on it, but the door would not budge. He stepped back and ran his flashlight along the doorjamb. He could see a few puckered places in the wood where big nails had been driven in. He swept the flashlight's beam around him. The windows in this room were all twenty feet above him. When had that changed? Maybe the windows had been that way for the past half hour. He began to run back the way he had come. The windows in the next room were the same, and the room after that. But at the portal between the next two rooms he saw the doors of another loading dock.

Barraclough hurried to the doors, set his spotter scope on the floor, stuck the flashlight in his pocket, slipped the bolt, and tried to slide the door open. He strained against it, but it only wobbled a little on its track. He tried to remember: wasn't this what Farrell had done to open one of these doors? He turned on his flashlight again and ran it around the edges of the door until he spotted another bolt that went into the floor. He lifted it and pushed the door. When it slid open, he tried to feel happy, but the relief only reminded him how frightened he had been only seconds ago.

He stepped out onto the loading dock and jumped down into the snow. He felt a wrenching pain as his ankle turned under him and he fell across something hard and cold. He cursed himself. He had jumped onto railroad tracks. How could he have forgotten the railroad tracks? The loading docks didn't have flat paved surfaces for trucks; they were for loading steel onto freight cars.

Barraclough sat up and tentatively shifted some weight onto his ankle. It hurt, but he could tell it wasn't broken. He was grateful, glad to be alive. He wasn't going to be trapped; he could still make it. He slipped the pistol into his belt and walked to the left, toward the edge of the factory, the tall fence, and the street beyond. Then he saw Jane's car parked near the side of the next building. For an instant he struggled to fathom how he could have come out of the huge building right where he had started, but then understanding settled on him. She had not been running through the building at all. She had driven along the outside to wait for him here.

Barraclough hobbled toward the fence, gasping terror into his chest with each freezing breath. He threw himself against the high fence, clung to the links with both hands, and stepped up. He stretched his arm to clutch higher links, then tried to feel for a footing he could maintain with his injured ankle.

The blast of the shotgun slapped his left arm against the fence and deadened it. He was falling. His back slammed the ground hard and made him gulp air to reinflate his lungs. He tried to push himself up, but his mangled left arm would not respond, and he could see his dark, warm blood soaking into the snow. As he struggled to rise, it occurred to him that he had already heard the *snick-chuff* of the shotgun slide. "Stop!" he screamed. The weak, pleading sound of his own voice sickened him. He bent his legs under him, bobbed up, and turned to see her standing in the snow ten feet from him. She was only a dark, shadowy shape against the luminous snow. He waited for the roar of the shotgun, the splash of bright sparks, but they didn't come.

He gripped his injured arm with his right hand and pulled it painfully toward the center of his body. "Listen to me!" If he could just hide the right hand behind the left to get a grip on the pistol in his belt, he had a chance. "You need a way out of this as much as I do. The minute you helped your first felon to evade prosecution, you were meat on the hoof. Somebody—local cops, F.B.I., it doesn't matter who—was going to notice you and hunt you down." His fingers closed numbly on the pistol. "Without a powerful friend, you're going to be somebody's dinner." He swung the pistol upward.

The shotgun blast blew through his chest. His body toppled backward to rattle the links of the fence, then lay still. "But not yours," said Jane. She turned and walked back through the snow to her car, put the shotgun in the trunk, and drove along the side of the building toward the gap in the fence.

J udge Kramer awoke from his dream. The house was dark, but the moon shone through the big magnolia tree outside his window, so small patches of gray-blue light fell on the bedspread. Something was wrong.

He heard the little voice and remembered that he had heard it in his dream and tried to ignore it. But it was all right. It was just the boy.

He swung his feet to the floor and walked out of the bedroom and down the hall to the guest room. He reminded himself that this was perfectly normal. A child who had seen what this one had was going to have night terrors. Kramer rubbed his eyes and struggled to wake up. He was going to have to be wise and strong and reliable. That was what this child needed right now. Adults came when you cried out in the night, and they told you everything was all right. If it wasn't all right, they damned well made it all right.

He stepped into the boy's room and said, "It's all right. Here I am, Timmy." He had barely uttered it when he realized he was wrong. The bed was empty. He looked around him. The boy was gone.

Kramer ran to the landing in time to see the triangular slice of moonlight appear on the floor of the foyer. The front door had opened. As he hurried down the first few stairs, he saw her step into the moonlight. "It's just me, Judge," said Jane Whitefield.

"What are you doing here?"

"I've come for Timmy."

"No," he said. He was shaking his head, but he knew she could not see it. "There are procedures for this. The law provides for it. You can't just . . ."

He could feel, not see, Jane Whitefield's eyes on him. "What does the law provide?" she asked.

"When it's safe, Children's Services will find him a suitable foster home."

"It's never going to be safe," said Jane. "Even if all the money is gone, there will be people who think more might turn up or who know how to get more just by using his name. Barraclough had a lot of people working on these side cases for him. They're still out there." She took a step with Timmy.

"You should know I have a gun." The judge reached into the pocket of his robe.

"So have I," Jane said. "I didn't bring mine either." She turned, took Timmy's hand, and then the slice of moonlight disappeared.

It was after midnight when Carey McKinnon turned his car onto the long gravel drive that ran up behind his old stone house in Amherst and parked his car in the carriage house that had, at some point in his grandfather's time, started being called "the garage." He swung the two doors closed and put the padlock on the hasp, not because anyone had ever tried to steal anything here but because the wind was cold tonight and by morning it would be strong enough to blow the old doors off their hinges if he didn't secure them. He had heard on the car radio that there was going to be another in the series of heavy snowstorms that had blown in, one after another, from the west, and he could already feel the cold front moving in.

Carey walked up the drive toward his house, looking down at his feet and trying to step in the spots where the snow had not drifted. He reached his front steps and stood under the eaves, stamping the snow off his shoes as he stuck his key into the lock, when he heard a car door slam. He looked over his shoulder at the street.

There was a person—a woman—walking away from her car across his front yard: Jane.

He stepped across the lawn to meet her. "Hey, I know you!" he said. "What happened—did your flight get grounded?"

She smiled as they met, and he tried to get his arms around her, but the brown paper bag she was carrying was between them, so he snatched it away and put his arm around her waist. "No." She stood on her tiptoes to kiss his cheek. "I'm home."

They walked together to his front door and he opened it. "Why didn't you call me? I'd have met you at the airport."

"Great idea, Carey," Jane said. "Then tomorrow while you were at work I could walk back there in a blizzard and get my car."

"Oh," he said. "Well, there must be some way that normal people do these things. I know some. I'll ask."

He flicked on the light and they stepped into the little old-fashioned entry. He set the bag on the bench, hung his coat on a hook, slipped hers off her shoulders and hung it beside his, then took her into his arms. They kissed in a slow, gentle, leisurely way, and then Jane put her hands on the sides of his face, held him a few inches away, and looked into his eyes. "You waiting for the wind to close the door?"

He shrugged, went to close the door, then came back and picked up the grocery bag. "Bring your laundry?"

She took the bag and pulled out a bottle of champagne. "There was a power failure in the store, so I thought this was Tabasco sauce. I figured you might be able to use it."

"A common mistake, but I can't launch the ship in this weather. Maybe we can drink it or something."

She reached into the bag again and pulled out a bouquet of white roses.

He looked at her for a moment, puzzled. Finally he said, "Oh, you brought my roses back. Thanks. It was getting to be about time, but I didn't want to say anything." He took the roses and sniffed them. "Held up pretty well, didn't they?"

"Remarkably," Jane said, but she barely got it out because he scooped her up and started to carry her toward the staircase.

He took her up the stairs, set her gently on the big bed, and began by taking off her shoes. He proceeded to undress her slowly. When he had finished, he sank down on the bed with her. He said quietly, "I love you, Jane," and before she could answer, his lips were on hers, and then by the time she could have spoken and remembered what she had wanted to say, words seemed unnecessary.

Hours later, Carey McKinnon awoke in his dark bedroom and moved his arm to touch her. She was gone. He stood up and walked down the hall. He found her downstairs, sitting on the couch in his big, thick bathrobe, looking away from him to stare at the fireplace. She looked tiny, like a child. He could tell she had heard him. "Hi, Carey," she said.

"What are you doing, figuring out how you're going to redecorate when your regime comes into power?"

"No. Come sit with me."

He walked down the stairs and sat beside her. He saw that she was not smiling. "What's wrong?"

She leaned over and kissed him, then said, "I've been thinking about your offer."

"You look like you've made up your mind."

"I have," she said. "One year from tonight, the tenth of January, you can set the date. If you'll give me some notice, I'll be there with something borrowed and something blue. If not, I'll just be there."

He grinned, but then his eyes began to look troubled. "Why a year from now? I mean, I guess what I want to say is, 'I'm happy. Ecstatic. I love you.' But what is there about it that takes so long? It's not as though we don't know each other."

Jane turned to face him. "I'm going to tell you a story. At the end of it, you'll say that you understand."

"I will?" he asked. "Then the year is to see if I really do understand. So it's that kind of story."

"I'm going to tell you about my trip."

Epilogue

In the spring of the year, as they had forever, Seneca women met at Tonawanda one evening at dusk to sing the Ohgiwe, the Dance for the Dead. Spring was the time when the dead came back. There were no drums, no rattles or flutes or bells, only the sad, beautiful voices of the women.

In the center of the big longhouse-shaped room, there were six lead singers who knew the ancient songs of the Ohgiwe best and had melodious voices strong enough to last through the night. They would sing the burden, and the women who danced along the walls of the longhouse would answer in chorus. Tonight the lead group included two who were not among the usual singers. One was Jane Whitefield, who had not been to Ohgiwe in some years, and the other was Martha McCutcheon, senior mother of the Wolf Clan in Oklahoma. She had been the one to sponsor Sarah Cartman in open council—not the Sarah Cartman everyone had known since birth, but the new Sarah, the one who had been adopted with her son, Timmy, in accordance with ancient practice.

The new Sarah Cartman danced along the wall in the circle with the other Nundawaono women. Six months ago she had been Mary Perkins. Six years ago she had called herself something else—maybe Stoddard or Stafford or Comstock—but she had done nothing under any of those names that she wanted to remember, so she did not think of them tonight. Instead, for a moment she anxiously wondered if she would be home in time to pack Timmy's lunch box for school tomorrow, then remembered that tomorrow was Sunday. When she had been Mary Perkins, she had neglected to develop the habits of mind that she considered necessary to a good mother, so sometimes she overcompensated. Still, she was becoming more comfortable as Sarah Cartman, and after a time she had even begun to feel safe. By then she already had a name, a job, a household to run, and a son to raise. Doing had made her Sarah Cartman; being was an afterthought. Through the long night, as her feet became accustomed to the dance steps and she repeated the words in the unfamiliar language, she began to forget that she had not always known them.

There were nearly a hundred other Nundawaono women, old grandmothers and young girls barely out of puberty, who danced for the dead on this night. Some wore modest spring dresses, as Sarah did. Others wore the traditional tunic, skirt, leggings, and moccasins, beaded and embroidered with all of the flowers that grew on the back of the great turtle that was the Seneca world. They wore them because women were the keepers and the source of life, the force that fought endlessly against the Being that is Faceless.

There were guests among the dead tonight too, and there were those in the longhouse who could feel their presence. The women sang the Ohgiwe for all of them together and for each in his own right. Some sang for the first Sarah Cartman, who had died in an automobile accident this winter at a young age. There was one who sang for Timmy Cartman's first parents, and for the couple who had taken him in and raised him. And she sang for Mona and Dennis, the lovers who had died in the fall.

The women sang the Ohgiwe and danced together as the grandmothers had, for the brave and the unselfish, for the protectors. They sang until dawn, when the spirits of the dead were satisfied and returned to their rest, where they would not be tempted to disturb the dreams of the living.

About the Author

THOMAS PERRY was born in Tonawanda, New York, in 1947. He received a B.A. from Cornell University in 1969 and a Ph.D. in English literature from the University of Rochester in 1974. He has been a laborer, maintenance man, commercial fisherman, weapons mechanic, university administrator and teacher, and television writer and producer. His other novels include *The Butcher's Boy,* 1982 (awarded an "Edgar" from the Mystery Writers of America); *Metzger's Dog,* 1983; *Big Fish,* 1985; *Island,* 1988; *Sleeping Dogs,* 1992; and *Vanishing Act,* 1995. He lives in southern California with his wife and two daughters.

About the Type

This book was set in Sabon, a typeface designed by the well-known German typographer Jan Tschichold (1902–74). Sabon's design is based upon the original letter forms of Claude Garamond and was created specifically to be used for three sources: foundry type for hand composition, Linotype, and Monotype. Tschichold named his typeface for the famous Frankfurt typefounder Jacques Sabon, who died in 1580.

THE HUNTED

Also by Brian Haig

Secret Sanction
Mortal Allies
The Kingmaker
Private Sector
The President's Assassin
Man in the Middle

THE HUNTED

BRIAN HAIG

GRAND CENTRAL
PUBLISHING

New York   Boston

Copyright © 2009 by Brian Haig

Grand Central Publishing
Hachette Book Group
237 Park Avenue
New York, NY 10017

Visit our Web site at www.HachetteBookGroup.com.

Printed in the United States of America

First Edition: August 2009
10 9 8 7 6 5 4 3 2 1

Grand Central Publishing is a division of Hachette Book Group, Inc.
The Grand Central Publishing name and logo is a trademark of Hachette Book Group, Inc.

Library of Congress Cataloging-in-Publication Data
Haig, Brian.
    The hunted / Brian Haig. — 1st ed.
        p. cm.
    ISBN 978-0-446-19559-1
    I. Title.
    PS3608.A54H86 2009
    813'.6—dc22   2008027873

Book design by Charles Sutherland

For Lisa, Brian, Pat, Donnie, and Annie.
Dedicated to Elena.

Acknowledgments

There are always very many people to thank when a book is finally slapped on the shelves for sale. Certainly my family: Lisa, Brian, Paddie, Donnie, and Annie, who are always my inspiration, especially since the kids are all facing college, and I have to pay the bills. Also my parents, Al and Pat Haig—they are in every way absolutely wonderful parents, and I love them both.

And of course everybody at Grand Central Publishing, from top to bottom, a remarkable collection of talented people who couldn't be more helpful or exquisitely professional: Jamie Raab, the lovely, warmhearted publisher; my overwhelmingly gifted and understanding editor, Mitch Hoffman; the very forgiving pair of Mari Okuda and Roland Ottewell, who do the too-necessary patchwork of repairing the horribly flawed drafts I send and somehow, remarkably, make them readable; and Anne Twomey and George Cornell, who designed this stunning cover.

Most especially I want to thank my trusted agent and dear friend, Luke Janklow, and his family. Every writer should have an agent like Luke.

Last, I want to thank my friend and favorite writer, Nelson DeMille, who in addition to being—in my view—America's best and most entertaining author, does more to help and encourage aspiring writers get a start than anybody. When I first met Nelson he generously offered this great advice: "You will only write so many books, so do your best to make each one as perfect as you can."

He does, I try to, and I very much hope you enjoy this latest effort.

THE HUNTED

Book One:
The Heist

1

November 1991

In the final days of an empire that was wheezing and lurching toward death, the aide watched his boss stare out the window into the darkness. Time was running out. The fate of the entire nation hinged on the next move at this juncture; the entire planet, possibly.

Any minute, his boss was due to pop upstairs and see Mikhail Gorbachev to deliver either a path to salvation or a verdict of damnation.

But exactly what advice do you offer the doctor who has just poisoned his own patient?

Only three short miles away, he knew, Boris Yeltsin had just uncorked and was slurping down his third bottle of champagne. Totally looped, the man was getting even more utterly hammered. A celebration of some sort, or so it appeared, though the aide had not a clue what lay behind it. A KGB operative dressed as a waiter was hauling the hooch, keeping a watchful eye on ol' Boris and, between refills, calling in the latest updates.

After seventy years of struggle and turmoil, it all came down to this; the fate of the world's last great empire hinged on a ti-tanic struggle between two men—one ordained to go down as the most pathetically naïve general secretary ever; the other an obnoxious, loudmouthed lush.

Gorbachev was frustrated and humiliated, both men knew. He had inherited a kingdom founded on a catechism of bad ideas and constructed on a mountain of corpses. What was supposed to be a worker's paradise now looked with unrequited envy at third world countries and pondered how it had all gone so horribly wrong. How ironic.

Pitiful, really.

For all its fearsome power—the world's largest nuclear arsenal, the world's biggest army, colonies and "client" nations sprinkled willy-nilly around the globe—the homeland itself was a festering pile of human misery and material junk.

Two floors above them in his expansive office, Gorbachev was racking his brain, wondering how to coax the genie back into the bottle. Little late for that, they both knew. He had unleashed his woolly-headed liberalizing ideas—first, that asinine glasnost, then the slam dunk of them all, perestroika—thinking a blitzkrieg of truth and fresh ideas would stave off a collapse that seemed all but inevitable; inevitable to him, anyway. What was he thinking?

The history of the Soviet Union was so thoroughly shameful—so pockmarked with murders, genocide, treachery, corruption, egomania—it needed to rest on a mattress of lies to be even moderately palatable. Fear, flummery, and fairy tales—the three F's—those were the glue that held things together.

Now everything was coming apart at the seams: the Soviet republics were threatening to sprint from the union, the Eastern Bloc countries had already made tracks, and communism itself was teetering into a sad folly.

Way to go, Gorby.

On the streets below them a speaker with windmilling arms and megaphones for tonsils was working up a huge rabble that was growing rowdier and more rambunctious by the second. The bulletproof thickened windows smeared out his exact words; as if they needed to hear; as if they wanted to hear. Same thing street-corner preachers were howling and exhorting from Petersburg to Vladivostok: time for democracy; long past time for capitalism. Communism was an embarrassing failure that needed to be flushed down the toilet of history with all the other old faulty ideas. Just rally around Boris. Let's send Gorby and the last of his wrinkly old apparatchiks packing.

His boss cracked a wrinkled knuckle and asked softly, "So what do I tell Gorbachev?"

"Tell him he's an idiot. Tell him he ruined everything."

"He already knows that."

Then tell him to eat a bullet, Ivan Yutskoi wanted to say. Better yet, do us all a big favor, shove him out the window and have that spot-headed idiot produce a big red splat in the middle of Red Square. Future historians would adore that punctuation point.

Sergei Golitsin, deputy director of the KGB, glowered and cracked another knuckle. He cared less for what this idiot thought. "Tell me you've finally found where Yeltsin's money's coming from."

"Okay. We have."

"About time. Where?"

"It's a little hard to believe."

"I'll believe anything these days. Try me."

"Alex Konevitch."

The deputy director gave him a mean look. After a full year of shrugged shoulders, wasted effort, and lame excuses, the triumphant tone in his aide's voice annoyed him. "And am I supposed to know this name?" he snapped.

"Well, no . . . you're not . . . really."

"Then tell me about . . . what's this name?"

"Alex Konevitch." Yutskoi stuffed his nose into the thick folder, shuffled a few papers, and withdrew and fixated on one typed sheet. "Young. Only twenty-two. Born and raised in an obscure village in the Ural Mountains you've never heard of. Both parents are educators, mother dead, father formerly the head of a small, unimportant college. Alex was a physics student at Moscow University."

Yutskoi paused for the reaction he knew was coming. "Only twenty two," his boss commented with a furious scowl. "He ran circles around you idiots."

"I've got photographs," said Yutskoi, ignoring that outburst. He withdrew a few blown-up eight-by-ten color photos from his thick file and splayed them like a deck of cards before his boss. Golitsin walked across the room, bent forward, adjusted his rimless glasses, and squinted.

The shots were taken, close up, by a breathtakingly attractive female agent who had entered Konevitch's office only the day before on the pretext of looking for a job. Olga's specialty was honeypot operations, the luring of victims into the sack for entrapment or the value of their pillow talk. She could do shy Japanese schoolgirls, a kittenish vixen, the frosty teacher in need of a role reversal, a doctor, a nurse, a wild cowgirl—whatever men lusted after in their most flamboyant yearnings, Olga could be it, and then some.

Olga had never been turned down. Not once, ever.

A top-to-bottom white blonde, she had gone in attired in an aggressively short skirt, low-cut blouse—not too low, though—and braless. Olga had pitch-perfect intuition about these things: no reason to doubt her instincts now. Demure, not slutty, she had artfully suggested. A few tactful hints, but sledgehammers were to be avoided.

Alex Konevitch was a successful businessman, after all; office games were the play of the day.

A miniature broadcasting device had been hidden in her purse, and every chance she had she snapped pictures of him with the miniature camera concealed inside her bracelet. Yutskoi reached into his folder and withdrew a tape recorder. The cassette was preloaded and ready to roll. "Olga," he mentioned casually, requiring no further introduction. "She was instructed merely to get a job and learn more about him. If something else developed, well, all the better."

Golitsin jerked his head in approval, and Yutskoi set the device down on the desk and pushed play.

Golitsin craned forward and strained to hear every word, every nuance.

First came the sounds of Alex Konevitch's homely middle-aged secretary ushering Olga into his office, followed by the usual nice-to-meet-you, nice-to-meet-you-too claptrap before the game began.

Very businesslike, Konevitch: "Why do you want to work here?"

Olga: "Who wouldn't? The old system's rotten to its core and ready to collapse. The corpse just hasn't yet recognized it's dead. We all know that. This is the best of the new. I'll learn a lot."

"Previous work experience?"

"Secretarial and statistical work, mostly. There were the two years I spent working at the State Transportation Bureau, helping estimate how many bus axles we would need next year. Bus axles? . . . Can you believe it? I nearly died of boredom. Then the Farm Statistics Bureau, where I'm stuck now. Do you know what it's like spending a whole month trying to project the demand for imported kumquats?"

"I can't imagine."

"Don't even try." She laughed and he joined her.

Back to business, Konevitch: "Okay, now why should I want you?"

A long and interesting pause. Stupid question—open your eyes, Alex, and use a little imagination.

Olga, sounding perfectly earnest: "I type eighty words a minute, take dictation, have good phone manners, and am very, very loyal to my boss."

Another interesting pause.

Then, as if Konevitch missed the point: "I have a very capable secretary already."

"Not like me, you don't."

"Meaning what?"

"I will make you very happy."

Apparently not, because Konevitch asked quite seriously, "What do you know about finance?"

"Not much. But I'm a fast study."

"Do you have a university degree?"

"No, and neither do you."

Another pause, this one long and unfortunate.

Konevitch, in a suddenly wary voice: "How do you know that?"

"I . . . your receptionist . . ." Long pause, then with uncharacteristic hesitance, "Yes, I believe she mentioned it."

"He. His name is Dmetri."

"All right . . . he. I misspoke. Who cares who told me?"

Konevitch, sounding surprisingly blasé: "What gave you the idea I'm looking to hire?"

"Maybe you're not. I'm fishing. My mother is desperately ill. Throat and lung cancer. Soviet medicine will kill her, and I need money for private treatments. Her life depends on it."

Nice touch, Yutskoi thought, admiring Olga's spontaneous shift of tack. Among the few details they *had* gleaned about Alex Konevitch was that his mother had passed away, at the young age of thirty-two, of bone cancer in a state sanitarium. Like everything in this country, Soviet medicine was dreadful. Yutskoi pictured Mrs. Konevitch in a lumpy bed with filthy sheets, writhing and screaming as her bone sores oozed and burned and her young son looked on in helpless agony.

Surely that pathetic memory rushed into Alex's head as he considered this poor girl and her ailing mother. Have a heart, Alex; you have the power to save her mama from an excruciating, all but certain death. She'll twitch and suffer and cough her lungs out, and it will be all your fault.

"I'm sorry, I don't think you'll fit in."

She had been instructed to get the job, whatever it took, and she had given it her best shot and then some. Olga's perfect record was in ruins.

Yutskoi slid forward in his seat and flipped off the recorder. A low grunt escaped Golitsin's lips, part disappointment, part awe. They leaned forward together and studied with greater intensity the top photograph of Alex Konevitch taken by Olga. The face in the photo was lean, dark-haired and dark-eyed, handsome but slightly babyfaced, and he was smiling, though it seemed distant and distinctly forced.

Nobody had to coerce a smile when Olga was in the room. Nobody. Golitsin growled, "Maybe you should've sent in a cute boy instead."

"No evidence of that," his aide countered. "We interviewed some of his former college classmates. He likes the ladies. Nothing against one-night stands, either."

"Maybe he subsequently experienced an industrial accident. Maybe he was castrated," Golitsin suggested, which really was the one explanation that made the most sense.

Or maybe he suspected Olga.

"Look at him, dressed like an American yuppie," Golitsin snorted, thumping a derisive finger on a picture. It was true, Konevitch looked anything but Russian in his tan slacks and light blue, obviously imported cotton button-down dress shirt, without tie, and with his sleeves rolled up to the elbows. The picture was grainy and slightly off-center. He looked, though, like he just stepped out of one of those American catalogues: a young spoiled prototypical capitalist in the making. Golitsin instantly hated him.

He had been followed around the clock for the past three days. The observers were thoroughly impressed. A working animal, the trackers characterized him, plainly exhausted from trying to keep up with his pace. The man put in hundred-hour workweeks without pause. He seemed to sprint through every minute of it.

Broad-shouldered, with a flat stomach, he obviously worked hard to stay in tip-top shape. Olga had learned from the receptionist that he had a black belt, third degree, in some obscure Asian killing art. He did an hour of heavy conditioning in the gym every day. Before work, too. Since he arrived in the office at six sharp and usually kicked off after midnight, sleep was not a priority. Olga had also remarked on his height, about six and a half feet, that she found him ridiculously sexy, and for once, the target was one *she* would enjoy boinking.

Yutskoi quickly handed his boss a brief fact sheet that summarized everything known to date about Alex Konevitch. Not much.

"So he's smart," Golitsin said with a scowl after a cursory glance. That was all the paucity of information seemed to show.

"Very smart. Moscow University, physics major. Second highest score in the country his year on the university entrance exam."

Alex had been uncovered only three days before, and so far only a sketchy bureaucratic background check had been possible. They would dig deeper and learn more later. A lot more.

But Moscow University was for the elite of the elite, and the best of those were bunched and prodded into the hard sciences, mathematics, chemistry, or physics. In the worker's paradise, books, poetry, and art were useless tripe and frowned upon, barely worth wasting an ounce of IQ over. The real eggheads were drafted for more socially progressive purposes, like designing bigger atomic warheads and longer-range, more accurate missiles.

Golitsin backed away from the photo and moved to the window. He was rotund with short squatty legs and a massive bulge under a recessed chin that looked like he'd swallowed a million flies. He had a bald, glistening head and dark eyes that bulged whenever he was angry, which happened to be most of the time. "And where has Konevitch been getting all this money from?" he asked.

"Would you care to guess?"

"Okay, the CIA? The Americans always use money."

Yutskoi shook his head.

Another knuckle cracked. "Stop wasting my time."

"Right, well, it's his. All of it."

Golitsin's thick eyebrows shot up. "Tell me about that."

"Turned out he was already in our files. In 1986, Konevitch was caught running a private construction company out of his university dorm room. Quite remarkable. He employed six architects and over a hundred workers of assorted skills."

"That would be impossible to hide, a criminal operation of such size and scale," the general noted, accurately it turned out.

"You're right," his aide confirmed. "As usual, somebody snitched. A jealous classmate."

"So this Konevitch was always a greedy criminal deviant."

"So it seems. We reported this to the dean at Moscow University, with the usual directive that the capitalist thief Konevitch be marched across a stage in front of his fellow students, disgraced, and immediately booted out."

"Of course."

"Turns out we did him a big favor. Konevitch dove full-time into construction work, expanded his workforce, and spread his projects all over Moscow. People are willing to pay under the table for quality, and Konevitch established a reputation for reliability and value. Word spread, and customers lined up at his door. When perestroika and free-market reforms were put in place, he cleaned up."

"From construction work?"

"That was only the start. Do you know what arbitrage is?"

"No, tell me."

"Well . . . it's a tool capitalists employ. When there are price differences for similar goods, an arbitrager can buy low, sell it all off at a higher price, and pocket the difference. Like gambling, he more or less bets on the margins in between. Konevitch's work gave him intimate familiarity with the market for construction materials, so this was the sector he first concentrated in."

"And this is . . . successful?"

"Like you wouldn't believe. A price vacuum was created when Gorbachev encouraged free-market economics. The perfect condition for an arbitrager, and Konevitch swooped in. There's a lot of construction and no pricing mechanism for anything."

"Okay."

That okay aside, Yutskoi suspected this was going over his boss's head. "Say, for example, a factory manager in Moscow prices a ton of steel nails at a thousand rubles. A different factory manager in Irkutsk might charge ten thousand rubles. They were all pulling numbers out of thin air. Nobody had a clue what a nail was worth."

"And our friend would buy the cheaper nails?" Golitsin suggested, maybe getting it after all.

"Yes, like that. By the truckload. He would pay one thousand rubles for a ton in Moscow, find a buyer in Irkutsk willing to pay five thousand, then pocket the difference."

Golitsin scrunched his face with disgust. "So this is about nails?" He snorted.

"Nails, precut timber, steel beams, wall board, concrete, roofing tiles, heavy construction equipment . . . he gets a piece of everything. A big piece. His business swelled from piddling to gigantic in nothing flat."

Sergei Golitsin had spent thirty years in the KGB, but not one of those outside the Soviet empire and the impoverishing embrace of communism. Domestic security was his bread and butter, an entire career spent crushing and torturing his fellow citizens. He had barely a clue what arbitrage was, didn't really care to know, but he nodded anyway and concluded, "So the arbitrager is a cheat."

"That's a way of looking at it."

"He produces nothing."

"You're right, absolutely nothing."

"He sucks the cream from other people's sweat and labor. A big fat leech."

"Essentially, he exploits an opening in a free-market system. It's a common practice in the West. Highly regarded, even. Nobody on Wall Street ever produced a thing. Most of the richest people in America couldn't build a wheel, much less run a factory if their lives depended on it."

Golitsin still wasn't sure how it worked, but he was damned sure he didn't like it. He asked, "And how much has he . . . this Konevitch character . . . how much has he given Yeltsin?"

"Who knows? A lot. In American currency, maybe ten million, maybe twenty million dollars."

"He had that much?"

"And then some. Perhaps fifty million dollars altogether. But this is merely a rough estimate on our part. Could be more."

Golitsin stared at Yutskoi in disbelief. "You're saying at twenty-two, he's the richest man in the Soviet Union."

"No, probably not. A lot of people are making a ton of money right now." Yutskoi looked down and toyed with his fingers a moment. "It would be fair to say, though, he's in the top ten."

The two men stared down at their shoes and shared the same depressing thought neither felt the slightest desire to verbalize. If communism went up in flames, their beloved KGB would be the first thing tossed onto the bonfire. In a vast nation with more than forty languages and dialects, and nearly as many different ethnic groups, there was only one unifying factor, one common thread—nearly every citizen in the Soviet Union had been scorched by their bureau in one way or another. Not directly, perhaps. But somebody dear, or at least close: grandfathers purged by Stalin; fathers who had disappeared and rotted in the camps under Brezhnev; aunts and uncles brought in for a little rough questioning under Andropov. Something. Nearly every family tree had at least one branch crippled or lopped off by the boys from the Lubyanka. The list of grudges was endless and bitter.

Yutskoi was tempted to smile at his boss and say: I hope it all does fall apart. Five years being your bootlicker, I've hated every minute of it. You'll be totally screwed, you nasty old relic.

Golitsin knew exactly what the younger man was thinking, and was ready to reply: You're a replaceable, third-rate lackey today, and you'll be a starving lackey tomorrow. Only in this system could a suck-up loser like you survive. The only thing you're good at is plucking fingernails from helpless victims. And you're not even that good at that.

Yutskoi: I'm young and frisky; I'll adapt. You're a starched lizard, a wrinkled old toad, an icy anachronism. Your own grandchildren fill their diapers at the sight of you. I'll hire you to shine my shoes.

Golitsin: I cheated and backstabbed and ass-kissed my way up to three-star general in this system, and I'll find a way in the next one, whatever that turns out to be. You, on the other hand, will always be a suck-up loser.

"Why?" asked Golitsin. As in, why would Alex Konevitch give Yeltsin that much money?

"Revenge could be a factor, I suppose."

"To get back at the system that tried to ruin him. How pedestrian."

"But, I think," Yutskoi continued, trying to look thoughtful, "mostly influence. If the union disintegrates, Yeltsin will wind up president of the newly independent Russia. He'll owe this guy a boatload of favors. A lot of state enterprises are going to be privatized and put on the auction block. Konevitch will have his pick— oil, gas, airlines, banks, car companies—whatever his greedy heart desires. He could end up as rich as Bill Gates. Probably richer."

Golitsin leaned back and stared up at the ceiling. It was too horrible to contemplate. Seventy years of blood, strain, and sweat was about to be ladled out, first come, first served—the biggest estate sale the world had ever witnessed. The carcass of the world's largest empire carved up and bitterly fought over. The winners would end up rich beyond all imagination. What an ugly, chaotic scramble that was going to be.

"So why didn't we find out about this Alex Konevitch sooner?" Golitsin snapped. Good question. When, three years before, Boris Yeltsin first began openly shooting the bird at Gorbachev and the Communist Party, the KGB hadn't worried overly much. Yeltsin was back then just another windbag malcontent: enough of those around to be sure.

But Yeltsin was a whiner with a big difference; he had once been a Politburo member, so he understood firsthand exactly how decrepit, dim-witted, incompetent, and scared the old boys at the top were.

That alone made him more dangerous than the typical blowhard.

And when he announced he was running for the presidency of Russia—the largest, most powerful republic in the union—the KGB instantly changed its mind and decided to take him dreadfully seriously indeed.

His offices and home were watched by an elite squad of nosy agents 24/7. His phones were tapped, his offices and home stuffed with enough bugs and listening gadgets to hear a fly fart. Several agents insinuated themselves inside his campaign organization and kept the boys at the center up to date on every scrap and rumor they overheard. Anybody who entered or left Yeltsin's offices was shadowed and, later, approached by a team of thugs who looked fierce and talked even fiercer. Give Boris a single ruble, they were warned, and you'll win the national lotto—a one-way ticket to the most barren, isolated, ice-laden camp in Siberia.

Concern, not worry, was the prevailing mood among the big boys in the KGB. This was their game. After seventy years of undermining democracy around the world, they knew exactly how to squeeze and strangle Yeltsin. An election takes money, lots of it; cash for travel and aides and people to carry and spread the message across the bulging, diverse breadth of a nation nearly three times the size of America.

Boris wasn't getting a ruble. Not a single ruble. He would rail and flail to his heart's content in empty halls and be roundly ignored. After being thoroughly shellacked in the polls, he would crawl under a rock and drink himself into the grave. So long, Boris, you idiot.

It was the inside boys who first raised the alarm. Hard cash was being ladled out by the fistful to campaign employees, to travel agencies, to advertisers, to political organizers. The conclusion was disquieting and inescapable: somewhere in the shadows a white knight was shoveling money at Yeltsin, gobs of it. Boris was spending a fortune flying across Russia in a rented jet, staying in high-class hotels, and to be taken more seriously, he had even traveled overseas to America, to introduce himself to the American president; Gorby was forced to call in a big favor, but he got Boris stiffed by a low-level White House flunky before he got within sniffing distance of the Oval Office. Boris's liquor bills alone were staggering.

Millions were being spent, tens of millions. Where was the mysterious cash coming from?

A task force was hastily formed, experts in finance and banking who peeked and prodded under all the usual rocks.

Nothing.

A team of computer forensics experts burgled Boris's campaign offices and combed the deepest crevices of every hard drive.

Not a trace.

Long, raucous meetings were held about what to do, with the usual backbiting, finger-pointing, and evasion of responsibility. This sneaky white knight, whoever he was, knew how to hide his fingerprints. Whatever he was doing to evade their most advanced techniques of snooping and detection had to be enormously clever. That level of sophistication raised interesting questions and dark misgivings. After much heated discussion, inevitably the preponderance of suspicion fell on foreign intelligence agencies. Surveillance of selected foreign embassies and known intelligence operatives was kicked up a notch and the squad of watchers increased threefold. Most of the foreign embassies were wired for sound anyway. And after seventy years of foreign spies lurking and sneaking around its capital, the KGB had a tight grip on every drop site and clandestine meeting place in Moscow.

More nada.

As Yeltsin's poll numbers climbed, frustration grew. The KGB was averse to mysteries—unsolved too long they turned into career problems. So the KGB chief of residency in Washington was ordered to kick the tires of his vast web of moles, leakers, and traitors in the CIA, DIA, FBI, NSA, and any other alphabet-soup agency he had his devious fingers in. Money, cash, lucre—that was America's preferred weapon. And even if America wasn't the culprit, the CIA or NSA, with their massive, sophisticated arsenals of electronic snoops, probably knew who was.

More nada, nada, nada. More wasted time, more wasted effort, more millions of dollars flooding out of nowhere, with more supporters flocking to Yeltsin's banner.

Yutskoi observed, "Actually, it's a miracle we found out at all. Konevitch is very, very clever."

"How clever?"

"In the private construction business, nearly everything's done in cash. And nearly all of it under the table. Compounding matters, right now, we're a mix of two economies: communist and free-market. The free-market guys know we don't have a good handle on them. They're inventing all kinds of fancy new games we don't know how to play yet. It's—"

"And what game did he play?" Golitsin interrupted in a nasty tone, tired of excuses.

"Everything was done offshore. It was smuggled out in cash, laundered under phony names at Caribbean banks, and from there turned electronic. He moved it around through a lot of banks—Swiss, African, American—divided it up, brought it back together, and just kept it moving until it became untraceable and impossible to follow."

"And how did he hand it over to Yeltsin's people?"

"That's the beauty of it. Not a single ruble ever touched the Soviet banking system. That's why we never saw it." He smiled and tried to appear confident. "What we now hypothesize was that he smuggled it back in as cash and handed it over in large suitcases." The truth was, they still had no idea, though he wasn't about to confess to that.

"Then who helped him?" Golitsin immediately barked, with a sizzling stare. Another good, unanswerable question. Soviet citizens knew zilch about international banking, money laundering, electronic transactions, or how to elude detection. The Soviet banking system was backward and shockingly unsophisticated. Besides, nobody had enough money to dream of getting fancy.

Or almost nobody—the Mafiya had money by the boatload. And they were masterminds at financial shenanigans; they had tried and perfected all kinds of underhanded tricks and scams. In the most oppressive state on earth, their survival depended on keeping their cash invisible. Golitsin waved a finger at his aide's folder. "Any evidence of that?"

"None. Not yet, anyway. It doesn't mean their crooked fingers aren't in it, just that we haven't found it."

"Keep looking. It has to be there."

After a moment, and totally out of the blue, Yutskoi mentioned, "I read a term paper he wrote as a freshman, something to do with Einstein's theory of relativity."

His boss had moved back to the window, restlessly watching the loud, angry crowd down on the street. Only a few years before the whole lot would already be in windowless wagons, trembling with fear on their way to Dzerzhinsky Square. They'd be worked over for a while, then shipped off to a uranium mine in the Urals where their hair and teeth would fall out.

The old days: he missed them already.

Yutskoi interrupted the pleasant reverie. "At least I *tried* to read his paper, I should say. I barely understood a word," he mumbled. "And all those complicated equations . . ." He trailed off, sounding a little stunned.

"What about it?" Golitsin asked absently. The crowd below was now dancing and chanting and growing larger by the minute. He felt weary.

"I sent it off to the director of the thermonuclear laboratory at the Kurchatov Institute. He said it was one of the most brilliant treatises he had read in years. Wanted to get it published in a few very prestigious international journals. You know, show the international community Soviet science still has what it takes. When I told him an eighteen-year-old college sophomore wrote it, he called me a liar."

His boss glanced back over his shoulder. "You already told me he's smart."

"I know I did. Now I'm saying he's more than smart."

They stared at each other a moment. Golitsin said, "He's only twenty-two."

"Yes, and that's the whole point. He's not hamstrung by old ideas. Nor has he lived long enough to have his brains and ambitions squeezed into radish pulp like everybody over thirty in this country."

Lost on neither of them was the ugly irony that they and their thuggish organ had done that squeezing. The average Russian could barely haul himself out of bed in the morning. The only social superlatives their nation boasted were the world's highest rate of alcoholism and the shortest life span of any developed nation. What a fitting tribute.

Yutskoi cleared his throat and asked, "So what will you advise Gorbachev?" He began stuffing documents and photos back into his expandable file.

Golitsin acted preoccupied and pretended he didn't hear that question. Yutskoi was an inveterate snoop and world-class gossip; if he let the cat out of the bag now, the news would be roaring around Moscow by midnight. Then again, Golitsin thought, so what? This news was too big to contain anyway. One way or another, it would be on the tip of every tongue in the world by morning. What difference would a few hours make?

He moved away from the window and ambled back in the direction of his aide. "On Gorbachev's desk is a document abolishing the Soviet Union. That jerk Yeltsin had the Congress vote on it this afternoon."

"And it passed?"

"By a landslide. If Gorbachev signs it, the Soviet Union is toast. History. Kaput."

"And if he doesn't?" asked Yutskoi, fully enlightened now about the cause of Yeltsin's drunken celebration that night: this was bound to be a bender of historic proportions. His tenders would have to pour Boris into bed. "What then?" he asked.

"What do you think will happen, idiot? We'll disband the mutinous Congress and crack down." He pointed a crooked, veiny finger through the window in the direction of the unruly crowd below. "We'll collect a few million malcontents and dissidents. Throw a million or so into the gulags. Shoot or hang a hundred or two hundred thousand to get everybody's attention."

"Won't that be fun," the aide blurted.

Golitsin shrugged. "Leave that file on Konevitch. I'll want to study him further."

Yutskoi stood and started to leave when he felt the old man's grip on his arm. "And keep me informed of what you learn about Konevitch. Spare no resources. I want to know *everything* about this young wunderkind. Everything."

2

The first team picked him up the moment he and his wife raced out the metal gate of their housing compound and stepped on the gas toward Sheremetyevo Airport. As usual, whenever the couple traveled around Moscow, a car with flashing blue lights rode in front, the shiny black armored Mercedes sedan was tucked securely in the middle, and a third car filled with heavily armed guards brought up the rear.

They followed at a discreet distance in a beaten-up rusted Lada sedan that blended in wonderfully, since it looked like all the other wretched junkheaps roaring around the streets of Moscow.

A totally excessive precaution, really. The plane tickets for the couple had been booked electronically; they knew the flight number, the departure time, his and her seat numbers, where they were going, and how long they planned to stay.

Why he was going wasn't in their briefing; nor did it matter, nor did they care. They knew why they were following him.

That's what mattered; all that mattered.

He and the Mrs. were booked in first-class side-by-side seats, and were picked up by a fresh team the instant they cleared customs and stepped onto the plane. Within moments after falling into their plush reclining seats, they ordered two flutes of bubbly and held hands as they sipped and chatted. A lovely couple, the second trail team agreed.

This new team, one male, one female, was positioned ten rows back, squished into cramped economy seats selected for the excellent view it gave them of their target. Nobody in first class ever glanced back at the deprived unfortunates in cattle class. Detection really wasn't an issue, but they worried about it anyway, and took every precaution possible. They munched on dried-out prunes, sipped bottled water, stayed quiet, and watched.

Another precaution that was totally useless, really. Wasn't like their targets could escape, flying twenty thousand feet above the earth, racing along at five hundred miles per hour.

Besides, a third team, much larger, about eight or ten people, would be in position an hour before landing at Ferihegy Airport outside Budapest.

Tedious work, but the watchers were professionals and never relaxed. They patiently spent their time hoarding mental notes that might come in handy later. Despite all the careful planning, rehearsals, and precautions, you never knew.

He, Alex Konevitch, was dressed in a superbly cut two-piece blue wool suit, obviously imported, probably from England, and just as obviously expensive. She, his wife, Elena, wore a lovely black wool pantsuit, also superbly tailored and definitely more expensive than his. From one of those faggy, la-di-da European design houses, they guessed, but the his-and-hers fancy rags were a big tactical mistake on their part. Russians and East Europeans in general are notoriously awful dressers and it set the couple apart.

After studying countless photographs of him, they agreed his likeness was a perfect match; he would be impossible to lose or misplace. His unusual height also worked heavily in their favor; even in the densest crowd, he would stick out.

No pictures of her were included in their file—a sloppy oversight in their professional judgment. What if the couple split up? What if they took separate cabs, he to his business meeting, and she maybe to a local plaza for a little noodling through stores?

They therefore focused mostly on her, collecting useful mental notes of her appearance, her distinguishing features. About his age, they estimated—possibly twenty-two, more likely twenty-four—though vastly shorter than him. Shoulder-length blonde hair, casually brushed, light on the makeup, and she really didn't need any, they both agreed. Delicious blue eyes, large, innocently doe-like, with a slightly upturned nose, and nice figure, but a little on the skinny side, in their view. All in all, though, a sweet number, very pretty, very sexy—and best of all, very difficult to miss.

They had been told little about her. Perhaps because little was known or maybe because her background was irrelevant. Why did they care?

She was with him.

That was the key.

Thirty minutes into the flight, he extended his lounger chair, unbuttoned his collar, loosened his tie, then dozed off. She handed the stewardess a few American dollars, plugged in her earphones, and intently watched a subtitled American action movie about an airplane hijacking, of all things.

He awoke from the siesta an hour later, refreshed, ready to dig in. He turned down an offer for a meal, withdrew a thick ream of papers from his briefcase, and got down to work. The file said he was a workaholic, driven, focused, and greedy. Looked about right.

But somewhere on this flight, they were almost certain, lurked a bodyguard. Possibly two, but no more than two: of this they were nearly certain. Alex Konevitch's life was in perpetual danger in Moscow, where it was open season on bankers, entrepreneurs, and rich businessmen. Nearly seven hundred had been whacked, bombed, or kidnapped that year alone, and there were still four months to go.

But the Wild East was behind him now; or so he believed. He would relax his precautions, as he always did when he left Mother Russia in the dust. And besides, Alex Konevitch, they had been confidently informed by their employer, regarded large bodyguard detachments as distasteful, ostentatious, and worse—bad for business. A large flock of elephant-necked thugs tended to up-set the Western investors and corporate types he dealt with.

But somewhere on this flight, they were quite sure, a body-guard or bodyguards were seated, like them, calm and unobtru-sive, waiting and watching. They held out little hope of detecting them, at least during the flight; these boys came from a well-heeled foreign private outfit with a first-class reputation, mostly former intelligence and police types who got paid big bucks not to make stupid mistakes. But the dismal odds aside, they were ordered to give it their best shot anyway; maybe they'd catch a lucky break. They agreed beforehand to look for anybody staring a little too possessively at Alex and his pretty little Mrs.

So the couple traded turns making idle passes through the cabin, trolling back and forth, mostly to the toilets. There were a few young men with tough faces and thick, muscular builds, but that seemed abnormally conspicuous for an elite security firm that loudly advertised its discreetness and invisibility.

At least the bodyguards wouldn't be armed; they were sure of this. Smuggling a weapon through a Russian airport was absurdly difficult. And detection would cause a public mess, the last thing a prestigious, supposedly ethical firm needed or wanted. No, they wouldn't be that stupid.

Besides, why risk getting caught when a better alternative was available?

Far easier to have somebody meet them in Budapest and dis-creetly hand over the heavy artillery.

On August 19, 1991, the old boys had their last desperate fling at preserving an empire hanging by its fingernails. Gorby, who had wrought so much damage with his flailing attempts at reform, was vacationing at his Black Sea resort when a clutch of rough-looking KGB officers stormed the building and took him hostage. In Moscow, a cabal including his chief of staff, vice president, prime minister, minister of defense, and KGB chairman promptly seized the organs of government.

A few thousand troops were rushed to the capital, the state television stations were seized, and water reservoirs secured; heavily armed guards were posted in front of food distribution centers to ensure a stranglehold on the city population. Tanks were littered at strategic intersections around the government section of the city—the usual signs of a beerhall putsch in progress.

Next, the cabal convened a hasty televised press conference to introduce themselves as the saviors of communism and the union. It was a disaster. They were wrinkled, sclerotic old men, unpleasant, nasty, and afraid. And it showed. Their hands trembled, their voices quivered and shook, no facial expression registered above a fierce scowl.

Never before had they smiled at their people: why start now?

Worst of all, they appeared disorganized, feeble, nervous, and ancient—as impressions go, at that precarious, decisive moment, the wrong one to convey to a fractious, anxious nation.

To say it was a glorious gift to Boris Yeltsin, a born opportunist and addicted rabble-rouser, would be an understatement. He rallied a band of fellow flamethrowers and issued a call for all Russians to join together and battle for their freedom. A large, unruly mob flocked to the Russian Congress building, heckling and chanting and daring the men who led the coup to do something about them. The cabal had been supremely confident their good citizens would respond in the best Soviet tradition—like scared, obedient sheep. The combative show of opposition caught the old boys totally by surprise.

Half argued strenuously to slaughter the whole bunch and hang their bodies from lampposts. A fine example, a paternal warning and long overdue, too. That wet noodle Gorby had been a sorry mollycoddler. The nation had grown soft and spoiled, they insisted; a good massacre was exactly the paternal medicine needed to whip it back in shape. The more dead wimps the better.

The other half wondered if a bloody spectacle might incite a larger rebellion. They weren't morally opposed by any means. In Lenin's hallowed words, as one of them kept repeating, as if anybody needed to hear it, omelets required broken eggs. But the nation had grown a little moody toward tyrants, they cautioned.

The wrong move at this brittle time and they, too, might end up
swinging on lampposts. Ignore the mob, they argued; in a day or
two, at the outside, the crowd would grow bored and hungry and
melt into the night.

Agreement proved impossible. Kill them or ignore them? Stomp
them like rodents or wait them out? The old men were cleanly
divided in their opinions, so they sat and squabbled in their gilded
Kremlin offices, brawling and cursing one another, drinking
heavily, collectively overwhelmed by the power they had stolen.

For two sleepless days the world held its breath and watched.
Boris's protestors turned rowdier and more daring by the hour.
They constructed signs. They howled protest chants and hurled
nasty taunts at the security guards sent to control them. They
erected camps, stockpiled food, heckled and sang, and prepared
to stay for the duration; the coup leaders argued more tumultu-
ously and drank more heavily.

Despite serious attempts to scare away the press, a small pesky
army of reporters had infiltrated the mob and was broadcasting
the whole infuriating standoff via satellite, smuggling out photographs and earning Pulitzers by the carton. The whole mess was
on display, in living color for the entire globe to see.

Yeltsin adored the spotlight, and was almost giddy at having
all the world as his stage. Televisions were kept on in the Kremlin offices 24/7. The old boys were forced to sit and watch as
Boris—miraculously sober for once—pranced repeatedly in front
of the cameras, calling them all has-beens and wannabe tyrants,
threatening to run them out of town. That clown was thumbing
his nose and shooting the bird at them.

For an empire in which terror was oxygen, it was humiliating;
worse, it was dangerous.

On the third day the old men had had enough. They ordered
the tanks to move, scatter the rabble, and crush ol' Boris. But after three hapless protestors were mowed down, the army lost its
stomach. As miscalculations go, it was a horrible one. Should've
sent in the ruffians from the KGB, they realized, a little sad, a little
late. Need a few bones snapped, a little blood spilled, the boys

from the Lubyanka were only too happy to oblige. Soldiers, on the other hand, had no appetite for flattening their own defenseless citizens. A handful of disgusted generals threw their support behind Yeltsin. A full stampede ensued.

The coup leaders were marched off in handcuffs, tired, defeated, disgruntled old men who had bungled their last chance. And Yeltsin, caught in the flush of victory, sprinted to the cameras and declared a ban on the Communist Party: a bold gesture, the last rite for a rotten old system that had run its course. The crowd roared its approval. It was also insane, and shortly thereafter was followed by an equally shortsighted act: the complete dissolution of the Soviet Union.

With a few swipes of ink the immense empire fractured into more than a dozen different nations.

For seventy years, communism had been the ingrained order—the legal system, the governing system, the economic apparatus of the world's largest nation. Lazy, wonderfully corrupt, and spitefully inefficient as they were, its millions of servants and functionaries were the veins and arteries that braided the country together. They kept it functioning. They doled out the food and miserly paychecks, assigned housing, mismanaged the factories and farms, maintained public order, distributed goods and services, kept the trains running. A terrible, horribly flawed system, for sure. Nonetheless, it was, at least, a system.

Yeltsin had given little serious thought to what would replace it, or them. A few vague notions about democracy and a thriving free market rattled around his brain, nothing more. Apparently he assumed they would sprout helter-skelter from the fertile vacuum he created.

Worse, it quickly became apparent that Yeltsin, so brilliant at blasting the system to pieces, was clueless about gluing the wreckage back together. He was a revolutionary, a radical, a demolitionist extraordinaire. Like most of the breed, he had no talent for what came after the big bang.

But Alex Konevitch definitely did. By this point, Alex already had built a massive construction business, a sprawling network of brokerage houses to administer an arbitrage business that began with construction materials and swelled to the whole range of national commodities, and a Russian exchange bank to manage the exploding finances of his hungry businesses. Amazingly, every bit of it was accomplished under the repressive nose of the communist apparatus. Dodging the KGB and working in the shadows, somehow he had self-mastered the alchemy of finance and banking, of international business.

The nation was not at all prepared for its overnight lunge into capitalism. But Alex was not only ready he was hungry.

With killer instinct, he rushed in and applied for a license to exchange foreign currency. The existing licenses had been granted by the government of the Soviet Union; whatever permissions or licenses had been endowed by that bad memory were insolvent, not worth spit. Anyway, the spirit of the day was to privatize everything, to disassemble the suffocating state bureaucracy, to mimic the West.

After a swift investigation, it turned out Alex's banks were the only functioning institutions with adequate experience and trained executives, and with ample security to safeguard what promised to be billions in transactions. Not only was the license granted, Alex ended up with a monopoly—every dollar, every yen, every franc that came or left Russia moved through his exchange bank. Cash flooded through his vaults. Trainloads from every direction, from Western companies scrambling to set up businesses in the newly capitalist country, and from wealthy Russians pushing cash out, trying to dodge the tax collector and hide their illicit fortunes overseas.

Millions of fearful Russians lined up at the doors to park their savings in Alex's bank, which happily exchanged their shrinking rubles for stable dollars or yen or deutsche marks, whatever currency their heart desired, and let them ride out the storm.

Overnight, Alex and his senior executives were setting the national exchange rates for all foreign currencies. Heady power for a young man, not yet twenty-five years old. Also, quite happily, a gold mine.

Alex took a slice of every ruble shuttled one way or the other, only two percent, but as the mountain of cash approached billions, he scraped off millions. Then tens of millions.

He saw another rich possibility and promised twenty percent interest to any Russian willing to park their savings at his bank for one year. Reams of advertisements flooded every TV station in Russia. A striking female model was used for certain pitches. She wiggled her pliant shoulders and gyrated her sinewy hips, and in a seductive whisper purred that her boyfriend was a sexy genius: his money was earning interest. Who knew it only took a little interest to get laid? To appeal to a different segment, a handsomely aged couple stood against the backdrop of a decrepit wooden cottage and in tearful voices thanked Alex's bank for ensuring their retirement funds were not only safe but actually growing by the day. Then, flash a year forward in time, and the same old couple were shown climbing sprightly into their gleaming Mercedes sedan parked in front of a charming seaside dacha.

It was unheard of. No Soviet bank ever advertised. None offered interest, not a single kopeck. Wasn't it enough that they protected their customers' money? Why should any bank dish out the bucks for its own generosity?

The commercials were vulgar and the promise of interest bordered on criminal negligence, the Soviet-era bankers growled among themselves and to whatever reporter would listen to their gripes. But twenty percent? Okay, one or two percent, maybe; but twenty? Konevitch would pay dearly for his bluster—he'd be bankrupt before a month was out.

Millions more investors lined up at the door. Billions more rubles flooded in. Alex took the deluge and hedged and bet it all against the unstable ruble, then watched as inflation soared above a thousand percent. At the end of a year, the investors took their twenty percent cut and considered themselves lucky indeed; at least their life savings hadn't melted into half a kopeck as happened to millions of miserable others. The remainder of the spread went to Alex. Nearly ninety percent of every ruble in his savings bank was his to keep. He cleaned up.

And as the economy limped from one catastrophe to another, as the disasters piled up, Boris reached out desperately for help. At the president's insistence, a telephonic hotline was installed between Boris and his trusted whiz kid, who seemed to have this whole capitalism thing figured out. Late-night calls became routine. A single push of the red button and the president would rail about this problem or that, long, whiny diatribes fueled by staggering amounts of liquor. Alex was a cool, sober listener; also a quick study with a mathematician's lust for numbers.

Yeltsin had little background and even less appetite for financial matters; all the economic prattle bored him to tears. Alex would talk him through the latest disaster—boil it all down to simple language—propose a reasonable solution, and Boris would pounce on his cabinet the next morning, issue a few brusque instructions, and a total meltdown would be avoided, or at least postponed for another day.

One night after a long rambling conversation about the evaporating foreign currency reserves, Yeltsin paused to catch his breath, then, seemingly out of the blue, asked Alex, "By the way, how's your house?"

"Nice. Very nice."

"Is it big?"

"Fairly large, yes. Why do you ask?"

"I heard it's huge."

"Okay, it is. Very, very big."

"How many bedrooms?"

"Six, I think. Maybe seven. Why?"

"Which is it, six or seven?"

"I honestly don't know. Could be ten for all I know. I've wandered through most of it, but there are rooms I've never seen. It was a wreck when I bought it, an old brick mansion constructed before 1917. According to local lore, it was built for a baron or maybe a wealthy factory owner to house his ten children. Poor guy. He was dragged out and executed by a Bolshevik firing squad three days after the last stud went in."

"Are you pulling my leg?"

"The bullet scars are still visible on the west side of the house. That adds a certain charm."

"And after that?"

"Well, I don't know about the early years. But the Ministry of Education owned it for decades. Occasionally it was used as a school for children of the elite, sometimes as a training center for school principals. Of course they neglected it disgracefully. The electrical wiring, even the plumbing had not been updated since it was built. The pipes were made of cast iron. Turn the spigot and chunky brown slush poured out."

"But you like it?"

Alex chuckled. "What's not to like?"

"You tell me," Boris replied.

"Not a thing. I used my own construction company to gut and rebuild with the best of everything. Voice-activated lighting, saunas in every bathroom, two mahogany-paneled elevators, the works. I even had an indoor pool installed, and a well-equipped gym. The attic is now a movie theater, twenty seats, with real popcorn machines and a ten-foot screen. A French chef and three servants live in the basement and take care of everything."

After a long moment, Yeltsin asked, in a suspiciously knowing tone, "And your wife, does she like it?"

"There are a few things she might like to change," Alex admitted, a loud understatement. Elena detested the house. He had bought and refurbished it before they met, a gift to himself after he made his first hundred million and regarded it as a neat way to pat himself on the back. A gay Paris decorator had been flown in and instructed to spare no expense. He did his best. He chartered a plane, flew around the world, slept in five-star hotels, loaded up on antiques from Asia, the Middle East, and Europe. He had drapes hand-sewn in Egypt, and furniture hand-manufactured by the best craftsmen in Korea.

As the bills piled up, Alex convinced himself that he wasn't being wasteful; it was a business expense, an unavoidable cost he couldn't do without. The big moneymen from Wall Street and

Fleet Street and Frankfurt did not talk business with anybody not like themselves, prosperous enough to show it off.

The house was cavernous and every nook and cranny was saturated with grandeur. But Elena liked things simple and small enough that you didn't have to shout across the room at each other. She didn't care for servants, either; she was reared to do things herself, and that's how she preferred it. If she even thought about a cup of coffee, a silver urn appeared out of nowhere. The flock of hired help violated their privacy. They made her feel guilty and spoiled.

The mansion sat on the corner of two furiously busy Moscow streets, for another thing. Traffic and pedestrians were always pausing to gawk at the impressive old home, and occasionally littered the property with letters strewn with vile curses and filthy threats. In a city populated largely with impoverished former communists—their families and few belongings suffocating in six-hundred-square-foot apartments—the newly rich and their expansive indulgences were not viewed fondly.

Any day, Elena expected a flotilla of Molotov cocktails to sail through her window.

After enough hateful letters, Alex built a small guard shack out front and posted guards around the clock to chase away disgruntled tourists. But it was, quite spectacularly, a mansion and thus a magnet for the growing breed of Moscow criminals. After two attempted break-ins, another guard shack was erected, more guards were added to the rear of the house, one was posted on the roof, and enough state-of-the-art surveillance systems were sprinkled around to give a porn studio fits of envy.

Elena began calling their home "The Fortress," without affection. Still, there was no doubt the house continued to pose serious security issues and little could be done about it.

They had had discussions, Alex and Elena. Not arguments, but mild disputes that were never settled. Elena was increasingly distressed about Alex's safety. He was famous now—more truthfully, infamous—a poster child of the gold-digging opportunists who were raking it in while most Russians slapped extra locks on their doors to keep the bill collectors at bay.

And their house was right there, on the street! A bazooka fired from a passing car could blast them all to pieces.

But the place was perfect for Alex. His office was only five minutes away, on foot. He was working twenty-hour days, seven days a week. Seconds were precious, minutes priceless. And everything he needed was right here, a floor or two above, or a floor or two below: a gourmet feast at the snap of a finger, that superb gym for his morning conditioning, the heated pool to unwind in after a long day of shoving millions around.

Elena had been raised in the country. She loathed the city and all its appendages—senseless crime, roaring traffic, the ever-present noise, the reeking smell and pollution. Most of all, she hated that disgruntled people walked by and spat angry hawkers on her property. She longed for clean air, lush forests, long, private walks around her property.

Long walks without a squadron of beefy guards shepherding her every step.

"Why do you ask?" Alex finally said.

"I want you closer," Boris replied. "No, I *need* you closer."

"I'm only forty minutes away. Call and I'll drop everything."

"Nope, that won't work. One minute I worry about foreign currency reserves, the next I'm dreaming of ways to get my nuclear missiles back from Kazakhstan. I'm a very spontaneous person, Alex. I have the attention span of a horny Cossack. I think you know that."

"Yes, I know that. So send a fast helicopter for me, Mr. President. The army's not doing anything these days. I think they have enough of them, and their pilots need a workout. I'll even foot the gas bill. Twenty minutes flat from my doorstep to yours."

"Not fast enough."

"Then describe fast enough."

"I want to reach out and touch you. Besides, you've been very good to me. I owe you more than I can express. Do me a favor, let me pay some of it back."

"Just fix this damned country. Finish what you started. Believe me, I'll be more than delighted."

Yeltsin chuckled. "You'll be old and senile before anything works in this land. I'll be dead and buried, with throngs of people lining up to pee on my grave for causing all this chaos. I'm giving you a house, Alex."

"I have a house already. Didn't we just go over that?"

Yeltsin ignored him. "Not quite as garish as yours. But big, and believe me, you'll love this place. It's out here, in the country, inside the presidential compound. A mere two-minute walk from my quarters—one minute if you sprint, which I expect you to do if I call. A gym and indoor pool. Six servants, a chef, and—hey, you'll love this part—they have separate quarters outside the house."

The president paused to let his sales pitch sink in, then threw out a little more ammunition. "Here's the kicker, Alex. My presidential security detail guards the entire compound. Even with your money, you couldn't touch the kind of security these goons provide."

Alex chuckled. "Is that a challenge?" He could not say it, but he abhorred the idea of living in walking, or even sprinting, distance of Boris. The man drank and partied until four every morning, frothy bacchanalias that consumed enormous amounts of liquor. He was notoriously social by nature and regarded it as sinful to get tanked alone. The idea of being dragged into those late-night orgies was appalling.

Yeltsin chuckled as well, then a loud belly laugh. What was he saying? With all that wealth, Alex could probably buy half the Russian army; maybe all of it. After a moment the laughing stopped. "I'm serious, Alex. My economic advisors are all boring idiots. Even that bunch of Harvard professors who've camped out here to tell me how to build a capitalist paradise—just stuffier idiots."

"All right, replace them."

"You're not listening. I'm trying to."

But Alex was listening, very closely. A week before he and Elena had attended a dull state dinner to honor the visiting potentate of some country where, apparently, everybody was short and squat, with bad teeth, horrible breath, and nauseating table manners. After the usual tedious speeches about eternal brotherhood and blah, blah, blah—along with a seriously overcooked meal—the party shifted to the ballroom, where Yeltsin promptly invited Elena to dance.

Boris had an eye for the ladies and Elena in a baggy sweatsuit could snap necks. But attired as she was, in a gold-embossed scarlet gown, she nearly sucked the male air out of the ballroom. And of course, three-quarters of a lifetime of ballet training had made her a splendid dancer who knew how to make her partner look graceful and better than he was. Yeltsin and Elena laughed and chatted and whirled gaily around the floor. All eyes were on them—Fred and Ginger, cutting the rug. One dance turned into two, then three.

Alex was sure he was listening to the echo of that third dance. Clearly Elena had whispered into Yeltsin's ear her growing concerns about Alex's safety. If her husband wouldn't heed her warnings, she would take matters over his head. He admired the effort and adored her for trying. He had absolutely no intention of humoring her.

He would just litter a few more guards around the property and hope it settled her nerves.

"Oh, one other thing," Yeltsin added, an afterthought, an insignificant little note to round out the pitch. "It happens to be Gorbachev's old house. The official quarters of the general secretary himself. I had him booted out the day after I took over. Didn't even give him time to clear the clothes from the closets. Ha, ha, ha. Had those shipped to him, later, with a nice personal note. 'I got the country, you keep the rags.' "

Alex suddenly went speechless. Had he heard that right? Yes! Gorbachev's home! Sure, his own mansion was grand, perhaps larger and more loaded with extravagances than the general secretary's residence—money, after all, was the great leveler. But some things money can't buy. Yeltsin was offering him the most storied home in Russia.

The thought of living in that home—How may bedrooms did Yeltsin mention? Who cared?—the thought of him and Elena basking in the general secretary's hot tub, making love in that bedroom, taking long, leisurely strolls around a property where legions of presidents and world leaders had stepped and stumbled, was simply exhilarating. Flushing the toilets would be a thrill.

It wouldn't hurt business, either. Alex could picture the amazed expressions of the Western investors he invited over for a light business dinner. Please don't chip the general secretary's china, he would tell them and watch their faces.

And so what if it was forty-five minutes from the office? The big Mercedes 600 was equipped with an office in the rear, a pull-down desk made of mahogany, a satellite carphone, enough gadgets that not one of the forty-five minutes would be idle or wasted. It might even be better, he thought: forty-five minutes of solitude, each way. Organize his thoughts on the way in; unwind from the daily turmoil on the way out.

And it was safe. Plus, it was in the country; Elena would love it.

Mistaking Alex's prolonged silence for indecision, Yeltsin prattled on. Like the politician he was, he couldn't stop selling. "Let me tell you, my boy, hell, I'd dearly love to live in it myself. Sometimes, at night, Naina and I wander around that house and dream of moving in. The chandeliers alone cost more than I make in a year. Of course, word would inevitably leak out to all these poor folk scraping by on a hundred rubles a month. There'd be another revolution. You know what, though? I don't think I'd enjoy this one as much as the last."

"My moving van will be there first thing in the morning," Alex blurted. He was too stunned to say "thanks."

Matching his speed, Yeltsin snapped, "Good, glad that's settled."

"It's definitely settled. Don't you dare make this offer to anyone else before nine o'clock tomorrow. By then, Elena and I will be seated on the front porch with shotguns to drive off the interlopers."

"Oh, one other thing. From now on, I want you along when I travel overseas. Russia needs as much money and foreign investors as we can get. I'm miserable at making that happen. You don't seem to have any problems in that department."

"Sure, whatever," Alex mumbled, dreaming of who to invite over first. Would they need furniture? Where would they get groceries? In his mind he was already moved in.

The instant they signed off, he rushed upstairs, awoke Elena, and broke the news about their incredible new home.

"Oh, isn't that wonderful," she replied, even managing to make the pretense of making her surprise look sincere.

At one o'clock, Bernie Lutcher crunched hard on his third NoDoz tablet and quickly washed it down with the bottled water he had carried onto the plane.

After twenty-five years as a successful cop in the NYPD intelligence bureau, retiring as a highly regarded lieutenant, he was now five years into his second life, five years that were nearly everything he hoped they would be.

The English security firm that employed him, Malcolm Street Associates, paid him one hundred grand a year, plus housing, plus car, *and* the chance for a twenty thousand annual bonus. Four for four in the bonus department, thus far. And the way this year was going, next year's was already in the bag and mentally spent. Supplemented by his NYPD pension, he was finally and faithfully putting away a little nest egg.

But not *exactly* as he always dreamed it would be. Cancer had struck five years before, had stolen his beloved Ellie, and only after it wiped out the paltry savings they had managed to scrimp from a meager cop's salary. His medical insurance had handled the prescribed treatments, but in the final months and weeks, as Ellie stubbornly wasted away, Bernie had thrown good money after bad, desperately investing in a plethora of unorthodox treatments and quackery, from Mexican miracle pills to an oddball dentist who swore that removing Elle's silver and mercury fillings would incite a complete remission. To no avail, it turned out. In the end, Elle had passed away, stuffed with all manner of phony cures and big holes in her teeth.

So now Bernie was rebuilding his life. No longer surviving one miserable day at a time, he was again viewing life as a promising future rather than a sad past. Both kids were grown, out of college, out on their own; the first grandkid was in the oven, and Bernie looked forward to many more.

Plus, he was living in Europe. Europe! He had acquired this dream in his late teens when Uncle Sam borrowed a few years of his life, making him a military policeman in Heidelberg, a gorgeous city in a lovely country that captured his heart. Other NYPD types had Florida fever; they dreamed of sweating out their idle years in tropical heat, blasting little white spheres around manicured lawns. Bernie hated golf, hated heat, and desperately hated the idea of spending his sunset years reliving the good old days—what was so good about them, anyway?—in a community saturated with retired cops. He had always yearned to return to Europe: the slower pace, the opportunity to travel, sip exotic coffees, and of course, the money was fantastic.

He hunched forward in his seat and noted, once again, the same wrinkled old biddy lurching and waddling down the aisle toward the lavatory. He had long ago learned not to ignore anything—not the innocuous, not the apparently innocent. The stakeout king, the boys in the NYPD had nicknamed him, with good reason—he had put more than a few banditos in the slammer by paying unusual attention to cars and pedestrians that appeared a little too often, often stickup artists and bank robbers reconning their targets. Pattern observation, it was called in the trade. Bernie wrote the book on it.

This was her fifth potty trip, by his count. A little suspicious: she did look old, though, and faulty kidneys couldn't be ruled out; or doctor's orders to keep her blood circulating; or just plain old-age restlessness.

In preparation for this job, the firm's experts had produced a thick folder detailing all known and presumed threats to the client. It was a wealthy firm with a big ego that could afford to be comprehensive and took it to the hilt.

Background checks were de rigueur for all prospective clients; unlike other firms, however, this was accomplished *before* a contract was signed. The client's ability to pay the firm's impressive bills was the principal topic of curiosity, of course. Also the nature of the client's business, types of threat, known enemies, special circumstances, and bothersome vulnerabilities.

British snobbery definitely weighed in. Unsavory clients were blackballed no matter how much they pleaded or offered.

But in a ferociously competitive business, reputation counted for everything. It all boiled down to two simple questions: How many lived? How many died?

The firm had dodged more than a few bullets by politely and firmly snubbing clients whose chance of survival was deemed subpar; in over thirty percent of those cases, the clients had been dead within a year, a striking piece of guesswork. A clutch of actuarial wizards lured from top insurance firms were paid a small fortune to be finicky. A computer model was produced, a maze of complex algorithms that ate gobs of information and spit out a dizzying spread of percentages and odds.

A client or two were lost every year, a better than average record for work of this nature, one the firm loudly advertised.

Regarding his current client, at the top of the threat chain were the usual suspects for a Russian tycoon: Mafiya thugs, hit men, and various forms of independent crooks or assassins intent on blackmail, or fulfilling a contract from a third party. They were effective and often lethal. They were also crude, obnoxiously brutal, notoriously indiscreet, and with their clownish affectation for black jeans and black leather jackets, usually ridiculously easy to spot. Bernie had already swept the cabin twice. No likely suspects of that ilk.

Next came business competitors who stood to benefit by eliminating an entrepreneurial juggernaut like Konevitch, followed closely by investors disgruntled for any number of reasons. His business was privately owned. Two limited partners, that was it. He owned eighty percent of the shares and neither partner was dissatisfied, as best the firm could tell. Really, how could they be? Konevitch had made them both millionaires many times over.

His estimated worth—a combination of cash and stock—now hovered around 350 million dollars—in all likelihood a lowball estimate—and growing by the hour, despite generous and frequent contributions to local charities and political causes. He had his fingers deeply into four or five mammoth businesses, was contemplating a move into two or three more, and his personal fortune was multiplying by the day. The construction firm he began had given birth to an arbitrage business—initially for construction materials only, then for all sorts of things—that bred a prosperous bank, then a sizable investment firm, part ownership in several oil firms, a car importing company, a real estate empire, ownership of two national newspaper chains, several restaurant chains, and myriad smaller enterprises that were expected to balloon exponentially as Russia fully morphed into a full-blown consumer society.

As fast as Alex made money, he poured it into the next project, the next acquisition, the next promising idea. Whatever he touched spewed profit, it seemed. In the estimation of the firm, that remarkable growth rested firmly on his own deft brilliance, his own impeccable instincts, his golden touch.

Take him out and Konevitch Associates would fold. Maybe not immediately, maybe it would limp along for a few anguished years. But with the brain dead, the body would atrophy. Eventually the pieces would shrivel and be sold off for a fraction of a pittance. Alex was a money-printing machine; surely his partners knew this.

Next came possible political enemies, and last, though not insignificantly, the obligatory threat for anyone with heaps of money—family members who might hunger for an inheritance and/or an insurance windfall.

Nearly all rich people dabbled in politics to a greater or lesser degree; this client was in it up to his neck. According to the dossier, Konevitch was very close to Yeltsin, had apparently backed his rise to the presidency, and he continued to throw cash by the boatload at Yeltsin's hungry political machine and a few of the reformist parties ambling in his wake.

The old commie holdovers were resentful, angry, and plentiful. Konevitch had played it smart and hid in the background—the mint behind the throne, an underground well of money—going to great lengths to keep his contributions invisible, or at the very least anonymous. But there were those who knew. And among them, it was assumed, were some powerful people who might wish to settle a historical score. A nasty political grudge couldn't be ruled out.

He had a serious ten million dollar term life policy with Carroythers & Smythe, a financially plump, highly regarded insurance company. That firm shared Malcolm Street Associates' intense concern for Alex's health and secretly informed its partner agency that his wife was the sole beneficiary. No brothers, no sisters, and his few cousins were distant, angry, avid communists, and unfriendly. His mother was long dead, leaving just a father, a former educator with few apparent wants and needs, who was wiling away his retirement from academia reading books that were formerly banned to Soviet readers.

Using his vast riches, the son set the old man up in a nice dacha in a resort town on the Black Sea with a tidy trust fund that would allow him to comfortably live out his life in pleasant surroundings. A bribe to the local hospital revealed the old man had incurable pancreatic cancer that was expected, shortly, to kill him. He was being treated with the best medicines imported from the States, but few had ever survived pancreatic cancer and time was not on his side. So what would the old man want with his son's fortune? Wasn't like he could take it with him.

Alex dutifully visited every few months. He and the old man spent hours in the garage, tinkering on old jalopies and knocking back imported beers. An odd relationship, given the wild differences between father and son. But they were close.

So it all boiled down to one intimate threat—his wife, Elena.

The firm had quietly observed their marriage: happy, healthy, and loving, or so it appeared. No indications of affairs or dalliances or even one-night regrets. Not for her, not for him. They had met a year and a half earlier. And from the best they could tell, from the opening instant, the couple could barely keep their hands off each other. A surface background check revealed that she had been a dancer, Bolshoi-trained. And though marvelously talented, with a technique that was deemed technically flawless, at only five foot and one inch she lacked the long limbs and extended torso demanded by audiences. She was offered a position as a full-time instructor, teaching giraffes with half her talent to prance and pirouette; she opted, instead, to retire her tutu. She put dance in the rearview mirror and majored in economics at

Moscow University, graduating five down from the top of her class. Bright girl.

A month after they met he had asked and she agreed, he suggesting a quick and efficient civil rite, she arguing vehemently for a traditional church wedding. She won and they were joined together, till death do they part, in a quiet ceremony by a hairy, bearded patriarch at a small, lovely Orthodox chapel in the pastoral countryside.

The firm regarded her fierce insistence on a church wedding as a hopeful sign—she had apparently been raised a closet Christian during the long years of godless communism; presumably, the sixth commandment meant something to her.

Her tastes were neither extravagant nor excessive. Some expensive clothing and a few costly baubles, though not by choice and definitely not by inclination: an outwardly prosperous image was necessary for business, he insisted, and he encouraged her to buy half of Paris. Day to day, she preferred tight American Levi's and baggy sweatshirts, limiting herself to a few elegant outfits that were mothballed except for social and business occasions. The couple never bickered, never fought. They enjoyed sex, with each other, nothing kinky, nothing weird, and it was frequent. The firm knew this for a fact.

The Konevitch apartment had been wired and loaded with enough bugs to fill an opera house, surreptitiously, of course, the day after Alex first contacted Malcolm Street Associates. All married applicants were electronically surveilled, at least during the opening weeks or months of a contract—this was never divulged to the clients, and the firm's prurience had never been discovered. Since part of its service was to sweep for listening and electronic devices, it would never be caught.

Statistically, the firm knew, a high number of rich men were murdered by their own wives, concubines, and mistresses. The reasons were mostly obvious: marital neglect, sexual jealousy, and, more often, outright greed. Nothing was harder to protect against, and the actuarial boys demanded a thorough investigation. The firm's gumshoes enthusiastically obliged; snooping in the bedrooms of the rich and famous, after all, was definitely more entertaining work than the normal tedium of tailing and watching.

But all evidence indicated that the marriage was strong. And Elena Konevitch, for now and for the foreseeable future, was rated low risk.

In January 1992, the first of what soon became a flood of newspaper stories about the amazing and mysterious Alex Konevitch appeared in the *Moscow Times*. Though other newly minted Moscow tycoons begged to be noticed, pleaded for publicity, actually, Alex had prodigiously tried his best to remain a complete nobody. Other fat cats blustered and bribed their way into every hot nightspot in town, rolling up in their flashy, newly acquired Mercedes and BMW sedans, a stunning model or two hanging on their arm—typically rented for the occasion—only too hungrily enthusiastic to strut the fruits of their newfound success, to show off their sudden importance.

Publicity management firms sprang up all over Moscow. Moguls and wannabe moguls lined up outside their doors, throwing cash and favors at anybody who could get them noticed, a few seconds of limelight, the briefest mention in the local rags. Under the old system everybody was impoverished, with little to brag about, and even less to show off; in any event, sticking one's head up was an invitation to have it lopped off. Now a whole new world was emerging from the ashes; old desires that had been cruelly repressed were suddenly unchained, flagrantly indulged. A thousand egos swelled and flourished, giddy with the impulse to show off. Donald Trump was their icon; they longed to live his life, to emulate his oversized image, to become famous simply for being obnoxiously famous.

Alex lived like a hermit, a man few knew and nobody knew well. He avoided parties and nightclubs, was rarely observed in public, and adamantly refused any and all requests for interviews. In his quest to remain anonymous, every employee of Konevitch Associates and its sprawling web of companies was required to sign a serious legal vow never to whisper a word about their reclusive employer. This only made the search for his story all the more irresistible. One of the richest men in the country, the kid millionaire they naturally called him. And he wanted to remain anonymous?

After several unfruitful attempts, a midlevel employee at his investment bank was secretly approached by a Moscow weekly and offered five thousand easy American dollars to chat a little about his employer. The employee confessed that he not only did not know Alex personally, he had actually seen him only twice in person—two fleeting glimpses of Alex speeding through the trading floor on his way to his office upstairs. Didn't matter, they assured him. Surely Alex's companies were rife with rumors, gossip, and anecdotes, concocted or otherwise. The price was kicked up to seven thousand and the employee was suddenly too eager to cough up a few confidences—as long as the check was good and, for sure, his name stayed out of it.

"Kid Midas" was the predictable headline that outed Alex, and it said it all and then some. It was rumored that Alex was Russia's richest man, its first fat-cat billionaire; he owned an armada of towering yachts; two hundred rare and exotic sports cars housed in a temperature-controlled underground garage and spitshined daily; a fleet of sleek private jets to ferry him to his sprawling estates in Paris, London, Rome, New York, and Hong Kong. The chatty employee had recently finished a spicy, newly translated, unauthorized biography about the marvelously perverse life of Howard Hughes, and he plagiarized liberally and imaginatively from that intoxicating tale to earn his seven grand.

Alex was a total schizoid paranoid, he'd said; he sat around his office nude, counting his rubles and hatching new businesses in between watching old black-and-white Katharine Hepburn flicks. He collected beautiful women by the carton, renamed them all Katharine, and was so germophobic that he boiled them before he slept with them. He was anti-Semitic, antisocial, ate only raw vegetables, drank only boiled water, was left-handed, was rumored to go both ways sexually, and had to be chloroformed by a squad of brawny assistants to get haircuts and his fingernails trimmed.

The resulting article was ridiculous, packed with bizarre lies, and viciously fascinating.

Fictitious or not, it incited an all-out frenzy and induced scores of Moscow reporters to join in the hunt. Sensationalized stories about Alex quickly became daily fare, more often than not outrageously fabricated nonsense. One enterprising weekly magazine initiated a column dubbed "Kid Midas Sightings" so the whole city could join in the fun: a five hundred dollar reward was offered to anybody who could produce a photograph of Alex, five thousand if he was nude, purportedly his normal state.

Alex's attorneys begged him to sue, promising to terrorize the publishing industry, as only lawyers can do. A flat, persistent refusal was his stubborn response. It would only generate more unwanted publicity, he insisted. And anyway, it was a novelty that would quickly wear off, he assured them, but he promptly hired his first security people. Six private bodyguards. All former Spetsnaz special forces warriors, who looked fierce and swore they would be loyal to the end.

Alex was still scribbling notes and poring over thick business files when, two hours later, the pilot's nasal voice launched the usual preparatory steps for landing. Seat backs were jolted forward, eating trays shoved back into position, a few people got up and stretched. The pair of watchers exchanged knowing winks.

Time for the fun to begin.

They followed Mr. and Mrs. Konevitch as they deplaned, he hauling their leather overnight bags casually slung over his broad shoulders; both of them totally clueless. Light packing for what the couple obviously assumed would be a brief and enjoyable business trip, in and out, a single night at most. Guess again, Alex.

The carry-on luggage was a welcome relief, nonetheless. Their instructions were stern and clear: avoid loose ends, anything that might make the authorities suspicious. The Hungarian police weren't known for nosiness or efficiency. Interference seemed unlikely. Still, unclaimed bags that were tagged with contact information might cause an unwanted problem or two.

At customs, Mr. and Mrs. Konevitch offered polite smiles to the green-uniformed customs guard, flashed their Russian passports, no problems there. Then they went directly through the sliding glass doors into the expansive lobby.

Midday. The foot traffic was sparse, which made the targets easy to track, but also made it harder for the reception team to blend in and hide.

Their briefing was unequivocal on this point—stay with the Konevitches every second of every minute. No respite until the arrival-and-reception team had matters firmly in hand. Same kind of job they had done hundreds or possibly thousands of times during the past fifty years, always successfully. Old age had slowed them down a few steps, but in their line of work the trade-off was more than equitable; nobody suspected a pair of doddering old geezers.

The customs agent barely gave them or their passports a glance as he waved them through. What possible threat could these wrinkled old wrecks pose to the Republic of Hungary? they were sure he was thinking. If only he knew. They had thirty confirmed kills to their credit, with six more they stubbornly claimed, though the corpses had been incinerated into ashes or fallen into deep rivers and washed away.

Mr. and Mrs. Konevitch were walking briskly through the lobby, straight for the taxi stand outside. The tail team followed at a safe distance, hobbling and creaking with every step.

At the taxi stand, three people were already lined up ahead of the Konevitches—a hatchet-faced lady struggling with her over-sized luggage, and two faces the tails instantly recognized, Vladimir and Katya.

Vladimir was the boss of the arrival-and-reception team, a man they all thoroughly feared and deeply loathed. Katya, like the rest of them, was vicious, cold-blooded, and unemotional, a veteran killer with a long and enviable list of hits—but always just business. Vladimir was a sadistic bastard with freakish appetites. He would've done this work for free; paid to do it, probably. Even the toughest killers in the unit felt a wash of pity for his victims.

The tail team from the airplane backed off, ignoring the Konevitches and redirecting their attention to trying to spot the private bodyguards. They had memorized as many faces from their flight as they could. Now they separated from each other, about twenty yards apart, stopped, pretended to fumble with their luggage, and watched for familiar faces.

The call came in at 2:37 p.m. and the secretary put it right through.

Sergei Golitsin checked his watch, right on time. He lifted the phone and barked, "Well?"

"Good news, they're here," the voice informed him. "Everything's under control."

"So you have them?"

"No, not yet. They're at the taxi stand two feet from Vladimir and Katya. Everything's on schedule, everything's in place. I'll call you in a few minutes when we do."

"Don't mess this up." Golitsin snorted.

"Relax. We won't."

There was a long pause. Golitsin, with barely suppressed excitement, asked, "Are the communications set up?"

"They are. The listening devices are state of the art. You'll get a crystal-clear feed into the phone lines and through your speakerphone. I tested it with your secretary an hour ago. Everything's fine." After a pause, the voice added, "Vladimir's going to handle this. It's going to be loud and ugly."

"It better be." Golitsin closed his eyes and smiled. "I want to hear every sound."

3

The old lady at the front of the line shoved two bags at a cabbie and crawled painfully into a blue BMW with TAXI splashed in bold letters across the side.

The couple directly in front of Alex and Elena stepped forward, and a black Mercedes sedan that had been idling by the far curb suddenly swerved in front of the other taxis and screeched to a noisy halt half a foot from the taxi stop. Vladimir, wearing the garb and collar of a Catholic priest, made a fast survey of the surroundings, then quickly threw open the rear door. The same instant, Katya, dressed as a nun, pushed out an ugly black pistol hidden inside the folds of her baggy sleeve and pointed it in Alex's face.

Her partner turned around. Coldly and in Russian he said to Alex, "It's a simple choice. Get into the car or die right here and right now."

Alex looked into his eyes. He had not the slightest doubt he meant every word. After a moment, he said, "Fine, I'll go. This young lady, however, you will leave alone. I don't know her. She's not with me."

"Don't be stupid, Konevitch. Katya will kill you, or your wife, or both of you. Doesn't matter to us."

Alex's face froze. His *name*. The man had used his name, and he *knew* Elena was his wife. For three years he had prepared himself for a moment like this. Dreamed about it. Dreaded it. Now it was actually happening, and he couldn't think or react.

Vladimir's thick hands shot out and grabbed Elena by the neck. He spun her around like a puppet; one hand slipped under her chin, the other against the back of her head. Elena squirmed and fought at first, but Vladimir was too large and strong. He tightened his grip, and she yelped with pain.

Vladimir said to Alex, "You have a black belt, I hear. Surely you recognize this stance. A quick shift of my weight and her neck will snap like a rotten twig. Now, will you *please* get into the cab?"

As they were sure he would, without hesitation or another word, Alex climbed inside. A moment later, Elena was shoved in beside him and landed awkwardly against his side. The man knew what he was doing; he was using her as a buffer from Alex's hands, and he squeezed into the backseat to her right. The woman in the nun's outfit, obviously anything but one of God's saintly servants, slipped into the front passenger seat with her pistol in Alex's face.

The driver, a trusted cohort and a skilled getaway man, gunned the engine, popped the clutch, and off they sped with a noisy screech. Nobody said a word. As if on cue, the lady in the front shifted her gun at Elena's face. The man in priest's garb said to Alex, "Hold up your hands, together."

Alex did as he was told. The man bent across Elena and efficiently slapped thick plastic cuffs on Alex's wrists, then with a show of equal dexterity, Elena's.

After a moment, Alex asked, "What do you want?"

"Be quiet," came the reply from Vladimir. He withdrew two black hoods and clumsily covered their heads.

In March 1992, two months after the press frenzy over Alex Konevitch began, the initial attacks on his companies were detected.

Somebody was making repeated highly sophisticated attempts to break into Konevitch Associates' computer networks. Quite successfully, or so it appeared. The Russian Internet backbone, like everything inherited from communism, was shockingly backward and inefficient. Alex had therefore hired an American company that specialized in these things and plowed millions into creating his own corporate network, a closed maze of servers, switches, and privately owned fiber-optic cable that connected his companies. The only vulnerabilities were in the interfaces between his private network and the Russian phone companies, interfaces that were, regrettably, unavoidable. Naturally this was precisely where the attacks occurred.

That discovery was made minutes after a new American antivirus software program was installed, a magical sifter that sorted gold from fool's gold. Tens of thousands of spyware programs were detected—like small tracking devices—that had penetrated and riddled the entire network. The programs were sophisticated little things, impossible to detect with homegrown software. They not only tracked the flow of Internet traffic, they caused each message to replicate and then forwarded copies to an outside Internet address.

Private investigators easily tracked the Internet address to a small apartment on the outer ring of Moscow and burgled their way into the flat. It was completely empty and wiped clean. Nothing, except a small table and dusty computer. The plug was pulled out. The hard disk had been removed.

What was going on? Alex had anxiously queried his technical specialists. Somebody is mapping your businesses and transactions, came the answer. For how long? he asked. Maybe weeks, more probably months, and it seemed fair to conclude that whoever launched this attack now had an avalanche of information regarding how his rapidly expanding empire came together, how one piece interfaced with the next, how and where the money flowed, even the identities of the key people who pushed the buttons. The computers in the human resources department, particularly, were riddled with enough spyware to feed a software convention.

The programs were wiped clean, gobs of money were thrown

at more protective software—all imported from America, all state of the art, all breathtakingly expensive—and nothing was heard from the originator of the attack. Corporate extortion or any of several forms of embezzlement had been anticipated—pay us off, the intercepted traffic will be destroyed, the attacks will stop. But after long weeks during which Alex's hired computer wizards held their breath and nobody approached the firm, a new, more hopeful scenario was reached. It was probably one of the expanding army of nettlesome computer nerds, his technical people speculated—nothing to be overly concerned with. This was an everyday problem in the United States, Alex was told, where hackers sat up all night and thought up ways to be bothersome for no greater reason than the idiotic satisfaction of imagining it made them something more than the insignificant little twits they were.

In fact, Alex was warned, it could have been much worse; the sneaks could've hacked in, crashed the entire system, and demolished mounds of irreplaceable information. A helpful and timely warning, actually—take better precautions, spend whatever it takes, and then some. Stay alert. Be thankful we detected the problem early and eliminated it, Alex was told by his head technician, an American imported and paid a small fortune for his erudition in these matters.

4

The old lady was merely daft, Bernie Lutcher concluded, at first.

She had jumped in front of him, repeating something loudly in Russian. At least it sounded like Russian. He understood not a word and shrugged his shoulders, and she switched to a different tongue, more quick bursts of incomprehensible gibberish—possibly Hungarian now—while he continued to shrug and tried to brush past her. To his rising impatience, she clutched his arm harder and ratcheted up the incoherent babble.

He recalled her from the plane, the old lady with apparent incontinence issues who made trip after trip to the potty. Maybe she was seeking directions to the air terminal ladies' room, he guessed. Or maybe she was a certified loony, a lonely human nuisance of the type found in every city in the world.

He tried to tug his arm away again and noticed how surprisingly strong she was. Ahead, he watched Alex and Elena pass through the electronic doors, and felt a sudden clutch of alarm. Depending on the length of the line outside, it might take only a few seconds for them to climb into a taxi and disappear into the vast, winding labyrinth of Budapest streets.

He knew their schedule and the name of their hotel: he could always catch up with them there. Unfortunately, he was pathologically honest and duty-bound to enter any coverage lapses in the report he assiduously completed and turned in after each job. In his mind he had already spent his annual bonus on a nice holiday in Greece, on a luxurious slow cruise through the sunbaked islands, sipping ouzo and ogling Scandanavian tourist girls in their Lilliputian bikinis; he now was watching it all go up in smoke.

He tried to recall any fragment of every language he knew and quickly blurted at the old lady, "Excuse me . . . *entschuldigen . . . excusez-moi . . . por favor . . .*" Nothing, no relief.

A large crowd began catching up to him, impatient travelers who had just cleared customs and now were plowing ahead and jostling for choice spots in the taxi line. He could hear their voices, but kept one eye on the old lady—who clutched his arm harder and acted increasingly distressed—and the other on the glass door Alex and Elena had just exited. He never turned around, never observed the old man who quickly approached his back.

The old lady continued prattling about something, more loudly frantic now, more mysteriously insistent, still stubbornly clasping his arm. Firm procedures were unequivocal about such situations: public scenes and embarrassments, indeed public attention in any form, were to be avoided at all costs. He reached down and gently tried to pry his arm loose from the old hag's grip, even as an old man approached from his rear aggressively swinging his arms with each step. Gripped tightly in the old man's right hand, and mostly obscured by an overly long coat sleeve, was a razor-thin, specially made thirteen-inch dagger.

One step back from the bodyguard's rear, it swung up. The blade entered Bernie Lutcher's back nearly six inches below his left shoulder blade, grazed off one rib, then immediately penetrated his heart.

The old man gave it a hard grind and twist, a signature technique honed decades before, one he was quite proud of, tearing open at least two heart chambers, ensuring an almost immediate death. In any event, the blade was coated with a dissolvable poison primed to instantly decrystallize and rush straight into Bernie's bloodstream. One way or another, he'd be dead.

Bernie's eyes widened and his lips flew open. At the same instant, the old lady gave him a hard punch—an expertly aimed blow to the solar plexus to knock the wind out of his lungs—and he landed heavily on his back, gasping for air and grasping his chest, as though he was suffering a heart attack, which he surely was.

The two assassins immediately scattered, moving swiftly to the departure area for a flight to Zurich that left thirty minutes later.

The first assassinations happened in the last three days of August 1992. The Summer Massacres, they were called afterward by the thoroughly cowed employees of Konevitch Associates.

Andri Kelinichetski, bachelor, bon vivant, and very popular vice president for investor relations, ended up first in the queue. A lifelong insomniac, he left his cramped apartment at two in the morning for a brisk walk in the cool Moscow air to clear the demons from his head. He had made it three blocks from his apartment when three bullets, fired from thirty feet behind his skull, cleared his head, literally. Andri stopped breathing before he hit the cement.

Five hours later, Tanya Nadysheva, divorced mother of two and a specialist in distressed companies, started up her newly purchased red Volkswagen sedan for the drive to work, triggering a powerful bomb. Her head landed half a block away; she had been operating her fancy new sunroof at the precise instant of detonation.

By ten o'clock that morning, six employees of Konevitch Associates lay in the morgue—one long-distance shooting, one short-distance, a hand grenade attack, one car bombing, one very grisly slit throat, and a notably devout employee who was literally fed a poisoned wafer as he stopped off at his local church for his habitual morning Communion.

Six victims. Six different types of murder. No failed attempts, no survivors, no witnesses. With the exception of the sliced throat and the fatal Communion wafer, the killers—obviously more than one—had struck from a distance, safely and anonymously. No forensic traces were found beyond spent bullets and bomb residue. The particles from the explosive devices were analyzed on the spot by a veteran field technician. In his opinion, the devices were so coarse and simple, virtually any criminal idiot could've built them.

A few hours later, a pair of special police investigators showed up, unannounced, at the headquarters of Konevitch Associates. They flashed badges, announced their purpose with a show of grim expressions, and were ushered hurriedly upstairs. They marched into Alex's office, where they found him and several of his more senior executives assembled, making hasty arrangements for the families of their dead friends and employees, plainly in shock over what had just happened. One executive, Nadia Pleshinko, was blowing snot into a white tissue, unable to stop weeping.

One officer was fat, mustachioed, and late-middle-aged, the other surprisingly young, runway skinny, with a face that looked glum even when he smiled. Laurel and Hardy, they were inevitably nicknamed by the boys at the precinct, a resemblance so glaring that even they celebrated the epithet.

They were both lieutenants with the municipal police, they informed the gathering, here to discuss what had been learned or not about the morning butchery.

"The Mafiya," the fat senior one opened his briefing. "That's who's behind this. It's not just you, it's happening all over Moscow. There have been over sixty murders in the city just this past month. Sixty!" he said, rolling his bloodshot eyes with wearied disgust. "Nearly all were businesspeople, bankers, and one or two news reporters who were getting too close to one of the mobs or to a corrupt politician on their payroll."

Skinny picked up where his partner left off. "Under the old system, the city averaged maybe three murders a month. And that was a bad month. Nearly always angry wives or husbands getting even for an affair or some marital slight or squabble."

"And the Mafiya is behind all these murders?" Alex asked, totally uninterested in a prolonged recounting of Moscow murderography. All that mattered was what happened to *his* people *that* morning. And what might happen tomorrow. Were the killers finished, or just warming up? Were these six the final toll?

Or should Alex buy bulletproof vests and begin building thick bunkers for his employees?

A serious nod from both officers and Skinny said, "In the old days they were into drugs, prostitution, the black market, that kind of funny stuff. Capitalism has given them a whole new lease. The big money these days is companies like yours. It's—"

"What do they want?" Alex interrupted.

"Hard to say," Fatty replied with a sad frown. "Usually it's a shake-down. Some variation of a protection or extortion racket. 'Pay us a few million, or give us a cut of the monthly profit, and we'll stop killing your people.' I'm afraid that's the optimistic scenario."

Alex paused for a moment, then reluctantly asked, "And what's the pessimistic one?"

Skinny took over and said, "It could also be that somebody—a competitor perhaps—is paying them to wipe you out. Or maybe to soften you up for an attempted takeover. Either way, they'll keep killing until you're out of business, or until they believe you're ready to meet their terms. These people are ambitious, creative, and vicious." He looked over at Fatty, who offered an approving nod. "For instance," he continued, "they hit a bank-ing company two months ago. Before you could say turnip soup, twelve executives were dead."

"The Mafiya," Alex said, rolling that ugly sound off his lips. "Aren't they organized into families or groups? It's not just one big mob, is it?"

"No, you're right," Skinny told him, warming to the subject. "Only two years ago we could've told you which syndicate was behind this, who headed the group, with an accurate, up-to-date, well-detailed manning and organization chart. These days there are so many mobs . . ." He trailed off.

He paused for a quick look at their beleaguered faces. "Even the ones we do know about multiply, merge, and divide so fast, we've lost count. They outnumber us, outgun us, and, worse, frankly, they're now smarter than we are."

"Can you protect us?" one of Alex's executives nervously asked, clearly speaking for them all.

It was a good question and the two officers looked at each other. Eventually, and with matched, timid expressions they turned back to Alex and his people. Fatty cleared his throat once or twice. "We can certainly give it our best try. Add more people to the investigation, make inquiries to local stoolies, throw a few uniformed guards outside your headquarters, that sort of thing. We're not in the bodyguard business, though. And frankly, you have too many employees to protect. That bank I mentioned a moment ago, we were doing our best to protect it." He rolled his eyes and sighed. "Twelve dead."

Before they could dwell on that, Skinny looked at Alex and asked, "Have you received any threats? Direct communications in any form from the killers?"

"No, not a word."

This was apparently a bad omen, as both policemen seemed to frown at the same time. As if by hidden cue, Fatty eventually shook his head and spoke up. "Not good. Typically they warn you beforehand. You do this, or we'll do that."

"Sometimes it's Chinese water torture," Skinny threw in, showing off his own mastery of the subject. "Other times it's a sledgehammer, and, to be perfectly frank, this has all the hallmarks of the latter. These people are professionals. They choose how and when to make their approach."

If they were trying to scare Alex and his employees, they were succeeding nicely. A few chairs were pushed back. One or two executives uttered loud groans.

After another quiet pause, Fatty said, "Here's the pattern we're seeing. Number one, they knew the names of your employees, their addresses, and their personal habits. I don't need to tell you what this implies. Your company has been under their eye for a long time, maybe even penetrated from the inside. Who knows how many of your people are on their payroll, or how many of you are targeted for hits. Number two, the potpourri of killing methods is a carefully scripted message in itself—they can kill you however and whenever they want, wherever you are, whatever you're doing."

The two officers continued batting around theories and chilling speculations, oblivious to the sheer horror they were inciting. Alex and his underlings exchanged piercing looks before Alex, with a discomfited shrug, looked away and contemplated a white wall. Nobody needed to say it: resentment cut like a knife through the room. Alex had all those layers of personal protection—those six beefy bodyguards, a private home with the best security systems money could buy, an armored Mercedes limousine, and a lifestyle that kept him off the streets, out of harm's way.

The four senior executives in the room, just like the rest of the employees of Konevitch Associates, were sitting ducks. Totally defenseless. Morgue meat, all of them.

And the cops were right. It took less than a year after the disintegration of the Soviet Union for Moscow to descend into chaos. Brutal murders were a daily event, soldiers were hawking their weapons and ammunition on street corners for a few measly rubles, unemployment had shot through the ceiling. In the clumsy rush to privatize, prices had climbed to dizzying heights, and public services, which had never been decent, deteriorated, then collapsed altogether. A long, fierce winter of misery set in. Hundreds of thousands of Muscovites couldn't afford oil to heat their homes, to buy decent food or clothing, and were turning to crime to make ends meet.

The newspapers were loaded with stories about the self-ennobling extravagances of the newly rich and famous, while hundreds starved or froze to death in Russia's arctic winter. Nobody was going to feel sorry for Konevitch Associates. No matter how many of its well-fed executives were shot, bombed, or chopped up, nobody would waste an ounce of pity. And the drumbeat of news stories about the shining toys and refurbished palaces of the newly rich worked like a tantalizing announcement to the criminals: "Here it is, boys! Come and get it."

When the two officers finished batting around the possibilities, Alex said, in an accusatory tone, "So you can't protect us?"

"To be honest, no," Fatty replied with a sad shake of the head and an earthquake of chin wobbles. "These days, we barely have enough manpower to haul the bodies to the morgue."

"What do you suggest, then?" Alex asked, avoiding the eyes of his executives, who looked ready to dodge from the room and flee for their lives.

"What we tell everybody who asks. Private security, Mr. Konevitch. You have a rich company. You can afford to hire the best."

Skinny looked like he wanted to say more and Alex glanced in his direction. "If you have something to add, we'd like to hear it."

"All right. Off the record. Between us. And just us, please. These are Mafiya people we're talking about. In case you haven't already gotten the message, they're tough, ruthless, and stubborn. But there is somebody who scares the shit out of these guys."

"Go on."

"KGB people. Former KGB people. They and the Mafiya have been at war for fifty years. Remember the old saying 'it takes one to know one'? A lot of highly trained former operatives are now out on the streets, unemployed, desperate for jobs and willing to work hard. Talented people, a lot of them. They have skills, experience, and attitude. To be blunt, the KGB people are even worse than the Mafiya types."

Alex spent a quiet, troubled moment thinking about the officer's suggestion. He had nothing but rotten memories of the KGB and was privately delighted that he had helped put them out of business. They had booted him out of college and nearly destroyed his life. They very nearly destroyed his country. Under communism, the Mafiya were nothing but a nasty irritant, two-bit gangsters engaged in shadowy enterprises that barely made a dent. The real mob was the KGB. It turned itself into the world's greatest extortion racket, a mass of faceless thugs who abused their power endlessly, living like spoiled princes while their people suffered in an asylum of terrified poverty.

No, he decided on the spot: not today, not tomorrow, not ever. No matter how bad it got, he would never employ a former KGB person to work in his company.

Fatty read his disapproving expression and withdrew a business card from his pocket that he smoothly slid across the table.

"In the event you change your mind, Sergei Golitsin is the man to call. He was the number two in the KGB, a retired three-star general. Whatever you need, believe me, he can take care of."

The next morning, after four more dead employees of Konevitch Associates were scraped off the cement and hauled to the morgue, Alex called Sergei Golitsin.

The door opened loudly and the room filled with noisy voices, a number of people, one or two women and several men, speaking crudely in Russian. Alex had no idea where he was—the car ride had lasted nearly half an hour—a fast trip filled with abrupt, jarring turns probably intended as much to disorient Alex and Elena as to elude any followers. He and Elena were pulled and shoved out of the backseat, then pushed and tugged through a doorway into a building that smelled cloyingly of oil and kerosene. The floor was hard concrete. By the loud echoes of their footsteps, the room was large, cavernous, and mostly empty.

A vacant warehouse, Alex guessed. Or possibly an abandoned garage.

From there, he and Elena were immediately split up and forced into separate rooms. Alex was rushed inside another, smaller room, laid out on what he guessed was a hard table or medical gurney, and the work began. A pair of strong hands untied his shoes, yanked them off his feet, and they landed with a noisy *clumpf* on the floor. A knife skillfully carved off his pants and shirt, leaving him naked except for his Jockeys.

A different pair of stronger hands efficiently clamped his arms and legs tightly with leather straps attached to the sides of the table. Because of the blindfold, he had not a clue what they had done with Elena, where they had taken her. The only thing Alex was sure of was this: it was no coincidence the kidnapping had taken place on one of the few occasions when they traveled together outside Russia, man and wife, on a business trip. This, more than anything, terrified him.

But he squeezed shut his eyes and somehow forced himself to think. Whoever these people were, they had somehow breached, then eliminated his security. Further, the simple yet elaborate kidnapping indicated they had advance knowledge, somehow, that he and Elena were traveling to Budapest. They were waiting for him. They knew his schedule and movements to a tee. And they were professionals—he was sure of this, for whatever it meant, for whatever it was worth.

What kind of professionals, though? Kidnappers out for a fat ransom? Or assassins? That was the urgent question.

They knew he was wondering and left him alone on the gurney to stew and suffer in isolation for nearly half an hour.

Then he heard two sets of footsteps approach, one pair moving lightly, the other heavy, making loud clumps. Probably hard-soled boots. Through the blindfold, he sensed somebody looking down on him, still not speaking, barely breathing. Alex's own breaths were pouring out heavily, his heart racing, his nightmares growing by the second. His mind told him they were allowing the terror to build and he should fight it. His heart would not allow it; he was utterly terrorized.

Without a word or warning, a fist struck him in the midsection; every bit of oxygen in his lungs exploded out of his mouth with a noisy *ooompf.* He sucked for air and tried to say, "What do—" when the fist struck again, this time in his groin. He couldn't even double over or writhe in agony. He screamed, and the beating continued, methodically, without pause, only the sounds of the fists striking against flesh and bone, and Alex howling and groaning in agony.

Vladimir stepped out of the room and slipped off the leather gloves that now were nearly saturated with blood, Alex's blood. He lifted the phone, and Golitsin, sounding like he was next door and experiencing an orgasm, said, "That was wonderful. Just wonderful. Thank you."

"You heard it all?"

"Every punch, every groan. What a treat. How did he look?"

"In shock, at first. He had not a clue why he was being beaten. Now he is merely miserable and confused. You heard him."

"I certainly did. Any broken bones?" he asked, sounding hopeful.

"A few ribs, I would think. Possibly the leg I banged with a chair. And I tore his left shoulder out of the socket. You must've heard the pop. It was certainly loud enough."

"Ah . . . I wondered what that was." Golitsin laughed. "As long as you didn't damage his precious right hand."

"No, no, of course not," Vladimir assured him, then waited, knowing Golitsin was calling the shots. If it was another beating, fine, though Vladimir needed at least ten minutes to catch his wind and rest his muscles.

After a moment, Golitsin asked, "Is he still conscious?"

"A little bit less than more. We had to revive him a few times. In twenty minutes or so the bruises will be swollen and his nerve endings will resensitize." He sounded like he'd done this many times.

"Good. Give him twenty minutes to recover, then mark him." There was a long pause before Golitsin stressed, "Slowly, stretch it out for all it's worth."

They were not going to kill him, Alex, in his moments of groggy consciousness, kept telling himself. Between the sounds of his own beating, he heard a voice, a woman's, deep and scornful, issuing occasionally stern reminders to the man torturing him. Soften the blows, she warned. Avoid damaging important organs, she reminded him. Twice she had loudly snarled that he had better stop choking Alex before their precious hostage had to be hauled out in a box.

So they needed him alive. They wouldn't kill him. They wanted something from him, and they would keep him breathing until they had it; whatever it was.

Then they might kill him.

The door opened loudly again, and two sets of footsteps approached. Same two pairs of feet, Alex thought, one light, one heavy. Were they going to beat him again? He totally forgot his earlier reasoning and wondered, maybe they *were* going to kill him?

The blindfold was ripped from his head. He blinked a few times. "What do you want?" he croaked, throat parched. No answer, not a peep. He tried to focus his eyes, which were blurry and unfocused though he was positive the hazy shapes before him were the same man and woman from the taxi. And probably the same pair who had inflicted the brutal beating.

"Please. Just tell me what you want."

The man, Vladimir, he had heard him called, bent down over his face, smiled, squeezed open his lids, and studied his pupils a moment. Vladimir then took two thick leather straps and, one at a time, stretched them across Alex's chest, strung them underneath the table, fastened them as he would a belt, and tightened them enough that they bit painfully into Alex's skin. Next he held something before his face—a handheld device. A machine of some sort. Oddly enough, it looked like a compact traveling iron for pressing clothes. "See this?" he asked Alex.

"Yes . . . what is it?"

"You'll learn in a moment."

"Where's Elena?" Alex demanded.

Vladimir laughed.

"Please," Alex pleaded. "Leave her out of this. She's done nothing to you."

"But you have," Vladimir informed him with a mean smile.

"I don't even know you." Sensing it was the wrong thing to say, Alex suggested, a little hopefully, "If it's money, let's agree on a price. Let her go. Keep me. She'll make sure you get paid."

"Are you proud of what you did?" Vladimir asked, backing away. He spit on the iron and enjoyed the angry hiss.

"I don't know what you're talking about."

The woman spoke up and said, "Most of us are former KGB. Career people, patriotic servants who protected Mother Russia. You ruined our lives."

"How?" Alex asked.

"You know how. You fed millions to Yeltsin and destroyed our homeland."

"How do you know about this?"

"We know all about you, Alex Konevitch. We've watched you for years. Watched you undermine our country. Watched you become rich off the spoils. Now it's time to return the favor."

Alex closed his eyes. Things had just gone from bad to worse. Not only did they know him, they knew *about* him. A simple kidnapping was bad enough. This was revenge on top of it, and both Vladimir and Katya allowed Alex a few moments to contemplate how bad this was going to get.

Vladimir held up the iron so they could jointly inspect it; the metal undertray was red-hot, glowing fiercely in the dimly lit room. He held it before Alex's face. "American cowboys branded their cattle. I hope you don't mind, but now we will brand you."

Without another word, Vladimir slipped a pair of industrial earphones over his head, thick black rubber gloves over his hands, then with a steady hand lowered the iron slowly toward Alex's chest. Watching it move closer, Alex squirmed and tried to evade it with all his might; the new belts totally immobilized him. The first hot prick of the iron seared the tender flesh above his left nipple—Vladimir used the recently sharpened edges of the iron and glided it slowly and skillfully around his skin.

Alex screamed and Vladimir pressed down firmly, though not too hard, etching a careful pattern: a long curve first, then another curve, meticulously connecting them into the shape of a sickle. The stench of burning flesh filled the room. Next, he began drawing a squarish shape—completing the hammer and sickle, the symbol of the once feared and mighty, now historically expired Soviet Union. Vladimir had done this before; this was obvious. Just as obviously, he was the kind of artisan who reveled in his work. The entire process lasted thirty minutes. Alex screamed until he went hoarse, piercing shrieks that echoed and bounced around the warehouse.

Katya stood and tried to watch, then, after two minutes, horrified, she gave up and fled.

5

By 3:30, Eugene Daniels was quaffing down the final dregs of his third Bavarian brew, a special, thick dunkel beer produced seasonally without preservatives that was totally unavailable in the States. Across the table, his wife, Maria, was stingily nursing her second wine, a Georgian pinot she had just explained, for the second time, with an excellent bouquet, overly subtle perhaps, but with fine, lingering legs and other insufferable claptrap she had obviously lifted from one of those snobbish wine books. How could anybody make so much of squished grapes? An attractive Hungarian waitress approached the table and, while Eugene wasn't looking, Maria quietly waved her off.

She toyed with the stem of her wineglass and reminded her husband, "Business meetings are best conducted sober."

"If Alex wanted me sober, he'd be here on time."

"Maybe he has something up his sleeve. Hundreds of millions are at stake, Eugene. Maybe he wants you loaded and stupid before he arrives." And maybe he's succeeding beyond his wildest dream, she thought and smiled coldly.

"You don't know Alex, obviously."

Rather than risk another squabble, Maria lifted a finely plucked eyebrow and insisted with a disapproving frown, "All the same, switch to coffee."

Eugene ignored this and took a long sip of beer. He checked his watch for the thirtieth time, then repeated the same thing he had said at least twenty times. "I've never known Alex to be late. He's punctual to a fault. Always."

"Maybe he has a Russian watch. I know for a fact, their craftsmanship is awful."

He was tempted to say: How would you know, you stupid spoiled twit? but swallowed the sentiment and instead noted, "No, something's wrong. I smell it."

"Yes, you're right. This whole thing is dreadfully wrong. We flew all the way from New York, he only had to come from Moscow, we're here, and he's not. This is rude and unprofessional. We should leave."

Eugene stared hard at his wife and fought the urge to stuff a napkin down her throat. Wife number four, actually—and without question, the biggest mistake of all. He was still on his third wife and making a decent go of it when Maria, a buxom brunette half his age and with a penchant for tight leather miniskirts, became his secretary. He'd chased her around the desk a few times, but not too many before she hit the brakes and made the pursuit pay off.

When it got out—with more than a little assistance from Maria, he only belatedly and after the fact realized—Wife Three stomped off into the sunset with a fifty million settlement and that big, ostentatious mansion in the Hamptons to quell her hurt pride. Word was she now had a shiny new red Rolls and a good-looking cabana boy to help her through the emotional relapses.

The house and money had been bad enough. What Eugene most sorely regretted was losing the one really capable secretary he ever had. Maria was pushy, curt, and anal, keeping him organized and punctual, and cleaning up behind him—qualities that now made her insufferable as a wife.

And now that she was bound to his money by a marriage license, any pretense of pleasantry had worn off. Even the sex had turned infrequent and limp.

He whipped out his cell and punched the preset for Alex's office in Moscow. The call went straight through to Alex's warm and efficient secretary, Sonja, who picked up on the second ring. Eugene and Alex had done a few very profitable deals together, he lining up American backers and bringing in the American greenbacks, while Alex plowed them into Russian enterprises that minted gold. Though he and Alex's secretary had never met face-to-face, Sonja never forgot a voice. She called him Mr. Daniels before he finished hello.

Eugene quickly explained his problem—Alex had scheduled a meeting with him, here, in the restaurant of the Aquincum Hotel for two hours before. "I know that," replied Sonja, who instantly turned equally perplexed and talkative. Alex was never tardy, she replied with considerable pride. Yes, she had made the travel arrangements herself, and no, Alex had not contacted her regarding delays or problems. They quickly exhausted the possibilities, and she eventually transferred Eugene to Alex's head of security, a former KGB general named Sergei Golitsin.

"What may I do for you?" Golitsin asked in heavily accented, stilted English.

Eugene slammed down his beer and came directly to the point. "Have you heard from Alex?"

"No."

"He's over two hours late for a meeting."

"Two hours?" he asked, only mildly interested.

"Yes, that's what I said."

"So what?"

"Alex is never late. That's the *what*."

"So maybe he makes an exception this time."

"Maybe he did. But wouldn't you know if he was diverted, or missed his flight, or had a car accident? Maybe he fell down a rabbit hole."

"Probably not."

"But shouldn't you *know*?"

"No, I should not. At Mr. Konevitch's insistence he employs an outside security company for foreign travel. I have strongly advised him against this dangerous practice many, many times.

Outside Mother Russia, his itinerary and security . . . well, they are out of my hands."

Eugene was dismayed by the too-bored-who-gives-a-damn tone at the other end of the line. If this guy was his chief of security, he thought, Alex better invest in plenty of body armor. He tried to swallow his exasperation and said, "Look, Alex and Elena are supposed to meet me here for a late lunch to discuss a pressing business deal. This deal has to close by tonight. Millions might be lost."

"I believe this is your problem."

"According to your job title, Alex's personal security is your problem."

"No," Golitsin replied with a nasty laugh, "that is Konevitch's problem."

"Can't you at least call the outside firm that handles Alex's security? Better yet, give me the number. I'll call."

"This is inside confidential information that cannot be divulged."

"All right, fine. Surely you won't mind if I call the local police and report Alex's disappearance."

The general's voice suddenly changed from a gruff blow-off to conciliatory. "No . . . there is no need to do that. Let me handle this."

"I don't think I trust you to handle it."

"I will. Give me your number. I will call the moment I have something."

"Call me even if you don't. I've got twenty million riding, my own cash, and four greedy partners who are throwing in another seventy mil each." He glanced at his watch. "If the deal's not going through, I'll have to cancel the bank order by five at the latest."

"Yes . . . of course."

Eugene gave him his number and the line went dead.

They let him rest for an hour after the branding was finished. A large industrial fan had been brought in and locked into high gear to push out the stench of roasted flesh. The iron had been pressed down hard enough that the best plastic surgeon in the world could not totally eliminate or disguise Vladimir's handiwork. Alex would spend the rest of his life tattooed with the symbol he had done so much to destroy.

At exactly 4:05, Vladimir and Katya reentered the room, herding a harried-looking doctor and a plump, greasy-haired lawyer who reputedly specialized in the rapidly changing Russian business legal codes. Vladimir and Katya stood and waited with indifferent expressions at the end of the gurney. The doctor checked Alex's pulse and monitored his breathing, then spent a while poking and prodding various body parts.

Eventually the doctor looked up and in high native Russian informed Vladimir, "Pulse count's a little high, no doubt the result of the trauma and fear. At least two ribs are broken and there's a terrible contusion on his leg. Without an X-ray I can't determine if it's broken."

The room was unheated and cold, and as nightfall moved in was becoming colder by the minute. Naked but for his underpants, Alex's teeth were chattering. His arms and legs would've been shivering except for the tight restraints. The doctor glanced again at the broken, bleeding body on the gurney, then, after wasting a horrified grimace at Vladimir, scuttled swiftly from the room.

Vladimir and Katya pulled over a long wooden bench and sat beside Alex. They had agreed beforehand they would play out their best imitation of the old good-cop/bad-cop routine.

Vladimir had already done a thoroughly credible job of establishing his credentials as the bad cop. Acting good wasn't exactly Katya's strong suit, either; as long as she sat beside Vladimir, though, she'd look like an angel. Vladimir slowly lit a foul-smelling French cigarette, exhaled loudly, and in his most blasé tone said to Alex, "You're probably wondering what this is about."

After toying with the idea of answering him, Alex decided against it. Finally they were getting down to business. They had beaten him to a pulp, branded him, had nearly killed him—at last they were going to tell him how much it would cost not to finish the job.

No use beating around the bush, and Vladimir in a command-ing voice came right out with it. "You're going to sign over your money and businesses to us."

"What?" Alex was sure he hadn't heard right. A demand for money had been expected. In fact, given the scale of this opera-tion and the brutal professionalism of his kidnappers, Alex had fully anticipated the initial demand to be huge: in all likelihood preposterous. They would threaten and insist, he would tell them whom to talk with, then the negotiations would begin in earnest. Eventually, the ransom experts at Alex's expensive English secu-rity firm would be brought into the game, there would be some haggling, a little give, a little take, threats and counterthreats, but sooner or later a reasonable price would be agreed upon and promptly paid. But sign over his businesses? Ludicrous.

These people were either stupid or crazy. Or both.

"You heard right," Vladimir insisted, very calmly, very seriously. He stood, bent over, and lowered his face within twelve inches of Alex's eyes. "It's simple. You sign a letter we've already prepared. Nothing fancy—you're tired, worn out, and frustrated from the crushing work and responsibilities. Then you sign a simple con-tract with a blank space for the name of the person we will des-ignate as your successor. You don't touch that—we will later. All you do is sign the bottom of the page."

"That simple?"

"Yes, that's it. My lawyer friend here will notarize it, and you and your wife are free to go." The shyster stood quietly in the cor-ner, and he nodded and smiled energetically, so damned pleased to be of service to both parties.

"And if I say no?" Alex asked.

"Then you and your wife are dead. Think about it. You lose your businesses either way."

Katya butted in and, taking her best stab at playing the good cop, informed him, "Vladimir will happily kill you and your wife. Believe me, he'll enjoy it. Don't be stupid, don't give him the excuse."

Alex took a long look at the dark ceiling. So this was what it was all about. His money *and* his businesses and his properties, the works—the greedy bastards were demanding everything he'd spent six years creating and building. He drew a heavy breath and, as firmly as he could, insisted, "Money you can have. Plenty of it, enough to live happily ever after. But no, you can't have my businesses."

Vladimir had expected this, in fact was fully prepared for it. He smiled and then turned around and looked at Katya. "Get the wife," he told her.

Katya rushed off. Vladimir sat back down on the wood bench and blew lazy smoke rings while Alex pondered his options. At least now he knew what they wanted. But what would they do to Elena? Had they already harmed her? He had been unconscious for a while and his imagination began playing with all the horrible things they might already have done during that interlude. The man on the bench was a monster, utterly without conscience. Maybe Elena had also been branded. Had she been molested? Tortured? Raped?

Moscow was filled with Vladimirs these days, murderous scum whose depravity and cruelty knew no limits. In the old days they were employed by the state as instruments for spreading terror and submission; they were now as much a part of Russia's free-market economy as potatoes and vodka. They wouldn't think twice about punishing a rich man's wife—they would *enjoy* it, in fact. Alex's mind filled with the ugly possibilities.

Eventually the door opened and Elena was led in by Katya, dragged along like a dog by a rope tied to her wrists. She was frightened out of her wits, and looked it. But on the surface, at least, she appeared healthy and unmarked. Then she took one long look at Alex on the gurney and lost it. She screamed, "You bastards!" at Vladimir and Katya. She yanked on her rope, trying to break free and move toward her battered husband.

Katya grabbed a large knot of her hair, gave it a hard jerk, and yanked her backward, nearly off her feet. So much for good cop.

Vladimir stood and moved toward Elena. He placed a gag in her mouth and tied it off behind her head.

"Leave her alone," Alex protested weakly.

"After I kill you," Vladimir informed him with cruel nonchalance, "I'll give her to the boys waiting outside. She's a very attractive lady. Imagine how much fun they'll have with her."

Eugene, halfway through his seventh beer, took the cell phone call at 4:10. It was Golitsin and he opened in a very reassuring tone, saying, "Good news, I've located Alex."

"Have you?"

"Yes, and he's fine."

"Glad to hear it. Where is he?"

"Apparently a more critically important meeting came up. He asked me to inform you that he needs to reschedule."

"Reschedule?"

"Yes, that's what he said. He suggested tomorrow afternoon. What do you think about tomorrow?"

"Out of the question. He knows that. Are you sure you spoke with Alex?"

"He's my boss. I believe I know his voice."

Eugene studied his fingers a moment. This made no sense. If this deal didn't close by five o'clock, the financing evaporated— by 5:01, there was no deal. Back in New York, a cluster of lawyers and accountants were huddled around a long conference table on a high floor of a massive tower, waiting impatiently for Eugene's call. They had been there all night, drinking stale coffee, munching stale pastries, telling stale jokes, drumming their fingers—and turning surlier with each passing moment.

Three months of sweat and hard work. Three long months of Eugene assuring and reassuring his anxious investors that it was safe to dive into Russia's crooked and rigged markets with Alex Konevitch as their guide. It was the Wild, Wild East, perilous and unruly for sure; but for those audacious few willing to jump in on the ground floor, colossal fortunes were waiting to be plucked. Three months of lengthy business plans, proposals, risk assessments, long boring briefings, and all the other tedious twaddle entailed in due diligence had taken place before this deal could be cobbled together.

Three insufferable months of sucking up to some of the biggest egos in New York.

All about to go down the drain. The thought of it was nauseating. This couldn't be happening. Over three hundred million electronic dollars were loaded and waiting to be fired into Alex's vaults. The investors were anxious and mistrustful, their commitments precarious at best. If one thing went wrong, they had collectively whispered in Eugene's ear—just one infinitesimally tiny thing—they would withdraw their dough and never take another call from him.

"I don't believe Alex told you to reschedule," Eugene spit into his phone in his best New York accusatory tone. "You're lying. I don't know why, but Alex is well aware this deal closes by five or it never closes."

A long silence followed while Golitsin recognized he had clumsily misplayed his hand. This pushy American on the other end was proving to be a big problem. If he alerted the Budapest police about the mysterious disappearance of Alex Konevitch, this whole operation could come unglued. There was the dead bodyguard at the airport to be factored in. The locals had already initiated an investigation, Golitsin had been informed by his well-placed sources. But the Hungarians had no idea of its relevance. And corpses don't complain or become impatient.

Once they learned, though, that Alex had disappeared from Ferihegy Airport at around the same time as the murder, they might put two and two together.

Alex was a rich, seriously important man, a celebrity back home, a big-time FOB—Friend of Boris. For sure, the Hungarians would not welcome the diplomatic noise and ugly publicity his disappearance would almost certainly ignite. A citywide manhunt would undoubtedly be initiated. The police would scour the airport for any witnesses who might have noticed anything. The Konevitches were an attractive couple and quite noticeable. Who knew what the cops might turn up?

His last report from that sicko freak Vladimir indicated he would need another hour to close the deal. Then another hour or two after that to tie up the nasty details like disposing of Alex's and Elena's corpses somewhere they would never be found. They would simply disappear and Golitsin would fuel rumors around Moscow that Konevitch had embezzled money from his own bank and eloped with it into nowhere. A brilliant plan, really, since Golitsin would embezzle the money himself, many, many millions, with dead Alex as his foolproof cover.

His bluff been called, though. Americans! The greediest, pushiest bastards on earth. No, the one on the other end wasn't going to let him off the hook. And too much was at stake for this to be mishandled at this stage.

"Do not call me a liar," Golitsin pushed back in his most threatening voice. "I am merely telling you what Alex told me. I'll call him again if you insist."

Eugene thought to himself: This guy is trying to jerk me off. He suggested, "Don't bother. Give me the number, I'll call and I'll speak with him."

"He told me he was not to be disturbed. He was very firm on this. No matter what."

"Fine. Why don't I just call the cops?"

"Don't. It would cause a public mess, an embarrassment. Alex would be most upset."

"Then have him call me. Five minutes or I'm on the phone to the locals." Without waiting for a reply, Eugene punched off, checked his watch, and ordered another beer from the buxom young waitress with the comely smile.

Maria was upstairs in the hotel suite, pouting and packing. Sometime during the middle of his sixth beer, Eugene had lost his temper and poured out his resentment on her. She had gotten fired up, replied in kind, and stormed off in a huff, threatening a divorce that would make the last three look like pleasant skirmishes.

Vladimir was just getting ready to hand Mrs. Konevitch over to the boys in the back when the clunky satellite phone on his waist began bleating. Every step that would lead to Konevitch's capitulation had been plotted well in advance by Vladimir, personally.

He was quite proud of his plan. He intended to let the boys have her as a plaything for an hour, and had encouraged them to do whatever they liked, as long as it produced plenty of screams and was not fatal. Konevitch would be forced to suffer the anguish of blindly listening to her shrieks and howls, knowing his own stubbornness was the cause; then she would be brought back in and tortured before his own eyes.

Vladimir hated to have his work interrupted, but the obnoxious satphone on his waist wouldn't quit. He uttered a loud curse, answered, listened for a moment, then stepped out of the room, away from prying ears, for this conversation.

"No," he told Golitsin in a reproachful tone, "not yet. Just say we're at the critical stage. You're interrupting progress."

"How long?" Golitsin hissed.

"Hard to say. He was really shaken when I told him we wanted everything. He thought it was only money. What a shock. You would've loved the look in his eyes when I told him what this was really about."

Golitsin was indeed very sorry he missed it. "Are we talking hours or minutes?"

Vladimir paused to consider this delicate question. Alex Konevitch had been horribly beaten, branded, and put under mind-crushing stress. With his considerable experience in these matters Vladimir prided himself on knowing his victims and their breaking points. Konevitch was tougher than most—probably too stubborn for his own good. Given five hours Vladimir could break anybody—make them plead and beg and roll over like dogs. That now was out of the question.

Then so be it; time to skip a few steps and accelerate the action. The boys in the back would have to wait their turn; his pretty little wife was about to get her leading role in the drama. Vladimir relished that thought, but her treatment would have to be paced just right. Too fast, and Alex would become enraged and dig in his heels. The emotional line between fury and surrender was brittle, and Vladimir had to calibrate, nudge, and terrorize Konevitch in just the right direction, at just the right speed.

Of course he would be angry, initially. He would put up his best front, would threaten and spit and yell profanities. But this was his wife's pain and degradation; ultimately, he would end up desperate, utterly helpless, and would cave in to every demand Vladimir imposed on him.

Yes, it had to be slow and quite horrible.

Then Alex would confront his only real choice: what was left of his wife, or his fortune and companies. "Three hours," Vladimir replied, very firmly. "With luck, two."

Golitsin exploded into the phone, calling Vladimir everything from incompetent to a moron. Vladimir pushed the phone away from his ear and let him vent and fume and spew whatever filthy invective he wanted. For a year now he had had to put up with the old man's abuse and derision. He was sorely tired of it and tried his best to ignore this latest diatribe. How tempted he was to just tell the old man to screw off. He eventually placed the phone back to his ear, smiled to himself, and said, "Maybe you want to come here and do it yourself."

"I don't like your impertinence," Golitsin barked back.

"Nobody ever does." He paused for a moment, then insisted, "Two, maybe three hours."

"That won't do."

"Fine. What will do?"

Golitsin explained the problem in rapid-fire fashion and Vladimir listened. Golitsin eventually asked, "Can you have him call this Eugene man and make up an excuse? He's a dangerous pest. Get rid of him."

"Give me the number," Vladimir confidently replied, then wrote it down. "If Konevitch says one wrong word, his wife dies. You understand the risks, though."

"No, tell me."

"If I have to kill her, we lose an irreplaceable leverage."

"I'm sure you'll find a way without her."

"Right now his mind is on one thing, and one thing only. His own misery. Relieve him of that thought, even for a brief moment, and I might have to start over."

"You mean . . . beat and torture him again?"

"Almost from the beginning."

"So what's wrong with that?"

The straps and belts were quickly unfastened, Alex was helped to sit up, and Katya positioned the cell phone by his ear; her forefinger hovered tensely over the disconnect button. His instructions and options had been explicitly and cruelly explained. "Make this man go away, or else," Vladimir had informed him. To help him comprehend the "or else," Vladimir placed a big knife against Elena's throat, poised on her jugular for a lethal slice.

Eugene answered on the second ring. Struggling to sound apologetic rather than terrified, Alex told him, "It's me, Alex. Sorry I'm late, Eugene. It was unexpected and, believe me, absolutely couldn't be helped."

Eugene replied in a simmering tone, "Check your damn watch, Alex. I've got a briefcase packed with contracts for your signature. In thirty minutes this deal goes through or I'm screwed."

"I understand, Eugene."

"Do you? Then what are you doing about it?"

"There's nothing I can do," Alex replied. "I'm tied up right now," he explained, speaking the unvarnished truth.

"In Budapest?"

"Yes."

"Fine. I'll come to you."

"No. Even if it were possible, it's not advisable."

"Make it possible, Alex. If this deal collapses I have to pay the partners a penalty of ten million. It was the only way I could get them to pony up. You know this."

"This isn't my call, Eugene. Believe me, I would help if I could."

"My last wife took me for fifty mil, Alex, and my mansion and even my dog. And Maria's upstairs right now scheming and counting how much she can make. I'm desperate here. I can't afford to lose *one* million right now. Ten will ruin me."

There was a long pause while both men considered their options. Eugene was brilliant and talented, and, like many of his ilk, his skill at business was matched only by his incredible ineptitude at romance. Three ex-wives, with now possibly a fourth in the making. But three already: three hefty alimony payments and seven needy children, four in obscenely expensive private colleges and three in equally rapacious private schools. And there was his own luxurious lifestyle to be considered. Not to mention Maria's, who thought designer clothes grew on trees. Eugene was burning through the cash faster than he could make it—almost faster than the U.S. Treasury could print it. This deal was make or break for him.

Alex glanced at Elena with the knife at her neck; she stared back, wide-eyed, plainly terrified. He felt a stab of gut-wrenching guilt that he had gotten her into this mess, and he tried with limited success to push that aside and figure out what was going on here. When he hadn't shown up for the scheduled meeting, Eugene had obviously called his office in Moscow, probably tossed around a threat or two, and gotten a concerned response. And then—somehow—somebody in Konevitch Associates had passed this news to Vladimir, who was now brandishing a knife at Elena's throat. With a blinding flash of the obvious he understood what this meant: an inside job. Somebody in his employ was a traitor.

No wonder they knew what flight he was on, that he was traveling with Elena, and how to bypass his security.

It dawned on him for the first time that definitely they intended to kill him and Elena. He could sign over his businesses and every last penny of his millions, the deeds to his homes, the titles to his cars, even the clothes off his back. Or he could refuse and tell them to go pound sand, they weren't getting a single penny.

It would make no difference. Absolutely none. He and Elena were dead either way.

Alex drew a long, deep breath. "All right, here's the deal," he blurted into the phone. "You remember the special clause? If Elena and I aren't in the restaurant in thirty minutes, invoke it. Both of us, or—"

A moment too late, Katya jerked the phone from his ear and with an angry forefinger punched the disconnect button.

"What was that about?" she hissed with a stare meant to kill.

Alex ignored her and looked at Vladimir and the knife at Elena's throat. He yelled, "Oh God . . . wait!" to Vladimir, then yelled at anyone who would listen, "Kill her, spill one drop of her blood, and you'll get nothing. I swear. Not a penny."

Vladimir played with carving a deep gash across her throat, but Katya barked, "Don't. Not yet." Obviously the smarter of the two—at least the less instinctively sociopathic—she awarded Alex a hard look and demanded, "What was that you told him?"

"It's very simple. Eugene is an American investor with three or four very wealthy backers in New York. It's called a joint venture. They are pooling hundreds of millions for this deal. They put up the cash, and I invest it for them, keeping a fair share of the profits for my trouble. In return I had to put up collateral."

Vladimir and Katya were in the wrong line of work to comprehend the meaning of this word, "collateral," and Vladimir snapped, "What are you talking about?"

"It's a common business term. In return for their trust and capital risk, I put my companies on the line. It's all stipulated in the contracts inside Eugene's briefcase. Every one of my businesses, right down to the final nail. If I fail to do my part, title to every business I own reverts to them."

"He's lying," Vladimir hissed at Katya.

"Am I?" Alex asked, definitely lying. He turned to the legal shyster who was hiding in the corner, watching this scene with nervous fascination. Alex asked him, "Have you ever heard of a business deal that did not involve collateral?"

The man frowned, stroked his chin, and tried to look thoughtful. He had small, crowded features and they pinched together; like a pug with hemorrhoids. And he was totally, irrevocably lost. He had been a criminal lawyer under the old Soviet system where the extent of his legal expertise was not lifting a finger or raising a squawk as his clients were ramrodded through the politically corrupt courts and crushed by the state. These days the big money was in corporate law, so he had hung out a new shingle and was avidly trying to cash in. Everything was crooked and rigged in

Moscow anyway and the shyster knew as well as anybody who needed to be bribed and/or threatened for a deal to go through.

In short, the man on the gurney had just tossed a pebble down an empty well. The thoughtful pause dragged on.

Well, he might not know squat about contracts, but he had a firm grasp on survival, he told himself. If he said no, this man is clearly a liar, and it turned out the shyster guessed wrong, everything would be lost—all those hundreds of millions of dollars. Naturally, they would hold him responsible. For well over an hour he had stood out in the warehouse, hearing Alex's anguished howls and shrieks echoing through the walls. He felt a sudden shiver as he considered how they might punish him.

But if he said Alex was telling the truth, well, whatever happened afterward—good, bad, or worse—they couldn't blame him.

Feeling quite Solomonic, and with a tone of utter conviction, he offered his best professional opinion. "No, never. As he says, it is typical to arrange collateral in these matters."

"And this is the special clause you referred to?" Katya asked Alex.

"That's right. In forty minutes, everything I own will revert to Eugene and his group of New York investors."

The lawyer walked over to the gurney and leaned in toward Alex. "But there is a way to void this clause, am I right?"

"I'd be an idiot if there weren't."

"Good. Tell me about it," the lawyer demanded, enjoying his sudden moment of importance.

"Put me through to whoever you work for. I'll tell him about it."

"Not a chance," Vladimir answered for all of them, sneering and sliding the knife back and forth against Elena's throat.

"Fine, your call," Alex replied, trying his best to look confident rather than terrified. He had done hundreds of high-pressure business negotiations, tense parleys upon which many millions of dollars hinged. They always involved a fair amount of posturing and bluffing, and Alex had become a master at it. This time, though, he was bargaining for Elena's life, and his own. He took a hard swallow, then forced a smile and said to Vladimir, "In forty minutes, everything will be gone. These are New Yorkers. Greedy bastards, every one of them. If they get their fingers on my properties, you can beat and torture me all you want. You'll never pry them back."

"Maybe we'll just go to the hotel and kill this Eugene man," Vladimir suggested, his preferred course for solving problems.

"That would be stupid. It won't make a difference," Alex told him. "Copies of all the contracts are with his partners in New York. In fact, they'll appreciate it. One less partner means more for them."

Vladimir nodded. Made sense.

"Also," Alex confided, sounding like an afterthought, a small, insignificant detail that meant nothing, "once I sign Eugene's contracts another three hundred million dollars will be electronically transferred to my investment bank."

"What?" Katya asked, suddenly hanging on every word.

"You heard me. When I sign the contract, Eugene and his investors will immediately wire-transfer their funds into my investment bank. Three hundred million American dollars. Cold cash."

Vladimir licked his lips and looked at Katya. Both were struggling to maintain the pretense that they were still in control. And both were clearly rattled and looking for a way out. When Golitsin learned about this, he would throw a tantrum of monumental proportions. But if they didn't call him and Konevitch's companies and properties slipped out of their fingers—much less losing the possibility of three hundred million more, in cash— well, neither of them wanted to think about what he would do to them. It would be horrible and slow, they both knew.

An unspoken signal passed, Vladimir removed the knife from Elena's throat, stepped out of the room, flipped open his clunky satphone, and dialed Golitsin.

"Why are you calling?" Golitsin asked with a ring of hope in his voice. "Is it done? Did he sign over the properties?"

"No. And now there is a new glitch," Vladimir replied, then quickly recounted the problem.

The moment he finished, Golitsin asked, "Is he telling the truth?"

"How would I know? The lawyer says it makes sense. Capitalists don't trust each other. What's new?"

Vladimir stopped talking and allowed this to sink in. He had done the smart thing, he decided; he had booted the problem upstairs. They would get only one chance at this, one shot at becoming unimaginably rich; just one shot at the biggest heist in Russian history. And Golitsin had done excruciating planning for every eventuality, had plotted and surmised and second-guessed every conceivable scenario—except this.

Golitsin knew what Vladimir was doing. But he wasn't at all sure what Konevitch was up to. Was this a trick? Did Konevitch have something up his sleeve?

On the other hand, another cool three hundred million in cash was there for the taking. Three hundred million!

Golitsin rolled that delicious number around his head. He spent a long moment relishing the new possibilities. In one swift swoop the overall take would nearly double. Better yet, this was cold cash, fluid money available for spending on fast cars, big homes, a sumptuous yacht, even a private jet—whatever his heart desired.

And the idea of ripping off a horde of greedy New Yorkers appealed to him mightily. He could hear their anguished howls when they learned their money was gone, stolen. Suddenly he could think of little else.

Eventually Golitsin said what needed to be said. "Take him to the hotel. And make sure he signs the contract." He thought about the extra three hundred million, and with palpable excitement added, "This is better. Much better. I can badly use that much cash."

"Yes, couldn't we all."

Golitsin didn't like the message but he absorbed it. "Pull this off, it will also mean another two hundred thousand for you. How many people do you and Katya have available?"

"Eight here, more than enough."

"He's a financial genius," Golitsin reasoned, as much to his listener as himself. "But he can't spell escape and evasion. A complete amateur."

"He doesn't worry me," Vladimir replied, bubbling with confidence. "Nabbing him was child's play. Besides, after his beating, he can barely walk."

"Still, if he does one thing wrong . . . if he even looks suspicious, kill the wife."

The doctor was rushed back into the room to hastily clean up Alex and make him presentable for the rich boy from New York. A relative term, of course—though Vladimir's blows had mostly been spent on Alex's body, there was a nasty open gash on his forehead, a broken nose, various welts, and some ugly swelling on his face. Six swiftly applied butterfly sutures took care of the nasty gash and a bandage was slapped on to hide it. The other wounds were wiped with medicinal alcohol and, where necessary, also bandaged. "Tell him you were in a car accident," Katya ordered Alex, again proving she was the smart one, the one to be watched. "You've been in the hospital getting checked out."

"All right."

Vladimir leaned in close and warned, "We'll be in the restaurant watching, close and personal. One false move . . . if I just become slightly bothered by the look in your eyes, your pretty wife dies."

"But if I sign the contract and everything goes fine, Elena and I will live. We're free to go. Right?"

"Yes, that's the deal," Vladimir said, dripping phony sincerity.

"How do I know you're telling the truth?" asked Alex. Of course, they were lying. They would take his money, his companies, his homes and cars, then kill the both of them.

"What choice do you have?"

The doctor was slathering a gooey yellow ointment on Alex's chest, a light analgesic. The burn went deep and covered nearly his whole upper left chest. It was raw, already blistering. It would be days before the wound scabbed over and the open nerve tissue was protected. Once they put a shirt on Alex, the material would rub and the pain would be serious. The doctor ordered Alex, "Stand up. Let's see if your leg works."

Alex slowly pushed himself off the gurney. He emitted a sharp yelp as he moved his dislocated left shoulder and stretched the tender skin around the burn. He put his left foot down on the hard floor, followed, more gingerly, by his right. A spike of pain from his right leg, where Vladimir had pounded it with a wooden chair, shot like a thousand-volt current instantly to his brain. A strangled gasp and he nearly collapsed. He would've collapsed except he focused on one overriding thought, one unyielding imperative: there would be no second chance, no do-overs. This was it. Get through it, whatever it took. Swallow the pain, don't let this opportunity slip away, he repeated to himself, over and over.

A man hauled in Alex's overnight bag, unzipped it, withdrew the spare fresh shirt and suit Alex had packed, and lazily tossed them on the gurney. "Get dressed," Vladimir ordered. "Hurry."

The doctor handed Alex a fistful of ibuprofen along with a bottled water, then instructed Alex to swallow them, all of them. Vladimir informed Alex, "Your wife will stay in the car in front of the hotel. She's our insurance. If I give the word, the boys will give her a Bulgarian necktie. Know what that is?"

Alex shook his head. It didn't sound pleasant.

Vladimir answered with a wicked laugh, "They'll slice her throat open and pull her tongue through the hole."

"That would be a big mistake," Alex said, swallowing his anger and carefully slipping a white dress shirt over his damaged shoulder. "I mean separating us. She has to be with me."

"Do you think we're stupid?" Katya asked.

Yes, he most certainly did. Stupid, crude, and impossibly cruel. But also, as he had just learned, afraid to make a move without instructions from their boss, who presumably was back in Moscow. But instead of saying that, Alex replied, "No, you're obviously quite smart. You're overlooking something, though."

"Are we?" Vladimir snarled.

"Think about it. Eugene's expecting Elena to accompany me. If I walk in, looking like I look—without Elena—he'll know something's wrong."

"So what?"

"A legally binding contract depends on both parties being of sound mind and operating of their own free will. People don't get rich being sloppy or stupid. And Eugene is a very, very shrewd and rich man. A flawed contract is worthless. If he suspects I'm under duress, or that something's not right, he'll balk." Alex looked pointedly at Katya, the good cop. "Three hundred million dollars will go out the door with him."

"Just tell him she was also injured and still in the hospital," said the lawyer, deciding to throw in his two cents. Suddenly, he was Mr. Big Shot, brimming with brilliance.

"What an idiotic suggestion," Alex said with a withering stare in the direction of the shyster. "I'd leave Elena seriously injured, in a hospital, just to attend to a business deal?"

"Sure," Vladimir replied, totally clueless. Why not? What husband wouldn't neglect his wife for money? "I don't see the problem."

"Because he'll know I'm lying. And he'll naturally ask why I didn't just invite him to join me at the hospital to sign these contracts."

They were all looking at one another. Nobody liked this idea. Really, though, what difference did it make? On second thought, it might in fact be even better. Just as easy to grease her in the restaurant as carve her throat in a car idling outside: it simplified things, really. With only eight gunmen, far easier to keep an eye on the couple together than split up.

Besides, with his beloved wife beside him, Konevitch would remember exactly what was at stake in the event he was tempted to try any funny business. Reminders were always helpful.

"And we need to carry our bags with us," Alex added, awkwardly knotting his tie with his one usable arm.

Vladimir kicked the base of the table. "Not happening," he snorted.

"Think again. Eugene knows we haven't checked into the hotel yet. I assume you want this to work. We need to look like we've just arrived."

"Think you're smart, don't you?" Vladimir replied, with a mean grin as he held up two tiny red booklets. "Go ahead, bring the bags. I've got your passports and your wallets. You won't escape, and you can't get out of Hungary, no matter what. But even if you do, we'll hunt you down and there won't be a second chance."

"I want this to work just as much as you. Probably more. I want to live," Alex assured him. "And three hundred million is a lot of money," he reminded him, as if anybody had forgotten, as if anybody could.

"We can live without it," Katya said, trying to sound indifferent and failing miserably. "But you're going to perform one small service before we set foot in that restaurant."

"Am I?"

"You definitely are. You're going to sign the letter of resignation and the contract that reassigns your businesses and properties to a new owner."

The show of confidence Alex had shown a moment earlier drained away. Now he looked crestfallen. "And if I say no?"

"That's your choice," Katya informed him. She looked over at Vladimir. "Count to five," she said, motioning her chin at Elena. "Then kill her."

"One . . . Two . . ."

Before he got to three, the lawyer was holding a sheaf of documents in front of Alex's nose and helpfully pointing out where to sign.

6

The black Mercedes, trailed by a pair of matching rental Ford Fiestas, pulled up to the entrance of the Aquincum Hotel. Two thugs hustled out of the nearest Fiesta, walked quickly through the entrance, strutted through the expansive lobby, and moved directly to the Apicius Restaurant located on the ground floor.

With a show of deliberate rudeness, they brushed past the attentive maître d', occupied the closest table to the exit, withdrew their pistols, placed them under the napkins on their laps, snapped at a waitress to bring them two bowls of steaming goulash, and waited.

After three minutes, Katya stepped out of the Mercedes, looked around to make sure the coast was clear, then signaled for Alex and Elena to get out, Elena first. Then Alex painfully hobbled out onto the curb. He slung their matched his-and-hers overnight bags over his good shoulder and waited. A moment later, Vladimir got out as well, taking a moment to stretch and slip the gun he had held at Elena's head into the belt behind his back.

A storm had moved in; thick, angry clouds covered the skies, and it was prematurely dark. With Katya leading, Alex and Elena in the middle, and Vladimir bringing up the rear, the parade entered the hotel and marched directly to the fancy restaurant on the ground floor.

Katya entered a little ahead of them and brusquely instructed the maître d' that a table for four was required, definitely in the middle of the room, make it quick. No problem. Hungarians are rigorously late sleepers and late eaters, and the crowd was subsequently sparse, mostly foreign guests of the hotel who didn't get the local customs.

Katya followed the maître d' to the table and sat. A moment later, Alex and Elena entered. Alex looked around, then spotted Eugene at the far-right corner table beside a plate-glass window where he could kill the boredom watching the pedestrians wander by. Alex took Elena's hand. They walked slowly across the room. With each step, his chest and leg radiated pain. He slowed his walk to a near crawl, shuffling like an old man.

It was their first chance to talk. He whispered to Elena, "They're going to kill us, no matter what."

"I know. It's not your fault," she replied.

Oh yes, it definitely was his fault, but this wasn't the time or situation to discuss it. At this stage, fault or fate or serendipity made no difference. Don't waste time; think quickly, he told himself. He squeezed her hand and said, "This is an opportunity—probably our only chance. We have to use it."

"Do you have a plan?"

"I'm thinking." He tried to smile reassuringly but it came across weakly. "If you think of anything, let me know." She squeezed his hand back, and made no reply.

Eugene had spotted them and jumped from his seat. He took in the gallery of bruises and abrasions on Alex's face, noted the severe limp, and his face turned instantly into a mass of concerned wrinkles. "My God, Alex, what happened to you?"

"Car accident," Alex replied with pretended indifference, slipping the overnight bags off his shoulder and placing them on the floor to free his one good arm for a lame handshake. His leg was killing him. His left arm hung limp and useless. The yellow ointment covering the burn was seeping through his white dress shirt. He forced a smile and said a little lamely, "You should see the other guy."

After a polite chuckle, Eugene asked, "That's why you're late?" It was a dumb question. Why ask? The answer was right before his eyes. He suggested, "It looks like the accident was damned serious," suddenly swimming in guilt that he had insisted on Alex coming here.

Elena explained, "Well, first there were the police reports. That took nearly an hour. Our taxi driver ran a red light, two other cars were involved, a complete mess. We went to the hospital afterward."

"The hospital?" Eugene echoed, still stunned by the condition of his friend. Elena looked fine; on the surface she appeared unharmed, anyway. Nervous and distressed, for sure—but considering the dreadful state of her husband, that was easily understandable.

"It's not as bad as it looks," Alex assured him. "I was lucky. A few cuts, some nasty bruises, a few broken ribs, I think."

Eugene stared at the floor, torn between empathy for his friend and sympathy for himself if he didn't get Alex's signatures on the contracts. Cuts and bruises heal. Ten million bucks are forever.

Only thirty minutes before, Maria had stormed back downstairs, suitcase in hand, and announced that she had booked a flight back to New York and scheduled a meeting with the most venomous East Coast divorce lawyer money can rent. A real loud-mouthed cutthroat with sterling references. Among those references, Eugene well knew, were wives two and three, whose divorces the lawyer had handled with appalling effectiveness. Practice makes perfect—how sadly true. Wife Three had walked away with twice what Wife Two got. Eugene shuddered to think how much Number Four might cost.

Alex stole a glance over his shoulder, took in the two boys by the exit, and noted that Vladimir had slipped in and joined Katya at her table in the center of the room. Vladimir and Katya were partially blocking the views of their pals by the exit.

Not that it mattered; they were arranged perfectly to keep him and Elena bottled up.

He needed time, and Alex looked at Eugene and said, "Incidentally, please call your friends in New York. Tell them I require another thirty minutes."

"Not possible, Alex."

"Please make it possible."

"You know the stakes. If this deal's not locked down by five tonight, I'm deeply, deeply screwed."

Alex and Eugene stared across the table at each other, frustration hanging in the air like mist. Alex eventually noted, "Surely your contract with them has an Act of God provision. Am I right?"

"Do I look stupid?"

"So use it, Eugene. I was an innocent victim, a hapless passenger in a taxi accident. That's a shining example of an Act of God." He pointed at his own face. Eugene needed no reminder.

"Alex, these contracts have been months in the making."

"I think I know that."

"I faxed copies to your office a week ago."

"And I can't tell you how much I appreciate it."

"Seven whole days. Surely you've had more than enough time to study them."

"I'm a slow reader."

"Damn it, Alex, I—"

"Look, Eugene, let me be honest. I once signed a contract my lawyers and I had examined only the day before. During the interim, without mentioning it, the other party slipped in a few clauses, a few very expensive clauses. I trusted them, Eugene. I signed the contract without noticing the changes. That little stunt cost me two million dollars."

"You're kidding."

No, not kidding; lying, definitely, though he offered a regretful shrug and lied again. "I swore I would never sign another contract I haven't read on the spot. Please get on the phone and buy me some time."

"This is me, Alex. Eugene Daniels."

Alex bent forward, inspected him closely. "Yes, no doubt about it."

"How many deals have we done together? Five? Six?"

"Four."

"All right, four. Have I ever cheated you? I'm telling you, nothing, not a word has been added or subtracted from the contracts I faxed you." He awarded Alex a look of complete bewilderment. "It's the same paper, Alex, identical, down to the commas. Don't you trust me?"

"Of course I do."

"Good. Then it's settled."

A brief pause. "You trust me, too, don't you, Eugene?"

"I'm here, aren't I?"

"Good. Then let's just dispense with those contracts. A useless waste of time. What's paper between friends? Let's just swap a few hundred million on a handshake."

Eugene lowered his head in defeat. "All right, all right, I'll try," he said, frowning tightly. "These people are absolute bastards, though."

"And right now, their mouths are watering for the easiest ten million they ever made. Your money, Eugene."

"But if I invoke the Act of God clause, they get nothing, right?" Eugene said, letting the words fall off his tongue. The frown began to melt. "Nothing, not a thing," he said, answering his own question, suddenly smiling. As hard as they had made him beg, work, and sweat to cobble this deal together—their nearly unending selfish demands, their noisy bickering over inane details, their lousy New York manners—and now, holding ten million of *his* dollars as ransom; well, the thought of suddenly yanking the rug from under *their* feet was exhilarating. What fun.

"That's right," Alex said, reading his thoughts. "The only people who will walk away from this richer and happier are the lawyers and accountants who prepared this deal."

Eugene wasn't drunk but he had inhaled enough thick German swill that any ability to think with real clarity was hours behind him. Alex was right, though. Every word made sense.

After all they'd put him through these past months, if the sharks in New York refused to give him another thirty minutes he'd tell them all to piss off. Take a flying leap and kiss your own fanny before you hit the floor.

"Please, make the call," Alex implored him, looking suddenly apologetic. He glanced quickly over his left shoulder: Vladimir and Katya were eyeing him closely. Once they saw Eugene stabbing numbers into his cell phone, things could instantly turn ugly. Alex put a hand on Elena's arm and smiled pleasantly at Eugene. "Excuse me. In all the excitement today, I never had a chance to use the bathroom."

Without waiting for an answer he stood and left Elena with Eugene. Eugene's plump fingers were already stabbing his cell phone. He couldn't wait. His only regret was that he couldn't watch their faces.

Alex approached the table where Katya and Vladimir sat. Both were glowering and trying to look utterly fierce. Why try? They could be wearing clown suits and sipping pink margaritas through striped straws; they would still smolder with menace. Alex stared directly at Vladimir and hooked a finger.

Katya was the smart one and he preferred to avoid her: Vladimir did his thinking with his fists and would be easier to fool. Not easy, but easier.

Vladimir had been watching the heavy American businessman at the table begin dialing numbers into his cell phone, and then— surprise—Alex standing up! Then walking in his direction! He turned to Katya. She shrugged noncommittally. Did the rich boy have a death wish? Where did he think he was going? Vladimir quickly pushed away from the table, stood, put a hand on the gun in his rear waistband, and trailed Alex.

The pair of hired guns by the exit were just lifting their pistols out of their laps when they saw Vladimir following behind Alex. They decided to sit and wait.

Alex offered a friendly nod as he walked past, then stopped beside a vacant pillar in the massive lobby and allowed Vladimir to catch up. The lobby, like the restaurant, was sparsely populated— it made it ridiculously easy for Alex to pick out Vladimir's people, a tough-looking couple lounging on comfort chairs right beside the entrance, smoking and glowering at anybody who passed by. And through the glass window, huddled directly beneath a fancy outdoor lantern, stood two more men in black jeans and black leather jackets. The moment Vladimir reached hearing distance, he hissed at Alex, "What in the hell are you doing?"

"What anybody in my position would do. The man at the table has to make a call to New York. It's not an option. I wouldn't want you to draw the wrong impression."

Vladimir opened his lips and was on the verge of speaking, but Alex cut him off. "His partners requested a thirty-minute extension. They want to add a few conditions. It's not uncommon. I probably should have warned you—antsy investors who come up with last-minute concerns, demands, and conditions. He's calling to nail down their issues."

Vladimir studied Alex. Nervous. Alex was fidgeting with his hands, his knees trembling so badly they were almost knocking together. Mr. Big Shot: all that money, all those businesses, one of the richest, most powerful men in Russia. Yet here he stood, nerves shot, ready to crumble. How utterly disappointing. Then again, Vladimir had worked damned hard to incite an earthquake of nervousness. In fact, he should be more worried if Alex seemed the least bit nonchalant. "If he's calling the police," Vladimir threatened, "he's arranging your death sentence."

"That's exactly why I'm talking to you right now. I knew you'd assume that."

"Is that right? Well, you're a bright guy, Konevitch, but don't think you can outsmart us. The local police will notify us the instant an alarm goes out about you," he warned. "There's no place you can go that we won't know. No place we won't catch you."

And it was true. During his long decades in the KGB, Sergei Golitsin had collected contacts and stoolies throughout Europe, all of whom now were struggling to create new lives in a new world, and wanted their dirty pasts as Moscow stooges and finks erased, buried, or forgotten. A fastidious bureaucrat with lethal instincts, over the decades Golitsin had kept every incriminating piece of paper he came in contact with. Within hours after

he was "retired with prejudice" from the KGB, three large vans
wheeled up in front of his old headquarters and were hurriedly
loaded with forty years' worth of pilfered files. Box after box.
Name after name, enough to fill several city-sized phone books.
It was all squirreled away in a clandestine warehouse a few miles
outside Moscow. Golitsin was sitting on enough dirt and compro-
mising material to coerce and blackmail many thousands.

Among the names were the deputy minister for internal security for Hungary, two captains and three senior inspectors in
the Budapest police, all of whom were operating under harsh
instructions to notify Golitsin the instant Alex Konevitch's disappearance, or death, became an item of police interest.

Vladimir thumped a threatening finger off Alex's forehead.
"You're way out of your league, boy. The only way out of this is to
get him to sign that money over to us."

"Believe me, I know that. I just want to survive this and get on
with my life."

From his face and eyes it appeared he did know. Still, Vladimir
thought it a good idea to rekindle his memory. With narrowed
eyes he said, "Your pretty bitch will go first. Remember that.
You'll have a moment to watch the blood draining from her head,
to hear her last pitiful breaths. And you'll know it's all your fault.
Then I'll kill you, too."

"I have to get back to the table," Alex told him, now looking
paralyzed with terror.

"You've got twenty-five minutes to finish this. Not a second
longer." He pointed at Alex's watch. "In twenty-five minutes and
one second, I write off the money and start blasting. Now, take a
few deep breaths," Vladimir said, "then get back in there and get
us our money."

"It worked," Eugene announced with a triumphal slap on the table the moment Alex returned to the table. The lawyers in New
York, a consortium of legal hit men who smelled an easy ten million for their clients, had yapped and howled a chorus of odious threats right up to the instant Eugene invoked the sacred Act

of God clause. Like that, the curses and bullying died in their throats. Total silence. After that moment of stunned stillness, suddenly they couldn't shut up. They talked over themselves to extend Alex however much time was needed. And how was the poor man's health? the suddenly compassionate throng wanted to know. Damn shame about that awful accident, they collectively agreed—they couldn't have felt more sorry or sincere.

Eugene euphorically snapped his cell phone shut and laid it on the table. "They gave us thirty more minutes to hammer this thing out." He took a long congratulatory sip of beer and smacked his lips.

"Do you mind if we order a little food first?" Alex replied, sliding gently into his seat. "We haven't eaten all day. We're famished."

"No, no, of course," Eugene replied, feeling regretful once more for putting his friend through this. Then he thought again of his money, of ten million sailing away to his despised partners. Like that, he got over it.

Alex asked Elena, "What would you like, dear?"

She gave the menu a cursory glance and settled on a table salad and spicy German sausage dish. Alex ordered lukewarm chicken broth and a warm cola. He was famished, though his lips were so scabbed and swollen that solid foods were out of the question; at least three teeth were cracked or broken with exposed nerves a hot or cold drink would have brutalized; his jaw muscles were so achy, the thought of chewing was sickening.

Eugene loudly ordered another dark beer, a celebratory one this time, and mentioned to Alex, "Why don't you get started on reviewing the contracts?" In other words: I pushed fate once for you, pal, now get started.

Trying hard to look focused, Alex hoisted the thick sheaf of papers over and began leafing through, thoughtfully scanning the pages. His head throbbed. His body howled with pain. He forced himself to concentrate on one overriding thought: How to get out of this alive. How to elude the team of professional assassins seated only fifty feet away, fingering their guns, ready to blast away.

At least he had bought twenty-four minutes of relative calm to

ponder his options—twenty-four minutes without anybody pummeling his body, or frying designs on his flesh, or uttering vile
threats into his ear.

Eugene and Elena made small talk. How did she like Budapest?
Lovely old city, didn't she think? Yes, very lovely indeed, she answered with a strained smile and firm nod—after what happened
to Alex she would curse this city to her dying breath. Did she
enjoy traveling with Alex? Oh, well, always quite an adventure,
she replied, tongue in cheek. And how was life in Moscow these
days? And so on and so forth.

The last thing Elena felt like doing was partaking in meaningless banter, but she had to buy time for Alex to think, and she
endured it with phony grace. Eugene seemed like a nice man, a
few rough New York edges aside—so why couldn't they sit there
and just enjoy each other's company in golden silence? He could
guzzle the beer he seemed to enjoy so much, and she could dwell
on their nightmare. Her heart was pounding. She was forced to
press her hands tightly together to keep them from shaking.

Her back was to Vladimir and Katya, yet she could sense—in
fact, nearly feel—a malevolent presence.

The food came. Between spoonfuls and slow, careful sips, Alex
maintained a pretense of studying the documents, occasionally
scribbling on a page, a notation here, a notation there—meaningless chicken scratch as he racked his brain for a way out of this.

Maybe he was overthinking this, he wondered. Maybe elaborate was the wrong approach; they should simply stand up and
walk out, thumb their noses at the gangsters, and flee. Maybe this
was all a big bluff. The more he thought about it, the more tempting that idea was. Would their kidnappers really open fire, here,
in the grand dining room of one of the best-known luxury hotels
in Hungary?

Back in Moscow, where such things were all too prevalent,
maybe: okay, yes, without a moment of vacillation, they would
blast everything in sight. But surely, in Budapest, the storied capital of a foreign nation, a peaceful, elegant old city renowned for
its sophistication and exotic charms, different rules applied.

He glanced over his shoulder and caught sight of the two dull-eyed thugs by the exit, engulfed in the dense cloud of cigarette smoke swimming over their table. And then, for a fleeting instant, he and Vladimir locked eyes. Stupid question, he realized. Of course they would. They would blow away Elena, Alex, probably Eugene, the waiters and waitresses, other customers, and for good measure they'd nail the doorman and run away with smiles on their faces.

It would be a total massacre, a bloodbath. And it would be Alex's fault.

He had already signed over his companies and properties, coerced statements that, if he survived, would be completely worthless. The moment he set foot in Moscow, he would hire the best lawyers money can rent and rescind everything; he then would use his immense fortune to hunt down every last one of them.

They would know this, of course. And they would know there was only one way to be sure that never happened.

And if that required a massacre, a flamboyant atrocity in a pleasant, peaceful city, it would only persuade the next millionaire they targeted that these were serious people who meant business.

7

With only eight minutes left on Vladimir's deadline—and Eugene noisily draining what he claimed, with a suspicious slur, was only his third stein of beer—Alex finally settled on a plan he thought had a chance of success. He had conceived, chewed over, and discarded at least a dozen different ideas, from dangerously complex to ridiculously simple—from standing up and screaming "Fire!" to collapsing on the floor and pretending to suffer a massive heart attack.

Impressive intelligence was not his kidnappers' forte. But what seemed to be an advantage in his favor was also, ironically, a double-edged sword. Sociopaths like Vladimir could not be depended upon to make cool, rational judgments in moments of stress. Whatever Alex tried had better be trigger-happy-proof.

He looked up from the papers and matter-of-factly asked Eugene, "How did you get from the airport to the hotel?"

"Automobile. Why?"

"How? Taxi? Limousine service?"

"I drove, actually."

"Then you rented a car?"

"Yes, a rusty old orange Trabant," Eugene said, referring to the automobile mass-produced by the East Germans under the old system. Trabants were notorious for their atrocious workmanship, nonexistent reliability, and cramped lack of comfort. The automotive equivalent of throwaway razors, they were called, and that was a compliment; even junkyards didn't want them. He leaned back in his chair and chuckled, enjoying a private joke.

Elena asked, "What's funny? Surely there were nicer cars on the lot."

"You're right. Shiny Mercedes and speedy Beemers all over the place."

"Then—"

"Because Maria is a typical, spoiled American, without the slightest thought of how awful things were under communism. I thought she should experience firsthand the quality of socialist manufacturing." The drive had taken forty-five minutes and Maria moaned and complained every inch of it. Well accustomed to his money and all the perks it could buy, whatever memories she had of life on a secretary's paycheck were long behind her. She was horrified by this sudden dip back into the pool of poverty. Eugene relished every minute of it. His sole regret was that he hadn't brought along a tape recorder so he could replay it again and again.

"That sounds like a novel concept," Elena noted, obviously wondering about Eugene's marital skills, or sanity.

"So is the car parked in the hotel lot?" Alex asked.

"The side lot. Why?"

"I'd like to borrow it," he said, rubbing the bandage over his eye and looking pained. "Elena and I have had enough taxi rides for the day. And as soon as we're done here we have to return to the hospital pharmacy for painkillers and fresh bandages."

"Of course."

"Also," Alex said, shifting from pained to apologetic, "I seem to have misplaced my wallet. The orderlies undressed me at the hospital to treat my injuries. It must have fallen out of my pocket. Do you happen to have some money I could borrow?"

"How much do you need?"

"I might have to cover the medical bills. How much do you have?"

"Two thousand in bills, another thousand in traveler's checks. American dollars, all of it. I exchanged two hundred into Hungarian forints, but Maria left with that."

"Dollars are fine. Two thousand should be enough."

Eugene dug into his pant pocket, withdrew the keys, then a fat wad of hundred-dollar bills, and slid them across the table. "About the car, only a strong hind wind will get you over thirty miles an hour, the shocks are nonexistent, springs are popping through the seats, and the windshield wipers flop all over the place." He smiled for a moment. "Other than that, great car."

"Before the wall came down," Alex noted with an ironic shrug, "we all had to place our names on long lists, then wait years for the privilege to buy a Trabant. Some people were smart enough to sign up every year."

"Every year?" Eugene asked.

"Well cared for and driven minimally, that's about how long they lasted."

They lifted their glasses and silently toasted the marvelous new world.

Alex waved for the waitress, the same cute one Eugene had been nakedly admiring all afternoon. When she arrived he spoke in a low rasp that forced her to bend deeply over to hear him. He spoke for about thirty seconds, then slipped a hundred-dollar bill into her palm—two weeks' salary and tips for her. An enthusiastic nod and she rushed off, beaming.

Alex checked his watch—five more minutes and New York would be calling Eugene. In six, Vladimir and Katya would be blasting away. He fought the temptation to turn around and look at Vladimir and Katya, lifted up another few pages, and pretended to return to his work.

"What's he doing now?" Golitsin inquired into Vladimir's satellite phone. Copies of Alex's resignation letter and the appending contract relinquishing his properties had been faxed by the lawyer and now were stacked in a tidy pile on his desk. They sat there, less than two feet away. Close enough to where he could reach out and caress them. He had read and reread them six times. He could barely keep his hands off them.

A courier on a night flight from Budapest was en route with a chain around his wrist attaching him to a briefcase containing the legally vital originals. Just scrawl his name onto those originals, designate himself as the handpicked successor to Alex's empire, and voilà—he, Sergei Golitsin, controlled 350 million dollars. Possibly more.

Years of plotting and scheming and putting the pieces together were about to pay off. A few drops of ink and he would be one of the ten richest men in Russia; but throw in another three hundred million in New York moolah, and, well . . . he might be *the* richest. In the new Russia, cash was king. He was about to be seated on a mountainous throne of cash.

"He's still reading the contract," Vladimir eventually answered in a tone saturated with annoyance. He was so tired of being checked up on. "His wife and the American banker are talking."

"Talking about what?"

"Who knows? Who cares?"

"Can't you hear what they're saying?"

"No."

After a brief pause meant to expose the seriousness of his concern, Golitsin asked very quietly, "Why can't you?"

"Because," Vladimir replied testily, "we're seated in the middle of the room, at a vantage where we can keep them from escaping."

"Maybe Konevitch and the banker are planning their escape."

"Possibly they are. So what?"

"I'll tell you *so what*. Hundreds of millions of dollars disappear with them, you idiot."

"Two men are positioned by the exit to the restaurant. Two more by the exit to the hotel. That's three layers of security they would have to make it past. Also I have the Konevitches' passports, and their wallets, and he's nearly crippled. I'm telling you, he's not going anywhere."

Silence.

Vladimir rolled his eyes. "No matter what they try, he's dead."

Golitsin let more silence register his disapproval.

After a long moment, Vladimir said, "I gave him twenty-five minutes to produce the signed contracts or I start shooting. That was twenty-two minutes ago. I think I can keep him from escaping within the next three minutes."

"I still don't like it."

Vladimir could almost see the condescending scowl on Golitsin's face. So far he, Vladimir, had taken all the risks and done every bit of the dirty work. Plotting and overseeing the murder of Alex's executives, the kidnapping, the torture, obtaining the invaluable signatures—his handiwork, all accomplished without a glitch. He was quite proud of it. He had made Golitsin a very, very rich man. Was there even a halfhearted grumble of thanks? How about: Good job, Vladimir my boy, you really pulled this one off?

But more than anything, Vladimir despised being second-guessed and scolded by this deskbound lizard. The old boy hadn't been in smelling distance of real fieldwork in decades. And here he was, sticking his big nose into everything

Then again, Golitsin had promised him a bonus of one hundred thousand dollars, U.S., the instant this job was finished, three hundred if they bagged an additional 300 million of New York dough. A year of lurking in the shadows, of watching and killing—the money was so close he could smell it. No way would he give Golitsin an excuse to snatch it away. Yes, he was tired of being lectured and reprimanded, of having to endure the old man's biting insults, but in a few more hours, he reminded himself, it would be over. A few more hours and he would take his money, and then tell the old man exactly where to stuff it.

He fought the impulse to say, "Shut up and mind your own business," and instead meekly said, "Don't worry, boss. Less than three minutes. We're fifty feet away, watching his every move."

"You're an overconfident idiot. Don't mess this up."

With slightly more than two minutes left before the deadline expired, the lights suddenly went out in the restaurant. Like that, the room was pitched into darkness.

Nearly simultaneously, the kitchen door flew open and out marched a long line of waiters and waitresses, one after another, ten in all. The cute waitress with the impressive bosom headed the procession, proudly hauling a chocolate cake with ten lit birthday candles. The marching line was loudly slaughtering "Happy Birthday," in English polluted by thick Hungarian accents, and moving at a fast clip directly toward the table in the center of the room. Then they came to an abrupt stop, positioning themselves directly between Vladimir, Katya, and the table by the window where Alex and Elena were seated with Eugene.

The moment the throng was in place, stamping their feet and singing in a brash routine imported from an American restaurant chain, Alex leaped up from his chair, lifted the empty chair beside him, and hurled it with as much force as he could muster directly at the big picture window ten feet away. He had rehearsed this throw over and over in his mind. Over and over he told himself, ignore the pain from his dislocated shoulder, forget the severe burn on his chest. No matter how agonizing, put everything he had into this one chance. There wouldn't be another.

The moment the chair launched, he shut his eyes, held his breath, and prayed.

The chair flew through the air, and then, with a loud satisfying crash, the large plate-glass window shattered into a thousand shards and crumbled to the floor.

Vladimir was still holding the satellite phone, still smarting from the conversation.

Katya had been eavesdropping. Her elbows were planted on the table, her head craned sideways in a wonderfully successful attempt to catch every word.

She loathed Vladimir and found huge enjoyment in overhearing the old man browbeat and humble him. She had no love for Golitsin either—a selfish, overbearing, snarling old tyrant she detested to her core. But she worked for him. She took his money and, without complaint, did whatever sordid work he asked of her. And why not? The money was damned good; actually it was merely adequate, but she wasn't about to complain. Two thousand a month in salary when thousands of KGB veterans were out on the street, wiping windshields of traffic-stalled cars and pleading for kopecks.

Plus he was cunning, corrupt, ambitious, and endlessly ruthless; in the bare-knuckle new Russia, with that résumé, she was betting the old coot would shoot quickly to the top. There were worse wagons to hitch her horses to, she reasoned. Besides, her other options were few and not overly hopeful. She had spent twelve years doing dirty work for the KGB before the wall tumbled down. Sadly, her skillset had prepared her for only one thing.

By twenty-six, she had thirty kills on five continents. All clean hits, all professionally flawless. Now thirty-one, her once lustrous hair had been peroxided, bleached, dyed and redyed so many times it hung in listless strands. Her skin resembled a snare drum in need of a rigorous tightening. Long years killing under the hot African and Afghan sun had prematurely aged her. She still had an attractive face, one that bordered on beauty, except for a detached iciness that chased men off. She cared less. Her tastes ran more toward women than men anyway.

Besides, sex didn't interest her generally, and emotions even less.

Unfortunately, that arctic demeanor was exactly what attracted Vladimir, who over the past year had come on to her more than a few times. Like many men with bulletproof egos, beating around the bush wasn't his preferred style of seduction. He barged right into the sweet talk, long, swaggering soliloquies of what he'd like to do to her. Much of it sounded physically impossible; all of it sounded vividly repulsive.

Katya encouraged him in the strongest terms to get lost or, barring that, try performing the acts on himself.

One dark night, while they were staking out a target from a parked van, he gave up on the subtle approach. Without ado, he rabbit-punched her twice on the side of the head, clamped his hands around her throat, and tried to rape her.

She wasn't entirely surprised by his foreplay. The brawl was brief. No quarter was given. His balls screamed with pain for weeks afterward.

She didn't nurse a grudge. Vladimir was an animal. Naturally, his urges lingered closer to the surface than most. She simply hated him a little more passionately than before.

And thus, at that moment, while Golitsin upbraided Vladimir on the phone, she smiled and hung on every word. Way to go, old boy. Oh please, don't forget my favorite part—call him an idiot again.

And thus, at the very moment the lights were extinguished, they both were preoccupied with their own thoughts, off guard and flat-footed. One instant the restaurant was brightly lit and humming with small groups engaged in polite conversation; then, without warning, it went dark and the calamitous mob of waiters and waitresses were clustered in front of their table, a gaggle of people in white uniforms stomping their feet and howling that stupid ditty at the top of their lungs.

A long hesitation. Then both drew their pistols and leaped to their feet. It was already too late.

They heard the glass crash and stretched their necks to look over the choir. They began hopping up and down, feeling like idiots. But between the darkness and the wall of kitchen staff, they were completely blinded.

Vladimir, who prided himself on being a man of action, for once was at a loss, frozen. Katya reacted first. She raised her pistol and fired three shots into the ceiling, rapid-fire—boom, boom, boom. It was absolutely effective—and totally the wrong move. The first shot unleashed a wild fiasco; the next two wildly reinforced it.

Between the thunderous crash of the glass shattering and the upsetting flash and bang of the pistol shots in a dark chamber, the entire dining room collapsed into instant bedlam. Half the waiters and waitresses fell to the floor. The other half fled, screaming and hollering and clawing past one another in the general direction of the kitchen. Customers leaped to their feet, shoving over tables and chairs, banging against each other, racing for sanctuary wherever they could find it. Wails and shrieks and flailing bodies bounced around the room.

After an interminable thirty seconds, somebody flipped the lights back on. Vladimir and Katya stared wide-eyed at Alex's table. "They're gone," Katya screeched, and indeed, they were. Quite gone.

They were dumbfounded. They stood, mute, wide-eyed, gripping their pistols and gawking at the empty table. They took in the gaping hole that had replaced the picture window. They observed the heavy chair that hung on the window frame, dangling precariously. They didn't need to confer, didn't need to voice a single theory or weigh any half-baked suspicions. The facts were right before their eyes, unmistakable. They had underestimated Konevitch. A stupid amateur's mistake, and they had made it: plain and simple.

Konevitch had obviously confided to the waitress that Vladimir and/or Katya were old pals celebrating a birthday, and obviously he persuaded, or more likely bribed, her to have the lights shut off and put on a little show to distract them. Just as obviously, he had faked the severity of his wounds. That harsh limp, that shambling gait, that lame shoulder: nobody that horribly mangled could've tossed that heavy chair, much less disappeared with such speed through the window frame. But he and his wife had successfully bypassed the layers of security. They had escaped, and were out there, on the streets of Budapest.

They were out there now, running for their lives.

Katya came to her senses and screamed at Vladimir, "Go out the window and find them. I'll get the others."

A response was a waste of time. He raced for the hole in the window and dove through, crashing hard on his knees on the concrete sidewalk outside. A loud curse exploded from his lips. The pain was sharp and intense. But his fury at being made into a fool hurt worse. He pushed himself to his feet, extended his pistol arm, spun on his heels, and scanned the surroundings.

Not a soul. Not out on the street. Not in the side parking lot. And not along the front of the hotel.

Alex and his party had vanished into the evening.

The hotel entrance was to his right and guarded by a pair of his men, making it unlikely, if not impossible, that Konevitch fled that way. He gripped his pistol hard and limped off in the other direction. There would be no warning this time. No second chance. He endured the pain from his bleeding knees and kicked it up to an all-out run.

Katya raced to the pair of thugs who were still seated by the restaurant exit, quietly congratulating themselves that they weren't in charge of this mess. When Golitsin learned about this screwup, heads were going to roll, literally.

She shrieked at them to follow her and went and collected the pair by the hotel entrance, then the two bored watchers outside. She ordered two of them to trail Vladimir before she set off, accompanied by the other four, in the opposite direction.

She signaled for the men to spread out, and issued one stern instruction. "Blow them to hell," she hissed.

8

A minute after Vladimir and Katya departed, the long white table-cloth was gently tugged back. Alex slowly raised his head and looked around. A waitress and two waiters loitered by the kitchen entrance, bantering about the bad people who had fired guns and chased all the customers away. The waitress was in tears, trau-matized. One waiter looked ready to faint or flee. Otherwise, the palatial dining room was empty.

Alex stood and glanced over at the table where Vladimir and Katya had been seated. No corpses littered the floor. There were no dead waiters, and from what he could detect, no wounded patrons bleeding on the expensive carpet. He nearly fainted with relief. The three shots he heard were warnings or misses. Prob-ably frantic or angered bullets fired out the broken window, he decided.

"Are they gone?" Elena asked from under the table, almost a whisper.

"Maybe. It looks that way," Alex replied in a tone that conveyed half hope and half doubt. "Stay where you are another moment." He walked over to a waiter by the kitchen, a tall young man, considerably less fazed than the other two. He asked where the shooters had gone. Out of the building, he was informed—one dove out the window and disappeared and the other raced out of the restaurant, collected her evil pals, and dashed outside. Nothing more to worry about, Alex was assured. The bad people were gone. The concierge called the police. Any minute, the place would flood with cops.

Alex rushed back to the table, hefted the overnight bags over his good shoulder, and informed Elena and Eugene it was safe. Elena came out first and threw her arms around Alex, a hug she immediately lessened when he winced and groaned.

Then Eugene emerged, loud, upset, and furiously disoriented. He kept asking Alex why he had grabbed him, wrestled him under the table, pinned him down, and slapped a hand over his mouth. Alex tried leading him out of the room, but Eugene refused to budge until he had a reply, and it better be damned good.

"Long story. I don't have time to explain everything," Alex replied in a hasty effort to put him off, looking around and wondering what to do next. Open and shut, his plan had started and stopped at getting the killers out of the restaurant. Divert them, send them off on a wild-goose chase. Then he and Elena would make a speedy getaway in Eugene's Trabant.

But now, how was he to get to the Trabant in the parking lot without blundering into Vladimir and his people? And, he realized, if he left Eugene here, they might return and take their fury out on him. Eugene's yapping was growing louder. Alex waved a hand for him to calm down and attempted another explanation. "They kidnapped Elena and me, beat me silly, and forced me to sign over my companies. Now they're after your money, too. Let's go."

"My money?"

"Yes, Eugene, that's what I said."

"You know them?"

"We just met this afternoon. I don't want to get to know them better. Come on, we have to hurry." Alex glanced at the doorway to the dining room. He did not have time for these questions.

"Who are these people?"

"Eugene, please, shut up and help me. They're out there. Right now, they're combing the street, hunting for us. In a few moments, they'll figure out they've been hoodwinked and they'll be back. They're professional assassins. Are you listening?"

In the past two minutes, Eugene had passed from inebriated verging on tipsy to frightened out of his wits with Alex nearly smothering him under the table; he was finally settling on an emotion he could live with. Upset. Very, very upset. "Dammit, I'm not going anywhere. Why don't you just wait for the police?"

"Because they might be in on it. There's a very good chance they are. These people are unbelievably well-connected, better than you can even imagine, Eugene, and I can't . . . Listen to me, it's time to leave, now."

Eugene still looked angry and dubious—it *was* a lot to absorb—and Alex decided it was time to be blunt, and possibly a little deceitful. "It's not just Elena and me, they're hunting you, too. They want to kidnap and torture you, to force you to get your partners to wire the cash into my corporate accounts. They made me sign over the title to my companies, and now they want to steal your three hundred million, all of it. After that, they'll kill you."

Eugene suddenly felt nauseated. "They want to kill me?" he asked in a high-pitched voice. This was too much. He leaned back against a table and, drawing a few labored breaths, struggled to regain his balance; recapturing his composure was out of the question. He couldn't seem to think. He deeply regretted all those beers. How many was it? Eight? Nine? However many, the answer was: too many.

Alex placed a hand on his arm. "Yes," he said very quietly. "After they beat and torture you, after they steal all your money, yes, Eugene, yes, they intend to kill you."

Elena had been standing quietly, listening, and decided the time was right to throw her two cents in. Only shock would get this man moving, and she provided it. "Look what they did to Alex. Look at his battered face. Look, they nearly killed him, Eugene. They beat him for hours and burned him with an iron. That's what they'll do to you, too. Now, please stop wasting time. Do what Alex says."

With that, it finally sank in and Eugene offered the one response that felt appropriate at that moment. He vomited, a huge, boisterous gusher that splashed across the floor. He bent over, sucked in a few deep breaths, wiped the sleeve of his hand-tailored, thousand-dollar suit across his mouth and nose, then mumbled his first intelligent words of the night. "Get me the hell out of here."

Alex walked over to the same waiter he had spoken with earlier, politely explained what he needed, handed him the keys to the rented orange Trabant, and stuffed a hundred-dollar bill into his palm with the promise of another hundred the second the job was done.

Vladimir raced down the long alleyway and fought to suppress his exploding anxiety. He should have caught up with them by now, he realized. By his calculation, after they fled the hotel, this was the only route Konevitch and his wife and their plump friend could've taken.

Even if Konevitch *had* faked the severity of his injuries, Vladimir was damn sure he was at least partially lame. He had personally slammed that chair across his leg. Had smashed it down with such pulverizing force that it splintered into pieces against Konevitch's muscle, tissue, and bone. It was a miracle Konevitch could walk; running was out of the question, he was sure of it.

Also that short wife and flabby American banker were accompanying him. Vladimir was a fitness fanatic, a former Spetsnaz soldier who spent long hours in the gym buffing his superb condition. He had been sprinting, nearly full-speed, for four, possibly five minutes now.

He slowed to a hesitant trot, then an angry stomp for a few yards before he came to a dead halt in his tracks. He was breathing heavily. No, this definitely did not add up. He stole a quick glance at his watch: six minutes.

Six minutes.

A gimp, a fatty, and a small woman—a woman!—no way were they a match for his speed. It simply wasn't possible, he concluded with excruciating insight.

He quickly reviewed the possibilities. It was a simple process of elimination; exactly the arithmetic he should've use six minutes before, he now knew. One, had they leaped out the window and run away in the other direction, the team posted outside the entrance would've seen them and blasted away. Two, had they instead exited through the lobby and out the hotel's front entrance, either of the two teams by the entrance would've bagged them. Open and shut.

There was, however, a third possibility. The least physically demanding possibility for a wounded man, as he thought about it—the most likely possibility, he realized with an ugly curse.

If only Katya hadn't barked at him to rush out the window. Stupid bitch. Like a snot-nosed rookie, she panicked. Rule number one: be sure what you *think* you see is what you're actually seeing. They should've yanked back all the curtains and peeked under all the tables.

Oh look, it's Alex and his friends playing peekaboo; ha, ha, ha—bang, bang, bang.

How simple that would've been. How deeply satisfying.

But no, they fell for Konevitch's cat-and-mouse game, and the mouse won. It was terribly stupid. But this blunder was definitely her fault, not his.

No, on second thought, the real blame fell on Golitsin's stooped shoulders. He approved the plan in the first place to drag Konevitch to the hotel. Okay, yes, Vladimir had claimed it would be easy. But of course there were risks. The greedy bastard knew that, but he wanted more money, money, money.

Konevitch baited the trap and the old geezer bit with every tooth in his mouth. He had nobody to blame but himself.

The satellite phone suddenly rattled at his waist. After a long hesitation, he pulled it off his belt and stared at it, consumed with dread, a new and surprisingly unwelcome emotion for Vladimir. Probably it was Golitsin. He would not answer it, not under any condition. He would just let it bleep and bleep until the old geezer got frustrated and gave up.

The thought of trying to explain this muddle, of trying to justify and excuse his stupidity, of confessing that he had allowed Konevitch to escape, was sickening.

On the other hand, maybe it was Katya. Maybe she was calling to say she had caught up with them; maybe Konevitch and his short wife and fat friend were already decomposing in a dark alley and out of their hair. Maybe their troubles were over. Oh, how he longed to hear those words.

So which was it? The devil or salvation? The bastard or the bitch?

He pushed the receive button and placed the phone firmly against his ear.

Golitsin said without a breath of emotion, "Your twenty-five minutes are long over. I'm assuming you lost him."

Vladimir felt a rush of fear bordering on panic. The voice was cold, so totally flat. For a moment he said nothing. He just stood there, tempted to throw the phone and flee as far and as fast as his feet could carry him. Find a new life in India or Zanzibar, for all he cared.

What could he say?

Golitsin snapped, "Your silence confirms it, you cretin. You were outsmarted by a complete dilettante."

"I still made you a fortune."

"So what?"

"Hundreds of millions. Doesn't that count for anything?"

"No." Just no.

"He hasn't escaped yet," Vladimir insisted, trying to sound convincing. The echo of his own bleating in the earphone, loud and whiny, shocked him.

"Oh, I think we both know he is long gone," Golitsin whispered, and he was right. "He and my three hundred million. All gone. Vanished. And it's your fault, you incompetent dimwit."

Vladimir stared into the dark, overcast skies. The alley was narrow and empty: no pedestrians; no lost tourists wandering in confusion; not even a smelly wino sleeping it off on a dark doorstoop. Just him, just a dead man sniveling into a clunky satphone. A scatter of small shops lined both sides of the street, all of which were locked and shuttered. Rain was pouring down in heavy sheets. A few lights burned in the apartments over the stores and the flickering glow from television sets refracted off several windows. The gloom contributed to his quickly deepening misery. "I'm sorry," he choked, mangling the words he had never before uttered in his life. He tried again, more clearly, more unctuously repentant, anything to mollify the menacing voice on the other end. "Truly, sir, I am very, very sorry."

"Are you?"

"Yes sir. Sorry, sorry, sorry. "

"Well, sorry won't do, idiot. Sorry is for spilling coffee on my carpet. But losing three hundred million dollars? For letting Konevitch escape from under your nose? Just sorry?" Golitsin paused for a moment, then laid down the verdict. "When I am done with you, you'll learn the real meaning of sorry."

Vladimir reached into his waistband and withdrew his pistol. He took a deep swallow and said, "That's where you're wrong. You'll never get your hands on me, you ugly old bastard."

"Listen closely, moron. Wherever you run, I'll find you. You'll last days, long, terrible days, I promise that."

Vladimir laughed and the sound echoed down the alley and bounced off the walls, bitter and scornful. A few lights popped on. Concerned faces appeared in the windows over the empty shops.

"You think this is funny?" Golitsin hissed.

"Yes, I do. Absolutely. I'm laughing because I lost you all that money. Now screw yourself." Vladimir aimed the pistol at his left temple, held the phone right next to it, screamed, "Good-bye, asshole!"—and blew his brains down the dark alleyway.

9

The orange Trabant came to a screeching halt under the hotel's grand entryway, less than an inch from the steep curb. Alex, Elena, and Eugene scrambled through the rotating glass doors, looked both ways, then made a mad bolt for the car. Alex stuffed another hundred in the waiter's outstretched hand, mumbled quick words of thanks, and they squeezed and fought their way inside the car. The keys were in the ignition, the engine running. Elena climbed behind the wheel and punched the gas with gusto.

With an angry sputter the car lurched and coughed away from the curb, every bit as unsightly and underpowered as advertised. Only two years off the production line, it didn't look a day over a hundred. From bumper to bumper, nothing but peeling paint, dents, and vast patches of oxidation.

Alex couldn't have cared less. The car was perfect. Every rattle, every belch and spit from the perforated muffler was just perfect. Nobody would expect a man of his means to be seen in such a creaky monstrosity.

For five minutes they drove without anybody saying a word. The rain battered the roof. Alex hunched down in his seat to disguise his height; Elena inched up in hers, straining to disguise her lack of it.

Thirty minutes of sitting under the watchful gaze of wicked

people who intended to kill them left them moody and edgy. They peeked through the rear window incessantly. They thought they saw cars on their tail and breathed with relief when the cars turned off. Elena zigzagged through narrow streets, going nowhere in particular. Just away from the hotel. Just as far as they could get from Katya and Vladimir and the other killers. At a red light at a large intersection, she finally asked Alex, "Where to?"

Without hesitation, he said, "Out of Hungary."

"Not so fast," Eugene offered in a newly concerned tone from the backseat. "Alex, you need to see a doctor before we go anywhere." Now that they were out of danger, his good manners were kicking back in. "You should see how you look. A concussion, broken bones, internal bleeding, who knows how serious the damage is."

"Not a good idea, Eugene. I told you, these people are connected everywhere. They're former KGB, for godsakes. You're American, you don't understand what that means."

"So tell me what it means."

"They used to rule these countries. They can pull strings you can't imagine. The moment they recover their senses, they might even put out an alert to the Hungarian border police. Our names, our descriptions, and probably some trumped-up charges to warrant our arrests. Getting out will be impossible."

Eugene and Elena sat quietly and stewed on Alex's warning.

"In fact," Alex said after thinking about his own words, "it's safe to assume the alert's already out."

Another moment of silence, longer than the last one. A nationwide manhunt suddenly seemed like a possibility. Only a few years earlier this was a police state; they didn't have a prayer.

"Then the train station and airport are out of the question," Elena observed sensibly. "They'll alert those places first."

Alex nodded. "But I think they'll check hospitals and doctor's offices before they do anything else." He squeezed Elena's leg. "The nearest land border is our best chance." He twisted around in the seat and peered at Eugene. "You still have your cell phone?"

Eugene patted himself down. "It's gone. It was still sitting on the table when you pulled me down. I'll bet it's still there."

"Of course."

"Our passports, Alex, they have them," Elena remembered with a jolt. "Maybe it would be better just to stay here. Find a safe place and hide."

"I don't think so." Alex held up a clutch of small red booklets and waved them in front of her. "These were packed in a hidden compartment of my overnight bag."

Elena shook her head. Her husband's cleverness had long since ceased to surprise her, but to insist on bringing the overnight bags for the restaurant meeting with Eugene was an amazing stroke of clear thinking. She didn't need to ask about the fistful of little booklets.

But Eugene did. "Are those legal?"

Elena caught his eye in the rearview mirror. "Whenever Alex accompanied Yeltsin on overseas trips he submitted his passport for the required visa. Now that Russians are free to travel overseas, seventy years of curiosity about the outside world demands to be instantly vented. The visa office of the Foreign Ministry is choked with requests. Mountains of paper everywhere. And more often than not, requests with the accompanying passports get lost or misplaced in the logjam. These are former Soviet bureaucrats we're talking about. It's a miracle they find their way home at night."

Alex continued, "Two or three days out, my office would call to complain, and liberally mention Yeltsin's name. Rather than hunt for a pin in a haystack, a clerk would just issue a new passport with the appropriate visa and send it by courier. That's the right expression, right? Pin in a haystack? Anyway, a month or two later, when the original turned up, it was returned by mail."

"Exactly how many do you have?" Eugene asked, enjoying his little peek into Russian inefficiency. A died-in-the-wool capitalist, he loved hearing about the sins of former commies.

"I honestly don't know."

"Guess."

"Ten. A dozen. Perhaps more."

Elena had twice gone along on Yeltsin's trips; she had three passports, one, of course, now inconveniently tucked in the back pocket of Vladimir's corpse. But Alex always shoved a few extras in his baggage, in the event the ones he or she were using got lost or stolen.

"There are two borders we can head for," Alex was saying, sharing the possibilities as he tried to think this through. "Austria to the south. Or due east, to Czechoslovakia."

"Okay, which?"

"I think Austria makes the most sense. It's closer. Also, I have part ownership of an advertising company in the capital. Illya Mechoukov is the president. A good man. I trust him. Better yet, the KGB had little influence there." He opened the window and took a deep breath. The night had turned cold. A frigid blast of air hit him in the face, but he felt dizzy. He briefly pondered the possibility that the exhaust was spewing carbon monoxide into the cabin. "Unfortunately, that border takes a visa. The Czechs and Slovaks, though, as former Bloc members, still have open borders for Russian passports."

"Where do you want to cross?" Elena asked, now that Austria was ruled out. She searched the rearview mirror. Nothing.

"Avoid the major arteries. Our best chance is a secondary or backcountry road. The guards at the smaller checkpoints will be the last ones alerted."

Eugene decided to join the discussion and leaned forward from the backseat. "Then what?"

"Then . . . directly to the nearest international airport. That would be Slovakia," Alex answered.

"Then Russia, right?"

"Maybe."

"I don't see that you have a choice, pal. You better get back there fast," Eugene advised.

"Do you think?"

"You better rescind those letters before anybody can act on them."

"I have other worries right now," Alex replied almost absently. He reached up and switched on the overhead light, which thankfully seemed to be the one thing in the car that functioned properly. He began flipping through passports and thumbing the pages.

"You know what?" Eugene announced, lurching forward in his seat.

"I think you're about to tell me what."

"Damn right I am. I think you got conked on the head harder than you realize. You're not thinking clearly. They could empty out your bank accounts in hours and, in a day or so, swipe all the investors' money in your banks."

"Don't you think that's a lot of cash to haul away?" Alex replied, curiously indifferent.

"You know damn well what I'm talking about. Come on, pal. They'll wire it all to a bank in the Azores or Switzerland. Then it'll shuttle around to a hundred banks and fall off the radar."

With no small amount of pleasure, Alex said, "I don't think so."

"Think harder."

"The people who forced me to sign those letters know nothing about banking. To move even a dollar they need my account numbers and the security codes."

"Oh."

"And those are all locked away in a safe in my office, guarded around the clock. They didn't know enough to ask about the numbers and I wasn't in the mood to educate them."

Elena reached over and patted her husband on the leg. "You're a genius."

His nose was stuffed back inside the passports.

Sergei Golitsin sat behind Alex Konevitch's massive hand-carved desk and stared across it at the ten hungry faces around the long conference table. The irony of using Alex's own office as a command post to track him down and kill him was too delicious.

A phone was positioned directly in front of each man. A yellow notepad and a slew of satphones were poised within arm's reach. Empty coffee mugs littered the table. Ashtrays overflowed with snuffed-out butts. A large, 10,000-to-1 map of Hungary was taped to a wall, with dozens of little yellow and red pins stuck here and there. Another map, even larger, displaying the entire European continent and punctured with a similar mixture of multicolored pins, was fastened to the adjoining wall.

The men inside the room knew the address of Konevitch's unpretentious but nicely located Parisian apartment. They knew what hotels he preferred when he traveled, as well as the address of each and every office and subsidiary of Konevitch Associates outside the Russian border. A pin for each one, with a man or two now lurking at each destination. A mushroom of cigarette smoke rose from the table and swirled in cancerous eddies just below the ceiling.

Below them, the six floors of Konevitch Associates were nearly deserted. A handpicked crew of security guards ambled around the building; otherwise, the employees were home, cleaning up after dinner, mixing it up with their lovers, or snoring loudly in their beds. A few hyperambitious souls had tried to work late, but the guards had chased them out and shut down their phones and computers.

A sign was posted on the front door downstairs announcing a two-day holiday. A squad of burly guards would be placed there in the morning to make sure everybody got the message.

At that second, for the first time in two frantic hours, only one noise interrupted the sound of breathing—a buzzing that emanated from a specialist and his assistant employing a noisy instrument of some sort to crack a wall safe. The specialist had twice reassured everybody it was going "super splendidly." No hitches. No surprises, and Golitsin had good reason not to doubt him.

Six months before, when Alex Konevitch had ordered a personal safe to be installed in his office, the job naturally landed on the desk of his corporate security chief. Golitsin promptly handed it off to a black job specialist who once worked under him at the KGB, a master thief with an encyclopedic knowledge of safes and locks. Golitsin's instructions were precise and contradictory.

Nothing but the best brand on the market for the boss. Something sturdy, something imposing in appearance, something with a tidy reputation for quality, he'd emphasized; in other words, something that would duly impress its owner.

Just be damn sure the model was one he was sure he could crack; within two hours or less would do the trick nicely.

Golitsin's top deputy, Felix Glebov, eventually broke the awkward silence. "It's been three hours. Where is he?"

"Still running," Golitsin said, eyes blazing down the table with a look that could curdle bowels. "A scared rabbit, fleeing for his life." He paused briefly to scratch his chin. "Successfully, apparently, because he's up against a bunch of incompetent twits."

One of the twits, large, with a neck that moved like a tank turret, spoke up, a nervous attempt to deflect blame from his overgrown shoulders. "I have ten good people at the Budapest train station. Twenty more at the airport, a man at each ticket counter. All former KGB or Hungarian secret police. Another squad is hanging out at the arrival gate at Sheremetyevo Airport in the event they make it this far." Eager to impress everybody with his efficiency, he added, "They all have color pictures."

"Good for you," replied the next twit in line, a man with a skinny, pockmarked face and puffy eyes who lost no time launching his own accomplishments. "Only two minutes ago I got off the phone with the deputy minister of Hungarian Security. He has two children in private school and is cracking heads to collect the hundred thousand bounty I promised if he catches them. An hour ago, a red alert went out to all customs offices. They and the police have been notified a murderer and his accomplices are trying to flee."

He paused to be sure everybody heard the next point. "Katya and one her people gave statements to the police. Said they witnessed Konevitch stick a knife in a man's back at the airport. Said they thought they recognized his face from photos in a Russian magazine, but couldn't remember if he was a movie star or what. Took them a while to figure it out, so now they're reporting it."

That last clever move was Katya's brainchild. Of course he felt no obligation to mention it now.

The next man, introduced by Golitsin to the others earlier that evening as Nicky—no last name, no formal introduction, just plain Nicky—sat for a moment, sucking deeply from a black cheroot, bored out of his mind, trying to entertain himself watching the safecrackers at work. Dressed head to toe in shiny black leather, down to his dapper biker boots, he was the only man present who did not get the executive-suite dress code. He was also the only non-employee of Konevitch Associates, the only one not hired by Golitsin over the past year for what they brought to this table.

Lacking a KGB background, he was also happily clueless about the reporting procedures.

Eventually the silence grabbed his attention and he noticed everybody staring at him. He crushed his cigarette on the tabletop, flashed an amused sneer, then held it long enough for everybody to get the message. Nicky came from a different world, one without silly protocols, a world with but one simple rule: rules are meant to be broken.

But even without the last name—despite never having seen him face-to-face—half the men around the table were sure they knew who he was. A photo of his face had hung in a place of honor on KGB walls long enough to grow mold. A much younger face, certainly. A little thinner, maybe, without the cute ponytail laced with gray that bounced when he strutted. One with considerably less scars, absent the gallery of tattoos on the neck, and certainly before the huge nose had been rearranged into a bent banana.

Nicky, aka Igor, aka Leon, or a half dozen other transient aliases he had used and thrown away in his illustrious career, was in fact one Nickolas Kozyrev, head of the largest crime syndicate in Russia.

How ironic that they were all now sharing the same table, smoking and sipping coffee like old pals. In their previous lives, they had spent countless hours chasing Nicky around the shadows. Typical gruntwork for the police ordinarily, except Nicky's kingdom had tentacles in every Russian city, webs that stretched across Europe and Asia, and bustling branch offices in Brighton

Beach and Miami. Nicky was known and wanted by police forces from New York to Timbuktu. Three different American presidents and an army of other world leaders had bombarded two different general secretaries with strong requests to get Nicky off the street.

Among assorted other enterprises, Nicky wholesaled kidnapped girls to whorehouses, owned a string of porn studios, blackmarketed, smuggled arms, traded in stolen cars, gems, artwork, pushed heroin and an assortment of other illegal pharmaceuticals, and most recently, was making a loud splash in Russia's burgeoning executive kidnapping market. Wherever there was illicit profit to be made, Nicky pushed his sticky fingers in. Contract murder had long been a mainstay of his repertoire. The sheer breadth, expanse, and outright violence of his operation proved too considerable for the police to handle; not to mention wildly exaggerated suspicions that Nicky owned half the senior police officers in the country.

A quarter was more like it.

Thus the KBG was brought into the hunt and encouraged to use every filthy trick in its arsenal.

And despite every effort, despite years of exhausting work, they had never come close. Not even close.

"Tell me again," Nicky opened, his eyes dancing playfully around the table, "exactly how this guy got away."

He knew damn well how Konevitch escaped. They had already been over it, in detail. Twice. But he despised these former KGB boys. He would keep asking again and again, because it amused him to rub their faces in it.

Making no effort to disguise his irritation, Golitsin said, "Why does it matter? He got away. Now we'll find him."

"It matters because I say it does."

"Is that right?"

"Yeah, I'm just trying to figure out how all your morons got made asses of." His lips curled and he watched Golitsin. "Remind me, how old is this Konevitch guy? Who trained him to be such a Houdini? The KGB? The army?"

"Vladimir was the moron who let this happen. He was your man, last time I checked."

"Yeah, on loan to you for the past year, last time I checked. When I sent you Vladimir, he was a real killing machine. Your cretins polluted him, turned him stupid and clumsy."

Golitsin held his breath and counted to ten. An hour before, they had sniped back and forth like this for a full fifteen minutes. He gathered as much patience as he could muster and said, "Tell me what your people are doing."

Nicky had broken his spell of boredom and gotten his blood; he could wait until the next opportunity rolled around. He fought back a smile and said, "All right. Word's been passed to all my guys in East Europe. Since we got their passports, they'll need new ones, right? So what are they gonna do? Try and buy phonies, right? Every counterfeiter and half-assed fabricator in Hungary's been warned to pass word the second they make contact."

Golitsin nodded. Sounded good.

Nicky pulled out another black cheroot and lit up. "I got pick-pocket teams working every train and plane station in Europe. They been told to keep a good eye out for a gimpy giant, a blonde runt, and a rich American fatty."

The twit who had just detailed his own efforts at corralling Alex at transportation terminals leaned forward and advised Nicky, "Consider giving them photographs instead. Our experience shows that visual representations always work better than verbal descriptions." He produced a crooked smile. "If you have fax machines, I'll provide copies."

He instantly regretted that he had opened his mouth. "Fax machines?" Nicky roared. He looked ready to bounce out of his seat and strangle the twit. "Oh, sure, moron. Hell, every pickpocket's got one. You know, stuffed in his back pocket." The other former agents at the table instantly hated the thick-necked dolt for his stupid remark. Little wonder they never caught Nicky.

Nicky planted his leather elbows on the table. "Listen up, ass-hole. They don't need no pictures. Pickpockets are . . . what? Ob-servant, right? It's what they do. All day, staring at people, sizing 'em up. They can tell in a blink if a mark's got ten bucks in their pocket and who's got a thousand."

Another withering glare at the fool and Nicky clammed up. Why cast pearls before swine? He lit another cigarette and collapsed back into his chair.

The next man in line, in an earlier life the Ministry of Interior's liaison to Interpol, squirmed for a moment, stared down at the table, picked at a scab on his nose, then as quietly as he could, mumbled, "I called my former colleagues and alerted them that a warrant for Alex's arrest would be coming their way within hours."

Time for the next man in line to speak up. Nobody did, and the silence quickly turned deafening.

The man stole a quick sideways peek at Golitsin, who was staring back with a mean scowl. "And what are they doing about it?" Golitsin snapped, his scowl deepening.

This was not the question the man wanted to hear. "And they . . . they listened."

"Listened?"

"Well . . . umh, yes. Interpol won't do anything until a formal request is launched through appropriate legal channels. Can't really. The protocol is written in stone. It's a very bureaucratic and—"

"You're saying Interpol won't do anything?"

"No. I'm . . . I'm not saying that."

The other sharks around the table were edging forward in their seats, waiting for the fireworks to erupt. Oh yeah, pal, that's what you're saying, no question about it. "Then explain to me what you meant," Golitsin barked.

"We . . . that is, we, as executives of Konevitch Associates, we don't, well . . . we don't exactly have the legal authority to demand an arrest. Interpol wants to see a legitimate warrant before it will act."

The man reached under the table and with both hands gripped his knees together to keep them from shaking. His face was red. A jackhammer was going off in his chest. With pleading eyes he

looked around the table for help, a meager sign of support, anything; a tepid nod of pity would be fine. Nine sets of eyes looked
elsewhere. At the table, the ceiling, the white walls.

"Did you offer your contacts money?" Golitsin asked.

"Money, women, cars, drugs. Yes, anything their hearts desire."
Complete silence.

"And they swore at me and hung up."

"Then you didn't offer enough, idiot."

Nervous snickers around the table. They had all, every last
man, heard the pistol shot reverberate through Golitsin's phone
in that fatal final conversation with Vladimir. What a moment.
Just the sound of Golitsin's throaty voice and that hardass Vladimir pumped a bullet into his own head. One for the record books,
definitely.

More to the point, they had collectively witnessed the old man's
response. He did not flinch or cringe or curse. Bang—not even a
wrinkle of surprise. Actually, he smiled.

It looked, in fact, remarkably like the unpleasant little smirk he
was offering Mr. Interpol at that moment. Wouldn't it be special
if that smile ignited a heart attack?

Golitsin cracked a knuckle, then in a hectoring tone said, "Listen to me, idiot. All you idiots listen up. Konevitch doesn't have a
game plan. He's improvising. If, somehow, they make it over the
Hungarian border, they could jump on a late-night train or plane
and end up anywhere in Europe. Only Interpol can issue orders
broad enough to cover the entire continent. Only Interpol has
instant access to charge card information. Only Interpol can forward warrants to police and border officials across Europe. Are
you getting this?"

The man was scribbling notes furiously in a small notebook.
Not a word had been said that he did not already know. If he
shrank any deeper into his chair, he would disappear.

Golitsin stood up and walked in his direction. He bent over, got
less than six inches from the man's ear, and muttered, "Get back
on the phone and offer more money, moron."

Golitsin headed for the door, kicked it open, and slammed it loudly after he left. The room nearly collapsed in relief; everybody except Nicky. Watching these boys squirm and sweat was more fun than he could remember.

They all grabbed their phones and began making more calls, frantic now to find Alex Konevitch.

Golitsin took the stairs one at a time, down one flight, then bounced along a short hallway that ended in a small, well-lit conference room. A young lady, shapely and wonderfully attractive in red business attire, tight jacket, and a provocatively short skirt was seated patiently at the end of the long table.

A stout bodyguard stood in the corner and kept his mouth shut.

She looked up as Golitsin entered and acknowledged his presence with a cold smile. "How's it going, Sergei?"

Not many people dared call him Sergei. General Golitsin was fine; plain General better yet. His own wife and children called him General to his face and The General behind his back; he liked that most of all, the singularity of it. That had been his rank, after all—a lifetime title, one that reeked of power, prestige, and authority. He particularly enjoyed the look in their eyes when people learned it was not army, but KGB rank.

The informality of Sergei, though, was reserved for his equals; in his mind, there weren't many. Tatyana Lukin certainly wasn't his equal; she was the special assistant to Yeltsin's chief of staff, the youngest one, his right hand and chief counsel.

Nothing about that impressed Golitsin.

The Kremlin had more special assistants than mice, clawing around and trying to look and act more important than the replaceable coatholders they definitely were. But Tatyana came with another qualification, a priceless one. She happened also to be the chief of staff's mistress, the person who planted the first whisper in his ear in the morning, with final say at night. The chief was a lazy bureaucrat, a man who adored the many perks of his position and detested the maddening grind of daily work. His major qualification for his lofty title was that he was a more than willing drinking buddy for this sorry lush of a president. The whole Kremlin staff knew it. Anything of importance was therefore passed through Tatyana, who more than compensated for her boss's steady indifference.

She held a law degree from Moscow University, where she had graduated top of her class. A background check performed by his people revealed that those professors she couldn't awe with her mastery of law she conquered with her body. That got her to number two. Number one was a young genius who ignored sleep and consumed libraries, with an elephantine memory and a talent for oratory that would make a southern preacher blanch with envy. Two weeks before graduation, the KGB received a late-night tip—a female caller, the records revealed, who naturally insisted on anonymity—to ransack his room. The contraband was discovered under the bed, a stack of kiddie-porn magazines and nauseating videos, all with American trademarks, making them doubly illegal—all of which he naturally protested he'd never laid eyes on in his life. The next day, he was forced to goose-step across a stage to a chorus of boos and hisses from the entire student body, then hauled straight to jail.

His fourth day in prison, he was beaten to death by a fellow prisoner with two young daughters and a hard-fisted aversion to perverts.

After that, three years as a state prosecutor. Tatyana never lost a case, not one. From the best his people could tell, she seduced at least two judges to acquire convictions of men who were flagrantly innocent. The rumors about her in Moscow's legal circles were rich and rife. She blackmailed and framed witnesses. She burned evidence contrary to her case, concocted false evidence, persuaded the police to force confessions, and so on. Golitsin believed every word of it. She was a scheming, conniving whore whose only scruple was to get ahead, whatever the cost. The old man admired her greatly.

Tatyana had the looks, the brains, the ambitions, and, more importantly, the chief of staff's balls in her hand. She could call him Sergei, or idiot, or toad for all he cared. He looked upon her as the daughter he wished he'd had, rather than the ugly cow he ended up with.

"Get lost," Golitsin barked at the guard, who shot out the door.

"Everything's on track," he informed Tatyana with a confident scowl. He moved around the room and collapsed into the chair at the other end of the table. "Just one unexpected glitch."

"Oh, do tell."

"Konevitch and his pretty little wife, they got away."

"Okay." Cool as ice, no shock, no histrionics. "Please explain that."

Golitsin launched into a brief recap. He left out a few embarrassing details, such as his own miserable role in dispatching Konevitch to the hotel. Nor did he feel it at all necessary to bring up the extra three hundred million that nearly fell in his lap, which he fully intended to keep for himself. When the doctored tale was done, he concluded, "We've initiated a manhunt. We're turning over all the usual rocks. I'm sure he'll turn up."

She had gorgeously thick black hair and was playing with a long strand next to her left ear. "And if he doesn't?" she asked, revealing no shock or surprise at this turn.

"Well, then he doesn't."

"But he signed the letters?"

"After a little persuasion, yes."

"And you now have the originals?"

"Signed, sealed, and delivered to my office an hour ago."

"And properly notarized by an attorney, I'm sure."

"Good assumption."

The lawyer in her seemed satisfied. "Does he know you're behind it yet?"

"Not yet, no. The name of his successor was left blank."

"Whose idea was that?"

"Who do you think?"

She raised an admiring eyebrow at that touch. As long as Konevitch didn't know who put this together, he wouldn't know who or what he was fighting. Time counted for everything. Hours were worth half a fortune. A full day was worth everything Konevitch owned.

It was brilliant, really. Keep him guessing and punching in the dark until they chose to expose themselves.

"Where do you think he'll go next?"

"If he's stupid, here. Moscow."

"But he's not stupid, is he?" she asked. A rhetorical question, really. The man was brilliant and full of surprises. Why else were they in this room, at this hour, rehashing his escape?

Golitsin grinned. "He was stupid enough to hire me."

"Good point." She laughed.

"Right now," Golitsin hypothesized in his usual way, as if it were a fact, "he's probably gone to ground. I think he's hiding someplace in Hungary. Trying to wait us out."

"Interesting. What makes you think that?"

"Deductive logic. We took their wallets, and we have his and his wife's passports. He can't get out. I limited the kidnap team to only ten people, and to the best of our knowledge, that's all he's seen. He has no idea how many more people are involved. But we won't underestimate him again. The torture was administered by one of Nicky's people, so Konevitch might reasonably guess the Mafiya is behind this. That alone will scare the crap out of him. He'll try to keep his head down, perhaps by driving around all night, or checking into a cheap fleabag long enough to lick his wounds. As long as he stays in Hungary, we're fine. In another ten hours it won't matter where he turns up."

She seemed to consider this. "Have you traveled overseas lately?"

"No."

"But Konevitch has, right?"

"You know he has. Between Yeltsin's trips and his own business, he's on the road more than he's here."

"Then it's safe to presume he has more passports."

"How do you know this?"

"Trust me. You know, I also usually accompany Yeltsin. I have seven passports with open visas myself."

A bored shrug. "So what? It really doesn't matter if he has a thousand. If he makes it to Austria or Czechoslovakia, we'll find him. Like I said, the key is keeping him away from here."

Tatyana stood up and moved around the table. She lit a cigarette as she walked, and a long trail of smoke curdled behind her. She came to a stop less than two feet from Golitsin. A small hop and she was on the table, seated, legs swaying loosely from side to side. Long, lovely legs. She crossed one knee over the other and leaned in toward the old man.

He could smell her perfume, something wicked and musky— probably French, definitely expensive, a gift from one of her well-heeled lovers, he guessed. She had left the top three buttons of her jacket undone, he noticed, offering a quick peek at the chief of staff's playthings.

He spent a long moment taking it all in, the aroma, the pose, the alluring flare of her nostrils. She was just so perfect—a perfect blend of Asiatic and Caucasian, perfect teeth, perfect black, uninhibited eyes, perfect body. She leaned a little lower. "Who do you think he'll call first? What's your hunch?"

"I know who he'll call. Sonja."

"And who's she? The mistress?"

"No, the secretary. Been with him since the beginning. He relies on her for everything, an old lady he trusts completely. Treats her like the mother he barely knew." He pushed his chair back and stretched his short arms over his head. He was too old, too tired, and too callous to be seduced. He definitely admired the effort, though.

The message was received, and she produced an elegant little shrug; even the shrug was a turn-on. She took another pull off her cigarette. "So where's this Sonja? At home?"

"She was, yes, before we dragged her back here. She's seated at her desk at this moment, with a garrote dangling loosely around her neck. If he calls, she'll ask for his location or the new necklace will become unbearably uncomfortable."

"You don't miss much, do you?"

"No, I don't. But in the event we don't catch him tonight, tomorrow will be your turn."

She bounced off the table and with one hand began nimbly rebuttoning her jacket. "Relax, Sergei. Yeltsin's in China trying to mend a thousand years of bad relations. He'll be kissing Chinese ass for the next three days, bouncing around landmarks and ceremonies, drinking himself into a stupor at every opportunity. He'll be impossible to reach." She headed toward the door. "Everything on my end is taken care of."

Malcolm Street Associates was an opulent firm with an operations room fashioned to impress. Only the rare visitor was ever allowed inside, but to a man, they walked out whistling and shaking their head. Large flashing screens overloaded the walls, lights blinked, faxes whirred, computers hummed, phones always jangling with agents reporting in. Day or night, it was a beehive of dizzying activity.

The Vault, as it was called by its stressed-out inhabitants, occupied the entire top floor of the London headquarters, a five-story, stone-faced building located two blocks off Trafalgar Square. According to the brass plaque beside the front entry it had been established in 1830.

The tradition of maintaining eternally expanding profits fell on Lord Eldridge Pettlebone, an intimidating former police superintendent, number eight in the short line of managing partners, and at that moment a man who was annoyed almost to the point of bother. Twenty minutes before, a courier had fought his way past the doorman of his club and dragged him here.

A dead agent, and a missing client. One or the other, maybe. A twofer was unheard of, and the entire firm was reeling with distress. He paced around the long table where the firm's best and brightest were gathered, trying to catch up on a fiasco that had a long head start and took off at a gallop. He stifled a yawn, squared his shoulders, and tried to appear steady for the troops.

He had handled serious crises before, plenty of them. Nearly all came late at night. Each arrived with its own unique twists and turns. The first reports were always wrong, the second and third reports only more so.

"Who exactly confirmed Bernie Lutcher's death?" he asked, staring directly at one of the bloodshot-eyed assistants crowded around the table. This particular man, as a sad result of his previous time at a backwater desk in MI6, had the rare misfortune to be nearly fluent in Hungarian. That peculiar distinction earned him a turn on the hotseat, but he had worked himself into a lather and felt eager and ready for whatever Number Eight threw at him.

The young man straightened his tie, gathered his wits, and sat up. "The coroner of the Budapest police. The body was called in by airport security at one-fifteen, Budapest time. The police arrived a few minutes later. Bernie's corpse was transported to the city morgue, then placed in cold storage until six, when the night shift came on. The preliminary workup was done by a Dr. Laszlo"—he conferred with his notes—"Massouri."

Lord Pettlebone nodded, not at anything the man had said but a gesture to speed this up.

"We requested a full and immediate autopsy, of course. They begged off until tomorrow. That's our Hungarian friends for you. Even a ghastly murder in their capital airport doesn't put a hop in their step. But the preliminary cause of death," the man continued, browsing through his notes, "was a small knife puncture in the back."

He reached over and with a brash forefinger pointed like a dagger scraped an X slightly below the left shoulder blade of the man beside him. He plowed ahead. "A slight tearing around the incision suggests a twisting of the blade. The weapon was a stiletto, twelve or perhaps fifteen inches in length, only a few centimeters in width. Not a garden-variety weapon, I should say, more a specialist's tool, and it went directly for poor Bernie's heart." He waited a beat before he revealed this next revelation. "But his pupils were widely dilated, and his face also had a purplish discoloration, the visual by-products of oxygen deprivation. But no scarring or lesions from ligatures or bruises on his neck. As you know, this could be suggestive of poisoning."

"Assume both. He was poked with a coated blade," Pettlebone concluded swiftly, before the assistant could voice that rather evident opinion himself. "Let's further assume, hypothetically, the assassin was professional."

"Sorry, sir. Did I mention the dark bruise slightly below Bernie's breastbone?"

"Right you are. A pair of assassins." He examined the other faces. Knowing nods all around. "Witnesses?"

"Yes, and here's where it gets interesting," the man said with a relieved grin: this tidbit had fallen in his lap only ten minutes before. "The Budapest police were contacted about two hours ago by a Russian lady and man claiming to be her boyfriend. She swore she observed Konevitch stab his bodyguard in the back, then flee outside and jump into a cab."

"The client? The client stabbed his own security escort and fled?" Pettlebone sniffed and scowled. This firm did not hire out bodyguards, it provided security escorts.

"Quite right, sir. Alex Konevitch. Claimed she recognized him clear as a bell from the newsie magazines back in Russia. Seems he's quite the celebrity back home, being filthy rich and all."

Pettlebone removed his glasses and rubbed his eyes. "But it took her ten hours to recall who he was?"

"So she says."

"I don't suppose the lady has a name?"

Back to the notes. A few pages were flipped. "Ah, here— according to her passport, Alisa Petrova. It might be a phony, though. I had a nice chat with the detective who received her statement. Not much of a lady, in his words. A rough piece of work."

"So she saw Konevitch stab our man. Did she also see who punched him in the gut?"

"She didn't mention it, no. Though it might be prudent to consider the possibility that her angle of observation precluded it."

"Is that your considered opinion?"

"Well, if her view was from the rear, Konevitch is quite tall, and Bernie very wide. Fat, actually."

"But is that your opinion?"

It was as close as he was going to come to one. The man

clammed up and stopped talking. He suddenly found the blinking lights on the far wall endlessly fascinating.

Pettlebone looked up and down the table again. "Can anybody here recall an instance where one of our clients murdered one of our employees? Anyone?"

A retired partner leaning on the far wall, an old man, who missed the excitement with apparently little better to do than hang around the headquarters, took the challenge. "Aye. Back in '59, if I recall properly, Clyde Witherspoon got offed by his man. Seemed Clyde was shagging the client's old lady. Got caught in flagrante and the client blew his pecker off." The old man shook his head and whistled in wonder. "Ten meters away, too. Quite a shot, that. Allowed poor Clyde a distressing moment or so to ponder the damage, then finished him with a shot between the eyes."

Pettlebone adjusted his glasses. "Yes . . . Well, thank you, Bertie."

After a quick survey of the young pups around the table Bertie smiled and replied, "My pleasure."

"Now, can anyone tell me why our client had only one bodyguard?"

"At his own insistence, I'm afraid," the head of scheduling replied with a disapproving frown. "We recommended four escorts in the strongest possible terms. The client wouldn't hear of it. Said it would be poor for business." He arched his thick eyebrows and looked up. "A record of that conversation is on tape, if you're interested."

Malpractice suits were rare in the trade, since potential claimants were usually dead, one of the few upsides in a business loaded with downsides. But they happened. The firm had been dragged through a highly publicized courtroom brawl eighteen years before. That experience still smarted: business did not recover for five years. Pettlebone was satisfied that the firm's backside was covered, and moved on. "And does anybody have a clue where our client disappeared to? Anybody?"

Apparently not. The best and brightest shuffled papers, sipped tea, and adjusted their striped ties.

"Right you are," Pettlebone said, placing his hands on the table and leaning forward, "Then let me hazard a guess."

The best and brightest collectively thought: Have at it, old boy. You always like your own theories better than ours anyway.

He lifted three long, bony fingers. "He's either running away from murder, kidnapped, or dead." They stared at the fingers and said not a word.

The collective response: Oh, spare me; a brain-dead copper two days out of the academy could summarize the obvious.

"But the former looks a little shaky, I should think we all agree." One finger flopped down.

The collective wisdom: You're getting warmer, old boy. That possibility was discarded by the rest of us well over two hours ago while you and your pathetic old chums were chugging sherry in your snooty, prehistoric club.

Another finger folded. "And the latter we can do little about but send a bucket of roses after the dust settles."

The collective rejoinder: In which case you'll fall back on your standard response—dodge for cover, shove the blame downward, and send three or four of us packing. The first report of Bernie's death was called into your office six hours ago; you fled for sanctuary in your club so fast there are burn marks on your office carpet. And how very convenient of you to forget your pager and cell phone, which we found conveniently stuffed in the bottom drawer of your desk, you sly old bastard.

"So why haven't we heard from his kidnappers yet?"

The collective response: twenty sets of eyes suddenly shifted upward, in the general direction of the ceiling. Why not, indeed?

Statistically, they all knew, kidnappers nearly always make their demands a few short hours after the fact. Like card players holding a blackjack, why let the pot get cold?

More shuffling of papers, more sipped tea, more tightening of ties. A recorder in the attic was silently capturing every word. The lads around the table had sat through Pettlebone's inquisitions before and to a man weren't taken in by his Socratic bullshit. The first fool who guessed wrong, on the record and imprinted forever on the device in the attic, would end up first on the chopping block when this crisis ended, one way or the other, and they shifted into the usual blamestorm.

Bertie, the retired partner, with nothing to lose, took a stab. "I don't suppose we'd hear anything if it's an inside job. These Russki millionaires are all surrounded by nasty chaps. Sleep with the wolves, one shouldn't wonder when one wakes up main course on a dinner plate. If it's insider work, the culprits aren't likely to bring in outside help, are they? What do you think?"

"Have we contacted his company?" Pettlebone asked, deliberately sidestepping Bertie's theory. The recorder in the attic was his own clever idea; he had no intention of leaving a magnetic trace that might not withstand scrutiny later.

Another of the bright lads in the middle of the table said, "I've spoken with his head of corporate security. Three or four times, in fact. Sergei Golitsin, a former KGB general. Not a nice sort. The conversations weren't all that pleasant. Kept insisting that Alex's security outside Russia was our concern, not his."

"Had he heard anything from the kidnappers? A demand for ransom, a threat, that sort of thing?"

"Well . . . I did ask, sir."

"And?"

"He laughed, then cursed me and hung up."

"We're not going back to Russia," Alex announced with a very firm frown. After ten minutes of staring intently out the window, interrupted by occasional searches through the stack of passports on his lap, tossing ideas back and forth, he had finally made up his mind. "Too obvious," he announced.

"What's that mean?" Eugene asked.

"They're expecting it. In fact, they're hoping we'll try. We got lucky. I don't want to depend on luck again."

"Who's they?" Elena asked. Good question but one Alex didn't have the answer to.

"Certainly more than just Katya and Vladimir and the other goons we saw," Alex answered grimly.

"Did you see more of them?" Eugene asked. After all, his ass was on the line as well; naturally he wanted to know what he was up against.

"No, but they were too ignorant to put this together. They're working for somebody. And there may be . . . no, there definitely are more where they came from." But who knew how many more were in on this? They could be Mafiya, or they could be independents partnered with the mob. For such a big score, there could be hundreds of them, possibly thousands.

And for sure, an employee, or a number of employees of Konevitch Associates, were in on it up to their larcenous necks. Somebody who knew Alex's travel plans. Somebody who knew the instant Eugene called his secretary to query about his whereabouts.

Alex knew exactly what this meant: somebody very high up in the corporate food chain was feeding the goons precious inside information and trying to put a noose around his neck.

He searched his mind, but quickly lost count of potential suspects. He now had several hundred former KGB people, more or less, on the payroll. Some were good people, smart, honest, and deeply relieved to be able to look themselves in a mirror without, for a change, wrinkling in self-disgust. Too many others were cutthroats in fancy suits. Nearly all were in security positions. Nearly all might have found a way to learn his travel plans. The security department was always notified in advance of his trips with a detailed agenda, a regrettable routine but one that was unequivocally necessary. Only a small handful, though, could've learned about Eugene's call to Sonja.

Where had it all gone wrong? Alex had once prided himself on personally hiring his chief lieutenants and a sizable number of his other employees as well. But the explosion of business happened so fast, Alex kept chasing more and more opportunities, and the need for more and more people became crushing. From one thousand to twenty thousand employees in less than two years. It was an old-fashioned gold rush: the lion's share went to the one who stampeded in with the most diggers and sifters. Supposedly qualified executives were being hired off their résumés, sans interviews, sans background checks, or even cursory calls to their former employers. Money beckoned. Each new opportunity begat others. Caution had long since been thrown out the window.

Greed. Money. He was printing it almost faster than they grew trees. They all wanted a piece of the action and too many were hustlers on the make. He swore to himself he would conduct a fierce purge when he got back and this was behind him. He could count on two hands the number of executives he fully trusted.

"Checkpoint's straight ahead," Elena announced, breaking into his deepening thoughts about who to sack.

Alex plucked two passports out of the stack, then carefully shoved the rest under his leg. Elena pumped the brakes and the car bounced and wrenched to a squealing halt. They held their breath and prayed.

The road was a two-lane, sparsely trafficked one surrounded by countryside and a light sprawl of quaint villages. The checkpoint itself was little more than a yellow crossbar, lightly manned, with a wood shack and a few flickering lampposts—nothing more than a hastily erected shelter placed there in the aftermath of the abrupt Soviet withdrawal and the helter-skelter opening of the borders.

A skinny young man in an ill-fitting green customs uniform approached from the passenger side. The sound of an angry generator, spitting and sputtering, came from behind the shack. No words were exchanged. He stuck out a hand and Alex, trying to match his air of lethargy, yawned and casually handed him two passports. Eugene shoved his out from the backseat as well.

The guard studied Eugene's first, then in awful English prodded, "You are American?"

"No, I'm from Brooklyn," Eugene replied with a stupid grin. The guard eyed him suspiciously, obviously unable to match a citizen from Brooklyn to the American passport. Just cool it with the wisecracks, Alex and Elena wanted to scream at him.

Eugene stuck his face out the window and smiled broadly. "Of course I am. Why, do you like Americans?"

"Oh yes. Americans good. Ronald Reagan is big hero for me. Every Slovakian loves this Reagan. He tells the Russians to go kiss his ass. You know him?"

The young guard was now smiling pleasantly. Not many Americans used this backcountry crossing—in fact, none ever had, come to think of it. The heavy man in the backseat was the first American he'd ever encountered in person. He was obviously delighted and enthusiastic to try out his very limited English. Under improved lighting he looked barely old enough to be in high school, much less securing his nation's boundaries, with a lanky frame, pimply-faced, a pumpkin-sized head his features hadn't yet grown to fit. America was such a small land, of course everybody knew everybody.

"Oh . . . well, he's a dear old friend of mine. A dear, dear friend," Eugene rambled. "Ronnie and I . . . his pals call him Ronnie, by the way. Anyway, yeah, you could say we're big buddies."

"Ronnie. Yes, is better I think than Ronald. More friendly, yes?" The young guard was flipping through the back pages of Elena's passport, for no particular reason, since a Russian passport didn't require a visa. "He is really your friend?"

"I love him," Eugene declared loudly, anxious to like anything this kid liked. Stalin?—adore him. Liver?—my favorite meal. But it helped that it was true. He was a rich Wall Streeter and lifelong Republican without an ounce of guilt over the fortunes he'd made. He had no kind thoughts for those traitors from his tribe of millionaires who called themselves Democrats and did their best to get those tax-gobbling thieves back into the White House. Besides, it seemed like a great topic to keep this young guard's mind on other matters. Eugene told him truthfully, "I was one of his biggest contributors. Gave him lots of moolah. He had me down to the White House a few times. Nice place."

The guard was now measuring Alex's passport photo against his face. It was totally unnecessary. He was obviously dawdling to drag out the conversation. Why couldn't Eugene keep his mouth shut? Freedom was only ten yards ahead of them—if only Eugene would shut his yap.

The boy began thumbing through Alex's passport again, visibly more attentive to Eugene's ramblings about his hero than his work. He asked, not all that casually, "So you are big friend of Reagan's. Why then, you must tell me, you are traveling with these Russians?"

"Russians" spat out of his lips loaded with enough contempt to make it sound like he wanted to pull his pistol and blow Alex and Elena back to the gates of Moscow.

"They're old friends," Eugene replied, thinking fast.

A troubled look on the boy's face. He scratched his unwashed hair, shuffled his feet, and stared glumly at the passport. "This name, Konevitch, I think I have heard before."

"No surprise there," Eugene conceded in a quick rush of words. "Alex is . . . was . . . a dissident, a very famous one. He wrote brilliant essays about the rot of communism, they were smuggled out and published in the West." Eugene pushed his face closer and confided, "Guess how we met? Come on, guess."

Bunched shoulders. No idea.

"Ronnie introduced us. Get this—he told me personally that Alex's essays inspired him to tell the Russians to haul their asses out of East Europe."

The guard bent over and studied Alex's face more closely. His eyes narrowed and his lips scrunched with curiosity. Eugene's expansive lie suddenly did not appear all that clever. Alex tried to appear relaxed, humble, and proud, anything to look convincing. Would he become curious about Alex's injuries? Maybe he wasn't buying Eugene's bullshit. Or maybe he remembered exactly why the name Konevitch sounded familiar. Alex and Elena fought an overwhelming urge to hop out of the car and make a run for it. Just run as fast as their feet could go, flee into the nearest field, and hope the boy's marksmanship was as awful as his English. They squeezed each other's hands and prayed. The examination seemed to go on forever. "If he so famous," the guard eventually asked, fingering the passports, "why then you are traveling in this very awful car?"

Elena wagged a finger at that backseat. "In honor of our American friend." A knowing wink and she flashed her cutest smile. "We thought it would be fun for him to experience the full splendor of communist quality. He hasn't stopped complaining the entire trip."

The guard laughed, handed the passports to Alex, took a step back, and waved his arm. "Welcome to the *independent* Slovakian Republic. Drive carefully, if you please."

10

The drive through Slovakia to the airport proved mercifully un-
eventful. Slovakia, the former half of Czechoslovakia before the
"velvet divorce" rendered it asunder, had at one time been its
industrial breadbasket, a cauldron of sprawling factories that
spewed out guns and bombs and other nasty devices for the Soviet army. That business had suddenly dried up: the country now
resembled a ghost town; having survived sixty years of communism, it wasn't clear it would survive capitalism. The huge factories no longer belched smoke out of towering chimneys. Little
traffic was on the roads.

They stopped at a roadside eatery and killed a few hours, en-
gulfing coffee and battling to stay awake. Alex insisted on it. But
even had Elena or Eugene considered it a terrible idea, they were
not about to object. One look and they could see Alex was on
his last legs. He slumped in the chair, could hardly lift his head,
and rubbed his dislocated shoulder and kneaded his sore leg constantly. They could barely imagine how horribly his fried chest
ached and throbbed.

The beating and torture had sapped his incredible energy. He
spoke little, only when absolutely necessary. The words came out
slurred in short sentences, almost a labored whisper.

Elena was worried about him. He should be in a hospital, for godsakes. Every bone in his body should be X-rayed, his wounds cleansed and rebandaged, his chest embalmed in a burn packet. Then he should be pumped full of miracle drugs until the grimness in his eyes melted, until laughing fairies were dancing inside his head. But a powerful sense of guilt was driving him, she knew. He blamed himself for this whole mess; for being rich enough that serious people would want to steal it; for not insisting that a hundred security men shadow him everywhere; especially, he was ravaged with regret for dragging her and Eugene into this.

And now he was shouldering full responsibility for getting them out of it.

The first round of coffee and pastries arrived. They dug in and ran through the situation. Alex summoned energy from some hidden reserve and summarized their situation. The easy passage across the border could be a sign that his fears were overblown, Alex told them; or it was just a fickle stroke of luck. So play it safe. Assume people were still out there, hunting, so they should drag it out awhile. With each passing hour, the searchers would become more tired. Tired meant sloppy. Better yet, it might mislead them into believing their prey had traveled much farther than they had. They would be forced to extend and widen their dragnet, increasing the chance of slipping through. When the time was right they would jump back into the car, drive straight to the airport, and have a quick look-see. If the airport was covered, this plan would go on the scrapheap, and they would devise another way to escape.

Elena wasn't sure Alex had enough left in him for this plan. A whole new one seemed out of the question.

So they sat and sipped coffee, the three of them, tense and keyed up. After the first cup, Alex excused himself and limped away from the table. By their fourth cup, Alex had returned. He collapsed into his seat and insisted they unwind and dwell on topics other than their troubles.

Eugene tried his best with lively tales about his slew of marriages, how they all belly-flopped into messy divorces. The stories were deliciously vulgar and quite funny. He had nicknames for each ex, wedded to a hysterical talent for mimicry. Number Two—Dallaszilla—apparently had an aggravating Texas twang, chewed loudly with her mouth open, and couldn't mutter a word without violently flapping her arms—a stuttering windmill stuck on overdrive. Eugene shucked his New York accent and produced an impersonation that was almost frightening.

This was the same ex who hired a PI to track her husband, then showed up at Eugene's suite at the Plaza, catching him red-handed with his newest mistress. The door burst open and Dallaszilla screamed and bellowed and howled with the unadulterated fury only a native Texan lady can manufacture. Her arms whipped around so hard, the mistress thought she was witnessing an epileptic fit and promptly dialed 911 for an ambulance. Eugene never spoke to the mistress again. He was furious with her. Forgiveness would never come. In court, he adhered to his lawyer's standard legal dictum—he denied, denied, denied—until three paramedics showed up to corroborate the affair. The judge happened to be a she, herself an aggrieved veteran of two nasty divorces with husbands who had philandered and then lied their way out of what she considered fair settlements.

His lawyer swore afterward that that gaffe cost him an additional five million dollars.

Elena found the stories hilarious. She laughed until it ached. For one brief, shining moment she almost forgot people were out there chasing, trying to murder them. Alex managed an occasional stiff smile, but had either heard the tales before or was preoccupied, or exhausted.

They were back on the road at two o'clock. An hour later, after twice getting lost, they turned off a highway and entered the airport complex. Elena pumped the brakes and said, "You two get down. I'll cruise the terminal. See how it looks."

Alex reminded Elena, for the fourth time, "Be sure to check the cars in the lot," then both men tried their best to melt into the seats.

Crawling at fifteen kilometers per hour, Elena made a slow

pass, quietly tapping the brakes and searching with quick shifts of her head. The airport turned out to be the aeronautic equivalent of a one-horse town, small, sleepy, with only one main building, and definitely shut down for the night. Few lights were on. A solitary janitor in loose gray coveralls was shoving a mop around the floor. That was it. She saw nobody else inside the terminal or loitering suspiciously in front of it.

Another twenty yards and a quick glance to her left. The parking lot contained only a few cars; all appeared dark and thankfully empty. Then, in one of them—yes!—in an otherwise dark car she could swear she saw the flicker of two burning cigarettes.

She slowed almost to a stop. She stared hard at the car, then came to her senses, sped up, and retreated back the way they came, toward the capital. Alex and Eugene straightened up. "It's closed," she informed them, obviously surprised, obviously disappointed. "But in one of the cars in the parking lot, somebody was inside, smoking. I saw at least two cigarettes."

"You think it's them?" Eugene asked, bending forward with the help of Alex's seatback.

Elena replied. "I think they're just lovers too cheap to buy a hotel room. What do you think?"

"Yeah, I think it's them, too," Eugene answered.

Alex asked her, "What kind of car?"

"You know I'm not good with that kind of thing."

"All right, what color? This is important, honey."

"White."

"Not tan?"

"No, white. I'm positive."

"Big car, small car, medium, what?"

"A sedan. Fairly large. Four doors. I thought I saw an ornament of some sort on the end of a long hood. But it was dark, and by then I was scared, so I'm not sure. The car looked expensive, too, but how would I know? Are we through playing thirty questions?"

"Almost. Could it have been a Jaguar?"

"No, it was definitely a car."

Obviously they were through.

They drove for about five minutes in silence. A light rain began falling, and the wipers flopped wildly back and forth, never close to touching the windshield.

Apropos of nothing, Alex observed, "If you're interested, the doors to the terminal open at seven. A flight for New York leaves at eight every morning."

Eugene asked, "You knew the airport would be closed?"

"I thought it would, yes."

"And you knew about the New York flight?"

"Would it make a difference if I'd told you?"

"I don't guess it would, nope."

"But New York?" Elena asked.

"Yes, well, for one thing, the only open visas that match in both our passports are for America. Second, it's the one destination in the world where we'll be safe from these people. It's only temporary, anyway, until I get this cleared up."

Eugene remarked, "I'd offer you my place, but Maria will be there, and it's going to be a war zone."

Alex wasn't really in a listening mode and added, "We're not going together, anyway. It's time to split up."

"What's that mean?" Eugene asked, afraid he knew exactly what it meant.

"They're hunting three people, Eugene. They believe we're amateurs and they believe we're afraid and insecure."

Believe? Well, they were certainly amateurs. And if insecure meant scared out of their wits, the bad people had it right on both counts.

Alex continued, "The point is, frightened amateurs stay in packs. They'll be looking for three of us, together, so it's time for us to divorce Eugene."

"You couldn't have picked a different word?" Eugene complained. Elena laughed, and Eugene joined her. Both were becoming giddy with exhaustion and the unrelenting tension.

Alex turned around and faced him, his face rigid with concern. "Eugene, you're a target because you're with us. They blew the chance to get your money. Nothing can bring it back, and they know that. Whoever they are, they're professionals. They don't care about you anymore."

"Hey, I'm having a ball being shot at, chased, and hunted by Mafiya goons," Eugene felt like saying. "This is the best idea I've heard all night, so fine, dump me off right here." But his conscience bothered him. Instead he said, "Look, what the hell, I'm in this up to my neck already. You're my friends and I'd like to make sure you're safe. Are you sure this is a good idea, Alex?"

"I'm not sure about anything at the moment."

"Except this, right?"

"Yes, and I won't change my mind. The very least I owe you is to get you out of this alive."

An unspoken thought lingered in that statement. Alex obviously wasn't optimistic about his own chances. Eugene looked at Alex and thought about arguing. It would be useless, though; Alex's mind was clearly made up. "What do I do?"

"Drop Elena and me off at the nearest big hotel in Bratislava. Find another hotel, check in for the day, catch up on sleep, find a nice restaurant with pretty waitresses, have a long leisurely meal, then drive back to Budapest and catch the first flight home. By that time, I assure you, the people hunting us will believe you're long gone." It was obvious he had thought this through.

"What about you?"

"We'll catch taxis from the hotel. Don't worry, I think I know what I'm doing."

Twenty minutes later, Alex and Elena stood beneath the overhang of a run-down hotel in downtown Bratislava. The streets were empty, the doorman was inside, napping. They watched Eugene putter off in the junkheap, spitting and spewing smoke out the noisy tailpipe.

Alex turned to Elena and said, "Now we can discuss our plan."

"We couldn't discuss it in Eugene's presence?"

"He's better off not knowing. If the people chasing us get their hands on him, it's his best defense. Ours, too."

For the next few minutes, they stood under the awning and Alex told Elena what he hoped would happen.

11

The two taxis arrived at the terminal thirty minutes apart.

Alex was dropped off first, at 6:45.

Elena stepped out onto the curb at 7:14, a minute earlier than she'd been instructed, though it turned out not to be relevant.

Her instructions were clear and precise: Drive by the front of the terminal. If Alex wasn't standing and waving, alone, then howl at her driver to keep going and don't look back. Once they had Alex, they wouldn't care about her anymore. They wanted her only to get to him; if they had him, she was old baggage they could care less about. What was left of Eugene's 2,000 American dollars was wadded up and folded inside her bra. Use it, he told her, to find her own way to America, then contact her parents for help. Start a new life and don't look back.

But Alex was there, about twenty feet from the doors, waving, not directly at her, it seemed, but at some invisible person off in the distance. She tried hard not to stare at Alex as she walked right past him, then through the glass door and straight to the Continental Air counter. Yes, she had a reservation, she assured the smiling lady behind the counter. She held her breath and handed her passport across the counter. She was reaching into her bra for the money when the woman politely announced that the ticket was already reserved and prepaid, first class—and did she care for an aisle seat or window? Boarding started in fifteen minutes; she was welcome to use the VIP lounge until then. She had no idea how Alex arranged this, it wasn't part of the plan, but she smiled with relief and pleasure as the lady behind the counter ruffled papers and prepared her boarding pass.

First class? After all they'd been through, the idea of making a grand escape sipping champagne and munching on caviar seemed too good to be true. She felt like crying.

She sensed him before she saw him. A middle-aged man in a nice gray wool suit was staring at her. A quick glance in his direction, and he looked away. She took the ticket envelope from the smiling Continental representative and walked briskly in the direction of the VIP room. She kept her back turned to him for a few moments, then performed a pirouette that would earn a standing ovation. She looked him dead in the eye. The man almost jumped, before, suddenly, he discovered something on the magazine rack more interesting than her.

Her first thought was to scream. Just aim her arm at the man in the suit and scream full blast until her lungs hurt, until airport security rushed over to see what the fuss was about.

She kept walking instead. There was a knot in her throat and she tried hard to ignore it. She was an attractive woman, after all. Men stared at her: so what? She usually just ignored them. She was just on edge, she told herself. Paranoid people see big toothy monsters with lethal claws where others see squirrels. Maybe that's all it was, a sad, lonely little squirrel checking out the talent and dreaming of what would never be. She arrived at the door to the VIP room, looked back over her shoulder again, and there he was again, brazenly walking toward her! A little smarter, because his face was covered with a magazine. But the gray suit was a dead giveaway.

She was just raising her arm and preparing an earthshaking scream, when a firm hand grabbed her from behind. Panic enveloped her chest. She spun around, ready to kick and slap and howl like hell—it was Alex. "Don't worry about him, honey. Come on, step inside."

She stepped through the doorway and followed Alex to a table by the near wall, far away from the windows. Another man, this one in a blue wool suit, was seated, with his back against the wall, looping peanuts into his mouth. "Good morning, Mrs. Konevitch," he said, grinning between hard crunches. "I'm Eric. That fella outside's Jacob. I don't want to imagine what you've been through the past eighteen hours, but your worries are over." Another peanut in the mouth. "Jacob's watching the door and inside this VIP lounge is my territory. No bragging, but we can handle whatever comes up." A gentle slap on his forehead for effect. "Oh yeah, we're your Malcolm Street boys." The accent and demeanor were obscenely American—a thick twang ruthlessly tortured the vowels, broad, confident smile, black hair, tall and well built. Eric was leaning back on the chair, trying to appear relaxed and carefree. But Elena, the dancer, missed nothing about the human form. The body was coiled, ready to leap the length of the room and snap necks if the situation required. Ruthless blue eyes that never stopped wandering even as he spoke to her.

"Come on, Mrs. Konevitch, relax. You're safe. Take a load off your feet, please." He shoved a chair back with one hand, while the other hand plopped another peanut into the air; it sailed a full six feet before it fell and landed effortlessly in his mouth. His eyes never stopped darting around the room.

Elena nearly fell on her knees and kissed him. Eric in the nicely tailored blue suit could probably shoot with both hands simultaneously, hurl knives with his feet, and work an impossibly difficult crossword puzzle without missing a vowel. Let the bad guys try anything now. Eric would stack their bodies like cordwood.

The peanut fling was Eric's favorite trick, one that never failed to put the client at ease. That big lapdog smile again. "Fix yourself a cup of coffee. Don't skip them pastries, either," he suggested. Another peanut in the air—whoosh, it landed and was instantly compacted between two fierce incisors.

Alex took her arm. "Let's get a cup of coffee and talk."

They moved hand in hand to another wall where a wooden table sagged under the weight of coffee and tea urns, an enormous stack of pastries, and large containers loaded with eggs, bacon, flatcakes, and a few mushy concoctions unidentifiable to anybody but a Slovakian native. The smell of fresh-ground coffee was impossible to ignore. The only thing keeping her on her feet was the five cups she had swallowed at the café.

That half-life had expired an hour before.

Alex handed her a cup and saucer. "When I called the headquarters of Malcolm Street last night, they were in the midst of a meeting about our situation. A witness claimed I murdered my own security escort back at the Budapest Airport. It's—"

"What? That's ridiculous, Alex. Who claimed that?"

"A woman. A Russian woman. Her story was corroborated by her Russian boyfriend."

"Ridiculous. They murdered your bodyguard and now they're blaming it on you?"

"Yes, with a poisoned dagger, probably at the same moment as the kidnap. The security firm is dispatching a team to clear this up with the Hungarian authorities. There are big holes in the story. The woman's passport is a phony. The hit was professional and I'm an amateur. They're confident they can make this disappear."

Elena filled a cup with coffee. She snatched a Danish off the tray, stole a tentative nibble, and followed it with a deep sip. She couldn't remember anything tasting better in her life. "And they sent Eric and his friend to watch over us?"

"Eric and Jacob were covering a client in Prague; they were ordered to drop everything and rush here. That was them in the white Jaguar sedan last night."

The careful nibbling was over. She took a powerful bite from the Danish, neatly amputating half of it. "That was them? Smoking inside the car?"

"Not exactly."

"Then who?" she asked.

"You don't want to know."

"If you ever expect to sleep with me again, you'll tell me." The other half of the Danish disappeared into her mouth and she chewed it with vigor.

"Okay. Eric and his partner arrived about an hour before us.

They drove by, just like we did. Two men were loitering outside the terminal. At nearly two o'clock, in front of a closed building, the killers couldn't have been more conspicuous or sloppy. Whoever's behind this apparently doesn't hold a high opinion of us. So Eric snuck back on foot, surprised the two men, and forced them at gunpoint into their car. The cigarettes belonged to the pair of thugs he captured. Eric was interrogating them."

"And what did they say?"

"They claimed they had no idea why. Just had orders from their boss to kill us."

"Who was this boss?"

"A name neither of us would recognize. It's irrelevant. They're part of a crime syndicate, gunmen at the bottom of a long chain doing what they were told."

"Where are they now?" At the bottom of a deep river, she hoped. After murdering one man, brutally torturing her husband, and trying their best to add three more kills to the tally, she hoped the weasels died slowly and horribly.

"I didn't ask," Alex replied. "I don't think either of us want to know."

"Don't be so civilized. I'd love to know."

"I doubt we would hear the truth, anyway."

Eric was suddenly standing at their side, as if he had materialized out of thin air. Tell me, did you kill them, she wanted to demand, and don't go light on the details. "Time to board," he said with that reassuring grin. "Jacob and I are on the flight, too. We don't get first-class freight, but we'll be tucked in the back in seats where we can observe you. So don't you worry. Kick back, drink all the champagne you can stand, eat till your stomachs are sore, then nap till that pilot says you're in New York."

The plane lifted off ten minutes after they boarded, at which point Alex and Elena were downing their second champagne, with plans to keep sipping until New York or they passed out, whichever came first.

Elena eased back into her seat and asked, "Will the bodyguards stay with us in New York?"

"No," Alex said, waving at the stewardess for a refill. "My company paid the bills. Somebody in the security division last night faxed a termination order to Malcolm Street, effective upon delivery. The people after us are thinking of everything."

Elena paused to think about that. "That's not a good sign, is it?"

"It's a terrible sign. Whoever's behind this obviously has control over my companies, for the moment anyway. But Eric and Jacob will stay with us until we're safely checked into a hotel. After that, we're on our own."

"And the crooks have all our money, right?"

Alex pushed back his seat, extending it fully to the reclined position; the champagne was working its medicinal magic and taking the edge off his physical pain. He closed his eyes. "Not without my account numbers and security codes, they don't. They're locked in my office safe. Until we get this cleared up, though, I can't access that money," he said. "Except for $2 million tucked in a Bermudan bank. A rainy-day fund I never imagined I would have to use. The account numbers for that fund are in my head, so no matter what, they can't touch it."

"Was that the best you could do?" she asked, laughing.

Alex was asleep already.

Three sets of steady fingers punched the keys in unison. The clack of computer keys was the loveliest sound Golitsin could remember, a rich symphony in synchronized harmony.

The operation lasted ten minutes. He stood, arms crossed over his stomach, watched over their shoulders, and enjoyed every minute of it. Clack, clack, clack—another five million sent here, another ten million there. Money was flying everywhere, massive electronic whirls of cash, shuttling from Konevitch's accounts to banks in Switzerland, Bermuda, the Caymans, and a few Pacific islands with tortuous names nobody could pronounce. Who cared to? The money would barely touch down, gather no dust, then clack, clack, clack—scatter off to the next bank. The wonderful process would proceed for hours.

Within ten minutes after opening time that morning, Alex

Konevitch's immense personal hoard of cash was gone. Nearly two hundred million sprinkled around the world like fairy dust. The operation had been planned with exacting precision and rehearsed until the fingers of the pianists peering into the terminals ached and stiffened.

At noon, it would all be bundled back together in a dark Swiss vault where nobody could touch it but Golitsin.

In his pocket was the secret code for a new account at yet another Swiss bank only he had access to. He would sneak upstairs, punch the number into a computer he would dispose of afterward, and transfer all that money into a hole nobody could find but him.

A thirty-minute break for lunch. At one o'clock, the computer wizards would reassemble and the process would start again. This time on the hoards of savers' money in Alex's banks. Clack, clack, clack—not all of it, only fifty million, but enough that Alex Konevitch would be charged with looting his own bank and absconding into the sunset with that pretty little girl bride of his.

Two business reporters from *Kommersant*, the Russian equivalent of the *Wall Street Journal*, were at that moment cooling their heels downstairs. They had been promised the story of the year, how that wunderkind Konevitch had proved to be a rotten crook but was thoughtful enough to leave behind a letter transferring his businesses and properties to his trusted former chief of security.

"Yes," Golitsin would tell them with an appropriately grave nod, "for the sake of the twenty thousand employees, and for our valued customers everywhere," he, General Sergei Golitsin, "would restore the blemished reputation and keep the business up and running." Maybe you noticed the new sign over the headquarters entrance?

Golitsin Enterprises—it has a nice ring, don't you think?

By close of business the haul would be complete. Two hundred million of Alex's cash, plus fifty million more stolen from his banks—$250 million in liquid cash. Then, Alex's shares in his companies would be split with his co-conspirators, leaving Golitsin with probably another hundred million in stock. A moving van was already parked in front of Alex's Moscow home, unloading the new owner's possessions.

Book Two:
The Exile

12

September 1993

The promised call from Moscow had not been returned at ten; it was now eleven, so it was likely another broken promise, one in a long string of dashed hopes. Alex stood by the hotel window and stared down at the chaotic street seven stories below. Among the wash of humanity below, his eyes picked out the businesspeople—the lawyers, the moneymen, the entrepreneurs, the two-bit hustlers—scurrying around this loud and important city in search of the next deal.

Alex's mind was locked firmly on the last deal.

From the bed, Elena kept a wary eye on him. She was deeply worried about him, but so far had not broached those thoughts. The bathrobe that hung loosely from his shoulders had not been removed in days. A man who put punctuation points on restless and driven, the past week had barely crawled out of bed. Ordinarily he required a mere three or four hours of sleep to recharge his juices; he was now edging toward twelve. The room-service meals were nothing short of delicious—at these prices, they better be. He shoved the food around on his plate. He squished everything into mush and rearranged it all into untidy puddles. The fork rarely left the plate; it even more rarely went near his lips. Elena calculated he had shed at least fifteen pounds.

He looked gaunt and haggard, thoroughly beaten. An insomniac in reverse; the excess sleep had left him listless and drained. The change since their arrival day in New York nearly three weeks before was more than alarming and there was no bottom in sight.

After they hopped off the plane at JFK Airport, they had dashed through customs and hijacked the first available taxi for a fast sprint into Manhattan, where they checked into this plush suite in the Plaza. After quick showers, they slept three hours. Then Alex dragged her out of bed and they flew out the door. They raced to and through a few local shops, pausing only long enough to stuff a few bags with new clothes, toothbrushes, razors, shaving cream—enough essentials, and no more, to squeeze through two fast and furious days, Alex insisted.

Moscow beckoned. Two days was pessimistic, he warned her; half a day was more like it. Yeltsin might even dispatch a military plane to haul them back. Should he request one? he openly wondered. No, he would demand it—along with an armed military escort to keep the bad guys at bay, an armored car for the ride home, and an army of investigators to round up the crooks. A quick dash around the corner and he darted into a crowded office supply store. Alex emerged a short while later loaded with furious determination, typing paper, a few notebooks, pens, a cell phone, a laptop, and somewhere in this frantic rush he found software to convert the computer fonts to Cyrillic.

That afternoon, fully armed, Alex began his all-out assault on Moscow. He set up camp in the nicely equipped business center on the ground floor of the hotel. With care, he selected a small desk in the far corner of the room where foot traffic was minimal. With his arsenal of pens and pencils, his supply depot of notepads and stacks of typing paper all neatly arranged, he plugged in his computer and launched in, daring anybody to poach on his turf.

For seven frenetic days, Alex lived there. He bombarded Moscow with phone calls and faxes. Between his new cell and the landline in the business center, he often had a phone loaded in each fist, sometimes speaking into both at once. His voice was enraged but controlled, precise, and quick. His ability to explain the story improved with each retelling, becoming shorter, honed to the gory essentials. Sometimes he juggled the listeners and bounced back and forth between conversations. The pace never withered except when Elena enforced a cease-fire long enough for hurried visits on doctors and dentists to repair the damage inflicted by Vladimir. If the ministrations took too long, Alex cursed and walked out. The leg was slow to heal. He lurched and hobbled from one lamppost to the next, in a crippled race back to the hotel. He couldn't wait to return to his battle station, to fire off another fusillade of phone calls to anybody who would listen, the next flurry of faxes to whoever promised to read them.

After seven long and exhausting days, the assault faltered almost as suddenly as it began. By day eight, it waned to a dull skirmish—a few aimless shots fired without energy or optimism. Nothing but lingering echoes of a battle that had been desperately waged and apparently conceded.

"Come back to bed," Elena told her husband, fluffing his pillow and giving it a loud, inviting smack.

"I'm not tired."

"Neither am I. We're in a glorious luxury suite in a great city. Make love to me, Alex."

"I'm not in the mood." A moment later, with his back still turned, "Sorry."

"Listen to me, Konevitch. I am so in the mood I caught myself winking at the toothless old homeless guy across the street. His name's Harry. He's heavy, and dirty, and has only one eye, but sort of a cute butt. Now get in this bed and do your damnedest to satisfy me before Harry shows up."

He never turned around—never even glanced at the skimpy black teddy she had secretly purchased the day before at Victoria's Secret and slipped into two minutes before in the bathroom. Two thimbles and a string would've been more modest. Nearly two hundred dollars for barely three ounces of fabric, but that was the whole point. She had painted her face, something she seldom did. Her golden locks were brushed to a high glean. She had saturated herself in so much perfume, a thick mist of vapors hovered around her skin. She was taking no chances. No corner had been unpampered or over-looked or spared. A bottle of ridiculously expensive champagne cooled its heels in a frosted bucket beside the side of the bed.

She had schemed and prepared this seduction. If she had to slam his head with a mallet, he would damn well get in the mood.

In a marriage that rarely passed three days without sex, Alex had not been Mr. Ready-and-Able since Budapest. He was in a black depression, trapped in a bottomless funk, and she would do her damnedest to bring him out of it.

She climbed out of bed and approached him from behind. She grabbed his arm and spun him around. "Look what I bought for you. And I damn well better hear a gasp," she ordered. With that, she pranced and strutted and flaunted her sculpted dancer's body shamelessly, like a brassy stripper.

Three weeks before she wouldn't have made two steps before he tossed her on the bed and the ravaging began.

Ten steps. Twenty steps. Thirty.

He crossed his arms and weathered the distraction.

The hussy routine came to an abrupt halt. She squared her shoulders, took a deep breath, and looked him dead in the eye. "Get on the bed, now," she demanded, pointing a finger in that general direction.

"I warned you, I'm not in the mood."

"I can see that, Konevitch. But I bought this silly outfit, and primped and plucked my eyebrows and shaved my legs, and now I look like a whore, but I did this for you. You're not getting out of this if I have to kill you."

He took in the flared nostrils, the sparks in the blue eyes, the gripped fists, and he made the only sensible choice: a swift, meek retreat to the bed. He sat stiffly on a corner, enough to placate her—enough also to signal his stubborn indifference.

She sat on the opposite corner. She crossed her legs and for a moment did not say a word. Then, "Tell me what's happening. It's my life, too, and you're keeping everything to yourself."

"I'd rather not talk about it."

"I'd rather you do. No, I insist."

"Are we having a fight?"

"Not yet." She pulled a pillow over and rested it against her back. "But we're about to have a bloody world war if you don't tell me what's going on. I'm not bluffing."

"I don't want to depress you."

"Your depression is depressing me. Frankly I don't care if we lost everything. I'd actually be quite pleased if somebody else is now living in that musty old mansion."

"It's a good thing. I did, I lost everything. The money, our homes, our companies . . . everything."

"I thought the money was safe."

"Apparently they found the account numbers and security codes. They were better prepared than I anticipated."

"Well . . . it's only money, dear."

"A million or two is *only* money, Elena. But two hundred million in cash, and stock worth another hundred million, I think that deserves a slightly better modifier than '*only* money,' don't you?"

She had no idea it was that much. "Yeltsin won't allow it. He owes you everything, Alex."

A long sigh. "I can't get through to him. And believe me, I've tried. I've called his office countless times, and flooded it with faxes."

"Maybe he's busy. I'm sure that's it. This is urgently important to us, but I think he has a few other problems on his plate."

"No, I'm being stonewalled. I call and get foisted from one unimportant assistant to another. I know damn well what's going on."

"Okay, what is going on?"

"Somebody inside is pulling strings. Somebody clever and powerful enough to block me from Yeltsin. Each time it's a fresh new assistant, each time I have to start over from scratch. They're taking turns. They're trying to wear me down, and it's worked."

"You're smarter than they are, sweetheart. Shift your approach."

"Do you think I haven't attempted that? I tried every path into the Kremlin I could think of. Among many others, I've contacted

the minister of security, the secretary of the Security Council, the
minister of finance, the mayor of Moscow, even the chairman of
the Central Bank."

"And what do they say?"

"They said it sounded terrible and promised to look into it." He
turned away from her and stared again at the window. "That was
last week's line. Now they won't take my calls."

She reached over and hauled the champagne bottle out of the
bucket. Over the long days and nights they had stayed cooped up
in the hotel she had managed to make only one friend, Amber
Lincoln, a large, warm-hearted black woman who ran the phone
bank in the basement. During Alex's week of furious activity, as
Alex ignored her and as the switchboard people in the basement
pulled hairs to keep up with his incessant requests for calls to
various numbers in Russia, Elena had considered it the least she
could do to reward their help by bringing food and an occasional
bottle of wine.

This had been her only respite from Alex's bout of frenetic activity, and now his dark mood.

Champagne and sex were long overdue.

Her tiny fingers worked the aluminum cover before she handed
off the bottle to Alex for the honors. "What do you think is going
on?"

"Sergei Golitsin."

"The security chief? That ugly old toad?"

"He put this together, he and all the KGB crooks he brought into
the company with him. He took over my company, and now has
the nerve to rename it after himself. He stole everything I built,
everything, Elena. He's now living fat and happy in our house."

He can have it, she thought, but said, "Everybody knows it's
your company. He can't just steal it."

"Last week he fired every vice president. Called them all into
my office, and ordered them to depart the building immediately.
Armed guards pushed and shoved them out onto the street. Remember Mishi? He said it was the most frightening moment of his
life. Even before they were called in, Golitsin's thugs already had

taken over their offices." Alex rubbed his eyes and stared off into space. "All those decent, hardworking people, now they're out on the street, unemployed. It's my fault."

"How was it your fault?"

"I was stupid. And worse, careless. I became desperate after the killings, so I brought Golitsin in to protect the company. I've thought about it for days, and the pieces have fallen into place. From the very beginning he was plotting to steal it. I'm a fool."

"No, you're brilliant. You're the most talented man I ever met, and the most decent. You just don't think like they do." He was gripping the bottle tightly, and she took it away from him. He was the least self-pitying man she'd ever met, but he was utterly miserable. Then again, everything he had built had been stolen, his life turned upside down. The frustration was boiling his soul. She went to work on the cork. She squinted and grunted and twisted with all her might.

Alex seized it back. A single hard wrench and—*POP*—gold liquid gushed over and dribbled onto the carpet. The bottle cost two hundred bucks. Every drop was precious. She bounced off the bed and made a hasty scramble for the flutes.

Alex said, "The story spent five days on the front page of every paper in Moscow. I'm accused of stealing from my own banks and running off with the money. Can you believe it? They stole my money and they're blaming it on me. The prosecutor's office in Moscow is conducting an investigation. I'm being framed, and I'm not there to defend myself. I'm sure they'll issue an indictment."

She handed him a pair of tall crystal flutes she had borrowed from the dining room downstairs. He slowly filled them, one for her, one for him. She grabbed her flute and inched a little closer. Little of what he was now telling her was news. Over the past few days she had sneaked downstairs to the privacy of Amber's office and made her own calls back to Russia. She had her own sources, and if her husband kept her in the dark, she would use them.

Her family and a few close friends had fully apprised her about what had happened, the whole ugly story. For a few terrible days, Alex had been the talk of Moscow, with considerable interest throughout the rest of Russia. The story was irresistible and the press lunged into a predictable frenzy—on TV, in newspapers, and in magazines, Alex was loudly tried and all but convicted. The millionaire genius was on the lam. He had stolen the money and fled. Behind the glitz and glamour, behind that mysterious façade of quiet brilliance, he was nothing but a two-bit crook, a highway robber with a swollen IQ in a nice suit.

The day the news broke there was a frenzied stampede on Alex's bank: after two frightening days, though, it quickly stagnated to a mild panic. Only fifty million was supposedly stolen—a small drop from a massive bucket. And twenty percent interest, after all, was still the sweetest deal in town. The commercials with the lovely girl who adored men with interest and the treacly old couple fondly eyeing their shiny Mercedes flooded back onto the airwaves. Much of the money that had raced out limped back in.

As usual, the initial spate of news stories was brief and shallow and disgracefully inaccurate. Few details were known beyond the basic fact: Alex Konevitch was a lying, conniving thief who took off with a fortune. But somebody kept dropping more and more tips, inflaming interest in a bonfire that required no fuel. The stories turned longer, the lies more sensational and deceitfully toxic. Alex stole fifty million, a hundred million, a billion! He was holding out in a jungle palace in Brazil, guarded by snarling bandistas, flipping the bird and daring anybody to come after him. Using a false identity, he had checked into one of those California detox clinics, and now was doing cumbaya with the doped-out, besotted dregs of Hollywood. He was hiding here, in Moscow, in a plush safehouse protected by fierce syndicate killers in exchange for a cut of the loot.

The theories about Alex's wheres and whys changed daily. Alex had snapped under the pressure and flew out the door, laughing deliriously, hauling grocery bags leaking cash. Alex had plotted this theft from the start. Everything he built and accomplished was only to create the edifice for a massive heist; the only mystery was why he waited so long. Alex was bipolar and Jekyll finally smothered Hyde. A war was waged on the front pages as each paper tried to outdo the newest disclosures, the wildest suspicions. The same paper that dubbed him "The Kid with the Midas Touch" rechristened him "The Kid with the Sticky Touch."

Fortunately for Alex, Russians are bred to be jaded and skeptical. After seventy years of communist manipulation and distortions, any news fit enough to print was bound to be twisted enough to disbelieve. Besides, fabricating conspiracies is part of the Russian national character, and this story hit the street pregnant with lush possibilities. Golitsin's long career in the KGB did not work to his favor. This sounded like something the bad boys from the Lubyanka would cook up; and as everybody knows, old toads don't change their warts. Rumors and theories flew around Moscow, and ran heavily in Alex's favor.

Foul play was suspected, though nobody could put a finger on exactly how Golitsin pulled it off.

But the incredible idea that Alex would plunder his own bank and, before racing out the door, take the trouble to legally transfer everything he owned—not to his partners, not to his businesspeople, but to his chief of security, of all people—smelled rotten. What sense did that make? Besides, why would he care who snatched up the crumbs he left behind? And only fifty million from his bank customers? For a man rumored to have billions? Why squander his reputation and name for pocket change? And if he was willing to snatch fifty million, why leave behind billions more?

Even among those skeptics, however, very few pitied Alex. A rich man brought down, big deal. It was funny, actually. Live by the dollar, die by the dollar, seemed to be the general sentiment among a nation of former communists. Besides, nothing satisfies the average Ivan more than the spectacle of a high-and-mighty chopped down to his knees. Alex's downfall was weighed and deliberated around dinner tables with no small measure of delight.

"So what's next?" Elena took a long sip from the flute.

"I honestly don't know. I've tried everything I can think of."

She was now pressed firmly up against him, and between sips and explanations, he was stealing furtive glances at her threadbare teddy. She lowered her left shoulder and encouraged a strap to slip off. "What's the worst that can happen to us, Alex?"

"This is the worst."

"No it's not. Not by a long shot. We could be back in Budapest, dead."

"True enough. But if we return to Moscow, that could still happen."

"But they can't drag us back to Russia, can they? Without an extradition treaty, they can't touch us. They can add a library of charges but you're here. If they try, we'll just stay here."

"You wouldn't miss Russia?"

"A little, sure. But alive anywhere with you is better than dead there. But one thing's going to change."

He turned and looked at her.

"We're in this together. I wasn't involved in your business back in Moscow, I didn't need to be, and frankly I never cared to be. But our lives are different now. Our marriage changes with it."

"What does that mean?"

"From now on, no matter how depressing, keep me informed of everything. I'm scared, but I'm not some breakable china doll, and I won't be treated like one."

"I'm sorry."

"Don't be sorry. I love you, and I want to help."

He put his arm around her. Elena slid back and dragged him down onto the bed. The champagne flutes tumbled to the floor. Three weeks of pent-up energy and the frustration of three hundred and fifty million in stolen dollars and stocks were compacted into the first long, smoldering kiss.

The expensive little teddy was quickly ripped off—it sailed through the air and landed on the lampshade. Alex paused only long enough to ask, "What time did you tell Homeless Harry to be here?"

13

The black limo idled in an otherwise empty parking lot that over-looked the ice-cold Moskva River. Mid-October. The sky was gray, overcast, and dreary; another winter that threatened to be long and harsh had produced its first cold snap. The driver had been ordered out of the car. He stood some twenty feet away in the bone-aching darkness, smoking, shivering, stamping his feet, and eyeing the heated car with considerable bitterness.

Three people sat in the rear.

They had agreed to meet like this, one or two days each week. They were bound together by the money and the single enduring emotion that thieves hold for one another: poisonous distrust. For obvious reasons, the three could not be seen together in public under any circumstances, so Golitsin took the initiative and ar-ranged the inconspicuous rendezvous.

Tatyana Lukin sat in the middle, her splendid legs skillfully folded, impossible to miss or ignore. The men who were seated on each side of her—Golitsin to her left, Nicky her right—could barely stand the sight of each other. Golitsin hated to have his authority questioned. Nicky detested authority generally, and loathed Golitsin's prickly brand of it particularly.

Both men were arrogant, selfish, pushy, ill-tempered, and crooked to the core. They had so much in common it was scary.

One was brains, one brawn, and for this to work they had to remain together. She was a woman; she could handle them. Without
her to referee, they would have their hands around each other's
throats in seconds flat. Tatyana liked to be needed.

She was saying, "I lost count of how many times he called.
More than a hundred, probably. We're running an office pool.
The operators in the basement are given a daily tag sheet of who
to put the calls through to. Yeltsin still has no idea Konevitch
is trying to reach him. He's seen the summaries of the news accounts, and heard—"

"And what was his response?" Golitsin interrupted.

"He called in my boss . . . the chief of staff," she added for
Nicky's edification. "Said this did not sound like Alex. He wanted
Konevitch tracked down so he could hear it straight from the
horse's mouth. Asked my boss what he thought."

Golitsin smiled and rubbed his hands. "I'm sure you had already explained to him what he thought."

The answer was too obvious to merit a response. "He told
Yeltsin he always considered Konevitch a conniving crook.
Charming and likable, perhaps. But for sure, nobody earns that
kind of money, they steal it. Warned him that he always believed
Yeltsin allowed Konevitch to get too close. Whatever emotional
or political bonds they shared, the only tangible connection was
money. Konevitch didn't contribute all that cash out of the good-
ness of his heart. Plus, the Congress is filled with mutinous former communists who want to cut Yeltsin's balls off. He's walking
a tightrope between trying to placate them and the frustrated re-
formers in his camp. They're always threatening to impeach him,
and here's Konevitch, making a huge splash on the front pages.
Exactly the kind of connection Yeltsin doesn't need."

Nicky yawned. Politics bored him to death. It made absolutely
no difference to him whether commies or democrats or pansies
in birthday suits were in charge. His business was bulletproof
regardless of whichever idiots ruled the land.

"Did Yeltsin buy it?" asked Golitsin.

"He wasn't *not* buying it. He knows he's got enough problems already. There are dirty rumors regarding his daughter flying all over the city. She has almost literally hung out a sign saying, I'm daddy's little girl—leave your bags of cash here and I'll twist old poppa around my pinkie and bring home the goods."

Nicky perked up at this hint of corruption in high places. "Is it true?"

"Yes, and stay away from her," Tatyana warned with a knowing wink. "She doesn't know it, but she's already being investigated by the chief prosecutor. Bugs and undercover cops surround her everywhere she goes."

Nicky laughed and slapped his thighs with a loud thump. At least his brand of crook made no pretenses.

Golitsin merely grunted. He already knew about Yeltsin's daughter, of course. He could in fact educate Tatyana about how much little Miss Piggy had stashed in a Swiss bank, the account numbers, who gave her the money, and why. It was invaluable knowledge he had no intention of sharing.

"Tell you what, babe," Nicky announced. He leaned toward her and his left hand landed with a lecher's grip high on Tatyana's right thigh. "You still gotta get Konevitch. Put up all the road-blocks you want, eventually he's gonna find a way to get through. You thought about that?"

A twitch of irritation crossed Golitsin's face. "We'll take care of it," he sneered in Nicky's direction.

"Yeah? Like you took care of him in the first place?" Nicky snapped back.

"Stick to your own business." The two men glared at each other, Golitsin's face glowing with anger, Nicky sneering, as if to say, "You couldn't find a needle if it was sticking in your ass."

Tatyana waited until the men cooled off, then said to Golitsin, "Where's the money?"

"Tucked away in a safe place."

"I know that. Where?"

"None of your business."

"Okay. Will you take a little advice?"

"That depends."

"Don't be that way, Sergei. I'm looking out for all our best interests."

Golitsin sniffed and stared straight ahead. Bullshit. Given half a chance she'd rob him blind. She was smart and beautiful, and utterly without a conscience.

Tatyana plowed on. "You know why Konevitch was so popular with Yeltsin and his people? Money. He bankrolled Yeltsin's election. He bought them all their jobs. Literally. An election is coming in another few years, and believe me, they're scared. Yeltsin is being blamed for the mess we're in. His popularity's in the toilet and it'll take a load of cash to get him out of it. They'll miss Mr. Moneybags."

"You're assuming he'll still be alive in another year."

"I assume nothing. I'm just telling you there's an opportunity for whoever's clever enough and rich enough. Somebody is going to pump cash into the big hole Konevitch left. Why not us?"

Golitsin thought about it a moment. What was there not to like? Nothing, really. A million a year could buy a world's worth of influence; a few million, in the right hands, at the right moments, and who knew? It was a no-brainer, actually—he was only surprised he hadn't thought of it himself. He puffed a few times, stretched out the contemplative pause, then nodded. "Let's do it."

"Good decision," Tatyana said. "Funnel it through me. I'll make sure everybody knows where the money came from." And who inside the Kremlin arranged this infusion as well, though of course there was no need to point that out.

"How much are we talking?" Golitsin asked, suddenly concerned because it was his money.

"Not much. Relax, Sergei. A hundred or two hundred thousand a month, for starters. As the election draws closer, we'll increase it, have a real impact."

She had clearly thought this through and prattled a bit about the details—plans for secret bank accounts, blind contacts, how the money would be laundered, and so forth and so on, the typical architecture for large-scale graft and bribery. The irony that they were using Alex's money to replace Alex was lost on none of them.

In fact, Golitsin had arrived at this meeting ready to pitch and hatch his own bright new idea about how to spend more of Alex's hoard of cash, and was waiting impatiently with his hands clasped to pop it. But Tatyana's suggestion fit right in, so he let her rattle on.

As soon as she finished, he said, "Do we all agree this has worked out beautifully?"

Nicky had been staring out the window. But he swallowed his usual nasty cynicism, looked over, and admitted, "Yeah, it's real sweet."

Tatyana merely nodded.

"Then why stop now?" Golitsin asked them, shifting in his seat and facing them. "There's lots of little Konevitches out there, building businesses and creating millions that are just waiting to be taken away."

Tatyana appeared thoughtful, though she had long held the same idea. The only surprise was that it took Golitsin so long to broach this rather obvious inspiration. In her mind, all along Alex Konevitch was just a guinea pig, a test case for them to see if they could pull this off and get away with it. Young millionaires were growing on trees these days, just waiting to be fleeced. But she played dumb and asked, "Do you really think that's a good idea?"

"It will even be easier next time, less risky. None of the other rich kids have Konevitch's warm relationship with Yeltsin. We now know how it works, and we've got plenty of money to use for whatever we try. We'll get even better at it."

Nicky replied, predictably, "What's in it for me?"

Tatyana, speaking as the lawyer she was, answered, "Right now, Nicky, you get what our agreement called for, your share of company stock, and Konevitch's banks to launder your money. But you and the rest of your syndicate pals are making a very big impression. You've turned Moscow into a bloody war zone. The Russian people are screaming for law and order. Believe me, it's a sore topic in the Kremlin these days. The world is paying close attention to your fun and games, too. Yeltsin is tired of being lectured by Americans and Germans about getting your ilk under control."

"Talk, talk, talk."

"Not much longer, believe me," she replied, wagging a finger in his face.

"They have to catch us first."

"Adapt to the new rules. People now vote, Nicky. They make their displeasure known at the polls. Yeltsin knows he has to show tangible progress on the law-and-order front, and soon. A big crackdown is around the corner. Believe me, plenty will be caught."

"The dumb ones."

"That's right. The smart ones, like you, will get ahead of the curve."

"I like what I'm doing now."

"How much do you score in a year?" she asked him.

"Plenty."

"Don't play games, Nicky. How much?"

"Millions. I don't know. Thirty, maybe fifty." Twenty was more like it, but with Golitsin in the car he wasn't about to sound like a small fry. He squirmed in his seat and tried to look sincere.

"Not bad," Tatyana commented, arching her eyebrows. "How much did Konevitch make last year?"

"A lot, I guess," Nicky replied through gritted teeth. "I don't know."

"Around two hundred million. And there are others, like him, who will soon be hauling in billions. All of it considered legal, too."

"Billions?"

"Billions," she repeated, with cool enunciation, as if the word picked up velocity the more slowly it was pronounced. "It's time to take your game up a notch, Nicky, climb out of the gutter. Keep your whorehouses and drug business if they amuse you. But the real thievery, the big money, will be in big business. Billions, Nicky, billions."

Nicky adored that word, "billions." It rolled out of her lips so beautifully. She could repeat as often as she liked.

They chatted on a while, and—while the driver's toes turned black—settled on an equitable division of labor and responsibilities. Golitsin would scout the possibilities, determine the targets, and apply his devious talents to designing the takeovers. They had done it once, and the blueprint was perfectly adaptable for

the next victim. Tatyana would build the political cover, grease
the right palms, and buy their way into the hearts of Yeltsin's
people. Nicky would continue to push whores and dope and gray-
market cars, and bide his time until he was told who needed to be
terrorized, or chased out of the country, or murdered.

The conversation ended right where it started, on the perplex-
ing issue of Alex Konevitch. Nicky wanted him dead—as soon
as it could be arranged, however it was arranged. Just dead. In a
business with few troublesome principles, Nicky steadfastly adhered to one: the fewer witnesses the better.

Golitsin, too, wanted Konevitch dead. Very, very dead. For a
man whose emotions generally veered between heartless dispas-
sion and expressive fury, he had developed a fatal preoccupation
with Alex Konevitch. It was unhealthy, he knew, he just couldn't
help himself. He enjoyed thinking about how Alex would die.

Also, though nobody needed to mention it, if Konevitch did
eventually make contact with his old pal Yeltsin, this whole thing
could come apart. The lush owed the boy wizard a huge debt.
And no matter how hard Tatyana schemed and conspired, eventually Alex would break through—there were too many loose
threads, too many suspicious connections, too many holes that
could spring leaks. And as with all criminal conspiracies, they
would inevitably be pitted against each other. The three of them
knew beyond a shadow of a doubt that they would gladly hang
the other two, if it came to that.

A legitimate investigation conducted by any halfway honest
and competent official would be a catastrophe.

Tatyana confidently assured her partners she had a plan for
their boy Alex, and ordered them to cool their heels until she told
them otherwise.

The combination of champagne and sex worked like magic. The
past three nights Alex had slumbered a more reasonable six
hours. He was eating again, even exercising for two hard hours
every morning in the nicely equipped hotel gym.

He was toweling off after a shower, preceded by a fierce early-morning workout. Elena lay on the bed nibbling toast and browsing through the morning paper. A delicious breakfast of eggs, bacon, toast, and fresh coffee had just been wheeled in for Alex when the phone erupted.

Elena was closest, and she lifted it up, expecting it to be room service. She listened for a moment, then in Russian said, "Yes, he's here," and handed the phone to Alex. "Some officer from the Ministry of Security."

Alex put the phone to his ear and identified himself.

"This is Colonel Leonid Volevodz, special assistant to the minister of security." The voice was deep, with the clipped, irritatingly authoritative bark of a career officer.

"What do you want?" Alex replied in kind, in Russian.

"I have your number because a week ago, the minister asked me to look into your complaint."

"Pass him my thanks." He squeezed his eyes shut, and for a brief moment found it hard to speak. "What have you found?"

"What have I found? Well, there are . . . shall we say, certain irregularities and incongruities in your story."

"You think I'm lying."

"Don't put words in my mouth, Mr. Konevitch. I think there also happen to be big holes in the reports about what happened."

"Then why don't we discuss those holes?"

"Fine. For starters, on the fifth, you flew on Flight 290 to Budapest. The—"

"Yes, I—"

"Don't interrupt me, Konevitch. I will talk and you listen until I ask you a question. Are we clear?"

The arrogance was so thick the man probably was exactly what he claimed to be, a high-ranking bureaucrat in an important ministry. Alex drew a long breath and said, "No more interruptions."

"One more and I'll hang up. Now, where was I? Ah yes . . . the flight manifest confirms this. Also, Hungarian customs show you arrived there at 1:05. Nothing shows that you reentered Russia, yet bank records indicate your personal accounts were emptied out the morning of the sixth. A few hours later, fifty million more was stolen from your customers. The terminals that ordered the transactions were traced back to your own headquarters." He paused a moment, then asked, "What am I to make of this?"

This was the first time Alex had heard the precise details of the thievery, and he spent a long painful moment taking it in. Oh, how he would love to have Golitsin seated in a chair in this room, to have his strong hands gripped around the old man's throat. He would squeeze and squeeze harder until every last detail poured out. How did you get into my safe? Where did you send my money? Who's in this with you, and where is it parked now? Alex said, "I was on a plane to New York during that time. If you read my fax, you'd know that. It's easily confirmed."

"I read your fax, Mr. Konevitch. But that's not the only possibility, is it? Maybe you had an accomplice who moved the money."

"But I didn't. Is that all?"

"Not quite. From the Central Bank, I obtained copies of the letters assigning your properties to Sergei Golitsin. One of our handwriting experts gave your signature a look."

"Go on."

"The writing is pinched, nonlinear, and extended. He believes it is your writing. But perhaps scrawled under conditions of discomfort or duress."

"After three hours of beating and torture, it wasn't my best work."

Elena handed Alex a piece of buttered toast and a cup of coffee. She raised her eyebrows. He answered with a wavering hand. He took a large bite and washed it down with coffee.

After a long pause, the colonel said, "About the fax you sent the minister, it raises many provocative questions. For instance, you implicate General Golitsin."

"I didn't implicate him, I said very clearly that he was behind this. He had people murdered, he had me kidnapped, he had me tortured, and he stole everything."

"We are talking here about a very distinguished man. A patriot who served this country nobly for many decades. These are serious charges. I need to question you directly."

"Fine. I'm in New York. Come and ask whatever you like."

"Not possible. My jurisdiction ends at the Russian border. My friends in foreign intelligence are understandably territorial. They become quite touchy if I forget my place."

"All right. We'll handle this by phone. Ask whatever you like."

"That is . . . unacceptable."

"Is it? Why?"

"For one thing, the case is very complicated and implicates some very important people. For a second thing, I like to see the face of the man I'm interrogating. And of course, everything will have to be checked out. Over the phone won't work."

"Neither will coming to Moscow, Colonel. They tried to kill me and they might want to finish the job. I explained that in the fax."

"I will personally provide for your security, Mr. Konevitch. Arrangements will be made. You have my word as an officer."

"I don't even know you."

"Look, the state prosecutor is preparing an indictment. Do you want your name cleared or not?"

"Don't ask stupid questions. I'm not setting foot in Russia until I read in the paper that Golitsin and his people are under arrest."

A long moment passed. It sounded to Alex like Colonel Volevodz had a hand over the mouthpiece while he conferred with somebody. Alex munched toast and drank his coffee.

Volevodz came back on and suggested, "Why don't we meet on neutral ground?"

"Who were you speaking with?"

"Are we having trust issues, Mr. Konevitch?"

"No, no issues. I don't trust you."

A long pause, then, "That was my secretary. Another call has come in that I need to take. Quickly, Mr. Konevitch, do you want to meet or not?"

"Make it a *very* neutral place, Colonel."

"Berlin. Is that neutral enough for you? You know Checkpoint Charlie?"

"Of course."

"Tomorrow, be there at three. Don't be late."

14

Colonel Volevodz had a crooked sense of humor; or, at the very least, a wicked conception of irony. Checkpoint Charlie, for four troubled decades, had been the fabled symbol of a divided world—socialism versus capitalism, the free world versus the chained one. This was where hooded prisoners had been exchanged between East and West, where tense, shadowy bargains had been fashioned that kept both sides from blowing each other into overradiated rubble.

Alex and Elena had caught an overnight, landed at stately old Tempelhof Airport, and took a fast taxi to a modest gasthaus near the city center, in a nontrendy neighborhood, an anonymous little place off the beaten track. They checked in under false names; they paid with cash.

The recently reunited Berlin was a boomtown. Towering cranes poked at the sky like a thick forest. Construction crews seemed to outnumber the city's population by two to one. Real estate prices in the eastern half of the city were racing to catch up with the inflated prices in the west. The West Germans were stumbling over themselves to gentrify their neglected, prodigal brothers to the east.

Alex stared glumly out the window during the taxi ride and fell ineluctably back into an old habit. Fortunes were being made all around him, new buildings being thrown up at a dizzying pace, a whole city being refashioned before his eyes. He conceived of ten ways he could edge himself into this market and produce millions. He felt like an Olympic sprinter whose legs had been amputated, seated in the bleachers, watching the rookies take their victory laps while he stared on in frustration, hobbled, unable to compete.

At three o'clock, Alex stood alone, at the west end of Checkpoint Charlie. The guardshacks, the lights, the swinging gates were still in place, unmanned though, and all too happily neglected. The long, narrow alley was now little more than a tourist trap, and a very popular one. People of all nationalities and complexions loitered around in herds, snapping pictures of the remains, wandering through the museum of a now dead era, pausing to ogle the graying old photographs of desperate people employing desperate, and often brilliant, means to escape the horrors of communism and make new lives in the West.

Volevodz kept Alex waiting twenty minutes. The message was unmistakable. You're an ex-mogul, a wanted felon, a sorry thief, a loser. I may be only a lowly colonel but I'm your only hope and you'll kiss my boots or else.

Colonel Volevodz finally marched around the corner of a short gray building, a middle-aged, tall, thin man in civilian clothes wrapped in a rumpled trench coat. Two young assistants dressed nearly identically accompanied him, both slightly behind, one to his left, one to his right. They strutted in step, like conquering military men, across Checkpoint Charlie from the east, no doubt attempting to concoct a cinematic entrance. The colonel stopped about two feet from Alex. They eyed each other suspiciously for a moment.

The colonel finally put out a hand. They shook without enthusiasm. Volevodz pointed at his two colleagues, who kept their hands in their pockets and edged a little closer. "Captains Kaputhcuv and Godunov. They're assisting me with this investigation."

"Thank you for coming," said Alex without a trace of warmth. He had dressed carefully for this meeting—the same tailored suit he had escaped in, cleaned and neatly pressed, with a stiffly starched, monogrammed shirt and silk tie completing the ensemble. He looked every bit the big-deal gazillionaire who could roil entire markets with a swipe of his pen.

"So, where is your wife?"

"Around."

"You are alone, then?"

"But you're not," Alex answered without really answering. "I'd like to see your identification."

"I don't believe you should be making demands, Mr. Konevitch. You're a wanted man in Russia."

"Welcome to the new Russia, Colonel. I'm a taxpayer with rights. You're my servant now. Identification, please."

"I can arrest you right now and drag you back to Russia. I'd be a big hero."

"Then welcome to Germany, too. You have no legal authority here."

The colonel's hands were in the pockets of his trench coat. Alex studied him carefully. He had a thin face, thin eyes, thin lips, and close-cropped hair molded to conceal a thinning spot on top. The face was neither mean nor nice, neither handsome nor ugly; the prototypically stonewashed face of a career Soviet functionary. He pushed one hand toward Alex—something round and hard poked forward against his trench coat. "Here's all the authority I need. My assistants are also armed. I can kill you right here." He paused to produce a hard grin. "Maybe I will."

Alex upped him with a tight smile. "A bad idea. For you and for me."

"To the contrary, it would be a great idea. It would solve a lot of problems."

"Look behind me at that big gray apartment building."

Volevodz's gaze left Alex's face.

"Keep going," Alex ordered, following the colonel's roving eyes. "Third window down on the right side. See the barrel pointed out the window?"

Volevodz's mouth nearly fell open when his eyes finally settled on something long, cylindrical, and dark poking out a window.

"Look long and hard, Colonel," Alex said. "That's one of three snipers I hired to protect me. If I lift my right arm, you're dead, all of you. If I die, you're dead. I had hoped not to do this, but . . ." He cranked his right arm halfway up, nearly to his waist.

Volevodz computed the new situation very quickly, then, in a fast rush of words, said, "Put it down! For godsakes, put your arm down."

"Hands out of your coats. Palms up. Shut up and do as I say. Show me your identification—then, maybe my arm will come down."

The hands popped out and so did the identifications. The hands were trembling. Alex glanced dismissively at the official-looking IDs in the fists of the two captains and snatched the colonel's for a closer inspection. It looked genuine enough, but what did he know? He threw it back.

Volevodz caught it and slipped it back inside his pocket. "You're not behaving like an innocent man, Mr. Konevitch."

"I wasn't treated like an innocent man."

"You've just threatened the lives of three officers of the Ministry of Security. This will be added to the already grave charges against you."

"You won't believe how much that worries me. Are you wired?"

"Why would I be wired?" Volevodz replied with a sneer.

"You wouldn't necessarily. I'd just like to be sure our frequencies don't interfere with each other."

"Oh . . . I see."

"You threatened to kill me. It's on tape. Who sent you?"

He stared at Alex a moment. Alex had chosen to stand in the middle of the checkpoint, well away from any walls or protective cover of any nature. Why was now clear. Volevodz and his assistants were trapped, out in the open, wildly vulnerable, and he briefly pondered the interesting question of how many bull's-eyes were painted on his forehead at that moment. He tried a smile and said, "I think we've gotten off on the wrong foot."

Alex crossed his arms and stopped smiling. "I'm here because you promised to help me. You show up instead with guns and threaten to kill me. You have an interesting definition of a wrong foot."

"All right, all right. I made a mistake, a big one. I'm sorry. Let's start over." He tried to force the smile, and tried his damnedest to make it look friendly and sincere. "Can I call you Alex?"

"Sure. Why not?"

"Okay. Alex, as I said yesterday, I'd like you to return with me to Russia. If, as you claim, you're innocent, you can clear this up in court."

"Don't make me laugh. I won't be alive long enough to make it to court."

It was obviously a waste of time for Volevodz to contradict him; he'd just threatened to do the honors, here, now, in Germany, in a supposedly neutral corner. It was even more foolhardy to attempt to worm his way into Alex's confidence. A group of blond-haired, blue-eyed tourists wandered past, gibbering in some strange tongue. The eyes inside the skinny slits danced around a moment, then Volevodz observed, "There's a lady over there filming us with a camera."

"It's about time you started paying attention. Yes, you're being filmed, yes, your voice is being recorded, and yes, a bunch of guns in the hands of seriously nervous people are being pointed at you. At least four of these tourists wandering around are my people. They're all armed to the teeth in the event you have friends lurking nearby. Don't try something stupid; I'm a very frightened, very desperate man. Any second I could maybe forget, and reach up, wipe the sweat from my forehead, and you'll all be dead. Now, why are we here?" Alex suddenly flapped his arms up and down, half slaps on his thighs like a penguin. "Quickly, Colonel."

"Settle down, Alex. I'm not here to kill you. I have a bargain for you."

"I'm listening."

"Stop that with the arms. It makes me nervous."

"Speak faster. My nose itches."

"All right, all right." He rubbed his eyes. Alex's preparations were not a total surprise. After being briefed on his unexpected escape from Hungary and the clever stunts he had pulled off, he had been warned to expect some sort of shenanigans. But Alex's eyes seemed to be boring into his soul, and he was having difficulty trying to maintain his nonchalance. "Certain friends are very impressed with your financial acumen. Frankly, it's a shame you've been chased out. You're a national asset for Russia. We admire what you accomplished."

"Who are your friends?"

"Powerful people."

"Give me some powerful names."

"Don't waste both our time. I don't know all the names, anyway."

"All right, go on."

"They would like to enlist you to manage their finances. The money is parked offshore. You never have to come to Russia. It's work you certainly know how to do."

"And what do I get out of this?"

"Twenty percent of the profit. The fund contains hundreds of millions right now, but eventually will grow to billions. Your take, obviously, will depend on how well you invest it. It will be a reasonable compensation."

"Is the money clean or dirty?" Alex asked, ignoring the offer.

Volevodz shrugged. "What's clean money in Russia these days? Anyway, why should you care?"

"I don't. What about the case against me?"

"As I said, these are powerful people."

"How powerful?"

"Arrangements can be made." His forehead wrinkled and he pretended to think about it awhile. He reached up and massaged his sore neck. Alex towered a good six inches over him and had chosen to stand nose-to-nose. Volevodz was a tall man himself, used to being looked up to, and he hated having the role reversed. "A few witnesses might materialize and clear your name. The state prosecutor assigned to your case is a very reasonable sort. For a judgeship and a healthy contribution to his retirement account he might be persuaded to declare the case a dead end."

"Stop lying. My story was spread all over the front pages for weeks. I find it hard to believe it could be easily disposed of."

The colonel enacted a small shrug. "Sadly our police and courts are so overburdened, there is little pressure to close cases. Besides, in Moscow these days, a new scandal always eclipses the last. Such are the times you helped bring about, Alex Konevitch."

"What about my money?"

"Don't think of it that way." He attempted a feeble smile and placed a hand on Alex's arm.

Alex shrugged it off and backed away a step. "I was beaten and nearly killed. My wife was kidnapped and threatened. Three hundred and fifty million dollars were stolen from me. My businesses have been ruined and I've been publicly disgraced. How should I think of it?" Alex asked carefully, coolly, without a trace of rancor—a businessman dispassionately listing the credits and debits from a register.

"Water under a bridge, if you're smart. Or, if you like, a down payment on a new future. You're an exceptionally talented man, Alex. We're offering you the chance to make it all back."

"How kind of you."

"Get over it. In a few years, with a little elbow grease, you'll be right where you started. Maybe richer."

This offer was the last thing Alex had expected, and he needed a pause to consider what he was hearing and learning. It was almost laughable. Almost. Volevodz obviously was another cog in the rapidly growing conspiracy that robbed his life. Now they were offering Alex the chance to take the money they stole from him, to invest and nurture it, and produce fabulous profits that would make them even richer.

In return he would get a fraction of what was already his. It wasn't enough that the sharks took everything from him; they now were offering to make him a slave to their financial interests. And it was slavery. They would own him, a deal with the devil, and once he was in there was no way out.

They had his money, his companies, his homes—they now wanted to own him.

In fact, it was beautiful—for them, anyway. Alex would be the offshore front for their illegal activities, he would launder their money, keep it hidden and growing, and if anyone got wind of it, Alex would be there, the disposable frontman, holding the bag.

"You're a liar and the people who sent you are thieves," Alex said very simply, a fact he managed to express without sentiment. "So why should I trust you?"

"Do we have a deal?"

"Not yet. You're moving a little fast for me."

"I'm offering you a chance to live. Let's say you don't take this deal, okay? We'll hunt you down and kill you."

"I thought we were negotiating. Now you're making threats."

"All right. Negotiate."

"Twenty percent is too cheap," Alex told him. "A deal like this needs to be structured. If I increase the value of the fund ten percent or less, twenty percent is all I deserve. But if I beat that, my percentage needs to increase accordingly. Cap it at thirty percent if the value increases by fifty percent or more."

"What if you lose money?"

"I won't."

"You're quite the optimist, aren't you?"

"I gave you the pessimistic scenario. And any smart businessman builds in incentives to encourage better performance. I'm more than confident that I will easily produce returns surpassing a hundred percent a year. In that case, I'd like a five million bonus on top of the thirty percent."

Volevodz turned and traded surprised looks with his two assistants. "The man has balls."

"If you weren't a fool, you'd know I'm being generous. Find yourself another man with a track record like mine, the terms will be even stiffer. There are people on Wall Street who demand thirty percent even if they don't make you a dime. And if they know the money is tainted, or in any way questionable, they'll demand at least sixty percent. Don't take my word for it, ask around."

Volevodz became fidgety. "I will have to discuss this with my friends."

"Of course you will. You're an errand boy," Alex said, twisting the knife a little deeper. "You and I are through speaking. The next conversation will be with your boss or no one," he added. "If it's another rude flunky I'll hang up and never take another call."

Volevodz's eyes narrowed. Oh, how he was tempted to whip out his gun and blow this impertinent punk back to New York. He would, too, would smile and blast away, except he was at a severe disadvantage with all the guns pointed at him. "I'll bring it up," he mumbled, biting his lip.

"One other matter I'd like to bring to their attention."

"What?"

"Given my history with these people, I want some form of assurance I'll get what I earn."

"Like what?"

"I'm not sure yet. I'll think about it." He backed two steps away from Volevodz, then stopped and, treating it like a careless afterthought, warned, "Move two feet or make any effort to follow me—so much as tug a cell phone out of your pocket—and the nervous people with guns have orders to blast you to pieces."

Volevodz's mouth gaped open. A team of five stalkers lurked around the corner, awaiting a call from their boss to jump on Konevitch's trail and track him to his lair, where they would add a little more pressure and help Alex make the right call.

He shifted his feet, suddenly remembered Alex's warning, and froze. He briefly pondered the amazing question of how he had been so thoroughly outwitted by a complete amateur. But before Alex could escape, he remembered to ask, "How do we reach you?"

"Same as before. Tell your boss to call my hotel in New York."

With that Alex turned his back and walked purposefully toward the west and freedom and Elena, who was pacing nervously behind the large gray apartment building, praying they had not overplayed their bluff. They held hands tightly and briskly walked two blocks, caught a taxi, got lost in the traffic, and eventually made their way back to the gasthaus.

Volevodz and his two aides stood in place, nervously wringing their hands. Their eyes never wavered from the window ledge six floors above. As long as the barrel never budged, neither would they. A flock of giggly Japanese tourists mistook them for tired old spies, perhaps sharing a reunion in a place of former glory, swapping lies and inflating old adventures. The tourists spent five minutes snapping pictures of the three scowling men in wrinkled trench coats. A bus arrived delivering a fresh batch of rambunctious tourists, who piled out and were instantly drawn to the attraction. Erupting with laughter, they yanked out the cameras and joined in the fracas. They were third-rate actors hired to lend a little authenticity to the site, one tour leader helpfully explained to his entourage, who laughed louder. "Absolutely third-rate!" one of the crowd yelled back. How badly the three men wanted to yank out the guns and start blowing holes through the crowd.

They felt like boneheads. Nobody spoke, nobody moved, they just gaped at the barrel pointed out the window.

After twenty excruciating minutes, they drew verbal straws. The taller of the two captains lost and gently inched forward, slow, limited scrapes across the cement, before he squeezed his eyes shut, uttered a loud curse, and hopped three rapid bounces. No shots were fired. No bodies bounced off the concrete. They threw caution to the wind and raced toward the base of the apartment house. They drew their guns and pounded heavily up the stairwell to the sixth floor. Puffing from exertion, they found Alex's hired sniper there, directly underneath a hallway window: a mop head rested on an overturned metal trash can, with its rusty metal pole poking out the window.

The three men stared at one another with disbelief that quickly turned into red-faced humiliation. No debate was required or entertained; agreement was quick and unanimous—this petty detail would obviously only add unnecessary clutter in their report to Tatyana Lukin.

They were tired of hotel rooms. They wanted to get out and wander around this glorious city that reeked with such historical significance, to venture out and feel the soul of the German people. But they wouldn't. They agreed that it was too dangerous. It made no sense at this point to risk being picked up by Volevodz and his goons. Room service was contacted and they ate a quiet dinner in the room together.

Over dessert and a glass of wine Alex shared the details of the offer. Elena listened and withheld comment. The pros and cons were obvious. They were tired of living on the run, tired of looking over their shoulders, tired of going to bed each night and awakening each morning imagining the worst. And no matter how much Alex exercised, he was a man of restless energy and incredible intellect that needed an outlet. But the offer was humiliating, a disgrace, really. Still, the prospect of neutralizing the bad people trying to kill them had its pluses.

"What will you do if they meet your demands?" she finally asked.

"I may take it."

"Do you think Golitsin is behind the offer?"

"I seriously doubt it. I think he wants me dead."

"Then who?"

"That's the question. There are so many possibilities. I know of only one way to find out."

"So you intend to take the offer to discover who's involved," she suggested.

"That's the idea. If I say yes, I'll look for a way to smoke them out."

"Why you?" she asked, sipping from her wine. Good question.

"Partly because they're still afraid of me. That's why they want me inside and neutralized. Why else are they still working overtime to keep me away from Yeltsin? Bring me in, and they buy my silence."

"What's the other partly?"

"Golitsin has a partner. That's obvious. Somebody inside Yeltsin's inner circle, I'm nearly certain. But think about this, Elena. We know the syndicates are involved. We know Golitsin and his KGB friends are involved. And now this man Volevodz and his deputies show up."

"You think he really is with the ministry?"

"I'm sure of it. I made a call to a friend in Moscow and had him checked out. He's former KGB, but he's now exactly what he claims to be. And he is, in fact, conducting the investigation."

"So this conspiracy is quite big."

"Getting bigger by the day. It would help to know exactly who and what we're up against."

"And then?" Elena asked.

"I find another way to get to Yeltsin. I'll have names and evidence to shove in his face. If they can do this to me, Elena, they can do it to anybody. I'm sure they will. And if that happens, the damage will be immeasurable. Nobody will want to put money in Russia."

She was dressed in a long tight dress with a slit that stretched all the way to her waist; it clawed even more provocatively higher when she moved. The dress was not expensive and didn't need to be; she could justify drools in kitchen rags. She entered the restaurant and wound her way through the tables, where her date for the evening awaited impatiently in a long cushioned booth in the back.

Golitsin had arrived ten minutes earlier. He was deep into his third scotch, a fine, imported blend he had acquired a taste for during his years in the KGB.

The restaurant was the most exclusive and most breathtakingly expensive in Moscow. At that moment, anyway: city hot spots fluctuated monthly, and after three weeks of endless lines, of thousand-dollar bribes to the owner for a reserved table, this place was peering at oblivion. The tables were filled with other crooks and entrepreneurs who were choking down caviar by the bushel and gulping enough champagne to float the Russian fleet. Enough cigarette smoke filled the air for an artillery duel. Beautiful women seemed to be littered around every table, hanging lustily on the arms of seriously rich men, laughing at full volume over the slightest ping of humor, generally working hard to ingratiate themselves enough to let the party last another day, another week, another month, before they were replaced by a more eager bimbo with longer legs and a louder, faster quick-draw giggle.

Long live capitalism.

"Nice place. You have good taste," Tatyana said, smiling nicely, not meaning a word of it.

Golitsin did not get up or even acknowledge the phony compliment. She slid into the booth across from him and offered a nice flash of thigh. Her blue blouse was cut precariously low—if she tripped, or stooped even one inch forward, her breasts would flop out.

"How are things in the Kremlin?" Golitsin asked.

"Tense. Always tense. Disaster always lurking around the corner."

The waiter rushed over. She ordered British gin, straight up, no water, no ice. Golitsin tipped his nearly empty glass and signaled for a refill. A small band sat in the corner, dressed as Cossacks, playing old Russian folk songs to an audience playing a new Russian game.

Golitsin informed her, "Let me tell you why we're here. I'm hearing rumors."

"What kind of rumors?"

"Bad ones for the lush."

"How bad?"

"The reactionary forces are going to take him down."

"They've been promising that for years."

"They're beyond promising. They're hiring hooligans off the streets, arming them, and preparing a showdown."

An eyebrow shot up. "How reliable are these rumors?"

"Believe them. My old KGB friends say it will happen any day."

"What about Rutskoi? He involved?" she asked in a low whisper, meaning, of course, Aleksandr Rutskoi, Yeltsin's vice president, a war hero from the Afghanistan debacle Yeltsin had taken aboard in the hope that Rutskoi could calm down the right-wing wackos and former communists who loathed Yeltsin with a passion that bordered on madness. But the marriage was ill-conceived and soured from the start. It sped bitterly downhill from there. They were very different kind of men: one malleable and political down to his underwear; the other the sort of military man who adored absolutes in everything but his own ethics. Aside from a few organs the only thing they shared in common was that they were both legendary blowhards with a bottomless lust for power. The two men now barely talked. Rutskoi schemed and plotted with his friends and allies in the Russian version of a Congress, undermining Yeltsin and his reforms at every turn. And Yeltsin worked hard to return the favor. Stealing a note from his American friends, he pushed his vice president into the shadows, and shoved him out the door every time there was a funeral anywhere in the world. "The Pallbearer," Yeltsin called him with considerable malice.

"In it up to his hips," Golitsin confirmed, finishing off his scotch.

Her gin arrived. She took a long, careful sip. "I know you hate him, but it would be bad luck for us and our plans if Yeltsin was toppled right now."

Barely paying attention, he now was looking over her shoulder at a man who had just swaggered through the entrance. Six leggy women of identical height and approximate weight and anorexic build were hanging off his arms, all with their hair died bright red, all dressed in identical red evening gowns. He thought at first he was seeing double, or triple, and it was time to cut back on the hooch. What a glorious time to be ridiculously rich and Russian.

"Maybe there's an opportunity in this for us," she suggested.

That got his attention. He shifted his rear and bent forward. "Like what?"

"Your old KGB friends now run the Ministry of Security and the security services. If there's bloodshed, they'll be Yeltsin's only hope."

"Yes, they will. What do we get in return?"

She was about to throw out an unconsidered answer when what had been a loud argument at the next table turned dangerously louder. Two millionaires were enjoying a heated argument over a business deal gone sour, both in full throttle about who had outcheated whom. One leaped from his chair and drew a gun. The two lovely blonde bimbos who were their evening entertainment screeched and hit the floor. The gunman was red-faced and howling curses, aiming the pistol in the face of the man across from him. It was such an everyday mess in Moscow business circles that the other patrons mostly ignored the fracas. They went about their meals, the girls laughed, the champagne flowed. Fortunately, like nearly every business in this raucous, crooked town, the restaurant had a protection contract with a crime syndicate. Two burly men hustled over, blackjacked the gun wielder into unconsciousness, kicked and pummeled him a few times out of habit, and dragged him out by the legs. Tatyana exploited the brief entertainment to ponder Golitsin's question more deeply.

The moment things settled down, she suggested, "How about this? In return we name the new attorney general."

It was a brilliant idea, of course. Golitsin saw the possibilities immediately. If they owned the attorney general, any potential Alex problems would go away. Nor, as they gobbled up other companies, would they have to look over their shoulders; they wouldn't worry about the legal authorities because they owned the head honcho. He bent farther forward and asked, "You think Yeltsin will bite?"

"If we time it just right, what choice will he have?"

He folded his hands behind his head and leaned back into his seat. "Wait till the blood is running, till the standoff reaches full pitch. Till he's absolutely desperate and has no choice. Great idea."

"Exactly. Can you deliver the Ministry of Security?"

He chuckled. Stupid question. "I'll appeal to their patriotism and I'll spread money around like there's no tomorrow. They may have demands of their own. I'll tell them to make a list."

The waiter arrived. It was nearly midnight, so they both went for the special, boar au gratin, which materialized almost instantly. Large slabs of it, buried under a ton of gooey white cheese and thick gravy. She drank measured sips of champagne with her meal, he stuck with scotch and drank without letup. She nibbled carefully and economically from the feast on her plate, he stuffed everything into his mouth and chewed with noisy vigor.

She stayed on small talk, but had another topic to discuss. A delicate one, and she wanted his stomach full and his incredible intelligence watered down with liquor before she made her move.

After desserts were delivered, she asked, "How do you like your new house?"

"It's wonderful." He tried to keep the nasty smile off his face, but couldn't help it. "I love sleeping in Konevitch's bed, knowing I took it from him. I hope he and his lovely brat are sleeping on a hard, bug-ridden bunk in a flophouse, surrounded by smelly winos and hacking dopers, and thinking about me."

"And how is business these days?" she asked, though she already knew the answer. She was sure he would lie.

As she guessed he would, he said, "Fine. Money's pouring through the doors."

She looked down and played with the silverware beside her plate. "I heard three of the subsidiaries are already bankrupt."

"Small setbacks," he replied smugly, waving for the waiter to haul over another glass of hooch. "We didn't want to be in hotels or restaurants, anyway. Lousy businesses. I'm getting rid of the bloat Konevitch left behind."

"Two more banks were just granted state licenses to exchange foreign currencies. You now have serious competition."

"They'll have to catch up to me. I won't make it easy."

"You kicked your price up to five percent for every ruble exchanged. They're offering two percent."

"Well, I give better service."

Better service, my ass, she wanted to say. Golitsin's posse of former KGB morons were ripping the guts out of Konevitch's business empire. The speed and efficiency was frightening. One of the twits had made the deplorable decision to shift the tourist company to a lower-fare airline. The first load of paying customers died horribly in a fiery plane crash. Worse, the passengers thought they were traveling to a sex vacation in Thailand; the plane was headed for a run-down health clinic in Poland.

The construction business was an unfolding disaster. Without

Alex's name on the letterhead, no new contracts had come in. Nor, after the latest stumble, were they likely to. A huge high-rise under construction on the outer ring had collapsed in a spectacular heap. Ten workers crushed to death, twenty more in the hospital. The cause was an incredible decision by another of the twits to use less expensive wood beams in place of the thick metal ones clearly stipulated by the now enraged architects. Tatyana managed to pull a few strings and have the investigation squelched. The damage was done, though. Half the construction workforce quit on the spot; the other half were making ugly sounds about a strike.

Another twit, this one in charge of the bank, ignored the growing spread between government bonds and interest rates. A small, momentary blip on a computer screen and, like that, a hundred million, gone. Amazing.

The list of problems was endless, horrible, and growing. The car importing company shipped five hundred Mercedes sedans to the wrong cities, then hiked up the prices so high that the inventory was rusting on the lots. The hundred Mercedes convertibles that ended up in Yakutsk, a frigid penal colony near the Arctic Circle, were going to be a bitch to move at any price. The complicated computer program confused him, that twit whined afterward. And another idiot, this one in the arbitrage business, had purchased two thousand tons of the most expensive iron ore in history. He misread the code, thought it was silver at a great price, he insisted after he annihilated any possibility of the arbitrage business having a profitable year.

Another few months at this hideous pace and there'd be nothing left.

As per the original deal, Tatyana was a partner in Golitsin Enterprises—a hidden partner, of course—and she was quietly seething. From the beginning Golitsin had demanded Konevitch's cash for himself. His idea, his brilliant plan, his inspirational leadership; the instant gratification was rightfully his, every bit of it, he insisted. She had neither objected nor debated that point—she hadn't seen a reason to—and now she sorely regretted it. Looking back, it seemed so naïve. Stupid. But by any reasonable measure, at the time her take was around fifty million in stock in companies that were wildly flourishing and threatening to double or triple in a few brief years. At the time, that struck her as ample restitution for her part in the heist.

She doubted she could unload her shares now at any price. The smart money had already sprinted out of the banks; even the dumb money was pawing the exits. Lawsuits were piling up over shoddy workmanship, false promises, missed deliveries, slipped deadlines, and of course the furiously grieving families of the people slaughtered by that fly-by-night excuse for an airline booked by Golitsin's twits. Who knew what awful disaster would happen next? She had no legal friends, but plenty of attorney acquaintances, all of whom were eyeing Golitsin Enterprises with considerable intensity. They were salivating to get a piece of the action.

But Tatyana was a realist. Nothing she could say would change things. Golitsin, for all his brilliance and canniness, had no interest or talent for commerce. And his thugs had as much business running a company as three-year-olds playing with nuclear warheads. Tugging fingernails out of helpless prisoners was one thing; squeezing profit out of finicky customers quite another.

"I contacted Konevitch," she said, almost in a whisper.

"You *what*?"

She bent forward. "You heard me, Sergei. Konevitch. I dispatched an officer of the Security Ministry to make him an offer."

"You must have a death wish. You have no business freelancing."

"Well . . . then forgive me. I'm looking out for both our interests." Even she couldn't make that sound authentic. Golitsin's face reddened, his eyes narrowed into angry slits.

"Answer me this, Sergei. How much interest are you getting from the bank where the money is stashed?"

"None of your business."

"It won't hurt to tell me. How much?"

"It's a big pile of money. A mountain, really. A little interest goes a long way."

"If it's a Swiss bank, about one percent, am I right?"

"Around there," he snarled—not that one percent of 250 million was anything to be ashamed of. Besides, one didn't go to the Swiss for the interest.

"What if Konevitch could double it every few years? He's a genius. It will be easy to build in a few safeguards. He'll never actually touch the money. For a small share in the profits we'll be buying his golden touch."

"Not interested."

"Why aren't you? Because you're making a fortune from Golitsin Enterprises?" she asked with a constricted smile.

Since it was a privately owned company there was no financial reporting or formalized information flowing to the shareholders. He briefly wondered how much she knew. Too much, judging by the shrewd tone of her voice. He pulled a long sip of scotch, then admitted, "There have been a few small setbacks."

"Does Nicky know yet?" she asked, thrusting the knife a little deeper. "He's also a partner, last time I checked."

Golitsin flicked a hand through the air as if it didn't bother him in the least. He wasn't happy that she brought it up, though. Nicky definitely was not the sort of partner you wanted to disappoint with bad news. "What's your point?" he asked nastily.

"Two points. One, Konevitch is very good at making money," she said, and the insinuation was clear and painful—Golitsin and his band of fools would alchemize gold into Silly Putty. "Two, if we employ him," she continued, "we own him. He won't run and tattle, because it won't be in his interest. And he'll be a co-conspirator."

"Where is he?"

"New York City."

"A big place. Where in New York?"

"I don't know exactly."

He knew she was lying. Her lips were moving, so of course she was lying. "If you don't know, how did you reach him?"

"Why does it matter? Are you in or out?"

"What do you get out of it?"

"A reasonable share of the profits. Nothing exorbitant, say thirty percent. It's my idea, after all."

Golitsin knew damn well what she was up to. She wanted to get her fingers on the money, the cash. His millions. She would set up this arrangement with Konevitch, then figure out a scheme to rob him blind.

Well, he knew damn well what he wanted, too. More than ever, more than anything, he wanted that boy dead. Just dead. That he was running Konevitch's companies into the ground—he was too painfully aware of the snickers and rumors roaring around the city—only made him detest the man all the more.

He sat back, drew a few heavy breaths, and struggled to clear his brain. Maybe killing him was the wrong approach. Maybe he was being impetuous and shortsighted. In fact, enlisting Konevitch in this scheme might be a great idea. It felt better by the moment—let the genius double or triple his money, get the boy's fingers nice and dirty, and if Konevitch made one wrong move, then find a way to blow the whistle and humiliate him once again. Why not?

He could always kill him.

He asked, innocently enough, but without commitment, "And how did he sound about the offer?"

"Interested. He made a few demands. Don't worry, I'll grind him down."

"All right," he growled, playing at phony reluctance. "Go ahead. Make the deal. See where it goes."

15

Early October 1993

Midnight, and Elena was lying awake, improving her English by watching an old American western. The tense gunfight was interrupted, midshot, by a tedious toothpaste commercial, so she casually flipped over to CNN for a quick peek at what was happening around the world, late-night. They were back in their suite in the Plaza, counting the days and waiting for whoever sent Volevodz to call.

She reached across the bed and shook her husband awake. "Alex, look what's happening," she said, almost yelling, aiming a finger at the flickering tube across the room.

Alex sat up and stretched, glanced briefly at the tube, and froze. At that instant, a line of tanks was pouring salvo after salvo at the Russian White House, Russia's rather less than elegant equivalent of a parliamentary building. The top floors burned brightly. Fresh shells were striking the sides of the building, sending showers of shattered glass and debris that bounced off the concrete apron.

An unseen male correspondent was providing commentary in a hurried, theatrical voice: "The Supreme Soviet, as the Russian Congress is still known, a week ago voted to impeach Boris Yeltsin and replace him with his hard-line vice president, Aleksandr Rutskoi.

A few hours ago, in this very building, Rutskoi signed a decree announcing his own presidency. The fencing that has gone back and forth for months, the largely communist and right-wing deputies voting first to emasculate Yeltsin's reforms and power, and now to replace him, has finally erupted in violence. The past week there have been scattered skirmishes around the capital. Now there are two presidents of Russia. And now . . . the fate of democracy hangs in the balance."

Elena reached for the phone, called room service, and ordered two pots of coffee, with a fresh pot to be delivered every hour until she notified them otherwise. The drama, with overheated updates, unfolded throughout the night. Alex and Elena never budged. They sipped coffee, munched toast, spoke little, and watched in fascination. The troops surrounding the White House were part of the Ministry of Security. The trigger-happy tanks were courtesy of the army.

Inside the building, Vice President Rutskoi and a band of mutinous deputies, as well as a large clutch of armed thugs, were making their last stand. For the second time in two years, Russia's future hung over a bitter standoff at this same building. This time, though, the roles were reversed. Instead of Yeltsin flipping the bird at the old boys in the Kremlin, he was the one being flipped, the one who dispatched the tanks to flatten his opposition.

At seven the next morning the television showed Rutskoi and his humbled lieutenants waving a desultory white flag and scurrying from the still burning building. They were quickly slapped in handcuffs, forced into waiting vans, and driven off to prison.

The American president immediately issued a statement lauding a great victory of democracy, and a painful but desperately necessary move by his dear, dear friend Boris.

The screen quickly filled with talking heads who, as so often was the case, proceeded with silky conviction and utter certitude to get it all incredibly wrong. One graying authority in oversized horn-rimmed glasses made an analogy to Hitler's failed putsch in Munich. Another crowed that Yeltsin was the Lincoln of this era, a decisive, principled man who had locked horns with the devil and kicked his butt. Russia was saved, democracy triumphed, Yeltsin the hero of the hour, was the common refrain across network world.

Alex watched it all in sheer disgust. "They have no idea what they've just seen," he whispered to Elena, who was nibbling on a piece of cold toast.

"No, they're idiots," she agreed between bites.

"You saw who saved Yeltsin?"

"The Security people and the army."

"Yes, all former KGB people. You know what this means? Yeltsin cut a deal with them."

"How much trouble are we in?" Elena asked, though she knew the answer.

"A lot. This is the end of our Russian experiment in democracy. From here on, the old boys will take back what Yeltsin took from them, and there's nothing to stop them. The people who stole our money now have no fear. Even if I got through to Yeltsin, he's in their pocket. "

"He won't lift a finger to help. He sold his soul," Elena said, finishing the thought.

The call came a full two days later. The voice was a woman's, Anna, throaty and sultry, no last name.

Alex cut off her attempt at pleasantries and opened the bidding. "You heard my requirements?"

"Volevodz explained everything."

"Good. What's your answer?"

"Thirty percent might be a reasonable compensation, but it will be structured differently. I'll draw up a contract that pegs your take a little more precisely." And along the way, I'll whack off as many points as I can get away with and add them to my own total, she thought, but didn't explain.

"I won't commit until I see the details," Alex told her very quickly.

"That's understandable. But forget the five million bonus. Out of the question."

"I considered it a reasonable request. Of course, I have no idea how big the base is. Volevodz mentioned several hundred million."

"So you were for shooting for the stars. I don't blame you. But let's say it's in the several hundred million range now. It will be more in the future, considerably more. Down the road, based on your performance, we can talk about a structured bonus. Not until we see how good you are."

"Who are you?" Alex asked.

Anna, actually Tatyana, laughed playfully. "Alex, you're smarter than that."

Yes, he was. Also a painfully good listener. She was playing it close to the vest, but she had already made one serious slip—"I'll draw up a contract." Alex took a moment and added it up. Female by sex, Anna obviously an imaginary name, a lawyer most certainly, from her voice late twenties, early thirties at the outside, and Alex guessed she probably worked in the Kremlin or held a senior government position of some sort. Also arrogant and pushy and sly—of course, that could fit almost any lawyer. From her tone of smug self-assurance, Alex suspected she was very pretty, possibly beautiful.

"Explain how this is supposed to work," Alex asked. "Obviously you have no intention of assigning me direct control over the money."

"Good guess. You'll work through a team of accountants and brokers who report to me. You tell them what you'd like to do, they inform me, not a penny gets moved until I approve it. You'll receive daily updates from them. Satisfactory?"

"It's not ideal, no."

"From your angle, I'm sure it's not. It looks perfect from mine."

"Listen to me. The best investments don't give warning. A difference between interest spreads, for instance, can last seconds. The same is true in the arbitrage game. It's a very narrow strike window—miss it, and you can forget about it. If you want spectacular returns, I can't be handicapped by time. How many people have to approve my decisions?"

"Nice try. Next question."

"Where's the money now?"

"Try again."

"How much is it earning?"

"You're starting to bore me."

"Am I? Look, I won't take this job if Golitsin is in the decision loop. I've read what he's done to my companies. What a disaster. He couldn't make two cents if it was raining dollars."

Another very serious mistake on her part. A long, revealing pause before she snapped, "Who and how the decisions are made is my business." Then, after another moment, "You'd better be done with your demands. Let me remind you, you're broke, on the run, and wanted for crimes here in Russia. But you can lose more, a lot more. I'm offering you a chance to make some of your money back."

"Your generosity chokes me up."

"I know. Do you want it or not, Alex?"

Alex glanced carefully at Elena, who was resting on the bed, biting her lip and trying her best to appear noncommittal and supportive of whatever choice he made—and failing miserably.

This was the moment; did he or didn't he? Yes or no?

"Not," he replied without hesitation.

"Don't be foolish. I'm offering you a great deal."

"A great deal for you. It stinks for me."

"Take a minute, Alex. Cool down and think like a businessman, be practical. You really have no clue of how powerful we are, do you? How easily we can reach you."

"I'll take my chances."

"You'll regret it. Believe me, I'll—"

"I'd say nice talking with you, but it wasn't," Alex interrupted and pushed disconnect.

The instant it hit the cradle, Elena lifted up the phone and immediately placed a call to the hotel switch in the basement.

Her friend Amber, the head operator, had a live-in boyfriend who happened to work for the phone service that tied the hotel to the outside world. Amber promised to get right back with the phone number of their recent caller.

Two minutes later, Amber called with the number, which Elena hastily scribbled on the hotel stationery. Alex took it, studied it a moment—he did not recognize it—then stuffed it inside his pant pocket.

Elena sat on the bed, quietly pleased that her husband had refused the offer. An enormously talented genius at business he might be, but she was sure he was over his head with these people. He'd been surprisingly successful to date, and she prayed he didn't delude himself about why. Too much of that success rested on underestimation and beginner's luck. With each success the underestimation wore off. And luck could run out. Also, his plan had relied on Boris Yeltsin, an ambitious man she had never fully trusted. Alex had seen him as an embattled figure struggling to end dictatorship and bring democracy to Russia. Elena was convinced that his own hopes had blinded him to the man's considerable faults. He was a politician, for all the good and bad that implied. Boris had grabbed a tiger by the tail, and the tiger was angry and hungry.

Boris would happily cram Alex into the tiger's jaws if that kept the resentful tiger from eating him.

"So what will we do?" she asked.

"Hire an investigator in Moscow. Mikhail Borosky always did great work for me. He's incredibly competent, and discreet. I trust him completely."

"I know Mikhail's good, but what's the point?"

"We won't know until he digs and finds out a little more. Maybe it'll help, maybe not. At least he'll have a few leads to go on."

"Do you want to get the companies back?"

He shook his head sadly. "You haven't been reading the business news online. What's left isn't worth owning. Golitsin is way over his head. Banking is a business built on confidence. In two short months, he's ruined everything."

"So what's the point of hiring Mikhail?"

"I want to learn more about these people."

"That will take time. Maybe a lot of time. What will we do in the meantime?"

"We're leaving. Right away."

"Are we in trouble again?"

"Big trouble. This sounded very much like a final offer. The lady became very threatening at the end of the call."

"Are you as frightened as I am?" Elena asked.

"Terrified," Alex admitted.

Alex went to the closet, lifted their suitcases and overnight bags, and hauled them over to the bed. Inside thirty seconds, they were cramming clothes and belongings into the bags.

"What's next?" Elena asked.

"Hire a lawyer and apply for political asylum here in America. I have a perfectly legitimate case. They'll kill me if I ever return to Russia."

"So we'll be Americans."

"Why not, it's a land of immigrants. We're young and we can adjust. What do you think?"

Elena was struggling to fold one of her new skirts, a red thing with a thousand pleats that defied her every effort. "It's different . . . but I think I'll like it," she said, a little tentatively, a little sad. Until this moment, she had never really believed that they had departed Russia for good. The thought of leaving their lives behind, permanently, was deeply unsettling.

"Is there someplace else you'd rather go?"

She shook her head. She would sorely miss her parents and her friends. And okay, sure, it would be difficult to adjust to America's peculiar ways—people here were so flagrantly casual, so obtrusively personal, and their sense of humor was so weird. But she loved Alex, had from the moment she laid eyes on him—and her instincts told her this was the one place in the world where he would be happy, the one place he could be productive, the one place they would be safe. "What will we do for a living?"

"Start over. Build a business of some sort."

"You know, Alex, if you could make a fortune in Russia, there's no reason you won't do the same thing here. I'll help you. In fact, it should be easier. America is a land of laws and respect for property. Rich people aren't despised here."

"We'll need a place to live," he said, and she readily agreed—just definitely not like the old one, she thought. A small, livable home, no servants, and definitely unpretentious enough that nobody made a point of spitting hawkers on their doorstep.

They began listing the requirements. A safe place, she said very firmly, with guards and doormen, where they could sleep without worrying about Golitsin's thugs. Great, but it would have to be in or very near a metropolis, he replied—a bustling, prosperous city where money grew on trees. Not too big a city, she countered, and that swiftly ruled out New York and Chicago and Atlanta. California and Florida, in fact the entire South, and the Southwest, were too hot and miserably humid for their thick Russian blood. The Midwest was too plainly American, too parochial, and they doubted they would fit in. They were quickly running out of real estate.

An idea popped into her brain and, since time was short, and all other options were evaporating, Alex quickly agreed.

Washington. They would settle in that charming city, not too small, not too large, filled with impressive monuments, noisy politicians, and gobs of money. The more they considered it, the better it looked. They would find a nice home, stuff it with furniture, make a normal life, and quickly—and quietly—gather another fortune.

Plus, it was a city of lawyers, after all. It should be easy to locate a good one with loads of experience and contacts in immigration matters and get the paperwork started.

Alex warned, "We'll have to cover our tracks."

That sobering thought brought Elena back from her rosy dreams of the future-to-be to the here and now. "They'll keep hunting for us, won't they?"

"For a while, yes." He paused and looked at the window. "We have to mislead them on our way out. I'll need your help."

"Will this go on forever, Alex?"

"No. Not if we disappear and leave them alone. I think they'll forget about us, eventually. The idea is to be sure we aren't worth their time or effort."

*   *   *

By six, they had rented a car, stocked it with maps, and loaded the trunk with everything they owned. For a former mogul and his wife, it was almost pitiful—Alex's office supplies and what little clothing and toiletries they had gathered since their arrival. Alex checked out, with cash, then, accompanied by Elena, headed for the phone bank in the basement, where they discussed their plan with Elena's friend Amber. Ignoring her protests, Alex stuffed three thousand dollars into her palm with orders to keep a thousand or two for herself and spread the rest around liberally to select members of the hotel staff.

Amber pecked Elena on the cheek, hugged her tightly, and wished them both luck.

Fourteen hours after they departed, the team of killers arrived. They pushed through the door and began prowling the lobby, looking for their prey. There were six of them in all, five men and one lady, Katya, their old tormentor from Budapest, who had arrived only hours before, after being dispatched on a swift overnight from Russia. She was along to brief the new boys about Konevitch's elusiveness and ensure positive confirmation once the deed was done. At least that was the reason Golitsin had offered her and his partners, Tatyana and Nicky. A more truthful reply was that he did not trust Nicky. He wanted some of his own muscle involved.

The other killers were Americanized Russians, immensely talented at murder, citizens of Brighton Beach, connected through two or three shell companies to Nicky's expansive organization.

It had been easy enough to trace the phone number Tatyana handed Nicky after Konevitch told her to piss off; a swift look-see through the Manhattan Yellow Pages led them straight to the Plaza.

Alex was here, they were sure of it. His room number was the one mystery, but they would learn it quickly. Two men would remain downstairs in the lobby, one by each exit to block any attempt at escape. The rest would rush upstairs, employ a crowbar to burst through the doors, and toss the Konevitches through the window down onto the busy street below. If it turned out the room was on a lower level, knives and garrotes would do the trick.

The people at the reception counter refused to offer any information no matter how much Katya pleaded or offered in bribes. Customer confidentiality was an obligation taken quite seriously at the Plaza. Fine. The killers fanned out and began accosting maids and waiters, employees on the lower end of the pay scale, who might, for the right price, entertain a slight breach of hospitality ethics.

Katya, with considerably more experience in assassination matters, had a better idea. She took the elevator to the basement where the phone bank was located. The door was locked, so she knocked. A young woman opened it and Katya agilely stepped inside before she could be stopped. A large black woman who apparently was in charge pushed her rear out of her chair, stepped away from the switch console, and approached her.

"Sorry, you have to leave right now. This is a restricted area," she squawked with a posture that brooked no objections.

Katya spoke flawless English, but she hammed it up a bit, pretending she didn't fully understand. She slathered on the accent and said, "I am for my little sister looking. She is staying here, I am sure."

The black lady squared her heels and crossed her arms. "Then you need to go upstairs. Talk to reception. This is an employee-only room."

"Please, you must help me," Katya said with a long, uncomprehending frown. "She is named Elena. Elena Konevitch. She is here with husband."

Amber's big face retracted into a thousand suspicious wrinkles. "How come you don't know where your sister is?"

"She and her husband, Alex, they fled Russia. Alex does bad things there. Now is hiding."

"Bad things?"

"Yes, very, very bad. But our mother, she is most desperately sick. Dying, I think. I come because Elena must learn this." A long, pleading look. "Please, please, please, you must be of help to me."

Elena's big sister, my big ass. Who the hell did this Russian bitch think she was fooling, Amber thought. Her hands landed on her hips. "You missed 'em. Yep, yesterday they checked out in a hurry. Said they were headed for Chicago."

"Chicago?" Katya repeated, a little stunned.

"Uh-huh, Chicago. Said they were tired of New York and planned to settle there."

"Did they leave a forwarding address? A phone number, maybe?"

Amber's large hand popped out. Katya at first looked befuddled. The hand stayed put and she got the message. She yanked a twenty out of her pocket and slammed it onto the palm. The hand stayed put. Welcome to America, bitch. Not until four more twenties hit the pot did the hand retract.

"Nope," Amber said.

"They left no word? None?"

"That's right, none."

"Did they go by car, train, plane?" Katya was so disturbed at missing them, her concocted accent was melting.

"If I had to guess, he and your sister are gonna make themselves scarce. Be damned hard to find, know what I'm saying?"

Katya stared into her face for a long moment, spun on her heels, and departed. The door shut with a loud, angry bang.

At that moment, Maria Sanchez, an upstairs maid, was fingering the hundred in her pocket and recounting the same lie to two of the men on the hit team. Chicago, she told them with absolute certainty. She had overheard the Konevitches discussing the city as she cleaned their room two days before. Stacks of Chicago maps and travel guides sat on their bedside table; they sounded thrilled and eager to get on the road.

Amber figured she had at least bought the Konevitches a little time. A few weeks, maybe. With luck, a few months. But if the killers were serious, they would eventually track them down.

16

John Tromble was a man in a hurry. He had raced through a few years as a federal prosecutor, then sprinted through five more of a federal judgeship, and now was midway in his third year as director of the Federal Bureau of Investigation—the youngest ever, he reminded you quickly, in the event you failed to bring it up. He quickly stretched his long legs and speed-read a little more of the thick dossier produced by his staff in preparation for this trip.

He planned to spend another two years in this job, make a big splash, then pole-vault to the next level. A vice presidential candidacy wasn't out of the question; a senatorship should be easy pickings. Or barring that, open a private security firm and quickly haul in millions. With a mountain of cash, he could do whatever he wished. He read quickly, ate quickly, slept in a hurry, even had sex at astonishing speed. Everything he did, full speed ahead.

The plane was thirty minutes out from Sheremetyevo Airport, which apparently was on the outskirts of Moscow. If he were flying this damn thing he'd sure as hell find a way to make it in fifteen minutes.

Having slept since Washington, he had woken up thirty minutes before, showered, shaved, and slapped on a freshly pressed suit. He stole a quick glance in the mirror before he left the special cabin of this very special plane to make his final preparations for this very special trip. The rear of the plane was stuffed with as many American reporters as his aides and cronies could entice or cajole and cram aboard. The press would be shoved off five minutes before him. Oh yes, there they would be, a large, impatient mob at the bottom of the steps, snapping away as he made his majestic descent, capturing shot after shot of his photogenic face. The remains of a low-cal breakfast sat on the tray above his lap. He was sipping quickly and noisily from a bottled water, nose buried in the dossier, straining to avoid conversation.

Across from him sat Laura Tingleman, attorney general, and putatively his boss. She had worked through the entire flight since they lifted off from Andrews Air Force base twelve hours before. She was crumpled into her seat with her nose stuffed in her BlackBerry. She looked wrinkled, tired, and wrung out. She was a large, heavy, unimpressive-looking type, fifty years old, though she appeared a very poorly kept sixty, with a broad face that managed, somehow, always to convey panic.

This first year in her job had been unfortunate. For one thing, she was, quite publicly, the president's fourth choice. This happened only after it was revealed that choice one was doing the bedsheet tango with his underage nanny; Tromble had seen her, and to the man's credit, the nanny did not in fact look at all as if she was only fourteen; more like sixteen. This happened only after it was disclosed that choice two had taken numerous fat bribes from several very crooked oil companies. This happened only after it was discovered that choice three, a superior court judge in California, had spent his misguided youth dodging the draft, calling cops pigs, stuffing all nature of questionable substances up his snout, and barbecuing American flags. Perfect qualifications for a judgeship in California, but the rest of the country did not embrace his background.

After these train wrecks, Laura Tingleman had been found tucked away in a backcountry Montana circuit court, a low-key, competent judge who handled mostly divorces and small-time land disputes. Little to no political experience, no national exposure, zero controversial decisions, no overturned verdicts—all in all, Laura Tingleman was as apt to raise as much controversy as chicken soup. No bad habits, as best they could tell. Never married, thus never divorced; in fact, the lead FBI investigator who rummaged through her background even surmised that she might be a fifty-year-old virgin, if such a thing existed. Best of all, she was a woman! The first ever nominated for attorney general, and feminist leaders around the country growled that whoever opposed her would face a backlash of historic proportions.

It helped that she was a nice person, if deeply out of her depth, polite, respectful, and deeply religious, though not a zealot. Her nomination sailed through without a hitch.

Tromble detested her. There was room for only one legal superstar in this administration, one shining protector of America from the crooks, terrorists, and perverts who lurked in the dark shadows. And he, after all, was the whiz kid who came up the hard way through intellectual brilliance, sharp elbows, and unrelenting work. Yale undergrad, Harvard Law, and he had done his time in the legal trenches; she had been plucked out of Nowhere, Montana, for the plain and simple reason that she had no disputable accomplishments, or indeed any accomplishments at all.

And though it was true he had not been a popular prosecutor or judge, he had been greatly feared. The exception was cops, who adored him because he hammered defense attorneys and meted out terrifying sentences. His record of overturned verdicts was shocking.

In fact, the New York appellate court, tired of an exhausting docket overloaded with his weekly brutality, was about to serve notice of a review hearing when news broke that he was somehow, incredibly, on the president's short list for FBI director. The appellate judges were appalled. They gathered together in a private chamber and considered whether to blow the whistle on a judge they regarded as little short of a Nazi. No, no, one wise, notably liberal senior justice advised with a deep smile; don't shovel manure in a gift horse's mouth; at least John Tromble would be out of their hair. They could look forward again to being home by dinnertime and Friday golf.

In the expiring days of his outgoing presidency, the incumbent's predecessor, normally a moderate who had appointed two mild liberals to the Supreme Court, had spent his last political capital on the Hill to get Tromble this job. He took charge of ushering the appointment personally, called in every chit, used up every threat, and bent elbows until the sound of arms cracking thundered around the Senate. It was his finest hour. Had he poured that kind of energy and spirited determination into running the country, that southern governor who shellacked him at the polls would be back chasing skirts around some small southern town.

He was leaving his successor a poisoned chalice—a bundle of combustible, no-holds-barred, law-and-order ambition who would steamroll anything or anybody in his path, he confided to his chief of staff in a giggly private moment. He intended to sit back in his retirement and laugh at all the trouble John Tromble caused that southern boy. It was going to be horrendous.

And now, after two fairly low-key years in office, two years that were sadly unacclaimed, Judge Tromble had decided the time had come to kick it up a notch. Crime rates had dropped substantially under his watch, but the liberal press loathed him and credited a hundred other causes—from a diminishing appetite for crack, to all the hardened crooks already rotting in prison, to a religious revival in the Deep South and Midwest. He needed something—anything—they could not misinterpret or take away from him. He needed a signature issue, and he turned his fiercely impatient eyes on America's newest threat—international crime, foreign crooks on American soil, or maybe a little off it. First up, the Russian Mafiya.

Unfortunately for Alex and Elena Konevitch, their fates now rested in the hands of an attorney general in search of sea legs, and an FBI director with omnivorous ambitions and a few fairly strange ideas about justice.

The long line of limos cruised to a stop on the cobblestone plaza. Tromble's aides and coatholders—the fanny-wiping brigade they were called by the jaded field agents—tumbled out in an unruly mass, took a moment to get organized, then were ushered quickly through the historic Kremlin doors, up two flights of stairs, and directly into the cavernous office of Anatoli Fyodorev, Russia's attorney general.

Introductions were handled briskly in a no-nonsense fashion. Several of Fyodorev's stone-faced assistants were gathered around the office walls, not introduced. Among them stood a very striking young lady in a breathtakingly short skirt who smiled nicely as the procession entered.

Fyodorev sat down on a tall chair behind a desk that looked bigger than Finland. Two chairs—little more than small stools, actually—were positioned before the desk. After a moment of confusion, Tingleman and Tromble edged precariously onto the chairs. Their knees were nearly in their faces, their elbows almost on the floor. They were forced to stare up at Fyodorev.

A representative from the American embassy took a standing position slightly behind them, notepad in one hand, pen poised in the other. They had been assured that Fyodorev's English was exceptional—translation was neither needed nor wanted. The embassy flunky's real job was to take detailed notes, and pay careful attention to anything the professional diplomats would have to clean up afterward. Shovel duty.

Fyodorev was the host and he opened with a long windy soliloquy about how, national differences aside, they were all in the same business. To wit, law enforcement. Spiritual brothers and sisters. Bonded by their common enmity to criminals, and so on, and so forth—etcetera and double etcetera.

Fyodorev eventually wrapped up and Tromble summoned his important face and, before Tingleman could utter a word, quickly announced, "We're here to discuss bilateral cooperation in matters of crime."

"A nice term," Fyodorev noted dryly. "What does it mean?"

"Well . . . for starters, I'd like to offer you a few slots each year for your people to attend our FBI Academy."

"Why? Is it better than ours?"

The State Department flunky dashed off a few heavy notes on

his legal pad. With limited success, he tried to keep the smirk off his face. Boy, this was going to be fun.

"I . . . well, yes, probably. It has a certain reputation. Also, we think you might want to place some of your people in our profiling center down at Quantico."

Fyodorev's elbows landed heavily on his desk. "Explain this term, 'profiling.'"

"It's, um, well, it refers to specialists who employ psychiatry to get inside criminal minds. We've found it quite effective. Serial killers, for example, tend to exhibit complementary patterns. If you can figure that out, you can stop them and find them."

A dismissive grin. "Russia has no serial killers."

"Works pretty good against serial rapists, also. Or serial arsonists, if you have any of those."

"We have neither. Those are American problems."

The State guy was now composing entire paragraphs.

Who is this guy kidding? Tromble thought. He was sure his leg was being pulled and he laughed. Fyodorev developed a very deep frown.

The hottie in the short skirt suddenly shoved herself off the wall and moved to a position beside Fyodorev's desk. She said to him, "Anatoli, we're being terrible hosts. It's been a long, tiring trip for our American guests. Maybe they would like coffee."

Whoever she was, she had an interesting relationship with Fyodorev, because his demeanor turned on a dime. The angered frown converted instantly into a gracious smile. "Yes . . . yes, you're right. Coffee, anybody?"

Tromble said yes, black, no sugar, no cream. Laura chose tea, doused with sugar and cream. One of the aides shoved off from the wall and scurried off to retrieve the refreshments.

The young lady with the glorious legs slid around the desk and, with a glowing smile and firm handshake, introduced herself. Tatyana something-or-other—she explained she worked not here, in the attorney general's office, but upstairs, for his boss. She was a lawyer who frequently advised Yeltsin on legal matters. This seemed to justify her presence.

"Why don't we all adjourn to the conference table?" she suggested, quite hospitably.

Why not? For sure, the current arrangement was a bust. They shifted from their stools and desks to comfortable chairs abutting a huge walnut block table by a large window. Tingleman and Tromble sat side by side, in an uncomfortable silence.

Miss Tatyana Whoever sat closely beside Fyodorev on the other side of the long, gleaming table. They made small talk about the flight and weather and a dozen other uninteresting topics. Once the coffees and teas were delivered and the room had cooled to a level of moderate tension, Tatyana said, "Let's not beat around the bush. What is it you'd really like to discuss?"

Tromble's briefing papers, prepared by a bunch of stuffy eggheads over at State, had stipulated that the Russians were consummate horse traders. Never arrive empty-handed: give a little, get a little. In that spirit, he had started—more accurately, he had tried to start—by offering them a few handsome concessions before he got down to his own request.

But if she could come right to the point, so could he. "Your Mafiya," he said very importantly.

"What about them?"

"Since the wall came down, they've become your biggest export. They're crawling all over our cities. They've turned Miami into a free-fire zone. Brighton Beach is a funeral parlor." Tromble worked up a nasty grimace. "They're a very nasty lot."

"Tell me about it," Fyodorev said, shaking his head with disgust. "Total vermin. The most ruthless, brutal criminals in the world."

"Yes, so we're learning," Tingleman replied, slightly irritated, not really clued in to what her FBI director had in mind for this visit. She had been told it was no more than a diplomatic meet-and-greet, part of the required protocol for her office, a chance to get away from the daily grind of Washington. "Our own Italian Mafiosi are civilized gentlemen compared to your guys. With your people, no finesse, no rules, no attractive traditions. They kill over nothing."

"We're not proud of them," Fyodorev replied with an uneven shrug.

"I'm under great pressure from my president to do something about them," Tromble insisted, regaining the initiative.

A lie. His president could care less about anything that didn't register in national polls and outside Hollywood, where a fresh species of frightening brutes was always a welcome addition; the average Joe knew nothing about Russia's Mafiya and could care less.

Fyodorev looked sympathetic.

"I need a favor," Tromble continued with a friendly smile. "As you know, we have a small FBI field station at our embassy here in Moscow. Yeltsin personally signed the agreement. That was two years ago."

Tatyana noted, "And it expires in a few months."

"Exactly. Now I'd like an extension. Say, another five years. And I want to triple the size."

"How many of your people are here now?" Fyodorev asked.

"Four. Four overworked, exhausted agents," Tromble said sourly. "Two broken marriages, one newly minted alcoholic, one attempted suicide. Sad to say, it has become the most unpopular posting in the Bureau."

"Twelve would be a lot," Fyodorev countered, obviously cool to the idea. "This is, after all, Russian soil."

"I know, I know. But your Mafiya is huge, and growing fast. Ambitious, too. They're blasting their way into everything. Dope, whores, kidnapping, extortion. The bodies are piling up. Four agents barely make a dent. Besides, I hoped we would work this problem together."

"Together?"

"Well, yes. Presumably your people have a better handle on your own Mafiya than we do."

"I would hope that's the case."

"What if some of my agents worked full-time with your people?"

"Like liaisons?" Tatyana suggested, nudging Fyodorev with her knee under the table.

"That's the general idea. At our end, we're dealing with Mafiya foot soldiers. That's not working. Take one off the street, and in days he's replaced with two more. We presume that the heads of all these organizations are here, in Russia." Nobody contradicted that obvious point and he pushed ahead. "And you can put some of your people at my headquarters. We'll share intelligence, share everything we learn and tip each other off. Maybe perform a few big busts together."

Tatyana maintained a straight face, but her heart was racing. Oh, what an incredibly great idea: yes, we can share intelligence, the more the better. Wait until Nicky heard what had just landed in her lap. He would know everything the FBI was up to. He would learn the names of every plant, every snitch, every stoolie. Through her, he could set up his opposition and exploit the FBI boys to squash their American operations. It would be a windfall. Nicky's American branch would grow by leaps and bounds.

And it would all depend on little old Tatyana. She liked to be needed. Service like that doesn't come cheap.

A slight nod from Tatyana to Fyodorev, who glanced in her direction every few seconds.

"Of course we'll share the headlines?" Fyodorev asked, showing he and Tromble were kindred spirits.

"Wouldn't dream otherwise," Tromble lied.

"Why only twelve agents?" Tatyana asked. "And why only five years? Our Mafiya have been around for seven decades. They're such an institution, I hardly think we'll defeat them in only five years. Make it twenty agents. Thirty, if you wish. And a ten-year extension strikes me as much more reasonable."

Tromble reached both hands under the table and steadied his knees. This was everything he'd hoped for, times two or three. Ol' J. Edgar may have created the FBI and put it on the map, but he was determined to claw out his own storied place in Bureau legend. He was going to take America's only national police force and turn it into an international juggernaut. It would be twice as big before he was through: maybe more, maybe much more. He intended to have his agents in every damn embassy in every damn country in the world. A bigger operations center would be necessary, a real monster with dozens of lit-up screens constantly flashing the latest updates about Chink Triads, and Jap Yakuzas, French wharf rats, and Tibetan whatever-the-hell-they-weres. He would have a big seat in the middle of it all, a throne from which he could survey his crime-busting kingdom.

He bit his lip. "That all sounds reasonable to me."

"Good," said Tatyana with the great legs. She started to stand, then lightly tapped her forehead. She slid back into her seat, frowning, distracted. "There is, uh, one thing you can do for us, John. A favor. A very, very important one."

"Name it."

It was a gamble, but why not? How much was this worth to Tromble? She said, "There is a certain criminal who fled Russia. Alex Konevitch. He's hiding out in your country. He ran a large bank here that laundered billions of dollars. Mafiya money, in fact. When he learned we were on to him, he absconded with hundreds of millions, in dollars. A real crook."

"And he's in America?"

"That's right. We had a thread on him, but he disappeared over a year ago. We had a lead that he was in Chicago. And maybe he is, but our best people have been unable to locate him."

"No problem. I'll put twenty agents on it tomorrow."

"You have your most wanted list"—she paused and looked him dead in the eye—"well, John, we have ours, too. He's number one on our list. The top dog, the most wanted bad guy in Russia. It's a great embarrassment that he has eluded us this long. He is unquestionably guilty. We want him back. Crooked bankers are a serious problem for us. We intend to make an example of him with a very big, very public trial."

"One week and he'll be in a Moscow slammer. I guarantee it."

The State Department representative coughed. "Uh, that might be a problem."

"Why's that?" Tromble asked, clearly irritated by the interruption.

"We don't share an extradition treaty with our Russian friends, I'm afraid."

"So what?"

That question, emerging from the lips of America's top law enforcement officer, a former federal judge no less, was unnerving. "It would be . . . well, you know, a big legal problem if Konevitch has diplomatic permission to remain in America. You can't just throw him on an airplane and ship him back here."

Tromble leaned over until their faces were inches apart. "I don't think this is any of your business."

Tatyana calmly watched this exchange. "He might be right," she said, twirling a strand of her gorgeous hair. "But let's be sure we're all clear on our deal. You can maintain your field station only if Alex Konevitch is returned to us. If not, there will be no cooperation. None."

The big black limo was parked in the small lot by the Moskva River. It was Tuesday. And they usually met on Tuesdays. The windows were cracked open. Cigar smoke billowed out. The car parked here once or twice a week. Week after week. Month after month.

The sheer sloppiness of it all amazed the man who sat and watched from a small nondescript car half a block away. He understood it, though. Hunters rarely looked back over their own shoulders. The people inside that car had every reason to be overconfident, and they were. He lit up an American Marlboro and cranked up his heater.

Tracking down Miss Tatyana Lukin had proven to be neither easy nor quick. Tracing the phone number Alex gave him to the Kremlin was simple enough—a small bribe to a phone technician was all it took. But the Kremlin was an immense factory of bureaucrats of all manner and forms. They were not a talkative lot. It was such a snakepit of conspiracy and political fratricide that they spoke, even among themselves, in whispers. Outsiders were cold-shouldered as a matter of course.

Month after month of stubborn digging ensued. Six Annas were found and swiftly vetted. Unfortunately, none fit the broader profile and all were quickly rejected as dead ends. Mikhail had other jobs he had to balance with Alex's request, and a long, tiring period of frustration ensued. Dozens of trails opened, then grew cold. Leads looked hot then fizzled into disappointment. The staff at the Kremlin turned over constantly as Yeltsin chewed through prime ministers and assistants like a slaughterhouse. The number of potential suspects alternated almost daily. Was she one of those casualties? Maybe, like so many successful and well-connected political people, she had simply jumped into the private sector for the big bucks.

Mikhail Borosky had first encountered Alex Konevitch years before when Alex's firm had been hit hard by a few in-house embezzlers. A grizzled former cop, now a private investigator, Mikhail had been hired to find the crooks. No problem, they were greedy idiots. They drove up to work in their shiny new BMW 730s, which they stupidly parked in the office lot. Why not just hang out signs that announced: Hey, we're your thieves if you're wondering.

But Alex had been impressed. Only two brief days and Mikhail named the thieves. Steady work followed, nearly all of which involved in-house shenanigans of one sort or another. Mikhail handled it all with brutal efficiency.

Alex had been generous with the bonuses, always paid promptly in cash. The two became fast friends. There were occasional dinners that usually ran late. In his long years as a cop, Mikhail had specialized in combating the Mafiya, part of a handpicked cadre that was vetted and watched constantly for its incorruptibility and ruthlessness. Mikhail's strong suit was gathering intelligence, figuring out the corrupting webs of mob activity, bugging, trailing, and observing, collecting enough dirt on the hoods and thugs to ensure their convictions.

Alex enjoyed hearing tales that had nothing to do with business. But nobody in Konevitch Associates knew of their relationship. This secrecy Mikhail insisted on from the beginning. As long as he stayed hidden in the shadows, they would leave lots of breadcrumbs in their wake and the cat-and-mouse game would be child's play. Pay me personally, never call from the office phone, never mention my name. It made it so much easier for the bloodhound to find their trails.

After over half a year of hard effort, Tatyana had fallen into his lap by a stroke of luck, a complete fluke. He had befriended a pair of lowly assistants to the minister of finance, frequently accompanying them to a bar, a favorite Kremlin hangout where the coatholders schmoozed and networked. He plied them with booze and encouraged them to introduce him to everybody they knew.

One night, a gentleman at the next table was complaining bitterly and, after inhaling his fourth vodka, very loudly, about another Kremlin bureaucrat. Another staffer had knifed him in the back, had gotten him sacked. That sorry bitch, he kept calling her. Mikhail's ears perked up. Yes, but a tasty bitch, his companion noted with a garrulous laugh. The insults and bad jokes poured out and Mikhail's eavesdropping turned serious. No wonder the chief of staff always looked so exhausted, one said. Ha, ha. Yeah, but she's such a ballbuster, it's a miracle he still had his dingaling. More ha, ha.

Mikhail edged over to the table and began buying rounds for everybody. The fired staffer was drunk, and in no time became utterly drunker. The man had a bottomless bladder, but around midnight he ambled off to the men's room. Mikhail trailed two steps behind him. Over side-by-side urinals Mikhail offered him a cool thousand if the man could point out the backstabbing bitch the next morning as she made her way into the Kremlin.

One look, and he knew he had his girl. Everything fit, except the name. Then again, Tatyana to Anna had a certain ring to it. Alex had predicted she probably was attractive; she was that, and then some. Plus, she had a law degree. Over the next two weeks he tailed her everywhere, and it was fun, though not overly productive. Three to four nights a week she and her boss checked into a hotel. They drove into work together, holding hands and smooching like horny newlyweds. But she also took lots of extended lunch breaks in downtown hotels, not with her chubby middle-aged boss but a handsome, fit-looking young lad who apparently offered a little more in the sack. Click, click went Mikhail's camera. A little research and the young lad turned out to be Sasha Komenov, a star striker on the national soccer team. A little more digging revealed a little more dirt. Turned out pretty boy Sasha and lovely Tatyana were from the same town, had flirted and dated and wrestled together in backseats throughout high school. Her Moscow affairs came and went but Sasha was always there, lurking in her locker room after the game.

Late into the third week, he'd watched her disappear into the rear of a long black limo that took off at a gallop. Click, click. He hit the gas and followed. Next stop was a seedy, run-down nightclub on the city outskirts. More click, click, click. A short man with a large bent nose and graying ponytail dashed out of the club and clambered inside.

From his former days as a Mafiya crimebuster, Mikhail instantly put the name Nicky to the furtive figure wrapped in black leather. The limo's license plate told the rest of the story. It was registered as a company car by Golitsin Enterprises.

Usually the meetings by the Moskva lasted no longer than fifteen to twenty minutes. Today's meeting dragged on for over an hour. Big things were afoot, Mikhail guessed. At one point, Nicky climbed out, stumbled uncertainly for a few steps, then he whipped it out and peed in the open. More click, click with Mikhail's long, wide-angled lens. He chuckled to himself.

The most feared thug in Russia, Nicky Kozyrev, had a teenie weenie.

He made his weekly telephonic report to Alex that night. The pictures were bundled into a large envelope and sent off to the Watergate apartment.

17

The apartment bought by Alex and Elena Konevitch was riverside, on the sixth floor of the sprawling co-op building, gazing fitfully over the brown muddy waters of the broad Potomac and within yelling distance of the majestic Kennedy Center. Even after a year, Alex remained dismayed by how preposterously small it was. A two-bedroom, one for sleep, the other converted to a tiny, cluttered office shared by the two of them. At an amazing cost of almost a million, it had to be the most expensive eight hundred square feet in the city.

But it was safe. Lots of important and famous folks made their nests inside this famous building—they demanded privacy and good security, they paid out the nose for it, and they got it.

Elena adored its simplicity. The small space suited her fine—it was easy to clean. Alex felt cramped, squeezed, slightly claustrophobic. He loved big, open spaces and frequently cursed Golitsin for stealing his home, for exiling him to an apartment that would be swallowed by his old bedroom.

The contract for the co-op, their phones, their cars, their insurance—everything was registered under Elena's maiden name. The name Konevitch disappeared from sight. On Mikhail's expert advice, to be on the safe side, every two months Alex flew in and out of Chicago, brief trips where he liberally sprinkled the Konevitch name around Russian nightclubs and neighborhoods. On the first visit he even signed up for local cell phone services with unlisted numbers. Maybe the bad people were still hunting them, maybe not.

Safe beats sorry every time, Mikhail advised him.

Alex and Elena were one year into their new life, and their new careers were flourishing. The requests for political asylum had come through ten months before. Their lawyer, Martie P. Jones, MP to friends, or to anybody, really, had been as good as advertised. Better, in fact. MP had started his career laboring in the trenches as a lawyer in the stodgy legal office at the Immigration Service. He knew exactly what buttons to push, with a Rolodex that would put the New York phone book to shame.

A few calls to the right people and Alex and Elena's request was stamped "expedite." A few weeks later they were ushered into a sterile room before a small panel of serious people, sworn to honesty, and asked to present an abbreviated version of their sad case. The panel looked bored and impatient initially. That quickly changed. For starters, Alex opened his shirt and offered a long, nauseating gaze at the hammer-and-sickle emblem fried on his chest. A minute later, out popped the photos of Alex's overall physical condition, blowups of the photos taken by the doctor two days after they landed at Kennedy International. They were color and close up. MP accompanied the visuals with vividly horrifying descriptions—see, this is where the chair broke on his leg; the bruised lumps here, well, those are fractured ribs; and so forth. The wounds were brutal. Several members of the panel gasped and looked away. The verdict was returned promptly.

Approved, but only conditionally—welcome to America, land of the free and the brave—now go out there and make us proud you're an American.

Just one glitch: you must have a job—a place of permanent employment before permission to apply for full residency was granted.

Any job with a domestic corporation was also easily traceable, and therefore out of the question, so Alex immediately contacted his old friend Illya Mechoukov. They had met four years before, when Illya was first toying with the idea of jumping into mass-market advertising. No such thing existed in the Soviet Union, at least not in the same sense as in the West, where big companies spent billions each year shoving their names out into the market-place. Illya was young, only twenty-five, and seized with the pro-gressive idea that he would mimic the huge Western advertising firms. His business would explode quickly, he was sure, and the money would pour in.

A great idea that instantly hit a brick wall. Illya was odd-looking, with a hooked nose, unbalanced features, long woolly hair, and a thick black beard that looked revolutionary. But he was filled with brilliant concepts that poured out of his lips in quick, nervous bursts. He was inventive and wildly creative; un-fortunately, he was also far ahead of his time. The former commu-nists had no idea what he was talking about, or why it mattered. People went to stores. They grabbed the item off the shelf. The very idea of spirited competition sounded confusing, possibly im-moral. The notion of trumpeting your own product struck them as haughty, self-indulgent, a blatant waste of money.

Three minutes into his initial pitch in Alex's office, Alex leaned across his desk. "Okay, I've heard enough. Here's the deal: I'm buy-ing you. Not just your advertising, you. I'll fund your company, but you'll service my accounts before all others. I'll be the chairman of the board, you'll be the president, the chief of daily operations, and the brains. It's your show to run, and I expect great results."

Illya tugged on his beard and briefly considered this remark-able offer. "You're kidding."

"Yes, it's a joke. That's why I am about to write a check for five million dollars. Buy the best film and printing equipment on the market, hire good people, and call me if you need more."

The company was legally incorporated in Austria, close to Rus-sia's border and surrounded by cutthroat Western competitors. Alex insisted on this. Rivalry was healthy. To survive, Illya and his people would be forced to absorb the best Western practices, sharpen their own wits, and bring that state-of-the-art knowledge to the Russian market.

Better yet, Orangutan Media, as Illya had named it, was not technically part of Konevitch Associates. To get through the doors of Alex's competitors the firm had to be notionally independent. The only legal documents that evidenced Alex's financial interests were filed with the Austrian authorities. Thus, Orangutan slipped under Golitsin's radar.

Alex now offered to represent the company in America, and the timing could not be better. The big American corporations were floundering in Russia. All those years of a wall separating the two worlds left the Americans clueless about the local culture, local wants, local psychology. What worked like magic in the good ol' USA, resoundingly belly-flopped in Russia. The Pepsi generation caused deep bouts of head-scratching; how could a generation be defined by some stupid soft drink? Doctors recommending this pill or that antidote were unconvincing. Russian medicine was dreadful; anything they recommended was promptly blacklisted from the family shopping cart. And as for all those sports stars hawking products, another bust; who cared what some muscle-bound freak gobbled or drank or rubbed on his body?

Alex would make the rounds of the big American companies and sell them on Orangutan Media—an all-Russian outfit with a native feel for how to pitch to a home audience.

Alex would work for commission only; he wouldn't hear otherwise. Illya was gaining traction with Russian companies, but the business remained an uphill struggle. Monthly payrolls were always uncertain. The costs of production in Austria were staggering. Russian companies remained skeptical about advertising, and proved hard-fisted and stingy. They undervalued it as a matter of habit.

Within six months Alex and Elena were bagging millions in new accounts. They opened ambitiously with all-out attacks against certain large American candy companies and gargantuan consortiums that produced everyday household products, among other things. Most signed on—small, hesitant contracts at first, but once the clients gained confidence in this no-name Russian start-up, they couldn't throw enough money at Illya.

To cover more ground, Alex and Elena split up. Weekends were reserved for each other: rarely, though, was a weekday spent in the same town. She hit the big movie studios in Los Angeles, he bounced around the oil patch in Houston. The next week, Alex trolled New York City; he signed fat contracts to serve as subcontractors for three large Madison Avenue firms who recognized that their own efforts in Russia were failing abysmally. Two days later, Elena snagged a large Tennessee drug company with a slew of dietary products. A day after that, she hooked a New Jersey luxury cosmetics outfit that was salivating to decorate Russia's new class of uninhibited wealth. And so it went, week after week. Illya was elated. He tripled his staff and shifted the operation into an expansive new sixty-thousand-square-foot warehouse in Austria. It was expensive and risky, but what the hell. Spend money to make money, he figured. He struggled to keep up with demands that seemed to double by the week.

Their new life in America was coming together nicely. Over a million in commissions that first year. Not bad, but not good enough. The second year, they promised themselves, would be three million. With a little luck and more elbow grease, four million. Elena was happy. Alex was restless as always, but that was his nature, and part of his charm.

It was Saturday, and they had just finished a leisurely lunch at an excellent Georgetown restaurant followed by a brisk stroll along the lovely tree-lined canal to burn off the calories. Harold, the doorman, gave them a distressed look as they passed through the entrance on the ground floor. "Hey, Mr. K," he said in almost a whisper, "you got guests upstairs."

"I'm not expecting any."

"Yeah, well you got 'em. Guys in suits. They flashed badges and . . . hey, I tried, I swear I did. They wouldn't take no. They been up there about thirty minutes now."

Alex and Elena exchanged horrified looks. A race for the elevator and Alex punched six. They sprinted down the hallway. Alex gently pushed Elena aside before he stuffed his key into the door. No need, it swung open. He stepped through the entry, tense and ready to swing.

What a mess. The couches were overturned and knifed open, their interiors gutted, drawers emptied on the floor, lamps broken, books torn apart. The place had been tossed with cruel deliberation. The new furniture and furnishings Elena had picked out with such loving care were ruined. Two men in gray suits loitered by the living room window, ignoring the glorious view of the river while they admired their own handiwork. They took quick looks at Alex and Elena but didn't budge.

"Who are you?" Alex demanded, making no effort to disguise his fury.

"FBI," came the prompt reply. Two sets of identification were quickly flashed, then quickly put away.

"Why are you here?"

"Welcome to America, pal," said one of them with a nasty sneer. "We had a tip you and the wife were harboring a fugitive."

"That's ridiculous."

"Yeah? Seemed real enough to us."

"Do you have a warrant?"

"What are you, a lawyer?"

"Show me your warrant or get out."

They rocked back on their heels and laughed. Take a strike at us, their body language screamed. Look what we did to your home, look at your wife's horrified face, and do what any real man would do. Go ahead, run across the room—throw your best punch. We'll slap your ass in cuffs, cart you off like trash, and, as an undesirable, have your ass on the next flight to Moscow.

Alex was mad enough to do it, but at that moment a third man strolled out of their bedroom. Alex glanced in his direction, and froze. The man was tall and thin, dressed in a rumpled trench coat, and wrapped in his arms was their home computer. He looked, in fact, remarkably like his old friend Colonel Volevodz—but it couldn't be. Not here, not now. This was America.

"Hello, Mr. and Mrs. Konevitch." Amazing—he even sounded like Volevodz, right down to the clipped arrogance.

Alex drew a few heavy breaths and struggled to get himself under control. He felt a large lump in his throat. He snapped at Volevodz, "I thought your friends in external security were territorial. What are you doing here?"

In Russian, Volevodz replied very coolly, "You're a wanted felon. I'm here to take you back."

"Then you're going to be disappointed," replied Alex in English.

"Am I?" Volevodz stayed with Russian so the Fibbies couldn't understand a word. He had arrived two weeks before, after a call from Tatyana to Tromble offering his services and expertise.

The Konevitches' year of dodging and ducking was over. No more hiding behind his wife's name. Nicky's boys had been chasing ghosts in Chicago for a year, cowering in an embattled outpost in a forlorn corner of the city, and coming up empty. What they could not do, the FBI handled with speed and ease. A polite inquiry to the INS revealed the Konevitch address, working situation, and immigration status. Another call to the IRS revealed the full details of their financial status. All information the FBI gave Volevodz that he passed on to Nicky, via Tatyana. Hide-and-seek was over, a new game was about to begin.

One way or another, dead or alive, but on a plane to Russia, Konevitch was going to lose.

"I don't think I will," Volevodz countered, arrogance rising to full pitch. "You've tangled with the wrong people. There will be no second chance, Konevitch. You're a fool, you should have taken the deal."

"Think again. I have political asylum."

"I strongly advise you to come along willingly. This is inevitable, believe me. Make it easier on all of us."

"Get out of my apartment. Now."

A switch to English. "What will you do, Konevitch? Call the police? These are the police," he said, nodding his sharp chin in the general direction of the two agents by the window.

They smiled and waved. Real smartasses.

Elena bared her teeth and said to the two agents, "You should be ashamed of yourselves. Even in Russia, citizens aren't treated this way anymore."

"How much did you pay for this place?" one of the agents asked without a trace of curiosity. It was a statement of fact, an accusation, or, worse, a verdict.

"None of your business," Elena shot back.

"Nine hundred and seventy thousand," the agent replied, scowling. "Almost a million bucks. Lotta money. Cash, too. Where'd it come from?"

Alex placed a hand on Elena's arm—they were deliberately goading her. It would do no good to answer, so she stifled her reply.

"You stole it," the agent said, directing a long finger at Alex. "You robbed your own investors. You fled with hundreds of millions of dollars. You're crooks who lied to the immigration board to procure your status. You're nothing but lying thieves."

Elena had passed the point of rage. She was going to have her say, no matter what. "That's a lie. I don't know what this man told you, but he's a liar. You're stupid and he's a liar. Get out."

More smiles from the two agents. Large slack jaws, bunched shoulders, simple responses—actually they did look a little stupid.

Before things escalated, Alex decided to put an end to this. He stared coldly at the pair of agents. "Am I under arrest?"

No reply.

"Under investigation?"

The start of a nod, before it quickly turned into a crick of the neck that needed to be rubbed.

"It's time to call my lawyer," Alex announced, moving with feigned confidence toward the phone.

About two seconds passed. "There'll be time enough for that later," one of the agents said. It sounded like a threat.

Alex kept moving toward the phone. The agents appeared nonchalant, but the threat of a loudmouthed attorney showing up at this scene clearly unnerved them. No wonder. Without a warrant they had broken into a private residence, vandalized thousands of dollars' worth of property, then begun questioning a suspect without reading his rights. Worse, a foreign official without any legal status had been invited to the smashmouth party.

Any lawyer worth his salt would have their balls on a plate.

Alex lifted the phone and faced the two agents. "Give me your names. My lawyer will want them," he demanded.

They shuffled their feet and seemed to shrink. They exchanged matching looks of confusion.

"We'll be going now," one of them mumbled, one foot planted, ready to bolt.

"Not with my computer, you won't," Alex insisted.

"We're seizing it as evidence. Have your lawyer take it up with our lawyers," one said derisively. Having gotten the last word, and after firing off a final set of contemptuous looks, they walked quickly out of the apartment. Volevodz had that thin smile as he filed past Alex and Elena.

Alex slammed the door behind them, a loud shot that shook the walls.

Elena couldn't take her eyes off the mayhem in their apartment. Her only photograph of her parents had been torn out of the frame; it was on the floor, ripped into dozens of tiny pieces. The vindictiveness of it turned her stomach.

"Alex, I'm scared."

"So am I."

"What does this mean?"

"It means it's not over."

"Why would the FBI allow that man inside our home?"

"I don't know."

"We need to see MP, right away."

Alex lifted the phone.

Elena began picking up.

MP was at home, babysitting the kids while his wife shopped for groceries. He promised to drop everything and meet them at his office in two hours.

18

The office of MP Jones was on the second floor of a seven-story commercial building, almost dead center in the middle of M Street. MP was a graduate of Georgetown Law, a prestigious school, though not top five. He did it the hard way, four years of night school while he slaved at two menial jobs. Four years of pinching pennies. Four years of sprinting from class to McDonald's, where he pushed the torts and contracts to the back of his brain and shoved Big Macs and greasy fries across the counter. Four years of the cruel monotony of mac and cheese, of sleepless nights, of vying with full-time kids from wealthy families and wondering if this was the right choice. But he made it.

He graduated bottom third, but at least he had no onerous student debts. No interviews with big firms landed in his lap; sadly, no interviews at all. He had, however, passed the very difficult D.C. bar exam the first time around.

The Immigration Service was hiring and nobody else took his calls. Why not, he figured. Spend as few years as practical learning immigration law, then hang out a shingle and get rich quick.

Now it was him, two other lawyers, three stressed-out paralegals, and one very rude secretary who hated her job and couldn't wait till something better opened up. They called themselves partners. They referred to their setup as a firm. Nothing could be further from the truth. They were three struggling, scrambling attorneys dividing up the rent, a clutter of secondhand office furniture, and a few second-rate employees. No casework was shared, no fat profits divvied up at the end of a prosperous year. There were no prosperous years.

Married, with two kids and an attractive wife six months pregnant with the third, MP had cold sweats that it might turn out to be twins. They lived in a tiny, shabby ruin of a house he rented in a modest, run-down South Arlington neighborhood across the river.

Immigration cases, MP learned the hard way, paid squat. Nearly all his clients were poor, desperate people whose language skills were rudimentary, their earning power zilch. Too many were indigents assigned by the court. Hopeless causes seemed to be his specialty. They were booted out with regularity, which did not incline them to pay their legal bills. Immigration law, he had learned the hard way, was a poor man's game. Wealthy clients were scarce. The very few, mostly millionaires fleeing legal or tax troubles in their own lands, were bitterly scrapped over by every immigration attorney in the city; usually the large firms with dozens of lawyers to throw at their defense landed them with ease. MP had long since stopped hoping for a big score. His livelihood depended upon a backbreaking log of cases, and the oft-disappointed prayer that half of his clients might pay their bills.

But Alex and Elena Konevitch were different. An odd case, he thought as he stared at them holding hands across his desk. These were seriously frightened people. Probably had a right to be.

"So then the FBI just left? Walked out the door?" MP asked after listening closely to their story. A yellow legal pad was splayed open in front of him on his desk. Ten pages were filled with scrawls, questions, and other musings.

"With our computer," Alex clarified. "Can we get it back?"

"They entered without a search warrant?"

"Alex asked about it," Elena replied. "They didn't give him an answer."

"Okay, they didn't have one," MP concluded with the sad con-

fidence earned through hard experience. Immigrants had few
if any rights in this country. The police knew it and too often
abused them in ways that would be unimaginable against a full-
fledged citizen. Yes, Alex and Elena had been granted asylum. But
what the government giveth, it can, and sometimes doth, taketh
away. MP had seen it before. That the Feds would act with such
callous abandon was not a good omen.

"You're sure you committed no crimes in Russia?" MP asked.
He had repeated this same question a hundred times in preparation for their asylum hearings a year before. It wouldn't hurt to
hear the answer again. He studied their faces, hard.

"None," Alex told him. "A traffic violation once. I parked ille-
gally and paid the fine."

Blushing slightly, Elena said, "When I was sixteen, I was with
a group who had been drinking and became a public nuisance. I
was brought before a judge and released."

"You're sure you didn't steal anything from the bank?" This
question, obviously, was directed at Alex.

"Not a penny. Fifty million was stolen, according to the Russian
news. But by the people who took away my bank, not me," Alex
answered quite resolutely.

MP seemed undecided for a moment. He ran his pen aimlessly
across a page, trying to decide what to do next. "Could you step
out for a moment while I make a call?"

They left and found seats in the small, cramped lobby. MP
worked the phone for almost twenty minutes. It was Saturday,
late afternoon. He was calling home numbers and getting the expected responses. The lawyers of INS were either out watching
their spouses shop, clubbing divots into the back nine, or observing their kiddies tumble around soccer fields. He finally caught
Tommy Kravitz, on a cell phone, apparently.

Kravitz was a lifer who did as little work as possible, an inveterate busybody who amused himself by knowing everybody else's
business. The roar of a baseball game, live, loud, and raucous,
made it difficult to hear.

"Who's winning?" MP yelled.

"Not the Orioles, damn it. Why do I root for these guys? I'm an idiot."

"You are an idiot, Tommy. Nineteen years in the INS trenches. You should've left ten years ago, gotten a life."

"Yeah? Hey, seriously, how's the money out there? Great, right?"

"Just okay. The kids love their new private schools, Terry considers our mansion in Great Falls to be too ostentatious, and I'm looking around to replace my six-month-old Jag with a Mercedes. The Jag picked up a small scratch on the bumper and it's just too embarrassing to be seen in. What do you think? Mercedes 500, or splurge and go all out for a 600? It gets better mileage, that's what I hear."

Tommy laughed. "You're a lousy liar. Still got that same tiny shoebox in Arlington?"

"Yeah. The air-conditioning compressor went on the fritz last year, but we Joneses are tough. We'll sweat it out until Terry wins the lottery."

"Don't depend on her luck, pal. She got herself knocked up on your fourth date."

"Thanks for pointing that out."

"And that dented-up Chrysler minivan? That clunker still getting by the inspectors?"

"What do they know? We're driving it, anyway. Hey, you ever hear of a guy named Konevitch? Alex Konevitch."

A long moment of silence. Amid a loud roar, Tommy finally answered in a low whisper, "He your client?"

"Who scored?"

"Damn—that was a Yankee bat boy. The Orioles, remember? He your client or not, MP? Curious minds demand to know."

"Yeah, he is."

"Drop him. Just drop him, and run far, buddy."

"What's going on, Tommy? Tell me."

"I don't care if you were my brother. It's hush-hush, times ten. No can do. Mucho trouble's about to land on his head. Your guy's got problems he can't begin to imagine."

"Like that, huh?"

"Insist on cash, and make him pay you up front, MP. He has the dough, believe me. And count it real close—he's a rotten thief."

"Who's handling him?"

"Kim Parrish. That's not good news for you, either, pal."

The name was familiar: a vague memory, though. She had come aboard during his final year, when MP was more concerned with putting the INS in the rearview mirror than acquainting himself with the new associates he intended to leave in the dust. Like all new attorneys, she started out with the soft cases where she wouldn't embarrass the service—immigrants who snuck over a border or allowed their green cards to expire or committed some petty offense. Inside six months—record time—she was bumped up to the big leagues, the narcotraffickers, the big-time tax cheats, high-profile cases reserved for the best and brightest. She was old for a starting attorney, forty-five, maybe fifty. She was also smart and good, very good. Single, no children, intense, and very married to the law.

In a knowing tone, MP asked, "Who's pushing the case?"

"Are you deaf? I can't tell, MP. I swear I can't."

"Tommy, Tommy. That Gonzalez case, remember it? The one where you let the ball drop and the director wanted your—"

"Damn it, MP, I know I owe you. I'm not gonna say. Can't, just can't."

"I understand. I really do."

"Good. Believe me, if there was any way, I'd tell you everything."

After a brief pause. "So what aren't you gonna say?"

"You're a dogged bastard, you know that?"

"I can barely stand to eat with myself. Spill it, Tommy."

"All right, all right. For starters, I'm not gonna say the director was dragged over to Justice last week. I'm not gonna say the attorney general and FBI director reamed him purple 'cause he let this slimeball lie and cheat his way into asylum. I'm definitely not gonna say that this guy has the entire machinery of the Justice Department after his ass. I hope you're listening, MP. He's toast."

"Thanks for everything you didn't say, Tommy. I'll sleep better tonight knowing it's such an easy case."

"He's going home."

"He's got me as a lawyer."

"I'm telling ya, he's going home. Nothing you do will stop it."

"Watch me."

"You'll hurt yourself, pal. You're jumping in front of a steamroller. The heat on this guy's nuclear. Take the cash up front, then take a fast dive. Don't still be standing for the second round."

Tommy punched off, but MP still felt compelled to say, "I owe you one."

He called Alex and Elena and they filed back into his office. MP paced behind his desk, trying not to look overly concerned. The wrinkles on his forehead told a different story. They held hands as they fell back into their chairs.

"It's bad isn't it?" Alex asked.

"I'll be frank. Yes."

"How bad, MP?"

"The director of the FBI and the attorney general want you gone." He let this sink in, then continued, "I'm wondering why. Any ideas?"

"Yes, a few. My enemies in Moscow have powerful allies inside the Kremlin. They've obviously pulled strings with your government."

"But they can't ship us back, can they, MP?" Elena rocked forward in her chair, her hands tightly clenched beneath her knees. "They gave us political asylum. And there's no extradition treaty. If they send Alex back to Russia, they'll kill him."

"Those are the obstacles in their path. Ordinarily they're very powerful," he said, nodding thoughtfully, trying to balance optimism with his growing awareness of how serious this might be. He battled a temptation to jump out of his seat and scream, "Pack your bags and race for Canada. You haven't got a prayer."

"But . . . ?" Alex said.

"But they'll look for ways around them."

"What are these ways?"

"Every case is different, Alex. I can't predict. But I advise you to get your affairs in order. This can get ugly."

The first blow arrived Monday morning. Elena went to the bank to cash a check. They wanted to stay and fight, but they were realists. Flight might become their only option. To exercise that option they would need money, a hoard of cash, enough to get across the border and get settled. A withdrawal of ten thousand or more would trigger an immediate report to the IRS, and Alex was losing faith in all American authorities; so $9,999 it was. The teller, a plump young girl with a polite smile, punched the account number into her computer. The smile disappeared. She looked up with a puzzled expression. "Sorry, I can't cash this."

"You . . . What do you mean?"

"Your account's frozen." She was pointing at the screen Elena couldn't see.

"Frozen? How is it frozen?" Elena thought maybe her English was failing her, that maybe "frozen" was some enigmatic banking term like "overdrawn." A minor inconvenience that could easily be cleared up. "We have hundreds of thousands in that account," she insisted.

"Yes, I know. But the police or somebody has ordered the bank not to disburse any money from your account. I'm very sorry."

She felt like crying. Not here, though—not in front of all these strangers. She rushed outside and called Alex on her cell. She explained what had happened. He told her not to get upset, this had to be a misunderstanding. He would call MP, who would work a little legal magic and fix it.

They hung up and Alex immediately placed a call to his bank in Bermuda where the vast bulk of their money was parked. He was thanking God he had kept the account offshore, deeply relieved that he had not moved all that cash to an American bank where the interest rates were impressively higher. His business brain told him it was costing him thousands of dollars a year in lost income. A reckless waste. He had been sorely tempted a dozen times to just do it. Now he was pleased he had followed some darker instinct.

An assistant manager answered and quickly placed Alex on hold. A senior manager came on the line. "I'm sorry, Mr. Konevitch."

"What do you have to be sorry about?"

"There was nothing we could do."

"About what?"

"Well . . ." A lame cough. "Your account, sir, it's frozen."

The discussion lasted five minutes. Only an hour before, the governor of Bermuda had called in the head of the bank and read him the riot act. He himself had just gotten off the phone with a senior American Justice Department official who kicked him around like a third world tin can. Though Bermudan banking laws were notoriously loose, he was told that, in this case, the rules would tighten up. Ugly threats were traded back and forth, but in the end the outcome was preordained. Neither the governor nor the Bermudan banks wanted to be listed as havens for criminal money. It mattered not that they were—being accurately labeled was what they deathly feared. Tourism would dry up. Bermudan exports would sit on American docks, rotting. Bermuda, so dependent on rich Americans, would shrivel to a wasteland of empty beaches and foreclosed hotels, massive numbers of angry, unemployed people, etcetera. The governor remained steadfast for about three seconds before he crumbled under the onslaught of threats.

The FBI now had a death grip on both of Alex's accounts.

Not thirty minutes later, Illya called from Austria. "Alex, what's going on?" he yelled, clearly at the outer edge of reason.

"I have no idea what you're talking about."

"No idea? The roof's falling in here."

"Settle down, Illya. Take a deep breath and tell me what's happening."

A long moment passed while his excitable protégé tried to order his harried thoughts. "This morning I was informed that our license to do business in Russia has been revoked. All day, we've been getting calls from clients canceling their contracts."

"On what basis?"

"The American clients were advised by the American FBI that we're a front for criminal operations."

"And the Russian clients?"

"No reason was given. They were just ordered by the Ministry of Security to terminate their relationships with us, or else."

Alex quietly cursed himself. The computer! He had password-coded his files, a false sense of security, he realized now, very unhappily, and a little after the fact. The FBI had talented specialists who probably could crack his password in seconds flat. He tried to recall what was in those files. Nothing. Everything. Too much. He had never imagined he would have to protect himself against this kind of police abuse. Not here. Not in America.

Everything he and Elena had done with Orangutan, the accounts they had brought in, the names of his contacts in Austria. What else? His bank records, of course—that accounted for how swiftly the FBI moved in and strangled their finances. A new thought struck him and his blood ran cold.

As coolly as he could, he said to Illya, "Pack your bags and get away, Illya."

"Why, Alex? I'm—"

"Don't ask questions I can't answer. Just get away, right now."

"Alex, I have three hundred employees. I can't. I have responsibilities and obligations here."

"Do you want to live?"

"Of course, but—"

"Use cash, Illya. Don't leave a trail. Don't call your family or friends. Find a place to hide where nobody will expect you."

Mysteriously, the line suddenly went dead.

The three men parked one block away in the white, unmarked van, turned down the volume, and sipped lukewarm coffee. They exchanged knowing winks and satisfied smiles. They were "press aides" assigned to the Russian embassy, a thin guise for intelligence operatives. Yes, run, Illya, run as fast as your legs can carry you. Dodge and hide, spend only cash, ignore your family and job, and disappear into the darkest hole in the universe. We'll still find you.

Volevodz had littered bugs in almost every square inch of the

Konevitch apartment. The two Fibbies had observed him, had idly watched as he wandered around the Konevitch home hiding a listening device here, a bug there. They never said a word. After a while, Volevodz dropped any pretense of caution. They obviously didn't care. They had orders from on high to allow the Russian as much latitude as he wanted—as long as he didn't kill anybody. This was America, after all: a land of laws and inalienable rights. Beatings were questionable, they figured, in a gray area; guess it depended how bad the thumping got, the two agents decided.

The house phone was bugged as well. The men in the van could barely contain themselves when Elena had called that morning with the surprise news about the bank. Alex, we have no money. Oh Alex, how will we pay our lawyer? Alex, how will we buy food? The questions and pulled hair would come soon. Probably that night.

Another van, similarly equipped, and also filled with Russian "press aides," was parked half a block up from their lawyer's office. His phones, too, both at home and at work, were riddled with bugs. His house had been burgled the day before. While he, his wife, and two kids were doing the prayer thing at church, a team had entered through the broken back door. It was easy. A bad, decaying neighborhood. His neighbors generally stayed inside and very specifically ignored what happened outside their doors. His office, too, was wired like a sound studio.

So they knew the lawyer hadn't come in yet, was apparently still wandering the halls at INS, trying to fathom how bad his client's situation was.

Bad, pal. Real bad.

Neither the lawyer nor the Konevitches had the slightest idea how awful this was about to get.

19

The loud knock on the door came that night, slightly after midnight. Elena was sleeping with a pillow over her head, and never budged. Alex tried to ignore it, but the hammering grew more obnoxiously insistent, until he could stand it no longer. He slipped on his bathrobe and tiptoed quietly to the door.

He peered through the peephole. A middle-aged stranger in a cheap blue suit stood there, nervously looking around. Definitely FBI, Alex thought, though the demeanor was flagrantly different than the agents who tumbled their apartment on Saturday. This man appeared tentative, actually afraid. Alex opened the door.

The man inspected Alex's face, then asked in a low, raspy whisper, "You're Konevitch, right?"

"You know that or you wouldn't be here."

"Yeah, guess I do."

"Should I invite you in or would you rather just burst inside like your comrades? There's not much left to damage. A few chairs in the dining room. Two pictures we put back on the walls. I'll point them out for you. Take your pick."

"Lower your voice, all right? Step into the hall. Please."

"I'd rather make you come inside and drag me out."

The mysterious man leaned closer and lowered his voice to barely a whisper. "Trust me. We can't talk . . . not here, definitely not inside your apartment." His hand did something funny with his left ear, apparently trying to signal something.

Alex took a chance and stepped out. The agent reached over and gently eased the door shut behind him. He walked about ten steps and Alex followed. He turned around and they faced each other less than a foot apart. "Who are you?" Alex demanded.

"Hold your voice down. I'd rather not say. Did you do what they say you did?"

"Why ask? Your people already convicted me."

"Because I'm asking, okay?" The sour odor of a recently smoked cigar was on the man's breath. It mixed badly with the cheap aftershave.

"All right. No, I'm being framed. I swear it."

The agent almost smiled. Right, how pitiful. Why couldn't anybody come up with something original? "Tell you what. I really don't care if you did, or you didn't. I just don't like what's going down."

"Which is what?"

He played with the top button on his jacket and appeared indecisive for a moment. Then he apparently resigned himself to tell Alex everything. "A bunch of Russkis working in our headquarters. Tromble, the director, arranged it. I worked counterintelligence for ten years, right? I can smell it. These guys have former KGB written all over them."

"Colonel Volevodz?"

"Yeah . . . him and about three of his guys. Your apartment's bugged, you know."

"No . . . I . . . I had no idea."

"Probably your phones, too. Be careful."

"Why are you telling me this?"

"I'm a career guy, okay."

"So what? Volevodz is also a career guy."

"Yeah, but it's different." He wiped a hand across his forehead in frustration, apparently annoyed by being compared with some cold-eyed KGB thug. "Look, I'm taking a big risk coming here. But whatever you did back there don't justify what's happening here. I'm just warning you, be real careful."

"All right, I'm warned."

If anything, the agent suddenly became more agitated. He glanced down the long hallway, a long, searching look that indicated a high level of paranoia. He avoided Alex's eyes. After a moment he whispered, "One last thing."

"I'm listening."

"The Russian mob's got a contract on you. Don't ask how I know, I just know."

Alex should not have been surprised by this unwelcome news, but he was. Surprised and deeply unnerved. A long day of disasters was just capped by the Mount Vesuvius of bad news. He leaned against the wall and stared down at the red-and-black carpet.

"It's a serious contract," the agent continued, shuffling his feet and avoiding Alex's eyes. "Over a million bucks," he claimed, looking up. "These guys usually get people whacked for about five thousand. Apparently, you're quite valuable to them."

"Should I feel honored?"

"Scared shitless is how you should feel, Konevitch."

"All right, I do."

"Best we can tell, three teams flew in over the past week. That don't even account for the local players, of which there are too many to count."

"Your people know this for a fact?"

"Wouldn't be telling you otherwise."

"Where did this information come from? Do you have a source inside the syndicates?"

He shrugged his shoulders. "It's real, okay? Believe me or not, it's your ass."

"If your people know, why don't you protect us?"

"Because people high up don't believe you deserve it. They figure you did something to piss off the mob. It's your problem, not ours."

"Is that all?"

"That's all."

"Thank you."

A few seconds passed. The agent seemed to be arguing with

himself before he blurted, "Look, forget about it. If things get tough, though, if you want advice or help, call me. Just not from your apartment. This is our little secret, okay?" He pressed a business card into Alex's palm. Special Agent Terrence Hanrahan, it read, with the usual array of office, cell, and fax numbers. "Remember, anytime you step outside, look both ways before you cross the street."

Alex nodded. The hand dropped and Special Agent Hanrahan walked quickly back down the hall, straight to the elevator. Alex returned to the apartment, stopped momentarily in his office, and rushed directly to the bedroom. Gently shaking her, he quietly awoke Elena. Placing a forefinger to his lip he handed her a notepad and pencil, keeping another of each for himself.

They spent the rest of the night writing each other notes.

Agent Terrence Hanrahan stepped off the elevator on the ground floor. The Watergate doorman watched as he was quickly surrounded by five agents of the Bureau; they pinned his arms behind his back and roughly hustled him out through the door. No words were exchanged. A shiny black limo idled beside the curb.

A rear door opened and Hanrahan was shoved inside. A lean figure was slumped on the other side of the seat. The overhead reading lamp was on: the figure was paging through a stack of documents with blistering speed. Hanrahan found it hard to believe the man understood a tenth of what he was reading.

Tromble finally looked up. "Well?"

"Went down perfect. He's scared out of his wits."

"And he trusts you?"

"He's a smart guy, so I doubt it."

"But he at least believed you?"

"No question about that."

"And you think he'll call you?"

"Maybe. Depends, I guess, on how desperate he gets."

"You warned him about the contracts?"

"I did. Is it true?"

"Absolutely. My Russian friends say he not only embezzled from his own bank, he also stole millions more, from the mob. As if he didn't have enough enemies already. They want him as badly as the Russian government." He scratched his nose. "You remembered to mention the bugs?"

Hanrahan nodded. "His face turned white as a baby's ass. Why let him in on that, though?"

A slight smile. "We don't want Volevodz and his people to have an unfair advantage, do we?"

"Jesus, his own government, and now the Russian mob. I guess the only question is who'll get him first."

"Not really," Tromble said, glancing out the darkened window. "We'll beat them to him. Your job's to make that happen, Terrence. Don't let me down."

"He and that wife are going to be paranoid."

"Yes, I believe they will. That's the idea. You just make sure they realize America is more dangerous for them than Russia. I want them so hopeless they'll be more than ready for our offer, when it comes. We'll be their only help."

Hanrahan thought about it a moment. He had been an agent for eighteen years; Tromble was the fifth director he had served. By far, he was the toughest and most heavy-handed, but there was no question he got results. "And if they don't fold?"

"No problem. We'll turn up the heat. Pull out the stops and ship them back."

20

The three men sat in the white van, swapping American girlie magazines, sucking on cigarettes, sipping stale coffee, bored out of their wits. After that initial day of heart-thumping surprises and emotional terror, things had quickly retreated to a dull grind.

During the days, surprisingly little took place in the Konevitch apartment. Long bouts of silence, broken occasionally by tedious discussions about incredibly inane things—the laundry, the latest stupid game show on TV, Oprah, and so on. On Tuesday, the wife, Elena, read to her husband, out loud, a stream of interminable passages from *War and Peace*. Wednesday was *Anna Karenina*'s turn, which proved even worse. The men inside the van contemplated suicide, or rushing upstairs to drive a gag down her throat.

The Konevitches never left their building, or even their apartment, the best the men could tell. This had been a sore topic with Volevodz, who popped by occasionally to gather updates. As long as the couple stayed inside, the three listeners were trapped inside the van, crammed in with all the electronic equipment and debris from their meals. It seemed to shrink by the day; they were peeing in bottles, for God's sake. Theories and conjectures rumbled around the rear of the van. It was unnatural to stay penned up so long inside that cramped apartment. On the other hand, the Konevitches no longer had jobs. And money—actually the sudden lack of it—was undoubtedly a serious factor in their minds. Wasn't like they could afford to splurge on the theater or an expensive restaurant. Why not a movie, though? Better yet, a nice long stroll along the canal, like they used to? How much could that cost?

When it turned dark, things picked up and turned slightly more interesting. The Konevitches were like rabbits. Every night, for hours, groans and giggles, sheets rustling, and an occasional scream or "oh my God" to cap off the festivities. The first few times the volume had been kicked up full blast. The three men tried to imagine what was going on in that bed. Why hadn't Volevodz been thoughtful enough to plant a camera? It would have been so easy, they whispered among themselves. Eventually, the constant lovemaking only contributed to the enveloping air of misery.

It was almost as if the Konevitches knew all about the three listeners, that they were taunting and rubbing it in.

The phone action had turned virtually nonexistent. A few frustrated calls from their lawyer, who complained constantly about being stonewalled by his old friends in the INS.

An occasional call to order pizza and Chinese deliveries—that was it.

"What are they doing out there?" asked the note Elena passed over the dining room table to Alex.

A glance at his watch—8:00 p.m.—and he scribbled a hasty response and flashed it to her. "Going nuts, I hope." After days of corresponding like this they had finally mastered the awkward art of balancing two conversations at once—inane verbal ramblings to mollify their listeners while they scrawled brief messages back and forth. It was tedious and slow, and absolutely necessary. They chatted in English and they wrote in Russian.

"Why didn't we buy a bigger place?!!!!" she scribbled back. "It's closing in on me, Alex. I can barely breathe."

Alex wrote, "At least the company's better in here than out there." Who knew how many Mafiya thugs were prowling nearby, trying their damnedest to collect the bounty? Volevodz knew their address—they had to assume he had somehow passed it along to

the cabal in Moscow. So the thugs now had a firm fix on their location and Alex was sure they were huddled somewhere nearby,
waiting. Going outside was out of the question. The first few days
they had tried to suppress their terror, to find ways to cope with
their anxiety and rearrange and repair their living conditions.
Day three Elena had gone on a mad hunt for electronic bugs. She
discovered six. They suspected there were more, plenty more,
and they were right.

On day four, they agreed upon a strategy—they would work
overtime to appear like they were going through the motions of a
normal life, battling boredom, praying, and waiting for MP to whip
a legal rabbit out of his hat and end this miserable nightmare.

They weren't fooling themselves, though. MP was a gnat battling giants. This was way over his head—over any lawyer's head,
probably. At any moment, the people outside would become
tired of this, and the next hammer would fall. And Alex, ever the
clearheaded businessman, was sure things would become worse,
whatever that meant.

With each succeeding day, the situation became more intolerable. Elena tried reading, watching TV, meditating—nothing
worked. Nothing. Alex walked endlessly around the apartment,
doing laps and searching for a solution. He thought best on his
feet, and was wearing out shoe leather to find a way out of this.

They had no money. They were trapped inside this building.
Unable to escape. Unable to communicate with anybody outside
without the mice listening in. If there was a way out, it was up
to them to find it. Alex patted Elena's knee and wrote, "Time for
the bedroom."

They got up and together made the short trek down the hall.
Alex loaded the tape they had produced the first night, carefully
and quietly inserted it into the cassette player, then cranked the
volume knob to maximum. He said to Elena, "Get your clothes
off. I'm in the mood again." Neither of them had been in anything
close to the mood since the visit from Agent Hanrahan with the
terrifying news about all the bugs and the thugs waiting outside
to kill them.

The idea that their every word was being overheard was sickening.

Elena kicked off her shoes, flung them hard against the wall, and made a point to sit heavily on the edge of the bed, with an accompanying groan from the springs. She opened the nightly banter. "You're always in the mood."

"And you're always beautiful."

"You're insatiable."

"And you're a doll." Then, "Take off your blouse."

"You first, with the shirt . . . that's it. Now the pants."

They went back and forth, trying their best to make the listeners gag, then Alex sat heavily on the bed, right beside her.

They stared at each other a moment. Without another word, Alex pushed start and the tape kicked in. The sounds of the two of them sexually mauling each other shot full-blast into the listening devices.

They had nearly killed each other producing that tape.

Elena leaned close to Alex and whispered, "How many more days do you think we have?"

"One . . . twenty. Who knows?"

"What are they waiting for?"

"For us to break. Or run out of money and start starving."

"Why? What do they hope to gain?"

"They want us desperate. They have our money, and they've made us too terrified to step outside. It's a box, and the only way out is to accept their condition. A one-way trip to Russia."

"Maybe we should try to just make a run for it."

"How?"

"Disguise ourselves. Sneak out. Early in the morning when they're tired and their senses are dull. Create a diversion of some kind." She pecked him on the cheek, then pulled back. "You pulled it off in Budapest. We'll do it again."

"And go where, Elena? They have our passports."

"Montana, Idaho, Nevada. I'm past caring, Alex. A town in the middle of nowhere. Hot, cold, dry, wet, it no longer matters. Someplace small, neglected. America has millions of illegal immigrants. We'll live in the underground economy, find a way to blend in."

"I'll open a lawn service, and you'll be a maid. Is that the idea?"

"We'll be alive, Alex. And free."

He leaned over and touched her shoulder. "Listen to me. All of those millions of illegal immigrants don't have the FBI hunting them. The FBI doesn't know their names, doesn't have their physical descriptions, and could care less about them. We'd be looking over our shoulder every day. One day we'd wake up to a bunch of men in gray suits."

"But I'm tired of sitting here, waiting."

"Well, I have an idea."

"I'm willing to try anything."

"Unfortunately, it will take time."

"How much time?"

"Probably a lot. Probably too much. It's a complete gamble, anyway, an outside shot with a million things that can go wrong."

She stared up at the ceiling. "A million things can go wrong here. Tell me about it."

They whispered back and forth, while the men in the van, tired of the monotony of love and lust in the Konevitch place, squelched the volume and napped.

One block away, the lady and two men stayed hunched inside the car and, through a pair of powerful binoculars, kept a close eye on the front entrance of the Watergate. The year of hunting for Alex in Chicago had not agreed with Katya.

Nicky had a modest, not overly prosperous operation in Chicago run by a half-crazy, doped-out boss who put up the hunter-killer team, along with five of his own people, in a cramped, run-down rowhouse in one of the most crime-infested sections of the South Side. He called it a safehouse. It was barely a house, and anything but safe. Black and Hispanic gangs roamed the surrounding streets at will. They did not particularly cater to these Russians who were trying, rather unsuccessfully, to muscle into the local action.

The rowhouse quickly became a prison, a quite miserable one. The gangs were large, mean, and tough. A tiny bodega was positioned on a corner across the street. They hung there, blacks and spics in variously colored bandanas, mixing freely together, never less than fifteen of them. They sipped from canned beers, rapped back and forth, shared menthols, and glowered at the rowhouse across the street. They seemed to be honoring a local cease-fire among themselves, a temporary alliance against a common foe. For decades, they had battled and scrapped with one another for these streets—every inch of concrete, every crackhouse and whore's corner was a victory, paid in blood. No way were they going to let these Ivan-come-latelys have a piece of the action. At night they sometimes sprayed the rowhouse with bullets. They scattered when the cops arrived, only to reappear the instant the last blue suit departed. Once, a pair of Molotov cocktails sailed through the windows.

The Russians slept on the floors, and crawled on their bellies every time they passed a window. A stack of portable fire extinguishers was stored in the kitchen. First aid kits were in every room in the house.

Katya and her crew ventured outside as infrequently as possible. Two left on a grocery run one night and never returned. They may have fled. Nobody blamed them.

A few weeks later, a box with four ears was left on the doorstep. They studied the shriveled things and debated at length, but nobody could be entirely certain they belonged to Dmitri and Josef. Dmitri did in fact have two earrings. And okay, yes, Josef's ears were sort of large and floppy; but no one knew for sure.

It constipated the search for the Konevitches terribly. The first few months, Katya and her comrades snuck out only in the wee hours of the morning, trying to elude the gangs. Their car had been shot at more than they could count as they sped down the street. Nicky's locals had a firm fix on the Russian immigrant pockets of the city; naturally, this was where the bulk of effort was placed. At some point, inevitably, the Konevitches would turn up.

Occasionally, they got word that Alex Konevitch had been seen

cruising a few local Russian clubs, flashing a wad of bills and bragging about the flourishing real estate empire he was establishing
in the city. It sounded like Mr. Big Shot. And after flashing photos
at various witnesses, they were sure it was him. Queries to the local phone companies had revealed a cell service account, though
the number was unlisted and the phone service stubbornly refused to provide the billing address. That was it. No matter how
hard they dug, no matter how many cops they paid for information, this was all they had.

Additional pictures of the couple were plastered everywhere.
Hundreds more were pressed into the hands of Russian expats
with vile threats about what would happen should they fail to
snitch on first sight.

After those first few months, the hunters became dispirited—
and worse, seriously frightened. The party outside the bodega
seemed to grow bigger by the day. The Russians took to cowering
in the rowhouse, contriving false reports back to Moscow, manufacturing hopeful leads that never existed. The lies would never
be caught, they were confident of this. Nobody would dare run
the gauntlet and pay them a visit.

Massive quantities of food and beer and vodka were stockpiled. They watched the same tired porn flicks, ate and drank
heavily, and bickered among themselves. The men outnumbered
Katya, and they cruelly exploited this advantage against her. They
pressed her into service as their cook, their laundry lady, their
maid.

Even the long year of killing in the Congo, her previous record
for unadulterated wretchedness, paled in comparison.

Oh, how she hated the Konevitches. The last iota of icy detachment had melted months before. Her pouched eyes now burned
with a scary intensity. It was all their fault, that awful couple.
Why couldn't they just let themselves be killed? It would've been
so much easier for everybody. How could they be so selfish?

When the call came from Moscow that the Konevitches had
been found, living in Washington—and in a luxury co-op, of all
places—she nearly cried. At four that morning, she and the rest of

her team eased out of the bullet-pocked rowhouse, hauling their bags, and dodging a few farewell bullets.

The first day in Washington, she made six furtive passes around the Watergate and the busy streets surrounding the huge complex. To her trained eyes, the competition stood out like sore thumbs. The unmarked white van with too many antennas. The dark FBI cars splayed around like a drive-in movie theater, everybody watching, everybody waiting for the Konevitches to make a move.

They were all going to be sorely disappointed. They couldn't have them, not even a piece of them: the Konevitches were hers.

She sat, gazing hatefully through the binos, dreaming up unpleasant ways to kill them.

Mrs. Edna Clarke was ninety-two and still sprightly. She had lived in the Watergate from the day it was built. Her husband, Arthur, had been a managing partner of a large, prestigious law firm, before he passed, God bless him, at the youthful age of eighty-two. The past decade, she had stayed in her apartment, alone but for the kindred company of her three precious cats. She read and knitted and waited patiently for the good Lord to call her. Her children had pleaded with her to consider a nursing home. She wouldn't hear of it. This was her home, a place filled with wonderful memories of Arthur and the family they had bred and raised, through good times and bad, but mostly good. She would leave in a hearse, she vowed.

She just adored that lovely young Russian couple across the hall. The day they moved in, she had promptly rapped on their door, gripping a bottle of good red wine wrapped in a bright red bow. A housewarming gift. Not that young people practiced such things these days: they knew nothing about good manners. The Konevitches, though, were certainly different. They uncorked the bottle on the spot and insisted she come in and share a glass. And afterward, on weekends, they frequently invited her over for quiet dinners.

She and Arthur had led interesting lives. They had met in Europe during the war, where Arthur had been a legal star at the

Nuremberg trials. They had dined with presidents and senators, as Arthur went on to work in civil rights and dozens of other things that were important and fascinating. At least fascinating at that time. Now they were just rotten old memories to most people. A pathetic old attic nobody cared to peek into. Not that Alex, though. He was so bright, so curious, such an accommodating listener. He sat on the edge of his chair and peppered her with questions until her brain grew tired and she creaked back across the hall to her bed.

On Edna's ninety-second birthday, they sprang for a ballet at the Kennedy Center—the Bolshoi on tour, no less! Edna had pushed and squeezed herself into a gown she hadn't worn since Arthur's death. Elena was friendly with a number of the dancers, and afterward she had escorted Edna backstage and introduced her around. What a lovely, lovely birthday. Her own children hadn't even sent gifts. Hadn't called, either.

So she did not think twice when Alex knocked and asked to borrow her cell phone. He promised to pay her back for any expenses incurred. Edna wouldn't hear of it, of course. Arthur had left her a bigger fortune than she could ever hope to spend. She had a perfectly good house phone, anyway. What did she need with that shrunken little excuse for a squawk box? She only bought it to see what all the fuss was about: a lot of hype and ado about nothing, she quickly decided. She could barely hear through it. Had to scream into it just to hear her own voice.

But Alex certainly seemed to be attached to that thing. She felt nosy, and guilty, but couldn't keep her eye away from that spyhole on her door. All day, day after day, it seemed, Alex was out there in the hallway, pacing back and forth, chattering like mad into that silly little device. Occasionally, he popped back into his apartment, only to reappear after a few minutes with that stupid thing nudged up against his ear again.

Odd behavior. A little suspicious, maybe; the way a man might behave were he, say, maybe having a secret affair. She drove that thought straight out of her mind. Such a nice, loving couple. He had to be talking business, she concluded; he was enough of a gen-

tleman not to do it in front of his wife. Lord knew she hated when
Arthur spent hours on the phone talking all that legal mumbo-
jumbo with his partners and clients like she wasn't even there.

Shortly after midnight, the apartment door was opened with a
skillful thrust of the pick, and gently pushed open.

Two men quietly entered, Mikhail Borosky first, then Igor
Markashvili, a fellow PI whom Mikhail trusted devoutly, and occasionally employed for special jobs. Throughout the previous
week, Mikhail and his client Alex had spoken over the phone
every day, sometimes for hours. Things were getting ugly for the
Konevitches back in America. Alex's patience with the people
chasing him was exhausted. He had tried peaceful coexistence,
forgive and forget, and they, apparently, wouldn't hear of it. Also
they were targeting Alex's beloved Elena again. Mikhail could
sense a deep change in his old friend. In place of Alex's cool,
sober intelligence simmered a quiet rage. After a long dialogue,
after many desperate ideas were thrown back and forth, they finally settled on a plan.

It would take time, though. Months, probably, if not longer.
Mikhail encouraged his friend and client to just stay alive long
enough to see it through.

The apartment was spacious, and also dark and empty. They
tiptoed quietly in their sneakers, flipped on small flashlights, and
fanned out. Nice place, high-ceilinged, wood-floored, furnished
with expensive antiques, and kept neat as a pin by the lady of
the house. The lady in question, Tatyana, was spending the night
with her boss. Mikhail went to work on the phones, while Igor
began littering listening devices at strategic locations around the
apartment. Mikhail inserted a bug inside the phone in the living
room, then another inside the phone on the bedside table. In less
than fifteen minutes the job was done.

They slipped out as quietly as they entered.

The bugs were manufactured by a German electronics firm,
highly sensitive, sound-activated little things that fed the noise to
a small recording box hidden in the basement of the apartment

building. There would be no need for Mikhail to conceal himself in a cubbyhole somewhere, battling sleep and boredom with an earphone pressed against his ear. He would stop in every few days, collect the old tape, reload a fresh one, then sit back in comfort over a cigar and scotch and listen for the dirt.

Only a few hours before, the two men had magnetically attached a small tracking device on the undercarriage of Golitsin's limo. Another, as well, was slapped on that cute little BMW convertible Golitsin had bought himself.

Breaking through the high-tech security system into Golitsin's mansion was close to impossible; also, frankly unnecessary. Who cared what the old man said, anyway?

At this stage of the operation, all that mattered was where he went.

Illya Mechoukov was soaking up the sun on a fold-out beach chair and gazing, without a serious thought in his head, through his shades at the Caribbean beach from the commanding perch of his balcony. In the four years since he founded Orangutan Media, he had not taken a single day of vacation. Not one. Just work, work, work. And even more work once Alex and Elena started roping in all those big U.S. firms.

He had no idea how exhausted he was, until this forced vacation landed in his lap. And this glorious little sun-drenched island filled with all manner of pleasantries was such a perfect place to unwind and forget all that pressure. The sun, the rum, the beaches, all those native girls and American tourist girls romping in the surf, competing to see who could show off the tinier bikini. At that moment, his eyes were feasting on two of the lovely little things down below, flaunting their bronzed bodies in little more than thin strings.

He never heard them enter his hotel room. Never knew of their presence until the garrote landed around his neck and was pulled back. The pain was vicious and unbearable. The garrote was held firmly in place for over a minute. His eyes bulged, his lips turned purple, as his hands clawed desperately at the rope.

Then darkness. He passed out, though he hadn't died. He was sure of this when they threw cold water on his body and revived him.

"What—" he tried to say before a big fist smashed against his lips.

He spit out two front teeth. He was on a bed, gagging and coughing up blood.

"We'll talk and you'll listen," a man told him in Russian. The man was a terrifying giant, nearly six and a half feet, with swollen muscles that stretched against his silly Bahamian shirt. Black curly hair covered his arms and half-exposed chest. In fact there were three men, Illya realized. The other two were dressed similarly in pink and yellow shorts, flowered shirts, dark socks, and leather sandals.

"Nice outfits," Illya mumbled, and was quickly rewarded with another fist.

"This is very easy. We have nothing against you," the one in pink shorts informed him. "All you have to do is sign a simple statement and you're free."

"A statement? What kind of statement?"

"Do you want to live?"

"Of course."

"Then what do you care what the statement says?"

He really didn't. Not at all. A sheet of paper, official-looking and typed neatly in Russian, was shoved in front of Illya's face. A pen was propped in his hand.

He barely had time for a brief glance before the garrote around his neck suddenly tightened—something about a confession that Orangutan Media was a front for criminal activities. And something more, something about Alex Konevitch, before the world around Illya became a gathering blur. Somehow he scrawled his name at the bottom of the page before he subsided into darkness again.

When he awoke, the bad men were gone.

21

Tromble was seated behind his large desk, ruffling papers, pretending to read, a trivial excuse to keep Hanrahan and his team leaders waiting along the far wall, a spiteful way of showing his deep displeasure at their failure to bag Alex Konevitch.

After five minutes of this, Hanrahan thought seriously about rushing across the room and pistol-whipping him.

Eventually the director glanced up at Hanrahan. "It's been two weeks. Why hasn't Konevitch called us yet?" he asked in a tone suggesting this was all Hanrahan's fault.

"I don't know." It was five o'clock, Friday. The end of two long frustrating weeks, and Hanrahan was sure there was a happy hour somewhere with his name on it. He pushed himself off the wall and moved closer to the big desk. "They haven't left the building since our little chat. They're ordering in food, tiptoeing around their home, hunkering down. They're scared to death. They'd be idiots not to be."

"Where are they getting the money? I thought we took care of that."

"My guess would be they had a little cash laying around. Not everybody lives off charge cards."

"How much money?"

Hanrahan said, "I have no idea. Probably not a lot. They're living off pizza and Chinese food. We've questioned a few of the delivery boys. They're using coupons, very spare with the tips. Indications are the kitty jar ain't all that full. They're trying to stretch it out."

"But you could be wrong?"

"Yes, I could be wrong."

"And this could drag out for months?"

"That's possible. Unlikely as hell, but I won't rule it out."

Tatyana from Yeltsin's office had been calling Tromble every other day. She was polite and courteous, but beneath that veneer, she was needling and nagging. She never missed a chance to remind him of his boast that Konevitch would be in Russia inside a week. He was tired of it. Twenty talented agents with hundreds of years of experience in battling organized crime had been identified and told to prepare for quick reassignments to Russia. Everything was ready to go, everything except this Konevitch guy.

"What are our Russian friends up to?" Tromble asked, leaning back and folding his hands behind his head.

"The white van's still here. Our guys snuck over and attached a very sensitive listening device on its side. The three boys inside are seriously unhappy campers. Starting to act a little strange. Get this. Yesterday they actually played a few rounds of Russian roulette." He shrugged. "I guess it's their national sport."

"What else?"

"The Mafiya's got a small presence. Last Tuesday, one of their people made a few fast laps around the area. She and two of their people are living inside a car about a block away. They sleep in it, eat in it, and wait."

The impatience on Tromble's face was palpable. Hanrahan, an old hand, was a veteran of countless stakeouts and several hostage situations. Patience is key. They take time. It's a psychological face-off, both sides playing mind games with the other. It's just a matter of who'll snap first. You can't rush it.

Almost predictably, Tromble said, "We need to do something different." After a pause that was meant to appear thoughtful, he pushed on. "Why don't you just arrest them?"

"On what grounds?" Hanrahan asked.

"I don't care. You tell me."

Hanrahan scratched his head. "Maybe some sort of immigration violation. Something simple. Overstaying their visas, maybe. From what the Russkis are saying, he lied to get his asylum. Maybe toss on a charge for fraud."

"Go with the overstayed visa."

"That's INS's territory," Hanrahan observed, quite rightfully.

"Good point. They have to get involved eventually. Why not now?"

Hanrahan slowly nodded. There was obviously more going on here than he was being told. The director was playing this close to the vest, but that wasn't unusual. In an effort to learn more, he asked dubiously, "So we pick him up on a simple immigration violation?"

"We'll throw on all the additional charges we want later. And we'll bring the press into this thing, maybe put out a statement that throws all kinds of dirt at Konevitch. I just want them in the judicial system for now."

"Them?" A brief pause and a look of disbelief. "Both of them?"

"Isn't that what I said?"

"What crime did she commit?"

"She married him."

Hanrahan cleared his throat and stood his ground. "So you want us to use her to pressure him? I wanna be sure I heard this right."

Tromble played with a paperweight on his desk. "Did I say that?"

Hanrahan didn't dare answer.

Tromble lifted up a document and pretended to read it.

Hanrahan wouldn't budge—they were skirting on the thin edge of the law already. Now Tromble was trying to shove him across it. He was two years from retirement. He had it all mapped out: a small home on a golf course in Florida, as little private consulting as he could get away with, divorce the hag he married, and find a new hottie who looked good in a skimpy bathing suit or wearing nothing at all. He wasn't about to put it all at risk. He wanted an unequivocal order in the presence of the two witnesses against the wall.

When it became clear they would stand against that wall all night, Tromble finally relented. Without looking up, he said, "He entered our borders under false pretenses. She accompanied him, and she participated in his falsified testimony for asylum. That makes her party to the conspiracy, and her role merits similar treatment."

"Got it. When is this supposed to happen?"

"Tonight. Late tonight. It's Friday and his lawyer won't be able to do anything until Monday."

The knock came at three in the morning. Alex threw on his bathrobe, again, and again tiptoed to the door. A quick peep through the spyhole—Marty Brennan, the co-op maintenance man, peered back with a worried expression.

Alex opened the door. "What is it, Ma—"

Marty was suddenly shoved aside by a crowd of eight people who barged inside, seven men and a stout woman dressed like a man. The agents fanned out and raced into every room in the apartment, which did not take long as it was so small.

From the bedroom, Elena screamed. Alex made a move in that direction before he was restrained by two men with thick shoulders and rough hands. They yanked his arms behind his back and with well-practiced efficiency fitted flex-cuffs around his wrists. "Who are you?" Alex yelled.

"Immigration Service," replied a voice from the small kitchen.

"We've done nothing wrong. We have political asylum."

"Past tense. You had asylum," the man corrected in a snarling tone, moving back into the room and positioning himself before Alex. "That's now suspended, pending review."

"Fine. We also have visas. The passports are in my briefcase," Alex told him, using his chin, awkwardly, to indicate the case resting precariously on the now three-legged living room table.

The man walked to the briefcase, deftly snapped it open, and withdrew two booklets. He flipped through until he came to the pages with the American visas—a millisecond of study before he looked up and frowned. "These are obvious forgeries."

"So is the American Constitution, apparently."

"Search the place," the man directed his people. Everybody but one man in the corner snapped to and began rummaging through drawers and overturning furniture, again.

Alex informed them, "The FBI tossed our place over two weeks ago. What do you expect to find?"

No answer. Alex turned away from the destruction and studied the one man who leaned against the wall, not participating. He wore a cheap gray suit like the others, though he was clearly more observer than participant. Alex directed his voice at him and said, "You must be FBI."

The man looked a little uncertain, then replied very amiably, "Good guess."

"I want to call my lawyer. He has all the papers regarding my asylum and legal status. I'm sure you want to see those papers, right?"

"Nope. Not tonight."

"What about my rights, sir?"

"Illegal immigrants don't enjoy rights."

"I want to be clear on this, sir. You're denying me the right to counsel?"

In one of many conversations with MP, the lawyer had advised him that something like this might happen. Ignore the indignities and offensive behavior, stay cool, don't get confrontational, no matter how bad the goading gets, MP had advised quite insistently. It won't sound good at an immigration board hearing, or in a courtroom, that Alex, an immigrant, lacked respect for American authorities. Stay firm and polite. Gently remind them of your rights, and remember how many legal procedures they violate; later, we'll drag them through all that dirt in a courtroom.

But at that moment, Elena was tugged out of the bedroom and into the small living room by the female agent who looked like a drag queen in reverse. Elena wore only her nightie, a skimpy, nearly transparent garment that left little to the imagination. A few of the male agents were openly leering at her. Elena didn't care. She stared back with a ferocity that would make an armored tank wilt with shame.

The FBI agent also was sneaking quick lurid peeks at her, at least he was before Alex snapped, "Even the KGB didn't employ so many perverts."

The agent, who was named Wilson, shifted his eyes to his shoes and turned slightly pink.

"Are you married?" Alex asked him. No answer, so Alex again prodded, "Do you have a wife?"

"Yes." Still staring down at his laces like a shamed child.

"Would you enjoy seeing your wife treated this way?"

"How were we to know what she was wearing?"

"But you know it now, sir. And like sick perverts you're all leering at my wife. If you had any decency you'd allow her to go into the bathroom and get dressed."

Agent Wilson could not stop staring at his shoes, the tips, the laces, the stitching along the sides. His orders were clear and brutal. Humiliate Konevitch. Goad and provoke him into doing something stupid—any pitiful attempt at resistance, disrespectful behavior toward the agents, or, better yet, some mild act of violence. The charges against him were precariously flimsy, trumped-up bullshit that was dangerously toothless, if truth be told. His boss, Hanrahan, had demanded something a real judge could sink his teeth into.

But that "pervert" word really stung. Now looking at anything *but* the nearly naked, gorgeous blonde in the room, he said to the female agent, "Let her get some clothes and change in the bathroom."

Elena was led off, stomping angrily down the hall.

Alex leaned against a wall and resigned himself to watching the INS agents tear his apartment apart. The few pieces that weren't already broken—and those he and Elena had carefully and lovingly repaired—were now destroyed beyond repair. It was hard, grim work and, to their credit, nobody smiled or laughed this time.

After about five more minutes of frantic homewrecking, the sounds of somebody pounding hard on a door at the rear of the apartment brought a sudden halt to the action. A deep woman's voice was frantically yelling, "What are you doing in there? Open up. I said, open this damned door! I mean it, I'm not fooling around."

The FBI agent, Wilson, suddenly lost his polished cool and dashed back to the rear bathroom. After a few moments of loud confusion accompanied by more ignored demands to open the door, Alex heard a loud crash. A moment later, Elena was dragged back into the living room, fully dressed now, in jeans, a loose sweatshirt, and a petulant expression.

"What were you doing in there?" the FBI agent demanded two inches from her face.

"I changed clothes."

"What else?"

Elena could not resist a big smirk. "Isn't that a rude question to ask a lady who was in the bathroom?"

Mr. FBI rolled his eyes and barked at the INS agents, "Search the bathroom."

Two minutes later, one of the agents reappeared, sheepishly gripping a wet cell phone in his hand. "This was hidden inside the toilet."

It was senseless to ask Elena if she had made a call. And equally a total waste to ask whom she had called. At that moment, their lawyer probably had his foot glued to the metal as he raced to the apartment.

"Slap her in cuffs," the FBI agent ordered. "Time to get out of here."

As they were led out the doors on the ground floor, somebody had obviously alerted the press. They were there in force, it was 3:15 in the morning, and they were swapping jokes about the infamous Watergate, sipping coffee, playing with the klieg lights, waiting for the fun to begin.

It had been a slow, dry week for the news cycle—the Hollywood brats were behaving surprisingly well; plenty of murders, but none gruesome or weird enough to break the threshold of public monotony with such things; and of course Washington hosted its usual political scandals involving graft and sex, but nobody cared about that anymore. The boys from the Bureau publicity machine had gone into overdrive and kicked up huge interest in this fast-breaking story. The Runaway Millionaire, they had called Konevitch. The number one most wanted man in Russia. A beautiful celebrity couple, and better yet, the news bureaus were promised all kinds of inside leaks and dirt to fan the public interest and give the story long legs.

A blonde woman lingered at the rear of the crowd, gripping a big pistol under her jacket, silently cursing that there were so many witnesses. The hell with them all, Katya swore to herself. Her orders from Golitsin were clear and unequivocal: make their deaths look like an accident, or a robbery gone wrong, or a joint suicide pact by the obviously distressed couple. But in her long, fruitful career of killing and assassinating, no target had ever pushed her buttons this way. The humiliation of the escape from Budapest was bad enough. But the full year of misery in Chicago, and to learn now that it was all because Mr. Smartass inside that big building had outsmarted her, again. Oh, she was long past caring what Moscow wanted. If she saw any chance for a clean shot, she would take it—just blast away with her forefinger glued to the trigger. Just keep firing until the Konevitches had more holes than a doughnut shop, then flee into the night and hop the fastest transport headed to Mexico. She rather enjoyed the idea that it would all be caught on camera.

She would somehow acquire a copy of that tape. She intended to spend the rest of her life watching herself blow them both to hell.

Suddenly, the doors flew open. Tightly surrounded by the clutch of agents, Alex and Elena were led outside, then halted for a brief cameo. Cameras flashed, film rolled, and dozens of unanswered questions were flung at the INS and FBI people. Katya tried pushing herself through the mob, but the reporters were veterans at this game; with the brutal skill of NFL linemen they shoved and pummeled her backward till she landed on her ass.

Alex and Elena were pushed through the crowd then shoved into the backseat of a large blue sedan. An FBI spokesman stepped forward and began issuing a statement as terse as it was obviously rehearsed: "Mr. Alex Konevitch is wanted for serious crimes back in Russia. He and his wife embezzled hundreds of millions from innocent investors and fled here. They've been living like jet-setters in America, hiding in one of the most luxurious buildings in the city, hiding from the Russian authorities and pretending—"

The door slammed shut and Alex could hear no more.

Next, a fast trip to the INS building, where the suddenly notorious couple were swiftly photographed, fingerprinted, and processed into the INS system for deportation.

Alex was handed a pair of orange coveralls and allowed to step into the men's room for a quick change. When he emerged, Elena was gone. He was led back outside and stuffed into a van, shackled to a floor bolt, then sped quickly to the Alexandria jail, where he was shoved into a holding cell filled with other miserable men, a mixture of Hispanics, Chinese, Albanians, and sundry other violators of the apparently whimsical immigration system.

22

The guard rattled his keys and called for Prisoner Konevitch to step forward. Alex pushed through the crowd of disconsolate men and appeared at the door. He had not showered in three days. He had barely slept, quick catnaps frequently interrupted by another prisoner stumbling over him, or a fresh internee being jammed into the overcrowded cell. He looked tired and unshaven, his hair greasy and limp. He smelled of stale sweat and urine.

He stepped through the door and two guards shackled his hands and feet before he was led in a series of awkward shuffles to the visitor area.

MP Jones was seated at a table, briefcase in lap, frowning and clutching his hands together. "Alex, I'm sorry this took so long."

"Elena called you Friday night, MP. Don't tell me you're sorry, tell me what happened."

"Games. I called every number I know at INS. Nobody would tell me where they took you. You should be in a D.C. cell. That's where you're domiciled and where you were arrested. Instead, they moved you here, to Alexandria, to throw me off the scent. Was it bad?"

"It hasn't been pleasant. I don't care about me. Get Elena out of this."

MP wouldn't look him in the eyes. "That's going to be difficult."

"Why? Arrange bail. Murderers get out on bail. Our apartment is paid for. Use it as collateral and get her out."

"Don't think I haven't already tried, Alex. Remember all those reporters outside the Watergate? The Feds are turning you into a showcase. You were big news over the weekend, all those crime and legal channels on cable had a field day. You got creamed in the papers and TV." He held up a picture cut from a newspaper. It showed Alex and Elena being led from the Watergate, cuffed and looking guilty as hell. "Apparently, they want the Russian government to know they're playing hardball."

"They want me, MP. Elena has done nothing wrong."

"The answer's no, Alex. They claim you're a flight risk."

"They can let her go. They'll still have me in jail."

"Alex, you're not listening. They want her in jail, too."

Understanding what MP was saying came slowly, but it finally struck with full force. He tried to swallow the huge knot in his throat. It wouldn't go away. The U.S. government was using Elena as a hostage, as leverage to force him back to Russia. He prayed her conditions were better than his. He hoped she was in a private cell. His cell was filthy and so thoroughly overcrowded that the men took turns sleeping on the hard floor. They fought with one another for a turn at the toilet, trading insults in an array of languages that only contributed to the frustration. The room was cold and noisy: between the sounds of a toilet constantly flushing and the constant drone of fearful men sharing loud complaints, sleep was nearly impossible. The food was awful, microwaved garbage mixed together on a tin tray.

MP pushed on. "By law, they can hold you four days before a release can be applied for. I've demanded a hearing tomorrow. They can't say no."

"What am I charged with?"

"An expired visa."

"But you can easily prove that's false?"

"Of course. As long as everybody sticks to the truth, it should be easy."

"Get Elena out, MP. I don't care about me, I don't care what it takes, get her out."

"I'll do my best."

Yuri Khodorin's first hint of trouble was anything but subtle; five of his corporate executives ended up splayed out on tables in various morgues around the city. In less than three hours, five dead. An array of methods had been used, from shootings to stabbings to poisonings. The swath of killings spread from Moscow to St. Petersburg; it made it impossible to determine where the next strike might land, or, indeed, if there would be another.

On day two, this question was answered with an unmistakable bang. Six more dead. For sure, it was no longer an unlikely coincidence, or a sated spike of revenge, or spent anger: the killings weren't incidental. They were deliberate, and they weren't about to stop.

At thirty-three, already Russia's second richest man, Yuri Khodorin was perched within one good, profitable year of landing at number one. Like Alex, he had started young and early, even before the crash of communism opened the door to huge money. He sprinted out of the starting block and cobbled together an aggressive empire as wildly diversified as it was vast, profitable, and hungry. Central Enterprises, it was named, an innocuous title for a holding company that had a grip on everything from oil fields to TV stations, including myriad smaller businesses, from fast food through hotels, and almost too many other things to count. It created or swallowed new companies monthly and spewed out an almost ridiculous array of products and services.

A pair of Moscow police lieutenants appeared unannounced at Yuri's Moscow office the morning after the second set of killings—an odd pair, one an oversized butterball, the other thin as a rail. They unloaded the bad news that the Mafiya was kicking sand in his face. And no, sorry about that, no way could the city cops protect him; they were stretched so thin they could barely protect their own stationhouses. But in an effort to be helpful they generously left behind the business card of somebody who surely could.

Day four opened with three of Yuri's corporate offices fire-bombed; suspiciously, the local firefighters were dispatched to the wrong addresses, and all three buildings burned to the ground. Insurance would cover the losses, but droves of his terrified employees were threatening to stop showing up for work. At the sad end of day four—having once more been refused municipal protection—Yuri bounced his problems up to the next rung. He placed a desperate call to the attorney general, Anatoli Fyodorev, and pleaded loudly and desperately for help. Fyodorev made lots of sympathetic noises, and promised an abundance of assistance of all sorts. He was just disturbingly vague about what that meant.

The best Yuri could tell, it meant nothing. Not when day five opened with a car bomb in his headquarters parking lot that slaughtered three more employees.

Late that evening, reeling from the brutally rolling shocks, Yuri sat in his office alone, brooding and speculating about the future. At this rate, there would be no future. He had been shuttling around to funerals all day, trying his best to console sobbing widows and their crying little children. His mood was ugly. He wanted to be left alone, to stew with self-pity.

His secretary interrupted this bout of dark depression and informed him that a man was waiting in the lobby. "Doesn't he have a name?" Yuri barked. He refused to give one, she replied. "Send him away," Yuri said. Think twice, she insisted; he claimed he might know a few things about the murders plaguing their firm.

"Nobody else seems to," Yuri muttered. "All right, show him in."

The man entered and fell into the seat across from Yuri's desk. There were no handshakes, no empty attempts at pleasantries.

Mikhail studied Yuri for a moment. Dark cropped hair, rimless glasses, an efficient-looking type with a mass of excess energy he couldn't control. Constantly shifting in his seat, intermittently twisting the wedding band on a long, skinny finger.

This was Yuri's office, and he'd be damned if he was going to be outstared by anybody. He stared right back at Mikhail with a show of great intensity. The harder he stared, the less he learned—just a normal-sized, nameless male of about forty-eight years, with a hard, weathered face, dressed casually and nondescriptly.

After they stared at each other long enough, Mikhail broke the ice. "Alex Konevitch informed me that you and he were old buddies."

"We did a lot of business together, Alex and I. I miss him. Trying to keep up with him was a ball. He a friend of yours?"

"A good friend."

Yuri relaxed a little. "Where is Alex now?"

"America. Washington, D.C."

Yuri clapped his hands together in delight. "I knew it. All those theories about Brazil, or detox clinics, I always said they were bunk." Yuri's face turned grim. "Too bad he stole that money. Like I said, I miss him."

"That what you think happened, he ran with the money?" A year before this had been the most popular game in town—the Alex quiz. Where was the money? Where was Alex? How much did he steal?

"Sure, of course." A furious nod. "That's what the news said happened."

"Great tale, isn't it? What's your theory about it?"

"I'm a big fan of the 'he snapped' camp."

"Just freaked out, grabbed as much he could haul, and fled, huh?"

"Yeah, something like that. It probably makes more sense to me than it might to you. Tell the truth, I sometimes dream of doing the same thing."

"Having all that money isn't fun, huh?"

"Twenty-hour days, thousands of people who depend on you, constant crises where everything's on the verge of crashing down on your head. Oh sure, it's a blast." A brief pause, accompanied by a few more hard twists on the wedding band. "Now, who are you, and what do you want?"

"Mikhail Borosky. I did a lot of private investigation work for Alex. Still do."

"And what? Alex asked you to drop by?"

"Yes." Mikhail stretched his legs out and leaned back in the chair. "Alex asked me to keep my eye on the news. See who's next. Apparently, you're the guy."

A slight flinch. "Next? What does that mean?"

"It means you're at stage one of the same treatment Alex got. For some reason, you're getting it a bit rougher than he got. And they're a lot sloppier. I'm not sure why. Guess they're a little over-confident this time."

"I have no idea what you're talking about."

"Did you receive a visit from two of Moscow's finest?" From his tone, Mikhail already seemed to know the answer.

"Yes."

"A blimp and a beanpole, right?" It wasn't really a question. From a parking lot across the street, Mikhail had watched the pair enter the headquarters the day before yesterday.

A slow nod.

"They give you a business card recommending somebody who could put a stop to all this?"

Yuri tried to hide his surprise but found it impossible. This strange man knew so much. The card in question, in fact, sat on Yuri's blotter, in easy reach of his fingers. Only three minutes before, he had been within seconds of dialing the number and pleading for help.

Yuri shoved the card across the table. Mikhail bent forward and studied it a moment. The name on the card was unrecognizable and meant nothing. But the name didn't matter. If he bothered to check, which he had no intention of doing, the résumé would reveal a long career in the KGB and some kind of deep attachment or connection to Sergei Golitsin.

"You know the old story about the Trojan horse?" Mikhail asked, pushing the card back in Yuri's direction.

A careful nod. "Sure, who doesn't?"

Mikhail directed a finger at the business card. "There's your

Trojan horse. Those two cops are crooked to the core. They were sent in to kick open the door. Once you call that number, the worm will find a way to let the barbarians inside your company."

"This is what they did to Alex?"

A knowing nod, and for the next twenty minutes Mikhail revealed everything that happened to Alex, how the scheme worked, the kidnap, the torture, being framed for the theft of everything he owned. The whole ugly tale. To verify his story, he passed Yuri morgue forms that confirmed the death of Alex's employees, as well as one of the statements prepared a year before by Alex that he had faxed to all the senior officials around Yeltsin.

Mikhail sat back and allowed Yuri time to read the evidence, to see the similarities, and to realize that he was indeed the newest target.

Long before he finished, Yuri looked sad, confused, and scared out of his wits. He gripped his hands together and studied his blotter for a long moment. "So what do I do now?"

"I think you got two options. One, take as much money as you can, and run."

After everything this man had just told him, option one sounded impossibly irresistible. Screw option two. He had millions stored in a Swiss vault, a hoard of cash large enough to live happily ever after. A fraction of his current fortune of course, but he'd at least be alive to spend it. His private jet was tucked in a private hangar at the airport, fueled up and ready to go. He could have breakfast at his spacious London flat, or lunch at his favorite Azores resort. That indecision lasted seconds. The British have always been so very civil and accommodating to wealthy Russian exiles who drop by for breakfast, and asylum.

Mikhail allowed him a moment to bask in this hopeful reprieve before he warned, "Course, that option's not quite as clean as it sounds."

"Why's that?"

"They're still trying to murder Alex. They've got teams of killers hanging in his shadows. Also, they've somehow fooled the American FBI into shipping him back here. He's long past the point where he can do anything to them. They don't care. They still want him dead."

"What's option two?" Yuri asked very quickly, very solemnly.

"Fight them."

"Don't be silly. I'm a businessman. I don't know what I'm up against, or even who these people are."

Mikhail stood and began pacing in front of the desk. "That's why I'm here. I do know who they are. And every time they meet, wherever they go, I learn more. They're very powerful, very dangerous people. And they're very, very corrupt. It's a large conspiracy with lots of money that gets bigger by the month."

"Is this supposed to be encouraging?"

"If you're listening carefully, yes. That size now works against them. And, as I mentioned, after Alex, they've become overconfident and incredibly sloppy. Understand that this thing works only when they have complete surprise. They have to be in the shadows, totally anonymous."

"So what am I supposed to do?"

"For starters, forget the name on that card. I'll leave you the number of a former police captain. He's competent, tough as nails, a born street fighter. Call him first thing in the morning, pay him whatever he asks, and don't anticipate overnight results. Expect a few more killings and bombings. Over time he'll find a way to protect you and your people. If he needs money, write the check without questions. It's not just a matter of a few more guards and extra precautions. Alex tried that, and look where it got him. He's going to have to bribe people, and he'll probably need to buy you a little help from a competing syndicate. He's going to fight fire with fire."

"What are you going to do?"

"Stay in the shadows. Keep my eye on them. Eventually, I might come to you for money. It might be expensive, but I promise it'll be the best money you ever spent."

"So you expect me to just stay tough."

"Way I see it, you can stay tough or get dead."

23

Tuesday, at 9:00 a.m., Alex was again called out of the cell and led to the booking area. Elena was already there—like him, she now was dressed in oversized orange coveralls. Chains ran around her leg irons, looped around her waist, and were connected to her hand-cuffs. This was so ridiculous, Alex thought; no, on second thought, not ridiculous, it was outrageous. She was being treated like a serial murderer when all she was accused of was an expired visa.

The guards set to work on him next. Within two minutes he and Elena stood side by side, in ugly orange suits and matching chains.

They were led outside and helped into the back of a long, windowless van. The chains were locked down to bolts on the floor before the guards left and shut the rear door.

It was their first chance to speak since Friday night. "I'm so sorry," Alex told her.

"Don't be silly. You've done nothing wrong."

He tried to rub his eyes but the chains wouldn't reach and forced him to bend over. Elena asked, "Are you all right?"

"I'm fine."

"Don't worry, Alex. They can't ship us home over this," Elena said trying to sound confident.

"I think they can do whatever they want." They wouldn't have long to speak, and Alex was avoiding her eyes, trying desperately to build up his nerve. He had spent the whole weekend considering this conversation. Rehearsing it. Playing with variations on the same theme.

There were no other alternatives, and he finally blurted it out. "Elena, I want a divorce."

She considered this a joke and laughed.

"I'm serious. We're getting a divorce."

"Forget it."

"I intend to ask MP to find a good lawyer to arrange it. Uncontested, it should sail through quickly. Don't fight me on this. My mind's made up."

"Alex, this is so stupid."

"I said don't fight me on this, Elena. They're using you to get to me. The moment we're divorced they'll forget about you."

"Did you meet somebody in lockup? Another man? I know how good you look in orange coveralls. I won't be thrown away for some weekend fling." She was laughing again.

"Damn it, I—"

"Shut up, Alex. Just shut up." She leaned back and closed her eyes. The van was moving. They bounced along in tense silence for a few interminable moments.

With her eyes still shut, Elena said, "We'll never have this conversation again. I mean it. I love you, and if you ever bring up the 'divorce' word again, I'll kill you. We're going to suffer through this together. I don't care what happens as long as we're together. Nod your head if you understand, or should I just kill you now?"

Alex bent forward and refused to look at her. The silence dragged on.

Alex eventually said, "You look good in orange, too."

"Check out my new jewelry." She rattled her chains, then bent over and they shared a kiss. Bad jokes, but neither was in the state to think up good ones.

After a moment, Alex said, "I think there's a chance you might get out on bail."

"Me? What about you?"

"MP's not hopeful. Neither am I. Jail might even be the best place for me right now. Did you recognize anybody in the crowd of reporters the other night?"

"From Budapest, that blonde she-bitch."

They probably had only a few minutes left. There was a lot Alex wanted to discuss and he began speaking quickly. "You'll have to go underground. And you'll have to sell our apartment," he told her. "I know you love it, and I'm sorry. But you'll need the money to survive."

"I hate that apartment. I'll be happy to unload it. After four days in a small, cramped cell, I suddenly love the idea of wide-open space."

"Set a low price and dump it quickly. Then find a cheap rental, one you can get out of quickly. You'll need all the money you can get your hands on. My legal costs are probably going to be enormous."

"What about Orangutan? No longer an option?"

"It's history. But I've got a new idea. Probably even better than Orangutan Media, something I've been toying with for a while."

The van was beginning to slow down. In a fast rush of words, Alex shared the rough details of his idea. Elena nodded. She would have to learn a lot quickly. The concept was great, though. It would mint money, if she could pull it off.

The van wheeled into an underground garage beneath the INS building. Alex and Elena were separated, taken upstairs in different elevators, then deposited in different cells and left alone to stew with worry.

Thirty minutes later, a guard arrived, unlocked the cell, and escorted Alex down several long, well-lit corridors to a small courtroom. Elena was already there, seated at a table beside MP. Their lawyer had his back turned to Elena and was engaging in a conversation with an attractive, older, dark-featured female seated at what Alex presumed was the prosecution table. A considerably younger male colleague in a dark suit sat to her right, looking nervous and out of place.

Alex sat beside MP, who quickly bent around him and said to the prosecutor, "Kim Parrish, I'd like you to meet my client, Alex Konevitch."

Alex held out his hand and looked her dead in the eye. "It's nice to meet you."

The room was small. They were about three feet apart. She nodded but took a step back, said nothing, and studiously avoided his hand. Go ahead, MP was thinking from the sideline—take a nice long look at the man you're about to persecute. You'll be responsible when he lands in a coffin. He's young and handsome, and his wife is young and beautiful—they have so much to live for—but go ahead, ignore your conscience. Get them killed.

She understood exactly what MP was doing. A long awkward moment, then she suddenly buried her nose in the blank legal pad on her table.

A moment later, the judge entered through a side door. There was none of the procedural rigmarole Alex had observed on American TV. No announcement, no standing. No long perorations or lawyers being introduced. Apparently, immigration cases adhered to a less formal pattern.

Judge John Everston IV presided. He spent a brief moment surveying his court to be sure everything was the way he liked it.

Alex's and Elena's eyes were glued to the face of the man who held their lives in his hands. He was neither handsome, impressive-looking, nor even mildly judicial-looking, with a long, droopy face, thick, arched eyebrows that lent an impression of severe fierceness, scarecrow gray hair, and small eyes hidden behind bifocals that seemed impossibly thick and bleary.

John Everston had started out as an immigration attorney thirty years before, a fine, precise, hardworking lawyer whose service was eventually rewarded with a judgeship. His lawyer career had been spent in the prosecution trenches. He came from a long line of deeply rooted, well-heeled southern Virginia aristocrats. And though everybody assumed otherwise, banishing immigrants had been a job he utterly loathed, and nearly always was ashamed to perform. He carefully hid a soft spot for the miserable masses who flocked to America for a thousand different reasons and suddenly found themselves at risk of being booted out. Left alone, they generally turned into perfectly respectable citizens. The law had forced him to separate families, to dispatch honest, hardworking people back to a life of hopeless squalor, and occasionally to send them back to conditions that meant certain death. Thirty years of practicing law on both sides of the bench had converted him from a mild liberal to a fairly rabid one.

And like every liberal judge in the country—in his opinion, like any judge with half a brain—Judge Everston detested John Tromble and he loathed the attorney general for failing to reel him in.

His eyes took in the court recorder, the bailiff at his station along the wall, the attorneys at their appropriate tables, and the young husband and wife huddled miserably in their atrocious orange prison apparel. He finally settled on a small group tucked in the back of the small visitors' section—a pair of bespoke gentlemen in nice suits and a young lady dressed decidedly more flippantly in ragged jeans, a torn T-shirt, and plastic flip-flops.

The judge directed a long finger in their direction. "It's not often I get visitors in this courtroom. When I do, I always like to make your acquaintance. You look like a reporter," he suggested to the young lady; from the way she was attired, she could be nothing but. Jeans and a ripped T-shirt—he had threatened lawyers with contempt just for wearing distasteful ties.

Sally, the court recorder, and Harry, the bailiff, exchanged curious glances. The judge had never, ever before even acknowledged visitors on the few rare occasions any showed up. Now he was actually conversing with them.

"I am," the lady answered promptly and proudly.

"What paper do you represent?"

"*New York Times.*"

He would've publicly laid into her about her indecorum, but the *Times* was so reliably and frantically liberal, she could wear a birthday suit for all he cared.

"Good for you," he pronounced. The judge's gaze slowly shifted to her left. "And you two gentlemen?" he asked, directing a bony finger at the men.

"FBI," the older one said, sort of shuffling his feet at the unexpected attention.

The judge's head reared back. He squinted through his thick glasses and peered down his long, skinny nose. "And to what do I owe the rare pleasure of a few of Mr. Tromble's boys in my court?"

"We're just . . . merely observing," he replied.

"Observing what?"

"It's . . ." The agent blinked a few times. He had a law degree, though admittedly, he had sailed straight into the Bureau after law school. Aside from a few occasions on a witness stand, he had never actually been forced to address a sitting judge. He took another stab, saying, "We, that is, the Bureau, has an interest in the status of this case, Your Honor."

"An interest. I see. And what interest would that be, Agent, uh . . . ?"

"Special Agent Wilson. It, uh, well—"

"Speak up, Agent Wilson. This is a small court, and I'd like very much to hear your replies. I'm actually dying to hear your reply. In ten years on this bench, I don't believe I've ever entertained visitors from your Bureau. This is a small, unimportant court, and the proceedings are normally quite tedious. I'm on the edge of my seat to learn what's so special about today."

It was becoming increasingly apparent that the judge was not overjoyed with their presence. Every eye in the small court was on Wilson. He desperately wanted to crawl under his seat.

"Your Honor, the accused is wanted for certain crimes in Russia, crimes that are under our scrutiny."

The long finger popped back up like a pistol. "In this court, he's not the accused, Agent Wilson. This is not a criminal trial and I don't want you to prejudice my judicial neutrality through any misleading impressions. In here, he's simply a man who may or may not have overstayed his visa."

"Yes, I under—"

"Does he have a criminal record in this country?"

"Uh . . . no." A brief pause. "Not that we've yet discovered anyway," Wilson said, implying otherwise, and visibly proud that he was recovering nicely.

"I see. Well, it is not my jurisprudence or interest to try crimes that might or might not have been committed on foreign soil. Unless I misunderstand the law, I believe the well-known prurience of your Bureau also ends at the water's edge. Surely an agent of your distinguished agency might understand that," he announced, looking far down his nose.

"What I meant—"

"I really don't care what you meant. I care only about what you say. Precise legal terminology is important. Surely they taught you something about that in that FBI school all you boys go through."

Wilson was silently cursing Hanrahan for making him be here.

The judge waved a thick folder in the air. "I took the opportunity to review this case file. All your statements are in here, seven INS agents and yours, Agent Wilson. Eight of you, altogether. Eight! Eight of you involved in arresting this young, frightened couple. They look harmless enough. And, as I understand it, the charge for my consideration deals with nothing more serious than expired visas. Am I missing something here? Please tell me I am, Agent Wilson. Have they smuggled in one of those suitcase nuclear bombs? Committed mass murder or run one of those odious rape camps in Bosnia? Surely, they have. Please assure me I'm missing something here."

No, you're not missing a thing, Wilson thought, now visibly miserable. Not a damn thing, you mean old goat. His back was rigid. He could barely force himself to keep his eyes on this judge. He had faced down Mafia thugs, kidnappers, dope pushers, and never blinked. He was plainly terrified of this judge.

"I am only here because I was ordered to attend, Your Honor."

"And who gave you this order?"

"I'd rather not say."

"You'd rather not?"

"That's right, Your Honor."

His Honor rested his elbows on the bench and placed his sharp chin in his hands. "Is this some pressing matter of national security?"

"Yes."

"Yes?" His small eyes bored into Wilson like rockets.

"Uh, no."

"Precision, Agent Wilson. Which is it, yes or no?"

"It's not. Uh, no."

"I see." His Honor toyed with his pen a moment. Wilson was examining the door. His legs were tensed, ready to bolt. It was barely ten feet away. He was almost certain he could be outside, sprinting to his car, before the judge could fire off another question.

His Honor slipped off his glasses and leaned far forward. "Let me make this clear, Agent Wilson. Listen closely and pass this on to those whose names cannot be uttered in this court. The freedom and dignity of two human beings are at stake here. They are guests in our land, so the reputation of our great nation is at stake. If I find any hint of remotely unethical behavior, I'll make you wish you never heard of Mr. and Mrs. Konevitch. I watched the news reports over the weekend, and frankly, I am dismayed and alarmed. I seriously hope nobody in this court was attempting to humiliate or pressure these poor people. Are we clear on this?"

"Yes, Your Honor."

"I mean it." The public whipping was over. Wilson looked thoroughly whipped. His Honor redirected his eyes toward MP. "Mr. Jones, you may begin now."

The sound of Wilson's sigh of relief echoed throughout the room.

Without rising or missing a beat, MP said, "Thank you, Your Honor. I'm sorry we're wasting your time this morning over such a trivial, ridiculous matter. The issue is whether or not my clients overstayed their visas." MP slapped his right hand with a theatrical thump on a pile of documents on the defense table. "I have here all the requisite forms proving they have valid visa status. Also documentation proving they applied for and were unanimously approved for permanent residency in the United States. I'd like to get this charge dismissed immediately so my clients can go on with their lives."

Kim Parrish suddenly bounced to her feet. "Your Honor, we've changed the charges."

His Honor stared at the ceiling a moment. Speaking in a generally upward direction, he said, "Miss Parrish, you heard what I just advised Agent Wilson?"

"Every word."

"You understand that this applies to you also?"

"It left little question in my mind."

"Then proceed. Carefully, Miss Parish."

"Thank you. In fact, we have now established that the Konevitches do possess entirely valid visas."

"I would have thought this rather simple fact could've been established before their arrests."

"As would I, sir." She frowned contemptuously at the younger colleague at her table, as if he was at fault for this stupid blunder. His role in this farce was apparently to take the blame, and he obediently shrank and cowered under the force of her fierce glare. She continued, "Regrettably, paperwork was misplaced. A simple administrative mistake. We were unable to confirm this fact until yesterday."

"And did you notify Mr. Jones, who is, after all, representing these people?"

MP decided this was a perfectly good moment to help her out with this difficult question. "No, this is the first I've heard of it. I'm caught between shock and surprise. As Miss Parrish is no doubt aware, I'm prepared only to contest the charges I've been made aware of." MP looked so sad and disgusted it was impossible not to feel an ocean of pity for him.

"What do you have to say to that, Miss Parrish?"

"I tried to reach Mr. Jones."

"Did you?"

"Yes."

"How?"

"Phone."

"Once? Twice? How often?"

"I made multiple good-faith efforts. I can't recall the precise number. Unfortunately, there was no answer at his office."

"Do you have an answering machine, Mr. Jones?"

"Yes."

"Is it left on after office hours?"

"Yes. Always."

"Miss Parrish?"

"Maybe I dialed the wrong number."

"I'm sure that explains it."

Now that it was firmly established that she was lying, she pressed on. "We're now charging the Konevitches with immigration fraud."

"Is this charge likely to change in the next few minutes?" MP asked, looking at the judge.

"It will not." She was getting creamed, and like a good lawyer, taking it in cool stride.

Alex was almost lost. English wasn't his native tongue, and the parries and thrusts shot around the small courtroom like lightning bolts. The questions and replies came without time to breathe or think. Not a word was wasted, no "uhs," no hesitations. Three first-rate legal minds were playing hardball with each other, with his life at stake.

The judge removed his glasses and rubbed his eyes. "As this is the first this court has heard of this new charge, can you honor us with a little more specificity?"

"Mr. Konevitch was heavily involved in criminal activity in Russia before he fled and came to America. He presented himself to the Immigration Service as a victim of political persecution. He deliberately constructed false facts to verify this status. Further, he claimed permanent employment with a company that has subsequently been discovered to be a fraud. It is, in fact, a front for criminal activities, including money laundering. Given those unlawful actions, we recommend that Mr. and Mrs. Konevitch be immediately deported back to Russia."

"Mr. Jones?"

"I'm not at all prepared to contest these absurd charges. They're obviously preposterous, and will be easily debunked."

"When will you be ready?"

"Two weeks, at a minimum."

"Then we'll reconvene in two weeks."

Like that, it was over. His Honor started to rise, before MP interrupted his progress. "I have another matter for your advisement, Your Honor."

His Honor sank back into his chair.

"My clients should be released on bond immediately. The charges that led to their arrest have already been disproved and disposed. They should not have to suffer a lack of freedom over what my colleague Miss Parrish has already confessed was gross negligence on the part of her department."

"Miss Parrish?"

"I did not state it was gross negligence. That's an outrageous distortion of what I said."

"Remind me. What did you say?"

"Simple bureaucratic oversight. Nearly two million immigrants a year enter our porous borders, legally or otherwise. As hard as our people work, well"—she stared down at her hapless associate again—"occasionally a few pieces of paper get misplaced in the shuffle."

The elbows landed on the bench again. "Miss Parrish, I admire your noble efforts to defend the reputation of your service. I surely do."

"Thank you, Your Honor."

"It is admirable and it definitely touches my heart. However, I spent fifteen long years in your shoes. So don't you ever utter such outlandish baloney in this court again. It was, unmistakably, gross negligence. The INS is overworked and severely understaffed, but that in no way excuses or ameliorates what happened here today. Now, what's your response to bond for these people?"

She never blinked. "We strongly advise that it be denied, Your Honor."

"Grounds?"

"According to the Russian attorney general, Mr. Konevitch embezzled many millions of dollars from the investors in his bank. He also fled with millions more that he stole from the Russian mob. He fled from there, and he will certainly flee from here. He is, by any stretch, a definite flight risk."

"Mr. Jones?"

MP paused and stared down at his legal pad for a long moment. Alex didn't have a prayer. MP knew this. Further, he knew better than to irritate the judge and risk losing his obvious sympathy by arguing otherwise. Alex seemed to understand this as well. He was vigorously nodding his head in Elena's direction.

"Mr. Jones?" the judge repeated, taking his tone up a notch.

"Those issues will be addressed in two weeks. Mrs. Konevitch, though, has been accused of nothing."

His Honor was tired of talking. He simply shifted his stare to Kim Parrish.

"The government," she replied, "would strongly prefer that she remain in custody as well."

"I do not react to preferences, Miss Parrish. You had better offer substantiation for denial."

"She's a flight risk as well."

"With her husband in jail?"

"Maybe."

"You need to do better than that, Miss Parrish."

"She was party to his falsehoods. She testified at his hearings, confirmed his lies, and served as his able co-conspirator."

His Honor bent far forward and peered down at his court reporter, who also happened to double as his appointments secretary. "Sally, what did I do last Sunday?"

"You played golf, Your Honor."

"I did?"

"Of course. You had your usual ten a.m. tee time at Washington Golf and Country."

"And were you to ask Mrs. Everston where I was, what do you think she'd say, Sally?"

Sally produced a shy smile and blushed nicely. "She'd say you were at your county school board meeting."

"Am I on the school board, Sally?"

"No, Your Honor. Not for about five years now. It's the same tired old alibi you give her every other Sunday."

He redirected his gaze to Kim Parrish. "Mrs. Everston and I have been married thirty-two years now. You'd think she'd be on to me by now, wouldn't you?"

"I have no idea. I'm not married."

"Then allow me to offer a little wisdom from the trenches. The state of matrimony, Miss Parrish, does not confer infinite or absolute knowledge of spousal activities. Believe it or not, lots of married people cheat on each other, hide money from each other, and, in cases, even have additional wives and husbands. So as much as you might wish it, the laws of this land do not yet assign mutual guilt on married couples. I am not responsible for the horrible quilts my wife knits and afflicts on our poor children every Christmas. She is certainly not responsible for the three times Sunday that I regrettably shifted the lay of my golf ball and thereby cheated my partners into buying my lunch."

"Moving a golf ball and stealing millions are wildly different offenses. I don't agree with your analogies, Your Honor."

"You don't?"

"Absolutely not."

"Bond will be set at $5,000."

"I protest, Your Honor."

"Of course you do."

Before Alex was led away, Elena squeezed his hand, but did not say, "I love you."

Instead she said, "Interactive Internet video?"

"Exactly. And call Mikhail for an update," he whispered before he was tugged away.

24

The destroyed remnants of a long working lunch were strewn around the table. The mess would be picked up by the secretaries shortly after the meeting ended. Laura Tingleman presided from the end of the long shiny table.

The chief lieutenants of the Justice Department were gathered on this Friday morning, as they were every Friday morning, for what had come to be known as the "Weekly Roundup," named in honor of her background as a Montanan. A city girl through and through, Laura Tingleman could barely tell the back end of a cow from the front.

The chief of the Civil Rights Division was just winding up a long, complicated report about the status of a suit brought by an Indian tribe nobody in the room had ever heard of. The tribe demanded the right to sue the shorts off anybody who used the name "Indian," or any variation thereof, or any reference thereto, or any image thereabout, in their product, team, school, or institution, or whatever.

The case had bounced around various lower courts for over a decade. A victory here. A successful appeal there and now it was on the verge of ascending to consideration by the Supreme Court. No fewer than ten civil rights lawyers had been involved full-time, dodging around the country every time the case changed jurisdiction. The tribe in question was quite small, comprising a husband and wife, a weird migratory couple who claimed they were pursuing the nomadic tradition of their forebears and could not be pinned down for any length of time. They claimed to be following buffalo herds, or locusts, or even slight changes in wind direction. Every move incited a new excuse. Coincidentally, their geographic shifts occurred every time they lost an appeal and needed to bounce the case to a different, more radically liberal venue; they staunchly insisted that their ancient native rights took precedence over the newly created White Man Rule, and some harebrained judge somewhere had ruled in their favor. They won legal permission for unlimited changes of venue along with infinite reasons for appeal.

The couple had once been named Antonelli, before they had it legally changed to Chief and Mrs. Stare at My Moon. They happened to be graduates of Yale Law.

The head of the Civil Rights Division and the solicitor general squabbled back and forth. Civil Rights wanted to hand this hot potato to the solicitor general on the grounds that it was within spitting distance of the Supreme Court. The Court had yet to determine whether this case belonged on their docket, the solicitor general shot back, with his loquacious lips pursed. Yes, but the head of Civil Rights wanted his ten lawyers sprung. Also if the couple won, they would go on a legal rampage, suing for billions from schools and companies that apparently were brutally insensitive to the terrible slights they were inflicting on Indians. The costs would be huge, the backlash staggering.

Unfortunately, the White House was putting unbearable pressure on the department to roll over. The president felt the pain of what had happened to American Indians and he wanted to make amends for three hundred years of atrocities, for white men sharing their awful diseases, for stealing Indian land, for decimating the proud tribes. More succinctly, he wanted their votes.

It was a definite no-win situation.

As usual, Laura Tingleman deferred the decision for later—later being when it somehow resolved itself without her fingerprints.

Time to bounce to the next issue, and Laura's chief of staff held up an article clipped, a few days earlier, from the *New York Times*. Said article concerned a Russian couple being prosecuted for immigration violations. Predictably for the *Times*, the article was slanted and not overly complimentary to the government's case. The word "railroad" was thrown around a few times by the defense attorney, who had been given suspiciously generous play by the *Times* reporter.

"Does anybody know what this is about?" Laura asked, searching the faces around the table.

Tromble bent forward. "I do, and so should you."

"I should?"

"Sure. From our Moscow trip, remember? This couple ripped off hundreds of millions and are hiding here. We specifically agreed we would return them to Russia for trial."

"I might have a vague recollection about it," Laura allowed. So much business passed through her office, she could barely keep it all straight.

"You were a little tired," Tromble allowed back. "You gave your word to the Russian attorney general. I'm just following through."

"How did it make the papers?" she asked.

Fortunately, Tromble had the answer. "The usual games, nothing to become concerned over. The defense attorney has no case. He knows it, too. He's trying to spin up the media and build sympathy. He and the *Times* reporter went to college together. She did him a big favor."

Nobody asked how he knew this. He wouldn't have told them if they had. If the Russians could tap and wire the lawyer's office, it was clearly a national security imperative for Tromble to have a few taps of his own. It was only fair to know what the Russians knew.

"Do we have a solid case?" Laura's chief of staff asked.

"It's in the hands of INS," he fibbed, smoothly and persuasively. "We're providing assistance from the side; only when they ask, though. Believe me, it's waterproof."

"How can you be so sure?" the aide countered. Every eye in the room swiveled to Tromble. How indeed?

Though the Justice Department was purportedly above the fray of politics, this was a liberal administration, and the White House had packed the senior appointed ranks with legions of die-hard, woolly-headed lefties. Tromble was the exception, the lone, fierce duck out of water. The others in the room detested him, and secretly, on a more ambivalent note, nearly all were convinced he was the right man for the right job—a tireless, efficient, ruthless hatchetman who ran his besuited stormtroopers hard. Behind his cover they could spout all the tree-hugging, abortion-loving, big government nonsense they wanted. In the first two years of his incumbency, national crime rates had plummeted a historic nine percent.

A Nazi he might be, but at least he was *their* Nazi.

"This guy Konevitch," Tromble explained with an air of authority, "was worth hundreds of millions before he fled. Nobody with clean hands makes that kind of money over there. Nobody. He's definitely a crook."

Heads nodding all around. Though few of them had ever set foot in Russia, the roomful of news junkies was well aware of Russia's sad descent into crooked madness. The rampant shootings in Moscow streets. The swift rise of the Mafiya. Vast fortunes being made by a handful of conniving thieves—a kleptocracy, Russia was now being called, and with good reason. Naturally this Konevitch man had to be crooked.

"He's the number one most wanted criminal in Russia. It's Russia, so that's saying something," he continued to the nodding heads. "There is no chance he is innocent. And from what we've learned from our Russian friends, he's already got a foothold here."

Laura was only too happy it was something so simple and straightforward for a change. She asked, "What help can I provide?"

One of her many legal advisors—a she, it happened—scraped forward in her chair, gazing suspiciously down the long table at Tromble. After carefully reading the article, she wasn't sure this was such a slam dunk. "We lack an extradition treaty with the Russians," she announced.

"So what's the best way to proceed?" her boss asked.

"Essentially, we have to prove the merits of Russia's case before an American judge," the aide answered.

"How hard is that?"

"It's been done before. Not with Russia inside this country, but we often use this strategy ourselves. In Colombia, for example, when we want a drug lord renditioned to our courts. We dispatch a legal team there, do a little show-and-tell before a Colombian judge, then they transfer custody to us."

"So we need a team of Russian prosecutors?"

"Pretty much. Assuming they have a good case, they display their evidence to our INS attorneys, and our people handle the heavy lifting in the courts. This takes time, though."

"How much time?"

"Sometimes years. Varies by case."

Tromble stared down the table at this busybody pushing her nose into his business. "The case will be heard again in one week. Konevitch doesn't have a leg to stand on."

"What if you're wrong?" his boss's legal aide asked, not backing down.

"No reasonable judge will decide against us."

"All right, consider an unreasonable one."

"Fine. If you insist, I'll call Russia and get a team over here right away," he conceded. The concession was of course entirely meaningless. He had not the slightest doubt that the Konevitches would land in Moscow long before a Russian team landed in D.C.

The meeting broke up with the solicitor general and head of Civil Rights in a corner, trading insults, and nearly fists, over Chief and Mrs. Stare at My Moon.

Tatyana was heavily preoccupied when her phone started ringing off the hook. She tried to ignore it, but eventually stopped what she was doing, rolled over, and put it to her ear. "What? Who is this," she snapped in Russian.

"Please hold for the director of the Federal Bureau of Investigation," a female voice stiffly instructed her in English.

The voice of John Tromble popped on a moment later. "Hello, Tatyana. Heard the news about your boy Konevitch? Made a big splash in the news on this side of the water."

"How did you get my home number?" she asked, unable to disguise her irritation.

"When I couldn't get you at the office, my boys in the embassy tracked it down."

"All right. Yes, I see that you've got him in jail. Why haven't you just shipped him here?"

"It's complicated. Not as easy as I thought. Listen, I need a big favor."

He explained what he needed, a team of Russian prosecutors, and Tatyana listened. Eventually, she replied, "Is this absolutely necessary?"

"Probably not. He goes back to court in a week. No way in hell he won't be deported. But the judge might act crazily. Call it a precaution, insurance."

"It will take time to get the case together."

"How much time?"

"A month or two, probably. Maybe a little longer."

"I thought you folks were already prepared to fry him in your courts. What's the problem?"

"John, please. The case is ready for Russian courts, not yours. Your rules of evidence are different, and we'll have to tailor it accordingly. There are also certain pieces of evidence we would find it embarrassing or troublesome to show foreigners. Dirty laundry we really don't want to showcase at a time when we're trying to attract foreign investment. Those problems will have to be cleaned up."

"Okay, yeah. I understand that."

"You can keep him in jail, can't you? A lot of powerful people here are opposed to letting you keep the FBI outpost in your embassy. I'm doing my best, but, John, it's a real uphill battle. Such a clear lack of mutual cooperation won't go over well."

Tromble started to say something, but she cut him off. "President Yeltsin asked me about this case just yesterday," she lied. "He keeps asking if he needs to discuss it with your president."

"Hey, we'll find a way. I don't care if I have to bribe the judge or kill his wife. I'll find a way."

"Whatever it takes, John, whatever it takes. I'll put together a team of prosecutors and get them over there as soon as possible."

They rung off. Tatyana stretched, then rolled over, back into the muscular arms of Sasha Komenov, her boytoy soccer star. He drew away. "Who was it?" he asked in a petulant mood. He didn't speak English and understood not a word.

"Just some idiot law enforcement administrator from America."

"Oh, you're screwing him, too?" Sasha snapped. Lately, he was turning a little sulky about Tatyana and her extracurricular sleeping habits. It had never bothered him before, but after discovering a gray hair a few weeks before, he found himself suddenly torn with possessive urges.

"You're cute when you're mad. Come on and screw me now." She laughed.

Sasha crossed his arms and pouted. "Don't joke. I'm tired of sharing you."

"You're a fool. You've seen my boss. He's bald and fat and not the least bit interesting. He's so terrible in bed I have to pinch myself just to stay awake. He's so disgusting, I become nauseated afterward. I'm only doing this for us, Sasha."

"You've been saying that for years."

"And it's true. Listen, we're moving in on a huge fortune right now. Billions, Sasha, billions. My cut will be hundreds of millions, and as soon as I have it, I'll dump that old moron and quit my job. You and I will buy a big yacht and sail around the world. We'll never be able to spend it all. We'll die rich and happy."

The recorder in the basement whirred and caught every word.

The limo had been cruising around Moscow for an hour. It wandered aimlessly, in no particular direction, eating up pavement until the meeting in the back was finished. After picking up Sergei Golitsin at his big brick mansion, it had sped crosstown, straight to the comparatively smaller home of Anatoli Fyodorev, Russia's attorney general. He climbed inside and off it sped.

The tracking device on the undercarriage made it too easy to trail. After an hour it pulled back up to the curb in front of Fyodorev's home. Out stepped the attorney general, stretching and straightening his suit. And then Golitsin's big head peeked out. The old man said something, they both laughed. He handed Fyodorev a thick envelope. Right there, on the curb, the idiot actually opened it so he could count the cash.

Click, click, went Mikhail's trusty camera.

25

Court reconvened at ten o'clock in the morning on the second. Elena had driven herself and parked in the underground INS garage. She was dressed not in orange but in a modest dark blue frock that complemented her beauty, her blonde hair, her slim figure. She sat directly behind Alex, who was in his usual orange jumpsuit. They exchanged quiet whispers and handwritten notes while they waited for the festivities to begin. Alex had been permitted to shower and shave this time—though only after MP threatened his jailers with a noisy lawsuit for deprivation of dignity.

Kim Parrish sat at her table with the same youthful assistant perched anxiously to her right. Piles of paper along with several large boxes were stacked off to the side.

MP had offered her a warm, friendly greeting when they entered. She met it with stony indifference. She was openly furious with him over that nasty, rotten, one-sided *Times* article— earlier in the week, Agent Wilson had confided to her how MP had called in a favor from the *Times* reporter and arranged her public thrashing. She could barely stand to be in the same room with him.

As before, Judge John Everston entered punctually through a side door, hustling along, anxious to begin. He studied his court again. No reporters this time. None of Tromble's punks, either, he noted with satisfaction—nobody but a plump, middle-aged, long-haired fellow in the visitors' section who was sipping noisily through a straw stuck in a Diet Coke.

"Who are you, sir?" His Honor asked.

"An author," the man replied in an almost indifferent manner. "I'm halfway into a legal thriller that involves a few immigration matters. Saw this case mentioned in the *Times*. Thought I'd pop in and pick up a little authentic juice."

The man looked seedy, wildly disorganized, and poorly groomed. His threadbare blue blazer bore long streaks of mustard stain, and he was vigorously scratching his fanny. Sure looked like a writer.

When the judge did not throw him out, the man quickly settled his ample rear back into his seat. He dug a notebook out of a side pocket and loudly flicked his pen open. On the frames of his glasses were two miniature cameras. Tucked in his breast pocket, a highly sensitive microphone was capturing every word. In a small office two floors above, three federal agents were huddled before video screens, watching and listening to the proceedings with great amusement.

Agent Wilson laughed, slapped a thigh, and bellowed, "Hah, you old bastard, who's the smart one now?"

With his usual judicial efficiency, His Honor cut right to the chase. "Mr. Jones, we left off with your assessment that you needed two more weeks to prepare your defense. Are you ready?"

"I believe I am, Your Honor. But as there is no requirement for discovery in immigration code, I reserve the right to hear what the prosecution presents."

This reference was to the requirement in criminal trials for the prosecution and defense to share advance notice about evidence and witnesses they intend to present. There was no such obligation in immigration court. MP's retort was old hat. The judge nodded accordingly. He shifted his attention to the prosecutor. "Miss Parrish, make your case."

Without hesitation she said, "We'll open with the government claim that Mr. Konevitch lied to the immigration board about his place of employment."

She nodded at her young assistant. He apparently had another impressive purpose than being the meek target of blame for things gone wrong. He hefted up a number of documents and hauled them to the bench.

Miss Parrish said, "I'm providing annotated transcripts from the statement made by Mr. and Mrs. Konevitch to an immigration panel on April 15, to wit, they both were employed by a company supposedly established in Austria. The company so named is Orangutan Media."

Judge Everston licked his fingers and began noisily thumbing through the documents. "Go on."

"You'll also note three statements signed by Russia's attorney general, Anatoli Fyodorev. They detail several investigations by Russian federal investigators into the true activities of Orangutan Media. The—"

MP quickly interrupted. "Your Honor, we have not seen those statements."

"And you already established that, Mr. Jones."

"Yes, and surely it won't hurt to remind the court that my client came to America as a result of political persecution. The same government that provided those statements wishes him dead."

"Then you believe these statements to be false?"

"I haven't seen them."

"Well, they're in Russian. Can't read them myself. But let's assume, momentarily, that Miss Parrish is telling the truth. That's a reasonable assumption, is it not, Miss Parrish?"

"It is."

"Mr. Jones? Is Russia's attorney general lying?"

"Probably. I'll withhold judgment for now."

The prosecutor flipped a quick sideways smile at MP. She wasn't through, and he definitely wasn't going to like her next move. Too bad your hack reporter friend's not here to see you gag and choke, she wanted to tell him. Her errand boy hauled a few more papers up to the judge. "Your Honor, these are sworn statements from employees of Orangutan Media. They confirm the nature of the company's criminal activities. Please note the top statement."

"So noted. What is it?"

"A confession signed by Illya Mechoukov."

MP had never heard the name so he glanced over at his client. Alex's mouth hung open. He appeared to be in shock. He was massaging his forehead, openly pained.

MP bent over and scribbled a brief, questioning note to Alex.

"And who would he be?" the judge was asking.

"Mr. Mechoukov is the CEO of Orangutan Media. Again, it's in Russian, but he details not only the company's connections to money laundering for a notorious criminal syndicate but, more specifically, Mr. Konevitch's direct role in the nefarious activities."

Alex furiously scribbled a note back to MP. "Ask if the FBI was present," it said with a large exclamation point.

The judge was shuffling through several papers. "And the rest of these statements, who are they from?"

"More employees of said company. They all verify or expand upon the statement provided by Mechoukov."

"And how did you come upon these materials?" MP asked from the side.

She paused at this question, but only briefly. "They were given to me by the FBI."

"The FBI's a large organization. Who exactly, in the FBI?"

"I don't believe this is relevant, Your Honor."

"Should I give you my robes, Miss Parrish? Mr. Jones's question is quite relevant. This might only be immigration court, but the rules pertaining to chain of evidence remain in force. So long as you're making up my mind for me, you might as well look the part."

"Does your paycheck come with it?" She smiled briefly—a stupid mistake, one she immediately regretted.

His Honor did not smile back. "Miss Parrish, who in the FBI?"

"Agent Wilson."

"The same fellow who was present in this court two weeks ago?"

"I believe so."

"You believe so?"

"It is . . . was . . . whatever."

MP quickly interjected. "Did the FBI directly interview these people?"

"I . . . I believe so."

His Honor scratched his chin and asked, "Then where inside this arsenal of material are the statements by these agents?"

"If they were only observers, that wouldn't be necessary," she shot back.

"I asked if they took these statements, Your Honor," MP snapped.

"I heard what he asked," Parrish answered.

"I would like an unqualified response. Yes or no? They took the statements or they did not. They were present for the interrogations or were not," MP demanded, peering sideways at the judge. "Your Honor, if the FBI was present in any capacity, I request the names of the agents involved. Further, I'd like them to be deposed to confirm the authenticity of those statements."

In a room two floors above, Agent Wilson was loudly cursing. He drove a fist into a desk and instantly regretted it. It felt like he broke at least two knuckles. He hated lawyers. Such smartasses.

"It's not relevant," Parrish insisted, clearly rattled, and trying to squirm out of this line of inquiry. "The statements were taken by Russian law enforcement authorities. We should extend them the same trust and legal latitudes we afford our own police."

It was her first real mistake, and it was a whopper.

MP launched out of his chair; he was hell-bent to make her pay dearly for it. Directing a finger at her, he said, "Miss Parrish, are you telling this court that Russia's police are as credible as our own?"

She had said it, and it was too late to back away. "Yes."

"Have you ever heard of gulags, kangaroo courts, Solzhenitsyn, purges, Potemkin villages, Stalin, the Cold War, show trials—"

"Thank you, Mr. Jones," the judge burst in. "You made your point."

MP relaxed. "Thank you, Your Honor. I was starting to bore myself." He brushed a hand through his hair and shook his head.

It was a sly dig, skillfully delivered. Even His Honor cracked a hint of a smile.

A large scowl was on Parrish's face. She knew full well she had said something pathetically stupid. And she knew, equally well, that she had no choice but to breaststroke in quicksand. "I have no idea what Mr. Jones is saying. Nor does it sound at all relevant."

"Well, she might be the only person in the world confused about this," MP said with a nasty smile. "So let me clear it up. I'm saying the Russian police frequently use tactics that are abhorrent. They torture witnesses, employ blackmail and coercion, are notoriously dishonest, and sometimes even forge documents. If Mrs. Parrish is so naïve as to not be aware of this, I will gladly call in dozens of expert witnesses from the CIA and State Department to educate her. Or I can locate thousands of U.S. citizens who were granted political asylum—by her own department, I might add—after Russian police brutally tortured them and their families."

His Honor asked very nicely, "Miss Parrish, will that be necessary or will you simply concede this point?"

Parrish spent a moment grinding her fingernails into her palms. Was this a jury trial the damage would be enormous, possibly insurmountable. Fortunately it was an immigration case in an immigration court with an immigration judge. The rules were different.

She drew a few deep breaths, then tried gamely to repair the damage. "The prosecution is willing to concede that Russian legal authorities might occasionally employ a little excess vigor in the pursuit of justice."

Alex mentioned to MP, very loudly, "She means they rip fingernails out of innocent people and force them to sign untrue statements."

"I can interpret her words without your help," the judge said with a mildly aggravated expression. "Now sit down, Mr. Jones."

MP sat.

The judge removed his glasses and rubbed his eyes for a moment. Eventually he said to the prosecutor, "Can you produce any FBI agents who witnessed these interrogations?"

"No."

He turned to MP. "Can you produce witnesses or evidence that these statements are tainted or were forced?"

"I haven't been given the opportunity. They were sprung on us only five minutes ago. My client vehemently denies them. We would request the time to track down the signatories to interview them directly."

His Honor swiveled his neck back to the prosecutor. "I hope you have other evidence or substantiation."

This time her young lackey hauled two enormous cardboard boxes up to the bench. They overflowed with paper. Parrish allowed the judge a moment to peek over the lids and witness the massive volume of material. It would take at least a month to read it all.

"Your Honor, these are newspaper and magazine clippings collected and translated by our Foreign Service concerning Mr. Konevitch's considerable criminal activities in Russia."

Alex began scribbling more furious notes for MP. Parrish prattled on, describing the depth, complexity, and utter depravity of Alex's schemes and crimes. She referred to her notes frequently. She quoted freely from several of the more damning articles. About the abhorrent nature of Konevitch's crimes. Choice tidbits about the people this Russian mountebank harmed through his crookedness. The bankrupted investors who trusted him and were ruined. The thousands of employees laid off after he fled. The shock to the entire Russian business world and its incipient stock market. She requested that the accounts be entered into the record. MP scrawled a few questions. Alex dashed off hurried replies.

The moment she finished, MP observed, "I believe the prosecutor is aware of our contention that Mr. Konevitch was framed for these crimes."

"It's a common alibi from guilty criminals," Parrish replied dismissively.

"You doubt his word?" MP asked, slightly incredulous.

"Of course I do. Mr. Konevitch is listed number one on Russia's most wanted list. The Russian attorney general has issued a warrant for his arrest. The news stories in those boxes confirm everything he did, that he's now claiming he didn't do. I believe he is outnumbered."

MP turned to the judge. "I don't believe I've ever heard of a case where newspaper articles were introduced as evidence."

The judge was interested in where MP was going with this. "Nor I. On the other hand, I'm inclined to accept her claim that the articles add a certain level of verification to the government claims."

MP smiled at His Honor and said, "Could I have a little latitude to explore this issue?"

"A very little, Mr. Jones."

He turned and faced Parrish. "Did you read the *New York Times* article published two weeks ago regarding this trial?"

"I may have."

"Would you like me to read it to you? I have a copy."

"No. I read it."

"All of it?"

"I just said I did. Every stupid word."

MP picked up the article from the table and waved it around for the judge to see. "Here's my favorite part," he said, smiling broadly. He read loudly and proudly, "Quote, 'This case is a travesty of injustice, a railroad, and the prosecutor is the chief engineer driving a train of lies and deceit,' remarked an anonymous source. 'If Konevitch is returned to Russia, he'll be murdered. His blood will be on the prosecutor's hands as surely as if she killed him herself.' End quote." MP smiled nicely at the court reporter. "Sally, please enter that into the record. Especially that literary part about driving the train of lies and deceit. I really like that line."

Parrish launched out of her chair. "I protest, Your Honor," she yelled, red-faced. "That obvious smear has no business being entered into the record."

His Honor briefly considered an intervention. There was no question about it; she was right, it definitely was a bald-faced smear. On the other hand, she was asking to have press clippings entered into evidence. Whether she liked it or not, she had given the defense attorney the opening to explore the issue: if he chose to crash through it in a Mack truck she had no complaint.

And frankly, such testy exchanges were rare for an immigration hearing. He pushed his chair back, folded his hands behind his head, and watched the interplay with huge enjoyment.

"Why not?" MP snapped back at her. "Didn't you agree with it?"

"I did not."

"Oh, come on, Miss Parrish. It was a great article. Well-reasoned, finely balanced."

"It was a shameful, slanted, slanderous piece of garbage, Mr. Jones. And you know it. It was too obvious the reporter was an old college friend of yours. She made no effort to get the government's side. Her behavior verges on professional misconduct."

For the briefest moment, MP paused. How did she know about their old college relationship? There was only one way she could, and MP pondered that ugly thought before he recovered his senses and pushed on.

"Then sue her," he snapped, struggling to keep his cool. How long had his phones been tapped? Who was listening in? How much had he divulged?

"I might sue you instead. You and I both know you provided that despicable quote."

"Fine. Sue me, then. I dare you." He waved the article like a matador with a red cape.

"I would love to. If it wasn't impossible to prove, I would take everything you own."

"Spare me the empty threats. Any lawyer worth their salt would end up owning the *New York Times* and shoving me into the poorhouse."

"Don't you dare patronize me. She'll hide behind the First Amendment. And you'll lie for all it's worth."

On a dime, MP was suddenly all warmth and compassion. He balled up the article and threw it on the floor. "You know what? I agree with you, Miss Parrish. What can be worse than being smeared and maligned by lies in the press? To have your reputation unfairly dragged through the mud? If a lawyer like you has no realistic recourse, what chance does a simple citizen have? He can sue, but what chance does he have? He can say it's all lies, but who'll believe him? Anonymous sources leak all the lying filth they want. The juicier the lie, the more quickly it spreads, picked up by one paper after another until it becomes an avalanche of lies. The more outrageous the lie, the more ink it captures, the more it's guaranteed to hit the front page, then another front page, then a magazine cover, and then . . . Well, it's all just so sad."

The constant use of "he" left no doubt he wasn't talking about her. Alex suddenly thrust a note into MP's hand. It read, "Ask if her bosses requested a team of Russian prosecutors to come here and prove the case." He read it, had no idea what Alex was talking about, or where this was coming from, but Alex *had* nailed it on the head about the FBI and Orangutan Media. He nodded.

Parrish decided she hated MP Jones. She had known exactly what he was doing from the beginning. It had just been impossible to ignore or deflect his assault in a casual manner. He had shoved her into a corner and forced her to battle her way out.

But at least he was finished, she thought with grim satisfaction. In fact, MP was just getting warmed up.

He said to the judge, "Your Honor, since Miss Parrish has asked to enter these news articles into evidence, I would like you to ask her, on the record, if she believes every word to be true and accurate. Is she confident these stories represent the truth?"

His Honor pondered this weighty request for a second. Was it fair and reasonable? Well, it was her idea to enter all this media rubbish into evidence. "Miss Parrish, for the record, do you believe these articles to be true and accurate?"

For a moment she froze. In a thoughtful, halting voice, she eventually replied, "I won't attest for every word or every statement in every article. In general, though, yes, the articles convey . . . well, a fairly accurate portrayal of Konevitch's deplorable activities and actions." A perfect response. She was proud of her answer, so carefully measured, so finely hedged. She was glad MP gave her the opening. He had lobbed her the perfect softball to repair the damage she had already inflicted upon herself.

MP said, very carefully also, "Your Honor, could you please ask the prosecutor if it's true Russia's attorney general is dispatching a prosecutorial team here to share evidence of Mr. Konevitch's activities with her legal department?"

Parrish's mouth suddenly went dry. She had been informed of this news only two days before. A precautionary move, she was told, in the event this judge got stupid and produced an outrageous decision. It was confided to her in the strictest confidence. How did Jones learn about it? Who leaked it? How damaging was this? How much did he know? A hundred unanswered questions pinged around her brain.

"Miss Parrish?"

She had no choice but to answer truthfully. "Yes."

"Please ask her why the need for such a team?" MP asked, uncertain how Alex learned this little tidbit, but pushing the point for all it was worth.

"It wasn't my decision. I don't know," she replied, trying to get off the hook.

"Not your decision?" His Honor asked incredulously.

She replied lamely, "It was a departmental decision."

MP went for the kill. "Your Honor, please ask her the basis of this decision."

His Honor was already kneading his temples. "Good idea. Why, Miss Parrish?"

"I have no idea."

Once again, MP generously came to her aid. "If it pleases the court, I'd like to help my colleague clear up this mystery."

"It might not please her. It would damn well please me, though," the judge replied, shoving aside his decorum. He was sorely tempted to cite her for contempt. He had caught her lying several times. Her credibility was in shambles. Now he questioned her sanity.

Speaking with all the confidence he could muster, MP claimed, "It's obvious her own service has doubts about the outlandish claims made in the Russian press about my client. As for her faith in Russia's attorney general, it's obvious her superiors feel otherwise. They asked the Russians to come over here to prove their case."

"Is this true?" Judge Everston asked her with a look that nearly peeled the skin from her face.

She toyed with a thousand responses she could give him. Yes, it was true. And also deliberately taken out of context. No, she better not say that, she promptly decided; Jones would demand to know the right context. The right context was the FBI director and attorney general wanted this Russian couple expelled, no matter what.

She hated this case. It was rammed down her throat at the last minute, accompanied by dozens of vile threats if she flopped. But her job was to represent the interests of the United States government as best she could.

"I have no idea," she snapped spitefully, wondering what her superiors would say when they read the transcript.

"I am placing this case in abeyance," the judge snapped. He looked long and hard at Kim Parrish. If stares had weight, she'd be crushed under a hundred tons of barely controlled fury. "This might be the shoddiest case I've ever had the displeasure to observe. I am not happy, Miss Parrish. You've asked me to pull the trigger for immediate deportation when the gun's not even loaded."

She summoned the last tiny bit of her courage. "The government requests that Mr. Konevitch remain in custody until we ascertain the full validity of Russia's claim."

The judge reeled back and pretended to be shocked. "Miss Parrish, do you recall the warning I issued two weeks ago?"

"I do, Your Honor."

"And now you're asking me to approve indefinite imprisonment while you sort out whether Mr. Konevitch is guilty of crimes back in Russia?"

"I didn't say indefinite. We'll move this as fast as we can and notify the court the moment we're prepared."

"And when might that be?"

"A few months at worst. Possibly weeks." She didn't have a clue.

"Mr. Jones?"

Predictably, MP looked like a jackhammer was pulverizing his big toe. "It is grossly unfair for my client to remain in custody because the government arrested him on such spurious grounds. It's outrageous and—"

Parrish cut him off. "The alternative is that we release a possible criminal to escape his crimes, and possibly sin again. He has the resources, and he has fled before. As the huge volume of news accounts attest, Mr. Konevitch is an infamous fugitive in Russia. A celebrity thief. His case is being monitored closely by Russia's highest leaders and by his own people. Russia has made clear that the handling of this case will merit a strong reciprocal response. Thousands of American citizens are in Russia. They're at risk. We recognize and apologize for any inconvenience this causes Mr. Konevitch. But we emphasize the needs of the state over his personal comfort."

The slew of news stories in the boxes two feet from the judge's long nose suddenly weighed ten legal tons. The judge stared at the boxes that attested very clearly to Konevitch's infamy in Russia. For once, she had a good point.

His Honor removed his glasses and leaned forward. "With considerable reluctance, I'll approve this request, until this thing gets sorted out."

"Thank you, Your Honor."

"Oh, don't thank me, Miss Parrish. But do listen closely. I want Mr. Konevitch transferred to a federal facility. Get him out of that nasty holding cell."

"I understand."

"Find him a nice, comfortable place. I want him not overly taxed by our obvious inefficiency. Is this clear?"

"You have my word."

He bent far forward. "One of those country clubs with tennis courts, big-screen TVs hooked to satellites, and all the good food he can stand. A nice, white-collar environment without walls or barbed wire, where the worst lowlife in there is a tax cheat."

"I understand."

"The next time I see Mr. Konevitch I want him fat and tanned. He better be bored with gardening, and listening to all those fat-cat Wall Street lizards brag about their schemes."

"You have my word."

"I protest," MP said.

"Of course you do," His Honor said quickly, as he lunged out of his seat and fled from his own court.

26

The thrashing was horrible. Nothing less than deeply humiliating. It was the first time Kim Parrish had met the attorney general and FBI director. Oh, let it be the last, she prayed as they verbally tore into her. She gritted her teeth and mentally cursed both of them. Neither was in her chain of command, but they were enormously powerful people, and it stung.

Her own director chose to stand off to the side, eyeing the line of fire and avoiding it at all costs.

She had turned fifty years old only two weeks before. Same age as the attorney general. Twelve years older than Tromble. Yet they lashed into her like a little schoolgirl who had failed to finish her homework.

"It's not all lost," Parrish protested weakly, almost vainly, avoiding their damning eyes. "He's still in custody. We'll have our day in court again."

"His ass should already be on a plane back to Russia," Tromble yelled, slapping a hand on a table. "You blew it. A knockdown case, and you just blew it."

"It wasn't my decision to bring in the Russian prosecutors. I had them on the ropes until Jones used that ace."

"How did Jones learn about it?" the attorney general asked, plainly puzzled.

Kim Parrish shrugged. "You tell me."

Tromble stared down at his shoes. The profligate product of the wiretaps on Jones's office had been quietly reviewed that afternoon by a team of ten agents. No mention of it. Not in Jones's phone calls. Not even in private conversations inside his office. Not a hint, not a word.

He glowered at the INS director. "Your operation leaks like a sieve. Wasn't this Jones guy once one of your lawyers? Obviously one of your people tipped him."

"Maybe it was one of your people," Parrish's boss punched back, just as nasty now that the thrashing shifted toward him. "Myself and Miss Parrish were the only ones who knew. I sure as hell didn't let him know."

"When do these Russians arrive?" Laura Tingleman asked, cutting off the discourse. She hated confrontation.

"Could be months," Tromble replied, and with that, he suddenly had a new idea.

"Then another month or two for them to pass off their knowledge to one of your attorneys," Tingleman calculated to the director of the INS, choosing her language carefully, deliberately avoiding Parrish's eyes. That pointed "one of your attorneys" line was a clear shot—this girl either kicks it up a notch or find a replacement.

"Sounds about right," Parrish's boss replied, notably not going to Parrish's defense.

"So this might take six months?" Tingleman asked.

Tromble smiled and nodded. "Maybe longer. A year is a possibility. You'll have to call this judge," he advised her. "Tell him to be patient. Emphasize the importance of this thing."

She nodded.

Parrish's boss said, "I'll assign two more attorneys to Parrish's team. That'll speed things up."

Tromble looked at him like he was an idiot. "No you won't."

"I won't?"

"As long as Konevitch is in custody, what's the rush?"

"Hey, I've been your whipping boy every day to get this thing done. Why the sudden change of heart?"

The question did not faze him in the least. "Miss Parrish has been under unbearable pressure. Look at her, she's obviously exhausted. But the timing's no longer in the defense attorney's hands, is it? She needs to take her time, get this thing done right."

The sudden shift to kindness was unnerving. Tromble walked across the room and slapped Kim Parrish on the back. "Good luck, Counselor. Knock a home run next time, or else."

The meeting was suddenly over, to everybody's surprise and Kim Parrish's complete delight. She nearly left a smoke trail she moved out so fast.

Then it was just Tromble and the attorney general. Alone. The two of them, together, all by themselves in the big office filled with overwhelming burdens and responsibilities.

Tromble turned to her and observed, "The judge released Konevitch to your custody. The second you give the word, he's going into a federal prison."

"Well, there's that very nice one in Pennsylvania. The one where all the Wall Street fat cats go. Out in the countryside. I hear it's lovely in a pastoral sort of way."

Tromble said, not very pleasantly, "You're not really going to let some pissant immigration hack boss you around, are you? Just roll over and bark for that guy?"

That stung. Tromble was right, though; he was a lowly immigration judge in a backwater court. And she was, after all, the attorney general. Her eyes were glued to his face. "What do you have in mind, John?"

"You understand how important this case is?"

"Remind me."

"The Russian mobs are climbing all over our coastal cities. They're the newest thing, and it's not pretty. They earn a ten on the viciousness scale. And now they're battling us, the Italian Mafia, and the black gangs, and the Colombians and Mexicans to get a foothold. The Russians are very good, and very, very violent. They learned how to thrive in the most totalitarian country on earth. Don't forget that. Imagine what they can accomplish in our wide-open liberal democracy. We're frighteningly vulnerable. Let them get traction, let them have an inch, they'll become another rooted criminal institution inside this country. Another cancer that's impossible to dislodge."

"And Konevitch is the key to this?" she asked, leaning on her plump elbows and watching him carefully.

"Yes, the Russians are quite clear on this. He's a very guilty man, Laura. The man stole hundreds of millions. They get Konevitch, and in turn we get twenty agents in Moscow, with full access to their intelligence about the Mafiya. They'll assign liaisons to us, and we'll trade information back and forth. It's a gold mine. We'll break the back of these Russian goons."

"I see."

"Understand this, too. This guy Konevitch is sticking his finger in our eye, Laura. It's a disgrace. The press is watching. A damned foreigner exploiting our own legal system to make you and me look like eunuchs. It's very dangerous for us."

She sank about two more inches into her seat. Her forehead added about ten wrinkles. Left unsaid was that Tromble himself had issued the boneheaded directive to cream the Konevitches on the front pages, and attracted all the public scrutiny. He regretted it now—it had been a terrible mistake—but the die was cast. If Konevitch wanted to make this a pissing contest, a waterfall was about to land on his head.

Tromble placed a hand on her shoulder. "You decide what damned prison he's going to. If he wants to play games with you, stick it to him."

"You're right," she said, feeling a sudden burst of something called determination.

"Pick the worst, festering pisshole in the federal system. Put him in with the worst scum in our society. Someplace hot as Hades, with crap for food, and unrelenting violence. Let him rot and suffer until he begs us to throw him out of this country."

"I suppose a little softening up might encourage him to see our side," she agreed.

*   *   *

Mikhail had managed at last to hide listening devices inside the big black limo. For months he had looked for a chance. There just had been no openings. And it had to be unquestionably fail-safe; getting caught would blow everything apart. But the driver had dodged into a coffee shop one cold afternoon, leaving the engine running and doors unlocked. Mikhail gently eased over, ducked down, and quietly opened a rear side door. He jammed one bug into the deep crevice between the rear cushions. For insurance, he attached another tightly to the undercarriage of the front seat.

The range was only half a mile, and that was on a clear day. It gave him two important edges, though. He could hear what they were saying and record every word. And he no longer had to keep the limo in sight during the weekly meetings on the Moskva. They were oblivious to his presence, so far. But Mikhail intended to die peacefully in his bed at a ripe old age.

The limo was parked there, right now, a few meters to the right of its regular spot overlooking the river. Mikhail was parked three blocks away, the receiver/recorder in his lap, volume turned up full blast. He was sipping carefully from a large thermos of coffee and listening intently. Golitsin, then Tatyana, then Nicky sat in the rear, in their usual order, performing their usual ritual, nursing drinks, arguing back and forth, plotting their next big heist.

Nicky, in his distinctively caustic tone: "I thought you said it was going to be easy. Kid's play."

Golitsin: "All right, I lied. So what?"

"So what? Nine of my guys dead. Two of my chophouses blown to pieces, that's what. Somebody's screwin' with my dope business, too. I had half a million stolen from a pusher last week. Every time I hit Khodorin's company, I get hit back, twice as hard."

Tatyana, in a soothing tone obviously intended to unruffle the feathers: "What makes you think Khodorin's behind it, Nicky? He's just a businessman."

" 'Cause we keep finding notes pinned on the corpses. 'Lay off Central Enterprises, or we'll kick your ass.' " A brief pause. "Hey, you know what? They *are* kicking my ass."

Golitsin, in an annoyed, slightly absent tone: "He never called."

Tatyana: "Who never called who, Sergei?"

"Yuri Khodorin. He never called my man to handle his company's security."

Nicky: "Yeah, well, sure as hell he called somebody. Somebody connected. I'll tell ya who he called. A real vicious prick."

Tatyana: "Well, we can't let him off the hook. Not now. The man is worth billions, Nicky."

"You know, you keep sayin' that. But I don't see your ass out on the street, takin' the lumps this guy's dishing out. I'm tellin' ya, this guy's smart."

Golitsin: "How smart?"

"Last week, a few of my guys went to lay a little dynamite in that warehouse. Same one we talked about last week. It was a massacre."

Mikhail laughed so hard he nearly choked on his coffee. He had overheard their plan the week before, and quietly passed it along to his old friend from police days who was now handling security for Khodorin—with brutal effectiveness, based upon what he was hearing.

Tatyana: "Is it possible another syndicate is going to war with you? That sometimes happens, doesn't it?"

"Oh, yeah, good point, I hadn't thought of that." A brief pause. "Stick with what you know. No syndicate leaves messages warning me to lay off this Khodorin guy."

Tatyana: "Come on, Nicky. We've invested months in this. Central Enterprises is perfect, just perfect. Five hundred million in cash reserves. Cash, Nicky, cash. We'd be idiots to walk away at this point."

Nicky: "It's his fault"—presumably pointing a finger at Golitsin—"wasn't he supposed to get one of his snoops inside? Whatever happened to that, huh?"

Yes, whatever did happen to that, Mikhail wanted to yell in their faces.

But for a few long moments there was silence. Mikhail chuckled. He'd almost do this job for free. He couldn't wait to share this tape with Captain Yurshenko, the recently appointed head of security at Central Enterprises. They would crack a bottle of vodka, sit back, and bust a nut over the poisonous frustration on the other side.

Eventually, Golitsin, turning the tables: "All right, I'll find a way to get some people inside. Now what's the story with Konevitch?"

Nicky, speaking to Tatyana in an accusatory sneer: "Yeah, thought you said he was taken care of."

Tatyana: "It's under control. Tromble called this morning. Konevitch is in a federal penitentiary in Atlanta. Tromble swore he placed our friend in the nastiest hole in the universe."

Nicky, who presumably knew something about this subject: "I hear they got some places over there that are just unbelievable."

Tatyana: "We're cooking up the case to be presented to their courts right now."

Golitsin: "I have experts with decades of experience in this. Why don't I help you?"

Tatyana: "I don't think that's a good idea. The team that manufactures this evidence has to go over and present it to their lawyers. If you build your own lies, you should know your own lies, don't you think?"

Loud chuckles all around.

Three days languishing at the federal transit center in Atlanta— while Justice hotly debated which of its many prisons was the most awful at that particular moment—proved to be a godsend. Despite frequent requests, nobody would tell Alex his eventual destination.

Two days after his appearance in court, he had been hustled out of the Alexandria jail by a pair of federal marshals whose only words to Alex were, "Say good-bye to the good life." A quick flight on a Bureau of Prisons 737 to a private hangar in Atlanta International was followed by a fast trip in a shiny black van to the sprawling prison facility in Atlanta. The moment he entered the transient center for what he was warned would be a brief stay,

Alex knew he wasn't headed for the pleasurable resort the judge had ordered.

He was locked in a small cell with a repeat sex offender named Ernie, who favored small boys but settled for little girls, depending on his mood at the moment. Ernie was a leper, a small, oddly ebullient man despised and avoided by everybody. Even Alex could not bring himself to speak with the twisted pervert.

The transient prisoners moving through this portal to hell were a mixture of hardened two- and three-timers, seasoned vets, and others like Alex, wide-eyed newbies about to be thrown into a frightening new world.

The old-timers adored the chance to show off their experience, and they acted like garrulous college kids returning from spring break. They hollered back and forth, spitting out stories, exchanging names of acquaintances in this prison or that. The only verboten topic was any mention of their newest crimes. Alex listened carefully to every word, every boast. He studied how they moved, their mannerisms, how they wore their prison garb. He took careful mental notes and absorbed every nuance. Head down, always, but stay alert. Avoid eye contact at all costs—a wrong glance in this milieu was an invitation to rape, or worse. Among enemies, among guards, among friends, it didn't matter—act indifferent, no matter what. Better yet, *be* indifferent, and trust no one. And the golden rule: never, ever, under any circumstances, snitch.

On day four, Alex's toe was jerked out of the water. He was led out of his transient cell by a pair of stone-faced guards, escorted through a number of cellblocks and hallways, across a large courtyard, and, after four hours of tedious processing—including another shower, another delousing, and another invasive body search—was shoved into his new home.

Ernie, his former cellmate, smiled and welcomed Alex to his new cell. The cold, unpleasant relations between Alex and Ernie had been duly noted by the authorities. Being trapped in a small cell with this pervert would surely kick up the misery level a few notches.

Ernie had arrived two hours earlier, enough time for a little interior decorating. The walls were already plastered with pictures of little boys and girls clipped from magazines.

Based on the most recent indices of prison violence and brutality—and only after the chief of Justice's Bureau of Prisons twice swore it was the pick of the litter—Atlanta's medium-security prison earned the booby prize.

The truth was that by almost every measure, Atlanta's high-security facility had an impressive edge over its adjoining medium-security counterpart—three more murders over the past year, eighty percent more vicious assaults, nearly thirty more days in lockdown, and an impressive seventy percent lead in reported AIDS cases.

That year, Atlanta's high-security prison was, without question, and by any conceivable measure, the worst canker sore in the entire federal system.

The medium-security facility, however, offered a big advantage, one that swung the argument in its favor. Because it was medium-security, Alex would be forced to mix freely and openly with the prison population. Two hours every day in the yard, socializing with killers, gangbangers, big-time dope dealers, rapists, child molesters, and assorted other criminals. Showers twice a week in a large open bay, with minimal supervision. Three meals every day in the huge mess, where violence was as pervasive as big southern cockroaches.

Alex Konevitch, they were sure, would be petrified. A rich boy from Russia who had pampered and spoiled himself silly with unimaginable luxuries. Nothing in his background had prepared him for this. They were sure he would panic and end up begging for a seat on the next plane to Russia. Or maybe he would run afoul of one of the inhabitants and be shipped home in a casket. Who cared? The Russians never stipulated dead or alive.

The tipping point, though, was the large concentration of Cuban criminals. The facility contained the usual toxic mix of Crips and Bloods, a large, swaggering White Power brotherhood, and an assortment of lesser bands that huddled together under a hodge-podge of quirky banners and social distinctions. But the Cubans ruled. They terrorized the other groups, ran roughshod over the guards, got a piece of all the prison drug traffic and black-market action, and generally did as they pleased.

The ringleaders were a long-term institution, a troupe of thirty cutthroats shipped over on a special boat by Castro at the tail end of the Mariel Boatlift. The Immigration Service had been tipped off about their impending arrival by a Cuban convict who hoped his little favor would be met by a bigger favor. This was Castro's biggest flip of the bird, he warned without the slightest exaggeration; a group of handpicked incorrigibles, men who had been killing and raping and stealing since they were in diapers. The dregs of the dregs—once loose on America's streets, the havoc would be unimaginable.

They were picked up the second they climbed off the boat onto a lovely beach just south of Miami, and sent straight to Atlanta's prison. It was unfortunate, but since they had been denied the opportunity to commit crimes on American soil, no legal justification existed to place them in a high-security lockup, where they clearly belonged.

On the second day of Alex's incarceration, a guard, acting on orders from the warden, tipped the Cubans that the new boy in cell D83 was worth a boatload of money. By Alex's third week in the new facility, the Choir Boys of Mariel, as they were known, decided it was time for the new arrival to make their acquaintance.

Alex was one minute into his shower when three men surrounded him. "What can I do for you boys?" he asked, trying to pretend polite indifference, when every cell in his body screamed run. Just run. Don't look back, don't even breathe, just run.

The jefe of the trio, a small, wiry man with greasy black hair laced with gray, and long ridges of knife scars on his forehead and left cheek, stepped closer to Alex. "What you in for?" he asked with a strong Cuban brogue.

"Nothing."

"Nothing. Just visiting, huh?"

"All right, I was framed."

A light chuckle sounding like chalk scratched on a blackboard. "You and all the rest of us."

"It's true. I haven't even been to trial yet."

"You're Russian," the man observed, shooting past the normal prisoner baggage and getting to the point.

"I was. Now I'm American."

The man took another step toward Alex, ending up about a foot away. "I'm Cubano," he announced with a nasty smile and his chest puffed up. "I hate Russians. Biggest pricks in the world. You kept that bastard Castro in power."

The prisoners around Alex suddenly began shutting down their showerheads and bolting for the towel room. A fire alarm at full blast could not have emptied the place faster. The three men surrounding Alex were fully clothed in prison coveralls, hands stuffed deep inside their pockets. They stank of old sweat and a thousand cigarettes. Apparently, they didn't visit the showers very often.

Alex swallowed his fear and kept rubbing soap in his armpits. "No, you mean the communists kept him in power," he said and glanced around. Act indifferent, he kept reminding himself. Don't look scared, don't crack a smile, control your breathing. Pretend that standing naked in front of these three goons is no more threatening than a lap around the prison track. The guard who had been loitering at the entrance had mysteriously disappeared, Alex suddenly noticed.

"And what? You weren't a commie?"

Alex shook his head. "Definitely not."

"Yeah, well, what's that?" He wagged a finger at the hammer and sickle on Alex's chest.

"A present from some angry former commies," Alex informed him, eyeing the other two men, who had fanned out a bit and now blocked his exit in any direction.

"For what?"

"Because I bankrolled Yeltsin's election to the presidency."

"You, by yourself?" A quick, derisive snicker directed at his friends. "Just you, eh?"

"That's right, just me. I gave him the money to defeat Gorbachev."

This revelation was intended to defuse the confrontation, but instead produced a nasty sneer. "And you know who I am?"

Alex soaped his arms and decided not to answer.

"Napoleon Bonaparte. You ended communism in Russia, and me . . . well, I'm the short little prick what conquered Europe."

The man laughed at his own stupid joke—his friends joined him, loud guffaws that bounced off the walls. Alex forced himself to smile. "Actually, you're Manuel Gonzalez. But you go by Manny. Born in a small village, Maderia, you're forty-six years old, thirty-six of which you've lived inside prison. You've killed with guns, rope, and knives, but prefer your bare hands. You like two sugars with your coffee, no cream. Your favorite TV show is *Miami Vice*, though I suspect you always root for the bad guys." He paused and broadened his smile. "Have you heard enough things you already know about yourself?"

Manny's mouth hung open for a second before he reacquired his normal aplomb and its accompanying sneer. The sneer had a violent edge to it. "Smart guy, huh?"

"I've asked around a bit." With as much casualness as he could muster, Alex placed the soap on the metal tray on the wall. "I suggest you do your homework, too." He stuck out his hand. "Alex Konevitch. Have one of your boys look me up on the Internet."

"Already did that," he said, ignoring the hand. "You're rich, Konevitch, filthy rich. You ripped off hundreds of millions. I'm impressed. That's why we're having this little mano-a-mano. Question is, are you also generous?"

"We seem to have a tense problem, Manny."

"Maybe my English is not so good. What's that mean?"

"A bunch of former KGB goons stole my money and my businesses. The little that was left was seized by the FBI. I was rich, and now I'm broke."

Manny did not appear overly pleased with that response. He pushed his face within an inch of Alex's. "I'm not a man you want to lie to."

"Believe me, I know that."

Manny looked ready to whip out whatever was inside his pocket. "Yeah? Then you better—"

"Slow it down, Manny. Think about it. A man with hundreds of millions, would he be here, in this rotten excuse for a prison? This is America, land of the free and the brave, of all the justice you can afford. The rich boys are all eating steak and getting nice tans in the federal country clubs. I'm here, with you. Put two and two together."

Rather than respond to that, Manny glanced at the man standing to Alex's left, a large, hairy monster named Miguel. Physical appearances aside, Manny was the muscle, Miguel the brain. They had been longtime compadres in Cuba, arrived on the same miserable little boat, and for almost two decades had shared a cramped, smelly cell on the second floor. Manny had the top bunk and stayed out front. He did the bullying, the enforcement, bought off the guards, and terrified the other gangs. Miguel slept on the bottom, and spent most of his time in the library thinking up schemes and scams. It was he who researched Alex's background after the guard tipped them off. And it was he who devised this coarse plot to shake Alex down.

After a moment, Miguel leaned forward and butted in. "Were you really the cashbox behind Yeltsin?" Not a word about that had been mentioned in any of the many articles about Konevitch Miguel had read on the Internet.

Sensing the sudden shift in power, Alex turned and faced Miguel. "Seemed like a good idea at the time."

"But maybe not, eh?"

"You're perceptive. After all, look where it got me," Alex replied, shrugging indifferently, as if he'd be as happy here, among these men, as lounging with a bunch of gorgeous ladies in skimpy bikinis at a Caribbean resort. He was nearly gagging on indifference. "The same former KGB thugs who stole my money put me here."

"Why they put you here, man?"

"They want me back in Russia, where they can get their hands on me, or dead."

"That right?" Miguel leaned his large bulk against the wall and thoughtfully twisted the small goatee at the end of his chin. With that admission this tall Russian had just made a fatal slip. A dozen questions suddenly popped into Miguel's mind. Would the Russians pay to have this guy whacked? Who did Miguel and his friends have to contact? How much was Konevitch worth dead? That was the big question.

Maybe the situation still held possibilities.

Alex was beginning to feel awkward. He was naked, vulnerable, and dripping wet. Who knew what they had hidden in those pockets? Any one of these three brutes would happily slit his throat and casually watch his blood spill down the drain. He reached over and shut off the spigot. "Mind if I get a towel and dry off?" he asked.

"Why not?" Miguel grunted and winked. "Who's stopping you?"

Alex began edging around him, carefully, in the direction of the towel room. "What do you want with money, anyway?" he asked over his shoulder. "You're in prison, what good does it do?"

The Cubans followed about a step behind. "Don't you know anything?" Miguel answered, wondering exactly how much this Russian, dead, might be worth. "Money's everything. Inside the joint, outside—makes no differences. Good lawyers, cigarettes, dope, smuggled-in girls, even guards."

Alex seemed to consider that a moment, then, rapidly changing the subject, asked, "Have you ever heard of AOL? America Online?"

Manny and the third, unnamed man exchanged puzzled looks. Totally clueless. Miguel thought he might've heard of it, a hazy recollection at best. But in an effort not to appear dumb, he produced a knowing nod. "Sure. What about it?" he asked, as if he could write a textbook on the subject.

"It's the new thing, an Internet company that's making money hand over foot. The stock could easily quadruple in the next few years, maybe more."

Miguel turned to his colleagues. "Advice from a hustler who

ripped off millions back in Russia. Does this guy think we're stupid, or what?"

"You're forgetting something. I also made hundreds of millions."

This got a slight nod. He'd read that on the Internet.

"Point is," Alex plowed ahead, grabbing a towel and wrapping it around his waist, "you're losing out. The stock market's on a tear. You're trying to squeeze a few dollars from losers on the inside. The easy money's outside, the big money. It's perfectly legal and above board."

"Cons in the joint ain't allowed to buy stock," Manny chimed in angrily, as if that ended the discussion. From everything Miguel had told him about this Russian, he had been expecting the once-in-a-lifetime payday all convicts live for. Manny had lain awake on his bunk the night before, sweating in the intense heat, dreaming of the money and what he could do with it.

Like the rest of the Mariel Boys, Manny had an appeal for release grinding its way through the courts. They had collectively pooled their resources to hire a lawyer, a distant third cousin of one of the gang. The cousin offered an impressive discount, bragged about his many legal victories, and made lots of rowdy promises. He turned out to be a total loser. Between booze and gambling, Mr. Loser lost track of their paperwork with disturbing regularity; the only thing he turned out to be good at was consistently missing the deadlines for filings.

Mr. Loser had to go.

Miguel had asked around until he found the perfect mouthpiece. Mr. Perfect was a cutthroat from Miami who billed four hundred an hour and produced miracles. He was owned by the Colombians, a gaudy loudmouth who had earned quite the reputation for keeping their killers, mules, and pushers out of jail. Legal mastery was part of it; knowing which judges and prosecutors to help with their home mortgages and kids' college bills, the larger part. In his spare time, he was allowed to freelance as much as he wanted.

It was an outside shot, at best. Mr. Perfect was quite expensive. The billable hours would pile up. The case could drag on for years. And for such a large group, a band of thugs who definitely had not distinguished themselves as model prisoners, the bribes would be mountainous.

Mr. Perfect, though, was their only hope. The Cubans talked endlessly of walking out the gate and retiring in a small, lazy southern Florida town. Life would be so good. They would muscle their way into a few strip clubs and pawnshops, drink cerveza from dusk to dawn, cavort with the strippers, and put the ugly old days behind them.

Alex kept a close eye on Manny, who looked angry and frustrated that their mark turned out to have shallow pockets. He grabbed another towel and began briskly rubbing his hair. "You mean you can't invest under your own name," he corrected Manny in an even tone. "Have a lawyer handle your money. They represent you, they can't blow the whistle. It's in their oath."

Miguel shot Manny a look that said: This sounds interesting, so cool it, for now. "And how would this work?" he asked.

"It's simple. Surely you already have money and maybe you already have a lawyer in mind."

"Maybe we do," Miguel replied, exchanging looks with his pals.

"I have a friend on the outside who will set up a trading account. I'm assuming you have a way to communicate with the outside. It needs to be instantaneous. We'll be buying and selling every day. Throw in whatever cash you have. I can name ten stocks right now that are set to explode, and the spreads in commodities have never been better."

"How do we know you won't lose our money?"

"You know what a stop-loss order is?"

Miguel was through pretending he knew things he had never heard of. A slow shake of the head.

"With each purchase, you designate a trigger price that he programs into his computer. If the stock falls to that level, the broker is required to sell." Alex jabbed the air with a finger. "One push of a button and he dumps everything."

"That's all we have to do?"

"I told you it's easy, Miguel," Alex assured him, leaving Miguel to ponder the interesting question of how Alex knew his name. They had not been introduced. Nobody had mentioned his name. How much did Konevitch know about the Mariel Boys? The suspicion struck him that the Russian had been expecting this shakedown, maybe even prepared for it.

No, nobody was that cunning.

Alex walked over to the clothing locker, picked up his underwear and dirty coveralls, and began dressing. "But don't worry," he continued. "The stocks I pick will never trigger a sell order. Tell your lawyer to watch the action for a month. If he likes what he sees, he can join the fun. Better yet, cut a deal. In return for handling his investments, he'll handle your case."

"And you," Manny asked. "What do you get?"

"Protection," Alex told him, tying his shoes. "Also use your influence to arrange a new cellmate. Ernie gets on my nerves. I'm tired of tearing down pictures of little children."

"Easy," Miguel answered for all of them. "One more question."

"Shoot."

A nice smile, followed by a quick shift of mood and demeanor. "You know what happens if you lose our money, Mr. Smart Guy?"

"I have a fair idea. Do I look worried?"

He really didn't. Not in the least.

The end of Elena's first month in the South Arlington rental apartment and she was beginning to feel at home.

The D.C. housing market was hot as a pistol and her real estate agent had pleaded with her not to drop a hundred thousand off the asking price. It was the Watergate, after all; why throw away money? Her neighbors would never forgive her; not to mention the Realtor's own bitter feelings about the seven grand shucked off her own fee. Elena dug in her heels and stood fast. Lured by the great discount, inside two days, ten couples lined up for a shot. A brief, vicious bidding war erupted. The escalation quickly shot through the roof. The dust settled $120K later, at least $20K more than average Watergate prices for a cramped two-bedroom.

The winners were a young Bolivian couple with no children but plenty of money and an open desire to tell everyone back home they were part of the la-di-da Watergate crowd. Elena drove a hard bargain. A hundred thousand down, in cash, she insisted, before the titles were checked and the closing moved along at its usual constipated pace. The young couple hesitated only briefly before Elena mentioned how much she liked the terms offered by the runner-up bidder. A hundred thousand in cash landed on the table.

Their business affairs had always been handled by Alex. She was proud she had done so well. She promptly put down twenty thousand on a top-of-the-line server built by Sun Microsystems, and arranged for furniture from a cheap rental warehouse. MP helped her locate an apartment, not far from his own shabby home in a run-down neighborhood. At seven hundred a month the price was right, and Elena signed the lease under the name Ellen Smith. A few of MP's clients with expertise in such matters swiftly produced a driver's license and social security card to match her new name. Charge cards could be traced, and therefore were too dangerous. She vowed to live on cash.

The landlord wasn't fooled and neither did he care. Half his tenants were illegal aliens. As long as they paid cash, in American bills, on time, they could claim to be Bill Gates for all he cared. The phone service, both cellular and home, and Internet service, were opened by and billed to MP's firm.

The only remaining trace of Elena Konevitch was her car insurance. She called the company, said she had moved, and gave MP's office as her new address.

The killers were out there. With Alex locked up, she was the only one they could reach, she thought. The killers were professionals with loads of experience. They knew countless ways to find her and would peek under every rock. She was on her own for the first time; every decision would be hers. She needed to be disciplined and careful.

In her college days, Elena had taken courses in computer language, and had been quite good at it. A fast trip to a local mall and her apartment quickly flooded with books about programming and all sorts of other computer esoterica.

She had one last thing left to do. Sipping from a cup of tea, she unfolded a note Alex had passed her in court. She dialed the number he had written out and waited patiently until the connection went through.

A male voice answered, "Mikhail Borosky, private investigations."

"Hello, Mikhail. It's Elena Konevitch. Alex asked me to call."

"Yeah, I just learned he's in prison," Mikhail replied. "He okay?"

"Fine. Probably safer inside than out here."

There was a pause for a moment before Elena said, "From now on, direct your calls and send all your materials to me, addressed to Ellen Smith." She quickly gave him her new apartment address, her e-mail account information, and then said, "The materials you've already sent are hidden in a safe-deposit box at a bank. I went through everything three days ago."

"It's incredible isn't it?"

"You're incredible, Mikhail."

"No, this is all Alex's idea. He's incredible."

Enough incredibles. "Things have changed," Elena told him, very businesslike. "I'm handling this now. Alex has kept me informed of your general activities, but it might be best if you filled me in on all the details."

"This could take a while."

"With Alex in prison, I find I have lots of time on my hands. Start from the beginning."

27

After an hour of wailing and gnashing, of fruitless attempts at denial accompanied by turbulent rantings and sulfurous threats directed at the messengers, the long procession of accountants finally packed up their books and spreadsheets and fled from his office. The door closed quietly, at last. Sergei Golitsin hunched down in his chair and stared at the blank white walls. He was angry and felt depressed. The number crunchers had been merciless. No punches pulled, no quarter given.

The export-import bank, the flagship of Golitsin Enterprises—and one of its last surviving companies—was careening off a financial cliff. The priceless monopoly on the exchanging of foreign currencies had long since expired. The competition had swooped in and undercut his rates with a vengeance. For a few months, the five percent fee he charged had pumped up the profits and hid the bad news: customers were fleeing in droves.

Then, almost overnight, as if a switch had been flipped, the customers melted away. One day small trickles were still coming through the door; then, without warning, severe business anorexia settled in. Golitsin had moved decisively and ordered an aggressive retreat on his inflated rates, four percent, then three, then two; as of a week ago, it was set at a paltry one percent. At that price it would take thousands of new customers pushing large fortunes through his vaults to keep the doors open. No respite. No flood of new clients, or even return business. The doors to his bank had grown cobwebs.

He now doubted he could lure any customers if he offered to pay *them* five percent.

Amazing, the damage caused by one unfortunate hiccup. One of his handpicked VPs, a magician in his former life in KGB counterintelligence, had gotten overconfident. Freewheeling with the bank's money, and reeling under unrelenting pressure from Golitsin to show a profit, he had made the bizarre decision to dabble in the speculation game. He made a brazen one billion bet on the unstable English pound. After a few short hours, it was nearly all swallowed in quicksand. A vindictive American currency speculator named Soros detected the move and whacked it with a thousand-pound sledgehammer. Seven hundred million was lost, according to the squinty-eyed accountants who had just spent an hour cruelly detailing the urgent case for bankruptcy. Seven hundred million!

Golitsin could not squeeze even an ounce of solace from the fact that the idiot speculator would spend the remainder of his sorry life in a wheelchair, sucking fluid through a straw. Two kneecaps shattered into bony pulp. A face now unrecognizable to his own children. Big deal! It hardly compensated for the carnage—seven hundred million down the drain. What a mess.

After a year of horrible news, followed by worse news, Golitsin had at last reached a decision. A painful decision, and certainly humiliating. But it was also necessary, practical, and long overdue. Shove vanity aside. Managing businesses was not his forte. There was so little left to manage anyway. A few emaciated skeletons in a swarming sea of wreckage. The construction business had cratered into bankruptcy months ago. The arbitrage firm sank under the weight of ten thousand tons of North Korean "garbage" iron ore of a quality so poor nobody would touch it, at any price. The car import business had sputtered out of existence. The hotels and restaurants had been put on the block months before to pay off the ruinous debts accumulated by other struggling branches.

In fact, the feverish struggle to keep Konevitch's companies afloat had distracted and dislodged him from his God-given gift. What a waste! All those interminable hours exhausted in useless business meetings, listening to his sorry underlings concoct lies and excuses for their utter stupidity. The unending stream of crises brought about by the hapless dolts below him. From now on, he would focus his brilliance where it belonged: stealing other people's fortunes and businesses.

He left his office, walked downstairs, and climbed purposefully into the rear of his big black limousine. He barked at his driver to get it in gear and drive around until he was told otherwise. The motion would help him clear the cobwebs. A little medicinal relief wouldn't hurt, either. He yanked a bottle of imported scotch from the bar against the front seat and jerked the cap off. He positioned a tumbler carefully in front of him. A hearty tilt of the bottle and it was filled to the lip.

Feeling a new sense of purpose, he lifted the carphone, dialed a number in the Kremlin, drained the first long burning sip of scotch, and waited. Tatyana picked up on the third ring.

They wasted a few minutes on mock pleasantries and obligatory political gossip. The prime minister was about to be sacked. He was an idiotic little pencil pusher, bereft of ideas to bail out the crippled economy, and by general consensus a jerk. The old prime minister who had been fired before him—an even bigger jerk—had the inside track for a return engagement.

Golitsin drummed his fingers and waited. Tatyana obviously enjoyed recounting the tawdry gossip, and he let her ramble awhile before he got down to business. "Don't you find it curious how Yuri Khodorin has resisted our overtures?"

"He is a tough nut to crack," Tatyana agreed. "Nicky's taking a terrible beating."

"He's not the only one. I finally placed two of my agents inside his companies. Both discovered, somehow."

"How do you know this?"

"I was meant to. The message was quite clear. One found in his car with his throat slashed, the other disappeared. Went to work one day and hasn't been heard from in three weeks."

"They must've gotten sloppy," she said very coldly.

"They were handpicked. Veteran agents, both of them, and they went in with perfect covers. I don't think so."

"Then what do you think?"

After a brief pause, fueled by another noisy sip, Golitsin told her, "Khodorin has been tipped off. It's the only explanation."

"It's a good explanation. Not the only one, though. But assuming it's right, who would be behind it?"

"Alex Konevitch."

"Impossible."

"Is it really? They were friends before Konevitch fled. Business competitors, but they sometimes chummed around."

Tatyana considered this theory before launching into her usual nit-picking. "How could he get word out? He's rotting in prison, Sergei."

"So what? Solzhenitsyn smuggled out full-length novels, and that was from our most remote Siberian gulag."

"I do remember reading about that. He wrote them on toilet paper or something."

"Anything's possible."

"But how did Konevitch learn we were going after Khodorin?"

"Maybe Khodorin contacted our boy. Maybe Konevitch was watching. I don't know. It doesn't really matter."

"That's two maybes," Tatyana, ever the lawyer, observed, but without conviction.

"Then let's dispense with the doubts. We've tried the same tricks on Khodorin. The computer hacking, the murders, the bombings, the police visit, the in-house spies, all of which succeeded spectacularly with Konevitch. Khodorin's been ready for every single one. He's clobbering us at our own game. It's not beginner's luck, and it's not coincidental."

Tatyana kicked off her shoes and planted her lovely feet on the desk. "So what do you suggest?"

"It's not a difficult problem."

"Then there must be an easy solution."

"There is. Konevitch, he has to die," Golitsin informed her. "And the sooner the better." His glass was empty and he refilled it with a flourish. It felt great to be back in the game, outthinking his opponents. He privately relished the vision of an OUT OF BUSINESS sign hanging on the bank in the morning. How nice it would be to wake up and have those worries behind him. He would hang the sign himself, he decided. Good riddance. "So where is our boy wonder now?" he asked, trying to suppress any hint of giddiness.

"A federal prison in Illinois. After seven months in Atlanta, it was felt he became too acclimated. Too comfortable."

"Too comfortable?"

"According to Tromble, Konevitch fit right into the life. Some band of Cuban heavyweights took him under their wing. He was living like a king. A security detail followed him everywhere. A Barcalounger in his cell. Special meals prepared in the prison mess hall. Can you believe it?"

Yes, he did. He was long past being surprised by Alex Konevitch. And, too, he was long past underestimating him. Probably, he decided, this explained how Konevitch blew the whistle on them to his old chum Khodorin—with help on the inside, there were a million ways Konevitch could communicate with the outside. "So you've failed to turn up the heat on him," Golitsin stated, but without his characteristic nastiness.

He had his own bad news to impart—bad news for her, anyway. No use getting her all worked up.

"Technically, Tromble failed. Not me," she insisted. "I've done everything I could. Our prosecution team arrived months ago. Konevitch should've been back in an American court a long time ago. The case is perfect."

"All right," he conceded very agreeably. "Then it's all Tromble's fault."

Suspicious from this burst of benevolence, Tatyana snapped, "What are you hiding, Sergei?"

Golitsin sank in his plush leather seat and cracked a small smile. She was so quick. He quickly recounted the sad tale about the rogue trader who shoved the export-import bank into insolvency. By nine the next morning, the bank would be shuttered. By ten, word would race around Moscow: Konevitch's once mighty empire had finally bled to death.

Tatyana's feet flew off the desk and landed on the floor. "Oh, that's just great," she moaned. "Your idiots ruined me. My stock is now worthless."

"Mine, too."

"Oh, spare me. You have Konevitch's money, his mansion, his cars, his luxury apartment in Paris. What do I have?"

He was tempted to answer truthfully: A hundred thousand shares of nothing; you're broke and desperate, living on a mangy government paycheck. I'm your only hope—you need me more than ever.

Instead, he tapped his fingers on the car seat and sipped patiently from his scotch as she swore and vented for a few more minutes.

Eventually, he uncorked the cure to her troubles. "All the more reason to take care of this Khodorin business quickly. We'll divide the cash this time. I promise. Five hundred million, perfectly even, a three-way split. Same with his shares. And this time, we'll sell everything as fast as we can. We'll easily bag another billion or more."

He paused to allow her a moment to accept the inevitability of her situation. She was broke, for the moment; but not hopeless. With the right moves, in no time at all she could light her cigarettes with thousand-dollar bills. "The best way to get inside Khodorin's head is to kill Konevitch," he suggested.

"It will be quite difficult. He's out of reach, behind bars."

"But not impossible. And if Khodorin wants to play games with us, he needs to be taught a lesson. There's no way for him to win."

"You're right," she mumbled. The brilliance of the suggestion finally dawned on her. "Meet our demands when the time comes, or we'll hunt you down. If the U.S. government can't protect Konevitch, there's no hope for you. Khodorin will collapse."

*   *   *

After a brief call on her cell phone to Nicky, and a long meeting with a few American specialists in the Foreign Ministry, Tatyana barked at the Kremlin switch to do whatever it took to connect her to the director of the American FBI. It took three operators thirty minutes to track him down. He happened to be in an FBI field office in northern Jersey, clustered with a team of agents who had just broken up a large counterfeiting ring. An inside informant had been turned a year before. Unlike so many other operations during Tromble's tenure, the investigation had been a model of law enforcement skill and restraint. Every nuance of legal limit had been adhered to, no shortcuts. The evidence was overwhelming and, in the view of the Justice Department's sharpest experts, virtually unchallengeable in court.

The three counterfeiters had been slapped in cuffs an hour before. Tromble had arrived just in time for the press conference where he would make the announcement and bask in the glory. The podium was already set up, the large flock of reporters and cameras waiting with growing impatience.

An aide entered the room where Tromble was being fed enough information to fool the press into believing he had personally doted on every detail of the case, had personally overseen this masterstroke of crimefighting at its best. The aide cupped a hand to his ear and signaled his boss. Tromble cursed, then stepped out of the room and accepted the proffered cell phone.

Without preamble, Tatyana launched right in. "What's going on with Konevitch?"

"Sorry, no change," he told her, eyeing his watch, impatient to begin his briefing. All the big networks were there, all the big East Coast papers. "He's still up in Chicago. Believe me, it's a nasty place. One of our two worst."

"He's been there two months now, John."

"Almost three, actually."

"And it's been almost a year since you promised to deliver him to me."

"I know, and I'm sorry. He's tougher than expected."

"And how are the reports from Chicago?"

"Not promising. It's very curious. Somehow, he's wormed his way inside the Black Power brotherhood."

"But he's white. Don't they discriminate?"

"Typically, yes. He's amazingly adaptable."

"All right, you've had your turn," she barked, suddenly turning aggressive. "Now I'd like to take my best shot."

"What are you talking about?"

"I consulted with a few of my experts about your prisons. I want someplace tougher. Much tougher, much more terrifying."

This greatly annoyed him and he made no effort to hide it. "I believe I know our prisons better than your so-called experts. Atlanta and Chicago are our worst."

"The worst *federal* prisons, you mean. Not your worst prisons, not by a long shot."

"That might be true, but the federal prisons are the ones I can influence."

She went on, unfazed. "It's my understanding that your Bureau of Prisons occasionally subcontracts with state prisons."

"Occasionally, yes. To alleviate overcrowding. Sometimes as a temporary measure until a prisoner can be moved. So what?"

"I further understand that the state prison in Yuma is unimaginably horrible. A nightmare of violence, killings, and rapes."

"Well . . . it's pretty bad. But Parchman down in Mississippi's probably a little worse."

"You don't seem to be listening, John. Like it or not, it's my turn to pick Konevitch's hellhole."

Tromble swallowed his anger. "So what do you want?"

"Switch him to Yuma. Do it immediately."

"He's barely been in Chicago three months."

"It's almost summertime, and the prison lacks air-conditioning. I want him sweltering in 120-degree heat, locked into a small cell he has to share with a complete sociopath. I want him mixed in with the general population, eating horrible food, and worried every minute of every day for his life. I want him more miserable than he's ever been."

"I think that can be arranged."

"If you want your agents in Moscow, you'll make damned sure it is. You've embarrassed me with my bosses, John. You owe me for a year of humiliation and lame excuses."

Before Tromble could say another word, Tatyana punched off. She leaned back into her chair and placed her feet back on her desk. The prison had been Nicky's choice. He knew of ten Russians inside Yuma, three of them hit men with impressive credentials. He swore that any one of them could do the job.

Courtesy of Golitsin's fat wallet, a bonus would be offered to sweeten the pot—$500K to whoever killed Konevitch. A way would be found to get this word inside. Quick results were expected.

The next idea was Tatyana's. To encourage speedy action, the price would decrease by $100K a month, until the job was done.

28

Warden Byron James leaned back in his seat and contemplated the glistening toes of his spitshined wingtips. He peered into the reflected face of Special Agent Terrence Hanrahan and informed him, "Won't take long."

"You're sure?"

"Damn sure. Ask around. This here prison's the rottenest sewer in America," he said very loudly, smacking his lips and looking quite proud about that boast.

"What have you done with him?"

A slow smile. "A week in solitary for starters. Moved him to D Wing today."

"What's that? High-security?"

The warden's feet hit the floor and he leaned forward. "Just say he's not in the best of company."

"Tell me more."

"D Wing's for the undesirables. Big-time dealers, gangbangers, Mafia hoods, Black Power brotherhood, and recalcitrants who can't seem to behave. Plus, he's got a special new cellmate, Bitchy Beatty."

"That supposed to mean something to me?"

"If you were an inmate . . . then yeah, damned sure it would."

Hanrahan was pretty certain it was best not to know. In the

event he was subpoenaed later, total ignorance was his best defense. Curiosity got the better of him, though, and reluctantly he asked, "Tell me about Bitchy . . . ?"

"Beatty. Bitchy Beatty. Guess you might know him better as Benny Beatty."

"Oh . . . *that* Beatty?"

"Same guy. You know, before that awful assault thing happened." Hanrahan vaguely recalled the case, about three years back.

Beatty, formerly of one of those big Kansas college football factories, and in his second year as an All-Pro tackle for Arizona, had rushed into the New York Jets locker room with a baseball bat after getting creamed in a championship game. Like a whirling dervish, he spun and bounced around the room and brutally assaulted fifteen of the Jets' top stars. By the time he was wrestled down, the locker room was filled with busted teeth and broken bones, three shattered kneecaps, and more gallons of blood than anybody cared to measure.

Beatty got more than the max, ten to twenty: turned out the judge was a rabid Jets season ticketholder; turned out it would be five to ten before the Jets could rebuild and field a reasonable team. The furious judge threw away the sentencing guidelines and gave Beatty double what he gave the Jets. An appeal was pending. The grounds were solid, but it would be heard in a New York appellate court, of all places. His lawyers weren't optimistic.

Hanrahan asked, "How'd he get that nickname?"

"Short for 'bitchmaker.' Ol' Beatty misses all those groupie sluts something awful." A broad smile at the faces in the room. "Guess you'd say his cellmates are his surrogates."

Two special agents leaned against the wall and joined in the laughter, halfheartedly, little more than forced chuckles. They stopped as soon as it seemed polite.

This was the third prison inside a year. And the third cocksure warden who swore he would break Konevitch like a swaybacked pony. Konevitch had adapted to each new facility quickly, with surprising ease. Go figure.

As a prisoner in the federal system, though, he enjoyed one

protected right they badly wished they could withhold: monthly visits from that pretty little wife, who appeared like clockwork. No matter where they moved him, no matter how closely the secret was kept, she somehow learned where he was. The Feds monitored his mail, an easy task, as there had been no mail—none coming in, none going out. That nosy lawyer of theirs peppered the system with requests for his location, but none had been answered. Somehow, though, she always knew where he was.

He attacked the library with curious regularity. The FBI accessed the records and followed his literary pursuits with their own deep interest. The law stacks were a common destination. Little surprise there. All prisoners fashioned themselves Clarence Darrows, able to outdo all those esquired incompetents who screwed up and got them in here. Every other day, it was books on computers, computer languages, FORTRAN and COBOL, and that new thing called the Internet all their kids were raving about. A few times a week, he hopped onto the library computer and typed away at blazing speed, nearly burning up the keyboard. Why, they had no idea.

Hanrahan turned away from the warden and, talking maybe at the wall, maybe at nobody, emphasized, "You know how important this is to us."

"Guess I do. I got a call from Fielder at headquarters. Said your guy, Tromble, wants this real bad."

Still looking away, like this wasn't a conversation. "Find a way to scale back his liberties. Turn up the heat as fast and hard as you like."

The warden, also now talking, not at Hanrahan but at some invisible spot on the ceiling, hypothesized, "Yeah, well, he could, I dunno, maybe misbehave or somethin'. I'd have to come down hard with a few necessary disciplinary measures."

"Yeah, but like what?"

"A few more weeks in solitary will get his attention."

"Don't. Believe me, don't. That was tried at both previous prisons. He folds himself into some kind of yoga posture and goes into a trance. Actually, he seems to enjoy the solitude."

"Two . . . ? Hey, I thought this guy was a cherry."

"Sorry, no, you're the third. The other two prisons he's shown a talent for building coalitions and finding people to protect him. He's clever. We have no idea how he does it."

The warden leaned back in his chair and threw his hands behind his head. "Well, your boy ain't met me yet," he boasted. "Ask around, fellas. The state always sends me the biggest hardasses. I got my ways of making 'em crack."

The two agents on the wall shared quiet smiles. It was the same speech, almost word for word, they had heard from both previous wardens. And in each prison, inside a few weeks, Konevitch was hanging out with the biggest badasses in the yard, getting extra food helpings in the mess hall, the recipient of all kinds of special largesse and favors, even from the guards.

As much as they hoped and plotted otherwise, somehow, some way, they feared Alex Konevitch would find a way to upstage this wingtipped, overconfident ass as well.

Bitchy missed football like crazy. All in all, though, prison wasn't all that bad, or even all that different. He more or less spent his time just as he did back in his cherished NFL days, eating voraciously, hoisting enormous weights out in the yard, and bashing heads whenever the impulse seized him. He had packed on another forty pounds of bad mood to the 350 he arrived with, all hard muscle.

Bitchy had scraped by with terrible grades in college, not because he was stupid, because he was smart. A full ride, with all the cute little cheerleaders he wanted, and bright little volunteers to stand in and take his tests. What dork would hide his nose inside books with all that fun to be had? Like many football hotshots, off the field Bitchy had always been spoiled rotten; it shouldn't surprise anybody that he now had a few serious impulse control issues. Anyway, the college was determined to graduate him phi beta pigskin, no matter what, even if he never went near class, which he seldom did.

The new boy was lying on the lower bunk with his nose stuffed inside a book, something about Web site construction. He was cute, real cute. A bit tall for Bitchy's usual taste maybe, but what the hell, variety was supposed to be spicy. So why not? He shifted his vast weight to the side of his bunk and peered down.

"Hey, I heard you're a transfer."

"Third prison this year."

"How come they moved you to this shithole?"

"Mutilation."

"What the hell's that?"

"I mutilated a man. I didn't kill him. Afterward, though, I suppose he wished I had." Alex absently flipped a page and continued reading.

Bitchy scratched his head. "That's a new one on me."

"In the statutes it sits between first- and second-degree assault. You see, in your American laws, it boils down to intent. I didn't want to kill him."

"What are you, a lawyer?" Bitchy hated lawyers. He'd been screwed royally by the five-hundred-buck-an-hour suit he'd hired to defend him, a pompous prick who barely protested when the judge doubled his sentence. He would dearly love to screw one back.

"Hardly."

Bitchy bounced off the top bunk. With incredible agility, both feet hit the floor at once, almost catlike. He was so damned big and blockish, his opponents habitually underestimated his speed, balance, and dexterity. But not after Bitchy got his huge paws on you—suddenly, everything about him came into terrifying focus.

He placed a hand on his zipper and was about to introduce his new cellmate to Mr. Johnson.

Alex calmly closed the book and looked at him. "I castrated a man," he informed Beatty simply, coldly. "He attempted to rape me in the shower. That night, after he fell asleep, I chopped it off. While he howled in pain, I cut it into small pieces. You know why, Benny?" He paused long enough to allow Benny time to consider this intriguing question. "It made it impossible to sew back on."

Bitchy's hand left his zipper and entered a deep pocket.

Alex said, "I hear you were a professional footballer."

A strange way to put it, but Bitchy answered, "Yeah. So what?"

"Did it pay well?"

This was getting weird. "Not well. It paid great."

"How great?"

"A five million signing bonus. Three million a year in salary. Why you askin'?"

"Where is all that money now?"

"None of your business."

Alex put the book down and leaned his back against the wall. "I suppose your legal costs consumed most of it."

Bitchy also leaned back against the wall. He was in the mood for a little man-love, but this guy seemed to want to chitchat a bit before they got down to action. At least he wasn't hollering and bouncing around the cell like his last cellmate. The Russian accent sure sounded cool.

"I got millions left. When it hits three mil, the lawyers can go screw themselves. The appeals stop."

"Smart. So how is it invested?"

"In the bank. Where else would it be?"

"Did nobody advise you that's stupid?"

Bitchy bounced off the wall. The hand came out of the pocket and suddenly balled into a beefy fist. "Watch your mouth. You're stupid if you call me stupid."

"Relax, Benny. I never said you were stupid. I said leaving the money in the bank is stupid."

"It'll still be there when I get out. How stupid is that?"

"A lot more of it could be there. Is that smart, my friend?"

"All right, Mr. I-know-so-much, what's smarter?"

"In the right stocks, it will multiply enormously. Real estate is a fairly good and safe investment also."

"That's not my thing."

"Have you ever heard of Qualcomm, Benny?"

Bitchy laughed. "Sure. I get it from the pharmacy whenever I get jock itch." He laughed harder.

"We'll look into jock-itch providers if you'd like. It's certainly a market you know well. That's more of a slow growth, long-term investment, though," Alex replied, very seriously. "It's a company that invented a brilliant new way to send sound and information down a wire, or even fiber-optic cable. The stock is set to quadruple. Do you understand time-division versus code-division encoding?"

Not a chance.

"Well, let me explain the deal. If you want me as a lover, I probably can't stop you. Of course you'll have to sleep with one eye open. When will that crazy Russian guy cut my dingee off?" Alex waved his hand up and down in the air. "He will, most definitely, he will . . . but when?"

It was said so matter-of-factly, Bitchy took no offense. Shifting to the third person helped; it took a little personal edge off the threat.

"Or," Alex pushed on, "I can be your investment advisor. I'll double or triple your money. That's a lowball estimate, incidentally. I know a great deal about the Russian market also. A little cash in the right ADRs would be very smart. Derivatives are doing quite well these days also."

Alex patted the mattress. Bitchy's broad rear landed on the bunk beside him and he said, "I have no idea what you're talking about."

"That's why you need me, Benny."

"Just for not raping you?"

"There are many attractive men in this prison. Do whatever you like, just not with me, okay?"

"Do I have to protect you?"

"That's not part of the deal, no."

"Make me that kind of dough and I'll slaughter whoever comes near you."

An indifferent shrug. "Probably a wise move on your part."

"So how's this work?"

"Easier than you might think. There are probably fifteen or twenty contraband cell phones in the block, am I right?"

Bitchy nodded. Fifty was more like it. The guards were always hunting for them, but as they grew smaller they became so much easier to conceal. Bitchy knew of at least four tucked away in the prison laundry, another six in the kitchen. Twist a few arms, and he'd have all he wanted. No was not a word Bitchy heard very often.

"Get me three of those phones, Benny. The batteries wear down quickly and can't be recharged inside our cell. You'll handle the expenses. Believe me, you'll be able to afford it. I use the phones to manage your money and whoever else I decide to call."

"And what if you mess up and lose my money?"

"I'll be on the bottom bunk. If I fail to keep my end of the bargain, you're not obligated to keep yours."

Bitchy crossed his arms and stared off at the far wall. Of the vast multitude of "investment advisors" at the pro draft who pounced hungrily on the newest batch of twenty-two-year-old, undereducated millionaires, not one of those greedy blabbermouths had offered a deal remotely resembling this. And if they lost it all through their own utter ineptitude, it was tough luck, pal, sayonara.

Really, how many investment advisors promised outright that if they failed in their promises, they'd bend over and take it, like they just gave it? "All right," Bitchy said, hands back in his pockets.

"Another thing. I'm going to teach you how to do this. If I make you all that money, I don't want you to turn around and lose it afterward."

"Will it hurt?"

"Only a little, Benny."

Benny laughed.

"One last thing," Alex said, returning to his book.

"Name it."

"Spread the word. The last two prisons, we pooled our money and increased our buying positions enormously. The more the better for you."

The day that marked the anniversary of eleven months since the Konevitch trial, Kim Parrish threw her long-overdue fit.

The team of state prosecutors had arrived from Russia six months before, four of them in all, all men, all wearing blockish suits made of a cheap, indescribable fabric. Only one spoke any semblance of English—just please, thank you, yes, but mostly no, and a dismaying variety of filthy curses.

The FBI paid for the works and put them up in the downtown Hilton. They immediately raised hell about the lousy accommodations. To shut them up, they were bounced a few blocks over to the Madison, a decidedly more upscale lodging. The complaints did not abate until the Madison succumbed and switched them each to thousand-dollar suites.

They ate breakfast, lunch, and dinner at the most expensive Georgetown restaurants, rented two Mercedes sedans, a snazzy black Corvette, and a shiny red Maserati. They spent their five-day weekends raising hell in California and Florida, before they fell deeply in love with Las Vegas and the legalized brothels nearby. They billed it all to the FBI—the first-class airfares, the whores, the gambling losses that quickly turned mountainous. Everything was billed directly to the Feds. They drank from dawn till dusk, got in fistfights in bars, picked up four DUIs, smashed up the Maserati, trashed one Mercedes sedan, and billed all that, too, to the FBI.

They arrived with two dozen large crates stuffed to the lids with documents. Everything in Russian. Everything, every word and comma, had to be meticulously and painfully translated into English.

Two more weeks were lost while Kim scoured the city for a competent translator. As the documents proved to be a thick maze of Russian legalese, not any translator would do. Kim interviewed a dozen candidates. Several American college graduates whose levels of fluency weren't nearly as impressive as their résumés. Five Russian émigrés who utterly failed the English test. A retired book editor who had translated two complete Tolstoy novels had seemed like her best bet. That one took a brief glance at the two dozen crates and bolted.

Eventually, Kim drove across to the river to the leafy, sprawling CIA headquarters at Langley. She had called ahead and was met by man from the Russian analysis section. Downstairs, in the large marble lobby, she briefly described her problem. Mr. Spook smiled reassuringly and claimed he knew the perfect guy. On a sheet of paper he wrote the name and number of a Russian expat, a man named Petri Arbatov, a major in the KGB before he defected to the U.S. Petri had a law degree from Moscow University and in the fifteen years since his defection, he had also picked up an American JD from Catholic University. Petri demanded $600 an hour, a price that would've impressed the most expensive firm in New York. He insisted he wouldn't translate "da" to "yes" for a penny less. The price was outrageous, far beyond what she had intended to pay. She promptly agreed.

What the hell: Petri, too, could send his rather impressive bills to the FBI. If the Fibbies could blow through all that dough on a bunch of Russian cowboys whooping it up like rich Arab playboys, they better not even blink about all-too-legitimate legal expenses.

Kim rented a small, furnished fourth-floor apartment on Connecticut Avenue, they hauled up the boxes, rolled up their sleeves, and dug in. Petri proved to be a rare combination, an unemotional perfectionist—a short, thin, sad-faced man of few words who concentrated deeply and absolutely on his work. He consumed only one meal a day, always a thin broth he brought from home that he carefully spooned into his mouth. On such little nourishment, it was a miracle he stayed alive, much less endured the backbreaking load of work. He surrounded himself with both Russian and English dictionaries and waded through each document, word for word. He dictated. Kim typed. At six hundred an hour, he and Kim avoided expensive banter. They made it through three-quarters of the crates at a furious pace because they wasted nothing: neither time nor words. After four months and twenty days of eighteen hours each, she had no idea whether Petri was married, had cancer, children, was rich or poor, or even whether he lived on the street.

Thus she was hugely surprised when he slammed down one of the documents and turned to her. "You and I need to talk."

"About what?"

"Do you know what I did for the KGB, Kim? You've never asked."

"You were a lawyer?"

"More or less. I was the KGB's idea of a lawyer."

"Okay. What does that mean?"

"I worked in a legal section that specialized in what were termed special cases."

"So what? Specialization is the name of the game. I specialize in immigration law."

"Ask my specialty."

She decided to humor him. She smiled. "What was your specialty, Petri?"

"Framing. I framed people, Kim." He let that nauseating confession sit for a moment, then pushed on. "Only high-value targets. And I was the best, Kim, a remarkably talented lawyer. I could build a seamless case against anybody. A general secretary, a highly decorated marshal of the Soviet Union, a poet with a Nobel Prize, it didn't matter. Literally anybody, Kim. They gave me a name and I went to work. When I was done, any jury or judge would believe the accused was a capitalist pig with ten million in a Swiss account who had sex with his own children and lived only to destroy the motherland."

"Is this why you defected, Petri? Conscience."

He looked away. "Oh, I wish I could say yes." He seemed to sink in his chair. "I'm not so noble, I'm afraid."

"What happened?"

"One day, I went to visit another man in my section, a good friend of twenty years, who worked only three doors down from my office. He had slipped out to go to the latrine. He did something incredibly stupid, he left his door unlocked. This was totally against procedure, you must understand. Inexcusably sloppy. So I walked in. Documents were strewn everywhere. On his desk, his floor, everywhere. He was obviously well along."

"With what?"

"With me, Kim. He was building a case against me."

She moved closer, almost in his face. "Why?"

He refused to look at her. "An hour later, I was hugging a CIA man from your embassy and begging for help. I cried, Kim. I promised anything his bosses wanted—anything. I was about to get what I had done to so many others, and I was suffocating with fear. No level of betrayal was ruled out. They whisked me out the next morning." In a sad, resigned tone Petri added, "So I never asked my old friend, you see."

"You must have some idea."

"Competition, I suppose. You see, I *was* the best, Kim. I could turn a saint into a whore, a pope into a pimp, whatever I wanted them to be. The chief-of-section job was coming open. We were both vying for the job and all that came with it. A larger apartment, a chauffeured car, two weeks a year in a seedy KGB guesthouse in Ukraine. That's how KGB people operate."

"I see."

He rolled forward in his chair and planted his skinny elbows on his bony knees. "Don't look down your nose at my work. You have no idea the expertise or artistry it requires. Everything must be perfect, Kim. Documents forged with just the right dates, matching fonts, identical signatures, all the witnesses coached and carefully choreographed. It's police work and lawyer work and theater work rolled into one. You have to imagine the crime, Kim, dream it up out of thin air. Then dig a moat and build a castle nobody can assail. No detail can be overlooked, no knot untied. I must tell you, Kim, it's so much more difficult than constructing a real case with real facts."

"Well, I wouldn't know about that."

Petri lifted the document and began reading it again. He floated out of his past, back to the present. Nearly an hour passed before he looked up and asked casually, "How do you consider this case against Konevitch?"

"You know what?" She put aside the document she was reading and glanced over at him. "I'm impressed. I thought those four clowns were just drunken miscreants. Totally useless."

"But now?"

"Well, I was wrong. They're good. Very, very good. They've really delivered the goods."

"Will your judge be persuaded?"

Kim smiled. "The Konevitches will be back in Moscow faster than they can blink." After a moment, she asked, "What do you think?"

"Probably so."

"I just wish I had all this material at the first trial."

Petri nodded as if to say: Of course you do. "And what do you believe will happen to them at home?"

"Not my problem, Petri."

"My apologies. I offended you. Of course you can't worry about the people you kick out."

They returned to their work. They fell back into their normal pattern and quietly ignored each other for another hour. Petri thumbed through his beloved dictionaries and scrawled long, messy notes in the margins of a document. Kim pecked away on her keyboard, forcing yet another translated document into her hard drive—or trying to, at least. She began making mistake after mistake. She corrected, then corrected the correction, then repeated the first mistake again. Her brain and her fingers seemed to be coming unglued from each other.

With a loud curse, she finally pushed away from her desk. She wheeled her chair across the floor until she ended up less than a foot from Petri. "All right. What will happen to them?"

He quietly closed the thick dictionary. "Tell me what you think."

"All right. They'll be tried in court. Probably convicted. They didn't kill anybody, so probably they'll end up in prison."

Petri made no reply.

"Look," Kim said, more forcefully and with a show of considerable indignation, "all these crates of evidence from the Russians. Proof of intention, right? Why go to such enormous lengths and trouble if they don't intend to put them on trial?"

"As you say," Petri replied with a slight grin. The answer was now so obvious, it was staring her in the eye. She knew it. After all these months of sweat and hard work, and of unrelenting pressure from her bosses, it was only natural for her to suppress it. But pieces of it kept bubbling to the surface. Little fragments. Niggling doubts and caustic uncertainties.

The frustration was killing her. "Damn it, Petri, Konevitch stole the money. He's guilty. He plundered his own bank, he ripped off hundreds of millions."

"Is that so?"

She waved a hand at the crates stacked neatly in the corner. "Bank records. Statements from his own employees. Computer printouts of his transactions, police reports, three full investigations from three different government agencies. What more do you want?"

"You're absolutely right, Kim. Who could want more? It's all here."

"Damn right it is."

"A perfect little package, gift-wrapped, and handed to you on a silver platter." This skinny little lawyer who once made his living building perfect cases just wouldn't let go.

"Too perfect, isn't it?" she asked, bending forward and rubbing her forehead.

"Tell me how many cases you've tried."

"Hundreds. I don't know."

"Any cases where every detail matched up so well? Every date coincides, every witness saw exactly the same thing, every investigator came to identical conclusions? Everything so perfectly, so amazingly lined up? For a supposedly brilliant man, Konevitch left behind an astonishing ocean of evidence."

She was suddenly more deeply miserable than she had ever felt. It was inescapable now. She was fighting back a flood of tears. "No case is ever perfect."

She had reached the end of the journey. Petri sat back for a moment, allowing her to ponder the ugly magnitude of her discovery. Americans were so naïve about these things.

He then commented, "We never actually tried the cases in court, you know. Not our job, Kim. We built the perfect little cases and handed them off to others. Those trial lawyers, they all loved us. Such flawless gifts we gave them. They couldn't lose."

"I don't understand. Why hand them off? You said you were a great lawyer. Since you created it, you knew the material better than anybody."

"I often wondered that, you know. They never told us why. Perhaps they thought the man who designs the guillotine shouldn't actually be forced to pull the lever and have to stare at the head in the basket. Communists. They could be so incoherently humane in completely inhumane ways."

Kim wanted to jump out of her chair and bolt. Just run away from this case. Run as fast and as far as her feet could carry her.

He rolled forward in his chair and placed a hand on her knee. "They'll murder them, Kim. Oh, they might go through the motions of a trial . . . or they might not. They'll kill them, though, as sure as you and I are sitting here."

There was one question left for her to ask, one dark mystery to solve. "But Konevitch could be guilty, couldn't he, Petri?"

"You know the golden rule of my old KGB section?"

She forced herself to stare into his dark, sad eyes, to hear the wisdom of a soul soiled and ruined long before they ever met.

"Never frame a guilty man."

The first run at Alex Konevitch came shortly after sunrise. It came three weeks to the day after he stepped out of the dark prison van in Yuma. It came in a large sweltering room filled with sweaty men, less than a minute after Alex loaded his tray with his usual selection of soggy French toast and watery scrambled eggs, only seconds after he sat in his usual seat, at his usual table.

The offer had been smuggled in to the Russians a week before by a balding, nervous-looking guard named Tim. A double divorcé drowning under a serious gambling addiction, Tim owed his bookie, Marty, five thousand bucks after a sure-thing pony did the big choke on the backstretch. Before he placed the bet, Tim had vaguely wondered if his bookie had mob connections. Good guess. Turned out Anthony "the Crusher" Cardozzi was Marty's second cousin, a lifelong business associate, and quite serious about men honoring their debts. A month overdue on his vig, Tim now was seriously wondering if his state medical insurance would cover the destruction. Thus, when Marty relayed the offer—a favor for a friend, Marty intimated—Tim almost suffocated with relief.

Five thousand bucks forgiven, and two perfectly functional kneecaps—incredible generosity, just for delivering a simple message. Sure, no problem, Tim replied, vowing to give up gambling, and knowing he wouldn't.

The offer ignited a bitter quarrel among the Russians. Day to day a loose-knit group, they were bound by two common traits— they all spoke Russian, and all had ties of one sort or another to the Russian underworld. The big question—indeed, the only question—was, who would get first crack at Alex Konevitch?

After two days of passing increasingly malicious notes back and forth, the Russians gathered in a tight swarthy huddle in a remote corner of the yard to discuss the offer—a cool half million to whomever killed him within thirty days, declining in value with each passing month. They spoke in Russian, and they sparred loudly and heatedly, with no concern at all about being overheard.

The sooner the better—this point seemed elemental and was quickly agreed among the ten men. Why wait and waste a hundred grand? Point two was almost as easily settled—the first crack would be their best shot. Catch Konevitch before he knew of their intention to kill him. Catch him before he had his guard up. Catch him at his most vulnerable.

If that flopped, future efforts would become increasingly difficult.

The experienced hit men raucously laid claim to the honor. The killing game wasn't as easy as it seemed, one explained, and the other killers nodded with great gravity and solemn agreement. An amateur making his first plunge was likely to do something unfathomably stupid. Two of the veterans confessed how they had choked on their first jobs. Seemingly insignificant details that suddenly ballooned into big problems. A wrong glance here, a careless stutter there, that alerted the target. A case of last-minute jitters that turned paralytic. A lot could go wrong, and often did.

The thieves and pushers and kidnappers weren't buying it. What was so hard? Bring something sharp, pick a vital organ, and poke it. No problem, as easy as cutting steak. The bickering intensified and verged on violence, before Igor, a clever accountant with a talent for money laundering, came to the rescue with a way to buy peace. One hundred grand from the bounty would be carved off and split among the nine Russians who didn't get to stab a hole in Alex.

Everybody wanted to argue about this for a while, but the compromise was irresistible, and inevitably accepted.

Now everybody benefited. And now everybody had a stake in doing it right.

Thus the lottery rapidly whittled down to four. Three had made a handsome living on the outside, killing people. Number four was a blowhard who loudly proclaimed two murders and launched into vulgar, descriptive bragging about his handiwork. They suspected he was lying, and they were right. Nobody could prove it, though; thus he had a tenuous, shaky seat at the table. But having settled on this logic, it was a short bounce to the next argument.

To nobody's surprise, this proposal came from the lips of Lev Titov, hands down the most productive killer in the group, if not the entire prison. It was plain common sense, Lev argued—the one with the most scalps on his belt should have the first shot. Having jumped off to an early start, at age fourteen, fulfilling every schoolboy's dream by strangling his math teacher, Lev went on to compile an impressive pedigree of homicides. He was legendary among certain circles, a remorseless assassin who killed without flair or even a telltale method. He had slain for himself, for the Russian army, for the Mafiya, and occasionally, when his short fuse got the better of him, for the hell of it. He was fussy and painstaking, and able to murder with a bewildering variety of weapons, from a deck of cards to sophisticated bombs. He once killed a man he suspected of cheating at chess by stuffing the checkmated king down his throat. Unpredictability and a certain amount of messiness were his only signatures.

A quick show of hands. Eight for. One puzzling abstention. Only the blowhard against.

Lev was the man.

One hundred grand would be split nine ways; the other four hundred would go into an account of Lev's choosing. A man who smiled rarely, Lev could not wipe the grin off his face. With seven years left on his sentence, he could at least look forward to a little gold at the end of the rainbow.

And so it was that at the moment Alex placed his tray on the table and casually fell onto the hard metal bench, Lev never even turned around. Why bother? After watching and studying his target for four days, he could write a book on Alex's culinary habits. He knew Alex would quietly sip his lukewarm coffee and wait for his big cellmate. Alex liked eggs, his cellmate adored French toast. It was a routine they shared, like an old married couple. The roommate would pour and scrape his runny eggs onto Alex's tray, and the French toast would land on the big guy's before they launched into their breakfasts.

The other nine Russians were strategically situated in a rough concentric pattern, precisely in accordance with the neat diagram Lev had meticulously sketched and handed out. Lev raised a clenched fist to signal the start. Immediately the other nine launched their trays in the air, then began indiscriminately pummeling every prisoner within reach. In a claustrophobic chamber filled with sweaty, grumpy men with a strong penchant toward violence, the spark was volcanic, the result horrific. It opened with an artillery duel of hundreds of hurled trays. Then four hundred men commenced an orgy of punching, kicking, tackling, biting, hollering, shoving, and general havoc.

Lev, seated almost directly to Alex's rear, watched with quiet amusement. He wouldn't budge until the riot approached full pitch. The sudden shift from order to madness overwhelmed the guards, who shuffled their feet and watched helplessly from the sidelines. From past riots, Lev knew he had three minutes before reinforcements equipped with batons and riot gear arrived to break up the fun.

Lev slowly stood and stretched. He drew a deep breath and steeled his nerves. From his right pant pocket he withdrew a ten-inch shaft, a masterpiece of lethal perfection he had lovingly honed in the prison shop. The tip was pointy as a pin. Edges that could shave a baby's ass. The hilt was attractively bound in a coarse, fingerprint-resistant cotton fabric, a throwaway tool, a stab-and-leave-it special. And because of the commotion, a fast, quiet stabbing would be lost in the sea of violence. The odds of witnesses were about nil; the odds anyone would snitch on Lev even less.

Lev eased away from his table and through a series of short, stealthy steps quickly closed the seven feet to Alex. His target was standing now, back turned to Lev, thoroughly fixated on the raucous festivities, totally oblivious that this little party was all about him. Lev gripped the knife low. An upward thrust would be best, he promptly decided—up though the rib cage, then straight for the heart, or lungs.

But just as the blade was swinging up, something hard and powerful banged Lev's forearm. A nasty cracking sound, and the arm snapped. The shiv popped out of his fist and was instantly lost in the wild scuffle of feet. The county coroner would later note that Lev's radius and ulna bones had both snapped and shattered. Simultaneous breaks with lots of splinters. A blow from a sledgehammer might account for it. A one-in-a-million kick from one of those big-time karate guys was another possibility.

One thing was sure—the force had been a ten on the Richter scale.

Lev yelped with pain and barely had to time to look to his left. A defense of any kind was out of the question anyway. A giant with frightening speed and gargantuan hands lifted him off the floor by his head. A quick jerk to the right, another snapping noise, Lev's neck this time, and he dropped to the floor like a discarded sack of disconnected bones.

His body was jerking involuntarily but Lev didn't feel a thing. No pain, no tingling, not even a mild sense of relief as his bowels and bladder emptied.

The big man was leaning over him, looking down into his eyes. "Hey, Alex," the man asked over his shoulder, "know this guy?"

"I've never seen him before."

"He knows you, for damn sure. He was about to shiv you."

In Russian, Lev managed to croak, "Call a doctor."

The big man looked bewildered. "What?"

Alex eased the big man aside and bent down until his face was two inches from Lev's. "Who are you?" he asked, also in Russian.

"Call a doctor. Please. My body's not working."

"Give me your name."

"Can't breathe," he managed to gasp, and he was right. His spinal cord was severed; his face was turning bluer by the second as spinal shock settled in. "Hurry."

"Why me?" Alex asked.

"Money," Lev confessed.

"From who?" Alex asked, not budging, not making the slightest move to save him.

"I . . ." Lev tried to force a breath, but his lungs no longer functioned. "No idea."

The big man tugged at Alex's arm. "Let's go. Don't be standing here when the guards come."

"One last question," Alex promised the big man, then, staring into Lev's dying eyes, asked, "Are there more of you?"

Lev did not answer. The final act of his miserable life would not include snitching on his colleagues. He would not give Konevitch the satisfaction.

It was in his eyes, though.

Oh yes, there were definitely more killers out there.

They waited until they were back in the privacy of their small cell before either said a word. They sat on the lower bunk, kicked off their shoes, and pretended for a moment that it had never happened. Benny had not just killed a man. Nobody was trying to execute Alex. Life was every bit as good as it was yesterday, and tomorrow would be the same.

Eventually, Alex started it off. "Benny, I owe you my life."

"Just protecting my investment," Bitchy grunted as though it was nothing. His face betrayed him; he was obviously quite pleased.

"How did you know?"

"Oh, that. Well, the riot. There's usually one before a killing in here."

"I meant how did you know I was his target?"

"Didn't, necessarily. Protecting my quarterback in large mobs is how I make my living. You get an eye, or you don't get a contract. Who was that guy?"

"A Russian. I never met him."

"Why'd he want to shiv you?"

"Money, Benny—somebody put a bounty on me."

"A big one?"

"Quite large, probably."

"That's not good."

"Tell me about it."

"Any idea who's fronting the cash?"

"A very good idea, yes."

"Can you make them back off?"

"Sure, after I'm dead."

"Anyone else know?"

"I have that impression. The boys who started the riot, for sure."

They pondered the walls for a moment. Benny obviously was wondering what he had gotten himself into, hooked up with a Russian with a sumptuous bounty on his head. And Alex, just as obviously, was analyzing the same issue. How had the Russians found him? After a moment, that question answered itself. Somebody in the U.S. government had tipped them off; no other possibility made sense. But why now? And why here, in this miserable excuse for a prison? He was incarcerated, awaiting trial. In all likelihood, his next date with a judge would be followed by a quick trip to Russia. He posed absolutely no threat—or none they should know about, anyway.

Wait a few more months, and they could kill him at their leisure, in Moscow, in a small cell, in the prison of their choice. Kill him however they wanted, slow or fast, where nobody would ask questions later. So why now?

Benny broke the prolonged silence. "Will they try again?"

"What do you think?"

"I think I should find another cellmate."

"Good idea. I won't hold it against you."

Another moment of quiet passed. Alex studied his bare toes. Bitchy stood up, stretched, and produced a loud yawn.

"Thing is, Alex, you're trapped in here with these guys," Benny said, stretching his immense arms over his big head. "You can hide for 364 days, and on the 365th they catch you alone, in the shower, on the john, walking out of a meeting with your lawyer. That's it, game over." Then, as if Alex wasn't listening, "It's too easy."

"I'm already scared out of my wits, Benny. Thanks for making me hopeless."

"Just thought you should know."

"Now I know."

By 9:00 p.m. that same night, when Kim and Petri finally were allowed into the power chamber, the inquisitors were already settled comfortably in their chairs. After spending thirty minutes crashing in quiet huddles about how to manhandle an unruly INS attorney who was threatening mutiny, they had reached a decision.

Tromble sat at the middle of the table, tapping a pen, boiling with barely controlled fury. The head of INS, and the assistant district director, with the distinctly unhappy honor of being Kim's immediate boss, hunched down to his left. To his right sat the slightly inebriated chief of the Russian prosecutorial team, and a Colonel Volevodz, who had been frantically dispatched by Tatyana after a disturbing call from Tromble.

All were seated with unpleasant expressions on one side of the conference table. The other side was barren.

Two empty chairs were arrayed in the middle of the floor across from them; the setting resembled a kangaroo court. In fact, it was. Kim and her translator were actually led in like prisoners by an FBI agent, one of Tromble's errand boys who in the hallway had coldly introduced himself as Terrence Hanrahan.

The arrangement was frightening. It was meant to make the hairs on the back of her neck stand up, and very briefly, it did.

Kim more or less stumbled timidly into one chair. Petri, with a sad, resigned expression, collapsed into the seat beside her. The INS director opened with a withering glare. "Miss Parrish, do you realize how much time, money, and effort's been put into this investigation?"

A cautious nod. "Of course I do. Nobody has worked harder on it than me."

"And now you say you want the case dropped?"

"That's exactly what I'm saying, sir."

"Because it's too perfect," he noted, dripping disbelief and skepticism all over the table.

"Because the whole thing is phony. The Konevitches are being framed by these people," she said, directing a finger at the two Russians at the table.

"What's the matter? Not enough evidence?"

"To the contrary, too much. It's too pat, too polished. It's obviously manufactured."

"Well, I heard of cases being dropped for lack of evidence. But for too much, and it's too good?" He shook his head from side to side, frowning tightly. "It's the stupidest thing I ever heard."

Petri and the two Russians glared across the table at each other. The lead Russian prosecutor suddenly lurched forward and snapped, "He is the one behind this." Other than an array of imaginative curses, in more than four months it was the most English Kim had heard pass his lips. And it was flawless, with barely a hint of an accent.

"Who's he?" Tromble asked, staring at the skinny, diminutive figure in the chair.

"That man," the Russian growled, directing a shaking finger at the small figure across from him. "The translator. The traitor. He defected fifteen years ago. His life's calling is to harm his motherland. If she's listening to him, she's crazy. He's obviously poisoning her brain."

Volevodz quickly jumped on the bandwagon and the two Russians spent about three minutes hurling insults and invective at the tiny Russian. Petri endured it with an unpleasant smile.

The river of castigations quickly became tedious, and Tromble eventually grew tired of it. He pushed forward and leaned across the table, redirecting the fire at the right source. "You're supposed to be a prosecutor, Miss Parrish, a lawyer. Remember your job. Leave the judgments to the men in robes."

The *men* in robes? She was already tired of all these boys ganging up on her. "I have an ethical responsibility to present an honest case. This is a travesty. You should all be ashamed to be taken in by these crooked Russians."

"The only people taken in were millions of poor Russians who trusted Konevitch. Of course the evidence is compelling. Guess why. He did it, he's guilty. He's a rotten slimy crook, who deserves whatever he gets. And when the Russians come along and prove it, you say they proved it too well. Do you have any idea how ridiculous that sounds?"

"Have you studied the evidence?" Kim asked, sounding frustrated, knowing full well how weak—no, how pathetically silly—her argument sounded. Toss this case away because it's watertight, too perfect, she seemed to be insisting.

"I have not, and I don't intend to." Tromble's elbows landed on the table, with his hands forming a steeple. "Why should I? I have you sitting right here telling me the evidence is rainproof, flawless in every way. No holes, no contradictions, no imperfections."

"I've made my position clear."

"Then I'll make mine clear. It's moving with or without you. Make your choice."

"Without me. Replace me. Find another lawyer."

The assistant director, Kim's immediate boss, was dismayed by how rapidly things were unraveling. Seven months of work about to spill down the drain. Another of his attorneys would have to replace her, then more months wasted while the new guy came up to speed. And frankly, Kim Parrish was the best he had. He produced a warm smile. "Kim, Kim, don't be hasty. You're a great lawyer. You have a fine record. A whole promising career ahead of you. Please, finish this case and put it behind you."

"I also have the prerogative to refuse participation in a case I believe to be fraudulent and shameful. Reassign me to another case."

Tromble was tired of this pussyfooting. He was unaccustomed to having his orders questioned, and he had an invitation to a big White House reception that evening his wife was dying to attend. He detested the president, a feeling that was deeply reciprocated, so this was the first invitation, and very likely the last. His wife had already spent two grand on a gown, dropped a cool five hundred on a faggy hairdresser, and threatened two years without sex if he was a minute late. It was long past time to put his big foot down. "Take this case, or you're fired."

"Then I quit."

"No you don't, you're fired."

"You can't fire me. I don't work for you."

The director of the INS had this one last chance to preserve the independence of his service, not to mention his own prerogative and prestige. Tromble had just violated the most sacrosanct Washington law—keep your fingers out of somebody's else's bureaucratic turf.

The director summoned forth every bit of his courage, looked Kim dead in the eye, and muttered, "Oh, you definitely are fired."

29

At 10:00 a.m., Elena arrived promptly for her monthly visit. She came in a rental car picked up at the local airport, a cramped bright purple economy model with a zippy little engine. She and Alex had done this routine fourteen times now. Different prisons, different states, different guards. But it was old hat. The routine rarely varied. Later, she would dump the car, hop a fast flight for Atlanta, wander through the huge terminal for a few hours trying to shake any followers, then at the very last minute hop another flight and bounce around the Midwest awhile. Everything paid for in cash. It would take her two days to return home but Alex emphasized that the time and money were worth it. This was not a game. People were out there, trying to kill her. No precaution was too great.

Her ID had been checked, she'd been patted down and searched, had her hand stamped, and was waiting quietly in a stiff plastic chair when Alex entered. The glass partition was perforated with dozens of small holes. An improvement, they thought, over the last prison, where they had been forced to whisper awkwardly over intercom phones. They were paranoid about bugs. It hampered their conversations terribly.

"You look beautiful," Alex told her. He did not mention the dark circles under her eyes. She looked exhausted and worn down by fourteen months of endless work, of living in the shadows, of leaping out of bed at the slightest creak of a floorboard. He was trying to hide how guilty it made him feel.

"I love you," she replied, her usual opening.

No need to ask how he was doing; how the new prison was working out; how he was being treated. Alex called almost every night from one of his three cell phones, and they chatted back and forth late into the night. She knew about Benny Beatty, and all about the "mutual fund" Alex was running for an ever-swelling pool of prisoners and guards. No different from the two previous prisons. Elena kept the records and managed the investments through a local Virginia broker she had picked for his efficiency and reliability. Checks arrived in the mail with great frequency from Alex's new clients in each prison, a trickle in the first month, before word spread and the floodgates opened. Elena promptly deposited the checks with the broker, and they were instantly invested. Every night Alex called with fresh instructions to be relayed to the broker the next morning. Execute this sell; buy five thousand shares of this; short this, long that. The stock market was roaring. The fund was beating it handsomely, and Alex's "clients" were elated. He couldn't walk ten steps in the yard without people pleading to join up.

The *Wall Street Journal* and *Investor's Business Daily* were delivered to his cell every morning by a guard who had emptied his entire 401(k) nest egg and handed it over to Alex's care.

Even Elena's broker was shadowing Alex's moves with his own money.

"How's Bitchy?" Elena asked.

"Fine. His appeal comes up next month."

"Does he have a chance?"

"I helped draft a letter for him to the court. It might help."

Over the past year, Alex had kept her well-informed about the characters he had met in prison. His ability to fit in with these rogues and villains and gangsters amazed her. The Choir Boys of Mariel with their relentless scheming to find a lawyer who could buy their way out. Mustafa, the glowering head of the Black

Power brotherhood in Chicago, who kept ominously reminding "Brother Konebitchie" what would happen should the investments go south.

Bitchy Beatty was the most baffling one yet. Inexplicably, he and her husband had grown quite close. Odd bedfellows, though perhaps that was a phrase best avoided.

"What does the letter say?"

"He deeply regrets the pain and suffering he caused. He found God, God found him. When he gets out he intends to send hundred-thousand-dollar checks to each man he injured."

"That sounds nice. They should be impressed."

"I wrote the letter and forged his signature. Benny loathes the Jets for stealing his championship ring. He doesn't regret a thing."

Alex smiled and she laughed.

Alex leaned a little closer and lowered his voice. "The guard in the back. The tall one with blond hair. Name's George. He's your man."

Elena fell back into her chair, waited a moment, then glanced quickly over her shoulder. Three guards were back there but George was ridiculously easy to spot. Tall guy with white-blond hair leaning against the wall, pretending to be bored. He caught Elena's eye and winked effusively.

When they were finished, George would escort her out to the large anteroom to collect her coat and purse. They would brush against each other, a light bump that lasted seconds. Elena would hand George a bundle of computer disks. George would hand back a bundle of disks from Alex. George was the one with his whole 401(k) in the fund; in two short months, it had already doubled. Whatever Alex wanted, George would bend over backward to provide.

"Any new clients?" Alex asked, referring to their other new business venture.

"A few. General Motors signed up yesterday. I left right after they called. There wasn't time to update you."

"You do good work, Mrs. Konevitch."

"If she could write code half as fast as Mr. Konevitch, Mrs. Konevitch would have a thousand new clients."

For the time being, such talk was as romantic as they got. Their new business was roaring out the gate. The entire Internet world was going crazy with start-ups sprouting like poppies in a compliant Afghan field. None, though, had developed multimedia advertising technology as brilliant as Alex. The beauty of it was, Elena hit up pretty much the same clients they had enlisted for Orangutan Media. Same Rolodex. Same marketing contacts. Only the pitch differed. Alex leaned closer, until his lips were nearly pressed up against the glass. "What does MP say? Any updates?"

"No, the situation hasn't changed. He's furious. Says he's never seen anything like this. Keeps calling it a disgrace."

Alex appeared disappointed, though he tried his best to stifle it with a forced smile. "Tell him to relax, it's not his fault. We're up against the American and Russian governments, and I don't think any lawyer could prevail. I couldn't be happier with him."

"He's demoralized, Alex. He feels responsible. He wrote another long, bitter letter to the judge. Same theme as the last six. What happened to those high-sounding instructions to the prosecutor about putting you in a nicer place than this?"

"I'm fine, Elena."

"No, you're—"

"Relax, I'm fine. I actually had wine with a late dinner last night. Pot roast, fresh corn and potatoes, cooked by a guard's wife, served in the cell. Me and Benny over candlelight. He still thinks I'm cute, incidentally."

"You are cute. But you're not fine, Alex Konevitch. And don't tell me differently. You're surrounded by murderers and rapists and nasty gangs. You could get shooked in the showers by some crazy killer just because you stepped on his toe."

"Shanked," Alex corrected her.

"Oh, shut up." A few months before Elena had done something deeply regrettable; once done, though, it was impossible to erase. She had gone on an all-out binge of prison flicks, a response to her curiosity about what her husband was going through. She watched them all, one after another, late into the night, night after night. For months afterward she was tormented by nightmares, waking up sweating and shivering. The images of brutal killings and chaotic beatings and jailhouse rapes came back to her constantly. Her precious husband was trapped inside a vicious building filled with barbaric monsters who snuffed lives for a pack of cigarettes.

Alex tried to shrug it off. Hollywood hooey, he called it. A bunch of cinematic nonsense, hyped-up tripe to shock and appall the ignorant public, he insisted.

He was lying. She knew better.

Thankfully, he had acquired no tattoos; none she could observe, anyway. But who knew what was lurking beneath that shirt, or under those baggy pants? And there was no doubt that Alex *looked* different. Harder, long greasy hair pulled back in a tight ponytail now, less expressive, a little slower to laugh, and his eyes darted around constantly, alert in a way that tore at her heart. Even his walk was different. No longer the old determined, upright clip straining to shave off a few extra seconds; it now resembled a slide more than a walk, slow, slumped, and slothful, with hands perpetually sunk to the bottom of his pockets. A survivor's walk. A way of saying he cared about nothing.

She understood but did not like it. Adapt, blend in with the natives, or you became bait to the strongest animals in the cage.

There was only one good thing about prison: sleep and exercise were plentiful. What else was there to do? Until this visit, anyway, Alex always looked remarkably refreshed and fit. He must've had a bad few nights, though, because this time he looked painfully exhausted. His eyes were bloodshot, with large bags underneath them. He hadn't slept well in days, possibly weeks.

"This is crazy, Alex," she uttered softly.

"It is what it is, Elena. Be patient."

"I've been patient for a year. I want you in my bed, where you belong. I'm tired of sleeping alone."

"I'm not all that crazy about sleeping with Benny, either. Have you ever heard an All-Pro lineman snore?"

"Stop it."

"And the smell. All that bulk. He comes back from his workouts in the yard, the paint falls off the walls."

Like Alex was an Irish rose himself. All the prisoners stank. They were oblivious to their own odors, but Elena was nearly flattened by the stench in the prison visitors' room. She wanted to bring Alex home and scrub a year of prison stink out of his skin. Then take him to bed and heal a year's worth of fear and misery and frustration and loneliness.

"Alex, are you sure you're okay?" she pressed, more emphatically this time. She was his wife. All this jokiness was an attempt to conceal something. He was far from okay.

Alex looked down and played with his fingers a moment—a slight twitch around his left eye, an almost imperceptible shift of tiny muscles, and she knew.

She bent forward until her face was pressed against the glass. "Stop lying. What's happening?"

"All right. Somebody tried to kill me yesterday."

"Yesterday . . . what happened?"

"In the yard, I was playing basketball when a man made a run at me. He was carrying a crude hatchet constructed in the prison shop. As attempts go it was stupid and clumsy. It had no chance."

Elena was perfectly motionless. This was the nightmare she had long dreaded. She watched him and waited.

"I was lucky," Alex informed her, trying to make it sound trifling, little more than a bad hand of cards. "Two of the cons on my team are investors in the fund. I threw the ball in his face, his nose shattered, he slowed down, they disarmed him. It wasn't all that dramatic." He left off the part about how his friends mauled the killer, stomping his hands and breaking both arms to be sure he wouldn't try again.

"Who was he? Why did he want to kill you?"

"A Russian. A former Mafiya gunman who obviously wasn't as handy with an axe."

"I asked *why* he wanted to kill you."

A momentary pause. "Apparently, the people in Moscow are

offering big money to whoever gets me." Then a more prolonged pause before he made the painful decision to tell Elena everything. "It was the second attempt."

"I see. And when was the first?"

"Two months ago."

"Two months? Why didn't you tell me before?"

"I've been quite careful since then. Benny follows me everywhere he can. I'm surrounded at every meal by a squad of our investors. A few of the guys watch over me when I shower, use the bathroom, use the library. They don't want their golden goose hauled out in a coffin. I'm only in danger when I leave my cell."

Elena reeled backward into her seat and struggled to fight her horror—she couldn't. "I'll call MP and have him insist on moving you to another prison. We'll raise hell. Hold a big obnoxious press conference. We'll—"

Before she could finish, Alex was already shaking his head. "I've already considered that. Don't. Don't even try."

"Why not?"

"I'm alive only because I've established a network here. At each new place, it takes three weeks to a month, at a minimum. I'd be completely naked."

"And if the investment fund for some reason has a bad month? A sudden market correction, for instance. That happens, Alex. How good will your protection be then?"

He forced a smile. "Believe me, I think about that every day. It certainly helps focus the mind."

She crossed her arms and did not acknowledge the smile. "And if you stay here, it's just a matter of time, isn't it? Say one of your new friends becomes distracted, or at the wrong moment bends over to tie a shoe. Maybe somebody slips a little poison in your food, or a little knife in your back."

"A lot could happen," Alex admitted, rubbing his temples. "They've been scared off a few times. A week ago, in the library, before some of my friends made a threatening move. Five days ago, in the shower, three men were approaching me when a guard showed up."

"I see."

"Look, I won't pretend I'm not worried. These are rough people, killers. They're watching me every day, looking for an opening. I know the odds."

"You have to get out of here, Alex."

"Believe me, that thought has crossed my mind. The past few weeks, I've lived in the law section of the library."

"There has to be something. You can't just let these people kill you."

About two cubicles down, a loud argument suddenly exploded between a prisoner and his wife. The woman was barely more than a child, maybe nineteen, dressed in a scant black leather skirt, black net stockings, a halter top that did more to reveal than conceal, false eyelashes that flopped like gigantic butterflies, and enough cosmetics to camouflage a battleship or capsize it. Only a moment before, she and the hubby had their faces pressed tightly against the glass panel, whispering sweet nothings back and forth, like they were ready to disrobe and grope each other through the divider. The husband suddenly recoiled backward, nearly tipping his chair to the floor.

"Oh yeah, you heard right. Your twin brother," the woman roared.

"My own brother. You're sleeping with my own brother," the husband wailed, slamming both fists like noisy gavels against the glass panel.

"Yeah, well . . . least I kept it in the family, since I know how much that word means to you. This time, anyways."

"You're a bitch. A whore. A backstabbin' whore."

She stood up and jammed her face up against the divider. "Hey, you noticed, finally. Guess what, idiot? I'm givin' it away to any fool who looks twice. They're thinkin' of naming a mattress after me. So what are you gonna do about it, huh?" she taunted.

Until this moment, the three guards in the room had looked on with an air of bemused boredom. Old hat, old story, happy days again in the visitors' room. A wife cheating on a locked-up hubby: what's new? A tired old scene the guards had observed a thousand times with few variations. Many marriages lasted a year, some more than two, very, very few beyond the third year of separation.

There was one inviolate rule, though, and this prisoner bashed it to pieces. He snapped, leaped to his feet, and, howling at the top of his voice, began trying to crawl and claw his way over the divider. Two guards lost their look of boredom and sprang into action. They yanked him off the glass, jerked his arms behind his back, and slapped cuffs on him. They began dragging him out as he hollered a bewildering array of curses at his wife.

His wife stood and loitered, arms crossed, watching it all with a smile that smacked of huge contentment.

Then, at the final moment before they yanked her husband through the door, she whipped down her halter, exposing two rather impressive breasts. With two hands, she cupped and then began juggling them. "Hey," she yelled at her husband, "remember these? Tonight your brother's gonna have a field day with 'em. And once I get bored with him, you know what? I'll bet I can get your father in the sack."

She tugged the halter back up, spun on her heels, and with a loud triumphant clack of high heels departed the room.

"Poor man," Elena remarked with a sympathetic frown after the tumult died down.

Alex bent forward and shook his head. "That's Eddie Carminza. He's up for bigamy. Five years in the joint, the max. She's one of four wives."

"My God, this place is crazy, Alex. You have to get out."

"Well, there is one thing we can try. Move the case out of immigration channels into a federal court. It's premature, though, and incredibly risky."

"You might prematurely die in here if we don't try something."

"I know. But there are two problems. Serious problems. One, federal court means different rules and procedures. MP isn't a criminal lawyer. Also he has no experience in the federal system. The rules of evidence and admissibility are stricter. It's too late to replace him, though."

"Can he handle it?"

"I'm not sure any lawyer can and MP is already holding a bad hand. And who knows how much ammunition our friends in Russia have provided the prosecutor over the past year."

"But Mikhail—"

"Mikhail hasn't found us the silver bullet. There's no legally acceptable proof that my money was stolen. No proof I'm being framed. Nothing to keep me from being shipped back to Russia."

"All right, what's two?"

"If we rush into federal court, and I lose, I'll be shipped right back here. We can try an appeal, and we will. But that takes time. I'll probably be dead long before."

"So it's a choice between very bad and awful?"

"More like between certain death and probable death."

"So what's this idea?"

"It's called a motion for habeas corpus. Technically, by shoving me into the federal prison system, they've created a loophole we should be able to exploit. It forces the government to show cause for my imprisonment. If a judge accepts it, the process happens very fast."

"How fast?"

"Three days after we launch it, we'll be in court."

"Oh . . . that fast." Elena stared at her shoes a moment. She began fidgeting with her hands. "Is it too fast?"

"Possibly," Alex told her. "We have a lot of enemies, here and in Russia. Everything has to happen at once. And everything has to succeed, or as my friend Benny puts it, it's game over. Also Mikhail will have to move up his time schedule. And we'll have to pray for a legal miracle."

"We're overdue for a miracle."

"I don't think it works that way. We'll have to produce our own."

"I'll call Mikhail the second I'm out of here."

"You have a busy weekend ahead of you. It's time to share everything with MP, then pray it's enough."

30

On September 18, 1996, one year and two months to the day since Alex's incarceration in federal prison, MP Jones bounced up the steps of the D.C. Federal Courthouse, one of the loveliest, most impressive buildings in a city littered to the gills with marble monuments. The day alternated between warmth and chill, the first hint that another long, humid summer in a city built in a swamp was coming to a close. Elena, along with a stout paralegal hauling a box of documents, accompanied him.

Two days before, Elena had called and frantically insisted on an emergency meeting. MP dropped everything and Elena arrived, pale, tired, angry, upset, and wildly determined. She told him Alex's idea and MP instantly launched a hundred objections.

It was too fast. Too risky. Federal court wasn't his thing. Besides, who knew what the Russian prosecutors and INS had cooked up, how much damning material they could throw at Alex? Elena insisted that she and Alex had entertained all the same reservations, told him about the four attempts on Alex's life, and that ended the discussion. MP called his clients with pressing cases over the next week and foisted their files off on other immigration specialists around town.

So they moved with deep nervousness through the wide, well-lit corridors, straight to the office of the federal clerk. MP signed in at the front desk, moved to the rear of the room, and waited patiently with Elena and his paralegal amid a clutter of other nervous lawyers until the clerk called his name.

He nearly sprinted to her desk. He proudly threw down a document and with a show of intense formality informed her, "I am introducing a motion for habeas corpus on behalf of my client Alex Konevitch. I ask the court for expeditious handling on behalf of said client, who has been incarcerated beyond any reasonable length and forced to endure immeasurable suffering."

The clerk, a large, feisty black woman, lifted up MP's motion and automatically plunked it into a deep wooden in-box, a vast reservoir filled to capacity with other such requests, motions, and lawyerly stuff. "First time here?" she asked without looking up.

"Uh . . . yes."

"This ain't no courtroom. Plain English works fine in here."

MP looked slightly deflated. "It's a habeas corpus motion." She chewed a stick of gum with great energy and stared intently into a computer screen. The sign on her desk suggested she was named Thelma Parker.

"I heard what you said," Thelma noted. "How long's your guy been in?"

"A year and two months."

"Uh-huh." Thelma did not appear overly impressed. "What facility he at?"

"At the moment, based on a federal contract, the state prison in Yuma. It's his third prison."

The reaction was delayed, but she slowly shifted her gaze from the screen and directed it at MP. "His third? Inside a year? That what you sayin'?"

"To be precise, inside fourteen months."

"What'd he do? Kill a warden?"

"An alleged visa violation."

"Come on, you bullshittin' me."

"On my momma's grave."

"That's an immigration matter. What's your guy doin' in a federal joint?"

"That's what we'd like the government to explain."

"He a U.S. resident?"

"That's one point of contention. The government said yes. Now it's saying no."

She poised her chin on a pencil. "That prison in Yuma, it's a badass place."

"So Alex tells me. He's locked up in D Wing, mixed in with the most rotten apples."

She leaned forward, almost across the desk. In a low, conspiring, all-knowing whisper, she said, "Truth now. Who'd your boy piss off?"

MP played along. He bent over and whispered back, "John Tromble."

"Figures." She picked MP's motion out of the pile and smacked it down on her blotter. She paged through it, frowning and considering the request with some care for a moment. "Gotta cousin works over at the Bureau," she eventually remarked.

A sharp pain suddenly erupted in MP's chest. Idiot. Why hadn't he just kept his big mouth shut?

After a moment Thelma Parker added, "He hates that Tromble. Says he's the worst thing happened since J. Edgar pranced around in a skirt. Tell you what, you done this before?"

After manning this desk for fifteen years, she had seen thousands of lawyers pass in and out of her office. One sniff and she could smell a cherry a mile away.

MP allowed as, "My usual cases are in immigration court."

"Thought so. You never done this before?"

"Pretty much."

A large, plump elbow landed on her desk and her large chin ended up poised on a curled fist. "Now, don't you worry. Way this works is, your motion goes to a judge. Now, you could maybe get lucky and it might end up in the box of, say, oh, Judge Elton Willis. He's a fair and judicious man. Then, assuming this thing gets stamped expeditious"—she winked at MP—"which might maybe happen about three seconds after you walk outta here . . . well, then the government gets three days to respond. Got all that?"

"Three days," MP said, winking back.

"Then it's show-and-tell time. This kinda motion moves fast. You got your stuff together?"

With all the humility he could muster, MP replied, "It's going to be an ass-kicking of historical proportions. They'll carry Tromble out on a stretcher."

"Uh-huh." A slow nod. "You got help? Sure hope you do."

"Pacevitch, Knowlton and Rivers. A classmate from law school's a partner over there. They're lending a hand, pro bono."

"Well, that's nice." Her eyes hung for a moment on the JCPenney polyester threads that hung loosely on MP's narrow frame. She smacked her lips and said, "No offense, but you gonna need a few thousand-dollar suits at your table."

In a career that alternated between roaring barn burners and droning recitations of intolerable boredom, Boris Yeltsin was producing the biggest thud yet. At least he was sober this time—what a rare and welcome change, his chief of staff was thinking, as he rocked back on his heels and briefly scanned the crowd. Nearly all of them were staring edgily at their watches. A few seemed to be asleep on their feet. He looked longer and harder, and for the life of him could not find one person who seemed to be listening to Yeltsin.

His boss liked him along for these things. Principally it gave him a reliable drinking partner for the long ride back to the Kremlin. Plus he could always rely on his trusted chief of staff to lie and say the speech was stirring and deeply inspiring. They were a pair of wicked old politicians. The lies flowed easily and landed comfortably.

A man in a black leather jacket bumped up against him. He took a quick step sideways, to get some room. The man edged closer.

The man suddenly turned and looked at him with a spark of vague recognition. "Hey, didn't I see you with Tatyana Lukin the other night?"

"Who?"

"Tatyana Lukin. You know, she works for you." The man studied his face more intently and continued, "I'm sure it was you. Walking into a hotel together on Tverskoy Boulevard. Same place you and she spend every Tuesday and Thursday together."

"You're mistaken," he replied in as much a hiss as a whisper. He tried unsuccessfully once more to edge away.

"No, there's no mistake. Here." The mysterious man pushed a plastic case into the hands of the chief of staff. All trace of phony uncertainty was gone. With a mocking smile, the mystery man whispered, "You'll want to listen to these alone. Believe me, you won't want company. You're mentioned a lot on these tapes."

Before he could reply, Mikhail jogged away in the direction of the road, where he jumped into an automobile with the engine running and sped off.

The chief thought about just tossing the case away. Fling it as far and as hard as he could; forget about it and walk away. Instead he opened the lid and peeked inside—just two unmarked cassette tapes and a few photographs. He tucked it into his inside coat pocket and decided he'd get rid of it after he got home. Who knew what was on those tapes? Why risk having some stranger find them? Who knows how bad it might be?

He arrived home at nine that night, fixed a tall glass of vodka, and removed his jacket. He felt the weight of the plastic packet; he had nearly forgotten it. He withdrew it from the inside pocket and walked directly to the trash can. He promptly dropped it inside, then stared down at the case for a moment. He should listen to it, he decided: maybe the man that afternoon was a blackmailer. Who knew?

The photos fell on the floor when he pulled the tapes out, and he let them lie there until he knew what this was about. He selected the first tape and inserted it into the cassette player on his desk, sat back into his desk chair, and sipped quickly from his vodka.

It whirred quietly for a moment before a petulant male voice he didn't recognize said, "Who was it?"

"Just some idiot law enforcement administrator from America."

This would be Tatyana: no doubt about it. He reached over and turned up the volume.

"Oh, you're screwing him, too?"

"You're cute when you're mad. Come on and screw me now." A loud laugh. Definitely Tatyana's throaty laugh.

"Don't joke. I'm tired of sharing you."

"You're a fool. You've seen my boss. He's bald and fat and not the least bit interesting. He's so terrible in bed I have to pinch myself just to stay awake. He's so disgusting, I become nauseated afterward. I'm only doing this for us, Sasha."

"You've been saying that for years."

"And it's true. Listen, we're moving in on a huge fortune right now. Billions, Sasha, billions. My cut will be hundreds of millions, and as soon as I have it, I'll dump that old moron and quit my job. You and I will buy a big yacht and sail around the world. We'll never be able to spend it all. We'll die rich and happy."

By then the chief of staff was choking and coughing violently. The vodka popped out his nostrils, dribbled out his mouth, and spilled down his double chin. He clutched his chest and thought he was having a heart attack.

He lurched from his chair and rushed to the cassette player. He punched stop, rewind, then listened again, and then repeated the sequence three more times.

He put the machine on pause and sat back and rubbed his temples. He felt the onset of a crushing brain-splitter. "Nauseated." "Terrible in bed." "Bald and fat, and not the least bit interesting." The torrent of nasty words kept tumbling in his mind. The headache quickly progressed from a five to a ten on the Richter scale.

That bitch. That lying, deceitful, two-timing, impertinent bitch.

Settle down, he told himself. He actually voiced it, out loud in the big, empty room—relax, take a few deep breaths. Get a grip, for God's sake. He walked over and refilled his glass with vodka, then sloppily filled a second and third glass; it never hurt to be on the safe side. He carried them back to his desk, positioned them carefully and in order, freshest to least freshest, pushed start on the cassette player, then settled back to hear everything. It was going to be horrible, he knew. And he swore he would endure every last word.

Halfway through, he rushed to the trash can and picked up the photos from the floor. The first showed a smiling, handsome young man dressed in the uniform of the national soccer team. He had no idea who he was, just a strong suspicion that it was his whiny voice on the first tape. The second showed the justice minister accepting a fistful of dollars from a man whose face he thought he recognized.

An hour later, after listening to the second tape, after repeating it once, as he had with the first tape, he knew more than he had ever cared to about Tatyana Lukin. The sheer stereotypicality of it was hard enough to swallow; he was just one more old, middle-aged, cuckolded fool, stewing with anger, self-pity, and regret. Worse, she had used him from the very start. There she was bragging to her boyfriend, Sasha, about how she was running the entire machinery of the Kremlin while her fat, drunken bore buddied up to his big pal Boris. There simply were too many barbs to remember; but also too many to forget.

"Well, guess what, bitch," he grumbled, lumbering drunkenly up the stairs for bed. "Tomorrow, the fun will begin."

The girl was tall and blonde with skinny legs that stretched from the ground to the sky, pretty blue eyes, and she was at least forty years younger than him. She was even younger than his two granddaughters. If it didn't matter to her, sure as hell it made no difference to him. She gripped his arm and squished her ample breasts against its soft plumpness.

"You are so funny, General, I just can't get enough of you."

"I'll bet," Golitsin slurred as they staggered and swayed, holding each other up, in the direction of his shiny little Beemer in the rear parking lot. The Lido was behind them, the newest city hot spot where the big-deal millionaires gathered in their relentless quest for the best orgy in town. Somewhere between his fifth and eighth scotch—such a blur that he lost count—the girl had become attached to his arm. Between his tenth or twelfth scotch, at some now indeterminate point, he decided they were deeply in love.

"What did you say your name was again?" he asked her.

"Nadya. Please remember it, General. I've told you ten times already. I really don't want you to ever forget me."

Golitsin was again admiring the streamlined legs that seemed to stretch up to her armpits, when three men stepped out of a dark alley. Two lunged straight for him. One banged his arms behind his back, the other shoved a filthy rag in his mouth and then, very quickly, a coarse dark hood over his head. The girl started to step back and scream before the third man clamped a hand over her mouth. "Shut your trap, tramp," he growled, and flashed a knife to show her the request was serious.

A black sedan pulled up, seemingly from nowhere, and squealed to a jarring stop three feet away. Golitsin was bundled roughly into the rear seat before two of the men spilled in beside him. The other man released Nadya. She stepped back and winked at him. He winked back, before she disappeared into the night. He climbed into the front passenger seat and they sped away.

Twenty minutes and ten miles later, Golitsin was shoved through a large doorway, dragged about forty steps, then shoved down hard onto a stiff wooden chair. His hands were tied, quickly and roughly, behind his back, and his chubby legs were roped to the legs of the chair.

The hood was removed and tossed onto the floor. With a loud spit, the filthy gag flew out of his lips, though it took a moment for his eyes to adjust. Another moment before he realized there were five of them in all. They were gathered in the middle of a large, empty warehouse with a high, corrugated ceiling and an oil-stained concrete floor. They wore dark jeans and black leather jackets. Rough faces all around. There were more tattoos and earrings and facial scars than he cared to count. A few misshapen noses.

Syndicate thugs, that's all, nothing to be overly alarmed about, Golitsin told himself.

And they had made a mistake, a big one. They were nothing more than common, everyday kidnappers who threw out a random net and stupidly dragged in the meanest shark in town. Oh yes, this was a real boner, one they would deeply regret, and he decided to inform them of this right away. He worked up his most scary sneer. "Do you punks know who you're messing with?"

"Punks," one of them answered. Whack!—Golitsin's head bounced to the side. A spray of blood shot out his nose.

"Don't you dare strike me again. You—"

Whack, whack, whack.

"All right, all right. Enough," Golitsin insisted.

Whack, whack.

"Please . . . I . . . I said that's enough."

One of them pulled over another wooden chair, reversed it, then eased into it. Their faces were three feet apart. He looked about fifty, older than the others, and carried himself like he was in charge. A hard, weathered face. Dark, piercing eyes. "Listen up, Sergei. This can be hard or it can be easy. Understand?"

The punk had called him Sergei. He knew his name! It wasn't a random kidnapping after all. Golitsin even, very briefly, entertained the notion of reminding this scum of his proper title: General. But maybe flexing his muscles at this instant wasn't such a good idea. Maybe it was a terrible idea, in fact. That last whack had left him with a splitting headache.

"Can we talk?" Golitsin asked, trying his best to sound reasonable and unctuous.

"Sure, Sergei." He leaned closer. "But it works like this. I'll talk and you'll listen."

The other four men slapped their thighs and roared with laughter. This was funny? This wasn't the least bit humorous. These punks were just begging for it. "Can I at least have your name?"

The man in the chair, said, "For tonight, Vladimir. Let's not worry about what to call me tomorrow. First, you have to give us a reason to let you live that long, Sergei."

"There's no need for these threats. What do you want?"

"Let's start with the easy one. Where's the money?"

"What money?"

A long sigh. "Do we really have to go through this, Sergei?"

"I'm a simple retired officer with a family. I am struggling to survive off my pension. It's not much. Perhaps we can work something out."

From somewhere behind his head, whack, whack, whack.

"Enough! That's enough!" he wailed.

"The money, Sergei. Where's the money?"

"What money?"

"Two hundred and fifty million. The money you stole, where is it?"

How did he know the exact amount? Golitsin briefly wondered. Only a handful knew: Tatyana, Nicky, and of course, the victim knew, not that it mattered. He was rotting in prison, after all, counting the days until his return to Russia.

"Maybe," Golitsin suggested—he squeezed his neck down, hunching his shoulders, trying to avoid another whack—"maybe if you told me who you're working for we can work something out."

Whack—the ducked head and bunched shoulders were a wasted defense. It felt like six hands were slapping the back of his head. He heard his own voice whining and pleading for them to stop.

And eventually the slaps did subside. But Vladimir allowed him no time to recover his wits. "Pay attention, Sergei. This is invaluable advice. You've never been on this side of the torture rack, always the other side, watching and enjoying the show. Fifty years of screaming victims begging for quick deaths. Are you listening, Sergei? Do you understand?"

The voice was so very cold, so flat, so casually captivating; amazing how mesmerizing a voice becomes when it controls the pain.

How many times had Sergei heard that same droll pattern over the years as he watched one victim after another suffer and scream their guts out, until they eventually snapped, until they signed whatever was put before them, signed anything to make the pain stop—accusing their own mothers, sentencing their own children, confessing sins they never came within ten miles of committing. Oh yes, he definitely understood.

He slowly nodded.

"You know how bad this can get, don't you?"

Another nod—yes, yes, of course he remembered. Tears were now rolling down his fat cheeks.

"The pain is going to become intense, Sergei. I don't want you surprised by it. You're going to wish you were dead. You'll beg us to end it. We won't kill you, though. You can't feel the pain unless you're alive. Sorry, but we need you to feel everything."

"Wait!" Something was bothering him. All this talk about torture, and the name of this cruel man. There was a connection there, he was sure of it.

"Why wait? Do you want to tell me where the money is?"

"Vladimir? Yes, Vladimir. Like the Vladimir who worked for me, right?"

A quick shift of the eyes to the floor. "I have no idea who or what you're talking about."

Golitsin stretched as far forward as he could. "He a friend of yours? Is that what this is about? I am so sorry for what happened to poor Vladimir. He killed himself, you know. Suicide. How tragic."

The interrogator jumped out of his chair. Turning to the other four men, he directed a finger at one and said, "Get the BP cuff and monitor his blood pressure. He's old and fat. We don't want him slipping away on us."

The man dashed off.

"Get the tools," he barked at another, who also disappeared into the darkness. To the other two, he said, "You look bored. Work on him while we wait."

They moved up and the slapping began again. No punches, everything open-handed, a relentless fusillade of girly slaps obviously meant to add shame to his pain. Golitsin wailed and screamed, all to no avail.

Vladimir walked to a corner of the large warehouse, yanked a cell phone out of a pocket, punched a number, then cradled it to his ear.

Golitsin was being slapped silly. His cheeks, the back of his head, occasionally his ears, which really stung. He howled and moaned, begging them to stop. Eventually, his chin sank to his chest. His head began lolling wildly with each smack.

He bit down hard on his tongue, choked back his screams, and played opossum for all he was worth. Just stop those infernal slaps, he prayed with all his might. And after a moment, the prayers were answered. They did stop. One yelled out, "Vladimir, he's out cold."

"Don't worry about it," Vladimir replied, sounding distracted, then returned to his phone conversation.

Golitsin fought to control his breathing and prayed they didn't catch on. He could overhear Vladimir speaking louder now, unconcerned about his ability to eavesdrop.

"No, don't worry. We've only gotten started." A long pause. "Look, I've done this before. I—" Another pause. "Nicky, you have my guarantee, he'll tell us everything. Everybody does. We start ripping off the body parts, and they all—" Pause, then a nasty laugh. "I know, I know, Nicky. Look, by the time he's got no fingers or toes, his kneecaps are pulp, he'll spill . . . Yeah, okay, you, too."

Vladimir flipped the phone shut and returned to the scene of torture. A scream was going off inside Golitsin's head. Nicky! That rotten son of a bitch. That lying, thieving, betraying bastard. These were his people, he realized, and he fought the urge not to scream and threaten these people, to unleash all the rage he could muster.

One of the boys returned a moment later with the BP monitor. He quickly slapped it around Golitsin's right arm and tightened it up. Then the other fellow reappeared lugging a large dark suitcase, which he set down on the floor.

"Open it. Get the tools ready," Vladimir told him.

Golitsin heard the locks snap open and the noise of the lid hitting the cement. He didn't want to look—he had no desire at all to see what terrible ghoulish instruments were inside that damned case—he tried to fight it, just squeeze his eyes shut, he told himself; ignore them and ignore it. But it couldn't be helped. The curiosity was just too irresistible; he had to know, had to see what they had in store for him. Slowly, ever so slowly, he cracked open his right eyelid, just a hair. A tiny, tiny sliver, and he peeked.

Vladimir and two of his boys were bent over the now open case, rummaging through the contents, apparently deciding which tool should lead off.

Oh, Christ. Oh, no. The bastards had bought out the entire torture store. Three or four razor-sharp saws of various sizes and types, wicked things, so sharp and shiny. A small blowtorch. An iron, just like the one Vladimir used to scorch the hammer and sickle on Konevitch. A slew of gleaming surgical instruments employable for everything from eyeball gouging to nut-crunching. Golitsin could put a name and use to every instrument: a vivid picture of their exact use.

How many nights had he spent watching with sick fascination as the boys in the basement at Dzerzhinsky Square found all sorts of inspired uses for these things? Every instrument in that case, he knew them all like a mechanic knows his shop tools.

He squeezed his eyes shut and bit his lip, but it just slipped out. A moan of fear just clawed its way up his throat, into his mouth, and it popped right through his lips.

Five sets of eyes instantly snapped in his direction.

Vladimir smiled. "Ah, Sergei, you're back." With a befuddled expression, he asked, sounding mildly frustrated, "Listen, I can't seem to make up my mind. How would you like us to start?"

"You keep those damned things away from me."

"Well, you see, we're a little past that point. Come on, Sergei, I'm trying to be generous here." He laughed and the others joined him. "So, what will it be?"

"I swear I don't have any more of the money."

"None?"

"It's gone."

"All of it? Two hundred and fifty million?" Vladimir asked, dripping skepticism.

"Yes, it's spent, every penny. I swear it." Golitsin wasn't about to hand over his fortune to Nicky, no matter what. They could cut and slice and dice him however they wanted—not a red cent.

Vladimir bent over, studied the contents inside the case for a moment, then made up his mind and picked up a saw. "Well, that's too bad," he muttered, shaking his head.

"Please, you have to believe me. I was stupid and greedy. I wasted it all on idiotic things. It's all gone."

Vladimir was now ten feet away. With a finger, he was testing the sharpness of the blade as he moved closer. Two of the boys were now hovering directly behind Golitsin. They pinned his arms and squeezed his neck. He squealed but their grips only tightened.

"Where to start, where to start, that's the big issue now," Vladimir said. The piercing, hard, dark eyes began searching Golitsin's body. "Why not toes?" he asked very reasonably. "Start at the bottom, start with the little things, and slowly work our way up."

He bent down and pulled off Golitsin's shoes, then yanked off his socks. The plump white toes were wiggling, trying to curl under his feet. Vladimir carefully selected the big toe on the right foot. Using two strong fingers, he clamped the toe, poised the saw, then looked up. "I should warn you that I get a little carried away. Once I take one, I generally get all ten. You can answer everything, and I just can't stop," he warned, looking slightly remorseful. "It's, oh, I don't know, something wrong inside my head."

"Okay, okay, I have the money. Don't . . . oh, please, don't touch that toe."

Vladimir gave the toe a little pinch. Golitsin nearly bucked out of the chair. "Switzerland. A Swiss bank," he muttered in a fast rush.

"You wouldn't be lying, would you? I hate liars."

"No, no, I swear. Switzerland."

"What bank?"

A momentary hesitation and Vladimir suddenly had the saw pressed firmly on the flesh, right at the base of the big toe. "Lucerne National. All of it. Every penny."

"How much?"

"Two hundred."

The saw bit ever so lightly into his flesh.

"All right, all right . . . 220."

"You blew thirty million already?" Vladimir looked like he was ready to just whack the toe off. Nothing to do with disbelief, just anger.

"I'm . . . I'm sorry."

"I'm sure you are, Sergei. Now the hard questions."

Golitsin couldn't take his eyes off the saw.

"Are you ready, or should I just cut now?"

"No, please no. Ask anything."

"The account and security code numbers. Concentrate. What are they?"

"I . . . I don't have them in my head. My office. We have to go to my office."

Whack, whack, whack.

"Oh, God, all right." And like that, a fast rush of numbers spilled out of his lips.

As he spoke, another man, this one hiding in a back room, punched the numbers into a laptop computer, and they shot like lightning bolts through the Internet, straight to a large mainframe in Zurich. It took two minutes before the money—225 million and change, it turned out—was shunted into a new account, in a different Swiss bank, coincidentally only two blocks down from Lucerne National.

The man with the computer stuck his large ponytailed head out of the doorway. He gave Vladimir a thumbs-up.

"What will you do with me?" Golitsin asked.

"Why would I do anything with you?"

"You mean you're not going to kill me?"

"You know what? My instructions aren't real clear on that point." Vladimir stroked his chin and played at indecision for a moment. "You're broke now. A fat has-been loser with nothing to fall back on but a tiny pension and the tragic memory that once you were rich. Should I worry about you?"

"No, absolutely not. Definitely, no. You're right, you've ruined my life. I'm nothing, a sorry loser. I don't even know who you are," he lied.

"Well, I'm not so sure." The man dug a hand deep into his coat pocket. He appeared to be fishing around for something. Perhaps a gun or a knife. "Maybe, just to be on the safe side, maybe I should—"

"No, please," Golitsin pleaded, and words kept spilling out his lips. "I'll leave Russia. I promise, I'll be on the next train. I'll disappear and you'll never hear from me again. Please let me live."

The man stared at him with an impenetrable expression for a moment, then finally he shrugged his thick shoulders. "I guess it saves the trouble of what to do with your big, fat corpse."

Golitsin nearly groaned with relief. "Yes, exactly. I don't want to be a burden to you."

"Around nine in the morning the workers in the factory across the street come to work. Scream loud and hard, Sergei. Who knows, maybe they'll come and save you."

The tools were packed back inside the case, and within five minutes Vladimir and his boys had turned off the lights and scattered into the night.

After half an hour, Golitsin tried his hardest to close his eyes and float away into sleep. He so badly wanted to sleep. The fear and terror left him drained and exhausted, but he couldn't shut his eyes. The anger and resentment kept bubbling up. By 9:30 the next morning, he would make Nicky pay dearly for every humiliating moment, and for every dollar the bastard stole. He wasn't sure just how yet. It would be slow and horrible, though. And very, very painful; he promised himself this.

He leaned back on the chair and dreamed of Nicky's death.

The rumor started early that evening. Moscow's underworld loved rumors almost as much as gossip, the juicier the better, and this one took off like a rabbit with its ass on fire. By midnight it was bouncing through brothels, thug hangouts, drug dens, was being murmured by pickpockets on the street, and becoming a consuming point of interest in the bars frequented by the city's syndicate chiefs, who at that hour were just starting their day.

Somebody wanted Nicky Kozyrev dead. Somebody deeply serious; serious in the way that counted most in this town, serious enough to back up this gripping desire with big money. This was the salient point. This kept the rumor roaring all night. Five million dollars—five million to make Nicky's heart stop. Unconditionally, up to the assassin's discretion, nothing off-limits, no bounds—by bullet, by car accident, by poison, who cared? A stake through his black heart had a nice ring but dead in any form was fine. Five million excellent reasons for Nicky Kozyrev to die.

Three syndicate chiefs had been contacted by a Chechen mob that had been hired as underwriters by the source of this generous venture. For good and obvious cause, the benefactor preferred to remain anonymous. A select group of witnesses were invited to a small apartment in the city center, five suitcases of cash were hauled out of a closet and opened for display, though it was far too much to count. But for sure it looked like more than enough. This is it, they were told—this is what five million dollars looks like, up close and personal. Not an empty promise, no bluff, the real deal. Now get out and spread the word.

In a city where five thousand bucks will buy you all the corpses you wish, five million was going to kick-start a gold rush of assassins.

A few bookies put their heads together and gave thought to creating a betting pool. Nope, why bother? There were no competing odds. Open and shut. At five million bucks, Nicky was dead.

At three that morning, Nicky's chief bodyguard—his most trusted lieutenant, a lifelong friend from the same impoverished back alley of Novgorod—gently eased open Nicky's bedroom door and peeked inside. They had raped and killed and pushed dope together for three long, enjoyable decades. They had dodged the cops and KGB, swindled, murdered, and beaten too many to remember. Oh, the warm memories they shared. He snuck quietly inside. He hugged the wall, crept ever so slowly, never setting foot off the carpet. Nicky liked dark rooms. Nicky wouldn't sleep anywhere with windows, and this one was like a coffin. Nicky's loud snores bounced off the walls. The whore sprawled across his legs was shot so full of heroin she wouldn't have heard a T-80 tank pass three inches from her ear.

A pistol was in the bodyguard's right hand with a round chambered and the silencer screwed on tight. A pencil flashlight was in his left hand, with a finger poised to turn it on at the last second. He was ten feet away. Then five and the pistol came up. At two feet away, he suddenly felt something kick him in the chest. He flew backward, smashed against the wall, and crumpled in a bleeding heap on the floor. It was funny, he thought; he never heard the blast until a millisecond after his left lung blew out his back.

A moment later, Nicky was over him, peering down through the darkness into his eyes.

"It hurt?"

"Yeah, like a bitch."

"Why?" Nicky asked.

"Five million," his best friend managed to grunt.

"From who?"

"Who knows? Who cares?"

"For real?"

"Oh, it's real, Nicky."

"Why you?"

"Stupid question."

"Five mil. Yeah, you're right."

"Yeah, and you're dead."

Nicky pumped two more bullets into his best friend's mouth, straightened up, then tossed the semicomatose whore out of his room.

He locked the door behind her and moved a large dresser in front of it. He stopped and thought for a moment. Who put the price on his head? Five million was a very big level of enthusiasm. Who hated him that much? Who had the motive? Who had that much money?

After a split second, a name popped into his brain. Golitsin. It made perfect sense; in fact, no other name made any sense. He lifted his cell phone and dialed a number from memory. A voice answered, and Nicky said, "Georgi, it's me."

"Hey, I heard you got a big friggin' problem." Georgi laughed.

"Word's gotten around, I guess."

"It's five million, Nicky. You're the talk of the town."

"Good point. Here's the deal, Georgi. You owe me two million for that dope deal, right?"

"Hey, I got it right here. Deal was you don't get it till tomorrow night."

"Scratch that."

"Seriously?"

"As a heart attack. Put out the word, one and a half million to anybody who whacks Sergei Golitsin. Rest is yours to keep."

"Maybe I'll whack Golitsin and keep all of it."

"Your option, Georgi. But Golitsin better be dead, or you're next." They rang off.

He returned to his bed, sat down, and cradled the pistol on his lap. Five million!

His best friend was right. Nicky was dead. It might take an hour, a day, maybe a week, but he was, without debate or uncertainty, a dead man walking.

By eight in the morning, Tromble had assembled the full team in his office. The usual cast of characters: his pair of compliant hey-boys, Agents Hanrahan and Wilson, Colonel Volevodz, and the head Russian prosecutor, and a fresh pool of INS legal jockeys, now backed up by a pair of eager youthful hotshots from Justice. They sat, pens gripped, notepads poised, and awaited guidance from the great man himself.

"Really, it was to be expected," said one of the Justice boys, named Bill. Bill's area of expertise happened to be anything that happened five minutes before.

"Well, I didn't anticipate it," remarked Jason Caldwell, wiping a remnant of his morning shave from behind his left ear. After the harsh dismissal of Kim Parrish, Caldwell had been handpicked personally by the INS director, a hotshot gunslinger flown in from the San Diego office, where he was legendary for booting Mexican ass back across the border. Caldwell was a loudmouthed blowhard pretty boy without an ounce of pity for anybody accused of anything. He did deliver, though. He took the toughest, most ambiguous, most troubling cases and never once thought twice about the truth or consequences.

He made his ambitions well-known among his peers, among whom he was not now, nor had he ever been, overly popular. The INS job was a stepping stone, a temporary government job from which he intended to run for Congress, and he intended to eventually head the immigration panel, and they would all have to line up to kiss his ass. He was, by every stretch of the imagination, perfect for this job.

He had spent one month reviewing the vast hoard of evidence compiled, translated, and organized so strenuously by Kim and Petri. The hard work had been done for him, a perfect slam dunk; all he had to do was show up in court and smile brilliantly for the cameras. The past month he had mainly strutted in front of full-length mirrors, rehearsing and polishing his lines, admiring his courtly prose, and gearing up to kick a little Russian ass.

The motion for habeas corpus and switch to a federal court came like a bolt out of the dark. No warning. No threats, no hints preceded it. But MP's sneak attack bothered him not in the least. He looked forward to it, actually. Glad Alex and his hired gun did it. The chance to escape from the largely ignored immigration courts into the federal big leagues, and with such a high-visibility case, appealed to him immensely. He had no doubts he would do great. He was Jason Caldwell—if Konevitch had any clue he was up against the scourge of Mexico he'd book his own flight to Russia.

Tromble brought the meeting to order briskly. A few comments about the importance of the case. A blistering reminder about the need for victory at all costs. A hard stare around the table as he dwelled on the somber imperative of sending Konevitch home to pay for his many sins.

The Russians listened without comment. Volevodz detested America—he wanted desperately to get back to Russia, where he expected to pin on a general's star in recognition for bringing home the bacon. The head Russian prosecutor hoped Caldwell would blow it. Just choke and fumble and get his ass kicked. He prayed the case would drag on forever. He and his three comrades all had lady friends out in Vegas, a bunch of big-breasted showgirls who partied without stop and weren't overly picky about their men. And after losing nearly a hundred grand in FBI dough at the tables, he and his pals were finally starting to win a little back.

"You. Who's the judge?" Tromble asked, squinting at the two Justice boys whose names he couldn't remember because frankly he didn't care to.

"Elton Willis," replied Bill, only too proud to be here in the office of the FBI director.

Tromble looked like a lemon had been stuffed in his throat. "Oh, not Willis."

"He has a fairly good reputation," Bill argued, obviously not getting it.

During his brief tenure as a judge, Tromble and Willis had attended a few legal conferences together and, on one sour occasion, had even shared a podium for a spirited debate on civil liberties, one of many legal topics about which they held diametrically different views. The audience were other judges and the results were predictable. Willis was intelligent, methodical, measured, with a former Jesuit's grasp and approach to law. To put it mildly, the scholars and justices in the audience didn't seem to grasp the subtlety of Tromble's theories. It wasn't the first or last time he'd been pelted with boos, but it was probably the loudest.

"He's a lefty wimp," Tromble growled, daring anybody to contest this conclusion. He leaned back in his chair and cracked his knuckles. "You ready for the show?" he asked Caldwell.

"It's a knockdown case. In and out inside one or two days."

Tromble traded glances with Hanrahan. "What's the one thing we've overlooked?"

No clue.

"Publicity. Press. We need to bang Konevitch on every front page," he said, almost predictably.

Caldwell loved this brainchild. "Great idea," he announced quite loudly. "If we don't, the defense will. Better to preempt them."

"Our Russian friends need to see we're serious. All this time, but we haven't forgotten them."

"I could hold a few press conferences," Caldwell agreeably offered.

Tromble cleared his throat. "Well, we'll see if we need you." He paused briefly. "Hanrahan, tell the boys downstairs to kick it in gear. See if *Nightline* or *Good Morning America* has an opening for me. And call that blonde lawyer over at Fox News, you know the one. She always has an opening for me."

"Pretty short notice. We've only got two more days, boss."

"Tell them it's the biggest trial of the year."

Hanrahan looked away and pondered the tabletop. "Maybe that will work, maybe not." Truth was the newspaper and TV people were tired of his boss and his unrelenting attempts to steal ink and camera time. He was a preening spotlight hog, a master at shoving himself before every camera in sight. The boys downstairs in the public affairs office were working eighty-hour weeks, but had flat run out of angles, lies, and lures to get him press time.

"All right," Tromble said, thinking up a fresh angle quickly. "Tell them I intend to be a witness at this trial. A historic occasion. First time an FBI director has ever been on the stand."

"Good idea," Hanrahan said.

Caldwell offered no objections. Go ahead, give it your best shot, he was tempted to shout. Bill this as the biggest trial of the century, if not forever. You'll be a witness, but I'm the prosecutor, it's my show, and I'll damn sure find a way to make you second fiddle.

The meeting broke among frothy promises to make sure Konevitch would at last have his long-overdue appointment with justice.

31

The front steps of the Federal Courthouse looked like a convention for something. A few dozen TV crews were gathered, klieg lights in place, cameras loaded and ready to roll. Another dozen print reporters milled around aimlessly, drawn and stoked by the buzz fed by the FBI's impressive publicity machine.

Inside the court another dozen journalists were already seated at the rear benches, pool reporters who would rush out and share the dirt and drama with their less privileged brethren.

At one table sat a clutch of five lawyers, led by Jason Caldwell, looking rather resplendent in his fine new five-hundred-buck Brooks Brothers suit, bought in honor of his breakout debut. It matched his blue eyes. It would look great on camera. A pair of INS colleagues sat to his left, and on the floor beside them rested a large stack of evidence. The two boys from Justice were banished to a shallow space on the far side, though their exact purpose in the trial was an open question, especially between themselves.

At the defense table, MP huddled importantly with a pair of well-dressed guns from Pacevitch, Knowlton and Rivers, one of many monster firms in a city where lawyers outnumbered ordinary citizens three to one. Directly to his right sat Matt Rivers, a law school classmate who had served as best man in the hastily

arranged wedding between MP and his by then noticeably pregnant bride.

Top of his class, in his third year, Matt had been wined and
dined by big firms from New York and Chicago. But he chose
PKR, as it was commonly known. He was drawn by its no-holds-
barred reputation, a feared powerhouse, a collection of divisions
that did many things from corporate through criminal, with
branch offices in six American cities, and ten more spread around
the globe. Notice that PKR was involved in a case often had the
terrifying effect of getting even the most recalcitrant opponents
to promptly initiate settlement talks. PKR's unwritten motto was
"pile it on," in honor of the firm's willingness to throw a hundred
lawyers at a troubled case. However many lawyers were committed against it, PKR doubled it and wrenched up the hours, drowning the competition in useless motions and watching it sink in
exhaustion. To put it mildly, PKR did not like to lose. Matt's competitive streak—aka his killer instinct—had been identified early
and carefully nurtured and cultivated. The cultivation included
partnership within five years: three hundred thousand a year,
plus bonus, plus car.

Though their lives and fortunes diverged, Matt and MP still
lunched together every few months and shared tales from the
opposite ends of the legal profession. There was one condition
that was strictly followed; Matt picked the eating hole and paid
the check. This law was laid down in the early years after MP
took Matt to Taco Bell; no longer accustomed to such fare, Matt's
stomach rebelled with horrible violence.

At Alex's behest, MP had approached his old pal a few months
before for a favor. MP was seriously outgunned, and Alex pres-
sured him to find some reinforcements, but since funds were
short, to find somebody willing to do the work for the promise
of the publicity it might generate. Tromble seemed to be doing
a masterful job at stoking that publicity, and Matt took MP's appeal to the firm's management committee. It was a simple and
quite common request; assign one or two lawyers on a pro bono
basis. The bulk of the work would be handled by MP: all he

really wanted was the firm there, in the background, throwing its weight around, striking fear in the opposition. A simple immigration matter failed to fuel the committee's enthusiasm until Matt launched into Alex Konevitch's fascinating background and the strange nature of his supposed crimes. Interest swelled, then the partners on the committee became curiously fired up about the whole idea.

Two years before, PKR had joined the pell-mell rush of Western firms pouring into the new market of democratic Russia and opened a small, struggling branch in Moscow. The PKR boys in Russia were immediately hired by a free-market oil company battling to fend off a vicious takeover by a shady consortium with heavy government contacts. One day before the first hearing, PKR was notified by the Ministry of Justice that its lawyers had just been disbarred, and its branch office was no longer welcome. The PKR lawyers were all booted out. The oil company was swallowed up two days later.

What a great way for PKR to shoot a big middle finger back at the Russian government, the senior partners agreed. Among its many fine attributes, PKR never forgot a slight.

Thus, seated to Matt's right was Marvin Knowlton, the K in PKR, a distinguished-looking eighty-year-old gentleman, a legendary scrapper talked out of retirement for this one brief return engagement. He cut a striking figure, with the deep tan of a permanent Florida golfer that contrasted nicely with his long silver mane. The old lion's presence in this court was a warning to whoever cared to pay attention. In his trial lawyer days, Marvin specialized in suits for defamation, rights violations, and libel. He sued at the drop of a hat. He rarely lost.

The strategy was simple. By introducing the motion for habeas corpus—thus forcing the government to show the constitutional basis for Alex's prolonged detention—Alex and MP were moving it out of immigration and into federal court, a system with more rights protections for the accused. Also, there were appeals in this system, a chance for a second, or even a third hearing. MP would take first crack at defending the Konevitches. If he lost, the cutthroats from PKR would take over, commit a dozen more lawyers, and go for blood.

For the time being, though, Matt and Marvin were expected only to look threatening, listen to MP's arguments, and be prepared to step in only after things went wrong, which, after reviewing the evidence, in their collective view, was the likely outcome.

To MP's rear sat Elena in a simple blue pantsuit and white pumps, clutching her hands, praying fervently. Occasionally she stopped talking to the Lord long enough to throw a hateful glare at the defense table, the people who had so cruelly persecuted her husband.

At the last moment, Alex was led through a side door by two big marshals straight to the defense table. He had been offered the chance to shower and change into something more presentable, like a suit and tie. He politely but insistently refused. He sported the same dirty white trousers, soiled white shirt, and grungy flip-flops he wore in prison. His face had accumulated at least four days of thick, dark stubble. His hair was still pulled back in a tight, greasy ponytail.

Even MP had argued otherwise, but Alex adamantly insisted—let the judge and all the reporters see what had been done to him. The sight of him in such a sorry state would displace any thought of a fat-cat millionaire. Whatever he had been before, now he was just another simple guy cruelly oppressed and abused by the state.

Alex shambled in fits and starts to his chair, shoulders slumped, head and eyes down. He feigned a pained expression and very gently began to ease himself into the chair. A lady in the third row leaned over to somebody a few seats down and muttered loudly and indignantly, "You see that? The poor guy's been gang-raped by those animals."

The cue was perfect. MP and Matt immediately jumped up and made a dramatic show of helping poor Alex get more comfortable. And as though she hadn't seen her husband in months, Elena clutched her throat and emitted a strangled wail that bounced around the courtroom walls.

At just that moment, the rear door flew open and in marched John Tromble, fresh from a fast flurry of interviews on the court-house steps. His eyes roved around the courtroom, settling finally on the prisoner at the defense table. It was his first look at Alex Konevitch, up close and personal, his first glance at this irritat-ing man who had occupied so much of his time and attention over the past fourteen months. He took in the prison garb, the shaggy beard, the unkempt ponytail, the exhausted eyes, and he responded instinctively—he smiled.

This response was fully observed by the dozen pool report-ers in the back rows, who launched into noisy whispers among themselves.

Tromble moved with important purpose to the front row where an aide held an empty seat for him. He had not been in a court-room since his days as a judge, but he felt his presence would send a strong message to the court.

A moment later, a side door quietly opened. Judge Elton Wil-lis walked out, black robes rustling, and moved straight to the bench. The bailiff announced him, everybody stood, the judge sat, and the court fell back into its seats.

Elton Willis was fifty-nine, surprisingly short, with jet black skin and dainty facial features. A former Jesuit priest, he awoke one morning and decided God's will wouldn't be settled in a church, but out on the streets where the battle between good and evil was waged with terrible force. He turned in his vestments and spent five years dishing slop in soup kitchens and mentor-ing young black children in Washington's brutal slums, before becoming deeply discouraged. Any illusion that he would save the world was crushed by crack, guns, and the unrelenting vio-lence of the streets. So many of the kids ended up dead or in the legal system, with poor representation, and were shunted off to prisons they would bounce in and out of for the rest of their lives. It was time to take the battle up another level. He finished law school at the University of Virginia, where the novelty of a former Jesuit studying a lower law greatly amused the faculty, then returned to Washington, where he established himself as a defense attorney to be reckoned with. Rich clients were banned. If a prospective client passed through his door dressed in a suit, he was promptly sent right back out the door.

As a federal judge, he now waged the battle between good and bad from a high bench. Jesuits tend to be hard men of great intelligence. Elton Willis happened to be harder and smarter than most.

His eyes wandered around the court for a moment. In a quiet voice, he quickly summarized the matter for consideration, and in a louder voice established a few ground rules. This was not a jury trial. In fact it wasn't a trial, it was a habeas corpus hearing mediated by a judge. He did not cater to theatrics, asked the attorneys to object only when absolutely necessary, and emphasized that brevity was next to godliness. He offered threatening scowls to both lawyers, underscoring these points.

Opening statements were made by both attorneys. Jason Caldwell led off and couldn't help himself. After months of primping and prepping, he was like a Hollywood starlet at her first premiere. He paced and pranced around the floor. Half his remarks were addressed to the judge, the other half to the yawning journalists in the back row. Unfortunately, he was also an effective attorney with a sharp tongue and a strong case, and, long before he was done, Alex Konevitch sounded like the personification of evil. He deserved to be in prison, and possibly executed. At the very least he should be dispatched to his own shores for a long-overdue appointment with justice.

With a final flash of his freshly bleached teeth at the reporters in the back, he returned to his seat.

MP pushed himself only halfway out of his chair and said very simply, "My client has endured fourteen miserable months in prison, convicted of nothing. I request an immediate release."

He sat. That was it, nothing more—a tiny drop in a vast ocean that screamed for a long and indignant rant.

Caldwell felt like standing up and applauding. He was going to pound MP Jones into dust. This was going to be so easy. He stood and called his first witness, Colonel Leonid Volevodz, to the stand.

The colonel marched to the witness box, was sworn in, and sat.

Caldwell sidled up to the witness stand, Perry Mason absent the wheelchair. "What's your position, sir?"

"I am the special assistant to Russia's minister of internal security."

"And this would be equivalent to our FBI?"

"You might describe it that way." He leaned back and coolly crossed his legs.

"What is your relationship to the investigations concerning Mr. Konevitch?"

"The lead investigator for my department. The crimes were so severe and crossed so many areas, eventually I was ordered to oversee the efforts of all three government investigations."

Caldwell turned around and nodded at one of the INS lawyers at the crowded table. The lawyer seized a bundle of papers and rushed to Caldwell's side. He selected then held up one clump of papers. Caldwell asked, "Can you please identify this?"

Volevodz bent forward. "That is an English translation of the Ministry of Justice investigation."

"And this?"

"The Ministry of Finance investigation."

"And this?"

"My own investigation."

"And do these three investigations draw similar conclusions?"

"Identical conclusions."

"Could you briefly describe those conclusions?"

"Briefly? Konevitch stole 250 million dollars. He gutted and bankrupted his company. He almost single-handedly ruined the credibility of the Russian banking model. It is impossible to summarize in a short statement."

Caldwell turned his back to the colonel and smiled at the peanut gallery. "Yes, I imagine it is. Do any of these investigations differ in any serious regard?"

"No. The facts were easily established. The evidence was overwhelming. Perhaps a hundred different investigators reached the exact same conclusion."

"That Konevitch is a crook?"

"A thief. A liar. A confidence man."

"Was Konevitch ever asked to return to Russia?"

"Yes, by me. I pleaded with him. Twice, on two separate occasions. I assured him of a fair trial. I offered my personal protection. If he was innocent, he could clear his name."

"Twice?"

"That's what I said."

"And how did he respond?"

"He laughed. He pointed out there was no extradition treaty between our countries. He stuck his finger in my chest and said he would hide behind your flag."

Caldwell couldn't resist that opening. "He would hide behind our flag? The Stars and Stripes?"

"His exact words."

Another document was held up and splayed open. Caldwell asked, "Can you identify this for the court?"

The thin eyes squinted again. "It's the indictment issued against Alex Konevitch for his crimes." He leaned forward, as if he needed a closer look. "It's signed by Anatoli Fyodorev, Russia's equivalent to your attorney general."

Caldwell looked at the judge. "Your Honor, we submit these investigations and indictments as evidence that Alex Konevitch committed serious crimes in Russia, and later he lied and covered up these crimes when he fled here."

The stack was handed off to the clerk, who quickly assigned a number to each one before she arranged them in an orderly stack on her desk. Alex was seated in his chair. He showed no surprise or even concern over the seriousness of the testimony.

His Honor looked at MP. "Would you care to cross-examine?"

"I would not, Your Honor," he answered without looking up.

Volevodz was released. The next witness was the chief Russian prosecutor, who was identified and properly sworn in.

He sat and Caldwell approached. "Could you please describe your role in this investigation?"

"I was ordered by the state attorney general to prepare the indictment and legal case against Alex Konevitch."

"He's a wanted man in Russia, I take it?"

"Number one on our most wanted list."

"Do you believe he's guilty?"

"That would be a matter for our courts to decide."

"But Mr. Konevitch claims your courts are unfair."

"Ridiculous. Under the old communist system, maybe. We are a democracy now. Our courts are every bit as judicious and fair as yours."

"So he would be allowed to hire a lawyer?"

"As many as he can afford. If he can't afford any, the state will appoint one."

"He would be allowed to present evidence on his own behalf?"

"Just like here, Mr. Caldwell. Konevitch will enjoy the full benefit of innocence until proven guilty."

"Are you aware that some Americans have a poor impression of your legal system?"

"Are you aware that some Russians have a poor impression of yours?"

"Touché." Caldwell decided to step out on a limb, directed his gaze at Alex, then asked, "Why would Mr. Konevitch feel he can't get an honest shake in Russia?"

The Russian also directed his gaze at Alex, who nodded politely but otherwise appeared indifferent.

"Maybe an honest shake, as you call it, is the last thing he wants."

Caldwell paused and waited for the loud but inevitable objection from MP Jones. He had led this witness. He had openly encouraged an act of naked conjecture—how could the chief prosecutor possibly know what Alex was thinking?

Silence. MP sat in his seat, doodling on a legal pad. He looked bored out of his mind. Beside him, Alex appeared to be studying MP's doodles, as transfixed as he would be by a da Vinci or a Picasso.

"Thank you," Caldwell said to his witness, then studied the ceiling a moment as though he needed a little help from the Lord to remember his next point. He snapped his fingers. "Oh, another question. The money Mr. Konevitch stole? Did you ever find it?"

The chief prosecutor looked at Alex. "Some of it, yes. We tracked a few million to a bank in Bermuda."

Another of Caldwell's aides hustled over and shoved a sheet of paper at the witness.

Caldwell asked with construed curiosity, "Would this be the account information?" What else could it be?

After a careful examination, "Yes, this is it."

"How much is currently in the account?"

"Two and half million dollars."

"That's it?"

"Yes, that's all."

"I thought he stole 250 million dollars. Where's the remainder of Konevitch's money?"

"It's not Konevitch's money, sir."

"No?" A look of surprise. "Well, whose money is it?"

"It's money he robbed from poor people in Russia. They trusted him and are now bankrupt. We won't know where he stashed it all until we get him home and he confesses. Only then can those poor people be repaid."

Caldwell let that fester a moment—all those miserable victims back home starving and freezing while they waited for Alex to give them back their money—then said, "Are you familiar with a company named Orangutan Media?"

"I most certainly am."

"How are you familiar with this company?"

"It became the subject of police interest a few years ago."

"How did this come about?"

"The result of a tip from a source inside one of our crime syndicates. A Chechen mob, a nasty group involved in a number of criminal activities, from kidnapping to drugs to murder."

"Sounds like our Mafia."

"You should be so lucky. Compared to these people, your Mafia's a Boy Scout group. After the tip, a wiretap was installed and the police heard Konevitch arranging payments and transfers of cash. He was using Orangutan as a front to launder syndicate money."

"What was the nature of Orangutan Media?"

"Reputedly it was an advertising company. And it was established in Austria to evade our scrutiny. The syndicate money came into the company under the guise of client contracts. Orangutan turned around and gave the same money right back to the syndicate as subcontractors. It was all very neat."

"It sounds quite elaborate."

"Not really. It's a very common shell game. Child's play for a sophisticated financial mastermind like Konevitch."

"And you have Mr. Konevitch on tape discussing these arrangements with a syndicate?"

"Right there on your table," he said, pointing at the defense table. "The taped discussions are in Russian, of course, so I left them back in Russia. They would be incomprehensible to you, anyway. I therefore turned over paper transcripts to your people."

"Yes, you did." The aide took the cue and hauled a bunch of papers to the bench. "We introduce these translated transcripts," Caldwell said very slowly, with another flash of teeth. "As well, I submit statements collected by state prosecutors from a number of Orangutan Media employees confessing to the schemes inside the company."

He held his breath and waited in anticipation for Jones to jerk out of his chair. Without the tapes there was no way to verify that the written transcripts were accurate, or indeed whether any tapes even existed. There had to be an objection this time—a noisy protest infused with enraged anger would follow, he was sure.

In fact, Jones looked ready to jump out of his seat before Alex reached over and grabbed his arm. Alex briefly whispered something into his ear. MP relented, relaxed back into his seat, and went back to doodling on a yellow legal pad.

Caldwell silently congratulated himself. A brilliant move, and he couldn't believe he got away with it. Having the chief prosecutor in the witness chair obviously nullified the discrediting strategy Jones had pulled off in immigration court. Welcome to the big leagues, pal.

Caldwell triumphantly announced, "I'm through with this witness," and returned to his seat.

Judge Willis peered down from his perch at MP. Jones was still focused intensely on his yellow legal pad, which now was cluttered with aimless squiggles and shapes. "Mr. Jones, do you wish to cross-examine?"

MP looked up. "What? . . . Uh, no, thank you, Your Honor."

"You're sure?"

"Yes, quite sure."

Willis rubbed his eyes for a moment. "You heard what the witness presented?"

"I did."

"And you're sure you don't want to ask him a few questions?"

"Very sure."

"Is this your first time in federal court, Mr. Jones?"

"Yes sir. Very first. It's much nicer than immigration court. Quite lovely."

"I'm glad it appeals to your tastes. Do you understand how our procedures work?"

"I believe I do, Your Honor."

"Once I release this witness, he cannot be recalled."

"Then please do it quickly. I don't know about you, but he was becoming tiresome, Your Honor."

This caused a twitter of laughter among the reporters.

His Honor did not appear to get the joke. "I advise you, Mr. Jones, to think harder about questioning the witnesses than trying to entertain us with humor."

"Can I be blunt, Your Honor?"

"You can try, Mr. Jones."

"I don't wish to waste your time."

"To the contrary, Mr. Jones, I'm here to listen to both sides. It's an adversarial system, by design. I encourage you to participate."

"Well, I don't want to encourage him to tell more lies."

"I see. The witness is released."

Caldwell rose to call his next witness, but the judge put up a hand. "Hold on a moment." His eyes turned to Alex. "Can you please rise?"

Alex stood.

Judge Willis leaned far forward on his elbows. "Are you aware your attorney has no experience in federal jurisdictions?"

"In fact, he emphasized the same thing last week."

"I'm sure you're in a great hurry to get out of prison, Mr. Konevitch. I'm just wondering if this hearing might be premature."

"On the contrary, my arrest and imprisonment were premature, Your Honor."

"Do you have adequate knowledge of our legal system?"

Alex directed a look at Tromble, who was seated, legs crossed. "I've been imprisoned the past fourteen months, without trial. You could say I am quite familiar with this legal procedure. Soviet law operated the same way."

Willis pinched his nose and forced himself not to scowl. "Are you content with your representation? The question is on the record, Mr. Konevitch. Because if you try to appeal my decision based upon incompetent representation, it will now be clear that you knowingly settled on Mr. Jones."

MP blinked a few times at what was obviously intended as a very public putdown. It was humiliating to be treated as a featherweight but that wasn't the most painful part. Worse, part of their strategy cooked up by him and the PKR boys relied on Alex having valid claim to poor representation. So far, MP had availed himself of every opportunity to portray utter incompetence. Let the prosecutor get away with as much as was legally advisable, do your best to sit and look stupid.

A great idea, in concept, that was suddenly falling apart.

After a moment, Alex stated very clearly, "I'm happy with my counsel," then collapsed into his chair.

And so it went for the remainder of the morning. An hour break for lunch before Caldwell resumed calling more witnesses who confirmed and reconfirmed and elaborated powerfully on the inescapable fact that Alex Konevitch was a crook, a flight risk, a criminal who had to be incarcerated or he would flee and never be heard from again. Three FBI agents were paraded to the stand, followed by two Foreign Service officers with recent experience in Russia, each of whom had observed firsthand the public furor caused when Konevitch disappeared with the money.

MP politely and firmly declined to cross-examine each one. The clock read 4:30 when the last prosecution witness was excused from the stand.

Judge Willis checked his watch, then said, "Sidebar with the opposing attorneys."

MP and Caldwell joined His Honor in a small, tight cluster beside the bench.

The judge glared at MP. "Did you not in fact submit this motion for habeas corpus?" he whispered.

"I certainly did, Your Honor," MP whispered back.

"Why, Mr. Jones?"

"Why? Because my client has been incarcerated in federal prison for fourteen months. He's been bounced through three different prisons, each progressively more hazardous and miserable than the last. He's been submitted to several bouts of solitary confinement, and deliberately assigned cellmates categorized as Level Five inmates. I'm sure you're aware that prisoners reach this distinctive category only after they prove they are a grave danger to other inmates and to the guards. In short, somebody in our federal government wants my client dead or willing to submit to instantaneous deportation."

"Those are grave charges."

"I believe that's an understatement."

"Now, may I be blunt with you?"

MP nodded.

Still in whispers, His Honor unleashed a day's worth of quiet anger. "Since you requested this hearing, you are supposed to do something other than sit and doodle on a yellow pad, Mr. Jones. The American legal system is designed to allow a spirited defense. You are obligated to occasionally object to statements that are challengeable, and cross-examine witnesses and poke holes in points you believe are contestable or unsubstantiated. I am dismayed by your behavior. I find it egregiously outrageous and, frankly, incompetent."

"I apologize. I promise I'll try to appear more engaged."

"I'm sure your client will appreciate that."

He turned to Caldwell, who was biting back a smile. He could barely contain himself. His bosses had warned him that Jones was wily and tough and full of surprises. This was the guy, after all, who booted Kim Parrish's ass out of the ballpark. "Hey, who's the tough guy now?" the scourge of Mexico wanted to ask. He was tempted to move two inches from Jones's face and just break out into laughter.

"Mr. Caldwell, do you have more witnesses?"

In fact, three more he planned to question that afternoon. But, hey, what the hell—he could dispense with all of them. After the catastrophic damage he had administered—none of it challenged, all cleanly admitted—why pile more humiliation on top of ten thousand tons of misery? They were nothing more than confirmation witnesses, here to build on already well-substantiated facts. The judge was ready to rule in his favor right now.

"One more. It can wait till morning."

"Then unless you gentlemen disagree I intend to adjourn until nine a.m. tomorrow."

Neither attorney objected in the least.

His Honor looked at MP again. The look was anything but kindly and compassionate. "You had better do some soul-searching tonight. You requested this hearing. If I don't see a spirited attempt on your client's behalf in the morning, I'll cite you for contempt."

The instant the judge dismissed the court and the side door closed behind him, the mad scramble was on. Like the shot that starts a race, Caldwell scuttled for the door. He raced through the wide hallways, shoved open the huge outer doors, and nearly lost his balance as he went careening down the big steps.

Three dozen cameras and reporters converged on him at once. He pushed back his hair and produced his most handsome smile for the friendly cameras. "Ladies and gentlemen, I'm Jason Caldwell, and I'm prosecuting this case. I'm sure you have lots of questions. One at a time, and don't interrupt my replies."

Tromble crashed out the doors just as Caldwell finished his windup. Without even glancing back, Caldwell very smoothly said, "Surely you all recognize our beloved FBI director. He has been providing assistance to me on this case. Limited assistance, though it has been somewhat helpful. I just want to express my appreciation. If you haven't heard, in fact, he will be my first witness tomorrow morning."

Tromble wanted to punch him. Grab his throat and begin throttling. Instead he forced a smile, produced a firm, dutiful salute for the cameras, and sprinted off to his limousine, yelling over his shoulder, "Sorry, I don't have time for questions."

Caldwell remained on the steps for two hours. No question was too trivial to answer. No reporter too insignificant for an endearing smile and a long, thoughtful reply. He bravely withstood the fury of interest until the reporters remembered their deadlines and wandered off into the Washington evening.

32

It was called the Tsar's Suite. At an enormous five thousand square feet, it was furnished with rare and wondrous antiques, loaded with marble and teak, and crammed to the rafters with a staggering array of personal luxuries. Two separate baths, either one big enough to swallow and wash a squadron of sweaty horses. An entire wall of picture windows overlooking the glorious Moskva River and Moscow's twinkling lights.

The sumptuous dinner had been prepared by a four-star chef and delivered by three waiters who hung over the table, willing to cut the meat and spoon-feed the thoroughly spoiled customers. Whatever they wished for, a dollop landed on their plate, delivered by a gold ladle. A sip of wine and the crystal goblet was instantly topped off.

By ten, the chief of staff and his mistress were stuffed and sated, slightly lightheaded from the wine and champagne, ready to retire to the sumptuous pillow bed in the gargantuan bedroom. The chief dispatched the waiters with huge tips.

Tatyana was cradling a snifter of sherry and staring wistfully out the window at the sky full of stars. "This was a wonderful idea," she said.

"Isn't it?"

"The most romantic thing we've ever done."

"What can I say? I love you."

"I love you, too."

"Do you?"

"Of course. I love you, love you, love you."

He stared across the table at her. "Will you marry me?"

"I would love to."

"You're sure?"

"Yes. Just . . . obviously not right now."

"Why not now?"

"Yeltsin needs you. The country needs you. I won't be a distraction from your important work."

"I can handle it. After all, we see each other at work."

They had been through this same argument a hundred times, a conversation they had rehearsed so often it was stale. A brief loving glance at her paramour. "But I'm not sure I can. We've been through this. In case you haven't noticed, darling, I stay pretty busy, too."

His elbows landed on the table. "You're sure there's nobody else?"

"Absolutely," she snapped. She fell back on her usual defense, a deep pout. "Now you're acting like a jealous idiot."

He reached into a pocket, withdrew a photograph, and casually tossed it across the table. "Recognize this guy?"

She glanced down and didn't flinch or so much as squint. "No."

"Look again. You're sure you don't know him?"

She picked up the picture. "Who is he? He looks sort of cute."

"Nobody. Just thought you might. Until yesterday, he was a star striker on our national soccer team."

"*Was?*"

The chief began playing with a small fork. "That's right, was. Seems he experienced a terrible accident. Collided with another player and broke his leg. Also destroyed ligaments in his knee . . . actually both knees, I'm told. Then somebody ran over him with cleats and broke his nose and kicked off an ear. Poor fellow. Such a rough sport. His soccer career is definitely over."

Tatyana gripped the photograph a little harder.

Her boss said very amiably, "Just thought you might know or at least remember him."

"I'm not a soccer fan. Why should I?"

"It seems he went to the same elementary and gymnasium as you. Same small village. Same age, too."

"What's his name?"

"Sasha Komenov."

"I have a vague memory of the name." A well-feigned expression of dawning recognition. "Oh, yes, I think I do remember. A chubby little boy covered with pimples. Obviously, he looks different now. We were all so young back then."

Her boss swallowed a deep sip of sherry, then bit down hard on his lip. "How about a little music before we retire, dear?"

"Something romantic would be nice." She sipped carefully from her sherry, trying not to vomit. Poor, poor Sasha. She stared out at the city lights and tried hard not to imagine how her boytoy looked with a blown-up nose and only one ear. She failed miserably. The image just wouldn't disappear.

Her boss moved to the entertainment console, gritted his teeth, punched play on the tape machine, and waited for the sound of romance to start.

A moment later came the sounds of Tatyana and her freshly disfigured Sasha thrashing in the sheets and prattling away about what a disgusting, nauseating dork her boss was.

Tatyana spun around. She and her boss looked at each other for a moment, he with his eyes narrowed into betrayed slits, she unable to close her mouth. The damning tape droned on.

Tatyana screamed, "What in the hell is that?" She knew damn well what it was. Disaster. Her apartment was bugged. Some nosybody had been listening and, worse, recording. But for how long? Who? How sloppy had she been, how much dirt was on those dreadful tapes?

She quickly ended up with the one question all lawyers ask at a moment like this: how screwed am I?

"That?" he answered, jerking down the volume. "Oh, just the sound of you being fired."

"What? You can't."

He smiled. "Yes, I definitely can. Listen, it's fun. I'll do it again—you're fired." He pushed stop, and they stared at each other. Then, once more, because he loved the sound of it, "You're fired."

The snifter of sherry tumbled out of her hand, landed on the marble floor, and crashed into a thousand tiny shards. An apt metaphor to what was happening to her life. She bounced out of her chair, stamped a foot, and said, "Don't be a fool. Without me, you won't last two minutes. I've been carrying you for three years."

"I won't deny it."

"While you and your pal Yeltsin have been keeping the vodka industry afloat, who do you think's been keeping the office running?"

"Won't deny that, either. You worked like a dog."

She tried a smile. "Look, darling, we can get past this."

"I already have. I hired your replacement this afternoon. A real clever young fellow with endless energy and an incredible knack for organization. He'll be happily seated behind your desk in the morning."

"You bastard."

"You bitch."

She grabbed her coat and began stomping for the door. She threw it open with a loud crash and immediately three men in blue uniforms lunged at her. They spun Tatyana around and slapped cuffs on her wrists. She tried screaming and thrashing, but it had no effect, and she soon stopped.

Her boss watched with fierce satisfaction, then mentioned to his former lover, "Ooops, did I fail to mention there's a second tape?"

A second tape? She was suddenly sure she was going to become sick.

"I turned it over to our new attorney general. It's you talking with your crooked friends about all your illegal schemes." He mocked her with a loud laugh. "Hey, you know what else? Maybe I failed to mention that your stooge Fyodorev was also fired and arrested this afternoon."

"You lousy bastard."

"A postcard from prison would be nice. Be sure to let me know where you land."

So many of them were gathered in such a tight two-block circumference, it resembled a convention of killers. There were strutting pros with big-league experience, an all-star team of deadly assassins. A clutch of third-rate mobsters ambling for their first kill. And a sprinkling of ambitious young amateurs hoping to get lucky. It was every man to himself, or herself—a few women's suffrage types were lurking in the shadows as well.

They hung out in parked cars and vans, smoking and sipping coffee, eyeing Nicky's hideout, waiting for a break. Going inside was ill-fated stupidity. This had been tried rather unsuccessfully by one bold idiot before he was driven off by a furious hail of bullets. About twenty of Nicky's bodyguards were in there, armed to the teeth, guarding their turf. Poachers weren't welcome. A few snipers were perched on rooftops, fighting off the cold. The apartment building across the street from Nicky's holdout, a real dump, had suddenly experienced an unaccustomed flood of subleases. Responding to loud knocks on the doors, the inhabitants found themselves confronted by tough-looking men shoving thousands into their fists for what was promised would be a brief dislocation. The far side of the hall, the one that did not face Nicky's safehouse, couldn't draw any interest at any price.

The street had only one coffee shop, a cramped, neglected little place run by a chubby old babushka with a million wrinkles and a toothless smile. She was suddenly rolling in customers, nasty-looking sorts who demanded coffee day and night. She struck a deal with a sandwich and soup joint six blocks down. She imported their goods, tripled the price, and made a killing. To date, she was the only one making a killing, literally or figuratively. She quietly rooted for Nicky to last another few weeks.

Late on Tuesday evening, a new car joined the party, a big, shiny black Mercedes that slid to a curb and idled for hours. Instantly, a dozen hungry sharks took note of this latest entrant in the Nicky sweepstakes.

Throughout the night, the car never budged from the curb. At four in the morning, four men stepped out. They stretched and looked around. All were dressed in nice suits, wildly out of character for this game.

A moment later, a fifth man embarked from the car and stepped out onto the curb. Short and fat, he wore a double-breasted blazer with a hundred gold buttons that sparkled in the moonlit night. He stretched his cramped legs, looked around very briefly, then waddled off in the direction of the coffee shop. The four men followed at a discreet distance, an obvious deference to their boss that marked him like a whale swimming among minnows.

Golitsin ran in the wrong circles. He had no clue that photos of him with a million and a half bucks painted on his backside were circulating throughout the city's heavily populated underworld. Later, the city coroner would find it impossible to discern exactly which of nearly a hundred bullets fired in the willy-nilly hailstorm was the precise cause of death. The five through the heart were certainly candidates, though the ten in the brain had the odds in their favor.

Six of those ten, however, were fired from different guns, different ranges, and different angles. Unfortunately the shattered brain gave up no clues as to which bullet struck first, or indeed, which produced the most lethal damage. Frankly there was too little brain left to consider. So much of it was scattered on the concrete, bits and pieces too small to scrape up.

The logjam was settled after an intense three-day bombardment of whispered threats and intense pleadings, when one of the shooters secretly offered to split the reward fifty-fifty—of the many other offers that poured in, nothing was over a third.

Three-quarters of a million dollars!

The coroner's last troubling doubt instantly vanished in a cloud of certainty.

*   *   *

The third day in his self-imposed bunker was the one that got to Nicky. Three days and two nights of sitting in the same pitch-dark room, cradling his gun in his lap, counting down the hours and wondering when it would end. Three days of waiting for the inevitable. His own bodyguards made an occasional foray. Day and night, Nicky could hear them out there, exhorting one another, loading up on booze and dope, trying to stoke up the nerve.

Early on the second day there had been a chaotic rush at the door—a stupid, clumsy attempt with bodies bashing against the reinforced wood. Nicky emptied his pistol and smiled blissfully at all the satisfying howls and screams.

Later that same night, a second attempt. Smarter this time. Well, slightly more sneaky, anyway. One of the idiots crawled up to the door, planted a hand grenade against the wood, pulled the pin, then scuttled away for his life. Nicky became dismayed and depressed by the stupidity of his own handpicked bodyguards. It was a miracle he had survived this long. Anticipating them was child's play. Everything in the room—the furniture, the mattress—everything was piled up against the door. The pile of junk absorbed the blast and shrapnel nicely. When the boys showed up, Nicky emptied his pistol again. Another lovely chorus of screams and howls, and Nicky laughed long after they had retreated back to their refuge.

They were through being careless and stupid. No more suicidal rushes, no more dragging bullet-riddled corpses down the hall and trying to figure out how to dispose of them. Now they were trying to wait him out: if he snoozed, he was dead. They took shifts and listened for his snores. There was no food in his room. The bathroom was across the hall so water was a problem, too. But there was heroin and cocaine in abundance. Nicky pulled a fresh snort every hour. Every fourth hour, the needle slid back into a vein. He sat on the floor, pumped up on dope, erupting with delirious chuckles that echoed down the hall.

His best friend's corpse was three feet away, bloated like an overinflated balloon. The smell was intolerable, but Nicky's nostrils were so crusted and blocked up with white powder he had no idea.

Late on the third day the idea took root in his exhausted, drug-addled brain. He thought about it more, and liked it more. No, he loved it. In a lifetime of great ideas, it would be such a grand finishing touch. Long after he was gone, they would still be admiring his final masterstroke. His last finger at all of them.

He reached over to his friend's dead hand and pried the flashlight out of the rigor-mortised fist. He found a piece of paper and pencil and scribbled a brief, perfunctory note.

Holding the note in one hand, he put the pistol in his mouth and without a moment of hesitation blew out the back of his head.

His bodyguards waited an hour before they drew straws. They dispatched the losers first, frightened scouts who scuttled past the door and prayed Nicky didn't blast them to pieces. Everybody had heard that last shot an hour before. The debates and quarrels were noisy and fierce, but they just weren't sure.

Nicky was so clever, so diabolical. It wouldn't be beneath him to fake his own suicide just to lure a few more of them into his sights.

Finally, they tiptoed down the hall, broke the door down, and crashed inside. Somebody flipped on the lights. Between the rotting corpse and the fact that Nicky had used the floor as a toilet, the stench was like a dropkick in the nostrils. They pinched their noses and eased over to Nicky's body against the wall.

The note was gripped tightly in his dead hand: "I, Nicky Kozyrev, claim the five million dollars for my own death. You pricks figure out which of my many bastard kids are first in line. Send it to him. Or her. I don't care."

33

The trial opened on time. By 9:15, John Tromble was seated in the witness chair, duly sworn to honesty, waiting impatiently for this snotty, pretty-boy, headline-robbing prosecutor to kick it in gear.

The moment was historic, unprecedented, actually. No FBI director had ever sat in a witness chair—or, more accurately, none not accused of crimes themselves. One more groundbreaking achievement to tack on to the growing legend.

The evening news the night before had been an Alex fest. Every morning paper on the East Coast led off with the story about the Russian runaway millionaire who had been dragged out of the Watergate—a national landmark of sorts, after all—and was fighting deportation and a long-overdue appointment with justice in his own land. Legal experts held sway on the evening and late-night talk shows, and were still there, sipping coffee and yammering away, for the morning shows as well. Maybe they slept at the networks.

The general consensus was that Alex's legal team was getting its tail kicked and the result appeared inevitable. The only objection came from a big-time radical, highly esteemed member of the Harvard Law faculty, who posed the perverse theory that if Alex Konevitch was a foreign citizen, American courts had no purview over him. After getting laughed off two shows he disappeared back to his classroom.

Alex himself was back at the defense table, looking, if anything, more tragically decrepit and miserably ill-kempt than the day before. His beard was thicker, darker, more pronounced. Heavy circles under his eyes betrayed another long, sleepless night.

From the stand, Tromble stole a quick look at him, then quietly suppressed another smile. A few of the morning articles had mentioned his instinctive reaction as he entered the court the day before and first saw Alex; the mentions weren't overly flattering.

The pretty boy ambled up to the witness stand. "Could you please tell the court your name and title?"

It was a stupid, fatuous question, but Tromble played along. "Judge John Tromble, director of the FBI."

"And that would make you the nation's top law enforcement officer?"

"Technically, that honor belongs to the attorney general," he said with a condescending smile as if everybody should know this.

"Do you believe Alex Konevitch committed crimes in Russia that merit deportation?"

"I wouldn't know about the crimes. Russia's courts will decide that."

"But you reviewed the evidence against him?"

"My people reviewed it. I've seen summaries." Another fatuous question—Tromble obviously had more important things on his hands than sifting through piles of evidence.

"Is this evidence compelling?"

"Overwhelming."

"What would happen if Mr. Konevitch were to escape?" A slight frown. "I mean, escape again."

Tromble appeared thoughtful, as though he had never considered this possibility. "Well, it would be a flat-out disaster."

"Why?"

"Because a great deal of modern crime is international these days. Just as our corporations and businesses have expanded across borders, so have criminal syndicates. International police forces have to rely on each other."

"And you believe Mr. Konevitch's escape would hinder this cooperation?"

"He is what we would call a high-profile criminal back home. If we let him slip away, we would hear about it from the Russians in a million unfortunate ways. It would probably cripple our efforts against the new wave of Russian criminals."

"This is called reciprocity, is it not?"

"That's one word for it. If we want them to hand over our crooks, we have to hand over theirs. If we want their help to combat crime in our streets, we need to help them."

"That seems like common sense," Caldwell remarked, as if anybody would argue otherwise. "Now, why was Mr. Konevitch placed in federal detention?" Avoiding the "prison" word was a nice touch. Detention sounded so much more pleasant: little more than a mild inconvenience for Alex while things were sorted out.

"My understanding is that the immigration judge ordered this step. You should ask him why."

"Would you care to guess?"

Another thoughtful pause. "All right. The escape rate from federal facilities is demonstrably lower than county facilities. Our Russian friends tell us that Konevitch has hundreds of millions stashed away. Sad to say, he could probably buy his way out of almost any county jail in the country. And if he disappears again, he won't make the same mistake of living out in the open next time. I expect he would flee the country, change his name, maybe get a face-job, and find haven in a more criminal-friendly country, say Brazil, or a Pacific island. He's got plenty of money to spread around and buy favors and protection. It might be impossible to find and bring him to justice."

"Should he remain in prison? As a former federal judge, you're certainly qualified to answer."

Judge Willis's head snapped up and jerked hard to his left. The question was rude and an impertinent breach of protocol. True, this was Caldwell's first performance in a federal court. But he should still know better. And Tromble definitely knew better. If he answered, either way, it was an unforgivable violation of legal courtesy. This was, after all, what Willis was here to decide. Judges, even former ones, do not prejudge or inhibit or attempt to preempt other judges. Certainly never in public. And above all, not in their own courtrooms.

Tromble pretended he didn't see Willis or understand the slight, though he betrayed himself with a slight smile. "It would be an unimaginable blunder to let him out before his immigration status is decided. Only a fool would even consider it."

Willis's eyes shifted from Tromble to MP Jones. He exerted every pound of silent pressure he could muster to encourage the attorney to rise from that chair and unleash a loud, heated objection. Come on, boy, for godsakes, let him have it. The question and answer begged for an objection. Willis *needed* that objection. He so badly wanted a chance to slap down Tromble right here, in the presence of the entire court, that he nearly screamed objection himself.

Jones just sat, wide-eyed, listening attentively with a flat expression. At least for a change he wasn't idiotically scrawling doodles on that stupid legal pad. But not a word. Not so much as a raised eyebrow or parted lips.

"Your witness," Caldwell said, and nearly strutted back to his table.

Judge Willis continued to stare at MP. In a clenched tone that managed to convey both disapproval and regret, he commented, "I imagine Mr. Jones, in the interest of saving our time, has no desire to cross-examine."

Very slowly, MP pushed himself out of his seat. "Maybe a few questions, Your Honor."

"Well"—for a moment the judge was almost too stunned to reply—"proceed then."

MP didn't budge from his table. He glanced down at Alex, who seemed to shrug as if to say: Okay, why not?

"Mr. Tromble," he began, openly ignoring the official title, "your presence today suggests this is a very important case to you."

"More important than some, less than others," Tromble said, grinning and choosing a nice middle ground.

"As FBI director, at how many other trials have you appeared as a witness?"

Tromble wasted a moment rubbing a forefinger across his lower lip, as though this question required considerable thought. "I guess none."

"You guess?"

"All right, none."

"How'd this case come to your attention?"

"I don't exactly recall."

"You don't? Being the director of the FBI and all, I thought you were a smart guy. You recall nothing?"

"It might surprise you, but the FBI handles tons of cases a year. Nobody expects me to remember every detail."

"Do you recall any conversations with any Russian government officials about Alex Konevitch?"

He scratched his head. "Not exactly."

"Inexactly would be fine."

"I don't recall any."

"Then may we assume you did have such conversations, but just can't recall them?"

"No, you may not."

"Again, Mr. Tromble, did you or did you not discuss the Konevitch issue with the Russian government? Yes or no."

"No. If I did, it was only a passing reference."

MP lifted up a piece of paper from the desk and pretended to read from it. Then, in an annoying tone suggesting he knew everything, he asked, "That Russian colonel and head prosecutor, how'd they get over here?"

It was an old lawyer trick meant to rattle the witness. Tromble, an observant judge in his day, had seen it a thousand times. He handled it coolly, leaning back into his seat and replying, "The Russians have a compelling interest in this case. They were sent to help us prepare his extradition."

"Extradition? Do we have such a treaty with the Russians?"

"No. I . . . I misspoke."

"You mean you spoke your mind."

Caldwell showed none of MP's inclination against objections. "Objection," he yelled, launching from his chair.

"Sustained."

MP turned back to the witness stand and shook his head. "All right, Mr. Tromble, describe your role in deciding which prisons Mr. Konevitch would be incarcerated in."

"That was decided by the attorney general."

"You had no input? None?"

"Believe it or not, I stay fairly busy running the FBI. Federal prisons aren't my bailiwick."

With a condescending roll of his eyes, MP said, "Oops. That was another of those troublesome yes-or-no questions, Mr. Tromble."

"All right, no." Strictly speaking, the truth, although he looked uncomfortable.

MP bounced back to the issue of Colonel Volevodz and the team of Russian prosecutors. "Who paid for their trip? Who handled their expenses?"

"How would I know?"

"That was going to be my next question," MP answered skeptically.

Tromble lived by the motto "better to give than receive," and the derisive tone from this pip-squeak immigration lawyer was starting to grate on him. He gripped the sides of his chair and snapped at MP, "Was that a question?"

"If it makes you uncomfortable, we'll come back to it later."

MP went on for another two hours, bouncing quickly from subject to subject, tossing in as many insinuations as he could get away with. Occasionally he returned to an old topic, forcing Tromble to plow and replow old ground. Same questions, repeated with minor variations, and saturated with a rising tone of disbelief.

Caldwell objected as often as he dared, most often simple harassment objections intended to disrupt the flow, but eventually the judge warned him to cool it.

After two hours, Tromble was tired of sitting in the same hard wooden chair. He was tired of this disrespectful lawyer, tired of this Russian crook fighting an overdue trip back to Russia, and tired of the rude questions. He was tired of the judge, tired of the entire routine. He regretted he had subjected himself to this. He squirmed in his chair but couldn't seem to find a comfortable position.

MP suddenly left his position behind the defense table and moved to a place about two feet from Tromble. He paused very briefly, then leaned in. "Mr. Tromble, I'm a forgetful type. Did I hear you take an oath to tell the truth on this stand?" MP paused for effect. "The whole truth, absent equivocations, quibbles, or bald deceptions."

That was it. Tromble shifted his bulk forward and nearly spit in Jones's face. "Don't you dare lecture me on integrity, you two-bit mouthpiece. I'm a respected public servant. I will not be addressed this way by you. If you have another question you will call me Judge or Mr. Director. Those are my titles."

MP smiled. "You may go, Mr. Tromble."

Tromble leaned back into the chair. He planted his feet and didn't budge, not about to let this third-rate legal loser boss him around.

After a moment, Judge Willis leaned over and said very loudly and very firmly, "Mr. Tromble, if you're not out of my witness chair in three seconds, I'll cite you for contempt."

Lunch was a welcome reprieve. Alex and Elena were led into a small conference room and allowed to share a quiet meal in privacy. Outside, two deputies manned the door. Ham sandwiches, a fat deli pickle, chips, and ice-cold sodas, all bought and delivered by the court, were waiting in paper bags on the long conference table.

MP and his PKR pals lunched in a separate conference room three doors down. After fourteen months apart, Alex and Elena deserved a little time together, they figured. Left unsaid was that it might be the last time, and they should be allowed this last chance to be alone.

Besides, MP had a few testy legal issues about rules of evidence he wanted to bang out with the guns from the big firm. He had picked up a few lazy habits in immigration court that could get the book thrown at him in a federal venue. The afternoon would be the decisive battle—it would be very touch and go—and the boys from PKR wanted to iron out any kinks.

Caldwell, they knew, was eating with a *Post* reporter in a fancy restaurant a few blocks over, conducting a premature tutorial about his brilliant and inevitable victory. A PI employed by PKR followed him every time he left the court, and via cell phone kept his bosses apprised. Easy work, since the INS prosecutor, shipped in from out west and acclimated to the relative geniality of immigration courts, was too naïve to understand how things were played in the big leagues. At that moment, the nosy PI was seated one table over, enjoying a cheeseburger and Coke; Caldwell was a loud braggart and PKR's gumshoe was whispering into a cell phone and relaying every word of importance to a junior PKR associate in the hallway, who raced in and informed his bosses inside the conference room. PKR played for keeps.

Caldwell was oblivious to what was coming. He should be in a tense, sweaty huddle with the best and brightest at Justice, preparing for the assault Alex had gone to over a year's worth of difficult trouble to prepare. While Caldwell munched away on a cucumber salad, sipped a large diet Pepsi, and prattled on about his courtroom mastery, a surprise attack was being prepared.

A last-ditch effort was the only way to describe it, a desperate throw of the dice they would never contemplate against a more seasoned and tested brawler. It was a wild-haired idea of the sort that could come only from a legal novice—Alex himself.

After five days of painful consideration, the pros from PKR warned that it should be attempted only as a last resort.

Its only chance was to catch the government flat-footed.

The moment the conference room door closed behind them, Alex and Elena kissed and hugged. Then Elena stepped back and said, "Mikhail called this morning. The news from Moscow is good."

"Describe good."

"Golitsin and Nicky Kozyrev were shot dead last night."

"How?" No smile, no satisfied grin—just "How?"

"Mikhail did everything you asked. He talked Yuri Khodorin into putting up five million for Nicky's death. An easy sell. You said it would be, and it was. Yuri was fed up with his people being butchered, and tired of Nicky Kozyrev trying to destroy his business."

"Who killed him?"

"He killed himself, Alex."

"How poetic. And Golitsin?"

"This is just a guess on Mikhail's part, okay?"

Alex nodded.

"Nicky learned about the bounty on his head. I mean, he was meant to learn about it, wasn't he? He apparently assumed Golitsin was behind it."

"No trust among thieves. Let me guess, Kozyrev repaid the favor?"

She nodded.

After a moment, Alex asked, "And Tatyana Lukin? What about her?"

"Fired and arrested. The tapes and photos Mikhail gave her former boyfriend worked like magic. He also sacked the attorney general."

Alex finally allowed himself a smile. He had caused two deaths and destroyed two lives. Of course, they had tried to kill him, numerous times, and made his life as miserable as they could. The smile was distant and cold, though—the grim smile of a very different man from a few years before. "So that's it," Alex said. "No more enemies in Moscow."

"We're safe from them forever, Alex. We only have to worry about here."

Alex stared down at his flip-flops a moment. He asked Elena, "How much time do we have left?"

She checked her watch. "Forty-five minutes, more or less."

He walked to the table and picked up a chair. He carried it to the door and jammed it quietly but firmly in place underneath the large brass knob.

He turned around and looked at Elena. "Are you hungry?"

"Not in the least. You?"

The food was shoved out of the way. Elena's pantsuit flew off in two seconds; the prison suit took even less time. They landed on the tabletop and put their heart and soul into using forty minutes to make up for fourteen months apart.

Left unsaid, but certainly understood by both of them, was that this might be their last time.

MP called his first witness.

The rear door of the courtroom opened and Kim Parrish walked quickly down the aisle. Caldwell's head spun around so fast he nearly snapped his neck. He traded a look with Tromble, now seated directly to his rear.

Neither man was the least bit happy to see her.

She was duly identified and sworn in, then sat perfectly still in the witness chair while MP warmed up.

"You're an attorney?"

"Yes."

"And you worked at the INS legal office?"

"Same place you used to work. The district office that includes the District of Columbia."

"And you once handled the case of Alex and Elena Konevitch?"

"At one time I was the lead attorney for their persecution—I mean, prosecution," Kim replied, deliberately mixing up her nouns. She looked at Alex. He smiled and offered a thankful nod.

"But no longer?"

"No."

"Why not? Isn't it unusual to be removed from a case you initiated and took to immigration court?"

"Nearly unheard of. I asked to be reassigned from the case."

MP raised an eyebrow. "You asked? From such a big, important case? Why? I imagine any INS lawyer would die for a case like this. All this attention, all those hungry reporters out on the steps. Mr. Caldwell, over there, is so giddy he can barely contain himself."

"Objection," Caldwell howled, scowling at MP.

"Sustained."

MP ignored Caldwell and acted like the objection was meaningless. "Why did you ask to be removed, Miss Parrish?"

"Because . . . because, over time, I became convinced Mr. Konevitch was being—"

"Objection!" Caldwell yelled again, nearly bouncing up and down in his chair.

"Grounds?"

"Miss Parrish is in violation of attorney-client privilege."

"Sidebar," the judge snapped. The huddle formed beside the bench.

MP brought Matt. Because he didn't want to be outnumbered, Caldwell brought Bill, one of the useless Justice boys who did his best to appear fierce and disguise his general sentiment, which was thoroughly confused. He had no idea who this lady was, what was at issue, and even less idea of his role in this case.

The judge examined the four faces, then whispered to Caldwell, "Make your argument."

"Her knowledge of this case was gained through her employment by her client, the state."

"Mr. Jones?"

"Her employment was terminated. She's free to testify as she likes."

"She remains bound by her oath as an attorney," Caldwell insisted.

"You should have thought about that before you people sacked her," MP shot back.

"I'm inclined to agree with Mr. Caldwell," the judge intervened, strongly wanting to do the opposite, but he couldn't will the law against Caldwell's side.

"I'll restrict my questions," MP said, trying to mask his disappointment. Matt nodded at him. Good move.

"She should be dismissed," Caldwell complained.

"She's a private citizen now. She can testify," His Honor said. "But within limits. Be careful, Mr. Jones."

"I'll be watching," Caldwell sneered at MP.

"Watch hard," MP sneered back. "I enjoy an attentive audience."

They returned to their respective seats. MP spent a moment rearranging his thoughts, then asked, "Miss Parrish, do you recall a team of Russians sent over to help with this case?"

"I do, yes. Five of them in all. An investigator and four prosecutors."

"And do you recall who paid for this?"

"The FBI."

"All of it?"

"Yes, their full expenses. They've been here about a year."

"Where are they staying? Such a long way from home, what are they doing? Don't they get bored?"

Kim's eyes narrowed. She sent her answer like a rocket straight at Tromble. "At the Madison Hotel. Four of them, in separate thousand-dollar-a-night suites. For almost a year now, and they've racked up incredible bills. They eat at our most expensive restaurants, fly away first-class to Vegas every weekend, whoring, gambling, and drinking unimaginable amounts of liquor. Every bit of it is billed to the FBI."

"A rough estimate. How much would you guess the FBI has wasted on these crooked clowns?"

"Objection, Your Honor."

"Sustained. Watch your language, Mr. Jones. How much, Miss Parrish?"

"Millions. Many millions of taxpayer money. As I said, they've been here a year, living like spoiled kings."

MP returned to his seat.

Frankly there was no reason on earth for Caldwell to cross-examine Kim Parrish. His earlier, well-timed objection had slipped a noose around MP and put her in a box. No real damage had been done. Who cared about the Russians? Let them impregnate half the showgirls in Vegas. Bet the whole national treasury and lose it in a bad roll of the dice. Big deal. It had nothing to do with whether Konevitch should remain in prison.

But he was angered that Kim Parrish chose to turn on her own department. It was betrayal and he damn well knew how to make her pay for it. Time for a little discreditation.

He stood and asked, "How did you become a defense witness?"

"I don't understand the question."

"It's very simple. Did Mr. Jones contact you, or vice versa?"

"I contacted him. After I was—"

Before she could finish that thought, Caldwell cut her off. "Are you still employed at the INS, Miss Parrish?"

"No, I quit."

"You mean you were fired. You went to Mr. Jones because you were angry and wanted revenge."

"I mean I quit. Then Mr. Tromble fired me."

"No, you were fired by the director of the INS."

"I don't recall you being in the room. I was fired by Mr. Tromble because he refused to allow me to resign from what I considered a shoddy case."

Caldwell immediately turned red. He looked at the judge. "Strike that response from the record."

"You asked the question," the judge replied, "and you challenged her to elaborate. I'll allow it."

A stupid mistake. But so what? The damage was minimal. An ambiguous little defeat in the midst of a big, clear-cut victory. At least his well-timed objection had smothered her from exposing the really damaging stuff.

Kim was dismissed and MP called his next witness. Parrish walked back up the aisle and was passed by a poorly dressed, diminutive man slowly shambling in the opposite direction.

Petri Arbatov was sworn and seated.

MP spent a moment walking him through his background—for the edification of the judge and audience, he dwelled on it at some length. KGB for twenty years before his sudden defection.

A law degree from Moscow University, but no mention of the law degree from Catholic University.

MP didn't ask, and Petri didn't offer.

The crowd in the court hung on every word. With few exceptions, none had ever seen a real live KGB agent, up close and personal. Petri was their first peek at a living, breathing KGB agent—and he looked so small, so crushed, so sad. Who could believe this was the fierce demon portrayed in all those Cold War cinema thrillers and spy novels? Why hadn't we won the Cold War thirty years earlier? Having spent no time in courtrooms, Petri looked nervous and his opening responses were halting.

Next, a few warm-up questions to put the witness at greater ease. How Petri came in contact with this case, his interview with Kim Parrish, and so forth.

MP said, "So you were hired to translate the documents given to the INS, via the FBI?"

"It is how I make my living these days. I translate for American firms doing business in Russia."

"Are you still a practicing attorney?"

"No. I quit the profession sixteen years ago."

"Why?"

"The work I did for the KGB, I suppose. It left a certain taste."

"What kind of work would that be?"

Petri looked around the court for a moment and let the suspense build. "My job, Mr. Jones, was to frame people," he answered slowly, drawing out the words.

Petri spoke quietly, and the reporters bent forward as they spent a few minutes delving into that legal specialty. Fascinating stuff. People were on the edge of their seats, and never budged. How to frame a perfectly innocent man, ten easy steps to a surefire trip to a gulag, or worse.

Then, from MP, "And what did you conclude after you reviewed the material about Konevitch from Russia?"

"Objection," Caldwell barked.

"Grounds?" Willis asked, leaning his chin on his fist.

"Uh . . . attorney-client privilege again."

His Honor peeked down at Petri. "Remind me, please. Are you still a practicing attorney, sir?"

"Not for many, many years. These days I'm a simple translator."

MP confidently asked, "Did you sign a contract that precluded you from sharing what you learned?"

"No. I merely stated my price and Miss Parrish hired me."

The judge said, "Then overruled. Please answer the first question."

Petri looked at Alex seated at the table. "After looking at everything, I concluded that Mr. Konevitch was being framed."

"Why?"

"There is a certain stench to such things, Mr. Jones."

"An odor? An actual smell? Explain that."

Petri directed a finger at Colonel Volevodz seated at the rear, now in his capacity as an official observer. "Take that man, Mr. Jones. He might tell you he works at the Ministry of Security, but he was definitely career KGB before this. He might claim he's merely enforcing the law, but his hands are covered with blood. It's a stink no shower will erase."

Every neck in the court craned to examine Volevodz. A more charming man might have smiled or chuckled disarmingly—at a minimum shaken his head in pretended disbelief. Volevodz tried to bore holes through Petri with his skinny, mean little eyes.

Oh yeah, no doubt about it. There's the guy from the Hollywood thrillers—KGB down to his undershorts.

"But the documents?" MP asked. "Did they actually smell?"

"Well, you see, the key is to produce a perfect case. These four prosecutors your FBI is caring for, they are experts at this. That's exactly what they did."

MP led him through this for a while, the craftsmanship of how to string a noose with lies, forgeries, and planted evidence. Then he shifted on a dime and asked, "Incidentally, were you present when Miss Parrish was fired?"

"I was there, yes. Seated right beside her. But she wasn't fired."

"The prosecutor claimed she was."

"He's wrong, or he's lying. She quit."

"Why did she quit?"

"She reported to her boss that this case was phony. Cooked up. A sham."

MP paused to allow this to sink in, then asked, "What happened?"

"She is an honorable person, Mr. Jones. She did something I never had the courage to do."

"Which was what, Mr. Arbatov?"

"She tried to get the case dropped."

MP affected a look of huge surprise. "The attorney in charge wanted it dropped?"

"Yes."

"Well . . . why wasn't it dropped?"

"She was brought into a room with that man"—he pointed out Tromble, who was trying desperately to ignore him—"and her INS bosses. She begged them to drop the case. They refused quite rudely. She then asked to be reassigned, as is the prerogative, indeed, the responsibility of any attorney who believes a case is improper. They yelled at her. She resigned, then that man"— another damning finger aimed at Tromble—"screamed at her that she was fired."

MP thanked him and walked away. Petri sat quietly and looked at Alex. Alex looked back, nodding his head, a silent acknowledgment to an old countryman who had refound his conscience.

When offered the chance to cross-examine, Caldwell passed. He knew next to nothing about Petri Arbatov. What he did know was that the man was a legal minefield, and further questioning would only reinforce the damage.

Besides, the damage wasn't really that bad. Tromble looked like a mean horse's ass; like that was news to anybody. And maybe he lied a little on the stand. But that was Tromble's problem, not Caldwell's.

Frankly, the more he thought about it, Caldwell was quite pleased. There was room for only one ego on this side of the case—one shining exemplar of truth and justice—and this skinny, tired little Russian just blew Tromble right out of the saddle.

When time came for the summary, Caldwell would strongly note how the Russian "expert" had offered an opinion—not a fact, but a baseless opinion pulled out of thin air after concluding the case was, in his own words, too perfect. And he was heavily outnumbered. The word of a self-confessed framer of innocent men against that of the entire Russian government; a reformed, democratic government, he would stipulate quite loudly, not the corrupt old dictatorship this Petri Arbatov had sent people to the gallows for.

The little Russian was released and he nearly bounced out of his chair. He and Volevodz exchanged hateful looks as Petri passed up the aisle. MP announced that he had no more witnesses.

MP remained standing, though. He looked at the judge and asked, "Could we have a moment, Your Honor?"

"Take all the time you need," Willis replied, strongly intimating that time was not on his side.

Alex stood, too, then Matt, and for a moment they gathered in a tight triangle and conferred in tense whispers.

"What do you think?" Alex asked MP.

"We're in trouble. Big trouble," MP told him bluntly. "Kim was our star witness. But Caldwell blocked us from unloading her most damaging testimony."

"You don't think Petri repaired that?" Alex asked, searching their faces.

Matt, the pro with years of big-time criminal experience answered for both lawyers. "Caldwell will cream him in his closing. I certainly would. The opinion of a man who admitted framing people against the word of an entire government. The issue is credence, Alex."

MP nodded at this candid observation. "That's exactly what he'll do. If I try to counter it in my closing, it'll only sound defensive."

"Then let's go with it," Alex stated very firmly.

MP and Matt exchanged looks. Both had badly hoped to avoid

Alex's proposal. Legally speaking, it was fraught with difficulties. After a moment, Matt mentioned to MP, "He hides it well, but I think the judge is sympathetic."

MP nodded. Not enthusiastically, but nonetheless it was a nod.

Alex said to both of them, "It's all or nothing. Bluff, and do your best."

"I hope you're the lucky type," Matt replied, clearly believing this was crazy.

"He wouldn't be here if he was lucky," MP replied dryly.

Alex and Matt fell into their seats. MP remained standing. Finally, he announced somewhat hesitantly, "I'd like to submit a little evidence."

Matt handed him a tape player, a compact Bose system with small but thunderously powerful speakers. Alex arranged the system on his table, carefully directing the speakers toward the prosecutor's table, while the bailiff strung an extension cord and plugged it in. Next Matt handed Alex a tray loaded with about twenty cassettes. Alex noodled through the tapes and finally settled on one that he carefully withdrew. MP took it and inserted it neatly into the recorder. Alex's finger hovered over the start button as MP said, "This is a phone call to Miss Tatyana Lukin, special assistant to the Kremlin chief of staff. She's a lawyer who also serves as legal advisor to Boris Yeltsin." Alex stabbed play.

First, the sound of a ringing telephone.

"What? Who is this?" A woman's voice in Russian, and the annoyed tone came across loud and clear.

"Please hold for the director of the Federal Bureau of Investigation." A female voice, bored, in English.

"Hello, Tatyana. Heard the news about your boy Konevitch? Made a big splash in the news on this side of the water."

"How did you get my home number?"

"When I couldn't get you at the office, my boys in the embassy tracked it down."

"All right. Yes, I see that you've got him in jail. Why haven't you just shipped him here?"

"It's complicated. Not as easy as I thought. Listen, I need a big favor."

"John, you promised me Konevitch."

"Well, just listen. Some of these judges here are pigheaded. I need you to cook up a case for me."

"Why?"

"Because I can't just throw his ass on a plane. Look, Tatyana, I really don't care about the details. Understand? Come on, your guys are supposed to be real good at this sort of thing."

"What sort of thing is that, John?"

A long silence. "Look, give me whatever you like, just be damned sure it sounds convincing."

"Is this absolutely necessary?"

"Probably not. He goes back to court in a week. No way in hell he won't be deported. But the judge might act crazily. Call it a precaution, insurance."

Caldwell finally came to his senses and, doing something he should've done a minute before, yelled, "Objection, objection."

Alex reached over and cranked the volume up full blast until it drowned out Caldwell's voice. The voices on the tape howled out of the speakers and filled the courtroom.

"You can keep him in jail, can't you? A lot of powerful people here are opposed to letting you keep the FBI outpost in your embassy. I'm doing my best, but, John, it's a real uphill battle. Such a clear lack of mutual cooperation won't go over well."

An unintelligible mumble from Tromble before she cut him off. "President Yeltsin asked me about this case just yesterday. He keeps asking if he needs to discuss it with your president."

"Hey, we'll find a way. I don't care if I have to bribe the judge or kill his wife. I'll find a way."

Caldwell was now on his feet, screaming "Objection!" at the top of his voice.

Alex pushed stop. The tape finally went quiet, though it seemed to echo for a long moment. He glanced around and studied the faces in the court.

Tromble was melting into this chair. Every eye in the court was on him.

Directly to his front, Caldwell spent a long moment in terrified confusion. Eventually he repeated, an octave higher but more quietly this time, "Objection, Your Honor."

"Sidebar," the judge replied and scrambled off his bench. Again Matt accompanied MP, and this time he added Alex to his entourage. Again one of the Justice boys accompanied Caldwell, who arrived red-faced and furious.

"Lawyer's meeting," Caldwell snapped, directing a finger at Alex. "He has no business here."

"His presence is necessary to establish the provenance of the tapes," MP answered very nicely. "This is a hearing, not a trial. What do you say, Your Honor?"

"That might be a good idea," Willis answered, still a little shocked by what he had heard.

"That's clearly an illegal, inadmissible tape," Caldwell snapped, at the judge, at MP, at anybody in earshot.

"To the contrary," MP argued in a voice dripping with phony confidence, "it's legal and quite admissible."

"Was it taped with the consent of the conversants?" Caldwell demanded.

"That's American law," MP replied with a smug smile, trying to bluff his way through.

Alex quickly interjected. "This tape was made in Russia. Russians are allowed to tape and wiretap to their heart's content. No law bans it. In fact, it's our national pastime."

Caldwell had no idea whether that was true or not. "Your Honor, please," he pleaded, "it's blatantly inadmissible. Obviously the product of a wiretap."

His Honor looked at MP. "Well?"

"Yesterday, the prosecution introduced into evidence a wiretap provided by the Russian chief prosecutor. It concerned the supposed activities of Orangutan Media. I didn't challenge him on whether the tape was the product of a legal warrant, and am now dismayed that he's even making this argument. He established the precedent. I should be accorded equal latitude."

"Do you have more tapes, Mr. Konevitch?"

"About twenty here. Another fifty or so in a safe-deposit box."

"Are you requesting to play all of them?"

"Not at all," Alex replied. "My wife and I picked out the most damning ones."

"These are all conversations between Tromble and this lady?"

"No, just one more of those," MP insisted, borrowing a bit of Alex's confidence. "I'd love to play it. It's the one where Tromble brags to this lady about all the terrible prisons he's sending Alex to. He promises her that he will keep my client suffering until he snaps, until he begs to be returned to Russia."

"And what material's on the rest of the tapes?"

"Tatyana Lukin had two . . . well, I guess you'd call them business partners."

"Go on."

"Nicky Kozyrev, a notorious syndicate chief. This is a guy with Interpol and Russian police records long enough to stock a library. And General Sergei Golitsin, a former KGB deputy director hired by Alex as his corporate chief of security."

"These are phone conversations?"

"Some," Alex replied. "Most were captured as the three of them sat in back of a fancy limousine."

"And their role in this affair?"

It was time for the lawyers to take over, and MP answered, "Glad you asked. They stole Alex's money and his companies. Then they framed him. Then they orchestrated his persecution here."

"And these tapes prove those accusations?"

"I'll leave that for you to decide."

"And how did you come by these tapes?"

"My client."

"And how did you acquire them?" he asked, peering now at Alex.

"I hired a private detective. He did the taping and sent them to me."

After a moment of quiet consideration, the judge suggested, "Let me tell you what worries me, Mr. Jones. For all I know, your client had those tapes produced by actors."

It was Matt Rivers's turn at bat and he opened with a mighty swing. "My firm had the tapes analyzed over the weekend by a reputable laboratory. A clip of Tromble doing a TV interview was compared against the tape you just heard. Perfect match. Identical voice print. That analysis is included in our submission."

"I see."

"Also, they compared Miss Lukin's voice from the tape you just heard against the remaining tapes. It's her speaking to Tromble, and it's her speaking with her co-conspirators."

"And these tapes are in Russian?"

Matt's turn again. "We hired three actors to role-play in English. We're submitting the originals as well. You can check the accuracy of the translations if you wish. No expense was spared. They're quite good."

Matt couldn't wait for the judge to plow through them. The actors were professionals, used by New York publishers to make audiobooks. Over a very busy weekend, they rehearsed together for hours. Not only did they reproduce the conversations with passion, conviction, and fluidity, but they captured the small but important details that add a certain verisimilitude. The sounds of Nicky's furious snorts. The menace in Golitsin's voice. The woman who did Tatyana was nothing short of spectacular, a purr so spot-on you could almost picture her seductiveness.

Caldwell looked like a whipped dog. It was obvious which way the judge was leaning. His case was falling apart before his eyes. He could do nothing to prevent it. The sad truth was, he was dying to hear the tapes himself.

The judge said, "I want to hear them in my chambers before I decide. I expect both of you want to be present," he said, looking at the lawyers, then at Alex. "Not you. This is a matter for lawyers to hash out."

Three minutes later, court was adjourned until further notice. The solemn-faced judge issued one last ominous instruction:

Tromble would be present when the court reconvened. It was an unchristian sentiment, and he felt mildly guilty about it, but Tromble had done him no favors, and he fully intended to repay it.

The judge and lawyers disappeared to his chambers. The reporters straggled out to join their colleagues on the front steps where they would share the incredible events of the morning and file as much as they could before court reconvened. Within minutes, the legal talking heads were back in the studios, on the air, sharing updates, squawking away, and shoving opinions and predictions at whoever cared to listen. The opinions were divided and, hotly debated.

Half thought the judge might make a rare exception since this was, after all, only a habeas corpus hearing, where the benefit of the doubt normally leaned toward the accused. The other half claimed the defense didn't have a prayer.

Court reconvened four hours later. The reporters were notified and they bickered and fought with one another for choice seats, or even standing room at the crowded rear of the room. Would the judge allow that first tape? If so, what was on the others? And the big question of the day was, how screwed was John Tromble, director of the FBI? The sense of curiosity was running at fever pitch. The studios were screaming for updates the moment a decision was rendered.

With grim faces, the lawyers marched out and fell into their chairs. Alex was led back to the defense table after four long hours of cooling his heels in a holding cell. He had, however, showered, shaved, trimmed his own hair, and changed into a respectable suit and tie. The time had come, he decided, to present a before-and-after shot for the viewers.

And the contrast between the downtrodden criminal and this towering, clean-cut, handsome man at the table was indeed striking. You saw what they did to me, his old self screamed—now look at what I was before the power of the state fell on my head.

The side door opened. Willis hefted his robes and walked up to his bench. He appeared sad, furious, shaken, and slightly nervous.

Court was brought to order and things settled down quickly.

Willis stared at the ceiling for a long moment, his usual habit before rendering his decisions. A powerfully affecting moment—the former priest searching for guidance and wisdom from on high. Tromble, by contrast, looked perfectly miserable, squirming in his seat, unable to get comfortable.

The eyes came down. "After listening to all the tapes and giving the issue due consideration, I've decided to accept the tapes into evidence."

Alex leaned far back into his chair. Elena actually released a squeal of joy.

But as the court had heard only one tape, the significance of this decision was mysterious. The reporters remained mute.

He looked at Alex. "Sir, will you please stand?"

MP squeezed Alex's arm. The "sir" seemed to be a good sign. He stood.

"Let me begin by expressing my deepest apologies." Willis adjusted his robes and paused briefly. "Let me add a strong personal recommendation. I expect you and your attorney to file a civil suit against the FBI and Department of Justice. You have been wronged, sir. No amount of money will make up for it but it won't hurt, either."

Tromble was seated in his chair, struggling to square the competing demands of appearing confident and powerful while trying also to be completely invisible.

The judge then began addressing the court, speaking quite loudly, and ever so clearly, so that even the farthest reporter in the back wouldn't miss a word or legal nuance. He began with a long summary of everything on the tapes. He had notes, though he referred to them only rarely, primarily when a precise quote was preferred over a generalized summary. There had been a conspiracy of staggering proportions in Moscow; Konevitch was its first victim. His fortune was stolen, his companies taken away, only after he was brutally tortured. The conspiracy reached into the highest offices in the Kremlin; "we have these problems ourselves sometimes," the judge explained, "Teapot Dome, Watergate, Iran-Contra, and so on.

This case represents another of those watershed historical embarrassments."

He shared the names of the conspirators, struggling with the Russian names, and outlined their scheme. Next he spent a few moments dwelling on how exactly American law enforcement got duped into being a tool for the conspirators. A good duping requires a gullible dupe, he pointed out; the director of the FBI was that man. A quick description of the quid pro quo: they get Alex, whatever the costs; Tromble gets to sprinkle a few more agents in Moscow. A brief summary of how Tromble violated countless laws and procedures to persecute Alex and Elena Konevitch. There were too many breaches for the judge to count, but a full accounting would be prepared later by competent figures with enough time to wade through all the tapes and other evidence.

In effect, the INS, the FBI, and the Justice Department—the very people represented by the attorneys at the prosecution table—were suddenly branch offices of a cabal of evil people in a foreign land. MP had offered the judge a few pointers back in the chambers, and he threw out some of the more egregious ones: the constant shuffling through increasingly miserable prisons to turn up the heat; punishments inflicted by various wardens under orders from Washington; wiretaps in their apartment; illegal searches; the senseless destruction of their home and property; their money seized by the federal government and their business enterprise shut down and bankrupted.

For ten minutes, not a soul looked bored or even mildly inattentive. Twice the director of the FBI tried to walk out—both times he made a meek retreat back to his position after a stern and angry judge issued a strong warning.

Jason Caldwell sulked in his chair and listened to the bright, shining future he had envisioned collapse in ruins. He could see the evening news that night; him holding forth on the courthouse steps, the picture of brimming confidence promising a quick, punishing victory; then flash to a bunch of mealymouthed legal monkeys dissecting his overwhelming destruction in court. He knew it was going to be horrible—absolutely horrible.

He was right; it was.

Judge Willis ended with another long apology to Alex, then ordered his immediate release from custody.

He grabbed his robes and left.

Tromble dug his heels in and rushed for the door, shoving aside reporters who were bombarding him with questions. He turned to a deputy in the hallway. "Is there a back entrance to this place?"

The deputy smiled. "Sure is."

"Where?"

"Find it yourself, you prick."

The kisses, hugs, and relieved expressions of appreciation at the defense table—along with a round robin of the usual victorious congratulations among Alex, Elena, MP, Matt, and Marvin—lasted five minutes. Marvin eventually lifted a stately arm and quieted them down. The old pro got a strong grip on Alex's arm and solemnly pledged he would personally file and oversee the suits against the FBI, Justice, and INS.

One big suit, a monstrous case for compensatory damages, he promised with a gleam in his eyes.

"What are our chances, and when's the payoff?" asked Alex, ever the businessman.

Marvin smiled and rubbed his hands. "It's not a question of chances or when," he replied. "How much is the only question." He would demand and fight with conviction for ten million; after enough blood was shed, he would give them a break and settle at five million.

"Still pro bono?" Alex asked.

Marvin flashed a ruthless grin. "Not a chance."

Elena said to Marvin, quite firmly, "But you will forget your usual third. You'll take twenty percent or I swear I'll hire another firm tonight."

One look at her and Marvin had absolutely no doubt she meant every word. "Deal."

A mob of reporters descended and was driven off only after MP solemnly vowed he would stand on the courtroom steps all night. They could ask questions to their heart's content and he would bloviate until the moon came out. Before the night was over, he would be booked on five talk shows, and take calls from six book agents and five movie studio chiefs.

Marvin called the lawyers together into a tight huddle. They spent a brief moment trading ideas back and forth, planning what would be a very busy morning of filings.

When they turned around, Alex and Elena were gone.

34

The snow was three feet deep and dry, and though it was only fall, the snow machines were roaring full-blast and tourists in Aspen were at high tide. Neither Alex nor Elena had ever been near skis, much less on them. Both were good athletes, though. After three weeks of mastering the art, they were roaring recklessly down the black slopes like they owned the place.

Elena had argued vigorously for someplace warm. Her preferred option had been a small, pleasant, neglected Caribbean island where the natives were friendly and had no idea who they were, and wouldn't care a whit if they did.

Her preferred option two was one of those private, gated resorts in Florida. A nice one with a thick forest of palm trees, a thousand holes of golf, a well-stocked bar, and a beach where they could drink themselves silly on rum and piña coladas and roast themselves into shriveled prunes.

Alex had experienced enough heat and wouldn't hear of it. A federal prison in Georgia, followed by another in the heart of Chicago, and finally, the worst oven of all, a scorching summer in Yuma.

His Russian roots screamed for someplace where icicles hung off your nose. Exploiting her desire for privacy, he had briefly argued for an Arctic expedition, but Elena did not warm to that idea. The argument shifted slowly southward, working its way through Alaska, then, one by one, through the provinces of Canada, and refused to budge another degree once it hit Colorado.

At the end of the second week, MP called. Elena answered. Alex picked up the other line.

"Have you heard the big news?" MP asked them.

Elena happily informed him, "The only newspaper we've touched all week was the one we used to get a fire started."

"The attorney general quit this morning. Apparently the cows in Montana are calling her back."

"And Tromble?" Alex asked.

"Boy, you are out of touch. Fired, five days ago. He fled to Puerto Rico and is taking no calls."

"And how are you doing, MP?" Elena asked.

"Great. I have an offer right here from PKR. They're offering a partnership. They don't currently handle immigration law, and they'd like me to set up a new division."

"Will you take it?"

"I don't think so. Terry and I talked it over. It's almost ridiculously generous, but I doubt I'll fit in."

"You won't miss the money?" Alex, the practical one, asked.

"I think I'll be fine. With all the hooplah about you, I've kicked my fee up to three hundred an hour. Nobody's said no yet."

They promised they'd all get together for dinner after Alex and Elena got tired of Aspen, or ran out of money. Truthfully, neither of them was the least bit tired of it. It was such a playground, and the restaurants and bars were great and plentiful.

Bitchy had popped in for a visit two days before. He flew in from Chicago, where he had just closed on a North Shore home. The appellate court that reviewed his case had recently been joined by two new justices: a pair of rabid Giants fans who sincerely enjoyed the misery of their die-hard Jets brethren on the court. Neither was the least bit appalled by Beatty's assault. Besides, his letter to the court sounded so gracious and repentant the judges were all deeply affected. And, after all, it was Bitchy's first offense.

He showed up in a yellow taxi that brought him from Denver International, lumbering out in a three-piece, tailored Brooks Brothers suit, looking like a Wall Street banker—or more like four or five bankers squished into the same suit. He lifted Elena off the ground with one arm and gave her a huge kiss. After months in a cell with Alex, he knew all about her. He hugged Alex and started to kiss him also, but that's where Alex drew the line.

Over a long dinner, Bitchy happily informed them he was now in talks with the Bears, while his lawyers haggled with the football commissioner about having him reinstated in time for spring camp. Bitchy was optimistic. The commish was playing hard to get, but the inside word was that it was all show. Bitchy was a two-year All-Pro, after all, and an ex-con to boot. That combination always did wonders for attendance and TV ratings. He was also confident the Bears would kick in another million on top of his old three million contract. His reputation alone was worth at least that—what team wouldn't think long and hard before taking on a team with Beatty on the roster?

Elena invited Bitchy to join them on the slopes that day, but he demurred and was resting in his hotel room. The truth was, Bitchy wouldn't go near a ski lift. He was terrified of heights.

So Alex and Elena were alone, at the top of the big mountain, staring down at the valley. The sun was out. The snow sparkled and glistened. Hundreds of skiers below them were doing all the silly things people do when balanced on two thin boards—collapsing, racing, struggling to stay upright, occasionally producing bone-crunching collisions.

Alex was in no hurry to get down the hill. He sat down and watched the sun move lethargically through the sky. Elena sat beside him. They held hands. Both knew the time had come for The Talk. It had been put off for weeks while they slept, nearly killed each other with sex, drank too much wine and champagne, ignored work, and remembered why they loved each other so much. But they sensed the differences. More than two years of being chased and hounded, terrorized and threatened, and then the long enforced separation, had changed them. The marriage needed time to adjust.

The year alone had created a more self-reliant, more independent and stubborn Elena. She had lived by herself, started a thriving business, and outsmarted the people who wanted to kill her. It was impossible to shrink back to her former self; nor did she care to.

As for Alex, the vestiges of brutal torture and fourteen months in prison were hard to shake off. Elena wasn't certain he ever would. The smiles came slowly, the eyes never stayed still. He watched strangers with distrust, eyeing their hands first; Elena was sure he was looking for a shank.

"Do you want to stay here?" Alex finally asked.

"You mean America?" Elena replied.

"There are other countries. We could take a chance on Russia again."

"My family's still there. All our friends, too."

"Those are important considerations."

"It wouldn't be good for you, though, would it?"

"I think not. Russia's changing, Elena. The crooks and KGB are taking over again. Yeltsin's a failure, a placeholder until they're ready to make their move."

"And we might have to go through the same thing again?"

"We'll be smarter next time."

"But so will they."

"Yes, they will. You pick. I just need someplace where I can make money."

"That's your problem, Konevitch."

"I didn't know I had a problem."

"You're looking at this backward. Think of it as someplace we can spend money."

"We're not rich yet, dear. Only two and a half million in the bank. It's not enough to live on forever."

"The lawsuit might net another five to ten million."

"The government will fight it to the bitter end. It could take a decade. We might lose."

"MP thinks a book and movie deal might bring in up to ten million."

"A book deal will take at least two years and might amount to very little. Movie deals aren't worth the paper they're written on."

"You're a pessimist."

"I'm a realist."

After a moment, Elena pointed at the small village below. "It's beautiful, isn't it?"

"Very beautiful. Like a small French or German village shipped over and planted in heaven."

"How about a house here?"

"A cramped two-bedroom apartment would cost at least a million. After fourteen months in a cell, I demand space."

She surveyed the town below. She pointed at a cluster of large chalets that climbed up the slopes on the west side. The homes were immense, spaced far apart, pine trees towering over the high roofs, no more than a ten-minute walk to the bottom slope. "How about that neighborhood?"

"At least ten million."

They fell back in the snow, held hands, and stared straight up at the sky. "Alex?" Elena said.

"What?" Alex said.

"I forgot to tell you something."

He squeezed her hand.

"Mikhail had a talk with Golitsin the day before he died."

"I know. Those were his instructions. Give Golitsin a good scare. Fool him into believing Nicky was behind it."

"Well, I told him to talk to Golitsin about something else, too. So Mikhail brought along a few of his friends, and they . . . well, they encouraged Golitsin to chat a little about our money." She paused to admire the sky. "You know how persuasive Mikhail can be."

Alex slowly sat up. "How persuasive was he?"

"Oh . . . enough. Golitsin gave him 225 million reasons to go away and leave him alone."

Alex turned and stared hard at his wife. "Mikhail found our money?"

"I let him keep five million. He more than earned it, you know."

"Where is it now?"

"Switzerland. I don't trust Bermudan banks anymore. Do you?"

Alex stood and spent several minutes staring down on the valley. Elena eventually stood and joined him.

They waited quietly until Alex asked, "Exactly which chalet on that hillside did you buy?"

"The big one almost exactly halfway up the slope." She tried to point it out. "The one with the four big stone chimneys."

"Is it big inside?"

"The neighbors call it the coliseum. The current owners use walkie-talkies so they don't have to scream at each other all day."

"Is it nice?"

"Crystal chandeliers, six or seven enormous fireplaces, a huge wine cellar, and a twenty-seat movie theater downstairs. If you like that sort of thing, yes, I guess it's nice."

"How many bedrooms?"

"I'm not sure. Six, seven, eight. They're sort of spread all over the place. Hard to count."

"Do they come with children?"

"No. The owner insisted we have to make our own."

"She pushed a hard bargain."

"She was quite tough on that point."

"When do we get one?"

"They're not exactly an impulse buy, dear. They have long delivery dates. Up to nine months, I hear."

After a moment Alex said, "I love you."

"I love you, too."

"Race you to the bottom?"

"You'll eat my dust, Konevitch."

"Snow, dear. You'll eat my snow."

"Oh, shut up, and try to catch me."

Author's Note

A few years ago, I received an interesting proposal on my Web site from a Russian expat who generously suggested that his adventure might inspire a captivating book. After recently reading my third novel, *Kingmaker*, he thought I had gotten a few things right about modern Russia, and wondered if I might be the right person to attempt a tale about him.

I soon met Alex and his wife, Elena, and quickly became curious, intrigued, and impressed. Not to mention deeply enchanted and enamored. So I dug in more.

The real Alex and Elena Konanykhin became the inspiration for this book and they are its animating force. In real life, they experienced fifteen years I wouldn't wish on my worst enemy— and I pray my worst enemy wouldn't wish upon me. A lovely couple; he, tall and darkly handsome; she, tiny, funny, and vividly, blondely beautiful. Both were strikingly intelligent, deeply in love, and stunned at what they had been forced to endure. Alex in fact wrote a superb nonfictional memoir of his long, amazing trial—a book called *Defiance*—a sad, joyful, engrossing, inspiring, terrifically written account. It's definitely worth reading if you enjoyed this book. My book, after all, is fiction, as are all its characters, except Alex, Elena, and a few historical figures.

Tragically, a year ago, Elena, who had weathered so many dark and bright days with Alex and who battled for his freedom, supported his brilliance, argued his innocence, risked her life, did jail time, and withstood fears and privations most of us could not imagine, died. Two weeks afterward, Alex e-mailed me.

"I am in agony," was all he could say.

As noted on the first page, this book is dedicated to Elena. I am so disappointed in myself that I failed to finish it before she left us.

But also to Alex, whom I am quite pleased to call an American, and a friend.

4413 SW 34th Ae

97239